D1488502

COLLECTED
GHOST STORIES

M. R. JAMES

COLLECTED GHOST STORIES

Edited with an Introduction and Notes by
DARRYL JONES

OXFORD
UNIVERSITY PRESS

Great Clarendon Street, Oxford OX2 6DP

Oxford University Press is a department of the University of Oxford.
It furthers the University's objective of excellence in research, scholarship,
and education by publishing worldwide in

Oxford New York

Athens Auckland Bangkok Bogotá Buenos Aires Calcutta
Cape Town Chennai Dar es Salaam Delhi Florence Hong Kong Istanbul
Karachi Kuala Lumpur Madrid Melbourne Mexico City Mumbai
Nairobi Paris São Paulo Singapore Taipei Tokyo Toronto Warsaw
with associated companies in Berlin Ibadan

Oxford is a registered trade mark of Oxford University Press
in the UK and in certain other countries

Editorial material © Darryl Jones 2011

British Library Cataloguing in Publication Data

Data available

Library of Congress Cataloging in Publication Data

Library of Congress Control Number: 2011934716

Typeset by RefineCatch Limited, Bungay, Suffolk
Printed in Great Britain
on acid-free paper by
Clays Ltd, St Ives plc

ISBN 978-019-956884-0

ACKNOWLEDGEMENTS

THIS edition could not have appeared without a lot of help. I am grateful first to Judith Luna at OUP for inviting me to undertake this project, and for her help, patience, and wisdom. The librarians of many great libraries have been invaluable, and I would particularly like to thank the archivists at the two institutions with which M. R. James was closely associated, King's College Cambridge, and Eton College. My thanks also to Charles Benson, Keeper of Early Printed Books at Trinity College Dublin. I am not the first editor James has had, and I have benefited greatly from the work done by all of my predecessors, but particularly Michael Cox, whom I never got to meet, but whose work as an editor and biographer was exemplary.

Part of the research for this volume was enabled by an Arts and Social Sciences Benefactions Fund Award from the Faculty of Arts, Humanities and Social Sciences, Trinity College Dublin, for which I am very grateful.

For advice, information, and support along the way, I would like to thank Chris Baldick, Ailise Bulfin, Steve Cadman, John Connolly, Helen Conrad-O'Briain, Nick Daly, Dara Downey, John Exshaw, Christopher Frayling, Kate Hebblethwaite, Paul Jackson, Maureen Jurkowski, Hilde Losnegård, Elizabeth McCarthy, Philip McEvansoneya, Ebony Morey, Bernice Murphy, John Nash, Sorcha Ní Fhlainn, Helen O'Connell, Eve Patten, John Scattergood, and Brenda Silver, and my students at Trinity College Dublin.

Particular thanks must go to my friend and colleague Jarlath Killeen for very many conversations on Victorian and Edwardian literature and culture, and on the supernatural, over very many years.

My deepest debt is to my wife, Margaret, and my daughter, Morgan, to whom this volume is dedicated.

CONTENTS

INTRODUCTION

Readers who are unfamiliar with the stories may prefer to treat the Introduction as an Afterword.

IT is Christmas Eve in King's College Cambridge, in the first decade of the twentieth century. In the Chapel—the finest, most beautiful, and most complete work of late Gothic perpendicular architecture in England—the famous choir, made up of choral scholars from the College and schoolboy choristers from nearby King's College School, have sung the carol service, opening with a beautiful rendition of 'Once in Royal David's City' (though the celebrated Festival of Nine Lessons and Carols for which the choir is today best known is not a tradition that will begin until 1918, when the College starts to heal itself after the devastation of the First World War, in which so many young Kingsmen lost their lives). The Fellows and Scholars then process to Hall, for dinner and tankards of hot spiced beer to ward off the cold and the dark.

To close the evening, a select few, a very few—friends, colleagues, former students—retire to the Provost's rooms, participants in an altogether more sinister Christmas ritual, but one intimately connected to the carols and the Chapel. This is a dark, Victorian Anglicanism, practised out there on the fens in the flat east of England, where the sky and the land seem part of one another, and where there is no horizon; far away from the concerns of the world. The Provost thinks of his own childhood, not too far from here, a world of isolated country houses in the Italian style, of Martello towers, shingle beaches, Anglo-Saxon burial mounds, witches . . .

Candles are lit, the Provost disappears into his bedroom; the friends talk, and drink their brandies or port, a little nervously. Perhaps someone plays a few bars on the piano, but always hesitantly, and never for long. At last, the Provost returns, clutching a manuscript covered in a spidery, illegible handwriting that might almost be a private cipher, the ink still wet upon the final pages, and blows out all the candles but one. It is gone eleven, nearer midnight, when the Provost begins to read, his clear, confident voice cutting through the dim, flickering light of candle and fire: 'By what means the papers out of which I have made a connected story came into my hands is the last point which the reader will learn from these pages . . .'[1]

By the time his ghost story readings became a Christmas ritual, Montague Rhodes James—Old Etonian and Kingsman, dean and provost of King's College Cambridge, future vice-chancellor of Cambridge University and, in semi-retirement, provost of Eton—was amongst the most distinguished scholars in the world. His prodigious body of work, on manuscript catalogues, on biblical apocrypha and the writings of the Church Fathers, on ecclesiastical architecture, and on whatever else happened to capture his imagination, would continue unabated until his death, aged 73, in 1936. Very occasionally, to entertain himself and his friends, he also wrote ghost stories. Even more occasionally, these were collected together and published in slim volumes. While his catalogues, in particular, remain indispensable to any serious scholar of medieval manuscripts, and are very unlikely to be superseded, it may have come as a surprise to Monty James that it was to be for his ghost stories that he would be best remembered and most revered. The *Collected Ghost Stories*, published under his supervision in 1931, has never been out of print—although it is not complete, as there were more stories to come in the last years of his life.

M. R. James was born in Goodnestone, Kent, on 1 August 1862, the youngest child of Herbert James, an Anglican clergyman of Evangelical leanings, and his wife, Mary Emily. Young Monty grew up surrounded by an atmosphere of religion and the supernatural, subjects which captivated him throughout his life. He was particularly drawn as a child to dread visions, be they of the gruesome martyrdoms of saints, or of the end of the world itself. Preaching a sermon in Eton in 1933, he recalled:

There was a time in my childhood when I thought that some night as I lay in bed I should suddenly be roused by a great sound of a trumpet, and that I should run to the window and look out and see the whole sky split across and lit up with glaring flame: and next moment I and everybody else in the

---

[1] This passage is a paraphrase, sometimes verbatim, of accounts given by a number of participants at MRJ's ghost story evenings, including H. E. Luxmoore, Oliffe Richmond, S. G. Lubbock, and MRJ himself. For the original sources, see Michael Cox, *M. R. James: An Informal Portrait* (Oxford, 1986), 133–4; Lubbock, *M. R. James* (Cambridge, 1939), 38–9.

house would be caught up into the air and made to stand with countless other people before a judge seated on a throne with great books open before him: and he would ask me questions out of what was written in those books—whether I had done this or that: and then I should be told to take my place either on the right hand or the left.[2]

(As James's stories testify again and again, books are dangerous things, to be opened with great care, and often at great cost.) These eschatological interests inform much of his scholarship, culminating in a major study of apocalyptic iconography, also published in 1931.[3] They also account for his recurring fascination with the millenarian sensibilities of the English seventeenth century, a period which plays a prominent part in many of his stories. More generally, themes and images of supernatural retribution and judgement recur throughout James's stories, clearly a central component of his artistic and scholarly preoccupations, his own aesthetic.

When Monty was 3, the family moved to the living of Great Livermere in rural Suffolk; he spent many of his summers at his grandmother's house in nearby Aldeburgh. The Suffolk landscape of his childhood, to which he returned throughout his life, was to inform his stories in a profound way. Aldeburgh, in particular, is a wild spot on the Suffolk coast which has long attracted artists of a bleak sensibility, including James himself. George Crabbe was born in Aldeburgh in 1754, and was curate of the flinty parish church of St Peter and St Paul's for a time from 1781; his long poem *The Borough* was set around Aldeburgh, and has as its most celebrated episode the story of the suicide of Peter Grimes, a fisherman in Slaughden, half a mile north of Aldeburgh. (Slaughden was lost to the sea in the nineteenth century, finally vanishing for good in the 1930s; all that remains of it now is the Martello tower, which was painted by Turner in 1826, and which features dramatically in James's own 'A Warning to the Curious'.) Benjamin Britten, a longtime Aldeburgh resident, adapted Crabbe's tale for his own austere masterpiece, *Peter Grimes*. The uncompromising sculptor Maggi Hambling, another Aldeburghian, has her brilliant, controversial monument to Britten, entitled *Scallop*, on Aldeburgh beach, facing out to the freezing North Sea. Behind it,

---

[2] Cox, *M. R. James*, 9.

[3] James, *The Apocalypse in Art* (London, 1931). This was a published version of the Schweich Lectures on Biblical Archaeology, which MRJ delivered to the British Academy in 1927.

the Sizewell nuclear power station looms. It is as remarkable a place now as it was during James's childhood. Numerous of his stories draw on this landscape, variously fertile and unforgiving, and on the folklore that has grown up around it: 'The Ash-Tree', 'The Tractate Middoth', 'Rats', and 'A Vignette' all make important use of East Anglian landscapes; while two of his most important stories, 'Oh, Whistle, and I'll Come to You, My Lad' and 'A Warning to the Curious', are informed very heavily, and perhaps totally, by this sense of place.

Even more than the East Anglian landscape, it is the presence and influence of educational institutions which dominate James's work. On 'a rainy day in September 1873', young Monty was deposited by his father in Temple Grove school, East Sheen, which 'had the reputation of being the oldest private school in England'.[4] From this moment, his life was an unbroken progress through educational institutions—Eton, King's, and (when the deaths of so many of his students in the War proved too much for him) back to Eton. Along the way, he garnered just about every academic and professional accolade for which he was eligible, from the King's Scholarship at Eton through to the Order of Merit (awarded to James in 1930). It was a comfortable life—some of his contemporaries, and some of his modern readers, have thought it rather too comfortable, and perhaps downright complacent. But without this institutional influence, James would probably never have written a word of his stories.

By modern standards, and probably also by the standards of his own time, M. R. James seems to have been a curiously incomplete man. It was for this reason, perhaps, that he was so drawn to the ghost story. His extraordinary intellectual capacities were matched by a commensurate anti-intellectualism which amounted, at times, to a genuine fear of ideas—a fear which his stories, with their consistent themes of the dangers of knowledge, reflect quite clearly. His father, Herbert James, advised exercising 'wholesome restraint' against 'ill-regulated speculation', and this is the kind of advice which the young Monty seems to have taken to heart.[5] While it is true that his students at Cambridge and Eton tended to be uncritical admirers, his academic

---

[4] James, *Eton and King's: Recollections, Mostly Trivial 1875–1925* (1926; Ashcroft, British Columbia, 2005), 8.

[5] Cox, Introduction to M. R. James, *Casting the Runes and Other Ghost Stories* (Oxford, 1987), p. xii.

friends and colleagues could often be more sceptical. His longtime King's colleague Nathaniel Wedd recalled James's admonishing two students who were discussing a philosophical problem: 'He rapped sharply on the table with his pipe, and called out: "No thinking gentlemen, please." "Thought" in this sense really did disturb Monty throughout his life.'[6] Another King's colleague, Oscar Browning, is credited with being the origin of the frequently repeated slur that 'James hates thought'.[7] James's friend A. C. Benson, provost of Magdalene College Cambridge, could be withering in his opinions:

[James's] mind is the mind of a nice child—he hates and fears all problems, all speculation, all originality or novelty of view. His spirit is both timid and unadventurous. He is *much* abler than I am, much better, much more effective—yet I feel that he is a kind of child.[8]

Browning's comment, in particular, can in part be put down to a common kind of academic rivalry and backbiting, the jealousy felt by a modestly successful academic towards a colleague whose institutional advancement appears seamless. Benson's consistent criticisms, in turn, may be informed by his lifelong clinical depression, which often made him see the world through the black lens of despair. Nevertheless, such remarks consistently accompanied James's academic life, and can certainly be borne out by the practice of that life.

'"Remember if you please," said my friend, looking at me over his spectacles, "that I am a Victorian by birth and education, and that the Victorian tree may not unreasonably be expected to bear Victorian fruit"' (p. 315) This remark, near the beginning of 'A Neighbour's Landmark', is highly significant. M. R. James understood himself to be a Victorian, sometimes at sea in, and often at odds with, the modern world. This, in great part, is why he so happily spent his entire life in educational institutions of a decidedly traditional bent: they provided for him a shelter from the pressures of modernity. The King's College to which James was admitted in 1882 had until relatively recently (1861) been a closed corporation, solely for the university education of Etonians.[9] While recent reforms had brought it somewhat more in tune with the modern world, it remained perhaps

---

[6] Cox, *M. R. James*, 97.
[7] Ibid. 174.
[8] Ibid. 125.
[9] Christopher Morris, *King's College: A Short History* (Cambridge, 1989), 46.

the most conservative college in a notably conservative university. Little wonder that that most anti-Victorian of Modernist intellectuals, Lytton Strachey, should have read James's memoir *Eton and Kings* (1925) with what seems like real disdain, believing it to be 'a dim affair', full of 'vapid anecdotes and nothing more. Only remarkable as showing the extraordinary impress an institution can make on an adolescent mind. It's odd that the Provost of Eton should still be aged sixteen. A life without a jolt.'[10]

Across a long career as an increasingly influential academic and university administrator, James seems to have opposed, and attempted to block where he could, every piece of progressive legislation and every really modern thinker that crossed his path, increasingly seeing (and using) Eton and King's as bulwarks against secular modernity. As a student at King's, he objected to the proposed appointment of the great evolutionary biologist T. H. Huxley as provost of Eton: 'a secularist, and a coarse nineteenth-century stinks man like Huxley don't do'.[11] As a young Fellow of King's, he opposed the candidature for provost of the distinguished political philosopher and psychical researcher Henry Sidgwick. In 1871, Sidgwick had been one of the founders of Newnham, a Cambridge college for women, which awarded certificates rather than degrees. When the issue of awarding degrees to women, and so allowing them full university membership, arose in 1897, James found himself part of a syndicate of fourteen academics charged with producing a report—which he attempted to obstruct at every stage, and refused to sign in any of its forms. In 1905, shortly after his election to the provostship of King's, James's colleague Oliffe Richmond described him as 'orthodox and womanhater'.[12] Women were not to be awarded Cambridge degrees until 1948.[13] James was also a consistent opponent of the abolition of

---

[10] Michael Holroyd, *Lytton Strachey: A Biography* (London, 1973), 920.

[11] Cox, *M. R. James*, 74–5.

[12] R. W. Pfaff, *Montague Rhodes James* (London, 1980), 220. This forms part of a comic verse which Richmond sent from Galicia in 1905.

[13] Ibid. 127. Collected amongst James's papers at King's is a photograph, presumably his own, of massed protestors against degrees for women outside Senate House in 1897, under a large banner with an adapted quotation from *Much Ado About Nothing*: 'Get you to Girton, Beatrice, get you to Newnham. Here's no place for you maids': KCC MS MRJ:F/1. (Girton was the other 19th-cent. Cambridge women's college.) Also amongst James's papers at King's is a flyer issued by his highly eccentric colleague J. H. Nixon, ostensibly opposing degrees for women from a position of reforming radicalism (KCC MS MRJ:D/Nixon).

compulsory Greek from the Cambridge curriculum, and of any form of modern or systematized thinking, from communism to German Higher Criticism (which strove for a formalized analysis of biblical textual sources) to the comparative mythography of his Trinity College Cambridge contemporary J. G. Frazer's *The Golden Bough*. Karswell, the rogue scholar and occultist of 'Casting the Runes', is himself a comparative mythographer, who 'seemed to put the *Golden Legend* and the *Golden Bough* exactly on a par, and to believe both: [his work was] a pitiable exhibition, in short' (p. 159). In 1917, James wrote a withering review of the Newnham classicist Jane Harrison's comparativist essay on 'The Head of John the Baptist'. By his own admission, after reading the article, James 'instantly took a pen and dipped it in gall and flayed her'.[14] James was normally a mild man, and so it is worth dwelling on the disproportionate venom of his response to Harrison's essay:

Her article cannot, I feel sure, be the result of very careful thought, and I regret to see that a researcher of her experience can allow herself to make public crude and inconsequent speculations of this kind, which go far to justify those who deny to Comparative Mythology the name and dignity of a science.[15]

Underlying what is unquestionably a genuine scholarly dispute (comparativists by their nature tend to work at a high level of generalization; James was obsessed by particulars and exceptions) are a series of interrelated anxieties. Harrison was a woman, a graduate and Fellow of Newnham, and a systematizing intellectual. M. R. James was in flight from all of these things throughout his life.

Indeed, James seems to have objected to *all* the modern thinkers and writers he encountered: Aldous Huxley, James Joyce (both 'a charlatan' and 'that prostitutor of life and language'[16]), Lytton Strachey, Bertrand Russell (a pacifist), Radclyffe Hall ('I believe Miss Hall's book [*The Well of Loneliness*] is about birth control or some kindred subject, isn't it. I find it difficult to believe either that it is a good novel or that its suppression causes any loss to literature'[17]),

---

[14] Letter to Gordon Carey, 28 Jan. 1917: KCC MS MRJ:F/4.
[15] James, 'Some Remarks on "The Head of John the Baptist"', *Classical Review*, 31/1 (Feb. 1917), 4.
[16] Pfaff, *James*, 401.
[17] Ibid.

J. B. S. Haldane (James voted to dismiss him from his university readership in biochemistry following his involvement in a case of adultery and divorce in 1926, though Haldane's appeal against dismissal was upheld; Haldane was also an outspoken socialist). Perhaps worst of all for James was John Maynard Keynes, who appears to have become something of a nemesis, and who may have been one contributing factor to his decision to leave King's in 1918. Keynes was both James's double and his antithesis: an Old Etonian, Fellow and bursar of King's, an outward-looking modernizer, and amongst the very greatest British intellectuals of the twentieth century. 'I've had a good look at this place,' Keynes remarked shortly after his arrival at King's, 'and come to the conclusion that it's pretty inefficient.'[18] When James became provost of King's in 1905, Benson recorded his concerns: 'He will simply be a Head on the old lines, reactionary, against novelty and progress. He will initiate nothing, move nothing. Monty has *no* intellectual, philosophical or religious interests really.'[19]

The potential that ideas have for opening up new worlds of possibility caused James lifelong anxiety. Thus, his research, phenomenal as it was, tended habitually towards apocrypha, ephemera, marginalia—towards forgotten and perhaps deliberately irrelevant subjects. James was happy to acknowledge this himself. As a schoolboy, his autobiography records, he became fascinated by 'blobs of misplaced erudition. . . . Nothing could be more inspiriting than to discover that St Livinus had his tongue cut out and was beheaded, or that David's mother was called Nitzeneth.'[20] In 1883, the first paper James delivered to the Chitchat Society in Cambridge (to whom he first read a number of his important early stories) was entitled 'Useless Knowledge'.[21] Amongst the very greatest of his scholarly achievements is his 1924 Oxford edition of *The Apocryphal New Testament*, a collection of marginal or excluded scriptural texts whose intrinsic worth, James admitted, was highly dubious.[22] The irresistible pull of

---

[18] Morris, *King's College*, 63.

[19] Cox, *M. R. James*, 174.

[20] James, *Eton and King's*, 13.

[21] Ibid. 58.

[22] M. R. James, ed. and trans., *The Apocryphal New Testament* (Oxford, 1924), pp. xi–xii: 'It will very quickly be seen that there is no question of any one's having excluded [the Apocryphal Gospels] from the New Testament. They have done that for themselves.'

the irrelevant for James was frequently remarked upon by his colleagues and contemporaries. His revered tutor at Eton, H. E. Luxmoore, noted the way in which James 'dredges up literature for refuse'; Edmund Gosse, the great Edwardian man of letters, and lecturer in English at Trinity College Cambridge, remarked on 'those poor old doggrell-mongers of the third century on whom you expend (notice! I don't say *waste*) what was meant for mankind'; A. C. Benson believed that 'no one alive knows so much or so little worth knowing'.[23]

But it is the very limitations of James's personal, social, and intellectual horizons that account for the brilliance of his ghost stories. The great effect and power of James's stories lies in their acts of exclusion, the ways in which they use scholarship, knowledge, institutions, the past, as a rearguard action to keep at bay progress, modernity, the Shock of the New. They are straitened, narrow, austere, limited. And it is precisely this lack of expansiveness that makes him a great short story writer, and the very greatest ghost story writer, as these limitations become narrative preoccupations, simultaneously obsessions and games. The ghost story tends to be a highly conventional, formalized, conservative form, governed by strict generic codes, which often themselves, as with James, reflect and articulate an ingrained social conservatism, an attempt to repulse the contemporary world, or to show the dire consequences of a lack of understanding of, and due reverence for, the past, its knowledge and traditions. These traditions, when violated or subjected to the materialist gaze of modernity, can wreak terrifying retribution.

The nearest James ever came to a statement of theoretical principle about his chosen form—albeit one couched in a characteristic reluctance towards abstraction—was in the introduction he wrote to V. H. Collins's anthology *Ghosts and Marvels*, published in 1924:

Often have I been asked to formulate my views about ghost stories and tales of the marvellous, the mysterious, the supernatural. Never have I been able to find out whether I had any views that could be formulated. The truth is, I suspect, that the *genre* is too small to bear the imposition of far-reaching principles. Widen the question, and ask what governs the construction of short stories in general, and a great deal might be said, and has been said. . . . The ghost story is, at its best, only a particular sort of

[23] Cox, *M. R. James*, 40, 111, 125.

short story, and is subject to the same broad rules as the whole mass of them. These rules, I imagine, no writer ever consciously follows. In fact, it is absurd to talk of them as rules; they are qualities which have been observed to accompany success. . . . Well then: two ingredients most valuable in the concocting of a ghost story are, to me, the atmosphere and the nicely-managed crescendo. (Appendix, p. 407)

It is a very revealing essay, not least because of its typically self-denying nature: can the ghost story be theorized, or not? The short story has 'broad rules', but 'no writer ever consciously follows' them. The ghost story also properly belongs in the *past*—not necessarily the distant past; but it is important that its setting and concerns be at least a generation out of date, in a world which pre-dates technological modernity:

The detective story cannot be too much up-to-date: the motor, the telephone, the aeroplane, the newest slang, are all in place there. For the ghost story a slight haze of distance is desirable. 'Thirty years ago,' 'Not long before the war,' are very proper openings. (pp. 407–8)

Writing in 1924, James clearly conceives of his chosen form—as he conceived of himself—as fundamentally Victorian ('Thirty years ago'), or at best Edwardian ('Not long before the war').

Like James himself, in fact, the ghost story is a characteristic product of nineteenth-century forces. It is a reaction to the secular, materialist, industrial modernity that animated the dominant, progressivist Victorian utilitarian ideology. As such it has clear relations with spiritualism and occultism (and their scientific offshoot, psychical research), the belief that the worlds of matter and of spirit interpenetrated, or were separated only by a thin veil, which could readily be pulled aside (by clairvoyants, for example) to allow communication with the Other World. As the social historian Janet Oppenheim has argued, spiritualism, extraordinarily widespread and permeating all sections of society, was *the* main Victorian response to secular modernity.[24] Debates about spiritualism and the occult were at the very centre of Victorian public and intellectual life: 'No major Victorian thinker or writer,' Jarlath Killeen writes in his history of nineteenth-century Gothic fiction, 'from the Brontës to the Brownings, from

---

[24] Janet Oppenheim, *The Other World: Spiritualism and Psychical Research in England, 1850–1914* (Cambridge, 1985).

Dickens to Darwin, was unconcerned about the occult.' 'The ghost', Killeen concludes, 'represents a breach in historical progression: in a stark reproach to the Victorian investment in notions of linearity and progress, the ghost is a manifestation of the "past-in-the-present"'.[25]

James's own position on the reality of the supernatural was typically ambivalent, or contradictory—or perhaps, as Julia Briggs suggests, he was simply undisturbed by (or even unaware of) the implications of what he wrote.[26] Towards the end of his life, writing the Preface to the *Collected Ghost Stories* (1931), he asked: 'Do I believe in ghosts? To which I answer that I am prepared to consider evidence and accept it if it satisfies me' (Appendix, p. 419). It is difficult to know which is more striking about this remark, its brevity or its evasiveness. James had little interest in psychical research, that attempt by some of the foremost intellectuals of his own generation to establish a basis for discovering the veracity of the supernatural, and to test it according to tough-minded empirical standards. The Society for Psychical Research (SPR), in fact, had its home in Trinity College Cambridge, right next door to King's. As we have seen, James was no admirer of Henry Sidgwick, the intellectual powerhouse behind the SPR; and the SPR itself makes a disguised appearance in 'The Mezzotint' as the 'Phasmatological Society', a collection of busybodies from whom news of the story's supernatural illustration must be kept at all costs. James, in fact, policed the boundaries between his own stories and the possible reality of an Other World quite rigorously: 'I have not sought to embody in [my stories] any well-considered scheme of "psychical" theory' (Preface to *More Ghost Stories of an Antiquary*, Appendix, p. 406). While he believed that it was appropriate for a ghost story to express an uncanny sense of epistemological indeterminacy—'a loophole for a natural explanation; but, I would say, let the loophole be so narrow as not to be quite practicable' (Introduction to *Ghosts and Marvels*, Appendix, p. 407)—this is quite clearly an aesthetic judgement on the ghost story rather than a statement about the existence of the supernatural. In one of his late essays on the ghost story, 'Ghosts—Treat Them Gently!', he makes the distinction very plain: 'I am

[25] Jarlath Killeen, *Gothic Literature, 1914–1925* (Cardiff, 2009), 124, 129.
[26] Julia Briggs, *Night Visitors: The Rise and Fall of the English Ghost Story* (London, 1977), 124.

speaking of the literary ghost story here. The story that claims to be "veridical" (in the language of the Society of Psychical Research) is a very different affair' (Appendix, p. 416).

It is worth reiterating the fact that the stories for which James is now best known, and rightly revered, were for him gentlemanly entertainments and occasional pieces, the amusing by-products of his magisterial scholarship in catalogues, manuscript studies, and editorial work. They were certainly not to be taken with any great seriousness. In the Preface to *More Ghost Stories of an Antiquary*, he acknowledges that 'I have not been possessed by that austere sense of the responsibility of authorship which is demanded of a writer of fiction in this generation' (p. 406). When in 1934, the ghost-story writer Mary Butts wrote a critical article entitled 'The Art of Montagu James [*sic*] James', his response was 'I knew not that I had any'.[27] This is a perhaps characteristically disingenuous remark, as James's stories are at their best extremely artfully constructed works. Yet they are also generic works, variations on a successful template: this is what James's Christmas audiences expected to hear.

In the typical James story, a bachelor don or antiquarian scholar discovers a lost manuscript or artefact which unleashes supernatural forces, often causing him to rethink his comfortable assumptions about the nature of reality. While on occasion this happens within what were to James the familiar confines of a university college ('The Mezzotint') or library ('The Tractate Middoth'), or one of James's own schools ('A School Story', set in a disguised version of James's prep school, Temple Grove; 'After Dark in the Playing Fields', set in Eton), more usually the stories take the scholar away from institutional security, and it is here that danger really lurks. It is for this reason that the hotel or inn features so heavily as the locus for horror in James—in 'Canon Alberic's Scrap-book', 'Number 13', 'Oh, Whistle, and I'll Come to You, My Lad', 'A Warning to the Curious', 'Rats', and others. To step outside of institutions is to court danger.

The lifelong appeal of institutions for James was that they provided the security of all-male environments. One of the reasons that the hotel provides such a consistent locus of anxiety is that it requires enforced encounters with women—landladies, chambermaids, and

---

[27] Mary Butts, 'The Art of Montagu James', *London Mercury*, 29 (Feb. 1934). For James's response, see Cox, *M. R. James*, 141.

other kinds of domestics—whom James tended, where possible, to avoid throughout his life. The issue of his sexuality is one about which many of James's biographers and commentators choose to maintain a decorous silence, or at best allude to discreetly.[28] Michael Cox, indeed, closes the matter authoritatively by asserting that 'Women figure rarely in James's stories, for this is a world where sex is not'.[29] And yet, to many modern readers James's sexuality, simultaneously unknowable and all-pervasive, may be the key issue to understanding his stories. We are all now, inevitably, post-Freudian readers—and Freudianism, lest we forget, was itself the product of (and interpretation of, and response to) the same Victorian world that produced M. R. James. Sigmund Freud himself, just six years older than James, was the last, and the greatest, of all writers of Victorian Gothic.

Much has been written about the erotics of male relations in the Victorian public school system of which James was a distinguished product. Readers of this volume may well conclude, as his biographers and commentators tend to imply, that James had no sexual feelings of any kind, at least not in any way that a modern sensibility would understand the concept. Whatever sexuality he did have was very probably unrecognized and certainly never articulated. And yet James's sexuality, and the attitudes to men and to women which it tended to produce, can be read in displaced form throughout his life and his stories.

His friend James McBryde, a student at King's in the 1890s, when James was already dean, seems to have been the love of M. R. James's life; the pair went, with friends, on holidays to France and to Denmark in the 1890s, and McBryde, a talented illustrator, worked on a series of illustrations to accompany the publication of *Ghost Stories of an Antiquary*. These were sadly never completed, as McBryde died in 1904 of complications arising from an appendix operation. The story of James at McBryde's funeral in Lancashire is an extremely

---

[28] Michael Cox, for example, believes that 'We can talk glibly about his being a "repressed homosexual", but this seems a hopelessly inadequate summation of the complex cultural and personal factors behind his resistance to marriage', and warns against 'psycho-critical speculation' (Cox, *M. R. James*, 165, 149). See also David G. Rowlands, 'M. R. James's Women', in S. T. Joshi and Rosemary Pardoe (eds.), *Warnings to the Curious: A Sheaf of Criticism on M. R. James* (New York, 2007), 138.

[29] Cox, 'Introduction', p. xxiv.

touching one, and a moment in which one can detect, albeit in a
highly symbolic form, a sense of genuine, heartbroken passion in this
otherwise very repressed Victorian. On hearing of McBryde's death,
James picked flowers—roses, lilac, and honeysuckle—from the
Fellows' Garden at King's, which he took with him on the train from
Cambridge to Lancashire. After all the other mourners had left,
James threw the flowers into McBryde's grave. In 1904, James
arranged for the publication, by Cambridge University Press (normally an austere publisher of academic monographs), of *The Story of
a Troll Hunt*, a children's book written and illustrated by McBryde,
and inspired by the holiday they had taken to Denmark in 1899.
James contributed an introduction to the book, which may be the
nearest he ever came to articulating his feelings: 'The intercourse of
eleven years,—of late, minutely recalled,—has left no single act or
word of his which I could choose to forget.'[30] A. C. Benson, who certainly understood the nature of repressed homosexual desire, wrote
in his diary of receiving

A sad and moving letter from MRJ telling me of McBryde's death. . . .
Monty's letter touched me very much; for he called me his oldest friend.
But there seemed a curious effort in the letter not to let himself go, not to
dive deep; to take the thing as lightly as was consistent with feeling it very
much—not to let it be a sad remembrance. He spoke strongly of McB as
being a friend who didn't want sentimentality. But here I believe Monty a
little deceives himself. He likes beautiful graceful people and what is that
but a refined sentimentality. He is not demonstrative and thinks that is
unsentimental.[31]

After McBryde's death, James carried on the relationship in displaced
form, with a lifelong and devoted attachment to his widow Gwendolen,
easily the most important friendship he had with a woman.

Relations between men could also encompass more directly physical exchanges. James was particularly fond throughout his life of
'ragging' and other forms of horseplay, as evinced by this account of
an incident with his student friend St Clair Donaldson:

I then called on St Clair . . . He eventually came to my rooms and I speed-
ily originated a rag by hanging his hat on the coal scuttle. Marshall and

---

[30] M. R. James, Introduction to James McBryde, *The Story of a Troll Hunt* (Cambridge, 1904).
[31] Cox, *M. R. James*, 128.

Thomas thought my book cases were falling and came to see if they could render any assistance. We were at that moment somewhat mixed on the hearthrug.

Cyril Alington, later headmaster of Eton, recalled Donaldson's account of rolling around on the floor 'with Monty James's long fingers grasping at his vitals', a story which Alington omitted from his description of the Cambridge TAF (Twice a Fortnight) Club, of which James was a member, 'for reasons of piety'. Even the occasions for reading James's stories could degenerate into ragging, as H. E. Luxmoore recalled: 'Last night Monty James read us a new story of the most blood curdling character, after which those played animal grab who did not mind having their clothes torn to pieces and their hands nailscored.'[32]

This last observation of Luxmoore's does imply an inherent connection between the stories themselves and public-school sexuality: an all-male community, all of whose activities seem sexualized. It also implies that the story and the 'animal grab' were two different (but related) kinds of all-male game or entertainment which took place in this institutional setting. Torn clothes and nailscorings are, in fact, a recurring feature in James's stories. The (male) demon who looms up from behind Dennistoun in his hotel room at the end of 'Canon Alberic's Scrap-book' has 'nails rising from the ends of the fingers and curving sharply down and forward, grey, horny and wrinkled' (p. 11), while the lamia of 'An Episode of Cathedral History' grabs at a woman's skirt, leaving 'a jagged tear extending some way into the substance of the stuff' (p. 259). Giovanni, the vengeful ghost boy of 'Lost Hearts' (a story about an older scholar preying on his young wards), has 'fearfully long', translucent nails, which scratch 'long, parallel slits, about six inches in length, some of them not quite piercing the texture of the linen' of young Stephen Elliott's nightgown, and leave 'marks and scratches . . . for all the world like a Chinaman's finger-nails' (pp. 18–21) down his bedroom door. It is with these nails that he tears out the heart of his murderer Mr Abney. One of James's most overtly homoerotic stories is 'The Residence at

---

[32] Ibid. 55, 59, 132. For an account of James which in some ways parallels my own thinking here and in my reading of 'Oh, Whistle and I'll Come to You, My Lad', see Mike Pincombe, 'Homosexual Panic and the English Ghost Story: M. R. James and Others', in Joshi and Pardoe (eds.). *Warnings to the Curious*, 184–96.

Whitminster', which recounts the relationship between two school-boys, Frank Sydall and Lord Saul Kildonan: 'Frank was looking earnestly at something in the palm of his hand. Saul stood behind him and seemed to be listening. After some minutes he very gently laid his hand on Frank's head, and almost insistently thereupon, Frank suddenly dropped what he was holding, clapped his hand to his eyes, and sank down on the grass' (pp. 224–5). Frank and Saul's 'curious play' has tragic consequences, as Frank is killed by occult means and Saul, pursued by supernatural agents, is found 'clinging desperately to the great ring of the [cathedral] door, his head sunk between his shoulders, his stockings in rags, his shoes gone, his legs torn and bloody'. They are buried together in 'a stone altar tomb in Whitminster churchyard' (p. 228).

As Mike Pincombe has suggested, there are discernible elements of 'homosexual panic' in 'Oh, Whistle, and I'll Come to You, My Lad'.[33] The very title of the story is taken from a Burns ballad about the seduction of a maid. This most famous of all James's ghosts arises from the bed in which Professor Parkins is expecting his colleague Rogers to sleep; its 'horrible, . . . intensely horrible, face *of crumpled linen* . . . was thrust close into his own' (p. 92), as if trying to kiss him. But more strikingly than this, it seems to me that what 'Oh, Whistle' really exhibits is a fear of *domesticity*. The locus of horror is, after all, a bedsheet. Jonathan Miller's celebrated 1968 television adaptation of the story brilliantly realizes this theme by opening with an extended scene of hotel chambermaids making beds. Women, on close observation, do feature frequently in James's stories, but not necessarily in the ways we might initially expect. They are often the ghosts themselves.

Sometimes these ghosts require no interpretation: they are unambiguously supernatural women. Mrs Mothersole in 'The Ash-Tree' wreaks what seems like justified retribution on the heirs of her persecutor Sir Matthew Fell. In 'Martin's Close', the spurned Ann Clark, her throat cut, rises out of the pond in which her body lies, to convict George Martin of her murder. 'A Neighbour's Landmark' features the restless ghost of Theodosia Bryan, Lady Ivie, condemned for eternity to walk the land she had unlawfully obtained during her life. The lamia of 'An Episode of Cathedral History' is the female

---

[33] Pincombe, 'Homosexual Panic', 188–91.

counterpart of the demon of 'Canon Alberic's Scrap-book': physically, they are virtually identical (though his eyes are yellow and hers red), both are imprisoned within cathedrals, and both are linked by a shared passage from Isaiah: 'The wild beasts of the desert shall also meet with the wild beasts of the island, and the satyr shall cry to his fellow, and the screech-owl also shall rest there, and find for herself a place of rest.' One of the ghosts of 'Wailing Well' is 'a terrible figure—something in ragged black—with whitish patches breaking out of it: the head, perched on a long thin neck, half hidden by a shapeless sort of blackened sun-bonnet' (p. 388).

Other ghosts are trickier, more elusive or complex, and of liminal or ambiguous gender. The bedsheet ghost of 'Oh, Whistle', for example, is an overdetermined symbol: that is, the site where a number of anxieties converge to create an abundance of meaning. It simultaneously represents homosexual anxieties (the bed in which Mr Rogers is to sleep), and a fear of domesticity and *women* given nightmare form; and for James, these anxieties are related ones. One of the most striking images of the panic caused by the irruption of the supernatural into a secure setting comes in 'Casting the Runes' when Mr Dunning, lying in bed at home with the power out and noises coming from his study, gropes for his matches: 'he put his hand into the well-known nook under the pillow: only, it did not get so far. What he touched was, according to his account, a mouth, with teeth, and with hair about it, and, he declares, not the mouth of a human being' (p. 155). This is a terrifying image—along with 'Oh, Whistle' 's spectral bedsheet, probably the most unnerving in all of James's writing. It offers, to begin with, a classic adumbration of the Freudian category of the *uncanny*, in which the seeming security of domesticity is revealed as shot through with anxieties (and for James, as we have seen, the domestic was always a source of anxiety). More than this, though, this image of the hairy, fanged mouth lurking 'in the well-known nook under the pillow' is a powerful symbol of sexual terror, a *vagina dentata*—a nightmare image of the monstrous-feminine intruding upon the story's cloistered, gentlemanly world of libraries and scholarship. Another image of the monstrous-feminine occurs, in grotesquely abject form, at the close of 'The Treasure of Abbot Thomas'. Exploring a dark cavity inside a well, the antiquarian treasure-hunter Mr Somerton encounters one of James's most shockingly corporeal horrors:

I believe I am now acquainted with the extremity of terror and repulsion which a man can endure without losing his mind. I can only just manage to tell you the bare outline of the experience. I was conscious of a most horrible smell of mould, and of a cold kind of face pressed against my own, and of several—I don't know how many—legs or arms or tentacles or something clinging to my body. (pp. 108–9)

The symbolic language of this scene—wells, dark cavities, 'foulness', an overwhelming sense of physical violation—does not require too much decoding here, and 'Abbot Thomas' is ultimately a tale of uncontrollable sexual terror, a quest which leads Mr Somerton to this nightmare vagina, and an encounter which he barely survives.[34]

While it may not always predominate, there is also a discernible element of sexual terror in James's two most characteristic symbols of horror, spiders and hair—and, worst of all, hairy spiders, as the two are interconnected symbols for him. It is in these terms that the stories' ghosts and demons are most frequently imagined. The prevalence of spidery monsters in his stories is in part a product of James's lifelong and well-attested arachnophobia. On one of their French bicycling holidays, James records McBryde's encounter with a particular monster: 'the courage which enabled him to seize by its sinewy leg the largest spider I have ever seen in a derelict bath at Verdun commanded the deepest respect'.[35] The demon of 'Canon Alberic's Scrap-book' is a kind of tarantula: 'a mass of coarse, matted black hair . . . hideously taloned . . . Imagine one of the awful bird-catching spiders of South America translated into human form' (p. 9). The ghost of Dr Rant in 'The Tractate Middoth' has 'a very nasty bald head . . . and the streaks of hair across it were much less like hair than cobwebs . . . and the eyes were very deep-sunk, and over them, from the eyebrows to the cheek-bone, there were *cobwebs*—thick' (p. 133). At the close of the story, John Eldred is attacked and killed by what may be a mass of spiders, or another of James's spiders in human form, while frantically trying to destroy an unfavourable will. The event is seen unclearly, from a distance:

---

[34] The analysis of these stories draws on important aspects of the feminist analysis of horror, in particular the ideas of Barbara Creed, and the hugely influential theories of Julia Kristeva. See e.g. Creed, *The Monstrous-Feminine: Film, Feminism, Psychoanalysis* (London, 1993); Kristeva, *The Powers of Horror: An Essay in Abjection*, trans. L. S. Roudiez (New York, 1982).

[35] Cox, *M. R. James*, 109.

Then he took hold of a leaf, and was carefully tearing it out, when two things happened. First, something black seemed to drop upon the white leaf and run down it, and then as Eldred started and was turning to look behind him, a little dark form appeared to rise out of the shadow behind the tree-trunk and from it two arms enclosing a mass of blackness came before Eldred's face and covered his head and neck. (p. 142)

Investigating the scene of Eldred's death the next day, Garrett sees 'a thick black mass of cobwebs; and, as he stirred it gingerly with his stick, several large spiders ran out of it into the grass' (p. 144). 'The Ash-Tree' is entirely and most explicitly a tale of supernatural arachnid vengeance, and also unambiguously of a vengeful woman, as the story's deadly giant spiders are the instruments of Mrs Mothersole's will, living inside the tree which seems to grow out of her corpse. When the ash tree burns, her skeleton is discovered in its roots, 'with the skin dried upon the bones, having some remains of black hair', the human form of the 'enormous spider[s], veinous and seared' with which she shares her grave (pp. 46, 37).

As well as arachnids, insects, too, provoke terror in James's stories: the sawflies, crane-flies, and ichneumon wasps of 'The Residence at Whitminster'; the flies and their master Beelzebub, Lord of Flies, in 'An Evening's Entertainment'; the truly unsettling image of the charred ghost crawling out of the plans of the maze in 'Mr Humphreys and his Inheritance', 'a *burnt* human face: and with the odious writhings of a wasp climbing out of a rotten apple there clambered forth an appearance of a form, waving black arms prepared to clasp the head that was bending over them' (p. 219).

And so, finally, to hair, which of all things seems most terrifying to James and his protagonists, most emblematic of an insecure, destabilized world. James's own hair, as a young man, was often on the verge of being too long, and the subject of frequent comment and rebuke from his Eton masters, notably Walter Durnford, who was to succeed James as provost of King's ('I can still hear him proclaiming that James, K.S., must get his hair cut before five o'clock school'[36]). James's ghosts have hair, too much hair, hair where there should be none. Mrs Mothersole's skeleton, we have seen, has 'some remains of black hair', and the skeletal, child-abducting spectre of 'The Mezzotint' has 'a white dome-like forehead and a few straggling

---

[36] James, *Eton and King's*, 25.

hairs' (p. 32). Both the demon of 'Canon Alberic' and the lamia of 'An Episode of Cathedral History' are entirely covered in hair. The entity occupying the non-existent room in 'Number 13' is glimpsed only as 'an arm . . . clad in ragged, yellowish linen, and the bare skin, where it could be seen, had long grey hair upon it' (p. 59). The very feel of hair is unsettling: as we have seen, Mr Dunning in 'Casting the Runes' feels 'a mouth, with teeth, and hair about it' under his pillow; while Dr Haynes in 'The Stalls of Barchester Cathedral', putting his hand on a carved wooden choir-stall, 'was startled by what seemed a softness, a feeling as of rather rough and coarse fur' (p. 172).

One story, in particular, seems to concentrate the anxieties discussed here into one image of terrifying domesticity, homosexual panic, and hairiness. 'The Diary of Mr Poynter' is a tale of haunted curtains (analogous to 'Oh, Whistle''s haunted bedsheet), based on a design which so captivates Miss Denton, the aunt of the story's antiquarian protagonist, that she quite forgets her earlier demand for chintz curtains: 'It is a most charming pattern . . . and remarkable too. Look, James, how delightfully the lines ripple. It reminds one of hair, very much, doesn't it?' (p. 246). The design is, it transpires, based on the hair of Sir Everard Charlett: 'He was a very beautiful person, and constantly wore his own Hair, which was very abundant, from which, and his loose way of living, the cant name for him was Absalom' (p. 251). This is an encoded statement of Sir Everard's homosexuality. Absalom, son of King David, was a beautiful rebel, as recorded in 2 Samuel:

But in all Israel there was none to be so much praised as Absalom for his beauty: from the sole of his foot even to the crown of his head there was no blemish in him.

And when he polled his head [i.e., cut his hair], (for it was at every year's end that he polled it, because the hair was heavy on him, therefore he polled it:) he weighed the hair of his head at two hundred shekels after the king's weight. (15: 25–6)

The pattern in the wallpaper assumes corporeal form in James Denton's room, in what is for James an unusually long and descriptive account of supernatural terror:

happening to move his hand which hung down over the arm of the chair within a few inches of the floor, he felt on the back of it just the slightest touch of a surface of hair, and stretching it out in that direction he stroked and patted a rounded something. But the feel of it, and still more the fact that instead of a responsive movement, absolute stillness greeted his touch, made him look over the arm. What he had been touching rose to meet him. It was in the attitude of one that had crept along the floor on its belly, and it was, so far as could be recollected, a human figure. But of the face which was now rising to within a few inches of his own no feature was discernable, only hair. Shapeless as it was, there was about it so horrible an air of menace that as he bounded from his chair and rushed from the room he heard himself moaning with fear: and doubtless he did right to fly. As he dashed into the baize door that cut the passage in two, and—forgetting that it opened towards him—beat against it with all the force in him, he felt a soft ineffectual tearing at his back which, all the same, seemed to be growing in power, as if the hand, or whatever worse than a hand was there, were becoming more material as the pursuer's rage was more concentrated. (pp. 249–50)

As M. R. James knew, the ghost story form is itself essentially Victorian. This certainly was the authorial tradition to which he understood himself, in a small way, to be a contributor, as he returned throughout his life to the works of his two great Victorian precursors, Charles Dickens and Sheridan Le Fanu. Writing in 1977, in what is probably the most influential of the very few full-length studies of the ghost story, *Night Visitors: The Rise and Fall of the English Ghost Story*, Julia Briggs lamented that 'the ghost story now seems to look back over its own shoulder. It has become a vehicle for nostalgia, a formulaic exercise content merely to recreate a Dickensian or a Monty Jamesian atmosphere. It no longer has any capacity for growth or adaptation.'[37]

Perhaps, yes—but Briggs also seems a little harsh on the ghost story here, and on M. R. James himself. What James's stories do, it seems, is to give articulation to a particularly English longing for the past. This might be the classic attitude of a late imperial writer, which James certainly was; but such a backward-looking tendency is not always damagingly reactionary. Modernity *is* terrifying, monstrous, demonic. James lived long enough to see the effects of the Age of Total War (to use Eric Hobsbawm's term), which obliterated a generation of his best students at Cambridge, and left others scarred and incapacitated, hollow men. The temptation in his old age to retreat into an idealized Etonian youth must have been overwhelming.

---

[37] Briggs, *Night Visitors*, 14.

M. R. James died peacefully on 12 June 1936. Five years later, in 1941, with German bombs dropping around him, George Orwell, a very different kind of Old Etonian from James, wrote his famous manifesto of Englishness, 'The Lion and the Unicorn'. In this great essay, written in the teeth of Total War, Orwell attempted to encapsulate what was most precious about the English, most worth fighting for—and also what was most stultifying and retrograde, least helpful. His conclusion was that these two qualities, the admirable and the infuriating, were indissociable in the national character: 'the English', Orwell believed, 'are not intellectual. They have a horror of abstract thought, they feel no need for any philosophy or systematic "world view".'[38] It was precisely this anti-intellectualism, Orwell believed, that was to save the nation, as the English, being impervious to ideas, were the only major European nation also impervious to fascism, a systematic ideology which they did not understand. Instead, Orwell suggested, the English were a nation of individualists, eccentrics, cranks, hobbyists, cultivators of the deliberately irrelevant. This was their gift to the world. It may have come as a surprise to Monty James to discover that, in the end, he was a most Orwellian Englishman.

[38] George Orwell, 'The Lion and the Unicorn: Socialism and the English Genius', in *Essays*, ed. John Carey (London, 2002), 293.

NOTE ON THE TEXT

THE text for the majority of the stories here is based on the 1931 *Collected Ghost Stories*, overseen by M. R. James for publication. Where there are obvious errors, I have silently corrected them. Where available, I have consulted original manuscript sources, and have discussed substantive differences between MS and published versions in the Explanatory Notes. For the last three stories, published after the appearance of the *Collected Ghost Stories* ('The Experiment', 'The Malice of Inanimate Objects', 'A Vignette'), I have used the earliest printed versions of the stories.

Details of composition and first publication can be found in the Explanatory Notes to the individual stories at the back of the book. Asterisks in the text refer to these notes; all footnotes are by M. R. James.

SELECT BIBLIOGRAPHY

Biography

Cox, Michael, *M. R. James: An Informal Portrait* (Oxford, 1986). The most invaluable work for any student of James.

Lubbock, S. G., *M. R. James* (Cambridge, 1939). A personal memoir, written shortly after MRJ's death.

Pfaff, Richard William, *Montague Rhodes James* (London, 1980). An exhaustive account of James's scholarship.

Critical Studies

Carroll, Jane Suzanne, 'A "dramar in real life": Freaky Dolls, M. R. James and Modern Children's Ghost Stories', in Helen Conrad O'Briain and Julie-Anne Stevens (eds.), *The Ghost Story from the Middle Ages to the Twentieth Century: A Ghostly Genre* (Dublin, 2010), 251–65.

Cowlinshaw, Brian, ' "A Warning top the Curious": Victorian Science and the Awful Unconscious in M. R. James's Ghost Stories', *Victorian Newsletter*, 94 (Fall 2000), 749–71.

Fielding, Penny, 'Reading Rooms: M. R. James and the Library of Modernity', *Modern Fiction Studies*, 46 (2000), 36–42.

James, M. R., *A Pleasing Terror: The Complete Supernatural Writings*, ed. Christopher Roden and Barbara Roden (Ashcroft, British Columbia, 2001), gathers together all of James's stories and relevant writings, plus many very useful scholarly essays on aspects of his work.

Joshi, S. T., and Pardoe, Rosemary (eds.), *Warnings to the Curious: A Sheaf of Criticism on M. R. James* (New York, 2007), is a collection of essays on James.

Mason, Michael, 'On Not Letting Them Lie: Moral Significance in the Ghost Stories of M. R. James', *Studies in Short Fiction*, 19 (1982), 253–60.

Michalski, Robert, 'The Malice of Inanimate Objects: Exchange in M. R. James's Ghost Stories', *Extrapolation*, 37 (Spring 1996), 46–62.

O'Briain, Helen Conrad, ' "The gates of hell shall not prevail against it": Laudian Ecclesia and Victorian Culture Wars in the Ghost Stories of M. R. James', in O'Briain and Stevens (eds.), *The Ghost Story*, 47–60.

Young, B. W., *The Victorian Eighteenth Century: An Intellectual History* (Oxford, 2000), contains a chapter on James's 'Hanoverian Hauntings'.

No writer on James can ignore the indefatigable work of Rosemary and Darroll Pardoe, editors of the M. R. James newsletter and journal *Ghosts & Scholars*, a mine of notes, observations, and textual archaeology.

On the Ghost Story and the Supernatural

Briggs, Julia, *Night Visitors: The Rise and Fall of the English Ghost Story* (London, 1977).

O'Briain, Helen Conrad, and Stevens, Julie-Anne (eds.), *The Ghost Story from the Middle Ages to the Twentieth Century: A Ghostly Genre* (Dublin, 2010).

Davies, Owen, *The Haunted: A Social History of Ghosts* (London, 2007).

Killeen, Jarlath, *Gothic Literature 1825–1914* (Cardiff, 2009).

Oppenheim, Janet, *The Other World: Spiritualism and Psychical Research in England, 1850–1914* (Cambridge, 1985).

Russell, Jeffrey Burton, *The Devil: Perceptions of Evil from Antiquity to Primitive Christianity* (Ithaca, NY, 1977).

Smith, Andrew, *The Ghost Story 1840–1920: A Cultural History* (Manchester, 2010).

Sullivan, Jack, *Elegant Nightmares: The English Ghost Story from Le Fanu to Blackwood* (Athens, Ohio, 1978).

Westwood, Jennifer, and Simpson, Jacqueline *The Lore of the Land: A Guide to England's Legends from Spring-Heeled Jack to the Witches of Warboys* (London, 2005).

Wolfreys, Julian, *Victorian Hauntings: Spectrality, the Gothic, the Uncanny and Literature* (London, 2001).

A CHRONOLOGY OF M. R. JAMES

Life	*Historical and Cultural Background*
1862 MRJ born in Goodnestone, Kent.	Wilkie Collins, *No Name*; Charles Kingsley, *The Water Babies*.
1865 James family move to Great Livermere, Suffolk.	Rudyard Kipling and W. B. Yeats born.
1873 Enters Temple Grove School.	Death of Sheridan Le Fanu; John Henry Newman, *Idea of a University*.
1876 Enters Eton as King's Scholar.	Alexander Graham Bell patents the telephone; George Eliot, *Daniel Deronda*.
1882 Newcastle Scholar, Eton; enters King's College, Cambridge.	Death of Charles Darwin; Society for Psychical Research (SPR) founded.
1885 Graduates with Firsts in both parts of the Tripos.	H. Rider Haggard, *King Solomon's Mines*; birth of D. H. Lawrence.
1886 Appointed assistant director of Fitzwilliam Museum, Cambridge.	Gladstone prime minister for third time; Thomas Hardy, *The Mayor of Casterbridge*; Haggard, *She*; Robert Louis Stevenson, *Strange Case of Dr Jekyll and Mr Hyde*.
1887 Awarded Fellowship at King's, for dissertation on the Apocalypse of Peter.	Queen Victoria's Golden Jubilee; first appearance of Sherlock Holmes, in Arthur Conan Doyle's *A Study in Scarlet*.
1889 Becomes dean of King's.	
1892 Visits St Bertrand de Comminges and St Michan's church, Dublin.	Gladstone prime minister for fourth time; death of Tennyson.
1893 Appointed director of Fitzwilliam Museum; reads 'Canon Alberic's Scrap-book' and 'Lost Hearts' to Chitchat Society.	
1895 Awarded D.Litt. degree; publishes first MS catalogue; 'Canon Alberic' and 'Lost Hearts' published.	Oscar Wilde trial; Marie Corelli, *The Sorrows of Satan*.
1899 Visits Denmark with James McBryde and Will Stone.	Boer War; Sigmund Freud, *The Interpretation of Dreams*; Conrad, *Heart of Darkness* and *Lord Jim*.

Life	*Historical and Cultural Background*
1900 Tutor of King's; second Danish holiday with McBryde and Stone.	Boxer Rebellion; British Labour Party founded; death of Oscar Wilde.
1901 Visits Sweden.	Death of Queen Victoria and accession of Edward VII; Doyle, *The Hound of the Baskervilles*.
1904 *Ghost Stories of an Antiquary*; death of James McBryde.	Conrad, *Nostromo*; Barrie, *Peter Pan*.
1905 Elected provost of King's; 'The Edwin Drood Syndicate'.	Albert Einstein, Special Theory of Relativity.
1911 *More Ghost Stories of an Antiquary*.	Conrad, *Under Western Eyes*; D. H. Lawrence, *The White Peacock*; Frances Hodgson Burnett, *The Secret Garden*; Albert Einstein, General Theory of Relativity.
1913 Becomes vice-chancellor of Cambridge University.	D. H. Lawrence, *Sons and Lovers*; Sax Rohmer, *The Mystery of Dr Fu-Manchu*; Edgar Rice Burroughs, *Tarzan of the Apes*; Marcel Proust, *Swann's Way*.
1918 Becomes provost of Eton.	First World War ends; Lytton Strachey, *Eminent Victorians*; Oswald Spengler, *The Decline of the West*.
1919 *A Thin Ghost and Others*.	Sigmund Freud, 'The "Uncanny" '; John Maynard Keynes, *The Economic Consequences of the Peace*.
1922 *The Five Jars*.	James Joyce, *Ulysses*; T. S. Eliot, *The Waste Land*; F. W. Murnau, *Nosferatu*; Benjamin Christensen, *Häxän*; Ludwig Wittgenstein, *Tractatus Logico-Philosophicus*; Irish independence and civil war; BBC formed.
1924 *The Apocryphal New Testament*.	Death of V. I. Lenin; Josef Stalin assumes power in Russia; E. M. Forster, *A Passage to India*; Thomas Mann, *The Magic Mountain*.
1925 *Abbeys*; *A Warning to the Curious*.	F. Scott Fitzgerald, *The Great Gatsby*; P. G. Wodehouse, *Carry On, Jeeves*; Virginia Woolf, *Mrs Dalloway*; Franz Kafka, *The Trial*; Adolf Hitler, *Mein Kampf*; Benito Mussolini declares himself dictator of Italy.

Life	*Historical and Cultural Background*
1926 *Eton and King's.*	British General Strike; Francisco Franco declares himself dictator of Spain; birth of Queen Elizabeth II; Ernest Hemingway, *The Sun Also Rises*; John Logie Baird demonstrates television.
1928 Limited edition of *Wailing Well.*	Radclyffe Hall, *The Well of Loneliness*; D. H. Lawrence, *Lady Chatterley's Lover*; H. P. Lovecraft, 'The Call of Cthulhu'; Hermann Hesse, *Steppenwolf*; Walt Disney, *Steamboat Willie.*
1930 Awarded the Order of Merit; *Suffolk and Norfolk.*	Haile Selassie crowned Emperor of Abyssinia; Dashiell Hammett, *The Maltese Falcon*; William Faulkner, *As I Lay Dying.*
1931 *The Collected Ghost Stories of M. R. James.*	Virginia Woolf, *The Waves*; James Whale, *Frankenstein*; Tod Browning, *Dracula.*
1936 MRJ dies on 12 June, at Eton.	Italy annexes Abyssinia; Berlin Olympics; Dylan Thomas, *Twenty-Five Poems*; Daphne du Maurier, *Jamaica Inn*; Aldous Huxley, *Eyeless in Gaza*; William Cameron Menzies, *Things to Come.*

THE GHOST STORIES

CANON ALBERIC'S SCRAP-BOOK

❧❧

S T. BERTRAND DE COMMINGES* is a decayed town on the
spurs of the Pyrenees, not very far from Toulouse, and still nearer
to Bagnères-de-Luchon. It was the site of a bishopric until the
Revolution, and has a cathedral which is visited by a certain number of
tourists. In the spring of 1883 an Englishman arrived at this old-world
place—I can hardly dignify it with the name of city, for there are not a
thousand inhabitants. He was a Cambridge man, who had come specially from Toulouse to see St. Bertrand's Church, and had left two
friends, who were less keen archæologists than himself, in their hotel at
Toulouse, under promise to join him on the following morning. Half
an hour at the church would satisfy *them,* and all three could then pursue their journey in the direction of Auch. But our Englishman had
come early on the day in question, and proposed to himself to fill a
notebook and to use several dozens of plates in the process of describing and photographing every corner of the wonderful church that
dominates the little hill of Comminges. In order to carry out this design
satisfactorily, it was necessary to monopolize the verger of the church
for the day. The verger or sacristan* (I prefer the latter appellation,
inaccurate as it may be) was accordingly sent for by the somewhat
brusque lady who keeps the inn of the Chapeau Rouge; and when he
came, the Englishman found him an unexpectedly interesting object
of study. It was not in the personal appearance of the little, dry, wiz-
ened old man that the interest lay, for he was precisely like dozens of
other church-guardians in France, but in a curious furtive, or rather
hunted and oppressed, air which he had. He was perpetually half
glancing behind him; the muscles of his back and shoulders seemed to
be hunched in a continual nervous contraction, as if he were expecting
every moment to find himself in the clutch of an enemy. The
Englishman hardly knew whether to put him down as a man haunted
by a fixed delusion, or as one oppressed by a guilty conscience, or as an
unbearably henpecked husband. The probabilities, when reckoned up,
certainly pointed to the last idea; but, still, the impression conveyed
was that of a more formidable persecutor even than a termagant wife.

However, the Englishman (let us call him Dennistoun)* was soon too deep in his notebook and too busy with his camera to give more than an occasional glance to the sacristan. Whenever he did look at him, he found him at no great distance, either huddling himself back against the wall or crouching in one of the gorgeous stalls. Dennistoun became rather fidgety after a time. Mingled suspicions that he was keeping the old man from his *déjeuner*, that he was regarded as likely to make away with St. Bertrand's ivory crozier, or with the dusty stuffed crocodile* that hangs over the font, began to torment him.

'Won't you go home?' he said at last; 'I'm quite well able to finish my notes alone; you can lock me in if you like. I shall want at least two hours more here, and it must be cold for you, isn't it?'

'Good heavens!' said the little man, whom the suggestion seemed to throw into a state of unaccountable terror, 'such a thing cannot be thought of for a moment. Leave monsieur alone in the church? No, no; two hours, three hours, all will be the same to me. I have breakfasted, I am not at all cold, with many thanks to monsieur.'

'Very well, my little man,' quoth Dennistoun to himself: 'you have been warned, and you must take the consequences.'

Before the expiration of the two hours, the stalls, the enormous dilapidated organ, the choir-screen of Bishop John de Mauléon,* the remnants of glass and tapestry, and the objects in the treasure-chamber, had been well and truly examined; the sacristan still keeping at Dennistoun's heels, and every now and then whipping round as if he had been stung, when one or other of the strange noises that trouble a large empty building fell on his ear. Curious noises they were sometimes.

'Once,' Dennistoun said to me, 'I could have sworn I heard a thin metallic voice laughing high up in the tower. I darted an inquiring glance at my sacristan. He was white to the lips. "It is he—that is—it is no one; the door is locked," was all he said, and we looked at each other for a full minute.'

Another little incident puzzled Dennistoun a good deal. He was examining a large dark picture that hangs behind the altar, one of a series illustrating the miracles of St. Bertrand. The composition of the picture is wellnigh indecipherable, but there is a Latin legend below, which runs thus:

'Qualiter S. Bertrandus liberavit hominem quem diabolus diu volebat strangulare.' (How St. Bertrand delivered a man whom the Devil long sought to strangle.)*

Dennistoun was turning to the sacristan with a smile and a jocular remark of some sort on his lips, but he was confounded to see the old man on his knees, gazing at the picture with the eye of a suppliant in agony, his hands tightly clasped, and a rain of tears on his cheeks. Dennistoun naturally pretended to have noticed nothing, but the question would not [go] away from him, 'Why should a daub of this kind affect anyone so strongly?' He seemed to himself to be getting some sort of clue to the reason of the strange look that had been puzzling him all the day: the man must be a monomaniac; but what was his monomania?

It was nearly five o'clock; the short day was drawing in, and the church began to fill with shadows, while the curious noises—the muffled footfalls and distant talking voices that had been perceptible all day—seemed, no doubt because of the fading light and the consequently quickened sense of hearing, to become more frequent and insistent.

The sacristan began for the first time to show signs of hurry and impatience. He heaved a sigh of relief when camera and notebook were finally packed up and stowed away, and hurriedly beckoned Dennistoun to the western door of the church, under the tower. It was time to ring the Angelus.* A few pulls at the reluctant rope, and the great bell Bertrande, high in the tower, began to speak, and swung her voice up among the pines and down to the valleys, loud with mountain-streams, calling the dwellers on those lonely hills to remember and repeat the salutation of the angel to her whom he called Blessed among women. With that a profound quiet seemed to fall for the first time that day upon the little town, and Dennistoun and the sacristan went out of the church.

On the doorstep they fell into conversation.

'Monsieur seemed to interest himself in the old choir-books in the sacristy.'

'Undoubtedly. I was going to ask you if there were a library in the town.'

'No, monsieur; perhaps there used to be one belonging to the Chapter, but it is now such a small place——' Here came a strange pause of irresolution, as it seemed; then, with a sort of plunge, he went on: 'But if monsieur is *amateur des vieux livres*,* I have at home something that might interest him. It is not a hundred yards.'

At once all Dennistoun's cherished dreams of finding priceless manuscripts in untrodden corners of France flashed up, to die down again the next moment. It was probably a stupid missal of Plantin's printing, about 1580.* Where was the likelihood that a place so near Toulouse would not have been ransacked long ago by collectors? However, it would be foolish not to go; he would reproach himself for ever after if he refused. So they set off. On the way the curious irresolution and sudden determination of the sacristan recurred to Dennistoun, and he wondered in a shamefaced way whether he was being decoyed into some purlieu to be made away with as a supposed rich Englishman. He contrived, therefore, to begin talking with his guide, and to drag in, in a rather clumsy fashion, the fact that he expected two friends to join him early the next morning. To his surprise, the announcement seemed to relieve the sacristan at once of some of the anxiety that oppressed him.

'That is well,' he said quite brightly—'that is very well. Monsieur will travel in company with his friends; they will be always near him. It is a good thing to travel thus in company—sometimes.'

The last word appeared to be added as an afterthought, and to bring with it a relapse into gloom for the poor little man.

They were soon at the house, which was one rather larger than its neighbours, stone-built, with a shield carved over the door, the shield of Alberic de Mauléon,* a collateral descendant, Dennistoun tells me, of Bishop John de Mauléon. This Alberic was a Canon of Comminges from 1680 to 1701. The upper windows of the mansion were boarded up, and the whole place bore, as does the rest of Comminges, the aspect of decaying age.

Arrived on his doorstep, the sacristan paused a moment.

'Perhaps,' he said, 'perhaps, after all, monsieur has not the time?'

'Not at all—lots of time—nothing to do till tomorrow. Let us see what it is you have got.'

The door was opened at this point, and a face looked out, a face far younger than the sacristan's, but bearing something of the same distressing look: only here it seemed to be the mark, not so much of fear for personal safety as of acute anxiety on behalf of another. Plainly, the owner of the face was the sacristan's daughter; and, but for the expression I have described, she was a handsome girl enough. She brightened up considerably on seeing her father accompanied by an able-bodied stranger. A few remarks passed between father and daughter, of which Dennistoun only caught these words, said by the sacristan, 'He was laughing in the church,' words which were answered only by a look of terror from the girl.

But in another minute they were in the sitting-room of the house, a small, high chamber with a stone floor, full of moving shadows cast by a wood-fire that flickered on a great hearth. Something of the character of an oratory was imparted to it by a tall crucifix, which reached almost to the ceiling on one side; the figure was painted of the natural colours, the cross was black. Under this stood a chest of some age and solidity, and when a lamp had been brought, and chairs set, the sacristan went to this chest, and produced therefrom, with growing excitement and nervousness, as Dennistoun thought, a large book, wrapped in a white cloth, on which cloth a cross was rudely embroidered in red thread. Even before the wrapping had been removed, Dennistoun began to be interested by the size and shape of the volume. 'Too large for a missal,' he thought, 'and not the shape of an antiphoner;* perhaps it may be something good, after all.' The next moment the book was open, and Dennistoun felt that he had at last lit upon something better than good. Before him lay a large folio, bound, perhaps, late in the seventeenth century,* with the arms of Canon Alberic de Mauléon stamped in gold on the sides. There may have been a hundred and fifty leaves of paper in the book, and on almost every one of them was fastened a leaf from an illuminated manuscript. Such a collection Dennistoun had hardly dreamed of in his wildest moments. Here were ten leaves from a copy of Genesis, illustrated with pictures, which could not be later than A.D. 700. Further on was a complete set of pictures from a Psalter,* of English execution, of the very finest kind that the thirteenth century could produce; and, perhaps best of all, there were twenty leaves of uncial writing* in Latin, which, as a few words seen here and there told him at once, must belong to some very early unknown patristic treatise. Could it possibly be a fragment of the copy of Papias 'On the Words of Our Lord,'* which was known to have existed as late as the twelfth century at Nîmes?[1] In any case, his mind was made up; that book must return to Cambridge with him, even if he had to draw the whole of his balance from the bank and stay at St. Bertrand till the money came. He glanced up at the sacristan to see if his face yielded any hint that the book was for sale. The sacristan was pale, and his lips were working.

---

[1] We now know that these leaves did contain a considerable fragment of that work, if not of that actual copy of it.

'If monsieur will turn on to the end,' he said.

So monsieur turned on, meeting new treasures at every rise of a leaf; and at the end of the book he came upon two sheets of paper, of much more recent date than anything he had yet seen, which puzzled him considerably. They must be contemporary, he decided, with the unprincipled Canon Alberic, who had doubtless plundered the Chapter library of St. Bertrand to form this priceless scrap-book. On the first of the paper sheets was a plan, carefully drawn and instantly recognizable by a person who knew the ground, of the south aisle and cloisters of St. Bertrand's. There were curious signs looking like planetary symbols, and a few Hebrew words, in the corners; and in the north-west angle of the cloister was a cross drawn in gold paint.* Below the plan were some lines of writing in Latin, which ran thus:

'Responsa 12^{mi} Dec. 1694. Interrogatum est: Inveniamne? Responsum est: Invenies. Fiamne dives? Fies. Vivamne invidendus? Vives. Moriarne in lecto meo? Ita.' (Answers of the 12th of December, 1694. It was asked: Shall I find it? Answer: Thou shalt. Shall I become rich? Thou wilt. Shall I live an object of envy? Thou wilt. Shall I die in my bed? Thou wilt.)

'A good specimen of the treasure-hunter's record—quite reminds one of Mr. Minor-Canon Quatremain in "Old St. Paul's," '* was Dennistoun's comment, and he turned the leaf.

What he then saw impressed him, as he has often told me, more than he could have conceived any drawing or picture capable of impressing him. And, though the drawing he saw is no longer in existence, there is a photograph of it (which I possess) which fully bears out that statement. The picture in question was a sepia drawing at the end of the seventeenth century, representing, one would say at first sight, a Biblical scene;* for the architecture (the picture represented an interior) and the figures had that semi-classical flavour about them which the artists of two hundred years ago thought appropriate to illustrations of the Bible. On the right was a King on his throne, the throne elevated on twelve steps, a canopy overhead, lions on either side—evidently King Solomon.* He was bending forward with outstretched sceptre, in attitude of command; his face expressed horror and disgust, yet there was in it also the mark of imperious will and confident power. The left half of the picture was the strangest, however. The interest plainly centred there. On the pavement before the throne were grouped four soldiers, surrounding a crouching figure which must be described in a moment. A fifth soldier lay dead on the pavement, his neck distorted, and his eyeballs starting from his head. The four surrounding guards were looking at the King. In their faces the sentiment of horror was intensified; they seemed, in fact, only restrained from flight by their implicit trust in their master. All this terror was plainly excited by the being that crouched in their midst. I entirely despair of conveying by any words the impression which this figure makes upon anyone who looks at it. I recollect once showing the photograph of the drawing to a lecturer on morphology*—a person of, I was going to say, abnormally sane and unimaginative habits of mind. He absolutely refused to be alone for the rest of that evening, and he told me afterwards that for many nights he had not dared to put out his light before going to sleep. However, the main traits of the figure I can at least indicate. At first you saw only a mass of coarse, matted black hair; presently it was seen that this covered a body of fearful thinness, almost a skeleton, but with the muscles standing out like wires. The hands were of a dusky pallor, covered, like the body, with long, coarse hairs, and hideously taloned. The eyes, touched in with a burning yellow, had intensely black pupils, and were fixed upon the throned King with a look of beast-like hate. Imagine one of the awful bird-catching spiders of South America translated into human form, and endowed with intelligence just less than human, and you will have some faint conception of the terror inspired by this appalling effigy. One remark is universally made by those to whom I have shown the picture: 'It was drawn from the life.'

As soon as the first shock of his irresistible fright had subsided, Dennistoun stole a look at his hosts. The sacristan's hands were pressed upon his eyes; his daughter, looking up at the cross on the wall, was telling her beads feverishly.

At last the question was asked, 'Is this book for sale?'

There was the same hesitation, the same plunge of determination that he had noticed before, and then came the welcome answer, 'If monsieur pleases.'

'How much do you ask for it?'

'I will take two hundred and fifty francs.'

This was confounding. Even a collector's conscience is sometimes stirred, and Dennistoun's conscience was tenderer than a collector's.

'My good man!' he said again and again, 'your book is worth far more than two hundred and fifty francs, I assure you—far more.'

But the answer did not vary: 'I will take two hundred and fifty francs, not more.'

There was really no possibility of refusing such a chance. The money was paid, the receipt signed, a glass of wine drunk over the transaction, and then the sacristan seemed to become a new man. He stood upright, he ceased to throw those suspicious glances behind him, he actually laughed or tried to laugh. Dennistoun rose to go.

'I shall have the honour of accompanying monsieur to his hotel?' said the sacristan.

'Oh no, thanks! it isn't a hundred yards. I know the way perfectly, and there is a moon.'

The offer was pressed three or four times, and refused as often.

'Then, monsieur will summon me if—if he finds occasion; he will keep the middle of the road, the sides are so rough.'

'Certainly, certainly,' said Dennistoun, who was impatient to examine his prize by himself; and he stepped out into the passage with his book under his arm.

Here he was met by the daughter; she, it appeared, was anxious to do a little business on her own account; perhaps, like Gehazi,* to 'take somewhat' from the foreigner whom her father had spared.

'A silver crucifix and chain for the neck; monsieur would perhaps be good enough to accept it?'

Well, really, Dennistoun hadn't much use for these things. What did mademoiselle want for it?

'Nothing—nothing in the world. Monsieur is more than welcome to it.'

The tone in which this and much more was said was unmistakably genuine, so that Dennistoun was reduced to profuse thanks, and submitted to have the chain put round his neck. It really seemed as if he had rendered the father and daughter some service which they hardly knew how to repay. As he set off with his book they stood at the door looking after him, and they were still looking when he waved them a last good night from the steps of the Chapeau Rouge.

Dinner was over, and Dennistoun was in his bedroom, shut up alone with his acquisition. The landlady had manifested a particular interest in him since he had told her that he had paid a visit to the sacristan and bought an old book from him. He thought, too, that he had heard a hurried dialogue between her and the said sacristan in the passage outside the *salle à manger*; some words to the effect that 'Pierre and Bertrand would be sleeping in the house' had closed the conversation.

All this time a growing feeling of discomfort had been creeping over him—nervous reaction, perhaps, after the delight of his discovery. Whatever it was, it resulted in a conviction that there was someone behind him, and that he was far more comfortable with his back to the wall. All this, of course, weighed light in the balance as against the obvious value of the collection he had acquired. And now, as I said, he was alone in his bedroom, taking stock of Canon Alberic's treasures, in which every moment revealed something more charming.

'Bless Canon Alberic!' said Dennistoun, who had an inveterate habit of talking to himself. 'I wonder where he is now? Dear me! I wish that landlady would learn to laugh in a more cheering manner; it makes one feel as if there was someone dead in the house. Half a pipe more, did you say? I think perhaps you are right. I wonder what that crucifix is that the young woman insisted on giving me? Last century, I suppose. Yes, probably. It is rather a nuisance of a thing to have round one's neck—just too heavy. Most likely her father has been wearing it for years. I think I might give it a clean up before I put it away.'

He had taken the crucifix off, and laid it on the table, when his attention was caught by an object lying on the red cloth just by his left elbow. Two or three ideas of what it might be flitted through his brain with their own incalculable quickness.

'A penwiper? No, no such thing in the house. A rat? No, too black. A large spider? I trust to goodness not—no. Good God! a hand like the hand in that picture!'

In another infinitesimal flash he had taken it in. Pale, dusky skin, covering nothing but bones and tendons of appalling strength; coarse black hairs, longer than ever grew on a human hand; nails rising from the ends of the fingers and curving sharply down and forward, grey, horny and wrinkled.

He flew out of his chair with deadly, inconceivable terror clutching at his heart. The shape, whose left hand rested on the table, was rising to a standing posture behind his seat, its right hand crooked above his scalp. There was black and tattered drapery about it; the coarse hair covered it as in the drawing. The lower jaw was thin—what can I call it?—shallow, like a beast's; teeth showed behind the black lips; there was no nose; the eyes, of a fiery yellow, against which the pupils showed black and intense, and the exulting hate and thirst to destroy life which shone there, were the most horrifying features in the whole vision. There was intelligence of a kind in them—intelligence beyond that of a beast, below that of a man.

The feelings which this horror stirred in Dennistoun were the intensest physical fear and the most profound mental loathing. What did he do? What could he do? He has never been quite certain what words he said, but he knows that he spoke, that he grasped blindly at the silver crucifix, that he was conscious of a movement towards him on the part of the demon, and that he screamed with the voice of an animal in hideous pain.

Pierre and Bertrand, the two sturdy little servingmen, who rushed in, saw nothing, but felt themselves thrust aside by something that passed out between them, and found Dennistoun in a swoon. They sat up with him that night, and his two friends were at St. Bertrand by nine o'clock next morning. He himself, though still shaken and nervous, was almost himself by that time, and his story found credence with them, though not until they had seen the drawing and talked with the sacristan.

Almost at dawn the little man had come to the inn on some pretence, and had listened with the deepest interest to the story retailed by the landlady. He showed no surprise.

'It is he—it is he! I have seen him myself,' was his only comment; and to all questionings but one reply was vouchsafed: 'Deux fois je l'ai vu; mille fois je l'ai senti.'* He would tell them nothing of the provenance of the book, nor any details of his experiences. 'I shall soon sleep, and my rest will be sweet. Why should you trouble me?' he said.[1]

We shall never know what he or Canon Alberic de Mauléon suffered. At the back of that fateful drawing were some lines of writing which may be supposed to throw light on the situation:

'Contradictio Salomonis cum demonio nocturno.
Albericus de Mauleone delineavit.

[1] He died that summer; his daughter married, and settled at St. Papoul. She never understood the circumstances of her father's 'obsession.'

V. Deus in adiutorium. Ps. Qui habitat.
Sancte Bertrande, demoniorum effugator, intercede pro me miserrimo.
Primum uidi nocte 12^{ml} Dec. 1694: uidebo mox
ultimum. Peccaui et passus sum, plura adhuc
passurus. Dec. 29, 1701.'[1]

I have never quite understood what was Dennistoun's view of the
events I have narrated. He quoted to me once a text from Ecclesiasticus:*
'Some spirits there be that are created for vengeance, and in their
fury lay on sore strokes.' On another occasion he said: 'Isaiah* was a
very sensible man; doesn't he say something about night monsters
living in the ruins of Babylon? These things are rather beyond us at
present.'

Another confidence of his impressed me rather, and I sympathized
with it. We had been, last year, to Comminges, to see Canon Alberic's
tomb. It is a great marble erection with an effigy of the Canon in a
large wig and soutane, and an elaborate eulogy of his learning
below. I saw Dennistoun talking for some time with the Vicar of
St. Bertrand's, and as we drove away he said to me: 'I hope it isn't
wrong: you know I am a Presbyterian—but I—I believe there will be
"saying of Mass and singing of dirges" for Alberic de Mauléon's
rest.' Then he added, with a touch of the Northern British in his
tone, 'I had no notion they came so dear.'

The book is in the Wentworth Collection at Cambridge.* The
drawing was photographed and then burnt by Dennistoun on the day
when he left Comminges on the occasion of his first visit.

---

[1] *I.e.*, The Dispute of Solomon with a demon of the night. Drawn by Alberic de
Mauléon. *Versicle.** O Lord, make haste to help me. *Psalm.* Whoso dwelleth (xci.).*

Saint Bertrand, who puttest devils to flight, pray for me most unhappy. I saw it first on
the night of Dec. 12, 1694: soon I shall see it for the last time. I have sinned and
suffered, and have more to suffer yet. Dec. 29, 1701.

The 'Gallia Christiana'* gives the date of the Canon's death as December 31, 1701, 'in
bed, of a sudden seizure.' Details of this kind are not common in the great work of the
Sammarthani.*

LOST HEARTS

❦

I T was, as far as I can ascertain, in September of the year 1811 that a post-chaise drew up before the door of Aswarby Hall, in the heart of Lincolnshire.* The little boy who was the only passenger in the chaise, and who jumped out as soon as it had stopped, looked about him with the keenest curiosity during the short interval that elapsed between the ringing of the bell and the opening of the hall door. He saw a tall, square, red-brick house, built in the reign of Anne; a stone-pillared porch had been added in the purer classical style of 1790; the windows of the house were many, tall and narrow, with small panes and thick white woodwork. A pediment, pierced with a round window, crowned the front. There were wings to right and left, connected by curious glazed galleries, supported by colonnades, with the central block. These wings plainly contained the stables and offices of the house. Each was surmounted by an ornamental cupola with a gilded vane.

An evening light shone on the building, making the window-panes glow like so many fires. Away from the Hall in front stretched a flat park studded with oaks and fringed with firs, which stood out against the sky. The clock in the church-tower, buried in trees on the edge of the park, only its golden weather-cock catching the light, was striking six, and the sound came gently beating down the wind. It was altogether a pleasant impression, though tinged with the sort of melancholy appropriate to an evening in early autumn, that was conveyed to the mind of the boy who was standing in the porch waiting for the door to open to him.

The post-chaise had brought him from Warwickshire, where, some six months before, he had been left an orphan. Now, owing to the generous offer of his elderly cousin, Mr. Abney, he had come to live at Aswarby. The offer was unexpected, because all who knew anything of Mr. Abney looked upon him as a somewhat austere recluse, into whose steady-going household the advent of a small boy would import a new and, it seemed, incongruous element. The truth is that very little was known of Mr. Abney's pursuits or temper. The

Professor of Greek at Cambridge had been heard to say that no one knew more of the religious beliefs of the later pagans than did the owner of Aswarby. Certainly his library contained all the then available books bearing on the Mysteries,* the Orphic poems,* the worship of Mithras,* and the Neo-Platonists.* In the marble-paved hall stood a fine group of Mithras slaying a bull, which had been imported from the Levant at great expense by the owner. He had contributed a description of it to the *Gentleman's Magazine*, and he had written a remarkable series of articles in the *Critical Museum** on the superstitions of the Romans of the Lower Empire. He was looked upon, in fine, as a man wrapped up in his books, and it was a matter of great surprise among his neighbours that he should even have heard of his orphan cousin, Stephen Elliott, much more that he should have volunteered to make him an inmate of Aswarby Hall.

Whatever may have been expected by his neighbours, it is certain that Mr. Abney—the tall, the thin, the austere—seemed inclined to give his young cousin a kindly reception. The moment the front door was opened he darted out of his study, rubbing his hands with delight.

'How are you, my boy?—how are you? How old are you?' said he—'that is, you are not too much tired, I hope, by your journey to eat your supper?'

'No, thank you, sir,' said Master Elliott; 'I am pretty well.'

'That's a good lad,' said Mr. Abney. 'And how old are you, my boy?'

It seemed a little odd that he should have asked the question twice in the first two minutes of their acquaintance.

'I'm twelve years old next birthday, sir,' said Stephen.

'And when is your birthday, my dear boy? Eleventh of September, eh? That's well—that's very well. Nearly a year hence, isn't it? I like—ha, ha!—I like to get these things down in my book. Sure it's twelve? Certain?'

'Yes, quite sure, sir.'

'Well, well! Take him to Mrs. Bunch's room, Parkes, and let him have his tea—supper—whatever it is.'

'Yes, sir,' answered the staid Mr. Parkes; and conducted Stephen to the lower regions.

Mrs. Bunch was the most comfortable and human person whom Stephen had as yet met in Aswarby. She made him completely at home; they were great friends in a quarter of an hour: and great friends they remained. Mrs. Bunch had been born in the neighbourhood some fifty-five years before the date of Stephen's arrival, and her residence at the Hall was of twenty years' standing. Consequently, if anyone knew the ins and outs of the house and the district, Mrs. Bunch knew them; and she was by no means disinclined to communicate her information.

Certainly there were plenty of things about the Hall and the Hall gardens which Stephen, who was of an adventurous and inquiring turn, was anxious to have explained to him. 'Who built the temple at the end of the laurel walk? Who was the old man whose picture hung on the staircase, sitting at a table, with a skull under his hand?' These and many similar points were cleared up by the resources of Mrs. Bunch's powerful intellect. There were others, however, of which the explanations furnished were less satisfactory.

One November evening Stephen was sitting by the fire in the housekeeper's room reflecting on his surroundings.

'Is Mr. Abney a good man, and will he go to heaven?' he suddenly asked, with the peculiar confidence which children possess in the ability of their elders to settle these questions, the decision of which is believed to be reserved for other tribunals.

'Good?—bless the child!' said Mrs. Bunch. 'Master's as kind a soul as ever I see! Didn't I never tell you of the little boy as he took in out of the street, as you may say, this seven years back? and the little girl, two years after I first come here?'

'No. Do tell me all about them, Mrs. Bunch—now this minute!'

'Well,' said Mrs. Bunch, 'the little girl I don't seem to recollect so much about. I know master brought her back with him from his walk one day, and give orders to Mrs. Ellis, as was housekeeper then, as she should be took every care with. And the pore child hadn't no one belonging to her—she told me so her own self—and here she lived with us a matter of three weeks it might be; and then, whether she were somethink of a gipsy in her blood or what not, but one morning she out of her bed afore any of us had opened a eye, and neither track nor yet trace of her have I set eyes on since. Master was wonderful put about, and had all the ponds dragged; but it's my belief she was had away by them gipsies, for there was singing round the house for as much as an hour the night she went, and Parkes, he declare as he heard them a-calling in the woods all that afternoon. Dear, dear! a hodd child she was, so silent in her ways and all, but I was wonderful taken up with her, so domesticated she was—surprising.'

'And what about the little boy?' said Stephen.

'Ah, that pore boy!' sighed Mrs. Bunch. 'He were a foreigner—Jevanny he called hisself—and he come a-tweaking his 'urdy-gurdy* round and about the drive one winter day, and master 'ad him in that minute, and ast all about where he came from, and how old he was, and how he made his way, and where was his relatives, and all as kind as heart could wish. But it went the same way with him. They're a hunruly lot, them foreign nations, I do suppose, and he was off one fine morning just the same as the girl. Why he went and what he done was our question for as much as a year after; for he never took his 'urdy-gurdy, and there it lays on the shelf.'

The remainder of the evening was spent by Stephen in miscellaneous cross-examination of Mrs. Bunch and in efforts to extract a tune from the hurdy-gurdy.

That night he had a curious dream. At the end of the passage at the top of the house, in which his bedroom was situated, there was an old disused bathroom. It was kept locked, but the upper half of the door was glazed, and, since the muslin curtains which used to hang there had long been gone, you could look in and see the lead-lined bath affixed to the wall on the right hand, with its head towards the window.

On the night of which I am speaking, Stephen Elliott found himself, as he thought, looking through the glazed door. The moon was shining through the window, and he was gazing at a figure which lay in the bath.

His description of what he saw reminds me of what I once beheld myself in the famous vaults of St. Michan's Church in Dublin,* which possess the horrid property of preserving corpses from decay for centuries. A figure inexpressibly thin and pathetic, of a dusty leaden colour, enveloped in a shroud-like garment, the thin lips crooked into a faint and dreadful smile, the hands pressed tightly over the region of the heart.

As he looked upon it, a distant, almost inaudible moan seemed to issue from its lips, and the arms began to stir. The terror of the sight forced Stephen backwards, and he awoke to the fact that he was indeed standing on the cold boarded floor of the passage in the full light of the moon. With a courage which I do not think can be common among boys of his age, he went to the door of the bathroom to ascertain if the figure of his dream were really there. It was not, and he went back to bed.

Mrs. Bunch was much impressed next morning by his story, and went so far as to replace the muslin curtain over the glazed door of the bathroom. Mr. Abney, moreover, to whom he confided his experiences at breakfast, was greatly interested, and made notes of the matter in what he called 'his book.'

The spring equinox was approaching, as Mr. Abney frequently reminded his cousin, adding that this had been always considered by the ancients to be a critical time for the young: that Stephen would do well to take care of himself, and to shut his bedroom window at night; and that Censorinus* had some valuable remarks on the subject. Two incidents that occurred about this time made an impression upon Stephen's mind.

The first was after an unusually uneasy and oppressed night that he had passed—though he could not recall any particular dream that he had had.

The following evening Mrs. Bunch was occupying herself in mending his nightgown.

'Gracious me, Master Stephen!' she broke forth rather irritably, 'how do you manage to tear your nightdress all to flinders this way? Look here, sir, what trouble you do give to poor servants that have to darn and mend after you!'

There was indeed a most destructive and apparently wanton series of slits or scorings in the garment, which would undoubtedly require a skilful needle to make good. They were confined to the left side of the chest—long, parallel slits, about six inches in length, some of them not quite piercing the texture of the linen. Stephen could only express his entire ignorance of their origin: he was sure they were not there the night before.

'But,' he said, 'Mrs. Bunch, they are just the same as the scratches on the outside of my bedroom door; and I'm sure I never had anything to do with making *them*.'

Mrs. Bunch gazed at him open-mouthed, then snatched up a candle, departed hastily from the room, and was heard making her way upstairs. In a few minutes she came down.

'Well,' she said, 'Master Stephen, it's a funny thing to me how them marks and scratches can 'a' come there—too high up for any cat or dog to 'ave made 'em, much less a rat: for all the world like a Chinaman's finger-nails, as my uncle in the tea-trade used to tell us of when we was girls together. I wouldn't say nothing to master, not if I was you, Master Stephen, my dear; and just turn the key of the door when you go to your bed.'

'I always do, Mrs. Bunch, as soon as I've said my prayers.'

'Ah, that's a good child: always say your prayers, and then no one can't hurt you.'

Herewith Mrs. Bunch addressed herself to mending the injured nightgown, with intervals of meditation, until bed-time. This was on a Friday night in March, 1812.

On the following evening the usual duet of Stephen and Mrs. Bunch was augmented by the sudden arrival of Mr. Parkes, the butler, who as a rule kept himself rather *to* himself in his own pantry. He did not see that Stephen was there: he was, moreover, flustered, and less slow of speech than was his wont.

'Master may get up his own wine, if he likes, of an evening,' was his first remark. 'Either I do it in the daytime or not at all, Mrs. Bunch. I don't know what it may be: very like it's the rats, or the wind got into the cellars; but I'm not so young as I was, and I can't go through with it as I have done.'

'Well, Mr. Parkes, you know it is a surprising place for the rats, is the Hall.'

'I'm not denying that, Mrs. Bunch; and, to be sure, many a time I've heard the tale from the men in the shipyards about the rat that could speak.* I never laid no confidence in that before; but to-night, if I'd demeaned myself to lay my ear to the door of the further bin, I could pretty much have heard what they was saying.'

'Oh, there, Mr. Parkes, I've no patience with your fancies! Rats talking in the wine-cellar indeed!'

'Well, Mrs. Bunch, I've no wish to argue with you: all I say is, if you choose to go to the far bin, and lay your ear to the door, you may prove my words this minute.'

'What nonsense you do talk, Mr. Parkes—not fit for children to listen to! Why, you'll be frightening Master Stephen there out of his wits.'

'What! Master Stephen?' said Parkes, awaking to the consciousness of the boy's presence. 'Master Stephen knows well enough when I'm a-playing a joke with you, Mrs. Bunch.'

In fact, Master Stephen knew much too well to suppose that Mr. Parkes had in the first instance intended a joke. He was interested, not altogether pleasantly, in the situation; but all his questions were unsuccessful in inducing the butler to give any more detailed account of his experiences in the wine-cellar.

We have now arrived at March 24, 1812.* It was a day of curious experiences for Stephen: a windy, noisy day, which filled the house and the gardens with a restless impression. As Stephen stood by the fence of the grounds, and looked out into the park, he felt as if an endless procession of unseen people were sweeping past him on the wind, borne on resistlessly and aimlessly, vainly striving to stop themselves, to catch at something that might arrest their flight and bring them once again into contact with the living world of which they had formed a part. After luncheon that day Mr. Abney said:

'Stephen, my boy, do you think you could manage to come to me to-night as late as eleven o'clock in my study? I shall be busy until that time, and I wish to show you something connected with your future life which it is most important that you should know. You are not to mention this matter to Mrs. Bunch nor to anyone else in the house; and you had better go to your room at the usual time.'

Here was a new excitement added to life: Stephen eagerly grasped at the opportunity of sitting up till eleven o'clock. He looked in at the library door on his way upstairs that evening, and saw a brazier, which he had often noticed in the corner of the room, moved out before the fire; an old silver-gilt cup stood on the table, filled with red wine, and some written sheets of paper lay near it. Mr. Abney was sprinkling some incense on the brazier from a round silver box as Stephen passed, but did not seem to notice his step.

The wind had fallen, and there was a still night and a full moon. At about ten o'clock Stephen was standing at the open window of his bedroom, looking out over the country. Still as the night was, the mysterious population of the distant moonlit woods was not yet lulled to rest. From time to time strange cries as of lost and despairing wanderers sounded from across the mere. They might be the notes of owls or water-birds, yet they did not quite resemble either sound. Were not they coming nearer? Now they sounded from the nearer side of the water, and in a few moments they seemed to be floating about among the shrubberies. Then they ceased; but just as Stephen was thinking of shutting the window and resuming his reading of *Robinson Crusoe*, he caught sight of two figures standing on the gravelled terrace that ran along the garden side of the Hall—the figures of a boy and girl, as it seemed; they stood side by side, looking up at the windows. Something in the form of the girl recalled irresistibly his dream of the figure in the bath. The boy inspired him with more acute fear.

Whilst the girl stood still, half smiling, with her hands clasped over her heart, the boy, a thin shape, with black hair and ragged clothing, raised his arms in the air with an appearance of menace and of unappeasable hunger and longing. The moon shone upon his almost transparent hands, and Stephen saw that the nails were fearfully long and that the light shone through them. As he stood with his arms thus raised, he disclosed a terrifying spectacle. On the left side of his chest there opened a black and gaping rent; and there fell upon Stephen's brain, rather than upon his ear, the impression of one of those hungry and desolate cries that he had heard resounding over the woods of Aswarby all that evening. In another moment this dreadful pair had moved swiftly and noiselessly over the dry gravel, and he saw them no more.

Inexpressibly frightened as he was, he determined to take his candle and go down to Mr. Abney's study, for the hour appointed for their meeting was near at hand. The study or library opened out of the front hall on one side, and Stephen, urged on by his terrors, did not take long in getting there. To effect an entrance was not so easy. The door was not locked, he felt sure, for the key was on the outside of it as usual. His repeated knocks produced no answer. Mr. Abney was engaged: he was speaking. What! why did he try to cry out? and why was the cry choked in his throat? Had he, too, seen the mysterious children? But now everything was quiet, and the door yielded to Stephen's terrified and frantic pushing.

*   *   *   *   *

On the table in Mr. Abney's study certain papers were found which explained the situation to Stephen Elliott when he was of an age to understand them. The most important sentences were as follows:

'It was a belief very strongly and generally held by the ancients—of whose wisdom in these matters I have had such experience as induces me to place confidence in their assertions—that by enacting certain processes, which to us moderns have something of a barbaric complexion, a very remarkable enlightenment of the spiritual faculties in man may be attained: that, for example, by absorbing the personalities of a certain number of his fellow-creatures, an individual may gain a complete ascendancy over those orders of spiritual beings which control the elemental forces of our universe.

'It is recorded of Simon Magus that he was able to fly in the air, to become invisible, or to assume any form he pleased, by the agency of the soul of a boy whom, to use the libellous phrase employed by the author of the *Clementine Recognitions*,* he had "murdered." I find it set down, moreover, with considerable detail in the writings of Hermes Trismegistus,* that similar happy results may be produced by the absorption of the hearts of not less than three human beings below the age of twelve years.* To the testing of the truth of this receipt I have devoted the greater part of the last twenty years, selecting as the *corpora vilia** of my experiment such persons as could conveniently be removed without occasioning a sensible gap in society. The first step I effected by the removal of one Phœbe Stanley, a girl of gipsy extraction, on March 24, 1792. The second, by the removal of a wandering Italian lad, named Giovanni Paoli, on the night of March 23, 1805. The final "victim"—to employ a word repugnant in the highest degree to my feelings—must be my cousin, Stephen Elliott. His day must be this March 24, 1812.

'The best means of effecting the required absorption is to remove the heart from the *living* subject, to reduce it to ashes, and to mingle them with about a pint of some red wine, preferably port. The remains of the first two subjects, at least, it will be well to conceal:* a disused bathroom or wine-cellar will be found convenient for such a purpose. Some annoyance may be experienced from the psychic portion of the subjects, which popular language dignifies with the name of ghosts.* But the man of philosophic temperament—to whom alone the experiment is appropriate—will be little prone to attach importance to the feeble efforts of these beings to wreak their vengeance on him. I contemplate with the liveliest satisfaction the enlarged and emancipated existence which the experiment, if successful, will confer on me; not only placing me beyond the reach of human justice (so-called), but eliminating to a great extent the prospect of death itself.'

Mr. Abney was found in his chair, his head thrown back, his face stamped with an expression of rage, fright, and mortal pain. In his left side was a terrible lacerated wound, exposing the heart. There was no blood on his hands, and a long knife that lay on the table was perfectly clean. A savage wild-cat might have inflicted the injuries. The window of the study was open, and it was the opinion of the coroner that Mr. Abney had met his death by the agency of some wild creature. But Stephen Elliott's study of the papers I have quoted led him to a very different conclusion.

THE MEZZOTINT

꒰ꉂ꒱

S OME time ago I believe I had the pleasure of telling you the story
of an adventure which happened to a friend of mine by the name
of Dennistoun,* during his pursuit of objects of art for the museum
at Cambridge.

He did not publish his experiences very widely upon his return to
England; but they could not fail to become known to a good many of
his friends, and among others to the gentleman who at that time presided over an art museum at another University.* It was to be expected
that the story should make a considerable impression on the mind of a
man whose vocation lay in lines similar to Dennistoun's, and that he
should be eager to catch at any explanation of the matter which tended
to make it seem improbable that he should ever be called upon to deal
with so agitating an emergency. It was, indeed, somewhat consoling to
him to reflect that he was not expected to acquire ancient MSS. for
his institution; that was the business of the Shelburnian Library.* The
authorities of that might, if they pleased, ransack obscure corners of
the Continent for such matters. He was glad to be obliged at the
moment to confine his attention to enlarging the already unsurpassed
collection of English topographical drawings and engravings possessed by his museum. Yet, as it turned out, even a department so
homely and familiar as this may have its dark corners, and to one of
these Mr. Williams was unexpectedly introduced.

Those who have taken even the most limited interest in the acquisition of topographical pictures are aware that there is one London
dealer whose aid is indispensable to their researches. Mr. J. W.
Britnell* publishes at short intervals very admirable catalogues of a
large and constantly changing stock of engravings, plans, and old
sketches of mansions, churches, and towns in England and
Wales. These catalogues were, of course, the ABC of his subject to
Mr. Williams: but as his museum already contained an enormous
accumulation of topographical pictures, he was a regular, rather than
a copious, buyer; and he rather looked to Mr. Britnell to fill up gaps
in the rank and file of his collection than to supply him with rarities.

Now, in February of last year there appeared upon Mr. Williams's desk at the museum a catalogue from Mr. Britnell's emporium, and accompanying it was a typewritten communication from the dealer himself. This latter ran as follows:

DEAR SIR,—
We beg to call your attention to No. 978 in our accompanying catalogue, which we shall be glad to send on approval.
Yours faithfully,
J. W. BRITNELL.

To turn to No. 978 in the accompanying catalogue was with Mr. Williams (as he observed to himself) the work of a moment, and in the place indicated he found the following entry:

'978.—*Unknown*. Interesting mezzotint:* View of a manor-house, early part of the century. 15 by 10 inches; black frame. £2 2s.'

It was not specially exciting, and the price seemed high. However, as Mr. Britnell, who knew his business and his customer, seemed to set store by it, Mr. Williams wrote a postcard asking for the article to be sent on approval, along with some other engravings and sketches which appeared in the same catalogue. And so he passed without much excitement of anticipation to the ordinary labours of the day.

A parcel of any kind always arrives a day later than you expect it, and that of Mr. Britnell proved, as I believe the right phrase goes, no exception to the rule. It was delivered at the museum by the afternoon post of Saturday, after Mr. Williams had left his work, and it was accordingly brought round to his rooms in college by the attendant, in order that he might not have to wait over Sunday before looking through it and returning such of the contents as he did not propose to keep. And here he found it when he came in to tea, with a friend.

The only item with which I am concerned was the rather large, black-framed mezzotint of which I have already quoted the short description given in Mr. Britnell's catalogue. Some more details of it will have to be given, though I cannot hope to put before you the look of the picture as clearly as it is present to my own eye. Very nearly the exact duplicate of it may be seen in a good many old inn parlours, or in the passages of undisturbed country mansions at the present moment. It was a rather indifferent mezzotint, and an indifferent mezzotint is, perhaps, the worst form of engraving known. It

presented a full-face view of a not very large manor-house of the last
century, with three rows of plain sashed windows with rusticated
masonry about them, a parapet with balls or vases at the angles, and a
small portico in the centre. On either side were trees, and in front a
considerable expanse of lawn. The legend 'A. W. F. sculpsit'* was
engraved on the narrow margin; and there was no further inscription.
The whole thing gave the impression that it was the work of an amateur. What in the world Mr. Britnell could mean by affixing the price
of £2 2s. to such an object was more than Mr. Williams could imagine. He turned it over with a good deal of contempt; upon the back
was a paper label, the left-hand half of which had been torn off. All
that remained were the ends of two lines of writing: the first had the
letters —*ngley Hall*; the second, —*ssex*.*

It would, perhaps, be just worth while to identify the place represented, which he could easily do with the help of a gazetteer, and then
he would send it back to Mr. Britnell, with some remarks reflecting
upon the judgment of that gentleman.

He lighted the candles, for it was now dark, made the tea, and supplied the friend with whom he had been playing golf (for I believe the
authorities of the University I write of indulge in that pursuit by way
of relaxation); and tea was taken to the accompaniment of a discussion
which golfing persons can imagine for themselves, but which the con-
scientious writer has no right to inflict upon any non-golfing persons.

The conclusion arrived at was that certain strokes might have been
better, and that in certain emergencies neither player had experienced that amount of luck which a human being has a right to expect.
It was now that the friend—let us call him Professor Binks*—took
up the framed engraving, and said:

'What's this place, Williams?'

'Just what I am going to try to find out,' said Williams, going to the
shelf for a gazetteer. 'Look at the back. Somethingley Hall, either in
Sussex or Essex. Half the name's gone, you see. You don't happen to
know it, I suppose?'

'It's from that man Britnell, I suppose, isn't it?' said Binks. 'Is it for
the museum?'

'Well, I think I should buy it if the price was five shillings,' said
Williams; 'but for some unearthly reason he wants two guineas for it.
I can't conceive why. It's a wretched engraving, and there aren't even
any figures to give it life.'

'It's not worth two guineas, I should think,' said Binks; 'but I don't think it's so badly done. The moonlight seems rather good to me; and I should have thought there *were* figures, or at least a figure, just on the edge in front.'

'Let's look,' said Williams. 'Well, it's true the light is rather cleverly given. Where's your figure? Oh yes! Just the head, in the very front of the picture.'

And indeed there was—hardly more than a black blot on the extreme edge of the engraving—the head of a man or woman, a good deal muffled up, the back turned to the spectator, and looking towards the house.

Williams had not noticed it before.

'Still,' he said, 'though it's a cleverer thing than I thought, I can't spend two guineas of museum money on a picture of a place I don't know.'

Professor Binks had his work to do, and soon went; and very nearly up to Hall time Williams was engaged in a vain attempt to identify the subject of his picture. 'If the vowel before the *ng* had only been left, it would have been easy enough,' he thought; 'but as it is, the name may be anything from Guestingley to Langley, and there are many more names ending like this than I thought; and this rotten book has no index of terminations.'

Hall in Mr. Williams's college was at seven. It need not be dwelt upon; the less so as he met there colleagues who had been playing golf during the afternoon, and words with which we have no concern were freely bandied across the table—merely golfing words, I would hasten to explain.

I suppose an hour or more to have been spent in what is called common-room after dinner. Later in the evening some few retired to Williams's rooms, and I have little doubt that whist was played and tobacco smoked. During a lull in these operations Williams picked up the mezzotint from the table without looking at it, and handed it to a person mildly interested in art, telling him where it had come from, and the other particulars which we already know.

The gentleman took it carelessly, looked at it, then said, in a tone of some interest:

'It's really a very good piece of work, Williams; it has quite a feeling of the romantic period. The light is admirably managed, it seems to me, and the figure, though it's rather too grotesque, is somehow very impressive.'

'Yes, isn't it?' said Williams, who was just then busy giving whisky-and-soda to others of the company, and was unable to come across the room to look at the view again.

It was by this time rather late in the evening, and the visitors were on the move. After they went Williams was obliged to write a letter or two and clear up some odd bits of work. At last, some time past midnight, he was disposed to turn in, and he put out his lamp after lighting his bedroom candle. The picture lay face upwards on the table where the last man who looked at it had put it, and it caught his eye as he turned the lamp down. What he saw made him very nearly drop the candle on the floor, and he declares now that if he had been left in the dark at that moment he would have had a fit. But, as that did not happen, he was able to put down the light on the table and take a good look at the picture. It was indubitable—rankly impossible, no doubt, but absolutely certain. In the middle of the lawn in front of the unknown house there was a figure where no figure had been at five o'clock that afternoon. It was crawling on all-fours towards the house, and it was muffled in a strange black garment with a white cross on the back.

I do not know what is the ideal course to pursue in a situation of this kind. I can only tell you what Mr. Williams did. He took the picture by one corner and carried it across the passage to a second set of rooms which he possessed. There he locked it up in a drawer, sported the doors of both sets of rooms,* and retired to bed; but first he wrote out and signed an account of the extraordinary change which the picture had undergone since it had come into his possession.

Sleep visited him rather late; but it was consoling to reflect that the behaviour of the picture did not depend upon his own unsupported testimony. Evidently the man who had looked at it the night before had seen something of the same kind as he had, otherwise he might have been tempted to think that something gravely wrong was happening either to his eyes or his mind. This possibility being fortunately precluded, two matters awaited him on the morrow. He must take stock of the picture very carefully, and call in a witness for the purpose, and he must make a determined effort to ascertain what house it was that was represented. He would therefore ask his neighbour Nisbet to breakfast with him, and he would subsequently spend a morning over the gazetteer.

Nisbet was disengaged, and arrived about 9.30. His host was not quite dressed, I am sorry to say, even at this late hour. During breakfast nothing was said about the mezzotint by Williams, save that he had a picture on which he wished for Nisbet's opinion. But those who are familiar with University life can picture for themselves the wide and delightful range of subjects over which the conversation of two Fellows of Canterbury College* is likely to extend during a Sunday morning breakfast. Hardly a topic was left unchallenged, from golf to lawn-tennis. Yet I am bound to say that Williams was rather distraught; for his interest naturally centred in that very strange picture which was now reposing, face downwards, in the drawer in the room opposite.

The morning pipe was at last lighted, and the moment had arrived for which he looked. With very considerable—almost tremulous—excitement, he ran across, unlocked the drawer, and, extracting the picture—still face downwards—ran back, and put it into Nisbet's hands.

'Now,' he said, 'Nisbet, I want you to tell me exactly what you see in that picture. Describe it, if you don't mind, rather minutely. I'll tell you why afterwards.'

'Well,' said Nisbet, 'I have here a view of a country-house—English, I presume—by moonlight.'

'Moonlight? You're sure of that?'

'Certainly. The moon appears to be on the wane, if you wish for details, and there are clouds in the sky.'

'All right. Go on. I'll swear,' added Williams in an aside, 'there was no moon when I saw it first.'

'Well, there's not much more to be said,' Nisbet continued. 'The house has one—two—three rows of windows, five in each row, except at the bottom, where there's a porch instead of the middle one, and——'

'But what about figures?' said Williams, with marked interest.

'There aren't any,' said Nisbet; 'but——'

'What! No figure on the grass in front?'

'Not a thing.'

'You'll swear to that?'

'Certainly I will. But there's just one other thing.'

'What?'

'Why, one of the windows on the ground-floor—left of the door—is open.'

'Is it really? My goodness! he must have got in,' said Williams, with great excitement; and he hurried to the back of the sofa on which Nisbet was sitting, and, catching the picture from him, verified the matter for himself.

It was quite true. There was no figure, and there was the open window. Williams, after a moment of speechless surprise, went to the writing-table and scribbled for a short time. Then he brought two papers to Nisbet, and asked him first to sign one—it was his own description of the picture, which you have just heard—and then to read the other which was Williams's statement written the night before.

'What can it all mean?' said Nisbet.

'Exactly,' said Williams. 'Well, one thing I must do—or three things, now I think of it. I must find out from Garwood'*—this was his last night's visitor—'what he saw, and then I must get the thing photographed before it goes further, and then I must find out what the place is.'

'I can do the photographing myself,' said Nisbet, 'and I will. But, you know, it looks very much as if we were assisting at the working out of a tragedy somewhere. The question is, Has it happened already, or is it going to come off? You must find out what the place is. Yes,' he said, looking at the picture again, 'I expect you're right: he has got in. And if I don't mistake there'll be the devil to pay in one of the rooms upstairs.'

'I'll tell you what,' said Williams: 'I'll take the picture across to old Green' (this was the senior Fellow of the College, who had been Bursar for many years). 'It's quite likely he'll know it. We have property in Essex and Sussex, and he must have been over the two counties a lot in his time.'

'Quite likely he will,' said Nisbet; 'but just let me take my photograph first. But look here, I rather think Green isn't up to-day. He wasn't in Hall last night, and I think I heard him say he was going down for the Sunday.'

'That's true, too,' said Williams; 'I know he's gone to Brighton. Well, if you'll photograph it now, I'll go across to Garwood and get his statement, and you keep an eye on it while I'm gone. I'm beginning to think two guineas is not a very exorbitant price for it now.'

In a short time he had returned, and brought Mr. Garwood with him. Garwood's statement was to the effect that the figure, when he had seen it, was clear of the edge of the picture, but had not got far across the lawn. He remembered a white mark on the back of its drapery, but could not have been sure it was a cross. A document to this effect was then drawn up and signed, and Nisbet proceeded to photograph the picture.

'Now what do you mean to do?' he said. 'Are you going to sit and watch it all day?'

'Well, no, I think not,' said Williams. 'I rather imagine we're meant to see the whole thing. You see, between the time I saw it last night and this morning there was time for lots of things to happen, but the creature only got into the house. It could easily have got through its business in the time and gone to its own place again; but the fact of the window being open, I think, must mean that it's in there now. So I feel quite easy about leaving it. And, besides, I have a kind of idea that it wouldn't change much, if at all, in the daytime. We might go out for a walk this afternoon, and come in to tea, or whenever it gets dark. I shall leave it out on the table here, and sport the door. My skip* can get in, but no one else.'

The three agreed that this would be a good plan; and, further, that if they spent the afternoon together they would be less likely to talk about the business to other people; for any rumour of such a transaction as was going on would bring the whole of the Phasmatological Society* about their ears.

We may give them a respite until five o'clock.

At or near that hour the three were entering Williams's staircase. They were at first slightly annoyed to see that the door of his rooms was unsported; but in a moment it was remembered that on Sunday the skips came for orders an hour or so earlier than on week-days. However, a surprise was awaiting them. The first thing they saw was the picture leaning up against a pile of books on the table, as it had been left, and the next thing was Williams's skip, seated on a chair opposite, gazing at it with undisguised horror. How was this? Mr. Filcher (the name is not my own invention) was a servant of considerable standing, and set the standard of etiquette to all his own college and to several neighbouring ones, and nothing could be more alien to his practice than to be found sitting on his master's chair, or appearing to take any particular notice of his master's furniture or pictures. Indeed, he seemed to feel this himself. He started violently when the three men came into the room, and got up with a marked effort. Then he said:

'I ask your pardon, sir, for taking such a freedom as to set down.'

'Not at all, Robert,' interposed Mr. Williams. 'I was meaning to ask you some time what you thought of that picture.'

'Well, sir, of course I don't set up my opinion again yours, but it ain't the pictur I should 'ang where my little girl could see it, sir.'

'Wouldn't you, Robert? Why not?'

'No, sir. Why, the pore child, I recollect once she see a Door Bible,* with pictures not 'alf what that is, and we 'ad to set up with her three or four nights afterwards, if you'll believe me; and if she was to ketch a sight of this skelinton here, or whatever it is, carrying off the pore baby, she would be in a taking. You know 'ow it is with children; 'ow nervish they git with a little thing and all. But what I should say, it don't seem a right picture to be laying about, sir, not where anyone that's liable to be startled could come on it. Should you be wanting anything this evening, sir? Thank you, sir.'

With these words the excellent man went to continue the round of his masters, and you may be sure the gentlemen whom he left lost no time in gathering round the engraving. There was the house, as before, under the waning moon and the drifting clouds. The window that had been open was shut, and the figure was once more on the lawn: but not this time crawling cautiously on hands and knees. Now it was erect and stepping swiftly, with long strides, towards the front of the picture. The moon was behind it, and the black drapery hung down over its face so that only hints of that could be seen, and what was visible made the spectators profoundly thankful that they could see no more than a white dome-like forehead and a few straggling hairs. The head was bent down, and the arms were tightly clasped over an object which could be dimly seen and identified as a child, whether dead or living it was not possible to say. The legs of the appearance alone could be plainly discerned, and they were horribly thin.

From five to seven the three companions sat and watched the picture by turns. But it never changed. They agreed at last that it would be safe to leave it, and that they would return after Hall and await further developments.

When they assembled again, at the earliest possible moment, the engraving was there, but the figure was gone, and the house was quiet under the moonbeams. There was nothing for it but to spend the evening over gazetteers and guide-books. Williams was the lucky one at last, and perhaps he deserved it. At 11.30 p.m. he read from Murray's *Guide to Essex** the following lines:

'16½ miles, *Anningley*. The church has been an interesting building of Norman date, but was extensively classicized in the last century. It contains the tombs of the family of Francis, whose mansion, Anningley Hall, a solid Queen Anne house, stands immediately beyond the churchyard in a park of about 80 acres. The family is now extinct, the last heir having disappeared mysteriously in infancy in the year 1802. The father, Mr. Arthur Francis, was locally known as a talented amateur engraver in mezzotint. After his son's disappearance he lived in complete retirement at the Hall, and was found dead in his studio on the third anniversary of the disaster, having just completed an engraving of the house, impressions of which are of considerable rarity.'

This looked like business, and, indeed, Mr. Green on his return at once identified the house as Anningley Hall.

'Is there any kind of explanation of the figure, Green?' was the question which Williams naturally asked.

'I don't know, I'm sure, Williams. What used to be said in the place when I first knew it, which was before I came up here, was just this: old Francis was always very much down on these poaching fellows, and whenever he got a chance he used to get a man whom he suspected of it turned off the estate, and by degrees he got rid of them all but one. Squires could do a lot of things then that they daren't think of now. Well, this man that was left was what you find pretty often in that country—the last remains of a very old family. I believe they were Lords of the Manor at one time. I recollect just the same thing in my own parish.'

'What, like the man in *Tess of the D'Urbervilles*?'* Williams put in.

'Yes, I dare say; it's not a book I could ever read myself. But this fellow could show a row of tombs in the church there that belonged to his ancestors, and all that went to sour him a bit; but Francis, they said, could never get at him—he always kept just on the right side of the law—until one night the keepers found him at it in a wood right at the end of the estate. I could show you the place now; it marches with some land that used to belong to an uncle of mine. And you can imagine there was a row; and this man Gawdy (that was the name, to be sure—Gawdy; I thought I should get it—Gawdy), he was unlucky enough, poor chap! to shoot a keeper. Well, that was what Francis wanted, and grand juries—you know what they would have been then—and poor Gawdy was strung up in double-quick time; and I've been shown the place he was buried in, on the north side of the church*—you know the way in that part of the world: anyone that's been hanged or made away with themselves, they bury them that side. And the idea was that some friend of Gawdy's—not a relation, because he had none, poor devil! he was the last of his line: kind of *spes ultima gentis**—must have planned to get hold of Francis's boy and put an end to *his* line, too. I don't know—it's rather on out-of-the-way thing for an Essex poacher to think of—but, you know, I should say now it looks more as if old Gawdy had managed the job himself. Booh! I hate to think of it! have some whisky, Williams!'

The facts were communicated by Williams to Dennistoun, and by him to a mixed company, of which I was one, and the Sadducean Professor of Ophiology* another. I am sorry to say that the latter, when asked what he thought of it, only remarked: 'Oh, those Bridgeford people will say anything'—a sentiment which met with the reception it deserved.

I have only to add that the picture is now in the Ashleian Museum; that it has been treated with a view to discovering whether sympathetic ink has been used in it, but without effect; that Mr. Britnell knew nothing of it save that he was sure it was uncommon; and that, though carefully watched, it has never been known to change again.

THE ASH-TREE

❧❧

EVERYONE who has travelled over Eastern England knows the smaller country-houses with which it is studded—the rather dank little buildings, usually in the Italian style, surrounded with parks of some eighty to a hundred acres. For me they have always had a very strong attraction: with the grey paling of split oak, the noble trees, the meres with their reed-beds, and the line of distant woods. Then, I like the pillared portico—perhaps stuck on to a red-brick Queen Anne house which has been faced with stucco to bring it into line with the 'Grecian' taste of the end of the eighteenth century; the hall inside, going up to the roof, which hall ought always to be provided with a gallery and a small organ. I like the library, too, where you may find anything from a Psalter of the thirteenth century to a Shakespeare quarto. I like the pictures, of course; and perhaps most of all I like fancying what life in such a house was when it was first built, and in the piping times of landlords' prosperity, and not least now, when, if money is not so plentiful, taste is more varied and life quite as interesting. I wish to have one of these houses, and enough money to keep it together and entertain my friends in it modestly.

But this is a digression. I have to tell you of a curious series of events which happened in such a house as I have tried to describe. It is Castringham Hall* in Suffolk. I think a good deal has been done to the building since the period of my story, but the essential features I have sketched are still there—Italian portico, square block of white house, older inside than out, park with fringe of woods, and mere. The one feature that marked out the house from a score of others is gone. As you looked at it from the park, you saw on the right a great old ash-tree growing within half a dozen yards of the wall, and almost or quite touching the building with its branches. I suppose it had stood there ever since Castringham ceased to be a fortified place, and since the moat was filled in and the Elizabethan dwelling-house built. At any rate, it had wellnigh attained its full dimensions in the year 1690.

In that year the district in which the Hall is situated was the scene of a number of witch-trials. It will be long, I think, before we arrive

at a just estimate of the amount of solid reason—if there was any—
which lay at the root of the universal fear of witches in old times.
Whether the persons accused of this offence really did imagine that
they were possessed of unusual powers of any kind; or whether
they had the will at least, if not the power, of doing mischief to their
neighbours; or whether all the confessions, of which there are so
many, were extorted by the mere cruelty of the witch-finders—these
are questions which are not, I fancy, yet solved. And the present
narrative gives me pause. I cannot altogether sweep it away as mere
invention. The reader must judge for himself.

Castringham contributed a victim to the *auto-da-fé*.* Mrs.
Mothersole* was her name, and she differed from the ordinary run of
village witches only in being rather better off and in a more influential
position. Efforts were made to save her by several reputable farmers
of the parish. They did their best to testify to her character, and
showed considerable anxiety as to the verdict of the jury.

But what seems to have been fatal to the woman was the evidence
of the then proprietor of Castringham Hall—Sir Matthew Fell.* He
deposed to having watched her on three different occasions from his
window, at the full of the moon, gathering sprigs 'from the ash-tree
near my house.'* She had climbed into the branches, clad only in her
shift, and was cutting off small twigs with a peculiarly curved knife,
and as she did so she seemed to be talking to herself. On each occasion Sir Matthew had done his best to capture the woman, but she
had always taken alarm at some accidental noise he had made, and all
he could see when he got down to the garden was a hare running
across the park in the direction of the village.

On the third night he had been at the pains to follow at his best
speed, and had gone straight to Mrs. Mothersole's house; but he had
had to wait a quarter of an hour battering at her door, and then she
had come out very cross, and apparently very sleepy, as if just out of
bed; and he had no good explanation to offer of his visit.

Mainly on this evidence, though there was much more of a less striking and unusual kind from other parishioners, Mrs. Mothersole was
found guilty and condemned to die. She was hanged a week after the
trial, with five or six more unhappy creatures, at Bury St. Edmunds.*

Sir Matthew Fell, then Deputy-Sheriff, was present at the execution. It was a damp, drizzly March morning when the cart made its
way up the rough grass hill outside Northgate, where the gallows

stood. The other victims were apathetic or broken down with misery; but Mrs. Mothersole was, as in life so in death, of a very different temper. Her 'poysonous Rage,' as a reporter of the time puts it, 'did so work upon the Bystanders—yea, even upon the Hangman—that it was constantly affirmed of all that saw her that she presented the living Aspect of a mad Divell. Yet she offer'd no Resistance to the Officers of the Law; onely she looked upon those that laid Hands upon her with so direfull and venomous an Aspect that—as one of them afterwards assured me—the meer Thought of it preyed inwardly upon his Mind for six Months after.'

However, all that she is reported to have said was the seemingly meaningless words: 'There will be guests at the Hall.' Which she repeated more than once in an undertone.

Sir Matthew Fell was not unimpressed by the bearing of the woman. He had some talk upon the matter with the Vicar of his parish, with whom he travelled home after the assize business was over. His evidence at the trial had not been very willingly given; he was not specially infected with the witch-finding mania, but he declared, then and afterwards, that he could not give any other account of the matter than that he had given, and that he could not possibly have been mistaken as to what he saw. The whole transaction had been repugnant to him, for he was a man who liked to be on pleasant terms with those about him; but he saw a duty to be done in this business, and he had done it. That seems to have been the gist of his sentiments, and the Vicar applauded it, as any reasonable man must have done.

A few weeks after, when the moon of May was at the full, Vicar and Squire met again in the park, and walked to the Hall together. Lady Fell was with her mother, who was dangerously ill, and Sir Matthew was alone at home; so the Vicar, Mr. Crome, was easily persuaded to take a late supper at the Hall.

Sir Matthew was not very good company this evening. The talk ran chiefly on family and parish matters, and, as luck would have it, Sir Matthew made a memorandum in writing of certain wishes or intentions of his regarding his estates, which afterwards proved exceedingly useful.

When Mr. Crome thought of starting for home, about half-past nine o'clock, Sir Matthew and he took a preliminary turn on the gravelled walk at the back of the house. The only incident that struck Mr. Crome was this: they were in sight of the ash-tree which I described as growing near the windows of the building, when Sir Matthew stopped and said:

'What is that that runs up and down the stem of the ash? It is never a squirrel? They will all be in their nests by now.'

The Vicar looked and saw the moving creature, but he could make nothing of its colour in the moonlight. The sharp outline, however, seen for an instant, was imprinted on his brain, and he could have sworn, he said, though it sounded foolish, that, squirrel or not, it had more than four legs.

Still, not much was to be made of the momentary vision, and the two men parted. They may have met since then, but it was not for a score of years.

Next day Sir Matthew Fell was not downstairs at six in the morning, as was his custom, nor at seven, nor yet at eight. Hereupon the servants went and knocked at his chamber door. I need not prolong the description of their anxious listenings and renewed batterings on the panels. The door was opened at last from the outside, and they found their master dead and black. So much you have guessed. That there were any marks of violence did not at the moment appear; but the window was open.

One of the men went to fetch the parson, and then by his directions rode on to give notice to the coroner. Mr. Crome himself went as quick as he might to the Hall, and was shown to the room where the dead man lay. He has left some notes among his papers which show how genuine a respect and sorrow was felt for Sir Matthew, and there is also this passage, which I transcribe for the sake of the light it throws upon the course of events, and also upon the common beliefs of the time:

'There was not any the least Trace of an Entrance having been forc'd to the Chamber: but the Casement stood open, as my poor Friend would always have it in this Season. He had his Evening Drink of small Ale in a silver vessel of about a pint measure, and to-night had not drunk it out. This Drink was examined by the Physician from Bury, a Mr. Hodgkins, who could not, however, as he afterwards declar'd upon his Oath, before the Coroner's quest, discover that any matter of a venomous kind was present in it. For, as was natural, in the great Swelling and Blackness of the Corpse, there was talk made among the Neighbours of Poyson. The Body was very much Disorder'd as it laid in the Bed, being twisted after so extreme a sort as gave too probable Conjecture that my worthy Friend and Patron had expir'd in great Pain and Agony. And what is as yet unexplain'd, and to myself the Argument of some Horrid and Artfull Designe in the Perpetrators of this Barbarous Murther, was this, that the Women which were entrusted with the laying-out of the Corpse and washing it, being both sad Persons and very well Respected in their Mournfull Profession, came to me in a great Pain and Distress both of Mind and Body, saying, what was indeed confirmed upon the first View, that they had no sooner touch'd the Breast of the Corpse with their naked Hands than they were sensible of a more than ordinary violent Smart and Acheing in their Palms, which, with their whole Forearms, in no long time swell'd so immoderately, the Pain still continuing, that, as afterwards proved, during many weeks they were forc'd to lay by the exercise of their Calling; and yet no mark seen on the Skin.

'Upon hearing this, I sent for the Physician, who was still in the House, and we made as carefull a Proof as we were able by the Help of a small Magnifying Lens of Crystal of the condition of the Skinn on this Part of the Body: but could not detect with the Instrument we had any Matter of Importance beyond a couple of small Punctures or Pricks, which we then concluded were the Spotts by which the Poyson might be introduced, remembering that Ring of *Pope Borgia*,* with other known Specimens of the Horrid Art of the Italian Poysoners of the last age.

'So much is to be said of the Symptoms seen on the Corpse. As to what I am to add, it is meerly my own Experiment, and to be left to Posterity to judge whether there be anything of Value therein. There was on the Table by the Beddside a Bible of the small size, in which my Friend—punctuall as in Matters of less Moment, so in this more weighty one—used nightly, and upon his First Rising, to read a sett Portion. And I taking it up—not without a Tear duly paid to him which from the Study of this poorer Adumbration was now pass'd to the contemplation of its great Originall—it came into my Thoughts, as at such moments of Helplessness we are prone to catch at any the least Glimmer that makes promise of Light, to make trial of that old and by many accounted Superstitious Practice of drawing the *Sortes*:* of which a Principall Instance, in the case of his late Sacred Majesty the Blessed Martyr King *Charles* and my Lord *Falkland*, was now much talked of. I must needs admit that by my Trial not much

Assistance was afforded me: yet, as the Cause and Origin of these Dreadful Events may hereafter be search'd out, I set down the Results, in the case it may be found that they pointed the true Quarter of the Mischief to a quicker Intelligence than my own.

'I made, then, three trials, opening the Book and placing my Finger upon certain Words: which gave in the first these words, from Luke xiii. 7, *Cut it down*; in the second, Isaiah xiii. 20, *It shall never be inhabited*; and upon the third Experiment, Job xxxix. 30, *Her young ones also suck up blood.*'*

This is all that need be quoted from Mr. Crome's papers. Sir Matthew Fell was duly coffined and laid into the earth, and his funeral sermon, preached by Mr. Crome on the following Sunday, has been printed under the title of 'The Unsearchable Way; or, England's Danger and the Malicious Dealings of Antichrist,' it being the Vicar's view, as well as that most commonly held in the neighbourhood, that the Squire was the victim of a recrudescence of the Popish Plot.*

His son, Sir Matthew the second, succeeded to the title and estates. And so ends the first act of the Castringham tragedy. It is to be mentioned, though the fact is not surprising, that the new Baronet did not occupy the room in which his father had died. Nor, indeed, was it slept in by anyone but an occasional visitor during the whole of his occupation. He died in 1735, and I do not find that anything particular marked his reign, save a curiously constant mortality among his cattle and live-stock in general, which showed a tendency to increase slightly as time went on.

Those who are interested in the details will find a statistical account in a letter to the *Gentleman's Magazine* of 1772, which draws the facts from the Baronet's own papers. He put an end to it at last by a very simple expedient, that of shutting up all his beasts in sheds at night, and keeping no sheep in his park. For he had noticed that nothing was ever attacked that spent the night indoors. After that the disorder confined itself to wild birds, and beasts of chase. But as we have no good account of the symptoms, and as all-night watching was quite unproductive of any clue, I do not dwell on what the Suffolk farmers called the 'Castringham sickness.'

The second Sir Matthew died in 1735, as I said, and was duly succeeded by his son, Sir Richard. It was in his time that the great family pew was built out on the north side of the parish church. So large were the Squire's ideas that several of the graves on that unhallowed side of the building had to be disturbed to satisfy his requirements. Among them was that of Mrs. Mothersole, the position of which was accurately known, thanks to a note on a plan of the church and yard, both made by Mr. Crome.

A certain amount of interest was excited in the village when it was known that the famous witch, who was still remembered by a few, was to be exhumed. And the feeling of surprise, and indeed disquiet, was very strong when it was found that, though her coffin was fairly sound and unbroken, there was no trace whatever inside it of body, bones, or dust. Indeed, it is a curious phenomenon, for at the time of her burying no such things were dreamt of as resurrection-men, and it is difficult to conceive any rational motive for stealing a body otherwise than for the uses of the dissecting-room.

The incident revived for a time all the stories of witch-trials and of the exploits of the witches, dormant for forty years, and Sir Richard's orders that the coffin should be burnt were thought by a good many to be rather foolhardy, though they were duly carried out.

Sir Richard was a pestilent innovator, it is certain. Before his time the Hall had been a fine block of the mellowest red brick; but Sir Richard had travelled in Italy and become infected with the Italian taste, and, having more money than his predecessors, he determined to leave an Italian palace where he had found an English house. So stucco and ashlar masked the brick; some indifferent Roman marbles were planted about in the entrance-hall and gardens; a reproduction of the Sibyl's temple at Tivoli* was erected on the opposite bank of the mere; and Castingham took on an entirely new, and, I must say, a less engaging, aspect. But it was much admired, and served as a model to a good many of the neighbouring gentry in after-years.

One morning (it was in 1754) Sir Richard woke after a night of discomfort. It had been windy, and his chimney had smoked persistently, and yet it was so cold that he must keep up a fire. Also something had so rattled about the window that no man could get a moment's peace. Further, there was the prospect of several guests of position arriving in the course of the day, who would expect sport of some kind, and the inroads of the distemper (which continued among his game) had been lately so serious that he was afraid for his reputation as a game-preserver. But what really touched him most nearly was

the other matter of his sleepless night. He could certainly not sleep in
that room again.

That was the chief subject of his meditations at breakfast, and after
it he began a systematic examination of the rooms to see which would
suit his notions best. It was long before he found one. This had a
window with an eastern aspect and that with a northern; this door the
servants would be always passing, and he did not like the bedstead in
that. No, he must have a room with a western look-out, so that the
sun could not wake him early, and it must be out of the way of the
business of the house. The housekeeper was at the end of her
resources.

'Well, Sir Richard,' she said, 'you know that there is but one room
like that in the house.'

'Which may that be?' said Sir Richard.

'And that is Sir Matthew's—the West Chamber.'

'Well, put me in there, for there I'll lie to-night,' said her master.
'Which way is it? Here, to be sure'; and he hurried off.

'Oh, Sir Richard, but no one has slept there these forty years. The
air has hardly been changed since Sir Matthew died there.'

Thus she spoke, and rustled after him.

'Come, open the door, Mrs. Chiddock. I'll see the chamber,
at least.'

So it was opened, and, indeed, the smell was very close and earthy.
Sir Richard crossed to the window, and, impatiently, as was his wont,
threw the shutters back, and flung open the casement. For this end of
the house was one which the alterations had barely touched, grown
up as it was with the great ash-tree, and being otherwise concealed
from view.

'Air it, Mrs. Chiddock, all to-day, and move my bed-furniture in
in the afternoon. Put the Bishop of Kilmore* in my old room.'

'Pray, Sir Richard,' said a new voice, breaking in on this speech,
'might I have the favour of a moment's interview?'

Sir Richard turned round and saw a man in black in the doorway,
who bowed.

'I must ask your indulgence for this intrusion, Sir Richard. You
will, perhaps, hardly remember me. My name is William Crome, and
my grandfather was Vicar here in your grandfather's time.'

'Well, sir,' said Sir Richard, 'the name of Crome is always a
passport to Castringham. I am glad to renew a friendship of two

generations' standing. In what can I serve you? for your hour of calling—and, if I do not mistake you, your bearing—shows you to be in some haste.'

'That is no more than the truth, sir. I am riding from Norwich to Bury St. Edmunds with what haste I can make, and I have called in on my way to leave with you some papers which we have but just come upon in looking over what my grandfather left at his death. It is thought you may find some matters of family interest in them.'

'You are mighty obliging, Mr. Crome, and, if you will be so good as to follow me to the parlour, and drink a glass of wine, we will take a first look at these same papers together. And you, Mrs. Chiddock, as I said, be about airing this chamber. . . . Yes, it is here my grandfather died. . . . Yes, the tree, perhaps, does make the place a little dampish. . . . No; I do not wish to listen to any more. Make no difficulties, I beg. You have your orders—go. Will you follow me, sir?'

They went to the study. The packet which young Mr. Crome had brought—he was then just become a Fellow of Clare Hall in Cambridge,* I may say, and subsequently brought out a respectable edition of Polyænus*—contained among other things the notes which the old Vicar had made upon the occasion of Sir Matthew Fell's death. And for the first time Sir Richard was confronted with the enigmatical *Sortes Biblicæ* which you have heard. They amused him a good deal.

'Well,' he said, 'my grandfather's Bible gave one prudent piece of advice—*Cut it down*. If that stands for the ash-tree, he may rest assured I shall not neglect it. Such a nest of catarrhs and agues was never seen.'

The parlour contained the family books, which, pending the arrival of a collection which Sir Richard had made in Italy, and the building of a proper room to receive them, were not many in number.

Sir Richard looked up from the paper to the bookcase.

'I wonder,' says he, 'whether the old prophet is there yet? I fancy I see him.'

Crossing the room, he took out a dumpy Bible, which, sure enough, bore on the flyleaf the inscription: 'To Matthew Fell, from his Loving Godmother, Anne Aldous, 2 September, 1659.'

'It would be no bad plan to test him again, Mr. Crome. I will wager we get a couple of names in the Chronicles. H'm! what have we here?

"Thou shalt seek me in the morning, and I shall not be."* Well, well!
Your grandfather would have made a fine omen of that, hey? No
more prophets for me! They are all in a tale. And now, Mr. Crome,
I am infinitely obliged to you for your packet. You will, I fear, be
impatient to get on. Pray allow me—another glass.'

So with offers of hospitality, which were genuinely meant (for
Sir Richard thought well of the young man's address and manner),
they parted.

In the afternoon came the guests—the Bishop of Kilmore, Lady
Mary Hervey, Sir William Kentfield, etc. Dinner at five, wine, cards,
supper, and dispersal to bed.

Next morning Sir Richard is disinclined to take his gun with the
rest. He talks with the Bishop of Kilmore. This prelate, unlike a good
many of the Irish Bishops of his day, had visited his see, and, indeed,
resided there for some considerable time. This morning, as the two
were walking along the terrace and talking over the alterations and
improvements in the house, the Bishop said, pointing to the window
of the West Room:

'You could never get one of my Irish flock to occupy that room,
Sir Richard.'

'Why is that, my lord? It is, in fact, my own.'

'Well, our Irish peasantry will always have it that it brings the
worst of luck to sleep near an ash-tree, and you have a fine growth of
ash not two yards from your chamber window. Perhaps,' the Bishop
went on, with a smile, 'it has given you a touch of its quality already,
for you do not seem, if I may say it, so much the fresher for your
night's rest as your friends would like to see you.'

'That, or something else, it is true, cost me my sleep from twelve
to four, my lord. But the tree is to come down to-morrow, so I shall
not hear much more from it.'

'I applaud your determination. It can hardly be wholesome to have
the air you breathe strained, as it were, through all that leafage.'

'Your lordship is right there, I think. But I had not my window
open last night. It was rather the noise that went on—no doubt from
the twigs sweeping the glass—that kept me open-eyed.'

'I think that can hardly be, Sir Richard. Here—you see it from this
point. None of these nearest branches even can touch your casement
unless there were a gale, and there was none of that last night. They
miss the panes by a foot.'

'No, sir, true. What, then, will it be, I wonder, that scratched and rustled so—ay, and covered the dust on my sill with lines and marks?'

At last they agreed that the rats must have come up through the ivy. That was the Bishop's idea, and Sir Richard jumped at it.

So the day passed quietly, and night came, and the party dispersed to their rooms, and wished Sir Richard a better night.

And now we are in his bedroom, with the light out and the Squire in bed. The room is over the kitchen, and the night outside still and warm, so the window stands open.

There is very little light about the bedstead, but there is a strange movement there; it seems as if Sir Richard were moving his head rapidly to and fro with only the slightest possible sound. And now you would guess, so deceptive is the half-darkness, that he had several heads, round and brownish, which move back and forward, even as low as his chest. It is a horrible illusion. Is it nothing more? There! something drops off the bed with a soft plump, like a kitten, and is out of the window in a flash; another—four—and after that there is quiet again.

'Thou shalt seek me in the morning, and I shall not be.'

As with Sir Matthew, so with Sir Richard—dead and black in his bed!

A pale and silent party of guests and servants gathered under the window when the news was known. Italian poisoners, Popish emissaries, infected air—all these and more guesses were hazarded, and the Bishop of Kilmore looked at the tree, in the fork of whose lower boughs a white tom-cat was crouching, looking down the hollow which years had gnawed in the trunk. It was watching something inside the tree with great interest.

Suddenly it got up and craned over the hole. Then a bit of the edge on which it stood gave way, and it went slithering in. Everyone looked up at the noise of the fall.

It is known to most of us that a cat can cry; but few of us have heard, I hope, such a yell as came out of the trunk of the great ash. Two or three screams there were—the witnesses are not sure which— and then a slight and muffled noise of some commotion or struggling was all that came. But Lady Mary Hervey fainted outright, and the housekeeper stopped her ears and fled till she fell on the terrace.

The Bishop of Kilmore and Sir William Kentfield stayed. Yet even they were daunted, though it was only at the cry of a cat; and Sir William swallowed once or twice before he could say:

'There is something more than we know of in that tree, my lord. I am for an instant search.'

And this was agreed upon. A ladder was brought, and one of the gardeners went up, and, looking down the hollow, could detect nothing but a few dim indications of something moving. They got a lantern, and let it down by a rope.

'We must get at the bottom of this. My life upon it, my lord, but the secret of these terrible deaths is there.'

Up went the gardener again with the lantern, and let it down the hole cautiously. They saw the yellow light upon his face as he bent over, and saw his face struck with an incredulous terror and loathing before he cried out in a dreadful voice and fell back from the ladder—where, happily, he was caught by two of the men—letting the lantern fall inside the tree.

He was in a dead faint, and it was some time before any word could be got from him.

By then they had something else to look at. The lantern must have broken at the bottom, and the light in it caught upon dry leaves and rubbish that lay there, for in a few minutes a dense smoke began to come up, and then flame; and, to be short, the tree was in a blaze.

The bystanders made a ring at some yards' distance, and Sir William and the Bishop sent men to get what weapons and tools they could; for, clearly, whatever might be using the tree as its lair would be forced out by the fire.

So it was. First, at the fork, they saw a round body covered with fire—the size of a man's head—appear very suddenly, then seem to collapse and fall back. This, five or six times; then a similar ball leapt into the air and fell on the grass, where after a moment it lay still. The Bishop went as near as he dared to it, and saw—what but the remains of an enormous spider, veinous and seared! And, as the fire burned lower down, more terrible bodies like this began to break out from the trunk, and it was seen that these were covered with greyish hair.

All that day the ash burned, and until it fell to pieces the men stood about it, and from time to time killed the brutes as they darted out. At last there was a long interval when none appeared, and they cautiously closed in and examined the roots of the tree.

'They found,' says the Bishop of Kilmore, 'below it a rounded hollow place in the earth, wherein were two or three bodies of these creatures that had plainly been smothered by the smoke; and, what is to me more curious, at the side of this den, against the wall, was crouching the anatomy or skeleton of a human being, with the skin dried upon the bones, having some remains of black hair, which was pronounced by those that examined it to be undoubtedly the body of a woman, and clearly dead for a period of fifty years.'

NUMBER 13

〜❦〜

AMONG the towns of Jutland, Viborg* justly holds a high place. It is the seat of a bishopric; it has a handsome but almost entirely new cathedral, a charming garden, a lake of great beauty, and many storks. Near it is Hald,* accounted one of the prettiest things in Denmark; and hard by is Finderup,* where Marsk Stig murdered King Erik Glipping on St. Cecilia's Day, in the year 1286. Fifty-six blows of square-headed iron maces were traced on Erik's skull when his tomb was opened in the seventeenth century. But I am not writing a guide-book.

There are good hotels in Viborg—Preisler's and the Phœnix are all that can be desired. But my cousin, whose experiences I have to tell you now, went to the Golden Lion* the first time that he visited Viborg. He has not been there since, and the following pages will perhaps explain the reason of his abstention.

The Golden Lion is one of the very few houses in the town that were not destroyed in the great fire of 1726, which practically demolished the cathedral, the Sognekirke, the Raadhuus,* and so much else that was old and interesting. It is a great red-brick house—that is, the front is of brick, with corbie steps on the gables and a text over the door; but the courtyard into which the omnibus drives is of black and white 'cage-work' in wood and plaster.

The sun was declining in the heavens when my cousin walked up to the door, and the light smote full upon the imposing façade of the house. He was delighted with the old-fashioned aspect of the place, and promised himself a thoroughly satisfactory and amusing stay in an inn so typical of old Jutland.

It was not business in the ordinary sense of the word that had brought Mr. Anderson* to Viborg. He was engaged upon some researches into the Church history of Denmark, and it had come to his knowledge that in the Rigsarkiv* of Viborg there were papers, saved from the fire, relating to the last days of Roman Catholicism in the country.* He proposed, therefore, to spend a considerable time—perhaps as much as a fortnight or three weeks—in examining and copying these, and he hoped that the Golden Lion would be able to give him a room of sufficient size to serve alike as a bedroom and a study. His wishes were explained to the landlord, and, after a certain amount of thought, the latter suggested that perhaps it might be the best way for the gentleman to look at one or two of the larger rooms and pick one for himself. It seemed a good idea.

The top floor was soon rejected as entailing too much getting upstairs after the day's work; the second floor contained no room of exactly the dimensions required; but on the first floor there was a choice of two or three rooms which would, so far as size went, suit admirably.

The landlord was strongly in favour of Number 17, but Mr. Anderson pointed out that its windows commanded only the blank wall of the next house, and that it would be very dark in the afternoon. Either Number 12 or Number 14 would be better, for both of them looked on the street, and the bright evening light and the pretty view would more than compensate him for the additional amount of noise.

Eventually Number 12 was selected. Like its neighbours, it had three windows, all on one side of the room; it was fairly high and unusually long. There was, of course, no fireplace, but the stove was handsome and rather old—a cast-iron erection, on the side of which was a representation of Abraham sacrificing Isaac, and the inscription, '1 Bog Mose, Cap. 22,'* above. Nothing else in the room was remarkable; the only interesting picture was an old coloured print of the town, date about 1820.

Supper-time was approaching, but when Anderson, refreshed by the ordinary ablutions, descended the staircase, there were still a few minutes before the bell rang. He devoted them to examining the list of his fellow-lodgers. As is usual in Denmark, their names were displayed on a large blackboard, divided into columns and lines, the numbers of the rooms being painted in at the beginning of each line. The list was not exciting. There was an advocate, or Sagförer, a German, and some bagmen* from Copenhagen. The one and only point which suggested any food for thought was the absence of any Number 13 from the tale of the rooms, and even this was a thing which Anderson had already noticed half a dozen times in his experience of Danish hotels. He could not help wondering whether the objection to that particular number, common as it is, was so widespread and so strong as to make it difficult to let a room so ticketed, and he resolved to ask the landlord if he and his colleagues in the profession had actually met with many clients who refused to be accommodated in the thirteenth room.

He had nothing to tell me (I am giving the story as I heard it from him) about what passed at supper, and the evening, which was spent in unpacking and arranging his clothes, books, and papers, was not more eventful. Towards eleven o'clock he resolved to go to bed, but with him, as with a good many other people nowadays, an almost necessary preliminary to bed, if he meant to sleep, was the reading of a few pages of print, and he now remembered that the particular book which he had been reading in the train, and which alone would satisfy him at that present moment, was in the pocket of his greatcoat, then hanging on a peg outside the dining-room.

To run down and secure it was the work of a moment, and, as the passages were by no means dark, it was not difficult for him to find his way back to his own door. So, at least, he thought; but when he arrived there, and turned the handle, the door entirely refused to open, and he caught the sound of a hasty movement towards it from within. He had tried the wrong door, of course. Was his own room to the right or to the left? He glanced at the number: it was 13. His room would be on the left; and so it was. And not before he had been in bed for some minutes, had read his wonted three or four pages of his book, blown out his light, and turned over to go to sleep, did it occur to him that, whereas on the blackboard of the hotel there had been no Number 13, there was undoubtedly a room numbered 13 in the hotel. He felt rather sorry he had not chosen it for his own. Perhaps he might have done the landlord a little service by occupying it, and given him the chance of saying that a well-born English gentleman had lived in it for three weeks and liked it very much. But probably it was used as a servant's room or something of the kind. After all, it was most likely not so large or good a room as his own. And he looked drowsily about the room, which was fairly perceptible in the half-light from the street-lamp. It was a curious effect, he thought. Rooms usually look larger in a dim light than a full one, but this seemed to have contracted in length and grown proportionately higher. Well, well! sleep was more important than these vague ruminations—and to sleep he went.

On the day after his arrival Anderson attacked the Rigsarkiv of Viborg. He was, as one might expect in Denmark, kindly received, and access to all that he wished to see was made as easy for him as possible. The documents laid before him were far more numerous and interesting than he had at all anticipated. Besides official papers, there was a large bundle of correspondence relating to Bishop Jörgen Friis,* the last Roman Catholic who held the see, and in these there cropped up many amusing and what are called 'intimate' details of private life and individual character. There was much talk of a house owned by the Bishop, but not inhabited by him, in the town. Its tenant was apparently somewhat of a scandal and a stumbling-block to the reforming party. He was a disgrace, they wrote, to the city; he practised secret and wicked arts, and had sold his soul to the enemy. It was of a piece with the gross corruption and superstition of the Babylonish Church that such a viper and blood-sucking *Troldmand** should be patronized and harboured by the Bishop. The Bishop met these reproaches boldly; he protested his own abhorrence of all such things as secret arts, and required his antagonists to bring the matter before the proper court—of course, the spiritual court—and sift it to the bottom. No one could be more ready and willing than himself to condemn Mag. Nicolas Francken if the evidence showed him to have been guilty of any of the crimes informally alleged against him.

Anderson had not time to do more than glance at the next letter of the Protestant leader, Rasmus Nielsen, before the record office was closed for the day, but he gathered its general tenor, which was to the effect that Christian men were now no longer bound by the decisions of Bishops of Rome, and that the Bishop's Court was not, and could not be, a fit or competent tribunal to judge so grave and weighty a cause.

On leaving the office, Mr. Anderson was accompanied by the old gentleman who presided over it, and, as they walked, the conversation very naturally turned to the papers of which I have just been speaking.

Herr Scavenius, the Archivist of Viborg, though very well informed as to the general run of the documents under his charge, was not a specialist in those of the Reformation period. He was much interested in what Anderson had to tell him about them. He looked forward with great pleasure, he said, to seeing the publication in which Mr. Anderson spoke of embodying their contents. 'This house of the Bishop Friis,' he added, 'it is a great puzzle to me where it can have stood. I have studied carefully the topography of old Viborg, but it is most unlucky—of the old terrier* of the Bishop's property which was made in 1560, and of which we have the greater part in the Arkiv, just the piece which had the list of the town property is missing. Never mind. Perhaps I shall some day succeed to find him.'

After taking some exercise—I forget exactly how or where— Anderson went back to the Golden Lion, his supper, his game of patience, and his bed. On the way to his room it occurred to him that he had forgotten to talk to the landlord about the omission of Number 13 from the hotel, and also that he might as well make sure that Number 13 did actually exist before he made any reference to the matter.

The decision was not difficult to arrive at. There was the door with its number as plain as could be, and work of some kind was evidently going on inside it, for as he neared the door he could hear footsteps and voices, or a voice, within. During the few seconds in which he halted to make sure of the number, the footsteps ceased, seemingly very near the door, and he was a little startled at hearing a quick hissing breathing as of a person in strong excitement. He went on to his own room, and again he was surprised to find how much smaller it seemed now than it had when he selected it. It was a slight disappointment, but only slight. If he found it really not large enough, he could very easily shift to another. In the meantime he wanted something—as far as I remember it was a pocket-handkerchief—out of his portmanteau, which had been placed by the porter on a very inadequate trestle or stool against the wall at the farthest end of the room from his bed. Here was a very curious thing: the portmanteau was not to be seen. It had been moved by officious servants; doubtless the contents had been put in the wardrobe. No, none of them were there. This was vexatious. The idea of a theft he dismissed at once. Such things rarely happen in Denmark, but some piece of stupidity had certainly been performed (which is not so uncommon), and the *stuepige** must be severely spoken to. Whatever it was that he wanted, it was not so necessary to his comfort that he could not wait till the morning for it, and he therefore settled not to ring the bell and disturb the servants. He went to the window—the right-hand window it was—and looked out on the quiet street. There was a tall building opposite, with large spaces of dead wall; no passers-by; a dark night; and very little to be seen of any kind.

The light was behind him, and he could see his own shadow clearly cast on the wall opposite. Also the shadow of the bearded man in Number 11 on the left, who passed to and fro in shirtsleeves once or twice, and was seen first brushing his hair, and later on in a night-gown. Also the shadow of the occupant of Number 13 on the right. This might be more interesting. Number 13 was, like himself, leaning on his elbows on the window-sill looking out into the street. He seemed to be a tall thin man—or was it by any chance a woman?—at least, it was someone who covered his or her head with some kind of drapery before going to bed, and, he thought, must be possessed of a red lamp-shade—and the lamp must be flickering very much. There was a distinct playing up and down of a dull red light on the opposite wall. He craned out a little to see if he could make any more of the figure, but beyond a fold of some light, perhaps white, material on the window-sill he could see nothing.

Now came a distant step in the street, and its approach seemed to recall Number 13 to a sense of his exposed position, for very swiftly and suddenly he swept aside from the window, and his red light went out. Anderson, who had been smoking a cigarette, laid the end of it on the window-sill and went to bed.

Next morning he was woke by the *stuepige* with hot water, etc. He roused himself, and after thinking out the correct Danish words, said as distinctly as he could:

'You must not move my portmanteau. Where is it?'

As is not uncommon, the maid laughed, and went away without making any distinct answer.

Anderson, rather irritated, sat up in bed, intending to call her back, but he remained sitting up, staring straight in front of him. There was his portmanteau on its trestle, exactly where he had seen the porter put it when he first arrived. This was a rude shock for a man who prided himself on his accuracy of observation. How it could possibly have escaped him the night before he did not pretend to understand; at any rate, there it was now.

The daylight showed more than the portmanteau; it let the true proportions of the room with its three windows appear, and satisfied its tenant that his choice after all had not been a bad one. When he was almost dressed he walked to the middle one of the three windows to look out at the weather. Another shock awaited him. Strangely unobservant he must have been last night. He could have sworn ten times over that he had been smoking at the right-hand window the last thing before he went to bed, and here was his cigarette-end on the sill of the middle window.

He started to go down to breakfast. Rather late, but Number 13 was later: here were his boots still outside his door—a gentleman's boots. So then Number 13 was a man, not a woman. Just then he caught sight of the number on the door. It was 14. He thought he must have passed Number 13 without noticing it. Three stupid mistakes in twelve hours were too much for a methodical, accurate-minded man, so he turned back to make sure. The next number to 14 was number 12, his own room. There was no Number 13 at all.*

After some minutes devoted to a careful consideration of everything he had had to eat and drink during the last twenty-four hours, Anderson decided to give the question up. If his sight or his brain were giving way he would have plenty of opportunities for ascertaining that fact; if not, then he was evidently being treated to a very interesting experience. In either case the development of events would certainly be worth watching.

During the day he continued his examination of the episcopal correspondence which I have already summarized. To his disappointment, it was incomplete. Only one other letter could be found which referred to the affair of Mag. Nicolas Francken. It was from the Bishop Jörgen Friis to Rasmus Nielsen. He said:

'Although we are not in the least degree inclined to assent to your judgment concerning our court, and shall be prepared if need be to withstand you to the uttermost in that behalf, yet forasmuch as our trusty and well-beloved Mag. Nicolas Francken, against whom you have dared to allege certain false and malicious charges, hath been suddenly removed from among us, it is apparent that the question for this time falls. But forasmuch as you further allege that the Apostle and Evangelist St. John in his heavenly Apocalypse describes the Holy Roman Church under the guise and symbol of the Scarlet Woman,* be it known to you,' etc.

Search as he might, Anderson could find no sequel to this letter nor any clue to the cause or manner of the 'removal' of the *casus belli*.* He could only suppose that Francken had died suddenly; and as there were only two days between the date of Nielsen's last letter—when Francken was evidently still in being—and that of the Bishop's letter, the death must have been completely unexpected.

In the afternoon he paid a short visit to Hald, and took his tea at Baekkelund;* nor could he notice, though he was in a somewhat nervous frame of mind, that there was any indication of such a failure of eye or brain as his experiences of the morning had led him to fear.

At supper he found himself next to the landlord.

'What,' he asked him, after some indifferent conversation, 'is the reason why in most of the hotels one visits in this country the number thirteen is left out of the list of rooms? I see you have none here.'

The landlord seemed amused.

'To think that you should have noticed a thing like that! I've thought about it once or twice myself, to tell the truth. An educated man, I've said, has no business with these superstitious notions. I was brought up myself here in the High School of Viborg, and our old master was always a man to set his face against anything of that kind. He's been dead now this many years—a fine upstanding man he was, and ready with his hands as well as his head. I recollect us boys, one snowy day——'

Here he plunged into reminiscence.

'Then you don't think there is any particular objection to having a Number 13?' said Anderson.

'Ah! to be sure. Well, you understand, I was brought up to the business by my poor old father. He kept an hotel in Aarhuus* first, and then, when we were born, he moved to Viborg here, which was his native place, and had the Phœnix here until he died. That was in 1876. Then I started business in Silkeborg,* and only the year before last I moved into this house.'

Then followed more details as to the state of the house and business when first taken over.

'And when you came here, was there a Number 13?'

'No, no. I was going to tell you about that. You see, in a place like this, the commercial class—the travellers—are what we have to provide for in general. And put them in Number 13? Why, they'd as soon sleep in the street, or sooner. As far as I'm concerned myself, it wouldn't make a penny difference to me what the number of my room was, and so I've often said to them; but they stick to it that it brings them bad luck. Quantities of stories they have among them of men that have slept in a Number 13 and never been the same again, or lost their best customers, or—one thing and another,' said the landlord, after searching for a more graphic phrase.

'Then, what do you use your Number 13 for?' said Anderson, conscious as he said the words of a curious anxiety quite disproportionate to the importance of the question.

'My Number 13? Why, don't I tell you that there isn't such a thing in the house? I thought you might have noticed that. If there was it would be next door to your own room.'

'Well, yes; only I happened to think—that is, I fancied last night that I had seen a door numbered thirteen in that passage; and, really, I am almost certain I must have been right, for I saw it the night before as well.'

Of course, Herr Kristensen laughed this notion to scorn, as Anderson had expected, and emphasized with much iteration the fact that no Number 13 existed or had existed before him in that hotel.

Anderson was in some ways relieved by his certainty but still puzzled, and he began to think that the best way to make sure whether he had indeed been subject to an illusion or not was to invite the landlord to his room to smoke a cigar later on in the evening. Some photographs of English towns which he had with him formed a sufficiently good excuse.

Herr Kristensen was flattered by the invitation, and most willingly accepted it. At about ten o'clock he was to make his appearance, but before that Anderson had some letters to write, and retired for the purpose of writing them. He almost blushed to himself at confessing it, but he could not deny that it was the fact that he was becoming quite nervous about the question of the existence of Number 13; so much so that he approached his room by way of Number 11, in order that he might not be obliged to pass the door, or the place where the door ought to be. He looked quickly and suspiciously about the room when he entered it, but there was nothing, beyond that indefinable air of being smaller than usual, to warrant any misgivings. There was no question of the presence or absence of his portmanteau to-night. He had himself emptied it of its contents and lodged it under his bed. With a certain effort he dismissed the thought of Number 13 from his mind, and sat down to his writing.

His neighbours were quiet enough. Occasionally a door opened in the passage and a pair of boots was thrown out, or a bagman walked past humming to himself, and outside, from time to time a cart thundered over the atrocious cobble-stones, or a quick step hurried along the flags.

Anderson finished his letters, ordered in whisky and soda, and then went to the window and studied the dead wall opposite and the shadows upon it.

As far as he could remember, Number 14 had been occupied by the lawyer, a staid man, who said little at meals, being generally engaged in studying a small bundle of papers beside his plate. Apparently, however, he was in the habit of giving vent to his animal spirits when alone. Why else should he be dancing? The shadow from the next room evidently showed that he was. Again and again his thin form crossed the window, his arms waved, and a gaunt leg was kicked up with surprising agility. He seemed to be barefooted, and the floor must be well laid, for no sound betrayed his movements. Sagförer Herr Anders Jensen, dancing at ten o'clock at night in a hotel bedroom, seemed a fitting subject for a historical painting in the grand style; and Anderson's thoughts, like those of Emily in the *Mysteries of Udolpho*,* began to 'arrange themselves in the following lines':

> 'When I return to my hotel,
>   At ten o'clock p.m.,
> The waiters think I am unwell;
>   I do not care for them.
> But when I've locked my chamber door,
>   And put my boots outside,
> I dance all night upon the floor.
> And even if my neighbours swore,
> I'd go on dancing all the more,
> For I'm acquainted with the law,
> And in despite of all their jaw,
>   Their protests I deride.'

Had not the landlord at this moment knocked at the door, it is probable that quite a long poem might have been laid before the reader. To judge from his look of surprise when he found himself in the room, Herr Kristensen was struck, as Anderson had been, by something unusual in its aspect. But he made no remark. Anderson's photographs interested him mightily, and formed the text of many autobiographical discourses. Nor is it quite clear how the conversation could have been diverted into the desired channel of Number 13, had not the lawyer at this moment begun to sing, and to sing in a manner which could leave no doubt in anyone's mind that he was either exceedingly drunk or raving mad. It was a high, thin voice that they heard, and it seemed dry, as if from long disuse. Of words or tune there was no question. It went sailing up to a surprising height, and was carried down with a despairing moan as of a winter wind in a hollow chimney, or an organ whose wind fails suddenly. It was a really horrible sound, and Anderson felt that if he had been alone he must have fled for refuge and society to some neighbour bagman's room.

The landlord sat open-mouthed.

'I don't understand it,' he said at last, wiping his forehead. 'It is dreadful. I have heard it once before, but I made sure it was a cat.'

'Is he mad?' said Anderson.

'He must be; and what a sad thing! Such a good customer, too, and so successful in his business, by what I hear, and a young family to bring up.'

Just then came an impatient knock at the door, and the knocker entered, without waiting to be asked. It was the lawyer, in deshabille and very rough-haired; and very angry he looked.

'I beg pardon, sir,' he said, 'but I should be much obliged if you would kindly desist——'

Here he stopped, for it was evident that neither of the persons before him was responsible for the disturbance; and after a moment's lull it swelled forth again more wildly than before.

'But what in the name of Heaven does it mean?' broke out the lawyer. 'Where is it? Who is it? Am I going out of my mind?'

'Surely, Herr Jensen, it comes from your room next door? Isn't there a cat or something stuck in the chimney?'

This was the best that occurred to Anderson to say, and he realized its futility as he spoke; but anything was better than to stand and listen to that horrible voice, and look at the broad, white face of the landlord, all perspiring and quivering as he clutched the arms of his chair.

'Impossible,' said the lawyer, 'impossible. There is no chimney. I came here because I was convinced the noise was going on here. It was certainly in the next room to mine.'

'Was there no door between yours and mine?' said Anderson eagerly.

'No, sir,' said Herr Jensen, rather sharply. 'At least, not this morning.'

'Ah!' said Anderson. 'Nor to-night?'

'I am not sure,' said the lawyer with some hesitation.

Suddenly the crying or singing voice in the next room died away, and the singer was heard seemingly to laugh to himself in a crooning manner. The three men actually shivered at the sound. Then there was a silence.

'Come,' said the lawyer, 'what have you to say, Herr Kristensen? What does this mean?'

'Good Heaven!' said Kristensen. 'How should I tell! I know no more than you, gentlemen. I pray I may never hear such a noise again.'

'So do I,' said Herr Jensen, and he added something under his breath. Anderson thought it sounded like the last words of the Psalter, '*omnis spiritus laudet Dominum*,'* but he could not be sure.

'But we must do something,' said Anderson—'the three of us. Shall we go and investigate in the next room?'

'But that is Herr Jensen's room,' wailed the landlord. 'It is no use; he has come from there himself.'

'I am not so sure,' said Jensen. 'I think this gentleman is right: we must go and see.'

The only weapons of defence that could be mustered on the spot were a stick and umbrella. The expedition went out into the passage, not without quakings. There was a deadly quiet outside, but a light shone from under the next door. Anderson and Jensen approached it. The latter turned the handle, and gave a sudden vigorous push. No use. The door stood fast.

'Herr Kristensen,' said Jensen, 'will you go and fetch the strongest servant you have in the place? We must see this through.'

The landlord nodded, and hurried off, glad to be away from the scene of action. Jensen and Anderson remained outside looking at the door.

'It *is* Number 13, you see,' said the latter.

'Yes; there is your door, and there is mine,' said Jensen.

'My room has three windows in the daytime,' said Anderson, with difficulty suppressing a nervous laugh.

'By George, so has mine!' said the lawyer, turning and looking at Anderson. His back was now to the door. In that moment the door opened, and an arm came out and clawed at his shoulder. It was clad in ragged, yellowish linen, and the bare skin, where it could be seen, had long grey hair upon it.

Anderson was just in time to pull Jensen out of its reach with a cry of disgust and fright, when the door shut again, and a low laugh was heard.

Jensen had seen nothing, but when Anderson hurriedly told him what a risk he had run, he fell into a great state of agitation, and suggested that they should retire from the enterprise and lock themselves up in one or other of their rooms.

However, while he was developing this plan, the landlord and two able-bodied men arrived on the scene, all looking rather serious and alarmed. Jensen met them with a torrent of description and explanation, which did not at all tend to encourage them for the fray.

The men dropped the crowbars they had brought, and said flatly that they were not going to risk their throats in that devil's den. The landlord was miserably nervous and undecided, conscious that if the danger were not faced his hotel was ruined, and very loth to face it himself. Luckily Anderson hit upon a way of rallying the demoralized force.

'Is this,' he said, 'the Danish courage I have heard so much of? It isn't a German in there, and if it was, we are five to one.'

The two servants and Jensen were stung into action by this, and made a dash at the door.

'Stop!' said Anderson. 'Don't lose your heads. You stay out here with the light, landlord, and one of you two men break in the door, and don't go in when it gives way.'

The men nodded, and the younger stepped forward, raised his crowbar, and dealt a tremendous blow on the upper panel. The result was not in the least what any of them anticipated. There was no cracking or rending of wood—only a dull sound, as if the solid wall had been struck. The man dropped his tool with a shout, and began rubbing his elbow. His cry drew their eyes upon him for a moment; then Anderson looked at the door again. It was gone; the plaster wall of the passage stared him in the face, with a considerable gash in it where the crowbar had struck it. Number 13 had passed out of existence.

For a brief space they stood perfectly still, gazing at the blank wall. An early cock in the yard beneath was heard to crow; and as Anderson glanced in the direction of the sound, he saw through the window at the end of the long passage that the eastern sky was paling to the dawn.

*   *   *   *   *

'Perhaps,' said the landlord, with hesitation, 'you gentlemen would like another room for to-night—a double-bedded one?'

Neither Jensen nor Anderson was averse to the suggestion. They felt inclined to hunt in couples after their late experience. It was found convenient, when each of them went to his room to collect the articles he wanted for the night, that the other should go with him and hold the candle. They noticed that both Number 12 and Number 14 had *three* windows.

Next morning the same party reassembled in Number 12. The landlord was naturally anxious to avoid engaging outside help, and yet it was imperative that the mystery attaching to that part of the house should be cleared up. Accordingly the two servants had been induced to take upon them the function of carpenters. The furniture was cleared away, and, at the cost of a good many irretrievably damaged planks, that portion of the floor was taken up which lay nearest to Number 14.

You will naturally suppose that a skeleton—say that of Mag. Nicolas Francken—was discovered. That was not so. What they did find lying between the beams which supported the flooring was a small copper box. In it was a neatly-folded vellum document, with about twenty lines of writing. Both Anderson and Jensen (who proved to be something of a palæographer)* were much excited by this discovery, which promised to afford the key to these extraordinary phenomena.

*   *   *   *   *

I possess a copy of an astrological work which I have never read. It has, by way of frontispiece, a woodcut by Hans Sebald Beham,* representing a number of sages seated round a table. This detail may enable connoisseurs to identify the book. I cannot myself recollect its title, and it is not at this moment within reach; but the fly-leaves of it are covered with writing, and, during the ten years in which I have owned the volume, I have not been able to determine which way up this writing ought to be read, much less in what language it is. Not dissimilar was the position of Anderson and Jensen after the protracted examination to which they submitted the document in the copper box.

After two days' contemplation of it, Jensen, who was the bolder spirit of the two, hazarded the conjecture that the language was either Latin or Old Danish.

Anderson ventured upon no surmises, and was very willing to surrender the box and the parchment to the Historical Society of Viborg to be placed in their museum.

I had the whole story from him a few months later, as we sat in a wood near Upsala,* after a visit to the library there, where we—or, rather, I—had laughed over the contract by which Daniel Salthenius* (in later life Professor of Hebrew at Königsberg) sold himself to Satan. Anderson was not really amused.

'Young idiot!' he said, meaning Salthenius, who was only an undergraduate when he committed that indiscretion, 'how did he know what company he was courting?'

And when I suggested the usual considerations he only grunted. That same afternoon he told me what you have read; but he refused to draw any inferences from it, and to assent to any that I drew for him.

COUNT MAGNUS

B Y what means the papers out of which I have made a connected story came into my hands is the last point which the reader will learn from these pages. But it is necessary to prefix to my extracts from them a statement of the form in which I possess them.

They consist, then, partly of a series of collections for a book of travels, such a volume as was a common product of the forties and fifties. Horace Marryat's *Journal of a Residence in Jutland and the Danish Isles** is a fair specimen of the class to which I allude. These books usually treated of some unfamiliar district on the Continent. They were illustrated with woodcuts or steel plates. They gave details of hotel accommodation, and of means of communication, such as we now expect to find in any well-regulated guide-book, and they dealt largely in reported conversations with intelligent foreigners, racy innkeepers and garrulous peasants. In a word, they were chatty.

Begun with the idea of furnishing material for such a book, my papers as they progressed assumed the character of a record of one single personal experience, and this record was continued up to the very eve, almost, of its termination.

The writer was a Mr. Wraxall. For my knowledge of him I have to depend entirely on the evidence his writings afford, and from these I deduce that he was a man past middle age, possessed of some private means, and very much alone in the world. He had, it seems, no settled abode in England, but was a denizen of hotels and boarding-houses. It is probable that he entertained the idea of settling down at some future time which never came; and I think it also likely that the Pantechnicon fire* in the early seventies must have destroyed a great deal that would have thrown light on his antecedents, for he refers once or twice to property of his that was warehoused at that establishment.

It is further apparent that Mr. Wraxall had published a book, and that it treated of a holiday he had once taken in Brittany. More than this I cannot say about his work, because a diligent search in

bibliographical works has convinced me that it must have appeared
either anonymously or under a pseudonym.

As to his character, it is not difficult to form some superficial opinion. He must have been an intelligent and cultivated man. It seems that
he was near being a Fellow of his college at Oxford—Brasenose, as I
judge from the Calendar. His besetting fault was pretty clearly that of
over-inquisitiveness, possibly a good fault in a traveller, certainly a
fault for which this traveller paid dearly enough in the end.

On what proved to be his last expedition, he was plotting another
book. Scandinavia, a region not widely known to Englishmen forty
years ago, had struck him as an interesting field. He must have lighted
on some old books of Swedish history or memoirs, and the idea had
struck him that there was room for a book descriptive of travel in
Sweden, interspersed with episodes from the history of some of the
great Swedish families. He procured letters of introduction, therefore, to some persons of quality in Sweden, and set out thither in the
early summer of 1863.

Of his travels in the North there is no need to speak, nor of his residence of some weeks in Stockholm. I need only mention that some
savant resident there put him on the track of an important collection
of family papers belonging to the proprietors of an ancient manor-
house in Vestergothland, and obtained for him permission to
examine them.

The manor-house, or *herrgård*, in question is to be called Råbäck*
(pronounced something like Roebeck), though that is not its name. It
is one of the best buildings of its kind in all the country, and the picture of it in Dahlenberg's *Suecia antiqua et moderna*,* engraved in
1694, shows it very much as the tourist may see it to-day. It was built
soon after 1600, and is, roughly speaking, very much like an English
house of that period in respect of material—red-brick with stone
facings—and style. The man who built it was a scion of the great
house of De la Gardie,* and his descendants possess it still. De la
Gardie is the name by which I will designate them when mention of
them becomes necessary.

They received Mr. Wraxall with great kindness and courtesy, and
pressed him to stay in the house as long as his researches lasted. But,
preferring to be independent, and mistrusting his powers of convers-
ing in Swedish, he settled himself at the village inn, which turned out
quite sufficiently comfortable, at any rate during the summer months.

This arrangement would entail a short walk daily to and from the manor-house of something under a mile. The house itself stood in a park, and was protected—we should say grown up—with large old timber. Near it you found the walled garden, and then entered a close wood fringing one of the small lakes with which the whole country is pitted. Then came the wall of the demesne, and you climbed a steep knoll—a knob of rock lightly covered with soil—and on the top of this stood the church, fenced in with tall dark trees. It was a curious building to English eyes. The nave and aisles were low, and filled with pews and galleries. In the western gallery stood the handsome old organ, gaily painted, and with silver pipes. The ceiling was flat, and had been adorned by a seventeenth-century artist with a strange and hideous 'Last Judgment,' full of lurid flames, falling cities, burning ships, crying souls, and brown and smiling demons. Handsome brass coronæ hung from the roof; the pulpit was like a doll's-house, covered with little painted wooden cherubs and saints; a stand with three hour-glasses was hinged to the preacher's desk. Such sights as these may be seen in many a church in Sweden now, but what distinguished this one was an addition to the original building. At the eastern end of the north aisle the builder of the manor-house had erected a mausoleum* for himself and his family. It was a largish eight-sided building, lighted by a series of oval windows, and it had a domed roof, topped by a kind of pumpkin-shaped object rising into a spire, a form in which Swedish architects greatly delighted. The roof was of copper externally, and was painted black, while the walls, in common with those of the church, were staringly white. To this mausoleum there was no access from the church. It had a portal and steps of its own on the northern side.

Past the churchyard the path to the village goes, and not more than three or four minutes bring you to the inn door.

On the first day of his stay at Råbäck Mr. Wraxall found the church door open, and made those notes of the interior which I have epitomized. Into the mausoleum, however, he could not make his way. He could by looking through the keyhole just descry that there were fine marble effigies and sarcophagi of copper, and a wealth of armorial ornament, which made him very anxious to spend some time in investigation.

The papers he had come to examine at the manor-house proved to be of just the kind he wanted for his book. There were family correspondence, journals, and account-books of the earliest owners of the estate, very carefully kept and clearly written, full of amusing and picturesque detail. The first De la Gardie appeared in them as a strong and capable man. Shortly after the building of the mansion there had been a period of distress in the district, and the peasants had risen and attacked several châteaux and done some damage. The owner of Råbäck took a leading part in suppressing the trouble, and there was reference to executions of ringleaders and severe punishments inflicted with no sparing hand.

The portrait of this Magnus de la Gardie was one of the best in the house, and Mr. Wraxall studied it with no little interest after his day's work. He gives no detailed description of it, but I gather that the face impressed him rather by its power than by its beauty or goodness; in fact, he writes that Count Magnus was an almost phenomenally ugly man.

On this day Mr. Wraxall took his supper with the family, and walked back in the late but still bright evening.

'I must remember,' he writes, 'to ask the sexton if he can let me into the mausoleum at the church. He evidently has access to it himself, for I saw him to-night standing on the steps, and, as I thought, locking or unlocking the door.'

I find that early on the following day Mr. Wraxall had some conversation with his landlord. His setting it down at such length as he does surprised me at first; but I soon realized that the papers I was reading were, at least in their beginning, the materials for the book he was meditating, and that it was to have been one of those quasi-journalistic productions which admit of the introduction of an admixture of conversational matter.

His object, he says, was to find out whether any traditions of Count Magnus de la Gardie lingered on in the scenes of that gentleman's activity, and whether the popular estimates of him were favourable or not. He found that the Count was decidedly not a favourite. If his tenants came late to their work on the days which they owed to him as Lord of the Manor, they were set on the wooden horse, or flogged and branded in the manor-house yard. One or two cases there were of men who had occupied lands which encroached on the lord's domain, and whose houses had been mysteriously burnt on a winter's night, with the whole family inside. But what seemed to dwell on the inn-keeper's mind most—for he returned to the subject more than once—was that the Count had been on the Black Pilgrimage,* and had brought something or someone back with him.

You will naturally inquire, as Mr. Wraxall did, what the Black Pilgrimage may have been. But your curiosity on the point must remain unsatisfied for the time being, just as his did. The landlord was evidently unwilling to give a full answer, or indeed any answer, on the point, and, being called out for a moment, trotted off with obvious alacrity, only putting his head in at the door a few minutes afterwards to say that he was called away to Skara,* and should not be back till evening.

So Mr. Wraxall had to go unsatisfied to his day's work at the manor-house. The papers on which he was just then engaged soon put his thoughts into another channel, for he had to occupy himself with glancing over the correspondence between Sophia Albertina in Stockholm and her married cousin Ulrica Leonora at Råbäck in the years 1705–1710. The letters were of exceptional interest from the light they threw upon the culture of that period in Sweden, as anyone can testify who has read the full edition of them in the publications of the Swedish Historical Manuscripts Commission.

In the afternoon he had done with these, and after returning the boxes in which they were kept to their places on the shelf, he proceeded, very naturally, to take down some of the volumes nearest to them, in order to determine which of them had best be his principal subject of investigation next day. The shelf he had hit upon was occupied mostly by a collection of account-books in the writing of the first Count Magnus. But one among them was not an account-book, but a book of alchemical and other tracts in another sixteenth-century hand. Not being very familiar with alchemical literature. Mr. Wraxall spends much space which he might have spared in setting out the names and beginnings of the various treatises: The book of the Phœnix, book of the Thirty Words, book of the Toad, book of Miriam, Turba philosophorum, and so forth;* and then he announces with a good deal of circumstance his delight at finding, on a leaf originally left blank near the middle of the book, some writing of Count Magnus himself headed 'Liber nigræ peregrinationis.'* It is true that only a few lines were written, but there was quite enough to show that the landlord had that morning been referring to a belief at least as old as the time of Count Magnus, and probably shared by him. This is the English of what was written:

'If any man desires to obtain a long life, if he would obtain a faithful messenger and see the blood of his enemies, it is necessary that he should first go into the city of Chorazin,* and there salute the prince. . . .' Here there was an erasure of one word, not very thoroughly done, so that Mr. Wraxall felt pretty sure that he was right in reading it as *aëris* ('of the air').* But there was no more of the text copied, only a line in Latin: 'Quære reliqua hujus materiei inter secretiora' (See the rest of this matter among the more private things).

It could not be denied that this threw a rather lurid light upon the tastes and beliefs of the Count; but to Mr. Wraxall, separated from him by nearly three centuries, the thought that he might have added to his general forcefulness alchemy, and to alchemy something like magic, only made him a more picturesque figure; and when, after a rather prolonged contemplation of his picture in the hall, Mr. Wraxall set out on his homeward way, his mind was full of the thought of Count Magnus. He had no eyes for his surroundings, no perception of the evening scents of the woods or the evening light on the lake; and when all of a sudden he pulled up short, he was astonished to find himself already at the gate of the churchyard, and within a few minutes of his dinner. His eyes fell on the mausoleum.

'Ah,' he said, 'Count Magnus, there you are. I should dearly like to see you.'

'Like many solitary men,' he writes, 'I have a habit of talking to myself aloud; and, unlike some of the Greek and Latin particles, I do not expect an answer. Certainly, and perhaps fortunately in this case, there was neither voice nor any that regarded: only the woman who, I suppose, was cleaning up the church, dropped some metallic object on the floor, whose clang startled me. Count Magnus, I think, sleeps sound enough.'

That same evening the landlord of the inn, who had heard Mr. Wraxall say that he wished to see the clerk or deacon (as he would be called in Sweden) of the parish, introduced him to that official in the inn parlour. A visit to the De la Gardie tomb-house was soon arranged for the next day, and a little general conversation ensued.

Mr. Wraxall, remembering that one function of Scandinavian deacons is to teach candidates for Confirmation, thought he would refresh his own memory on a Biblical point.

'Can you tell me,' he said, 'anything about Chorazin?'

The deacon seemed startled, but readily reminded him how that village had once been denounced.

'To be sure,' said Mr. Wraxall; 'it is, I suppose, quite a ruin now?'

'So I expect,' replied the deacon. 'I have heard some of our old priests say that Antichrist is to be born there; and there are tales——'

'Ah! what tales are those?' Mr. Wraxall put in.

'Tales, I was going to say, which I have forgotten,' said the deacon; and soon after that he said good night.

The landlord was now alone, and at Mr. Wraxall's mercy; and that inquirer was not inclined to spare him.

'Herr Nielsen,' he said, 'I have found out something about the Black Pilgrimage. You may as well tell me what you know. What did the Count bring back with him?'

Swedes are habitually slow, perhaps, in answering, or perhaps the landlord was an exception. I am not sure; but Mr. Wraxall notes that the landlord spent at least one minute in looking at him before he said anything at all. Then he came close up to his guest, and with a good deal of effort he spoke:

'Mr. Wraxall, I can tell you this one little tale, and no more—not any more. You must not ask anything when I have done. In my grandfather's time—that is, ninety-two years ago—there were two men who said: "The Count is dead; we do not care for him. We will go to-night and have a free hunt in his wood"—the long wood on the hill that you have seen behind Råbäck. Well, those that heard them say this, they said: "No, do not go; we are sure you will meet with persons walking who should not be walking. They should be resting, not walking." These men laughed. There were no forest-men to keep the wood, because no one wished to hunt there. The family were not here at the house. These men could do what they wished.

'Very well, they go to the wood that night. My grandfather was sitting here in this room. It was the summer, and a light night. With the window open, he could see out to the wood, and hear.

'So he sat there, and two or three men with him, and they listened. At first they hear nothing at all; then they hear someone—you know how far away it is—they hear someone scream, just as if the most inside part of his soul was twisted out of him. All of them in the room caught hold of each other, and they sat so for three-quarters of an hour. Then they hear someone else, only about three hundred ells off.

They hear him laugh out loud: it was not one of those two men that laughed, and, indeed, they have all of them said that it was not any man at all. After that they hear a great door shut.

'Then, when it was just light with the sun, they all went to the priest. They said to him:

' "Father, put on your gown and your ruff, and come to bury these men, Anders Bjornsen and Hans Thorbjorn."

'You understand that they were sure these men were dead. So they went to the wood—my grandfather never forgot this. He said they were all like so many dead men themselves. The priest, too, he was in a white fear. He said when they came to him:

' "I heard one cry in the night, and I heard one laugh afterwards. If I cannot forget that, I shall not be able to sleep again."

'So they went to the wood, and they found these men on the edge of the wood. Hans Thorbjorn was standing with his back against a tree, and all the time he was pushing with his hands—pushing something away from him which was not there. So he was not dead. And they led him away, and took him to the house at Nykjoping, and he died before the winter; but he went on pushing with his hands. Also Anders Bjornsen was there; but he was dead. And I tell you this about Anders Bjornsen, that he was once a beautiful man, but now his face was not there, because the flesh of it was sucked away off the bones. You understand that? My grandfather did not forget that. And they laid him on the bier which they brought, and they put a cloth over his head, and the priest walked before; and they began to sing the psalm for the dead as well as they could. So, as they were singing the end of the first verse, one fell down, who was carrying the head of the bier, and the others looked back, and they saw that the cloth had fallen off, and the eyes of Anders Bjornsen were looking up, because there was nothing to close over them. And this they could not bear. Therefore the priest laid the cloth upon him, and sent for a spade, and they buried him in that place.'

The next day Mr. Wraxall records that the deacon called for him soon after his breakfast, and took him to the church and mausoleum. He noticed that the key of the latter was hung on a nail just by the pulpit, and it occurred to him that, as the church door seemed to be left unlocked as a rule, it would not be difficult for him to pay a second and more private visit to the monuments if there proved to be more of interest among them than could be digested at first. The building, when he entered it, he found not unimposing. The monuments, mostly large erections of the seventeenth and eighteenth centuries, were dignified if luxuriant, and the epitaphs and heraldry were copious. The central space of the domed room was occupied by three copper sarcophagi, covered with finely-engraved ornament. Two of them had, as is commonly the case in Denmark and Sweden, a large metal crucifix on the lid. The third, that of Count Magnus, as it appeared, had, instead of that, a full-length effigy engraved upon it, and round the edge were several bands of similar ornament representing various scenes. One was a battle, with cannon belching out smoke, and walled towns, and troops of pikemen. Another showed an execution. In a third, among trees, was a man running at full speed, with flying hair and outstretched hands. After him followed a strange form; it would be hard to say whether the artist had intended it for a man, and was unable to give the requisite similitude, or whether it was intentionally made as monstrous as it looked. In view of the skill with which the rest of the drawing was done, Mr. Wraxall felt inclined to adopt the latter idea. The figure was unduly short, and was for the most part muffled in a hooded garment which swept the ground. The only part of the form which projected from that shelter was not shaped like any hand or arm. Mr. Wraxall compares it to the tentacle of a devil-fish,* and continues: 'On seeing this, I said to myself, "This, then, which is evidently an allegorical representation of some kind—a fiend pursuing a hunted soul—may be the origin of the story of Count Magnus and his mysterious companion. Let us see how the huntsman is pictured: doubtless it will be a demon blowing his horn."' But, as it turned out, there was no such sensational figure, only the semblance of a cloaked man on a hillock, who stood leaning on a stick, and watching the hunt with an interest which the engraver had tried to express in his attitude.

Mr. Wraxall noted the finely-worked and massive steel padlocks— three in number—which secured the sarcophagus. One of them, he saw, was detached, and lay on the pavement. And then, unwilling to delay the deacon longer or to waste his own working-time, he made his way onward to the manor-house.

'It is curious,' he notes, 'how on retracing a familiar path one's thoughts engross one to the absolute exclusion of surrounding objects. To-night, for the second time, I had entirely failed to notice where I was going (I had planned a private visit to the tomb-house to copy the epitaphs), when I suddenly, as it were, awoke to consciousness, and found myself (as before) turning in at the church-yard gate, and, I believe, singing or chanting some such words as, "Are you awake, Count Magnus? Are you asleep, Count Magnus?" and then something more which I have failed to recollect. It seemed to me that I must have been behaving in this nonsensical way for some time.'

He found the key of the mausoleum where he had expected to find it, and copied the greater part of what he wanted; in fact, he stayed until the light began to fail him.

'I must have been wrong,' he writes, 'in saying that one of the padlocks of my Count's sarcophagus was unfastened; I see to-night that two are loose. I picked both up, and laid them carefully on the window-ledge, after trying unsuccessfully to close them. The remaining one is still firm, and, though I take it to be a spring lock, I cannot guess how it is opened. Had I succeeded in undoing it, I am almost afraid I should have taken the liberty of opening the sarcophagus. It is strange, the interest I feel in the personality of this, I fear, somewhat ferocious and grim old noble.'

The day following was, as it turned out, the last of Mr. Wraxall's stay at Råbäck. He received letters connected with certain invest-ments which made it desirable that he should return to England; his work among the papers was practically done, and travelling was slow. He decided, therefore, to make his farewells, put some finishing touches to his notes, and be off.

These finishing touches and farewells, as it turned out, took more time than he had expected. The hospitable family insisted on his staying to dine with them—they dined at three—and it was verging on half-past six before he was outside the iron gates of Råbäck. He dwelt on every step of his walk by the lake, determined to saturate himself, now that he trod it for the last time, in the sentiment of the place and hour. And when he reached the summit of the churchyard knoll, he lingered for many minutes, gazing at the limitless prospect of woods near and distant, all dark beneath a sky of liquid green. When at last he turned to go, the thought struck him that surely he must bid farewell to Count Magnus as well as the rest of the De la Gardies. The church was but twenty yards away, and he knew where the key of the mausoleum hung. It was not long before he was standing over the great copper coffin, and, as usual, talking to himself aloud. 'You may have been a bit of a rascal in your time, Magnus,' he was saying, 'but for all that I should like to see you or, rather——'

'Just at that instant,' he says, 'I felt a blow on my foot. Hastily enough I drew it back, and something fell on the pavement with a clash. It was the third, the last of the three padlocks which had fastened the sarcophagus. I stooped to pick it up, and—Heaven is my witness that I am writing only the bare truth—before I had raised myself there was a sound of metal hinges creaking, and I distinctly saw the lid shifting upwards. I may have behaved like a coward, but I could not for my life stay for one moment. I was outside that dreadful building in less time than I can write—almost as quickly as I could have said—the words; and what frightens me yet more, I could not turn the key in the lock. As I sit here in my room noting these facts, I ask myself (it was not twenty minutes ago) whether that noise of creaking metal continued, and I cannot tell whether it did or not. I only know that there was something more than I have written that alarmed me, but whether it was sound or sight I am not able to remember. What is this that I have done?'

Poor Mr. Wraxall! He set out on his journey to England on the next day, as he had planned, and he reached England in safety; and yet, as I gather from his changed hand and inconsequent jottings, a broken man. One of several small notebooks that have come to me with his papers gives, not a key to, but a kind of inkling of, his experiences. Much of his journey was made by canal-boat, and I find not less than six painful attempts to enumerate and describe his fellow-passengers. The entries are of this kind:

'24. Pastor of village in Skåne. Usual black coat and soft black hat.
'25. Commercial traveller from Stockholm going to Trollhättan.* Black cloak, brown hat.
'26. Man in long black cloak, broad-leafed hat, very old-fashioned.'

This entry is lined out, and a note added: 'Perhaps identical with No. 13. Have not yet seen his face.' On referring to No. 13, I find that he is a Roman priest in a cassock.*

The net result of the reckoning is always the same. Twenty-eight people appear in the enumeration, one being always a man in a long black cloak and broad hat, and the other a 'short figure in dark cloak and hood.' On the other hand, it is always noted that only twenty-six passengers appear at meals, and that the man in the cloak is perhaps absent, and the short figure is certainly absent.

On reaching England, it appears that Mr. Wraxall landed at Harwich,* and that he resolved at once to put himself out of the reach of some person or persons whom he never specifies, but whom he had evidently come to regard as his pursuers. Accordingly he took a vehicle—it was a closed fly—not trusting the railway, and drove across country to the village of Belchamp St. Paul.* It was about nine o'clock on a moonlight August night when he neared the place. He was sitting forward, and looking out of the window at the fields and thickets—there was little else to be seen—racing past him. Suddenly he came to a cross-road. At the corner two figures were standing motionless; both were in dark cloaks; the taller one wore a hat, the shorter a hood. He had no time to see their faces, nor did they make any motion that he could discern. Yet the horse shied violently and broke into a gallop, and Mr. Wraxall sank back into his seat in something like desperation. He had seen them before.

Arrived at Belchamp St. Paul, he was fortunate enough to find a decent furnished lodging, and for the next twenty-four hours he lived, comparatively speaking, in peace. His last notes were written on this day. They are too disjointed and ejaculatory to be given here in full, but the substance of them is clear enough. He is expecting a visit from his pursuers—how or when he knows not—and his constant cry is 'What has he done?' and 'Is there no hope?' Doctors, he knows, would call him mad, policemen would laugh at him. The parson is away. What can he do but lock his door and cry to God?

People still remembered last year at Belchamp St. Paul how a strange gentleman came one evening in August years back; and how the next morning but one he was found dead, and there was an inquest; and the jury that viewed the body fainted, seven of 'em did, and none of 'em wouldn't speak to what they see, and the verdict was visitation of God; and how the people as kep' the 'ouse moved out that same week, and went away from that part. But they do not, I think, know that any glimmer of light has ever been thrown, or could be thrown, on the mystery. It so happened that last year the little house came into my hands as part of a legacy. It had stood empty since 1863, and there seemed no prospect of letting it; so I had it pulled down, and the papers of which I have given you an abstract were found in a forgotten cupboard under the window in the best bedroom.

'OH, WHISTLE, AND I'LL COME TO YOU, MY LAD'

❦

'I SUPPOSE you will be getting away pretty soon, now Full term is over, Professor,' said a person not in the story to the Professor of Ontography, soon after they had sat down next to each other at a feast in the hospitable hall of St. James's College.*

The Professor was young, neat, and precise in speech.

'Yes,' he said; 'my friends have been making me take up golf this term, and I mean to go to the East Coast—in point of fact to Burnstow*—(I dare say you know it) for a week or ten days, to improve my game. I hope to get off to-morrow.'

'Oh, Parkins,' said his neighbour on the other side, 'if you are going to Burnstow, I wish you would look at the site of the Templars' preceptory,* and let me know if you think it would be any good to have a dig there in the summer.'

It was, as you might suppose, a person of antiquarian pursuits who said this, but, since he merely appears in this prologue, there is no need to give his entitlements.

'Certainly,' said Parkins, the Professor: 'if you will describe to me whereabouts the site is, I will do my best to give you an idea of the lie of the land when I get back; or I could write to you about it, if you would tell me where you are likely to be.'

'Don't trouble to do that, thanks. It's only that I'm thinking of taking my family in that direction in the Long,* and it occurred to me that, as very few of the English preceptories have ever been properly planned, I might have an opportunity of doing something useful on off-days.'

The Professor rather sniffed at the idea that planning out a preceptory could be described as useful. His neighbour continued:

'The site—I doubt if there is anything showing above ground— must be down quite close to the beach now. The sea has encroached tremendously, as you know, all along that bit of coast. I should think, from the map, that it must be about three-quarters of a mile from the Globe Inn, at the north end of the town. Where are you going to stay?'

'Well, *at* the Globe Inn, as a matter of fact,' said Parkins; 'I have engaged a room there. I couldn't get in anywhere else; most of the lodging-houses are shut up in winter, it seems; and, as it is, they tell me that the only room of any size I can have is really a double-bedded one, and that they haven't a corner in which to store the other bed, and so on. But I must have a fairly large room, for I am taking some books down, and mean to do a bit of work; and though I don't quite fancy having an empty bed—not to speak of two—in what I may call for the time being my study, I suppose I can manage to rough it for the short time I shall be there.'

'Do you call having an extra bed in your room roughing it, Parkins?' said a bluff person opposite. 'Look here, I shall come down and occupy it for a bit; it'll be company for you.'

The Professor quivered, but managed to laugh in a courteous manner.

'By all means, Rogers; there's nothing I should like better. But I'm afraid you would find it rather dull; you don't play golf, do you?'

'No, thank Heaven!' said rude Mr. Rogers.

'Well, you see, when I'm not writing I shall most likely be out on the links, and that, as I say, would be rather dull for you, I'm afraid.'

'Oh, I don't know! There's certain to be somebody I know in the place; but, of course, if you don't want me, speak the word, Parkins; I shan't be offended. Truth, as you always tell us, is never offensive.'

Parkins was, indeed, scrupulously polite and strictly truthful. It is to be feared that Mr. Rogers sometimes practised upon his knowledge of these characteristics. In Parkins's breast there was a conflict now raging, which for a moment or two did not allow him to answer. That interval being over, he said:

'Well, if you want the exact truth, Rogers, I was considering whether the room I speak of would really be large enough to accommodate us both comfortably; and also whether (mind, I shouldn't have said this if you hadn't pressed me) you would not constitute something in the nature of a hindrance to my work.'

Rogers laughed loudly.

'Well done, Parkins!' he said. 'It's all right. I promise not to interrupt your work; don't you disturb yourself about that. No, I won't come if you don't want me; but I thought I should do so nicely to keep the ghosts off.' Here he might have been seen to wink and to nudge his next neighbour. Parkins might also have been seen to become pink. 'I beg pardon, Parkins,' Rogers continued; 'I oughtn't to have said that. I forgot you didn't like levity on these topics.'

'Well,' Parkins said, 'as you have mentioned the matter, I freely own that I do *not* like careless talk about what you call ghosts. A man in my position,' he went on, raising his voice a little, 'cannot, I find, be too careful about appearing to sanction the current beliefs on such subjects. As you know, Rogers, or as you ought to know; for I think I have never concealed my views——'

'No, you certainly have not, old man,' put in Rogers *sotto voce*.

'——I hold that any semblance, any appearance of concession to the view that such things might exist is equivalent to a renunciation of all that I hold most sacred. But I'm afraid I have not succeeded in securing your attention.'

'Your *undivided* attention, was what Dr. Blimber* actually *said*,'[1] Rogers interrupted, with every appearance of an earnest desire for accuracy. 'But I beg your pardon, Parkins: I'm stopping you.'

'No, not at all,' said Parkins. 'I don't remember Blimber; perhaps he was before my time. But I needn't go on. I'm sure you know what I mean.'

'Yes, yes,' said Rogers, rather hastily—'just so. We'll go into it fully at Burnstow, or somewhere.'

In repeating the above dialogue I have tried to give the impression which it made on me, that Parkins was something of an old woman—rather hen-like, perhaps, in his little ways; totally destitute, alas! of the sense of humour, but at the same time dauntless and sincere in his convictions, and a man deserving of the greatest respect. Whether or not the reader has gathered so much, that was the character which Parkins had.

On the following day Parkins did, as he had hoped, succeed in getting away from his college, and in arriving at Burnstow. He was made welcome at the Globe Inn, was safely installed in the large double-bedded room of which we have heard, and was able before retiring to rest to arrange his materials for work in apple-pie order upon a commodious table which occupied the outer end of the room, and was surrounded on three sides by windows looking out seaward; that is to say, the central window looked straight out to sea, and those on the left and right

---

[1] Mr. Rogers was wrong, *vide Dombey and Son*, chapter xii.

commanded prospects along the shore to the north and south respectively. On the south you saw the village of Burnstow. On the north no houses were to be seen, but only the beach and the low cliff backing it. Immediately in front was a strip—not considerable—of rough grass, dotted with old anchors, capstans, and so forth; then a broad path; then the beach. Whatever may have been the original distance between the Globe Inn and the sea, not more than sixty yards now separated them.

The rest of the population of the inn was, of course, a golfing one, and included few elements that call for a special description. The most conspicuous figure was, perhaps, that of an *ancien militaire*, secretary of a London club, and possessed of a voice of incredible strength, and of views of a pronouncedly Protestant type. These were apt to find utterance after his attendance upon the ministrations of the Vicar, an estimable man with inclinations towards a picturesque ritual, which he gallantly kept down as far as he could out of deference to East Anglian tradition.

Professor Parkins, one of whose principal characteristics was pluck, spent the greater part of the day following his arrival at Burnstow in what he had called improving his game, in company with this Colonel Wilson: and during the afternoon—whether the process of improvement were to blame or not, I am not sure—the Colonel's demeanour assumed a colouring so lurid that even Parkins jibbed at the thought of walking home with him from the links. He determined, after a short and furtive look at that bristling moustache and those incarnadined features, that it would be wiser to allow the influences of tea and tobacco to do what they could with the Colonel before the dinner-hour should render a meeting inevitable.

'I might walk home to-night along the beach,' he reflected—'yes, and take a look—there will be light enough for that—at the ruins of which Disney* was talking. I don't exactly know where they are, by the way; but I expect I can hardly help stumbling on them.'

This he accomplished, I may say, in the most literal sense, for in picking his way from the links to the shingle beach his foot caught, partly in a gorse-root and partly in a biggish stone, and over he went. When he got up and surveyed his surroundings, he found himself in a patch of somewhat broken ground covered with small depressions and mounds. These latter, when he came to examine them, proved to be simply masses of flints embedded in mortar and grown over with turf. He must, he quite rightly concluded, be on the site of the preceptory he had promised to look at. It seemed not unlikely to reward the spade of the explorer; enough of the foundations was probably left at no great depth to throw a good deal of light on the general plan. He remembered vaguely that the Templars, to whom this site had belonged, were in the habit of building round churches,* and he thought a particular series of the humps or mounds near him did appear to be arranged in something of a circular form. Few people can resist the temptation to try a little amateur research in a department quite outside their own, if only for the satisfaction of showing how successful they would have been had they only taken it up seriously. Our Professor, however, if he felt something of this mean desire, was also truly anxious to oblige Mr. Disney. So he paced with care the circular area he had noticed, and wrote down its rough dimensions in his pocket-book. Then he proceeded to examine an oblong eminence which lay east of the centre of the circle, and seemed to his thinking likely to be the base of a platform or altar. At one end of it, the north-ern, a patch of the turf was gone—removed by some boy or other creature *feræ naturæ*.* It might, he thought, be as well to probe the soil here for evidences of masonry, and he took out his knife and began scraping away the earth. And now followed another little discovery: a portion of soil fell inward as he scraped, and disclosed a small cavity. He lighted one match after another to help him to see of what nature the hole was, but the wind was too strong for them all. By tapping and scratching the sides with his knife, however, he was able to make out that it must be an artificial hole in masonry. It was rectangular, and the sides, top, and bottom, if not actually plastered, were smooth and regular. Of course it was empty. No! As he withdrew the knife he heard a metallic clink, and when he introduced his hand it met with a cylindrical object lying on the floor of the hole. Naturally enough, he picked it up, and when he brought it into the light, now fast fading, he could see that it, too, was of man's making—a metal tube about four inches long, and evidently of some considerable age.

By the time Parkins had made sure that there was nothing else in this odd receptacle, it was too late and too dark for him to think of undertaking any further search. What he had done had proved so unexpectedly interesting that he determined to sacrifice a little more of the daylight on the morrow to archæology. The object which he now had safe in his pocket was bound to be of some slight value at least, he felt sure.

Bleak and solemn was the view on which he took a last look before starting homeward. A faint yellow light in the west showed the links, on which a few figures moving towards the club-house were still visible, the squat martello tower, the lights of Aldsey* village, the pale ribbon of sands intersected at intervals by black wooden groynes, the dim and murmuring sea. The wind was bitter from the north, but was at his back when he set out for the Globe. He quickly rattled and clashed through the shingle and gained the sand, upon which, but for the groynes which had to be got over every few yards, the going was both good and quiet. One last look behind, to measure the distance he had made since leaving the ruined Templars' church, showed him a prospect of company on his walk, in the shape of a rather indistinct personage, who seemed to be making great efforts to catch up with him, but made little, if any, progress. I mean that there was an appearance of running about his movements, but that the distance between him and Parkins did not seem materially to lessen. So, at least, Parkins thought, and decided that he almost certainly did not know him, and that it would be absurd to wait until he came up. For all that, company, he began to think, would really be very welcome on that lonely shore, if only you could choose your companion. In his unenlightened days he had read of meetings in such places which even now would hardly bear thinking of. He went on thinking of them, however, until he reached home, and particularly of one which catches most people's fancy at some time of their childhood. 'Now I saw in my dream that Christian had gone but a very little way when he saw a foul fiend coming over the field to meet him.'* 'What should I do now,' he thought, 'if I looked back and caught sight of a black figure sharply defined against the yellow sky, and saw that it had horns and wings? I wonder whether I should stand or run for it. Luckily, the gentleman behind is not of that kind, and he seems to be about as far off now as when I saw him first. Well, at this rate he won't get his dinner as soon as I shall; and, dear me! it's within a quarter of an hour of the time now. I must run!'

Parkins had, in fact, very little time for dressing. When he met the Colonel at dinner, Peace—or as much of her as that gentleman could manage—reigned once more in the military bosom; nor was she put to flight in the hours of bridge that followed dinner, for Parkins was a more than respectable player. When, therefore, he retired towards twelve o'clock, he felt that he had spent his evening in quite a satisfactory way, and that, even for so long as a fortnight or three weeks, life at the Globe would be supportable under similar conditions— 'especially,' thought he, 'if I go on improving my game.'

As he went along the passages he met the boots* of the Globe, who stopped and said:

'Beg your pardon, sir, but as I was a-brushing your coat just now there was somethink fell out of the pocket. I put it on your chest of drawers, sir, in your room, sir—a piece of a pipe or somethink of that, sir. Thank you, sir. You'll find it on your chest of drawers, sir—yes, sir. Good night, sir.'

The speech served to remind Parkins of his little discovery of that afternoon. It was with some considerable curiosity that he turned it over by the light of his candles. It was of bronze, he now saw, and was shaped very much after the manner of the modern dog-whistle; in fact it was—yes, certainly it was—actually no more nor less than a whistle. He put it to his lips, but it was quite full of a fine, caked-up sand or earth, which would not yield to knocking, but must be loosened with a knife. Tidy as ever in his habits, Parkins cleared out the earth on to a piece of paper, and took the latter to the window to empty it out. The night was clear and bright, as he saw when he had opened the casement, and he stopped for an instant to look at the sea and note a belated wanderer stationed on the shore in front of the inn. Then he shut the window, a little surprised at the late hours people kept at Burnstow, and took his whistle to the light again. Why, surely there were marks on it, and not merely marks, but letters! A very little rubbing rendered the deeply-cut inscription quite legible, but the Professor had to confess, after some earnest thought, that the meaning of it was as obscure to him as the writing on the wall to Belshazzar.* There were legends both on the front and on the back of the whistle. The one read thus:

$$\text{FUR} \quad \overset{\text{FLA}}{\underset{\text{FLE}}{}} \quad \text{BIS}$$

The other:

$$\maltese \text{QUIS EST ISTE QUI UENIT} \maltese$$

'I ought to be able to make it out',* he thought; 'but I suppose I am a little rusty in my Latin. When I come to think of it, I don't believe I even know the word for a whistle. The long one does seem simple enough. It ought to mean, "Who is this who is coming?" Well, the best way to find out is evidently to whistle for him.'

He blew tentatively and stopped suddenly, startled and yet pleased at the note he had elicited. It had a quality of infinite distance in it, and, soft as it was, he somehow felt it must be audible for miles round. It was a sound, too, that seemed to have the power (which many scents possess) of forming pictures in the brain. He saw quite clearly for a moment a vision of a wide, dark expanse at night, with a fresh wind blowing, and in the midst a lonely figure—how employed, he could not tell. Perhaps he would have seen more had not the picture been broken by the sudden surge of a gust of wind against his casement, so sudden that it made him look up, just in time to see the white glint of a sea-bird's wing somewhere outside the dark panes.

The sound of the whistle had so fascinated him that he could not help trying it once more, this time more boldly. The note was little, if at all, louder than before, and repetition broke the illusion—no picture followed, as he had half hoped it might. 'But what is this? Goodness! what force the wind can get up in a few minutes! What a tremendous gust! There! I knew that window-fastening was no use! Ah! I thought so—both candles out. It's enough to tear the room to pieces.'

The first thing was to get the window shut. While you might count twenty Parkins was struggling with the small casement, and felt almost as if he were pushing back a sturdy burglar, so strong was the pressure. It slackened all at once, and the window banged to and latched itself. Now to relight the candles and see what damage, if any, had been done. No, nothing seemed amiss; no glass even was broken in the casement. But the noise had evidently roused at least one member of the household: the Colonel was to be heard stumping in his stockinged feet on the floor above, and growling.

Quickly as it had risen, the wind did not fall at once. On it went, moaning and rushing past the house, at times rising to a cry so desolate that, as Parkins disinterestedly said, it might have made fanciful people feel quite uncomfortable; even the unimaginative, he thought after a quarter of an hour, might be happier without it.

Whether it was the wind, or the excitement of golf, or of the researches in the preceptory that kept Parkins awake, he was not sure. Awake he remained, in any case, long enough to fancy (as I am afraid I often do myself under such conditions) that he was the victim of all manner of fatal disorders: he would lie counting the beats of his heart, convinced that it was going to stop work every moment, and would entertain grave suspicions of his lungs, brain, liver, etc.—suspicions which he was sure would be dispelled by the return of daylight, but which until then refused to be put aside. He found a little vicarious comfort in the idea that someone else was in the same boat. A near neighbour (in the darkness it was not easy to tell his direction) was tossing and rustling in his bed, too.

The next stage was that Parkins shut his eyes and determined to give sleep every chance. Here again over-excitement asserted itself in another form—that of making pictures. *Experto crede*,* pictures do come to the closed eyes of one trying to sleep, and are often so little to his taste that he must open his eyes and disperse them.

Parkins's experience on this occasion was a very distressing one. He found that the picture which presented itself to him was continuous. When he opened his eyes, of course, it went; but when he shut them once more it framed itself afresh, and acted itself out again, neither quicker nor slower than before. What he saw was this:

A long stretch of shore—shingle edged by sand, and intersected at short intervals with black groynes running down to the water—a scene, in fact, so like that of his afternoon's walk that, in the absence of any landmark, it could not be distinguished therefrom. The light was obscure, conveying an impression of gathering storm, late winter evening, and slight cold rain. On this bleak stage at first no actor was visible. Then, in the distance, a bobbing black object appeared; a moment more, and it was a man running, jumping, clambering over the groynes, and every few seconds looking eagerly back. The nearer he came the more obvious it was that he was not only anxious, but even terribly frightened, though his face was not to be distinguished. He was, moreover, almost at the end of his strength. On he came; each successive obstacle seemed to cause him more difficulty than the last. 'Will he get over this next one?' thought Parkins; 'it seems a little higher than the others.' Yes; half climbing, half throwing himself, he did get over, and fell all in a heap on the other side (the side nearest to the spectator). There, as if really unable to get up again, he remained crouching under the groyne, looking up in an attitude of painful anxiety.

So far no cause whatever for the fear of the runner had been shown; but now there began to be seen, far up the shore, a little flicker of something light-coloured moving to and fro with great swiftness and irregularity. Rapidly growing larger, it, too, declared itself as a figure in pale, fluttering draperies, ill-defined. There was something about its motion which made Parkins very unwilling to see it at close quarters. It would stop, raise arms, bow itself toward the sand, then run stooping across the beach to the water-edge and back again; and then, rising upright, once more continue its course forward at a speed that was startling and terrifying. The moment came when the pursuer was hovering about from left to right only a few yards beyond the groyne where the runner lay in hiding. After two or three ineffectual castings hither and thither it came to a stop, stood upright, with arms raised high, and then darted straight forward towards the groyne.

It was at this point that Parkins always failed in his resolution to keep his eyes shut. With many misgivings as to incipient failure of eyesight, overworked brain, excessive smoking, and so on, he finally resigned himself to light his candle, get out a book, and pass the night waking, rather than be tormented by this persistent panorama, which he saw clearly enough could only be a morbid reflection of his walk and his thoughts on that very day.

The scraping of match on box and the glare of light must have startled some creatures of the night—rats or what not—which he heard scurry across the floor from the side of his bed with much rustling. Dear, dear! the match is out! Fool that it is! But the second one burnt better, and a candle and book were duly procured, over which Parkins pored till sleep of a wholesome kind came upon him, and that in no long space. For about the first time in his orderly and prudent life he forgot to blow out the candle, and when he was called next morning at eight there was still a flicker in the socket and a sad mess of guttered grease on the top of the little table.

After breakfast he was in his room, putting the finishing touches to his golfing costume—fortune had again allotted the Colonel to him for a partner—when one of the maids came in.

'Oh, if you please,' she said, 'would you like any extra blankets on your bed, sir?'

'Ah! thank you,' said Parkins. 'Yes, I think I should like one. It seems likely to turn rather colder.'

In a very short time the maid was back with the blanket.

'Which bed should I put it on, sir?' she asked.

'What? Why, that one—the one I slept in last night,' he said, pointing to it.

'Oh yes! I beg your pardon, sir, but you seemed to have tried both of 'em; leastways, we had to make 'em both up this morning.'

'Really? How very absurd!' said Parkins. 'I certainly never touched the other, except to lay some things on it. Did it actually seem to have been slept in?'

'Oh yes, sir!' said the maid. 'Why, all the things was crumpled and throwed about all ways, if you'll excuse me, sir—quite as if anyone 'adn't passed but a very poor night, sir.'

'Dear me,' said Parkins. 'Well, I may have disordered it more than I thought when I unpacked my things. I'm very sorry to have given you the extra trouble, I'm sure. I expect a friend of mine soon, by the way—a gentleman from Cambridge—to come and occupy it for a night or two. That will be all right, I suppose, won't it?'

'Oh yes, to be sure, sir. Thank you, sir. It's no trouble, I'm sure,' said the maid, and departed to giggle with her colleagues.

Parkins set forth, with a stern determination to improve his game.

I am glad to be able to report that he succeeded so far in this enter-prise that the Colonel, who had been rather repining at the prospect of a second day's play in his company, became quite chatty as the morning advanced; and his voice boomed out over the flats, as certain also of our own minor poets have said, 'like some great bourdon in a minster tower.'*

'Extraordinary wind, that, we had last night,' he said. 'In my old home we should have said someone had been whistling for it.'

'Should you, indeed!' said Parkins. 'Is there a superstition of that kind still current in your part of the country?'

'I don't know about superstition,' said the Colonel. 'They believe in it all over Denmark and Norway, as well as on the Yorkshire coast; and my experience is, mind you, that there's generally something at the bottom of what these country-folk hold to, and have held to for generations. But it's your drive' (or whatever it might have been: the golfing reader will have to imagine appropriate digressions at the proper intervals).

When conversation was resumed, Parkins said, with a slight hesitancy:

'Apropos of what you were saying just now, Colonel, I think I ought to tell you that my own views on such subjects are very strong. I am, in fact, a convinced disbeliever in what is called the "supernatural."'

'What!' said the Colonel, 'do you mean to tell me you don't believe in second-sight, or ghosts, or anything of that kind?'

'In nothing whatever of that kind,' returned Parkins firmly.

'Well,' said the Colonel, 'but it appears to me at that rate, sir, that you must be little better than a Sadducee.'

Parkins was on the point of answering that, in his opinion, the Sadducees were the most sensible persons he had ever read of in the Old Testament; but, feeling some doubt as to whether much mention of them was to be found in that work, he preferred to laugh the accusation off.

'Perhaps I am,' he said; 'but—— Here, give me my cleek,* boy!—Excuse me one moment, Colonel.' A short interval. 'Now, as to whistling for the wind, let me give you my theory about it. The laws which govern winds are really not at all perfectly known—to fisher-folk and such, of course, not known at all. A man or woman of eccentric habits, perhaps, or a stranger, is seen repeatedly on the beach at some unusual hour, and is heard whistling. Soon after-wards a violent wind rises; a man who could read the sky perfectly or who possessed a barometer could have foretold that it would. The simple people of a fishing-village have no barometers, and only a few rough rules for prophesying weather: What more natural than that the eccentric personage I postulated should be regarded as having raised the wind, or that he or she should clutch eagerly at the reputation of being able to do so? Now, take last night's wind: as it happens, I myself was whistling. I blew a whistle twice, and the wind seemed to come absolutely in answer to my call. If anyone had seen me——'

The audience had been a little restive under this harangue, and Parkins had, I fear, fallen somewhat into the tone of a lecturer; but at the last sentence the Colonel stopped.

'Whistling, were you?' he said. 'And what sort of whistle did you use? Play this stroke first.' Interval.

'About that whistle you were asking, Colonel. It's rather a curious one. I have it in my—— No; I see I've left it in my room. As a matter of fact, I found it yesterday.'

And then Parkins narrated the manner of his discovery of the whistle, upon hearing which the Colonel grunted, and opined that, in Parkins's place, he should himself be careful about using a thing that had belonged to a set of Papists, of whom, speaking generally, it might be affirmed that you never knew what they might not have been up to. From this topic he diverged to the enormities of the Vicar, who had given notice on the previous Sunday that Friday would be the Feast of St. Thomas the Apostle,* and that there would be service at eleven o'clock in the church. This and other similar proceedings constituted in the Colonel's view a strong presumption that the Vicar was a concealed Papist, if not a Jesuit; and Parkins, who could not very readily follow the Colonel in this region, did not disagree with him. In fact, they got on so well together in the morning that there was no talk on either side of their separating after lunch.

Both continued to play well during the afternoon, or, at least, well enough to make them forget everything else until the light began to fail them. Not until then did Parkins remember that he had meant to do some more investigating at the preceptory; but it was of no great importance, he reflected. One day was as good as another; he might as well go home with the Colonel.

As they turned the corner of the house, the Colonel was almost knocked down by a boy who rushed into him at the very top of his speed, and then, instead of running away, remained hanging on to him and panting. The first words of the warrior were naturally those of reproof and objurgation, but he very quickly discerned that the boy was almost speechless with fright. Inquiries were useless at first. When the boy got his breath he began to howl, and still clung to the Colonel's legs. He was at last detached, but continued to howl.

'What in the world *is* the matter with you? What have you been up to? What have you seen?' said the two men.

'Ow, I seen it wive at me out of the winder,' wailed the boy, 'and I don't like it.'

'What window?' said the irritated Colonel. 'Come, pull yourself together, my boy.'

'The front winder it was, at the 'otel,' said the boy.

At this point Parkins was in favour of sending the boy home, but the Colonel refused; he wanted to get to the bottom of it, he said; it was most dangerous to give a boy such a fright as this one had had, and if it turned out that people had been playing jokes, they should suffer for it in some way. And by a series of questions he made out this story: The boy had been playing about on the grass in front of the Globe with some others; then they had gone home to their teas, and he was just going, when he happened to look up at the front winder and see it a-wiving at him. *It* seemed to be a figure of some sort, in white as far as he knew—couldn't see its face; but it wived at him, and it warn't a right thing—not to say not a right person. Was there a light in the room? No, he didn't think to look if there was a light. Which was the window? Was it the top one or the second one? The seckind one it was—the big winder what got two little uns at the sides.

'Very well, my boy,' said the Colonel, after a few more questions. 'You run away home now. I expect it was some person trying to give you a start. Another time, like a brave English boy, you just throw a stone—well, no, not that exactly, but you go and speak to the waiter, or to Mr. Simpson, the landlord, and—yes—and say that I advised you to do so.'

The boy's face expressed some of the doubt he felt as to the likelihood of Mr. Simpson's lending a favourable ear to his complaint, but the Colonel did not appear to perceive this, and went on:

'And here's a sixpence—no, I see it's a shilling—and you be off home, and don't think any more about it.'

The youth hurried off with agitated thanks, and the Colonel and Parkins went round to the front of the Globe and reconnoitred. There was only one window answering to the description they had been hearing.

'Well, that's curious,' said Parkins; 'it's evidently my window the lad was talking about. Will you come up for a moment, Colonel Wilson? We ought to be able to see if anyone has been taking liberties in my room.'

They were soon in the passage, and Parkins made as if to open the door. Then he stopped and felt in his pockets.

'This is more serious than I thought,' was his next remark. 'I remember now that before I started this morning I locked the door. It is locked now, and, what is more, here is the key.' And he held it up. 'Now,' he went on, 'if the servants are in the habit of going into one's room during the day when one is away, I can only say that—well, that I don't approve of it at all.' Conscious of a somewhat weak climax, he busied himself in opening the door (which was indeed locked) and in lighting candles. 'No,' he said, 'nothing seems disturbed.'

'Except your bed,' put in the Colonel.

'Excuse me, that isn't my bed,' said Parkins. 'I don't use that one. But it does look as if someone had been playing tricks with it.'

It certainly did: the clothes were bundled up and twisted together in a most tortuous confusion. Parkins pondered.

'That must be it,' he said at last: 'I disordered the clothes last night in unpacking, and they haven't made it since. Perhaps they came in to make it, and that boy saw them through the window; and then they were called away and locked the door after them. Yes, I think that must be it.'

'Well, ring and ask,' said the Colonel, and this appealed to Parkins as practical.

The maid appeared, and, to make a long story short, deposed that she had made the bed in the morning when the gentleman was in the room, and hadn't been there since. No, she hadn't no other key. Mr. Simpson he kep' the keys; he'd be able to tell the gentleman if anyone had been up.

This was a puzzle. Investigation showed that nothing of value had been taken, and Parkins remembered the disposition of the small objects on tables and so forth well enough to be pretty sure that no pranks had been played with them. Mr. and Mrs. Simpson further-more agreed that neither of them had given the duplicate key of the room to any person whatever during the day. Nor could Parkins, fair-minded man as he was, detect anything in the demeanour of master, mistress, or maid that indicated guilt. He was much more inclined to think that the boy had been imposing on the Colonel.

The latter was unwontedly silent and pensive at dinner and throughout the evening. When he bade good night to Parkins, he murmured in a gruff undertone:

'You know where I am if you want me during the night.'

'Why, yes, thank you, Colonel Wilson, I think I do; but there isn't much prospect of my disturbing you, I hope. By the way,' he added, 'did I show you that old whistle I spoke of? I think not. Well, here it is.'

The Colonel turned it over gingerly in the light of the candle.

'Can you make anything of the inscription?' asked Parkins, as he took it back.

'No, not in this light. What do you mean to do with it?'

'Oh, well, when I get back to Cambridge I shall submit it to some of the archæologists there, and see what they think of it; and very likely, if they consider it worth having, I may present it to one of the museums.'

' 'M!' said the Colonel. 'Well, you may be right. All I know is that, if it were mine, I should chuck it straight into the sea. It's no use talking, I'm well aware, but I expect that with you it's a case of live and learn. I hope so, I'm sure, and I wish you a good night.'

He turned away, leaving Parkins in act to speak at the bottom of the stair, and soon each was in his own bedroom.

By some unfortunate accident, there were neither blinds nor curtains to the windows of the Professor's room. The previous night he had thought little of this, but to-night there seemed every prospect of a bright moon rising to shine directly on his bed, and probably wake him later on. When he noticed this he was a good deal annoyed, but, with an ingenuity which I can only envy, he succeeded in rigging up, with the help of a railway-rug, some safety-pins, and a stick and umbrella, a screen which, if it only held together, would completely keep the moonlight off his bed. And shortly afterwards he was comfortably in that bed. When he had read a somewhat solid work long enough to produce a decided wish for sleep, he cast a drowsy glance round the room, blew out the candle, and fell back upon the pillow.

He must have slept soundly for an hour or more, when a sudden clatter shook him up in a most unwelcome manner. In a moment he realized what had happened: his carefully-constructed screen had given way, and a very bright frosty moon was shining directly on his face. This was highly annoying. Could he possibly get up and reconstruct the screen? or could he manage to sleep if he did not?

For some minutes he lay and pondered over the possibilities; then he turned over sharply, and with all his eyes open lay breathlessly listening. There had been a movement, he was sure, in the empty bed on the opposite side of the room. To-morrow he would have it moved, for there must be rats or something playing about in it. It was quiet now. No! the commotion began again. There was a rustling and shaking: surely more than any rat could cause.

I can figure to myself something of the Professor's bewilderment and horror, for I have in a dream thirty years back seen the same thing happen; but the reader will hardly, perhaps, imagine how dreadful it was to him to see a figure suddenly sit up in what he had known was an empty bed. He was out of his own bed in one bound, and made a dash towards the window, where lay his only weapon, the stick with which he had propped his screen. This was, as it turned out, the worst thing he could have done, because the personage in the empty bed, with a sudden smooth motion, slipped from the bed and took up a position, with outspread arms, between the two beds, and in front of the door. Parkins watched it in a horrid perplexity. Somehow, the idea of getting past it and escaping through the door was intolerable to him; he could not have borne—he didn't know why—to touch it; and as for its touching him, he would sooner dash himself through the window than have that happen. It stood for the moment in a band of dark shadow, and he had not seen what its face was like. Now it began to move, in a stooping posture, and all at once the spectator realized, with some horror and some relief, that it must be blind, for it seemed to feel about it with its muffled arms in a grop-ing and random fashion. Turning half away from him, it became sud-denly conscious of the bed he had just left, and darted towards it, and bent over and felt the pillows in a way which made Parkins shudder as he had never in his life thought it possible. In a very few moments it seemed to know that the bed was empty, and then, moving forward into the area of light and facing the window, it showed for the first time what manner of thing it was.

Parkins, who very much dislikes being questioned about it, did once describe something of it in my hearing, and I gathered that what he chiefly remembers about it is a horrible, an intensely horrible, face *of crumpled linen*. What expression he read upon it he could not or would not tell, but that the fear of it went nigh to maddening him is certain.

But he was not at leisure to watch it for long. With formidable quickness it moved into the middle of the room, and, as it groped and waved, one corner of its draperies swept across Parkins's face. He could not—though he knew how perilous a sound was—he could not keep back a cry of disgust, and this gave the searcher an instant clue. It leapt towards him upon the instant, and the next moment he was half-way through the window backwards, uttering cry upon cry at the utmost pitch of his voice, and the linen face was thrust close into his own. At this, almost the last possible second, deliverance came, as you will have guessed: the Colonel burst the door open, and was just in time to see the dreadful group at the window. When he reached the figures only one was left. Parkins sank forward into the room in a faint, and before him on the floor lay a tumbled heap of bed-clothes.

Colonel Wilson asked no questions, but busied himself in keeping everyone else out of the room and in getting Parkins back to his bed;

and himself, wrapped in a rug, occupied the other bed for the rest of the night. Early on the next day Rogers arrived, more welcome than he would have been a day before, and the three of them held a very long consultation in the Professor's room. At the end of it the Colonel left the hotel door carrying a small object between his finger and thumb, which he cast as far into the sea as a very brawny arm could send it. Later on the smoke of a burning ascended from the back premises of the Globe.

Exactly what explanation was patched up for the staff and visitors at the hotel I must confess I do not recollect. The Professor was somehow cleared of the ready suspicion of delirium tremens, and the hotel of the reputation of a troubled house.

There is not much question as to what would have happened to Parkins if the Colonel had not intervened when he did. He would either have fallen out of the window or else lost his wits. But it is not so evident what more the creature that came in answer to the whistle could have done than frighten. There seemed to be absolutely nothing material about it save the bed-clothes of which it had made itself a body. The Colonel, who remembered a not very dissimilar occurrence in India, was of opinion that if Parkins had closed with it it could really have done very little, and that its one power was that of frightening. The whole thing, he said, served to confirm his opinion of the Church of Rome.

There is really nothing more to tell, but, as you may imagine, the Professor's views on certain points are less clear cut than they used to be. His nerves, too, have suffered: he cannot even now see a surplice hanging on a door quite unmoved, and the spectacle of a scarecrow in a field late on a winter afternoon has cost him more than one sleepless night.

THE TREASURE OF ABBOT THOMAS

꤮

I

'VERUM usque in præsentem diem multa garriunt inter se
Canonici de abscondito quodam istius Abbatis Thomæ
thesauro, quem sæpe, quanquam adhuc incassum, quæsiverunt
Steinfeldenses. Ipsum enim Thomam adhuc florida in ætate existen-
tem ingentem auri massam circa monasterium defodisse perhibent;
de quo multoties interrogatus ubi esset, cum risu respondere solitus
erat: "Job, Johannes, et Zacharias vel vobis vel posteris indicabunt";
idemque aliquando adiicere se inventuris minime invisurum. Inter
alia huius Abbatis opera, hoc memoria præcipue dignum iudico quod
fenestram magnam in orientali parte alæ australis in ecclesia sua
imaginibus optime in vitro depictis impleverit: id quod et ipsius
effigies et insignia ibidem posita demonstrant. Domum quoque
Abbatialem fere totam restauravit: puteo in atrio ipsius effosso et
lapidibus marmoreis pulchre cælatis exornato. Decessit autem, morte
aliquantulum subitanea perculsus, ætatis suæ anno lxxii^do, incarna-
tionis vero Dominicæ mdxxix°.'

'I suppose I shall have to translate this,' said the antiquary to himself, as he finished copying the above lines from that rather rare and
exceedingly diffuse book, the 'Sertum Steinfeldense Norbertinum.'*[1]
'Well, it may as well be done first as last,' and accordingly the following rendering was very quickly produced:

'Up to the present day there is much gossip among the Canons
about a certain hidden treasure of this Abbot Thomas, for which
those of Steinfeld have often made search, though hitherto in vain.
The story is that Thomas, while yet in the vigour of life, concealed a
very large quantity of gold somewhere in the monastery. He was
often asked where it was, and always answered, with a laugh: "Job,

---

[1] An account of the Premonstratensian abbey of Steinfeld, in the Eiffel, with lives of
the Abbots, published at Cologne in 1712 by Christian Albert Erhard, a resident in the
district. The epithet *Norbertinum* is due to the fact that St. Norbert was founder of the
Premonstratensian Order.

John, and Zechariah* will tell either you or your successors." He
sometimes added that he should feel no grudge against those who
might find it. Among other works carried out by this Abbot I may
specially mention his filling the great window at the east end of the
south aisle of the church with figures admirably painted on glass, as
his effigy and arms in the window attest. He also restored almost
the whole of the Abbot's lodging, and dug a well in the court of it,
which he adorned with beautiful carvings in marble. He died rather
suddenly in the seventy-second year of his age, A.D. 1529.'

The object which the antiquary had before him at the moment was
that of tracing the whereabouts of the painted windows of the Abbey
Church of Steinfeld. Shortly after the Revolution, a very large quantity of painted glass made its way from the dissolved abbeys of
Germany and Belgium to this country, and may now be seen adorn-
ing various of our parish churches, cathedrals, and private chapels.
Steinfeld Abbey was among the most considerable of these involun-
tary contributors to our artistic possessions (I am quoting the somewhat ponderous preamble of the book which the antiquary wrote),
and the greater part of the glass from that institution can be identified
without much difficulty by the help, either of the numerous inscriptions in which the place is mentioned, or of the subjects of the
windows, in which several well-defined cycles or narratives were
represented.

The passage with which I began my story had set the antiquary on
the track of another identification. In a private chapel—no matter
where—he had seen three large figures, each occupying a whole light
in a window, and evidently the work of one artist. Their style made it
plain that that artist had been a German of the sixteenth century; but
hitherto the more exact localizing of them had been a puzzle. They
represented—will you be surprised to hear it?—JOB PATRIARCHA,
JOHANNES EVANGELISTA, ZACHARIAS PROPHETA, and each of
them held a book or scroll, inscribed with a sentence from his writings. These, as a matter of course, the antiquary had noted, and had
been struck by the curious way in which they differed from any text
of the Vulgate* that he had been able to examine. Thus the scroll in
Job's hand was inscribed: 'Auro est locus in quo absconditur' (for
'conflatur');[1] on the book of John was: 'Habent in vestimentis suis

---

[1] There is a place for gold where it is hidden.*

scripturam quam nemo novit"[1] (for 'in vestimento scriptum,' the following words being taken from another verse); and Zacharias had: 'Super lapidem unum septem oculi sunt'[2] (which alone of the three presents an unaltered text).

A sad perplexity* it had been to our investigator to think why these three personages should have been placed together in one window. There was no bond of connection between them, either historic, symbolic, or doctrinal, and he could only suppose that they must have formed part of a very large series of Prophets and Apostles, which might have filled, say, all the clerestory* windows of some capacious church. But the passage from the '*Sertum*' had altered the situation by showing that the names of the actual personages represented in the glass now in Lord D——'s chapel had been constantly on the lips of Abbot Thomas von Eschenhausen* of Steinfeld, and that this Abbot had put up a painted window, probably about the year 1520, in the south aisle of his abbey church. It was no very wild conjecture that the three figures might have formed part of Abbot Thomas's offering; it was one which, moreover, could probably be confirmed or set aside by another careful examination of the glass. And, as Mr. Somerton was a man of leisure, he set out on pilgrimage to the private chapel with very little delay. His conjecture was confirmed to the full. Not only did the style and technique of the glass suit perfectly with the date and place required, but in another window of the chapel he found some glass, known to have been bought along with the figures, which contained the arms of Abbot Thomas von Eschenhausen.

At intervals during his researches Mr. Somerton had been haunted by the recollection of the gossip about the hidden treasure, and, as he thought the matter over, it became more and more obvious to him that if the Abbot meant anything by the enigmatical answer which he gave to his questioners, he must have meant that the secret was to be found somewhere in the window he had placed in the abbey church. It was undeniable, furthermore, that the first of the curiously-selected texts on the scrolls in the window might be taken to have a reference to hidden treasure.

Every feature, therefore, or mark which could possibly assist in elucidating the riddle which, he felt sure, the Abbot had set to

---

[1] They have on their raiment a writing which no man knoweth.*
[2] Upon one stone are seven eyes.*

posterity he noted with scrupulous care, and, returning to his Berkshire manor-house, consumed many a pint of the midnight oil over his tracings and sketches. After two or three weeks, a day came when Mr. Somerton announced to his man that he must pack his own and his master's things for a short journey abroad, whither for the moment we will not follow him.

II

Mr. Gregory, the Rector of Parsbury,* had strolled out before breakfast, it being a fine autumn morning, as far as the gate of his carriage-drive, with intent to meet the postman and sniff the cool air. Nor was he disappointed of either purpose. Before he had had time to answer more than ten or eleven of the miscellaneous questions propounded to him in the lightness of their hearts by his young offspring, who had accompanied him, the postman was seen approaching; and among the morning's budget was one letter bearing a foreign postmark and stamp (which became at once the objects of an eager competition among the youthful Gregorys), and was addressed in an uneducated, but plainly an English hand.

When the Rector opened it, and turned to the signature, he realized that it came from the confidential valet of his friend and squire, Mr. Somerton. Thus it ran:

HONOURD SIR,—

Has I am in a great anxiety about Master I write at is Wish to Beg you Sir if you could be so good as Step over. Master Has add a Nastey Shock and keeps His Bedd. I never Have known Him like this but No wonder and Nothing will serve but you Sir. Master says would I mintion the Short Way Here is Drive to Cobblince* and take a Trap. Hopeing I Have maid all Plain, but am much Confused in Myself what with Anxiatey and Weakfulness at Night. If I might be so Bold Sir it will be a Pleasure to see a Honnest Brish Face among all These Forig ones.

I am Sir

Your obed^t Servt

WILLIAM BROWN.

P.S.—The Villiage for Town I will not Turm It is name Steenfeld.

The reader must be left to picture to himself in detail the surprise, confusion, and hurry of preparation into which the receipt of such a letter would be likely to plunge a quiet Berkshire parsonage in the year of grace 1859. It is enough for me to say that a train to town was caught in the course of the day, and that Mr. Gregory was able to secure a cabin in the Antwerp boat and a place in the Coblentz train. Nor was it difficult to manage the transit from that centre to Steinfeld.

I labour under a grave disadvantage as narrator of this story in that I have never visited Steinfeld myself,* and that neither of the principal actors in the episode (from whom I derive my information) was able to give me anything but a vague and rather dismal idea of its appearance. I gather that it is a small place, with a large church despoiled of its ancient fittings; a number of rather ruinous great buildings, mostly of the seventeenth century, surround this church; for the abbey, in common with most of those on the Continent, was rebuilt in a luxurious fashion by its inhabitants at that period. It has not seemed to me worth while to lavish money on a visit to the place, for though it is probably far more attractive than either Mr. Somerton or Mr. Gregory thought it, there is evidently little, if anything, of first-rate interest to be seen—except, perhaps, one thing, which I should not care to see.

The inn where the English gentleman and his servant were lodged is, or was, the only 'possible' one in the village. Mr. Gregory was taken to it at once by his driver, and found Mr. Brown waiting at the door. Mr. Brown, a model when in his Berkshire home of the impassive whiskered race who are known as confidential valets, was now egregiously out of his element, in a light tweed suit, anxious, almost irritable, and plainly anything but master of the situation. His relief at the sight of the 'honest British face' of his Rector was unmeasured, but words to describe it were denied him. He could only say:

'Well, I ham pleased, I'm sure, sir, to see you. And so I'm sure, sir, will master.'

'How *is* your master, Brown?' Mr. Gregory eagerly put in.

'I think he's better, sir, thank you; but he's had a dreadful time of it. I 'ope he's gettin' some sleep now, but——'

'What has been the matter—I couldn't make out from your letter? Was it an accident of any kind?'

'Well, sir, I 'ardly know whether I'd better speak about it. Master was very partickler he should be the one to tell you. But there's no bones broke—that's one thing I'm sure we ought to be thankful——'

'What does the doctor say?' asked Mr. Gregory.

They were by this time outside Mr. Somerton's bedroom door, and speaking in low tones. Mr. Gregory, who happened to be in front, was feeling for the handle, and chanced to run his fingers over the panels. Before Brown could answer, there was a terrible cry from within the room.

'In God's name, who is that?' were the first words they heard. 'Brown, is it?'

'Yes, sir—me, sir, and Mr. Gregory,' Brown hastened to answer, and there was an audible groan of relief in reply.

They entered the room, which was darkened against the afternoon sun, and Mr. Gregory saw, with a shock of pity, how drawn, how damp with drops of fear, was the usually calm face of his friend, who, sitting up in the curtained bed, stretched out a shaking hand to welcome him.

'Better for seeing you, my dear Gregory,' was the reply to the Rector's first question, and it was palpably true.

After five minutes of conversation Mr. Somerton was more his own man, Brown afterwards reported, than he had been for days. He was able to eat a more than respectable dinner, and talked confidently of being fit to stand a journey to Coblentz within twenty-four hours.

'But there's one thing,' he said, with a return of agitation which Mr. Gregory did not like to see, 'which I must beg you to do for me, my dear Gregory. Don't,' he went on, laying his hand on Gregory's to forestall any interruption—'don't ask me what it is, or why I want it done. I'm not up to explaining it yet; it would throw me back— undo all the good you have done me by coming. The only word I will say about it is that you run no risk whatever by doing it, and that Brown can and will show you to-morrow what it is. It's merely to put back—to keep—something—— No; I can't speak of it yet. Do you mind calling Brown?'

'Well, Somerton,' said Mr. Gregory, as he crossed the room to the door, 'I won't ask for any explanations till you see fit to give them. And if this bit of business is as easy as you represent it to be, I will very gladly undertake it for you the first thing in the morning.'

'Ah, I was sure you would, my dear Gregory; I was certain I could rely on you. I shall owe you more thanks than I can tell. Now, here is Brown. Brown, one word with you.'

'Shall I go?' interjected Mr. Gregory.

'Not at all. Dear me, no. Brown, the first thing to-morrow morning—(you don't mind early hours, I know, Gregory)—you must take the Rector to—*there*, you know' (a nod from Brown, who looked grave and anxious), 'and he and you will put that back. You needn't be in the least alarmed; it's *perfectly* safe in the daytime. You know what I mean. It lies on the step, you know, where—where we put it.' (Brown swallowed dryly once or twice, and, failing to speak, bowed.) 'And—yes, that's all. Only this one other word, my dear Gregory. If you *can* manage to keep from questioning Brown about this matter, I shall be still more bound to you. To-morrow evening, at latest, if all goes well, I shall be able, I believe, to tell you the whole story from start to finish. And now I'll wish you good night. Brown will be with me—he sleeps here—and if I were you, I should lock my door. Yes, be particular to do that. They—they like it, the people here, and it's better. Good night, good night.'

They parted upon this, and if Mr. Gregory woke once or twice in the small hours and fancied he heard a fumbling about the lower part of his locked door, it was, perhaps, no more than what a quiet man, suddenly plunged into a strange bed and the heart of a mystery, might reasonably expect. Certainly he thought, to the end of his days, that he had heard such a sound twice or three times between midnight and dawn.

He was up with the sun, and out in company with Brown soon after. Perplexing as was the service he had been asked to perform for Mr. Somerton, it was not a difficult or an alarming one, and within half an hour from his leaving the inn it was over. What it was I shall not as yet divulge.

Later in the morning Mr. Somerton, now almost himself again, was able to make a start from Steinfeld; and that same evening, whether at Coblentz or at some intermediate stage on the journey I am not certain, he settled down to the promised explanation. Brown was present, but how much of the matter was ever really made plain to his comprehension he would never say, and I am unable to conjecture.

III

This was Mr. Somerton's story:

'You know roughly, both of you, that this expedition of mine was undertaken with the object of tracing something in connection with some old painted glass in Lord D——'s private chapel. Well, the starting-point of the whole matter lies in this passage from an old printed book, to which I will ask your attention.'

And at this point Mr. Somerton went carefully over some ground with which we are already familiar.

'On my second visit to the chapel,' he went on, 'my purpose was to take every note I could of figures, lettering, diamond-scratchings on the glass, and even apparently accidental markings. The first point which I tackled was that of the inscribed scrolls. I could not doubt that the first of these, that of Job—"There is a place for the gold where it is hidden"—with its intentional alteration, must refer to the treasure; so I applied myself with some confidence to the next, that of St. John—"They have on their vestures a writing which no man knoweth." The natural question will have occurred to you: Was there an inscription on the robes of the figures? I could see none; each of the three had a broad black border to his mantle, which made a conspicuous and rather ugly feature in the window. I was non-plussed, I will own, and but for a curious bit of luck I think I should have left the search where the Canons of Steinfeld had left it before me. But it so happened that there was a good deal of dust on the surface of the glass, and Lord D——, happening to come in, noticed my blackened hands, and kindly insisted on sending for a Turk's head broom* to clean down the window. There must, I suppose, have been a rough piece in the broom; anyhow, as it passed over the border of one of the mantles, I noticed that it left a long scratch, and that some yellow stain instantly showed up. I asked the man to stop his work for a moment, and ran up the ladder to examine the place. The yellow stain was there, sure enough, and what had come away was a thick black pigment, which had evidently been laid on with the brush after the glass had been burnt, and could therefore be easily scraped off without doing any harm. I scraped, accordingly, and you will hardly believe—no, I do you an injustice; you will have guessed already—that I found under this black pigment two or three clearly-formed capital letters in yellow stain on a clear ground. Of course, I could hardly contain my delight.

'I told Lord D—— that I had detected an inscription which I thought might be very interesting, and begged to be allowed to uncover the whole of it. He made no difficulty about it whatever, told me to do exactly as I pleased, and then, having an engagement, was obliged—rather to my relief, I must say—to leave me. I set to work at once, and found the task a fairly easy one. The pigment, disintegrated, of course, by time, came off almost at a touch, and I don't think that it took me a couple of hours, all told, to clean the whole of the black borders in all three lights. Each of the figures had, as the inscription said, "a writing on their vestures which nobody knew."

'This discovery, of course, made it absolutely certain to my mind that I was on the right track. And, now, what was the inscription? While I was cleaning the glass I almost took pains not to read the lettering, saving up the treat until I had got the whole thing clear. And when that *was* done, my dear Gregory, I assure you I could almost have cried from sheer disappointment. What I read was only the most hopeless jumble of letters that was ever shaken up in a hat. Here it is:

Job.   DREVICIOPEDMOOMSMVIVLISLCAVIBASBAT
           AOVT

St. John.   RDIIEAMRLESIPVSPODSEEIRSETTAAESGIAV
           NNR

Zechariah. FTEEAILNQDPVAIVMTLEEATTOHIOONVMC
           AAT.H.Q.E.

'Blank as I felt and must have looked for the first few minutes, my disappointment didn't last long. I realized almost at once that I was dealing with a cipher or cryptogram; and I reflected that it was likely to be of a pretty simple kind, considering its early date. So I copied the letters with the most anxious care. Another little point, I may tell you. turned up in the process which confirmed my belief in the cipher. After copying the letters on Job's robe I counted them, to make sure that I had them right. There were thirty-eight; and, just as I finished going through them, my eye fell on a scratching made with a sharp point on the edge of the border. It was simply the number xxxviii in Roman numerals. To cut the matter short, there was a similar note, as I may call it, in each of the other lights; and that made it plain to me that the glass-painter had had very strict orders from Abbot Thomas about the inscription, and had taken pains to get it correct.

'Well, after that discovery you may imagine how minutely I went over the whole surface of the glass in search of further light. Of course, I did not neglect the inscription on the scroll of Zechariah—"Upon one stone are seven eyes," but I very quickly concluded that this must refer to some mark on a stone which could only be found *in situ*, where the treasure was concealed. To be short, I made all possible notes and sketches and tracings, and then came back to Parsbury to work out the cipher at leisure. Oh, the agonies I went through! I thought myself very clever at first, for I made sure that the key would be found in some of the old books on secret writing. The "*Steganographia*" of Joachim Trithemius, who was an earlier contemporary of Abbot Thomas, seemed particularly promising; so I got that, and Selenius's "*Cryptographia*" and Bacon "*de Augmentis Scientiarum*,"* and some more. But I could hit upon nothing. Then I tried the principle of the "most frequent letter," taking first Latin and then German as a basis. That didn't help, either; whether it ought to have done so, I am not clear. And then I came back to the window itself, and read over my notes, hoping almost against hope that the Abbot might himself have somewhere supplied the key I wanted. I could make nothing out of the colour or pattern of the robes. There were no landscape backgrounds with subsidiary objects; there was nothing in the canopies. The only resource possible seemed to be in the attitudes of the figures. "Job," I read: "scroll in left hand, forefinger of right hand extended upwards. John: holds inscribed book in left hand; with right hand blesses, with two fingers. Zechariah: scroll in left hand; right hand extended upwards, as Job, but with three fingers pointing up." In other words, I reflected, Job has *one* finger extended, John has *two*, Zechariah has *three*. May not there be a numeral key concealed in that? My dear Gregory,' said Mr. Somerton, laying his hand on his friend's knee, 'that *was* the key. I didn't get it to fit at first, but after two or three trials I saw what was meant. After the first letter of the inscription you skip *one* letter, after the next you skip *two*, and after that skip *three*. Now look at the result I got. I've underlined the letters which form words:

DREVICIOPEDMOOMSMVIVLISLCAVIBASBATAOVT

RDIIEAMRLESIPVSPODSEEIRSETTAAESGIAVNNR

FTEEAILNQDPVAIVMTLEEATTOHIOONVMCAAT.H.Q.E.

'Do you see it? "*Decem millia auri reposita sunt in puteo in at . . .*" (Ten thousand [pieces] of gold are laid up in a well in . . .), followed by an incomplete word beginning *at*. So far so good. I tried the same plan with the remaining letters; but it wouldn't work, and I fancied that perhaps the placing of dots after the three last letters might indicate some difference of procedure. Then I thought to myself, "Wasn't there some allusion to a well in the account of Abbot Thomas in that book the '*Sertum*'?" Yes, there was: he built a *puteus in atrio* (a well in the court). There, of course, was my word *atrio*. The next step was to copy out the remaining letters of the inscription, omitting those I had already used. That gave what you will see on this slip:

RVIIOPDOOSMVVISCAVBSBTAOTDIEAMLSIVSPDEER
SETAEGIANRFEEALQDVAIMLEATTHOOVMCA.H.Q.E.

'Now, I knew what the three first letters I wanted were,—namely, *rio*—to complete the word *atrio*; and, as you will see, these are all to be found in the first five letters. I was a little confused at first by the occurrence of two *i*'s, but very soon I saw that every alternate letter must be taken in the remainder of the inscription. You can work it out for yourself; the result, continuing where the first "round" left off, is this:

"rio domus abbatialis de Steinfeld a me, Thoma, qui posui custodem super ea. Gare à qui la touche."

'So the whole secret was out:

"Ten thousand pieces of gold are laid up in the well in the court of the Abbot's house of Steinfeld by me, Thomas, who have set a guardian over them. *Gare à qui la touche.*"*

'The last words, I ought to say, are a device which Abbot Thomas had adopted. I found it with his arms in another piece of glass at Lord D——'s, and he drafted it bodily into his cipher, though it doesn't quite fit in point of grammar.

'Well, what would any human being have been tempted to do, my dear Gregory, in my place? Could he have helped setting off, as I did, to Steinfeld, and tracing the secret literally to the fountain-head? I don't believe he could. Anyhow, I couldn't, and, as I needn't tell you, I found myself at Steinfeld as soon as the resources of civilization could put me there, and installed myself in the inn you saw. I must tell you that I was not altogether free from forebodings—on one hand of disappointment, on the other of danger. There was always the possibility that Abbot Thomas's well might have been wholly obliterated, or else that someone, ignorant of cryptograms, and guided only by luck, might have stumbled on the treasure before me. And then'—there was a very perceptible shaking of the voice here—'I was not entirely easy, I need not mind confessing, as to the meaning of the words about the guardian of the treasure. But, if you don't mind, I'll say no more about that until—until it becomes necessary.

'At the first possible opportunity Brown and I began exploring the place. I had naturally represented myself as being interested in the remains of the abbey, and we could not avoid paying a visit to the church, impatient as I was to be elsewhere. Still, it did interest me to see the windows where the glass had been, and especially that at the east end of the south aisle. In the tracery lights of that I was startled to see some fragments and coats-of-arms remaining—Abbot Thomas's shield was there, and a small figure with a scroll inscribed "Oculos habent, et non videbunt" (They have eyes, and shall not see), which, I take it, was a hit of the Abbot at his Canons.

'But, of course, the principal object was to find the Abbot's house. There is no prescribed place for this, so far as I know, in the plan of a monastery; you can't predict of it, as you can of the chapter-house, that it will be on the eastern side of the cloister, or, as of the dormitory, that it will communicate with a transept of the church. I felt that if I asked many questions I might awaken lingering memories of the treasure, and I thought it best to try first to discover it for myself. It was not a very long or difficult search. That three-sided court southeast of the church, with deserted piles of building round it, and grass-grown pavement, which you saw this morning, was the place. And glad enough I was to see that it was put to no use, and was neither very far from our inn nor overlooked by any inhabited building; there were only orchards and paddocks on the slopes east of the church. I can tell you that fine stone glowed wonderfully in the rather watery yellow sunset that we had on the Tuesday afternoon.

'Next, what about the well? There was not much doubt about that, as you can testify. It is really a very remarkable thing. That curb is, I think, of Italian marble, and the carving I thought must be Italian also. There were reliefs, you will perhaps remember, of Eliezer and Rebekah, and of Jacob opening the well for Rachel,* and similar subjects; but, by way of disarming suspicion, I suppose, the Abbot had carefully abstained from any of his cynical and allusive inscriptions.

'I examined the whole structure with the keenest interest, of course—a square well-head with an opening in one side; an arch over it, with a wheel for the rope to pass over, evidently in very good condition still, for it had been used within sixty years, or perhaps even later, though not quite recently. Then there was the question of depth and access to the interior. I suppose the depth was about sixty to seventy feet; and as to the other point, it really seemed as if the Abbot had wished to lead searchers up to the very door of his treasure-house, for, as you tested for yourself, there were big blocks of stone bonded into the masonry, and leading down in a regular staircase round and round the inside of the well.

'It seemed almost too good to be true. I wondered if there was a trap—if the stones were so contrived as to tip over when a weight was placed on them; but I tried a good many with my own weight and with my stick, and all seemed, and actually were, perfectly firm. Of course, I resolved that Brown and I would make an experiment that very night.

'I was well prepared. Knowing the sort of place I should have to explore, I had brought a sufficiency of good rope and bands of webbing to surround my body, and crossbars to hold to, as well as lanterns and candles and crowbars, all of which would go into a single carpet-bag and excite no suspicion. I satisfied myself that my rope would be long enough, and that the wheel for the bucket was in good working order, and then we went home to dinner.

'I had a little cautious conversation with the landlord, and made out that he would not be overmuch surprised if I went out for a stroll with my man about nine o'clock, to make (Heaven forgive me!) a sketch of the abbey by moonlight. I asked no questions about the well, and am not likely to do so now. I fancy I know as much about it as anyone in Steinfeld: at least'—with a strong shudder—'I don't want to know any more.

'Now we come to the crisis, and, though I hate to think of it, I feel sure, Gregory, that it will be better for me in all ways to recall it just as it happened. We started, Brown and I, at about nine with our bag, and attracted no attention; for we managed to slip out at the hinder end of the inn-yard into an alley which brought us quite to the edge of the village. In five minutes we were at the well, and for some little time we sat on the edge of the well-head to make sure that no one was stirring or spying on us. All we heard was some horses cropping grass

out of sight farther down the eastern slope. We were perfectly unob-
served, and had plenty of light from the gorgeous full moon to allow
us to get the rope properly fitted over the wheel. Then I secured the
band round my body beneath the arms. We attached the end of the
rope very securely to a ring in the stonework. Brown took the lighted
lantern and followed me; I had a crowbar. And so we began to descend
cautiously, feeling every step before we set foot on it, and scanning
the walls in search of any marked stone.

'Half aloud I counted the steps as we went down, and we got as
far as the thirty-eighth before I noted anything at all irregular in the
surface of the masonry. Even here there was no mark, and I began
to feel very blank, and to wonder if the Abbot's cryptogram could
possibly be an elaborate hoax. At the forty-ninth step the staircase
ceased. It was with a very sinking heart that I began retracing my
steps, and when I was back on the thirty-eighth—Brown, with the
lantern, being a step or two above me—I scrutinized the little bit of
irregularity in the stone-work with all my might; but there was no
vestige of a mark.

'Then it struck me that the texture of the surface looked just a little
smoother than the rest, or, at least, in some way different. It might
possibly be cement and not stone. I gave it a good blow with my iron
bar. There was a decidedly hollow sound, though that might be the
result of our being in a well. But there was more. A great flake of
cement dropped on to my feet, and I saw marks on the stone underneath. I had tracked the Abbot down, my dear Gregory; even now I
think of it with a certain pride. It took but a very few more taps to
clear the whole of the cement away, and I saw a slab of stone about
two feet square, upon which was engraven a cross. Disappointment
again, but only for a moment. It was you, Brown, who reassured me
by a casual remark. You said, if I remember right:

'"It's a funny cross; looks like a lot of eyes."'

'I snatched the lantern out of your hand, and saw with inexpressible pleasure that the cross *was* composed of seven eyes, four in a
vertical line, three horizontal. The last of the scrolls in the window
was explained in the way I had anticipated. Here was my "stone with
the seven eyes." So far the Abbot's data had been exact, and, as I
thought of this, the anxiety about the "guardian" returned upon me
with increased force. Still, I wasn't going to retreat now.

'Without giving myself time to think, I knocked away the cement all round the marked stone, and then gave it a prise on the right side with my crowbar. It moved at once, and I saw that it was but a thin light slab, such as I could easily lift out myself, and that it stopped the entrance to a cavity. I did lift it out unbroken, and set it on the step, for it might be very important to us to be able to replace it. Then I waited for several minutes on the step just above. I don't know why, but I think to see if any dreadful thing would rush out. Nothing happened. Next I lit a candle, and very cautiously I placed it inside the cavity, with some idea of seeing whether there were foul air, and of getting a glimpse of what was inside. There *was* some foulness of air which nearly extinguished the flame, but in no long time it burned quite steadily. The hole went some little way back, and also on the right and left of the entrance, and I could see some rounded light-coloured objects within which might be bags. There was no use in waiting. I faced the cavity, and looked in. There was nothing immediately in the front of the hole. I put my arm in and felt to the right, very gingerly. . . .

'Just give me a glass of cognac, Brown. I'll go on in a moment, Gregory. . . .

'Well, I felt to the right, and my fingers touched something curved, that felt—yes—more or less like leather; dampish it was, and evidently part of a heavy, full thing. There was nothing, I must say, to alarm one. I grew bolder, and putting both hands in as well as I could, I pulled it to me, and it came. It was heavy, but moved more easily than I had expected. As I pulled it towards the entrance, my left elbow knocked over and extinguished the candle. I got the thing fairly in front of the mouth and began drawing it out. Just then Brown gave a sharp ejaculation and ran quickly up the steps with the lantern. He will tell you why in a moment. Startled as I was, I looked round after him, and saw him stand for a minute at the top and then walk away a few yards. Then I heard him call softly, "All right, sir," and went on pulling out the great bag, in complete darkness. It hung for an instant on the edge of the hole, then slipped forward on to my chest, and *put its arms round my neck*.

'My dear Gregory, I am telling you the exact truth. I believe I am now acquainted with the extremity of terror and repulsion which a man can endure without losing his mind. I can only just manage to tell you now the bare outline of the experience. I was conscious of a most horrible smell of mould, and of a cold kind of face pressed against my own, and moving slowly over it, and of several—I don't know how many—legs or arms or tentacles or something clinging to

my body. I screamed out, Brown says, like a beast, and fell away back-
ward from the step on which I stood, and the creature slipped downwards, I suppose, on to that same step. Providentially the band round
me held firm. Brown did not lose his head, and was strong enough to
pull me up to the top and get me over the edge quite promptly. How
he managed it exactly I don't know, and I think he would find it hard
to tell you. I believe he contrived to hide our implements in the
deserted building near by, and with very great difficulty he got me
back to the inn. I was in no state to make explanations, and Brown
knows no German; but next morning I told the people some tale of
having had a bad fall in the abbey ruins, which, I suppose, they
believed. And now, before I go further, I should just like you to hear
what Brown's experiences during those few minutes were. Tell the
Rector, Brown, what you told me.'

'Well, sir,' said Brown, speaking low and nervously, 'it was just
this way. Master was busy down in front of the 'ole, and I was 'olding
the lantern and looking on, when I 'eard somethink drop in the water
from the top, as I thought. So I looked up, and I see someone's 'ead
lookin' over at us. I s'pose I must ha' said somethink, and I 'eld the
light up and run up the steps, and my light shone right on the face.
That was a bad un, sir, if ever I see one! A holdish man, and the face
very much fell in, and larfin, as I thought. And I got up the steps as
quick pretty nigh as I'm tellin' you, and when I was out on the ground
there warn't a sign of any person. There 'adn't been the time for anyone to get away, let alone a hold chap, and I made sure he warn't
crouching down by the well, nor nothink. Next thing I hear master
cry out somethink 'orrible, and hall I see was him hanging out by the
rope, and, as master says, 'owever I got him up I couldn't tell you.'

'You hear that, Gregory?' said Mr. Somerton. 'Now, does any
explanation of that incident strike you?'

'The whole thing is so ghastly and abnormal that I must own it
puts me quite off my balance; but the thought did occur to me that
possibly the—well, the person who set the trap might have come to
see the success of his plan.'

'Just so, Gregory, just so. I can think of nothing else so—*likely*, I
should say, if such a word had a place anywhere in my story. I think it
must have been the Abbot. . . . Well, I haven't much more to tell you.
I spent a miserable night, Brown sitting up with me. Next day I was
no better; unable to get up; no doctor to be had; and, if one had been

available, I doubt if he could have done much for me. I made Brown write off to you, and spent a second terrible night. And, Gregory, of this I am sure, and I think it affected me more than the first shock, for it lasted longer: there was someone or something on the watch outside my door the whole night. I almost fancy there were two. It wasn't only the faint noises I heard from time to time all through the dark hours, but there was the smell—the hideous smell of mould. Every rag I had had on me on that first evening I had stripped off and made Brown take it away. I believe he stuffed the things into the stove in his room; and yet the smell was there, as intense as it had been in the well; and, what is more, it came from outside the door. But with the first glimmer of dawn it faded out, and the sounds ceased, too; and that convinced me that the thing or things were creatures of darkness, and could not stand the daylight; and so I was sure that if anyone could put back the stone, it or they would be powerless until someone else took it away again. I had to wait until you came to get that done. Of course, I couldn't send Brown to do it by himself, and still less could I tell anyone who belonged to the place.

'Well, there is my story; and if you don't believe it, I can't help it. But I think you do.'

'Indeed,' said Mr. Gregory, 'I can find no alternative. I *must* believe it! I saw the well and the stone myself, and had a glimpse, I thought, of the bags or something else in the hole. And, to be plain with you, Somerton, I believe my door was watched last night, too.'

'I dare say it was, Gregory; but, thank goodness, that is over. Have you, by the way, anything to tell about your visit to that dreadful place?'

'Very little,' was the answer. 'Brown and I managed easily enough to get the slab into its place, and he fixed it very firmly with the irons and wedges you had desired him to get, and we contrived to smear the surface with mud so that it looks just like the rest of the wall. One thing I did notice in the carving on the well-head, which I think must have escaped you. It was a horrid, grotesque shape—perhaps more like a toad than anything else, and there was a label by it inscribed with the two words, "Depositum custodi." '[1]

---

[1] 'Keep that which is committed to thee.'

A SCHOOL STORY

Two men in a smoking-room were talking of their private-school days. 'At *our* school,' said A., 'we had a ghost's footmark on the staircase. What was it like? Oh, very unconvincing. Just the shape of a shoe, with a square toe, if I remember right. The staircase was a stone one. I never heard any story about the thing. That seems odd, when you come to think of it. Why didn't somebody invent one, I wonder?'

'You never can tell with little boys. They have a mythology of their own. There's a subject for you, by the way—"The Folklore of Private Schools." '

'Yes; the crop is rather scanty, though. I imagine, if you were to investigate the cycle of ghost stories, for instance, which the boys at private schools tell each other, they would all turn out to be highly-compressed versions of stories out of books.'

'Nowadays the *Strand* and *Pearson's*,* and so on, would be extensively drawn upon.'

'No doubt: they weren't born or thought of in *my* time. Let's see. I wonder if I can remember the staple ones that I was told. First, there was the house with a room in which a series of people insisted on passing a night; and each of them in the morning was found kneeling in a corner, and had just time to say, "I've seen it," and died.'

'Wasn't that the house in Berkeley Square?'*

'I dare say it was. Then there was the man who heard a noise in the passage at night, opened his door, and saw someone crawling towards him on all fours with his eye hanging out on his cheek. There was besides, let me think—— Yes! the room where a man was found dead in bed with a horseshoe mark on his forehead, and the floor under the bed was covered with marks of horseshoes also; I don't know why. Also there was the lady who, on locking her bedroom door in a strange house, heard a thin voice among the bed-curtains say, "Now we're shut in for the night." None of those had any explanation or sequel. I wonder if they go on still, those stories.'

'Oh, likely enough—with additions from the magazines, as I said. You never heard, did you, of a real ghost at a private school? I thought not; nobody has that ever I came across.'

'From the way in which you said that, I gather that *you* have.'

'I really don't know; but this is what was in my mind. It happened at my private school thirty odd years ago, and I haven't any explanation of it.

'The school I mean was near London.* It was established in a large and fairly old house—a great white building with very fine grounds about it; there were large cedars in the garden, as there are in so many of the older gardens in the Thames valley, and ancient elms in the three or four fields which we used for our games. I think probably it was quite an attractive place, but boys seldom allow that their schools possess any tolerable features.

'I came to the school in a September, soon after the year 1870; and among the boys who arrived on the same day was one whom I took to: a Highland boy, whom I will call McLeod. I needn't spend time in describing him: the main thing is that I got to know him very well. He was not an exceptional boy in any way—not particularly good at books or games—but he suited me.

'The school was a large one: there must have been from 120 to 130 boys there as a rule, and so a considerable staff of masters was required, and there were rather frequent changes among them.

'One term—perhaps it was my third or fourth—a new master made his appearance. His name was Sampson.* He was a tallish, stoutish, pale, black-bearded man. I think we liked him: he had travelled a good deal, and had stories which amused us on our school walks, so that there was some competition among us to get within earshot of him. I remember too—dear me, I have hardly thought of it since then!—that he had a charm on his watch-chain that attracted my attention one day, and he let me examine it. It was, I now suppose, a gold Byzantine coin; there was an effigy of some absurd emperor on one side; the other side had been worn practically smooth, and he had had cut on it—rather barbarously—his own initials, G.W.S., and a date, 24 July, 1865. Yes, I can see it now: he told me he had picked it up in Constantinople: it was about the size of a florin, perhaps rather smaller.

'Well, the first odd thing that happened was this. Sampson was doing Latin grammar with us. One of his favourite methods—perhaps it is rather a good one—was to make us construct sentences out of our own heads to illustrate the rules he was trying to make us learn. Of course that is a thing which gives a silly boy a chance of being impertinent: there are lots of school stories in which that happens—or anyhow there might be. But Sampson was too good a disciplinarian for us to think of trying that on with him. Now, on this occasion he was telling us how to express *remembering* in Latin: and he ordered us each to make a sentence bringing in the verb *memini*, "I remember." Well, most of us made up some ordinary sentence such as "I remember my father," or "He remembers his book," or something equally uninteresting: and I dare say a good many put down *memino librum meum*, and so forth: but the boy I mentioned—McLeod—was evidently thinking of something more elaborate than that. The rest of us wanted to have our sentences passed, and get on to something else, so some kicked him under the desk, and I, who was next to him, poked him and whispered to him to look sharp. But he didn't seem to attend. I looked at his paper and saw he had put down nothing at all. So I jogged him again harder than before and upbraided him sharply for keeping us all waiting. That did have some effect. He started and seemed to wake up, and then very quickly he scribbled about a couple of lines on his paper, and showed it up with the rest. As it was the last, or nearly the last, to come in, and as Sampson had a good deal to say to the boys who had written *meminiscimus patri meo** and the rest of it, it turned out that the clock struck twelve before he had got to McLeod, and McLeod had to wait afterwards to have his sentence corrected. There was nothing much going on outside when I got out, so I waited for him to come. He came very slowly when he did arrive, and I guessed there had been some sort of trouble. "Well," I said, "what did you get?" "Oh, I don't know," said McLeod, "nothing much: but I think Sampson's rather sick with me." "Why, did you show him up some rot?" "No fear," he said. "It was all right as far as I could see: it was like this: *Memento*—that's right enough for remember, and it takes a genitive,—*memento putei inter quatuor taxos*." "What silly rot!" I said. "What made you shove that down? What does it mean?" "That's the funny part," said McLeod. "I'm not quite sure what it does mean. All I know is, it just came into my head and I corked it down. I know what I *think* it means, because just before I wrote it down I had a sort of picture of it in my head: I believe it means 'Remember the well among the four'—what are those dark sort of trees that have red berries on them?" "Mountain ashes, I s'pose you mean." "I never heard of them," said McLeod; "no, *I'll* tell you—yews." "Well, and what did Sampson say?" "Why, he was jolly odd about it. When he read it he got up and went to the mantel-piece and stopped quite a long time without saying anything, with his back to me. And then he said, without turning round, and rather quiet, 'What do you suppose that means?' I told him what I thought; only I couldn't remember the name of the silly tree: and then he wanted to know why I put it down, and I had to say something or other. And after that he left off talking about it, and asked me how long I'd been here, and where my people lived, and things like that: and then I came away: but he wasn't looking a bit well."

'I don't remember any more that was said by either of us about this. Next day McLeod took to his bed with a chill or something of the kind, and it was a week or more before he was in school again. And as much as a month went by without anything happening that was noticeable. Whether or not Mr. Sampson was really startled, as McLeod had thought, he didn't show it. I am pretty sure, of course, now, that there was something very curious in his past history, but I'm not going to pretend that we boys were sharp enough to guess any such thing.

'There was one other incident of the same kind as the last which I told you. Several times since that day we had had to make up examples in school to illustrate different rules, but there had never been any row except when we did them wrong. At last there came a day when we were going through those dismal things which people call Conditional Sentences, and we were told to make a conditional sentence, expressing a future consequence. We did it, right or wrong, and showed up our bits of paper, and Sampson began looking through them. All at once he got up, made some odd sort of noise in his throat, and rushed out by a door that was just by his desk. We sat there for a minute or two, and then—I suppose it was incorrect—but we went up, I and one or two others, to look at the papers on his desk. Of course I thought someone must have put down some nonsense or other, and Sampson had gone off to report him. All the same, I noticed that he hadn't taken any of the papers with him when he ran out. Well, the top paper on the desk was written in red ink—which no one used—and it wasn't in anyone's hand who was in the class. They all looked at it—McLeod and all—and took their dying oaths that it wasn't theirs. Then I thought of counting the bits of paper.

And of this I made quite certain: that there were seventeen bits of paper on the desk, and sixteen boys in the form. Well, I bagged the extra paper, and kept it, and I believe I have it now. And now you will want to know what was written on it. It was simple enough, and harmless enough, I should have said.

'"*Si tu non veneris ad me, ego veniam ad te*," which means, I suppose, "If you don't come to me, I'll come to you."'

'Could you show me the paper?' interrupted the listener.

'Yes, I could: but there's another odd thing about it. That same afternoon I took it out of my locker—I know for certain it was the same bit, for I made a finger-mark on it—and no single trace of writing of any kind was there on it. I kept it, as I said, and since that time I have tried various experiments to see whether sympathetic ink had been used, but absolutely without result.

'So much for that. After about half an hour Sampson looked in again: said he had felt very unwell, and told us we might go. He came rather gingerly to his desk, and gave just one look at the uppermost paper: and I suppose he thought he must have been dreaming: anyhow, he asked no questions.

'That day was a half-holiday, and next day Sampson was in school again, much as usual. That night the third and last incident in my story happened.

'We—McLeod and I—slept in a dormitory at right angles to the main building. Sampson slept in the main building on the first floor. There was a very bright full moon. At an hour which I can't tell exactly, but some time between one and two, I was woken up by somebody shaking me. It was McLeod; and a nice state of mind he seemed to be in. "Come," he said,—"come! there's a burglar getting in through Sampson's window." As soon as I could speak, I said, "Well, why not call out and wake everybody up?" "No, no," he said, "I'm not sure who it is: don't make a row: come and look." Naturally I came and looked, and naturally there was no one there. I was cross enough, and should have called McLeod plenty of names: only—I couldn't tell why—it seemed to me that there *was* something wrong— something that made me very glad I wasn't alone to face it. We were still at the window looking out, and as soon as I could, I asked him what he had heard or seen. "I didn't *hear* anything at all," he said, "but about five minutes before I woke you, I found myself looking out of this window here, and there was a man sitting or kneeling on

Sampson's window-sill, and looking in, and I thought he was beckoning." "What sort of man?" McLeod wriggled. "I don't know," he said, "but I can tell you one thing—he was beastly thin: and he looked as if he was wet all over: and," he said, looking round and whispering as if he hardly liked to hear himself, "I'm not at all sure that he was alive."

'We went on talking in whispers some time longer, and eventually crept back to bed. No one else in the room woke or stirred the whole time. I believe we did sleep a bit afterwards, but we were very cheap next day.

'And next day Mr. Sampson was gone: not to be found: and I believe no trace of him has ever come to light since. In thinking it over, one of the oddest things about it all has seemed to me to be the fact that neither McLeod nor I ever mentioned what we had seen to any third person whatever. Of course no questions were asked on the subject, and if they had been, I am inclined to believe that we could not have made any answer: we seemed unable to speak about it.

'That is my story,' said the narrator. 'The only approach to a ghost story connected with a school that I know, but still, I think, an approach to such a thing.'

    *   *   *   *   *

The sequel to this may perhaps be reckoned highly conventional; but a sequel there is, and so it must be produced. There had been more than one listener to the story, and, in the latter part of that same year, or of the next, one such listener was staying at a country house in Ireland.

One evening his host was turning over a drawer full of odds and ends in the smoking-room. Suddenly he put his hand upon a little box. 'Now,' he said, 'you know about old things; tell me what that is.' My friend opened the little box, and found in it a thin gold chain with an object attached to it. He glanced at the object and then took off his spectacles to examine it more narrowly. 'What's the history of this?' he asked. 'Odd enough,' was the answer. 'You know the yew thicket in the shrubbery: well, a year or two back we were cleaning out the old well that used to be in the clearing here, and what do you suppose we found?'

'Is it possible that you found a body?' said the visitor, with an odd feeling of nervousness.

'We did that: but what's more, in every sense of the word, we found two.'

'Good Heavens! Two? Was there anything to show how they got there? Was this thing found with them?'

'It was. Amongst the rags of the clothes that were on one of the bodies. A bad business, whatever the story of it may have been. One body had the arms tight round the other. They must have been there thirty years or more—long enough before we came to this place. You may judge we filled the well up fast enough. Do you make anything of what's cut on that gold coin you have there?'

'I think I can,' said my friend, holding it to the light (but he read it without much difficulty); 'it seems to be G.W.S., 24 July, 1865.'

THE ROSE GARDEN

❦

MR. and Mrs. Anstruther were at breakfast in the parlour of Westfield Hall, in the county of Essex.* They were arranging plans for the day.

'George,' said Mrs. Anstruther, 'I think you had better take the car to Maldon and see if you can get any of those knitted things I was speaking about which would do for my stall at the bazaar.'

'Oh well, if you wish it, Mary, of course I can do that, but I had half arranged to play a round with Geoffrey Williamson this morning. The bazaar isn't till Thursday of next week, is it?'

'What has that to do with it, George? I should have thought you would have guessed that if I can't get the things I want in Maldon I shall have to write to all manner of shops in town: and they are certain to send something quite unsuitable in price or quality the first time. If you have actually made an appointment with Mr. Williamson, you had better keep it, but I must say I think you might have let me know.'

'Oh no, no, it wasn't really an appointment. I quite see what you mean. I'll go. And what shall you do yourself?'

'Why, when the work of the house is arranged for, I must see about laying out my new rose garden. By the way, before you start for Maldon I wish you would just take Collins to look at the place I fixed upon. You know it, of course.'

'Well, I'm not quite sure that I do, Mary. Is it at the upper end, towards the village?'

'Good gracious no, my dear George; I thought I had made that quite clear. No, it's that small clearing just off the shrubbery path that goes towards the church.'

'Oh yes, where we were saying there must have been a summer-house once: the place with the old seat and the posts. But do you think there's enough sun there?'

'My dear George, do allow me *some* common sense, and don't credit me with all your ideas about summer-houses. Yes, there will be plenty of sun when we have got rid of some of those box-bushes. I know what you are going to say, and I have as little wish as you to strip the place bare. All I want Collins to do is to clear away the old seats and the posts and things before I come out in an hour's time. And I hope you will manage to get off fairly soon. After luncheon I think I shall go on with my sketch of the church; and if you please you can go over to the links, or——'

'Ah, a good idea—very good! Yes, you finish that sketch, Mary, and I should be glad of a round.'

'I was going to say, you might call on the Bishop; but I suppose it is no use my making *any* suggestion. And now do be getting ready, or half the morning will be gone.'

Mr. Anstruther's face, which had shown symptoms of lengthening, shortened itself again, and he hurried from the room, and was soon heard giving orders in the passage. Mrs. Anstruther, a stately dame of some fifty summers, proceeded, after a second consideration of the morning's letters, to her housekeeping.

Within a few minutes Mr. Anstruther had discovered Collins in the greenhouse, and they were on their way to the site of the projected rose garden. I do not know much about the conditions most suitable to these nurseries, but I am inclined to believe that Mrs. Anstruther, though in the habit of describing herself as 'a great gardener,' had not been well advised in the selection of a spot for the purpose. It was a small, dank clearing, bounded on one side by a path, and on the other by thick box-bushes, laurels, and other evergreens. The ground was almost bare of grass and dark of aspect. Remains of rustic seats and an old and corrugated oak post somewhere near the middle of the clearing had given rise to Mr. Anstruther's conjecture that a summer-house had once stood there.

Clearly Collins had not been put in possession of his mistress's intentions with regard to this plot of ground: and when he learnt them from Mr. Anstruther he displayed no enthusiasm.

'Of course I could clear them seats away soon enough,' he said. 'They aren't no ornament to the place, Mr. Anstruther, and rotten too. Look 'ere, sir'—and he broke off a large piece—'rotten right through. Yes, clear them away, to be sure we can do that.'

'And the post,' said Mr. Anstruther, 'that's got to go too.'

Collins advanced, and shook the post with both hands: then he rubbed his chin.

'That's firm in the ground, that post is,' he said. 'That's been there a number of years, Mr. Anstruther. I doubt I shan't get that up not quite so soon as what I can do with them seats.'

'But your mistress specially wishes it to be got out of the way in an hour's time,' said Mr. Anstruther.

Collins smiled and shook his head slowly. 'You'll excuse me, sir, but you feel of it for yourself. No, sir, no one can't do what's impossible to 'em, can they, sir? I could git that post up by after tea-time, sir, but that'll want a lot of digging. What you require, you see, sir, if you'll excuse me naming of it, you want the soil loosening round this post 'ere, and me and the boy we shall take a little time doing of that. But now, these 'ere seats,' said Collins, appearing to appropriate this portion of the scheme as due to his own resourcefulness, 'why, I can get the barrer round and 'ave them cleared away in, why less than an hour's time from now, if you'll permit of it. Only——'

'Only what, Collins?'

'Well now, it ain't for me to go against orders no more than what it is for you yourself—or anyone else' (this was added somewhat hurriedly), 'but if you'll pardon me, sir, this ain't the place I should have picked out for no rose garden myself. Why look at them box and laurestinus, 'ow they reg'lar preclude the light from——'

'Ah yes, but we've got to get rid of some of them, of course.'

'Oh, indeed, get rid of them! Yes, to be sure, but—I beg your pardon, Mr. Anstruther——'

'I'm sorry, Collins, but I must be getting on now. I hear the car at the door. Your mistress will explain exactly what she wishes. I'll tell her, then, that you can see your way to clearing away the seats at once, and the post this afternoon. Good morning.'

Collins was left rubbing his chin. Mrs. Anstruther received the report with some discontent, but did not insist upon any change of plan.

By four o'clock that afternoon she had dismissed her husband to his golf, had dealt faithfully with Collins and with the other duties of the day, and, having sent a campstool and umbrella to the proper spot, had just settled down to her sketch of the church as seen from the shrubbery, when a maid came hurrying down the path to report that Miss Wilkins had called.

Miss Wilkins was one of the few remaining members of the family from whom the Anstruthers had bought the Westfield estate some few years back. She had been staying in the neighbourhood, and this was probably a farewell visit. 'Perhaps you could ask Miss Wilkins to join me here,' said Mrs. Anstruther, and soon Miss Wilkins, a person of mature years, approached.

'Yes, I'm leaving the Ashes to-morrow, and I shall be able to tell my brother how tremendously you have improved the place. Of course he can't help regretting the old house just a little—as I do myself—but the garden is really delightful now.'

'I am so glad you can say so. But you mustn't think we've finished our improvements. Let me show you where I mean to put a rose garden. It's close by here.'

The details of the project were laid before Miss Wilkins at some length; but her thoughts were evidently elsewhere.

'Yes, delightful,' she said at last rather absently. 'But do you know, Mrs. Anstruther, I'm afraid I was thinking of old times. I'm *very* glad to have seen just this spot again before you altered it. Frank and I had quite a romance about this place.'

'Yes?' said Mrs. Anstruther smilingly; 'do tell me what it was. Something quaint and charming, I'm sure.'

'Not so very charming, but it has always seemed to me curious. Neither of us would ever be here alone when we were children, and I'm not sure that I should care about it now in certain moods. It is one of those things that can hardly be put into words—by me at least—and that sound rather foolish if they are not properly expressed. I can tell you after a fashion what it was that gave us—well, almost a horror of the place when we were alone. It was towards the evening of one very hot autumn day, when Frank had disappeared mysteriously about the grounds, and I was looking for him to fetch him to tea, and going down this path I suddenly saw him, not hiding in the bushes, as I rather expected, but sitting on the bench in the old summer-house—there was a wooden summer-house here, you know—up in the corner, asleep, but with such a dreadful look on his face that I really thought he must be ill or even dead. I rushed at him and shook him, and told him to wake up; and wake up he did, with a scream. I assure you the poor boy seemed almost beside himself with fright. He hurried me away to the house, and was in a terrible state all that night, hardly sleeping. Someone had to sit up with him, as far as I remember. He was better very soon, but for days I couldn't get him to say why he had been in such a condition. It came out at last that he had really been asleep and had had a very odd disjointed sort of dream.* He never *saw* much of what was around him, but he *felt* the scenes most vividly. First he made out that he was standing in a large room with a number of people in it, and that someone was opposite to him who was "very powerful," and he was being asked questions which he felt to be very important, and, whenever he answered them, some-one—either the person opposite to him, or someone else in the room—seemed to be, as he said, making something up against him. All the voices sounded to him very distant, but he remembered bits of the things that were said: "Where were you on the 19th of October?" and "Is this your handwriting?" and so on. I can see now, of course, that he was dreaming of some trial: but we were never allowed to see the papers, and it was odd that a boy of eight should have such a vivid idea of what went on in a court. All the time he felt, he said, the most intense anxiety and oppression and hopelessness (though I don't suppose he used such words as that to me). Then, after that, there was an interval in which he remembered being dread-fully restless and miserable, and then there came another sort of pic-ture, when he was aware that he had come out of doors on a dark raw morning with a little snow about. It was in a street, or at any rate among houses, and he felt that there were numbers and numbers of people there too, and that he was taken up some creaking wooden steps and stood on a sort of platform, but the only thing he could actually see was a small fire burning somewhere near him. Someone who had been holding his arm left hold of it and went towards this fire, and then he said the fright he was in was worse than at any other part of his dream, and if I had not wakened him up he didn't know what would have become of him. A curious dream for a child to have, wasn't it? Well, so much for that. It must have been later in the year that Frank and I were here, and I was sitting in the arbour just about sunset. I noticed the sun was going down, and told Frank to run in and see if tea was ready while I finished a chapter in the book I was reading. Frank was away longer than I expected, and the light was going so fast that I had to bend over my book to make it out. All at once I became conscious that someone was whispering to me inside the arbour. The only words I could distinguish, or thought I could, were something like "Pull, pull. I'll push, you pull."

'I started up in something of a fright. The voice—it was little more than a whisper—sounded so hoarse and angry, and yet as if it came from a long, long way off—just as it had done in Frank's dream. But, though I was startled, I had enough courage to look round and try to make out where the sound came from. And—this sounds very foolish, I know, but still it is the fact—I made sure that it was strongest when I put my ear to an old post which was part of the end of the seat. I was so certain of this that I remember making some marks on the post—as deep as I could with the scissors out of my work-basket. I don't know why. I wonder, by the way, whether that isn't the very post itself. . . . Well, yes, it might be: there *are* marks and scratches on it—but one can't be sure. Anyhow, it was just like that post you have there. My father got to know that both of us had had a fright in the arbour, and he went down there himself one evening after dinner, and the arbour was pulled down at very short notice. I recollect hearing my father talking about it to an old man who used to do odd jobs in the place, and the old man saying, "Don't you fear for that, sir: he's fast enough in there without no one don't take and let him out." But when I asked who it was, I could get no satisfactory answer. Possibly my father or mother might have told me more about it when I grew up, but, as you know, they both died when we were still quite children. I must say it has always seemed very odd to me, and I've often asked the older people in the village whether they knew of anything strange: but either they knew nothing or they wouldn't tell me. Dear, dear, how I have been boring you with my childish remembrances! but indeed that arbour did absorb our thoughts quite remarkably for a time. You can fancy, can't you, the kind of stories that we made up for ourselves. Well, dear Mrs. Anstruther, I must be leaving you now. We shall meet in town this winter, I hope, shan't we?' etc., etc.

The seats and the post were cleared away and uprooted respectively by that evening. Late summer weather is proverbially treacherous, and during dinner-time Mrs. Collins sent up to ask for a little brandy, because her husband had took a nasty chill and she was afraid he would not be able to do much next day.

Mrs. Anstruther's morning reflections were not wholly placid. She was sure some roughs had got into the plantation during the night. 'And another thing, George: the moment that Collins is about again, you must tell him to do something about the owls. I never heard anything like them, and I'm positive one came and perched somewhere just outside our window. If it had come in I should have been out of my wits: it must have been a very large bird, from its voice. Didn't you hear it? No, of course not, you were sound asleep as usual. Still, I must say, George, you don't look as if your night had done you much good.'

'My dear, I feel as if another of the same would turn me silly. You have no idea of the dreams I had. I couldn't speak of them when I woke up, and if this room wasn't so bright and sunny I shouldn't care to think of them even now.'

'Well, really, George, that isn't very common with you, I must say. You must have—no, you only had what I had yesterday—unless you had tea at that wretched club house: did you?'

'No, no; nothing but a cup of tea and some bread and butter. I should really like to know how I came to put my dream together—as I suppose one does put one's dreams together from a lot of little things one has been seeing or reading. Look here, Mary, it was like this—if I shan't be boring you——'

'I *wish* to hear what it was, George. I will tell you when I have had enough.'

'All right. I must tell you that it wasn't like other nightmares in one way, because I didn't really *see* anyone who spoke to me or touched me, and yet I was most fearfully impressed with the reality of it all. First I was sitting, no, moving about, in an old-fashioned sort of pan-elled room. I remember there was a fireplace and a lot of burnt papers in it, and I was in a great state of anxiety about something. There was someone else—a servant, I suppose, because I remember saying to him, "Horses, as quick as you can," and then waiting a bit: and next I heard several people coming upstairs and a noise like spurs on a boarded floor, and then the door opened and whatever it was that I was expecting happened.'

'Yes, but what was that?'

'You see, I couldn't tell: it was the sort of shock that upsets you in a dream. You either wake up or else everything goes black. That was what happened to me. Then I was in a big dark-walled room, pan-elled, I think, like the other, and a number of people, and I was evidently——'

'Standing your trial, I suppose, George.'

'Goodness! yes, Mary, I was; but did you dream that too? How very odd!'

'No, no; I didn't get enough sleep for that. Go on, George, and I will tell you afterwards.'

'Yes; well, I *was* being tried, for my life, I've no doubt, from the state I was in. I had no one speaking for me, and somewhere there was a most fearful fellow—on the bench; I should have said, only that he seemed to be pitching into me most unfairly, and twisting everything I said, and asking most abominable questions.'

'What about?'

'Why, dates when I was at particular places, and letters I was supposed to have written, and why I had destroyed some papers; and I recollect his laughing at answers I made in a way that quite daunted me. It doesn't sound much, but I can tell you, Mary, it was really appalling at the time. I am quite certain there was such a man once, and a most horrible villain he must have been. The things he said——'

'Thank you, I have no wish to hear them. I can go to the links any day myself. How did it end?'

'Oh, against me; *he* saw to that. I do wish, Mary, I could give you a notion of the strain that came after that, and seemed to me to last for days: waiting and waiting, and sometimes writing things I knew to be enormously important to me, and waiting for answers and none coming, and after that I came out——'

'Ah!'

'What makes you say that? Do you know what sort of thing I saw?'

'Was it a dark cold day, and snow in the streets, and a fire burning somewhere near you?'

'By George, it was! You *have* had the same nightmare! Really not? Well, it is the oddest thing! Yes; I've no doubt it was an execution for high treason. I know I was laid on straw and jolted along most wretchedly, and then had to go up some steps, and someone was holding my arm, and I remember seeing a bit of a ladder and hearing a sound of a lot of people. I really don't think I could bear now to go into a crowd of people and hear the noise they make talking. However, mercifully, I didn't get to the real business. The dream passed off with a sort of thunder inside my head. But, Mary——'

'I know what you are going to ask. I suppose this is an instance of a kind of thought-reading. Miss Wilkins called yesterday and told me of a dream her brother had as a child when they lived here, and something did no doubt make me think of that when I was awake last night listening to those horrible owls and those men talking and laughing in the shrubbery (by the way, I wish you would see if they have done any damage, and speak to the police about it); and so, I suppose, from my brain it must have got into yours while you were asleep. Curious, no doubt, and I am sorry it gave you such a bad night. You had better be as much in the fresh air as you can to-day.'

'Oh, it's all right now; but I think I *will* go over to the Lodge and see if I can get a game with any of them. And you?'

'I have enough to do for this morning; and this afternoon, if I am not interrupted, there is my drawing.'

'To be sure—I want to see that finished very much.'

No damage was discoverable in the shrubbery. Mr. Anstruther surveyed with faint interest the site of the rose garden, where the uprooted post still lay, and the hole it had occupied remained unfilled. Collins, upon inquiry made, proved to be better, but quite unable to come to his work. He expressed, by the mouth of his wife, a hope that he hadn't done nothing wrong clearing away them things. Mrs. Collins added that there was a lot of talking people in Westfield, and the hold ones was the worst: seemed to think everything of them having been in the parish longer than what other people had. But as to what they said no more could then be ascertained than that it had quite upset Collins, and was a lot of nonsense.

Recruited by lunch and a brief period of slumber, Mrs. Anstruther settled herself comfortably upon her sketching chair in the path leading through the shrubbery to the side-gate of the churchyard. Trees and buildings were among her favourite subjects, and here she had good studies of both. She worked hard, and the drawing was becoming a really pleasant thing to look upon by the time that the wooded hills to the west had shut off the sun. Still she would have persevered, but the light changed rapidly, and it became obvious that the last touches must be added on the morrow. She rose and turned towards the house, pausing for a time to take delight in the limpid green western sky. Then she passed on between the dark box-bushes, and, at a point just before the path debouched on the lawn, she stopped once again and considered the quiet evening landscape, and made a mental note that that must be the tower of one of the Roothing* churches that one caught on the skyline. Then a bird (perhaps) rustled in the box-bush on her left, and she turned and started at seeing what at first she took to be a Fifth of November mask* peeping out among the branches. She looked closer.

It was not a mask. It was a face—large, smooth, and pink. She remembers the minute drops of perspiration which were starting from its forehead: she remembers how the jaws were clean-shaven and the eyes shut. She remembers also, and with an accuracy which makes the thought intolerable to her, how the mouth was open and a single tooth appeared below the upper lip. As she looked the face receded into the darkness of the bush. The shelter of the house was gained and the door shut before she collapsed.

Mr. and Mrs. Anstruther had been for a week or more recruiting at Brighton before they received a circular from the Essex Archæological Society, and a query as to whether they possessed certain historical portraits which it was desired to include in the forthcoming work on Essex Portraits, to be published under the Society's auspices. There was an accompanying letter from the Secretary which contained the following passage: 'We are specially anxious to know whether you possess the original of the engraving of which I enclose a photograph. It represents Sir ——— ———, Lord Chief Justice under Charles II,* who, as you doubtless know, retired after his disgrace to Westfield, and is supposed to have died there of remorse. It may interest you to hear that a curious entry has recently been found in the registers, not of Westfield but of Priors Roothing, to the effect that the parish was so much troubled after his death that the rector of Westfield summoned the parsons of all the Roothings to come and lay him; which they did. The entry ends by saying: "The stake is in a field adjoining to the churchyard of Westfield, on the west side." Perhaps you can let us know if any tradition to this effect is current in your parish.'

The incidents which the 'enclosed photograph' recalled were productive of a severe shock to Mrs. Anstruther. It was decided that she must spend the winter abroad.

Mr. Anstruther, when he went down to Westfield to make the necessary arrangements, not unnaturally told his story to the rector (an old gentleman), who showed little surprise.

'Really I had managed to piece out for myself very much what must have happened, partly from old people's talk and partly from what I saw in your grounds. Of course we have suffered to some extent also. Yes, it was bad at first: like owls, as you say, and men talking sometimes. One night it was in this garden, and at other times about several of the cottages. But lately there has been very little: I think it will die out. There is nothing in our registers except the entry of the burial, and what I for a long time took to be the family motto;

but last time I looked at it I noticed that it was added in a later hand and had the initials of one of our rectors quite late in the seventeenth century, A. C.—Augustine Crompton. Here it is, you see—*quieta non movere.** I suppose——— Well, it is rather hard to say exactly what I do suppose.'

THE TRACTATE MIDDOTH

※

TOWARDS the end of an autumn afternoon an elderly man with a thin face and grey Piccadilly weepers* pushed open the swing-door leading into the vestibule of a certain famous library,* and addressing himself to an attendant, stated that he believed he was entitled to use the library, and inquired if he might take a book out. Yes, if he were on the list of those to whom that privilege was given. He produced his card—Mr. John Eldred—and, the register being consulted, a favourable answer was given. 'Now, another point,' said he. 'It is a long time since I was here, and I do not know my way about your building; besides, it is near closing-time, and it is bad for me to hurry up and down stairs. I have here the title of the book I want: is there anyone at liberty who could go and find it for me?' After a moment's thought the doorkeeper beckoned to a young man who was passing. 'Mr. Garrett,' he said, 'have you a minute to assist this gentleman?' 'With pleasure,' was Mr. Garrett's answer. The slip with the title was handed to him. 'I think I can put my hand on this; it happens to be in the class I inspected last quarter, but I'll just look it up in the catalogue to make sure. I suppose it is that particular edition that you require, sir?' 'Yes, if you please; that, and no other,' said Mr. Eldred; 'I am exceedingly obliged to you.' 'Don't mention it I beg, sir,' said Mr. Garrett, and hurried off.

'I thought so,' he said to himself, when his finger, travelling down the pages of the catalogue, stopped at a particular entry. 'Talmud: Tractate Middoth, with the commentary of Nachmanides, Amsterdam, 1707.* 11.3.34. Hebrew class, of course. Not a very difficult job this.'

Mr. Eldred, accommodated with a chair in the vestibule, awaited anxiously the return of his messenger—and his disappointment at seeing an empty-handed Mr. Garrett running down the staircase was very evident. 'I'm sorry to disappoint you, sir,' said the young man, 'but the book is out.' 'Oh dear!' said Mr. Eldred, 'is that so? You are sure there can be no mistake?' 'I don't think there is much chance of it, sir; but it's possible, if you like to wait a minute, that you might meet the very gentleman that's got it. He must be leaving the library soon, and I *think* I saw him take that particular book out of the shelf.' 'Indeed! You didn't recognize him, I suppose? Would it be one of the professors or one of the students?' 'I don't think so: certainly not a professor. I should have known him; but the light isn't very good in that part of the library at this time of day, and I didn't see his face. I should have said he was a shortish old gentleman, perhaps a clergyman, in a cloak. If you could wait, I can easily find out whether he wants the book very particularly.'

'No, no,' said Mr. Eldred, 'I won't—I can't wait now, thank you— no. I must be off. But I'll call again to-morrow if I may, and perhaps you could find out who has it.'

'Certainly, sir, and I'll have the book ready for you if we——' But Mr. Eldred was already off, and hurrying more than one would have thought wholesome for him.

Garrett had a few moments to spare; and, thought he, 'I'll go back to that case and see if I can find the old man. Most likely he could put off using the book for a few days. I dare say the other one doesn't want to keep it for long.' So off with him to the Hebrew class. But when he got there it was unoccupied, and the volume marked 11.3.34 was in its place on the shelf. It was vexatious to Garrett's self-respect to have disappointed an inquirer with so little reason: and he would have liked, had it not been against library rules, to take the book down to the vestibule then and there, so that it might be ready for Mr. Eldred when he called. However, next morning he would be on the look out for him, and he begged the doorkeeper to send and let him know when the moment came. As a matter of fact, he was himself in the vestibule when Mr. Eldred arrived, very soon after the library opened, and when hardly anyone besides the staff were in the building.

'I'm very sorry,' he said; 'it's not often that I make such a stupid mistake, but I did feel sure that the old gentleman I saw took out that very book and kept it in his hand without opening it, just as people do, you know, sir, when they mean to take a book out of the library and not merely refer to it. But, however, I'll run up now at once and get it for you this time.'

And here intervened a pause. Mr. Eldred paced the entry, read all the notices, consulted his watch, sat and gazed up the staircase, did all that a very impatient man could, until some twenty minutes had run

out. At last he addressed himself to the door-keeper and inquired if it was a very long way to that part of the library to which Mr. Garrett had gone.

'Well, I was thinking it was funny, sir: he's a quick man as a rule, but to be sure he might have been sent for by the libarian, but even so I think he'd have mentioned to him that you was waiting. I'll just speak him up on the toob and see.' And to the tube he addressed himself. As he absorbed the reply to his question his face changed, and he made one or two supplementary inquiries which were shortly answered. Then he came forward to his counter and spoke in a lower tone. 'I'm sorry to hear, sir, that something seems to have 'appened a little awkward. Mr. Garrett has been took poorly, it appears, and the libarian sent him 'ome in a cab the other way. Something of an attack, by what I can hear.' 'What, really? Do you mean that someone has injured him?' 'No, sir, not violence 'ere, but, as I should judge, attacted with an attack, what you might term it, of illness. Not a strong constitootion, Mr. Garrett. But as to your book, sir, perhaps you might be able to find it for yourself. It's too bad you should be disappointed this way twice over——' 'Er—well, but I'm so sorry that Mr. Garrett should have been taken ill in this way while he was obliging me. I think I must leave the book, and call and inquire after him. You can give me his address, I suppose.' That was easily done: Mr. Garrett, it appeared, lodged in rooms not far from the station. 'And, one other question. Did you happen to notice if an old gentleman, perhaps a clergyman, in a—yes—in a black cloak, left the library after I did yesterday. I think he may have been a—I think, that is, that he may be staying—or rather that I may have known him.'

'Not in a black cloak, sir; no. There were only two gentlemen left later than what you done, sir, both of them youngish men. There was Mr. Carter took out a music-book and one of the prefessors with a couple o' novels. That's the lot, sir; and then I went off to me tea, and glad to get it. Thank you, sir, much obliged.'

Mr. Eldred, still a prey to anxiety, betook himself in a cab to Mr. Garrett's address, but the young man was not yet in a condition to receive visitors. He was better, but his landlady considered that he must have had a severe shock. She thought most likely from what the doctor said that he would be able to see Mr. Eldred to-morrow. Mr. Eldred returned to his hotel at dusk and spent, I fear, but a dull evening.

On the next day he was able to see Mr. Garrett. When in health Mr. Garrett was a cheerful and pleasant-looking young man. Now he was a very white and shaky being, propped up in an arm-chair by the fire, and inclined to shiver and keep an eye on the door. If, however, there were visitors whom he was not prepared to welcome, Mr. Eldred was not among them. 'It really is I who owe you an apology, and I was despairing of being able to pay it, for I didn't know your address. But I am very glad you have called. I do dislike and regret giving all this trouble, but you know I could not have foreseen this—this attack which I had.'

'Of course not; but now, I am something of a doctor. You'll excuse my asking; you have had, I am sure, good advice. Was it a fall you had?'

'No. I did fall on the floor—but not from any height. It was, really, a shock.'

'You mean something startled you. Was it anything you thought you saw?'

'Not much *thinking* in the case, I'm afraid. Yes, it was something I saw. You remember when you called the first time at the library?'

'Yes, of course. Well, now, let me beg you not to try to describe it—it will not be good for you to recall it, I'm sure.'

'But indeed it would be a relief to me to tell anyone like yourself: you might be able to explain it away. It was just when I was going into the class where your book is——'

'Indeed, Mr. Garrett, I insist; besides, my watch tells me I have but very little time left in which to get my things together and take the train. No—not another word—it would be more distressing to you than you imagine, perhaps. Now there is just one thing I want to say. I feel that I am really indirectly responsible for this illness of yours, and I think I ought to defray the expense which it has—eh?'

But this offer was quite distinctly declined. Mr. Eldred, not pressing it, left almost at once: not, however, before Mr. Garrett had insisted upon his taking a note of the class-mark of the Tractate Middoth, which, as he said, Mr. Eldred could at leisure get for himself. But Mr. Eldred did not reappear at the library.

William Garrett had another visitor that day in the person of a contemporary and colleague from the library, one George Earle. Earle had been one of those who found Garrett lying insensible on the floor just inside the 'class' or cubicle (opening upon the central alley of a spacious gallery) in which the Hebrew books were placed, and Earle had naturally been very anxious about his friend's condition. So as soon as library hours were over he appeared at the lodgings. 'Well,' he said (after other conversation), 'I've no notion what it was that put you wrong, but I've got the idea that there's something wrong in the atmosphere of the library. I know this, that just before we found you I was coming along the gallery with Davis, and I said to him, "Did ever you know such a musty smell anywhere as there is about here? It can't be wholesome." Well now, if one goes on living a long time with a smell of that kind (I tell you it was worse than I ever knew it) it must get into the system and break out some time, don't you think?'

Garrett shook his head. 'That's all very well about the smell—but it isn't always there, though I've noticed it the last day or two—a sort of unnaturally strong smell of dust. But no—that's not what did for me. It was something I *saw*. And I want to tell you about it. I went into that Hebrew class to get a book for a man that was inquiring for it down below. Now that same book I'd made a mistake about the day before. I'd been for it, for the same man, and made sure that I saw an old parson in a cloak taking it out. I told my man it was out: off he went, to call again next day. I went back to see if I could get it out of the parson: no parson there, and the book on the shelf. Well, yesterday, as I say, I went again. This time, if you please—ten o'clock in the morning, remember, and as much light as ever you get in those classes, and there was my parson again, back to me, looking at the books on the shelf I wanted. His hat was on the table, and he had a bald head. I waited a second or two looking at him rather particularly. I tell you, he had a very nasty bald head. It looked to me dry, and it looked dusty, and the streaks of hair across it were much less like hair than cobwebs. Well, I made a bit of a noise on purpose, coughed and moved my feet. He turned round and let me see his face—which I hadn't seen before. I tell you again, I'm not mistaken. Though, for one reason or another I didn't take in the lower part of his face, I did see the upper part; and it was perfectly dry, and the eyes were very deep-sunk; and over them, from the eyebrows to the cheek-bone, there were *cobwebs*—thick. Now that closed me up, as they say, and I can't tell you anything more.'

What explanations were furnished by Earle of this phenomenon it does not very much concern us to inquire; at all events they did not convince Garrett that he had not seen what he had seen.

*

Before William Garrett returned to work at the library, the librarian insisted upon his taking a week's rest and change of air. Within a few days' time, therefore, he was at the station with his bag, looking for a desirable smoking compartment in which to travel to Burnstow-on-Sea, which he had not previously visited. One compartment and one only seemed to be suitable. But, just as he approached it, he saw, standing in front of the door, a figure so like one bound up with recent unpleasant associations that, with a sickening qualm, and hardly knowing what he did, he tore open the door of the next compartment and pulled himself into it as quickly as if death were at his heels. The train moved off, and he must have turned quite faint, for he was next conscious of a smelling-bottle being put to his nose. His physician was a nice-looking old lady, who, with her daughter, was the only passenger in the carriage.

But for this incident it is not very likely that he would have made any overtures to his fellow-travellers. As it was, thanks and inquiries and general conversation supervened inevitably; and Garrett found himself provided before the journey's end not only with a physician, but with a landlady: for Mrs. Simpson had apartments to let at Burnstow, which seemed in all ways suitable. The place was empty at that season, so that Garrett was thrown a good deal into the society of the mother and daughter. He found them very acceptable company. On the third evening of his stay he was on such terms with them as to be asked to spend the evening in their private sitting-room.

During their talk it transpired that Garrett's work lay in a library. 'Ah, libraries are fine places,' said Mrs. Simpson, putting down her work with a sigh; 'but for all that, books have played me a sad turn, or rather *a* book has.'

'Well, books give me my living, Mrs. Simpson, and I should be sorry to say a word against them: I don't like to hear that they have been bad for you.'

'Perhaps Mr. Garrett could help us to solve our puzzle, mother,' said Miss Simpson.

'I don't want to set Mr. Garrett off on a hunt that might waste a lifetime, my dear, nor yet to trouble him with our private affairs.'

'But if you think it in the least likely that I could be of use, I do beg you to tell me what the puzzle is, Mrs. Simpson. If it is finding out anything about a book, you see, I am in rather a good position to do it.'

'Yes, I do see that, but the worst of it is that we don't know the name of the book.'

'Nor what it is about?'

'No, nor that either.'

'Except that we don't think it's in English, mother—and that is not much of a clue.'

'Well, Mr. Garrett,' said Mrs. Simpson, who had not yet resumed her work, and was looking at the fire thoughtfully, 'I shall tell you the story. You will please keep it to yourself, if you don't mind? Thank you. Now it is just this. I had an old uncle, a Dr. Rant. Perhaps you may have heard of him. Not that he was a distinguished man, but from the odd way he chose to be buried.'

'I rather think I have seen the name in some guide-book.'

'That would be it,' said Miss Simpson. 'He left directions—horrid old man!—that he was to be put, sitting at a table in his ordinary clothes, in a brick room that he'd had made underground in a field near his house. Of course the country people say he's been seen about there in his old black cloak.'

'Well, dear, I don't know much about such things,' Mrs. Simpson went on, 'but anyhow he is dead, these twenty years and more. He was a clergyman, though I'm sure I can't imagine how he got to be one: but he did no duty for the last part of his life, which I think was a good thing; and he lived on his own property: a very nice estate not a great way from here. He had no wife or family; only one niece, who was myself, and one nephew, and he had no particular liking for either of us—nor for anyone else, as far as that goes. If anything, he liked my cousin better than he did me—for John was much more like him in his temper, and, I'm afraid I must say, his very mean sharp ways. It might have been different if I had not married; but I did, and that he very much resented. Very well: here he was with this estate and a good deal of money, as it turned out, of which he had the abso-lute disposal, and it was understood that we—my cousin and I—would share it equally at his death. In a certain winter, over twenty years back, as I said, he was taken ill, and I was sent for to nurse him. My husband was alive then, but the old man would not hear of *his* coming. As I drove up to the house I saw my cousin John driving away from it in an open fly and looking, I noticed, in very good spir-its. I went up and did what I could for my uncle, but I was very soon sure that this would be his last illness; and he was convinced of it too.

During the day before he died he got me to sit by him all the time, and I could see there was something, and probably something unpleasant, that he was saving up to tell me, and putting it off as long as he felt he could afford the strength—I'm afraid purposely in order to keep me on the stretch. But, at last, out it came. "Mary," he said,— "Mary, I've made my will in John's favour: he has everything, Mary." Well, of course that came as a bitter shock to me, for we—my husband and I—were not rich people, and if he could have managed to live a little easier than he was obliged to do, I felt it might be the prolonging of his life. But I said little or nothing to my uncle, except that he had a right to do what he pleased: partly because I couldn't think of anything to say, and partly because I was sure there was more to come: and so there was. "But, Mary," he said, "I'm not very fond of John, and I've made another will in *your* favour. *You* can have everything. Only you've got to find the will, you see: and I don't mean to tell you where it is." Then he chuckled to himself, and I waited, for again I was sure he hadn't finished. "That's a good girl," he said after a time,—"you wait, and I'll tell you as much as I told John. But just let me remind you, you can't go into court with what I'm saying to you, for *you* won't be able to produce any collateral evidence beyond your own word, and John's a man that can do a little hard swearing if necessary. Very well then, that's understood. Now, I had the fancy that I wouldn't write this will quite in the common way, so I wrote it in a book, Mary, a printed book. And there's several thousand books in this house. But there! you needn't trouble yourself with them, for it isn't one of them. It's in safe keeping elsewhere: in a place where John can go and find it any day, if he only knew, and you can't. A good will it is: properly signed and witnessed, but I don't think you'll find the witnesses in a hurry.'

'Still I said nothing: if I had moved at all I must have taken hold of the old wretch and shaken him. He lay there laughing to himself, and at last he said:

' "Well, well, you've taken it very quietly, and as I want to start you both on equal terms, and John has a bit of a purchase in being able to go where the book is, I'll tell you just two other things which I didn't tell him. The will's in English, but you won't know that if ever you see it. That's one thing, and another is that when I'm gone you'll find an envelope in my desk directed to you, and inside it something that would help you to find it, if only you have the wits to use it."

'In a few hours from that he was gone, and though I made an appeal to John Eldred about it——'

'John Eldred? I beg your pardon, Mrs. Simpson—I think I've seen a Mr. John Eldred. What is he like to look at?'

'It must be ten years since I saw him: he would be a thin elderly man now, and unless he has shaved them off, he has that sort of whiskers which people used to call Dundreary* or Piccadilly something.'

'—— weepers. Yes, that *is* the man.'

'Where did you come across him, Mr. Garrett?'

'I don't know if I could tell you,' said Garrett mendaciously, 'in some public place. But you hadn't finished.'

'Really I had nothing much to add, only that John Eldred, of course, paid no attention whatever to my letters, and has enjoyed the estate ever since, while my daughter and I have had to take to the lodging-house business here, which I must say has not turned out by any means so unpleasant as I feared it might.'

'But about the envelope.'

'To be sure! Why, the puzzle turns on that. Give Mr. Garrett the paper out of my desk.'

It was a small slip, with nothing whatever on it but five numerals, not divided or punctuated in any way: 11334.

Mr. Garrett pondered, but there was a light in his eye. Suddenly he 'made a face,' and then asked, 'Do you suppose that Mr. Eldred can have any more clue than you have to the title of the book?'

'I have sometimes thought he must,' said Mrs. Simpson, 'and in this way: that my uncle must have made the will not very long before he died (that, I think, he said himself), and got rid of the book immediately afterwards. But all his books were very carefully catalogued: and John has the catalogue: and John was most particular that no books whatever should be sold out of the house. And I'm told that he is always journeying about to booksellers and libraries; so I fancy that he must have found out just which books are missing from my uncle's library of those which are entered in the catalogue, and must be hunting for them.'

'Just so, just so,' said Mr. Garrett, and relapsed into thought.

No later than next day he received a letter which, as he told Mrs. Simpson with great regret, made it absolutely necessary for him to cut short his stay at Burnstow.

Sorry as he was to leave them (and they were at least as sorry to part with him), he had begun to feel that a crisis, all-important to Mrs. (and shall we add, Miss?) Simpson, was very possibly supervening.

In the train Garrett was uneasy and excited. He racked his brains to think whether the press mark of the book which Mr. Eldred had been inquiring after was one in any way corresponding to the numbers on Mrs. Simpson's little bit of paper. But he found to his dismay that the shock of the previous week had really so upset him that he could neither remember any vestige of the title or nature of the book, or even of the locality to which he had gone to seek it. And yet all other parts of library topography and work were clear as ever in his mind.

And another thing—he stamped with annoyance as he thought of it—he had at first hesitated, and then had forgotten, to ask Mrs. Simpson for the name of the place where Eldred lived. That, however, he could write about.

At least he had his clue in the figures on the paper. If they referred to a press mark in his library, they were only susceptible of a limited number of interpretations. They might be divided into 1.13.34, 11.33.4, or 11.3.34. He could try all these in the space of a few minutes, and if any one were missing he had every means of tracing it. He got very quickly to work, though a few minutes had to be spent in explaining his early return to his landlady and his colleagues. 1.13.34. was in place and contained no extraneous writing. As he drew near to Class 11 in the same gallery, its association struck him like a chill. But he *must* go on. After a cursory glance at 11.33.4 (which first confronted him, and was a perfectly new book) he ran his eye along the line of quartos which fills 11.3. The gap he feared was there: 34 was out. A moment was spent in making sure that it had not been misplaced, and then he was off to the vestibule.

'Has 11.3.34 gone out? Do you recollect noticing that number?'

'Notice the number? What do you take me for, Mr. Garrett? There, take and look over the tickets for yourself, if you've got a free day before you.'

'Well then, has a Mr. Eldred called again?—the old gentleman who came the day I was taken ill. Come! you'd remember him.'

'What do you suppose? Of course I recollect of him: no, he haven't been in again, not since you went off for your 'oliday. And yet I seem to—there now. Roberts 'll know. Roberts, do you recollect of the name of Heldred?'

'Not arf,' said Roberts. 'You mean the man that sent a bob over the price for the parcel, and I wish they all did.'

'Do you mean to say you've been sending books to Mr. Eldred? Come, do speak up! Have you?'

'Well now, Mr. Garrett, if a gentleman sends the ticket all wrote correct and the secketry says this book may go and the box ready addressed sent with the note, and a sum of money sufficient to dee-fray the railway charges, what would be *your* action in the matter, Mr. Garrett, if I may take the liberty to ask such a question? Would you or would you not have taken the trouble to oblige, or would you have chucked the 'ole thing under the counter and——'

'You were perfectly right, of course, Hodgson—perfectly right: only, would you kindly oblige me by showing me the ticket Mr. Eldred sent, and letting me know his address?'

'To be sure, Mr. Garrett; so long as I'm not 'ectored about and informed that I don't know my duty, I'm willing to oblige in every way feasible to my power. There is the ticket on the file. J. Eldred, 11.3.34. Title of work: T—a—l—m—— well, there, you can make what you like of it—not a novel, I should 'azard the guess. And here is Mr. Heldred's note applying for the book in question, which I see he terms it a track.'*

'Thanks, thanks: but the address? There's none on the note.'

'Ah, indeed; well, now . . . stay now, Mr. Garrett, I 'ave it. Why, that note come inside of the parcel, which was directed very thought-ful to save all trouble, ready to be sent back with the book inside; and if I *have* made any mistake in this 'ole transaction, it lays just in the one point that I neglected to enter the address in my little book here what I keep. Not but what I dare say there was good rea-sons for me not entering of it: but there, I haven't the time, neither have you, I dare say, to go into 'em just now. And—no, Mr. Garrett, I do *not* carry it in my 'ed, else what would be the use of me keeping this little book here—just a ordinary common notebook, you see, which I make a practice of entering all such names and addresses in it as I see fit to do?'

'Admirable arrangement, to be sure—but—all right, thank you. When did the parcel go off?'

'Half-past ten, this morning.'

'Oh, good; and it's just one now.'

Garrett went upstairs in deep thought. How was he to get the address? A telegram to Mrs. Simpson: he might miss a train by waiting for the answer. Yes, there was one other way. She had said that Eldred lived on his uncle's estate. If this were so, he might find that place entered in the donation-book. That he could run through quickly, now that he knew the title of the book. The register was soon before him, and, knowing that the old man had died more than twenty years ago, he gave him a good margin, and turned back to 1870. There was but one entry possible. 1875, August 14th. *Talmud: Tractatus Middoth cum comm. R. Nachmanidæ.* Amstelod. 1707. Given by J. Rant, D.D., of Bretfield Manor.'*

A gazetteer showed Bretfield to be three miles from a small station on the main line. Now to ask the doorkeeper whether he recollected if the name on the parcel had been anything like Bretfield.

'No, nothing like. It was, now you mention it, Mr. Garrett, either Bredfield or Britfield, but nothing like that other name what you coated.'

So far well. Next, a time-table. A train could be got in twenty minutes—taking two hours over the journey. The only chance, but one not to be missed; and the train was taken.

If he had been fidgety on the journey up, he was almost distracted on the journey down. If he found Eldred, what could he say? That it had been discovered that the book was a rarity and must be recalled? An obvious untruth. Or that it was believed to contain important manuscript notes? Eldred would of course show him the book, from which the leaf would already have been removed. He might, perhaps, find traces of the removal—a torn edge of a fly-leaf probably—and who could disprove, what Eldred was certain to say, that he too had noticed and regretted the mutilation? Altogether the chase seemed very hopeless. The one chance was this. The book had left the library at 10.30: it might not have been put into the first possible train, at 11.20. Granted that, then he might be lucky enough to arrive simultaneously with it and patch up some story which would induce Eldred to give it up.

It was drawing towards evening when he got out upon the platform of his station, and, like most country stations, this one seemed unnaturally quiet. He waited about till the one or two passengers who got out with him had drifted off, and then inquired of the stationmaster whether Mr. Eldred was in the neighbourhood.

'Yes, and pretty near too, I believe. I fancy he means calling here for a parcel he expects. Called for it once to-day already, didn't he, Bob?' (to the porter).

'Yes, sir, he did; and appeared to think it was all along of me that it didn't come by the two o'clock. Anyhow, I've got it for him now,' and the porter flourished a square parcel, which a glance assured Garrett contained all that was of any importance to him at that particular moment.

'Bretfield, sir? Yes—three miles just about. Short cut across these three fields brings it down by half a mile. There: there's Mr. Eldred's trap.'

A dog-cart drove up with two men in it, of whom Garrett, gazing back as he crossed the little station yard, easily recognized one. The fact that Eldred was driving was slightly in his favour—for most likely he would not open the parcel in the presence of his servant. On the other hand, he would get home quickly, and unless Garrett were there within a very few minutes of his arrival, all would be over. He must hurry; and that he did. His short cut took him along one side of a triangle, while the cart had two sides to traverse; and it was delayed a little at the station, so that Garrett was in the third of the three fields when he heard the wheels fairly near. He had made the best progress possible, but the pace at which the cart was coming made him despair. At this rate it *must* reach home ten minutes before him, and ten minutes would more than suffice for the fulfilment of Mr. Eldred's project.

It was just at this time that the luck fairly turned. The evening was still, and sounds came clearly. Seldom has any sound given greater relief than that which he now heard: that of the cart pulling up. A few words were exchanged, and it drove on. Garrett, halting in the utmost anxiety, was able to see as it drove past the stile (near which he now stood) that it contained only the servant and not Eldred; further, he made out that Eldred was following on foot. From behind the tall hedge by the stile leading into the road he watched the thin wiry figure pass quickly by with the parcel beneath its arm, and feeling in its pockets. Just as he passed the stile something fell out of a pocket upon the grass, but with so little sound that Eldred was not conscious of it. In a moment more it was safe for Garrett to cross the stile into the road and pick up—a box of matches. Eldred went on, and, as he went, his arms made hasty movements, difficult to interpret in the shadow of the trees that overhung the road. But, as Garrett followed cautiously, he found at various points the key to them—a piece of string, and then the wrapper of the parcel—meant to be thrown *over* the hedge, but sticking in it.

Now Eldred was walking slower, and it could just be made out that he had opened the book and was turning over the leaves. He stopped, evidently troubled by the failing light. Garrett slipped into a gate-opening, but still watched. Eldred, hastily looking around, sat down on a felled tree-trunk by the roadside and held the open book up close to his eyes. Suddenly he laid it, still open, on his knee, and felt in all his pockets: clearly in vain, and clearly to his annoyance. 'You would be glad of your matches now,' thought Garrett. Then he took hold of a leaf, and was carefully tearing it out, when two things happened. First, something black seemed to drop upon the white leaf and run down it, and then as Eldred started and was turning to look behind him, a little dark form appeared to rise out of the shadow behind the tree-trunk and from it two arms enclosing a mass of blackness came before Eldred's face and covered his head and neck. His legs and arms were wildly flourished, but no sound came. Then, there was no more movement. Eldred was alone. He had fallen back into the grass behind the tree-trunk. The book was cast into the roadway. Garrett, his anger and suspicion gone for the moment at the sight of this hor-rid struggle, rushed up with loud cries of 'Help!' and so too, to his enormous relief, did a labourer who had just emerged from a field opposite. Together they bent over and supported Eldred, but to no purpose. The conclusion that he was dead was inevitable. 'Poor gen-tleman!' said Garrett to the labourer, when they had laid him down, 'what happened to him, do you think?' 'I wasn't two hundred yards away,' said the man, 'when I see Squire Eldred setting reading in his book, and to my thinking he was took with one of these fits—face seemed to go all over black.' 'Just so,' said Garrett. 'You didn't see anyone near him? It couldn't have been an assault?' 'Not possible—no one couldn't have got away without you or me seeing them.' 'So I thought. Well, we must get some help, and the doctor and the police-man; and perhaps I had better give them this book.'

It was obviously a case for an inquest, and obvious also that Garrett must stay at Bretfield and give his evidence. The medical inspection showed that, though some black dust was found on the face and in the mouth of the deceased, the cause of death was a shock to a weak heart, and not asphyxiation. The fateful book was produced, a respectable quarto printed wholly in Hebrew, and not of an aspect likely to excite even the most sensitive.

'You say, Mr. Garrett, that the deceased gentleman appeared at the moment before his attack to be tearing a leaf out of this book?'

'Yes; I think one of the fly-leaves.'

'There is here a fly-leaf partially torn through. It has Hebrew writing on it. Will you kindly inspect it?'

'There are three names in English, sir, also, and a date. But I am sorry to say I cannot read Hebrew writing.'

'Thank you. The names have the appearance of being signatures. They are John Rant, Walter Gibson, and James Frost, and the date is 20 July, 1875. Does anyone here know any of these names?'

The Rector, who was present, volunteered a statement that the uncle of the deceased, from whom he inherited, had been named Rant.

The book being handed to him, he shook a puzzled head. 'This is not like any Hebrew I ever learnt.'

'You are sure that it is Hebrew?'

'What? Yes—I suppose. . . . No—my dear sir, you are perfectly right—that is, your suggestion is exactly to the point. Of course—it is not Hebrew at all. It is English, and it is a will.'

It did not take many minutes to show that here was indeed a will of Dr. John Rant, bequeathing the whole of the property lately held by John Eldred to Mrs. Mary Simpson. Clearly the discovery of such a document would amply justify Mr. Eldred's agitation. As to the partial tearing of the leaf, the coroner pointed out that no useful purpose could be attained by speculations whose correctness it would never be possible to establish.

The Tractate Middoth was naturally taken in charge by the coroner for further investigation, and Mr. Garrett explained privately to him the history of it, and the position of events so far as he knew or guessed them.

He returned to his work next day, and on his walk to the station passed the scene of Mr. Eldred's catastrophe. He could hardly leave it without another look, though the recollection of what he had seen there made him shiver, even on that bright morning. He walked round, with some misgivings, behind the felled tree. Something dark that still lay there made him start back for a moment: but it hardly stirred. Looking closer, he saw that it was a thick black mass of cob-webs; and, as he stirred it gingerly with his stick, several large spiders ran out of it into the grass.

There is no great difficulty in imagining the steps by which William Garrett, from being an assistant in a great library, attained to his present position of prospective owner of Bretfield Manor, now in the occupation of his mother-in-law, Mrs. Mary Simpson.

CASTING THE RUNES

✺

April 15th, 190–.

D EAR SIR,—I am requested by the Council of the —— Association to return to you the draft of a paper on *The Truth of Alchemy*, which you have been good enough to offer to read at our forthcoming meeting, and to inform you that the Council do not see their way to including it in the programme.

I am,

Yours faithfully,

—— *Secretary*.

April 18th.

DEAR SIR,—I am sorry to say that my engagements do not permit of my affording you an interview on the subject of your proposed paper. Nor do our laws allow of your discussing the matter with a Committee of our Council, as you suggest. Please allow me to assure you that the fullest consideration was given to the draft which you submitted, and that it was not declined without having been referred to the judgment of a most competent authority. No personal question (it can hardly be necessary for me to add) can have had the slightest influence on the decision of the Council.

Believe me (*ut supra*).*

April 20th

The Secretary of the —— Association begs respectfully to inform Mr. Karswell* that it is impossible for him to communicate the name of any person or persons to whom the draft of Mr. Karswell's paper may have been submitted; and further desires to intimate that he cannot undertake to reply to any further letters on this subject.

'And who *is* Mr. Karswell?' inquired the Secretary's wife. She had called at his office, and (perhaps unwarrantably) had picked up the last of these three letters, which the typist had just brought in.

'Why, my dear, just at present Mr. Karswell is a very angry man. But I don't know much about him otherwise, except that he is a person of wealth, his address is Lufford Abbey, Warwickshire,* and he's an alchemist, apparently, and wants to tell us all about it; and that's about all—except that I don't want to meet him for the next week or two. Now, if you're ready to leave this place, I am.'

'What have you been doing to make him angry?' asked Mrs. Secretary.

'The usual thing, my dear, the usual thing: he sent in a draft of a paper he wanted to read at the next meeting, and we referred it to Edward Dunning—almost the only man in England who knows about these things—and he said it was perfectly hopeless, so we declined it. So Karswell has been pelting me with letters ever since. The last thing he wanted was the name of the man we referred his nonsense to; you saw my answer to that. But don't you say anything about it, for goodness' sake.'

'I should think not, indeed. Did I ever do such a thing? I do hope, though, he won't get to know that it was poor Mr. Dunning.'

'Poor Mr. Dunning? I don't know why you call him that; he's a very happy man, is Dunning. Lots of hobbies and a comfortable home, and all his time to himself.'

'I only meant I should be sorry for him if this man got hold of his name, and came and bothered him.'

'Oh, ah! yes. I dare say he would be poor Mr. Dunning then.'

The Secretary and his wife were lunching out, and the friends to whose house they were bound were Warwickshire people. So Mrs. Secretary had already settled it in her own mind that she would question them judiciously about Mr. Karswell. But she was saved the trouble of leading up to the subject, for the hostess said to the host, before many minutes had passed, 'I saw the Abbot of Lufford this morning.' The host whistled. '*Did* you? What in the world brings him up to town?' 'Goodness knows; he was coming out of the British Museum gate as I drove past.' It was not unnatural that Mrs. Secretary should inquire whether this was a real Abbot who was being spoken of. 'Oh no, my dear: only a neighbour of ours in the country who bought Lufford Abbey a few years ago. His real name is Karswell.' 'Is he a friend of yours?' asked Mr. Secretary, with a private wink to his wife. The question let loose a torrent of declamation. There was really nothing to be said for Mr. Karswell. Nobody knew what he did with himself: his servants were a horrible set of people; he had invented a new religion for himself, and practised no one could tell what appalling rites; he was very easily offended, and never forgave anybody: he had a dreadful face (so the lady insisted, her husband somewhat demurring); he never did a kind action, and whatever influence he did exert was mischievous. 'Do the poor man justice, dear,' the husband interrupted. 'You forget the treat he gave the school children.' 'Forget it, indeed! But I'm glad you mentioned it, because it gives an idea of the man. Now, Florence, listen to this. The first winter he was at Lufford this delightful neighbour of ours wrote to the clergyman of his parish (he's not ours, but we know him very well) and offered to show the school children some magic-lantern slides. He said he had some new kinds, which he thought would interest them. Well, the clergyman was rather surprised, because Mr. Karswell had shown himself inclined to be unpleasant to the children—complaining of their trespassing, or something of the sort; but of course he accepted, and the evening was fixed, and our friend went himself to see that everything went right. He said he never had been so thankful for anything as that his own children were all prevented from being there: they were at a children's party at our house, as a matter of fact. Because this Mr. Karswell had evidently set out with the intention of frightening these poor village children out of their wits, and I do believe, if he had been allowed to go on, he would actually have done so. He began with some comparatively mild things. Red Riding Hood was one, and even then, Mr. Farrer said, the wolf was so dreadful that several of the smaller children had to be taken out: and he said Mr. Karswell began the story by producing a noise like a wolf howling in the distance, which was the most gruesome thing he had ever heard. All the slides he showed, Mr. Farrer said, were most clever; they were absolutely realistic, and where he had got them or how he worked them he could not imagine. Well, the show went on, and the stories kept on becoming a little more terrifying each time, and the children were mesmerized into complete silence. At last he produced a series which represented a little boy passing through his own park—Lufford, I mean—in the evening. Every child in the room could recognize the place from the pictures. And this poor boy was followed, and at last pursued and overtaken, and either torn in pieces or somehow made away with, by a horrible hopping creature in white, which you saw first dodging about among the trees, and gradually it appeared more and more plainly. Mr. Farrer said it gave him one of the worst nightmares he ever remembered, and what it must have meant to the children doesn't bear thinking of. Of course this was too much, and he spoke very sharply indeed to Mr. Karswell, and said it couldn't go on. All *he* said was: 'Oh, you think it's time to bring our little show to an end and send them home to their beds? *Very* well!' And then, if you please, he switched on another slide, which showed a great mass of snakes, centipedes, and disgusting creatures with wings, and somehow or other he made it seem as if they were climbing out of the picture and getting in amongst the audience; and this was accompanied by a sort of dry rustling noise which sent the children nearly mad, and of course they stampeded. A good many of them were rather hurt in getting out of the room, and I don't suppose one of them closed an eye that night. There was the most dreadful trouble in the village afterwards. Of course the mothers threw a good part of the blame on poor Mr. Farrer, and, if they could have got past the gates, I believe the fathers would have broken every window in the Abbey. Well, now, that's Mr. Karswell: that's the Abbot of Lufford, my dear, and you can imagine how we covet *his* society.'

'Yes, I think he has all the possibilities of a distinguished criminal, has Karswell,' said the host. 'I should be sorry for anyone who got into his bad books.'

'Is he the man, or am I mixing him up with someone else?' asked the Secretary (who for some minutes had been wearing the frown of the man who is trying to recollect something). 'Is he the man who brought out a *History of Witchcraft* some time back—ten years or more?'

'That's the man; do you remember the reviews of it?'

'Certainly I do; and what's equally to the point, I knew the author of the most incisive of the lot. So did you: you must remember John Harrington; he was at John's* in our time.'

'Oh, very well indeed, though I don't think I saw or heard anything of him between the time I went down and the day I read the account of the inquest on him.'

'Inquest?' said one of the ladies. 'What has happened to him?'

'Why, what happened was that he fell out of a tree and broke his neck. But the puzzle was, what could have induced him to get up there. It was a mysterious business, I must say. Here was this man—not an athletic fellow, was he? and with no eccentric twist about him that was ever noticed—walking home along a country road late in the evening—no tramps about—well known and liked in the place—and he suddenly begins to run like mad, loses his hat and stick, and finally shins up a tree—quite a difficult tree—growing in the hedgerow: a dead branch gives way, and he comes down with it and breaks his neck, and there he's found next morning with the most dreadful face of fear on him that could be imagined. It was pretty evident, of course, that he had been chased by something, and people talked of savage dogs, and beasts escaped out of menageries; but there was nothing to be made of that. That was in '89, and I believe his brother Henry (whom I remember as well at Cambridge, but *you* probably don't) has been trying to get on the track of an explanation ever since. He, of course, insists there was malice in it, but I don't know. It's difficult to see how it could have come in.'

After a time the talk reverted to the *History of Witchcraft*. 'Did you ever look into it?' asked the host.

'Yes, I did,' said the Secretary. 'I went so far as to read it.'

'Was it as bad as it was made out to be?'

'Oh, in point of style and form, quite hopeless. It deserved all the pulverizing it got. But, besides that, it was an evil book. The man believed every word of what he was saying, and I'm very much mistaken if he hadn't tried the greater part of his receipts.'

'Well, I only remember Harrington's review of it, and I must say if I'd been the author it would have quenched my literary ambition for good. I should never have held up my head again.'

'It hasn't had that effect in the present case. But come, it's half-past three; I must be off.'

On the way home the Secretary's wife said, 'I do hope that horrible man won't find out that Mr. Dunning had anything to do with the rejection of his paper.' 'I don't think there's much chance of that,' said the Secretary. 'Dunning won't mention it himself, for these matters are confidential, and none of us will for the same reason. Karswell won't know his name, for Dunning hasn't published anything on the same subject yet. The only danger is that Karswell might find out, if he was to ask the British Museum people who was in the habit of consulting alchemical manuscripts: I can't very well tell them not to mention Dunning, can I? It would set them talking at once. Let's hope it won't occur to him.'

However, Mr. Karswell was an astute man.

This much is in the way of prologue. On an evening rather later in the same week, Mr. Edward Dunning was returning from the British Museum, where he had been engaged in Research, to the comfortable house in a suburb where he lived alone, tended by two excellent women who had been long with him. There is nothing to be added by way of description of him to what we have heard already.* Let us follow him as he takes his sober course homewards.

A train took him to within a mile or two of his house, and an electric tram a stage farther. The line ended at a point some three hundred yards from his front door. He had had enough of reading when he got into the car, and indeed the light was not such as to allow him to do more than study the advertisements on the panes of glass that faced him as he sat. As was not unnatural, the advertisements in this particular line of cars were objects of his frequent contemplation, and, with the possible exception of the brilliant and convincing dialogue between Mr. Lamplough and an eminent K.C. on the subject of Pyretic Saline,* none of them afforded much scope to his imagination. I am wrong: there was one at the corner of the car farthest from him which did not seem familiar. It was in blue letters on a yellow ground, and all that he could read of it was a name—John Harrington—and something like a date. It could be of no interest to him to know more; but for all that, as the car emptied, he was just curious enough to move along the seat until he could read it well. He felt to a slight extent repaid for his trouble; the advertisement was *not* of the usual type. It ran thus: 'In memory of John Harrington, F.S.A., of The Laurels, Ashbrooke.* Died Sept. 18th, 1889. Three months were allowed.'*

   The car stopped. Mr. Dunning, still contemplating the blue letters on the yellow ground, had to be stimulated to rise by a word from the conductor. 'I beg your pardon,' he said, 'I was looking at that advertisement; it's a very odd one, isn't it?' The conductor read it slowly. 'Well, my word,' he said, 'I never see that one before. Well, that is a cure, ain't it? Someone bin up to their jokes 'ere, I should think.' He got out a duster and applied it, not without saliva, to the pane and then to the outside. 'No,' he said, returning, 'that ain't no transfer; seems to me as if it was reg'lar *in* the glass, what I mean in the substance, as you may say. Don't you think so, sir?' Mr. Dunning examined it and rubbed it with his glove, and agreed. 'Who looks after these advertisements, and gives leave for them to be put up? I wish you would inquire. I will just take a note of the words.' At this moment there came a call from the driver: 'Look alive, George, time's up.' 'All right, all right; there's somethink else what's up at this end. You come and look at this 'ere glass.' 'What's gorn with the glass?' said the driver, approaching. 'Well, and oo's 'Arrington? What's it all about?' 'I was just asking who was responsible for putting the advertisements up in your cars, and saying it would be as well to make some inquiry about this one.' 'Well, sir, that's all done at the Company's orfice, that work is: it's our Mr. Timms, I believe, looks into that. When we put up to-night I'll leave word, and per'aps I'll be able to tell you to-morrer if you 'appen to be coming this way.'

This was all that passed that evening. Mr. Dunning did just go to the trouble of looking up Ashbrooke, and found that it was in Warwickshire.

Next day he went to town again. The car (it was the same car) was too full in the morning to allow of his getting a word with the conductor: he could only be sure that the curious advertisement had been made away with. The close of the day brought a further element of mystery into the transaction. He had missed the tram, or else preferred walking home, but at a rather late hour, while he was at work in his study, one of the maids came to say that two men from the tramways was very anxious to speak to him. This was a reminder of the advertisement, which he had, he says, nearly forgotten. He had the men in—they were the conductor and driver of the car—and when the matter of refreshment had been attended to, asked what Mr. Timms had had to say about the advertisement. 'Well, sir, that's what we took the liberty to step round about,' said the conductor. 'Mr. Timms 'e give William 'ere the rough side of his tongue about that: 'cordin' to 'im there warn't no advertisement of that description sent in, nor ordered, nor paid for, nor put up, nor nothink, let alone not bein' there, and we was playing the fool takin' up his time. "Well," I says, "if that's the case, all I ask of you, Mr. Timms," I says, "is to take and look at it for yourself," I says. "Of course if it ain't there," I says, "you may take and call me what you like." "Right," he says, "I will": and we went straight off. Now, I leave it to you, sir, if that ad., as we term 'em, with 'Arrington on it warn't as plain as ever you see anythink—blue letters on yeller glass, and as I says at the time, and you borne me out, reg'lar *in* the glass, because, if you remember, you recollect of me swabbing it with my duster.' 'To be sure I do, quite clearly—well?' 'You may say well, I don't think. Mr. Timms he gets in that car with a light—no, he told William to 'old the light outside. "Now," he says, "where's your precious ad. what we've 'eard so much about?" " 'Ere it is," I says, "Mr. Timms," and I laid my 'and on it.' The conductor paused.

'Well,' said Mr. Dunning, 'it was gone, I suppose. Broken?'

'Broke!—not it. There warn't, if you'll believe me, no more trace of them letters—blue letters they was—on that piece o' glass, than—well, it's no good *me* talkin'. *I* never see such a thing. I leave it to William here if—but there, as I says, where's the benefit in me going on about it?'

'And what did Mr. Timms say?'

'Why 'e did what I give 'im leave to—called us pretty much anythink he liked, and I don't know as I blame him so much neither. But what we thought, William and me did, was as we seen you take down a bit of a note about that—well, that letterin'——'

'I certainly did that, and I have it now. Did you wish me to speak to Mr. Timms myself, and show it to him? Was that what you came in about?'

'There, didn't I say as much?' said William. 'Deal with a gent if you can get on the track of one, that's my word. Now perhaps, George, you'll allow as I ain't took you very far wrong to-night.'

'Very well, William, very well; no need for you to go on as if you'd 'ad to frog's-march me 'ere. I come quiet, didn't I? All the same for that, we 'adn't ought to take up your time this way, sir; but if it so 'appened you could find time to step round to the Company's orfice in the morning and tell Mr. Timms what you seen for yourself, we should lay under a very 'igh obligation to you for the trouble. You see it ain't bein' called—well, one thing and another, as we mind, but if they got it into their 'ead at the orfice as we seen things as warn't there, why, one thing leads to another, and where we should be a twelvemunce 'ence—well, you can understand what I mean.'

Amid further elucidations of the proposition, George, conducted by William, left the room.

The incredulity of Mr. Timms (who had a nodding acquaintance with Mr. Dunning) was greatly modified on the following day by what the latter could tell and show him; and any bad mark that might have been attached to the names of William and George was not suffered to remain on the Company's books; but explanation there was none.

Mr. Dunning's interest in the matter was kept alive by an incident of the following afternoon. He was walking from his club to the train, and he noticed some way ahead a man with a handful of leaflets such as are distributed to passers-by by agents of enterprising firms. This agent had not chosen a very crowded street for his operations: in fact, Mr. Dunning did not see him get rid of a single leaflet before he himself reached the spot. One was thrust into his hand as he passed: the hand that gave it touched his, and he experienced a sort of little shock as it did so. It seemed unnaturally rough and hot. He looked in passing at the giver, but the impression he got was so unclear that, however much he tried to reckon it up subsequently, nothing would come. He was walking quickly, and as he went on glanced at the paper. It was a blue one. The name of Harrington in large capitals caught his eye. He stopped, startled, and felt for his glasses. The next instant the leaflet was twitched out of his hand by a man who hurried past, and was irrecoverably gone. He ran back a few paces, but where was the passer-by? and where the distributor?

It was in a somewhat pensive frame of mind that Mr. Dunning passed on the following day into the Select Manuscript Room of the British Museum, and filled up tickets for Harley 3586,* and some other volumes. After a few minutes they were brought to him, and he was settling the one he wanted first upon the desk, when he thought he heard his own name whispered behind him. He turned round hastily, and in doing so, brushed his little portfolio of loose papers on to the floor. He saw no one he recognized except one of the staff in charge of the room, who nodded to him, and he proceeded to pick up his papers. He thought he had them all, and was turning to begin work, when a stout gentleman at the table behind him, who was just rising to leave, and had collected his own belongings, touched him on the shoulder, saying, 'May I give you this? I think it should be yours,' and handed him a missing quire. 'It is mine, thank you,' said Mr. Dunning. In another moment the man had left the room. Upon finishing his work for the afternoon, Mr. Dunning had some conversation with the assistant in charge, and took occasion to ask who the stout gentleman was. 'Oh, he's a man named Karswell,' said the assistant; 'he was asking me a week ago who were the great authorities on alchemy, and of course I told him you were the only one in the country. I'll see if I can't catch him: he'd like to meet you, I'm sure.'

'For heaven's sake don't dream of it!' said Mr. Dunning, 'I'm particularly anxious to avoid him.'

'Oh! very well,' said the assistant, 'he doesn't come here often: I dare say you won't meet him.'

More than once on the way home that day Mr. Dunning confessed to himself that he did not look forward with his usual cheerfulness to a solitary evening. It seemed to him that something ill-defined and impalpable had stepped in between him and his fellow-men—had taken him in charge, as it were. He wanted to sit close up to his neighbours in the train and in the tram, but as luck would have it both train and car were markedly empty. The conductor George was thoughtful, and appeared to be absorbed in calculations as to the number of passengers. On arriving at his house he found Dr. Watson, his medical man,* on his doorstep. 'I've had to upset your household arrangements, I'm sorry to say, Dunning. Both your servants *hors de combat.** In fact, I've had to send them to the Nursing Home.'

'Good heavens! what's the matter?'

'It's something like ptomaine poisoning,* I should think: you've not suffered yourself, I can see, or you wouldn't be walking about. I think they'll pull through all right.'

'Dear, dear! Have you any idea what brought it on?'

'Well, they tell me they bought some shell-fish from a hawker at their dinner-time. It's odd. I've made inquiries, but I can't find that any hawker has been to other houses in the street. I couldn't send word to you; they won't be back for a bit yet. You come and dine with me to-night, anyhow, and we can make arrangements for going on. Eight o'clock. Don't be too anxious.'

The solitary evening was thus obviated; at the expense of some distress and inconvenience, it is true. Mr. Dunning spent the time pleasantly enough with the doctor (a rather recent settler), and returned to his lonely home at about 11.30. The night he passed is not one on which he looks back with any satisfaction. He was in bed and the light was out. He was wondering if the charwoman would come early enough to get him hot water next morning, when he heard the unmistakable sound of his study door opening. No step followed it on the passage floor, but the sound must mean mischief, for he knew that he had shut the door that evening after putting his papers away in his desk. It was rather shame than courage that induced him to slip out into the passage and lean over the banister in his nightgown, listening. No light was visible; no further sound came: only a gust of warm, or even hot air played for an instant round his shins. He went back and decided to lock himself into his room. There was more unpleasantness, however. Either an economical suburban company had decided that their light would not be required in the small hours, and had stopped working, or else something was wrong with the meter; the effect was in any case that the electric light was off. The obvious course was to find a match, and also to consult his watch: he might as well know how many hours of discomfort awaited him. So he put his hand into the well-known nook under the pillow: only, it did not get so far. What he touched was, according to his account, a mouth, with teeth, and with hair about it, and, he declares, not the mouth of a human being. I do not think it is any use to guess what he said or did; but he was in a spare room with the door locked and his ear to it before he was clearly conscious again. And there he spent the rest of a most miserable night, looking every moment for some fumbling at the door: but nothing came.

The venturing back to his own room in the morning was attended with many listenings and quiverings. The door stood open, fortunately, and the blinds were up (the servants had been out of the house before the hour of drawing them down); there was, to be short, no trace of an inhabitant. The watch, too, was in its usual place; nothing was disturbed, only the wardrobe door had swung open, in accordance with its confirmed habit. A ring at the back door now announced the charwoman, who had been ordered the night before, and nerved Mr. Dunning, after letting her in, to continue his search in other parts of the house. It was equally fruitless.

The day thus begun went on dismally enough. He dared not go to the Museum: in spite of what the assistant had said, Karswell might turn up there, and Dunning felt he could not cope with a probably hostile stranger. His own house was odious; he hated sponging on the doctor. He spent some little time in a call at the Nursing Home, where he was slightly cheered by a good report of his housekeeper and maid. Towards lunch-time he betook himself to his club, again experiencing a gleam of satisfaction at seeing the Secretary of the Association. At luncheon Dunning told his friend the more material of his woes, but could not bring himself to speak of those that weighed most heavily on his spirits. 'My poor dear man,' said the Secretary, 'what an upset! Look here: we're alone at home, absolutely. You must put up with us. Yes! no excuse: send your things in this afternoon.' Dunning was unable to stand out: he was, in truth, becoming acutely anxious, as the hours went on, as to what that night might have waiting for him. He was almost happy as he hurried home to pack up.

His friends, when they had time to take stock of him, were rather shocked at his lorn appearance, and did their best to keep him up to the mark. Not altogether without success: but, when the two men were smoking alone later, Dunning became dull again. Suddenly he said, 'Gayton, I believe that alchemist man knows it was I who got his paper rejected.' Gayton whistled. 'What makes you think that?' he said. Dunning told of his conversation with the Museum assistant, and Gayton could only agree that the guess seemed likely to be correct. 'Not that I care much,' Dunning went on, 'only it might be a nuisance if we were to meet. He's a bad-tempered party, I imagine.' Conversation dropped again; Gayton became more and more strongly impressed with the desolateness that came over Dunning's face and bearing, and finally—though with a considerable effort—he asked him point-blank whether something serious was not bothering him. Dunning gave an exclamation of relief. 'I was perishing to get it off my mind,' he said. 'Do you know anything about a man named John Harrington?' Gayton was thoroughly startled, and at the moment could only ask why. Then the complete story of Dunning's experiences came out—what had happened in the tramcar, in his own house, and in the street, the troubling of spirit that had crept over him, and still held him; and he ended with the question he had begun with. Gayton was at a loss how to answer him. To tell the story of Harrington's end would perhaps be right; only, Dunning was in a nervous state, the story was a grim one, and he could not help asking himself whether there were not a connecting link between these two cases, in the person of Karswell. It was a difficult concession for a scientific man, but it could be eased by the phrase 'hypnotic suggestion.' In the end he decided that his answer to-night should be guarded; he would talk the situation over with his wife. So he said that he had known Harrington at Cambridge, and believed he had died suddenly in 1889, adding a few details about the man and his published work. He did talk over the matter with Mrs. Gayton, and, as he had anticipated, she leapt at once to the conclusion which had been hovering before him. It was she who reminded him of the surviving brother, Henry Harrington, and she also who suggested that he might be got hold of by means of their hosts of the day before. 'He might be a hopeless crank,' objected Gayton. 'That could be ascertained from the Bennetts, who knew him,' Mrs. Gayton retorted; and she undertook to see the Bennetts the very next day.

It is not necessary to tell in further detail the steps by which Henry Harrington and Dunning were brought together.

The next scene that does require to be narrated is a conversation that took place between the two. Dunning had told Harrington of the strange ways in which the dead man's name had been brought before him, and had said something, besides, of his own subsequent experiences. Then he had asked if Harrington was disposed, in return, to recall any of the circumstances connected with his brother's death. Harrington's surprise at what he heard can be imagined: but his reply was readily given.

'John,' he said, 'was in a very odd state, undeniably, from time to time, during some weeks before, though not immediately before, the catastrophe. There were several things; the principal notion he had was that he thought he was being followed. No doubt he was an impressionable man, but he never had had such fancies as this before. I cannot get it out of my mind that there was ill-will at work, and what you tell me about yourself reminds me very much of my brother. Can you think of any possible connecting link?'

'There is just one that has been taking shape vaguely in my mind. I've been told that your brother reviewed a book very severely not long before he died, and just lately I have happened to cross the path of the man who wrote that book in a way he would resent.'

'Don't tell me the man was called Karswell.'

'Why not? that is exactly his name.'

Henry Harrington leant back. 'That is final to my mind. Now I must explain further. From something he said, I feel sure that my brother John was beginning to believe—very much against his will— that Karswell was at the bottom of his trouble. I want to tell you what seems to me to have a bearing on the situation. My brother was a great musician, and used to run up to concerts in town. He came back, three months before he died, from one of these, and gave me his programme to look at—an analytical programme: he always kept them. "I nearly missed this one," he said. "I suppose I must have dropped it: anyhow, I was looking for it under my seat and in my pockets and so on, and my neighbour offered me his: said 'might he give it me, he had no further use for it,' and he went away just afterwards. I don't know who he was—a stout, clean-shaven man. I should have been sorry to miss it; of course I could have bought another, but this cost me nothing." At another time he told me that he had been very uncomfortable both on the way to his hotel and during the night. I piece things together now in thinking it over. Then, not very long after, he was going over these programmes, putting them in order to have them bound up, and in this particular one (which by the way I had hardly glanced at), he found quite near the beginning a strip of paper with some very odd writing on it in red and black—most carefully done—it looked to me more like Runic letters* than anything else. "Why," he said, "this must belong to my fat neighbour. It looks as if it might be worth returning to him; it may be a copy of something; evidently someone has taken trouble over it. How can I find his address?" We talked it over for a little and agreed that it wasn't worth advertising about, and that my brother had better look out for the man at the next concert, to which he was going very soon. The paper was lying on the book and we were both by the fire; it was a cold, windy summer evening. I suppose the door blew open, though I didn't notice it: at any rate a gust—a warm gust it was—came quite suddenly between us, took the paper and blew it straight into the fire: it was light, thin paper, and flared and went up the chimney in a single ash. "Well," I said, "you can't give it back now." He said nothing for a minute: then rather crossly, "No, I can't; but why you should keep on saying so I don't know." I remarked that I didn't say it more than once. "Not more than four times, you mean," was all he said. I remember all that very clearly, without any good reason; and now to come to the point. I don't know if you looked at that book of Karswell's which my unfortunate brother reviewed. It's not likely that you should: but I did, both before his death and after it. The first time we made game of it together. It was written in no style at all—split infinitives, and every sort of thing that makes an Oxford gorge rise. Then there was nothing that the man didn't swallow: mixing up classical myths, and stories out of the *Golden Legend** with reports of savage customs of to-day—all very proper, no doubt, if you know how to use them, but he didn't: he seemed to put the *Golden Legend* and the *Golden Bough** exactly on a par, and to believe both: a pitiable exhibition, in short. Well, after the misfortune, I looked over the book again. It was no better than before, but the impression which it left this time on my mind was different. I suspected—as I told you—that Karswell had borne ill-will to my brother, even that he was in some way responsible for what had happened; and now his book seemed to me to be a very sinister performance indeed. One chapter in particular struck me, in which he spoke of "casting the Runes" on people, either for the purpose of gaining their affection or of getting them out of the way—perhaps more especially the latter: he spoke of all this in a way that really seemed to me to imply actual knowledge. I've not time to go into details, but the upshot is that I am pretty sure from information received that the civil man at the concert was Karswell: I suspect—I more than suspect—that the paper was of importance: and I do believe that if my brother had been able to give it back, he might have been alive now. Therefore, it occurs to me to ask you whether you have anything to put beside what I have told you.'

By way of answer, Dunning had the episode in the Manuscript Room at the British Museum to relate. 'Then he did actually hand you some papers; have you examined them? No? because we must, if you'll allow it, look at them at once, and very carefully.'

They went to the still empty house—empty, for the two servants were not yet able to return to work. Dunning's portfolio of papers was gathering dust on the writing-table. In it were the quires of small-sized scribbling paper which he used for his transcripts: and from one of these, as he took it up, there slipped and fluttered out into the room with uncanny quickness, a strip of thin light paper. The window was open, but Harrington slammed it to, just in time to intercept the paper, which he caught. 'I thought so,' he said; 'it might be the identical thing that was given to my brother. You'll have to look out, Dunning; this may mean something quite serious for you.'

A long consultation took place. The paper was narrowly examined. As Harrington had said, the characters on it were more like Runes than anything else, but not decipherable by either man, and both hesitated to copy them, for fear, as they confessed, of perpetuating whatever evil purpose they might conceal. So it has remained impossible (if I may anticipate a little) to ascertain what was conveyed in this curious message or commission. Both Dunning and Harrington are firmly convinced that it had the effect of bringing its possessors into very undesirable company. That it must be returned to the source whence it came they were agreed, and further, that the only safe and certain way was that of personal service; and here contrivance would be necessary, for Dunning was known by sight to Karswell. He must, for one thing, alter his appearance by shaving his beard. But then might not the blow fall first? Harrington thought they could time it. He knew the date of the concert at which the 'black spot'* had been put on his brother: it was June 18th. The death had followed on Sept. 18th. Dunning reminded him that three months had been mentioned on the inscription on the car-window. 'Perhaps,' he added, with a cheerless laugh, 'mine may be a bill at three months too. I believe I can fix it by my diary. Yes, April 23rd was the day at the Museum; that brings us to July 23rd. Now, you know, it becomes extremely important to me to know anything you will tell me about the progress of your brother's trouble, if it is possible for you to speak of it.' 'Of course. Well, the sense of being watched whenever he was alone was the most distressing thing to him. After a time I took to sleeping in his room, and he was the better for that: still, he talked a great deal in his sleep. What about? Is it wise to dwell on that, at least before things are straightened out? I think not, but I can tell you this: two things came for him by post during those weeks, both with a London postmark, and addressed in a commercial hand. One was a woodcut of Bewick's,* roughly torn out of the page: one which shows a moonlit road and a man walking along it, followed by an awful demon creature. Under it were written the lines out of the 'Ancient Mariner'* (which I suppose the cut illustrates) about one who, having once looked round—

> 'walks on,
> And turns no more his head,
> Because he knows a frightful fiend
> Doth close behind him tread.'

The other was a calendar, such as tradesmen often send. My brother paid no attention to this, but I looked at it after his death, and found that everything after Sept. 18 had been torn out. You may be surprised at his having gone out alone the evening he was killed, but the fact is that during the last ten days or so of his life he had been quite free from the sense of being followed or watched.'

The end of the consultation was this. Harrington, who knew a neighbour of Karswell's, thought he saw a way of keeping a watch on his movements. It would be Dunning's part to be in readiness to try to cross Karswell's path at any moment, to keep the paper safe and in a place of ready access.

They parted. The next weeks were no doubt a severe strain upon Dunning's nerves: the intangible barrier which had seemed to rise about him on the day when he received the paper, gradually developed into a brooding blackness that cut him off from the means of escape to which one might have thought he might resort. No one was at hand who was likely to suggest them to him, and he seemed robbed of all initiative. He waited with inexpressible anxiety as May, June, and early July passed on, for a mandate from Harrington. But all this time Karswell remained immovable at Lufford.

At last, in less than a week before the date he had come to look upon as the end of his earthly activities, came a telegram: 'Leaves Victoria by boat train Thursday night. Do not miss. I come to you to-night. Harrington.'

He arrived accordingly, and they concocted plans. The train left Victoria at nine and its last stop before Dover was Croydon West. Harrington would mark down Karswell at Victoria, and look out for Dunning at Croydon, calling to him if need were by a name agreed upon. Dunning, disguised as far as might be, was to have no label or initials on any hand luggage, and must at all costs have the paper with him.

Dunning's suspense as he waited on the Croydon platform I need not attempt to describe. His sense of danger during the last days had only been sharpened by the fact that the cloud about him had perceptibly been lighter; but relief was an ominous symptom, and, if Karswell eluded him now, hope was gone: and there were so many chances of that. The rumour of the journey might be itself a device. The twenty minutes in which he paced the platform and persecuted every porter with inquiries as to the boat train were as bitter as any he had spent. Still, the train came, and Harrington was at the window. It was important, of course, that there should be no recognition: so Dunning got in at the farther end of the corridor carriage, and only gradually made his way to the compartment where Harrington and

Karswell were. He was pleased, on the whole, to see that the train was far from full.

Karswell was on the alert, but gave no sign of recognition. Dunning took the seat not immediately facing him, and attempted, vainly at first, then with increasing command of his faculties, to reckon the possibilities of making the desired transfer. Opposite to Karswell, and next to Dunning, was a heap of Karswell's coats on the seat. It would be of no use to slip the paper into these—he would not be safe, or would not feel so, unless in some way it could be proffered by him and accepted by the other. There was a handbag, open, and with papers in it. Could he manage to conceal this (so that perhaps Karswell might leave the carriage without it), and then find and give it to him? This was the plan that suggested itself. If he could only have counselled with Harrington! but that could not be. The minutes went on. More than once Karswell rose and went out into the corridor. The second time Dunning was on the point of attempting to make the bag fall off the seat, but he caught Harrington's eye, and read in it a warning. Karswell, from the corridor, was watching: probably to see if the two men recognized each other. He returned, but was evidently restless: and, when he rose the third time, hope dawned, for something did slip off his seat and fall with hardly a sound to the floor. Karswell went out once more, and passed out of range of the corridor window. Dunning picked up what had fallen, and saw that the key was in his hands in the form of one of Cook's* ticket-cases, with tickets in it. These cases have a pocket in the cover, and within very few seconds the paper of which we have heard was in the pocket of this one. To make the operation more secure, Harrington stood in the doorway of the compartment and fiddled with the blind. It was done, and done at the right time, for the train was now slowing down towards Dover.

In a moment more Karswell re-entered the compartment. As he did so, Dunning, managing, he knew not how, to suppress the tremble in his voice, handed him the ticket-case, saying, 'May I give you this, sir? I believe it is yours.' After a brief glance at the ticket inside, Karswell uttered the hoped-for response, 'Yes, it is; much obliged to you, sir,' and he placed it in his breast pocket.

Even in the few moments that remained—moments of tense anxiety, for they knew not to what a premature finding of the paper might lead—both men noticed that the carriage seemed to darken about them and to grow warmer; that Karswell was fidgety and oppressed;

that he drew the heap of loose coats near to him and cast it back as if it repelled him; and that he then sat upright and glanced anxiously at both. They, with sickening anxiety, busied themselves in collecting their belongings; but they both thought that Karswell was on the point of speaking when the train stopped at Dover Town. It was natural that in the short space between town and pier they should both go into the corridor.

At the pier they got out, but so empty was the train that they were forced to linger on the platform until Karswell should have passed ahead of them with his porter on the way to the boat, and only then was it safe for them to exchange a pressure of the hand and a word of concentrated congratulation. The effect upon Dunning was to make him almost faint. Harrington made him lean up against the wall, while he himself went forward a few yards within sight of the gangway to the boat, at which Karswell had now arrived. The man at the head of it examined his ticket, and, laden with coats, he passed down into the boat. Suddenly the official called after him, 'You, sir, beg pardon, did the other gentleman show his ticket?' 'What the devil do you mean by the other gentleman?' Karswell's snarling voice called back from the deck. The man bent over and looked at him. 'The devil? Well, I don't know, I'm sure,' Harrington heard him say to himself, and then aloud, 'My mistake, sir; must have been your rugs! ask your pardon.' And then, to a subordinate near him, ' 'Ad he got a dog with him, or what? Funny thing: I could 'a' swore 'e wasn't alone. Well, whatever it was, they'll 'ave to see to it aboard. She's off now. Another week and we shall be gettin' the 'oliday customers.' In five minutes more there was nothing but the lessening lights of the boat, the long line of the Dover lamps, the night breeze, and the moon.

Long and long the two sat in their room at the 'Lord Warden.'* In spite of the removal of their greatest anxiety, they were oppressed with a doubt, not of the lightest. Had they been justified in sending a man to his death, as they believed they had? Ought they not to warn him, at least? 'No,' said Harrington; 'if he is the murderer I think him, we have done no more than is just. Still, if you think it better— but how and where can you warn him?' 'He was booked to Abbeville only,' said Dunning. 'I saw that. If I wired to the hotels there in Joanne's Guide,* "Examine your ticket-case, Dunning," I should feel happier. This is the 21st: he will have a day. But I am afraid he has gone into the dark.' So telegrams were left at the hotel office.

It is not clear whether these reached their destination, or whether, if they did, they were understood. All that is known is that, on the afternoon of the 23rd, an English traveller, examining the front of St. Wulfram's Church at Abbeville,* then under extensive repair, was struck on the head and instantly killed by a stone falling from the scaffold erected round the north-western tower, there being, as was clearly proved, no workman on the scaffold at that moment: and the traveller's papers identified him as Mr. Karswell.

Only one detail shall be added. At Karswell's sale a set of Bewick, sold with all faults, was acquired by Harrington. The page with the woodcut of the traveller and the demon was, as he had expected, mutilated. Also, after a judicious interval, Harrington repeated to Dunning something of what he had heard his brother say in his sleep: but it was not long before Dunning stopped him.

THE STALLS OF BARCHESTER CATHEDRAL

✺❧✺

THIS matter began, as far as I am concerned, with the reading of a notice in the obituary section of the *Gentleman's Magazine* for an early year in the nineteenth century:

'On February 26th, at his residence in the Cathedral Close of Barchester,* the Venerable John Benwell Haynes, D.D., aged 57, Archdeacon of Sowerbridge and Rector of Pickhill and Candley. He was of —— College, Cambridge, and where, by talent and assiduity, he commanded the esteem of his seniors; when, at the usual time, he took his first degree, his name stood high in the list of *wranglers*. These academical honours procured for him within a short time a Fellowship of his College. In the year 1783 he received Holy Orders, and was shortly afterwards presented to the perpetual Curacy of Ranxton-sub-Ashe by his friend and patron the late truly venerable Bishop of Lichfield.* . . . His speedy preferments, first to a Prebend, and subsequently to the dignity of Precentor* in the Cathedral of Barchester, form an eloquent testimony to the respect in which he was held and to his eminent qualifications. He succeeded to the Archdeaconry upon the sudden decease of Archdeacon Pulteney in 1810. His sermons, ever conformable to the principles of the religion and Church which he adorned, displayed in no ordinary degree, without the least trace of enthusiasm, the refinement of the scholar united with the graces of the Christian. Free from sectarian violence, and informed by the spirit of the truest charity, they will long dwell in the memories of his hearers. (Here a further omission.) The productions of his pen include an able defence of Episcopacy, which, though often perused by the author of this tribute to his memory, afford but one additional instance of the want of liberality and enterprise which is a too common characteristic of the publishers of our generation. His published works are, indeed, confined to a spirited and elegant version of the *Argonautica* of Valerius Flaccus, a volume of *Discourses upon the Several Events in the Life of Joshua*,* delivered in his Cathedral, and a number of the charges which he pronounced at various visitations to the clergy of his Archdeaconry. These are distinguished by etc., etc. The urbanity and hospitality of the subject of these lines will not readily be forgotten by those who enjoyed his acquaintance. His interest in the venerable and awful pile under whose hoary vault he was so punctual an attendant, and particularly in the musical portion of its rites, might be termed filial, and formed a strong and delightful contrast to the polite indifference displayed by too many of our Cathedral dignitaries at the present time.'

The final paragraph, after informing us that Dr. Haynes died a bachelor, says:

'It might have been augured that an existence so placid and benevolent would have been terminated in a ripe old age by a dissolution equally gradual and calm. But how unsearchable are the workings of Providence! The peaceful and retired seclusion amid which the honoured evening of Dr. Haynes' life was mellowing to its close was destined to be disturbed, nay, shattered, by a tragedy as appalling as it was unexpected. The morning of the 26th of February——'

But perhaps I shall do better to keep back the remainder of the narrative until I have told the circumstances which led up to it. These, as far as they are now accessible, I have derived from another source.

I had read the obituary notice which I have been quoting, quite by chance, along with a great many others of the same period. It had excited some little speculation in my mind, but, beyond thinking that, if I ever had an opportunity of examining the local records of the period indicated, I would try to remember Dr. Haynes, I made no effort to pursue his case.

Quite lately I was cataloguing the manuscripts in the library of the college to which he belonged. I had reached the end of the numbered volumes on the shelves, and I proceeded to ask the librarian whether there were any more books which he thought I ought to include in my description. 'I don't think there are,' he said, 'but we had better come and look at the manuscript class and make sure. Have you time to do that now?' I had time. We went to the library, checked off the manuscripts, and, at the end of our survey, arrived at a shelf of which I had seen nothing. Its contents consisted for the most part of sermons, bundles of fragmentary papers, college exercises, *Cyrus*,* an epic poem in several cantos, the product of a country clergyman's leisure, mathematical tracts by a deceased professor, and other similar material of a kind with which I am only too familiar. I took brief notes of these. Lastly, there was a tin box, which was pulled out and dusted. Its label, much faded, was thus inscribed: 'Papers of the Ven. Archdeacon Haynes. Bequeathed in 1834 by his sister, Miss Letitia Haynes.'

I knew at once that the name was one which I had somewhere encountered, and could very soon locate it. 'That must be the Archdeacon Haynes who came to a very odd end at Barchester. I've read his obituary in the *Gentleman's Magazine*. May I take the box home? Do you know if there is anything interesting in it?'

The librarian was very willing that I should take the box and examine it at leisure. 'I never looked inside it myself,' he said, 'but I've always been meaning to. I am pretty sure that is the box which our old Master once said ought never to have been accepted by the college. He said that to Martin years ago; and he said also that as long as he had control over the library it should never be opened. Martin told me about it, and said that he wanted terribly to know what was in it; but the Master was librarian, and always kept the box in the lodge, so there was no getting at it in his time, and when he died it was taken away by mistake by his heirs, and only returned a few years ago. I can't think why I haven't opened it; but, as I have to go away from Cambridge this afternoon, you had better have first go at it. I think I can trust you not to publish anything undesirable in our catalogue.'

I took the box home and examined its contents, and thereafter consulted the librarian as to what should be done about publication, and, since I have his leave to make a story out of it, provided I disguise the identity of the people concerned, I will try what can be done.

The materials are, of course, mainly journals and letters. How much I shall quote and how much epitomize must be determined by considerations of space. The proper understanding of the situation has necessitated a little—not very arduous—research, which has been greatly facilitated by the excellent illustrations and text of the Barchester volume in Bell's *Cathedral Series*.*

When you enter the choir of Barchester Cathedral now, you pass through a screen of metal and coloured marbles, designed by Sir Gilbert Scott,* and find yourself in what I must call a very bare and odiously furnished place. The stalls are modern; without canopies. The places of the dignitaries and the names of the prebends have fortunately been allowed to survive, and are inscribed on small brass plates affixed to the stalls. The organ is in the triforium, and what is seen of the case is Gothic. The reredos and its surroundings are like every other.

Careful engravings of a hundred years ago show a very different state of things. The organ is on a massive classical screen. The stalls are also classical and very massive. There is a baldacchino* of wood over the altar, with urns upon its corners. Farther east is a solid altar screen, classical in design, of wood, with a pediment, in which is a triangle surrounded by rays, enclosing certain Hebrew letters in gold. Cherubs contemplate these. There is a pulpit with a great sounding-board at the eastern end of the stalls on the north side, and there is a black and white marble pavement. Two ladies and a gentleman are admiring the general effect. From other sources I gather that the archdeacon's stall then, as now, was next to the bishop's throne at the south-eastern end of the stalls. His house almost faces the west front of the church, and is a fine red-brick building of William the Third's time.

Here Dr. Haynes, already a mature man, took up his abode with his sister in the year 1810. The dignity had long been the object of his wishes, but his predecessor refused to depart until he had attained the age of ninety-two. About a week after he had held a modest festival in celebration of that ninety-second birthday, there came a morning, late in the year, when Dr. Haynes, hurrying cheerfully into his breakfast-room, rubbing his hands and humming a tune, was greeted, and checked in his genial flow of spirits, by the sight of his sister, seated, indeed, in her usual place behind the tea-urn, but bowed forward and sobbing unrestrainedly into her handkerchief. 'What—what is the matter? What bad news?' he began. 'Oh, Johnny, you've not heard? The poor dear archdeacon!' 'The archdeacon, yes? What is it—ill, is he?' 'No, no; they found him on the staircase this morning; it is so shocking.' 'Is it possible! Dear, dear, poor Pulteney! Had there been any seizure?' 'They don't think so, and that is almost the worst thing about it. It seems to have been all the fault of that stupid maid of theirs, Jane.' Dr. Haynes paused. 'I don't quite understand, Letitia. How was the maid at fault?' 'Why, as far as I can make out, there was a stair-rod missing, and she never mentioned it, and the poor archdeacon set his foot quite on the edge of the step—you know how slippery that oak is—and it seems he must have fallen almost the whole flight and broken his neck. It *is* so sad for poor Miss Pulteney. Of course, they will get rid of the girl at once. I never liked her.' Miss Haynes's grief resumed its sway, but eventually relaxed so far as to permit of her taking some breakfast. Not so her brother, who, after standing in silence before the window for some minutes, left the room, and did not appear again that morning.

I need only add that the careless maid-servant was dismissed forthwith, but that the missing stair-rod was very shortly afterwards found *under* the stair-carpet—an additional proof, if any were needed, of extreme stupidity and carelessness on her part.

For a good many years Dr. Haynes had been marked out by his ability, which seems to have been really considerable, as the likely successor of Archdeacon Pulteney, and no disappointment was in store for him. He was duly installed, and entered with zeal upon the discharge of those functions which are appropriate to one in his position. A considerable space in his journals is occupied with exclamations upon the confusion in which Archdeacon Pulteney had left the business of his office and the documents appertaining to it. Dues upon Wringham and Barnswood have been uncollected for something like twelve years, and are largely irrecoverable; no visitation has been held for seven years; four chancels are almost past mending. The persons deputized by the archdeacon have been nearly as incapable as himself. It was almost a matter for thankfulness that this state of things had not been permitted to continue, and a letter from a friend confirms this view. 'ὁ κατέχων,' it says (in rather cruel allusion to the Second Epistle to the Thessalonians),* 'is removed at last. My poor friend! Upon what a scene of confusion will you be entering! I give you my word that, on the last occasion of my crossing his threshold, there was no single paper that he could lay hands upon, no syllable of mine that he could hear, and no fact in connection with my business that he could remember. But now, thanks to a negligent maid and a loose stair-carpet, there is some prospect that necessary business will be transacted without a complete loss alike of voice and temper.' This letter was tucked into a pocket in the cover of one of the diaries.

There can be no doubt of the new archdeacon's zeal and enthusiasm. 'Give me but time to reduce to some semblance of order the innumerable errors and complications with which I am confronted, and I shall gladly and sincerely join with the aged Israelite in the canticle* which too many, I fear, pronounce but with their lips.' This reflection I find, not in a diary, but a letter; the doctor's friends seem to have returned his correspondence to his surviving sister. He does not confine himself, however, to reflections. His investigation of the rights and duties of his office are very searching and business-like, and there is a calculation in one place that a period of three years will just suffice to set the business of the Archdeaconry upon a proper footing. The estimate appears to have been an exact one. For just three years he is occupied in reforms; but I look in vain at the end of that time for the promised *Nunc dimittis*. He has now found a new sphere of activity. Hitherto his duties have precluded him from more than an occasional attendance at the Cathedral services. Now he begins to take an interest in the fabric and the music. Upon his struggles with the organist, an old gentleman who had been in office since 1786, I have no time to dwell; they were not attended with any marked success. More to the purpose is his sudden growth of enthusiasm for the Cathedral itself and its furniture. There is a draft of a letter to Sylvanus Urban (which I do not think was ever sent) describing the stalls in the choir. As I have said, these were of fairly late date—of about the year 1700, in fact.

'The archdeacon's stall, situated at the south-east end, west of the episcopal throne (now so worthily occupied by the truly excellent prelate who adorns the See of Barchester), is distinguished by some curious ornamentation. In addition to the arms of Dean West, by whose efforts the whole of the internal furniture of the choir was completed, the prayer-desk is terminated at the eastern extremity by three small but remarkable statuettes in the grotesque manner. One is an exquisitely modelled figure of a cat, whose crouching posture suggests with admirable spirit the suppleness, vigilance, and craft of the redoubted adversary of the genus *Mus*.* Opposite to this is a figure seated upon a throne and invested with the attributes of royalty; but it is no earthly monarch whom the carver has sought to portray. His feet are studiously concealed by the long robe in which he is draped: but neither the crown nor the cap which he wears suffice to hide the prick-ears and curving horns which betray his Tartarean* origin; and the hand which rests upon his knee is armed with talons of horrifying length and sharpness. Between these two figures stands a shape muffled in a long mantle. This might at first sight be mistaken for a monk or "friar of orders gray,"* for the head is cowled and a knotted cord depends from somewhere about the waist. A slight inspection, however, will lead to a very different conclusion. The knotted cord is quickly seen to be a halter, held by a hand all but concealed within the draperies; while the sunken features and, horrid to relate, the rent flesh upon the cheek-bones, proclaim the King of Terrors. These figures are evidently the production of no unskilled chisel; and should it chance that any of your correspondents are able to throw light upon their origin and significance, my obligations to your valuable miscellany will be largely increased.'

There is more description in the paper, and, seeing that the woodwork in question has now disappeared, it has a considerable interest. A paragraph at the end is worth quoting:

'Some late researches among the Chapter accounts have shown me that the carving of the stalls was not, as was very usually reported, the work of Dutch artists, but was executed by a native of this city or district named Austin. The timber was procured from an oak copse in the vicinity, the property of the Dean and Chapter, known as Holywood. Upon a recent visit to the parish within whose boundaries it is situated, I learned from the aged and truly respectable incumbent that traditions still lingered amongst the inhabitants of the great size and age of the oaks employed to furnish the materials of the stately structure which has been, however imperfectly, described in the above lines. Of one in particular, which stood near the centre of the grove, it is remembered that it was known as the Hanging Oak. The propriety of that title is confirmed by the fact that a quantity of human bones was found in the soil about its roots, and that at certain times of the year it was the custom for those who wished to secure a successful issue to their affairs, whether of love or the ordinary business of life, to suspend from its boughs small images or puppets rudely fashioned of straw, twigs, or the like rustic materials.'

So much for the archdeacon's archæological investigations. To return to his career as it is to be gathered from his diaries. Those of his first three years of hard and careful work show him throughout in high spirits, and, doubtless, during this time, that reputation for hospitality and urbanity which is mentioned in his obituary notice was well deserved. After that, as time goes on, I see a shadow coming over him—destined to develop into utter blackness—which I cannot but think must have been reflected in his outward demeanour. He commits a good deal of his fears and troubles to his diary; there was no other outlet for them. He was unmarried, and his sister was not always with him. But I am much mistaken if he has told all that he might have told. A series of extracts shall be given:

'*Aug.* 30, 1816.—The days begin to draw in more perceptibly than ever. Now that the Archdeaconry papers are reduced to order, I must find some further employment for the evening hours of autumn and winter. It is a great blow that Letitia's health will not allow her to stay through these months. Why not go on with my *Defence of Episcopacy*? It may be useful.

'*Sept.* 15.—Letitia has left me for Brighton.

'*Oct.* 11.—Candles lit in the choir for the first time at evening prayers. It came as a shock: I find that I absolutely shrink from the dark season.

'*Nov.* 17.—Much struck by the character of the carving on my desk: I do not know that I had ever carefully noticed it before. My attention was called to it by an accident. During the *Magnificat** I was, I regret to say, almost overcome with sleep. My hand was resting on the back of the carved figure of a cat which is the nearest to me of the three figures on the end of my stall. I was not aware of this, for I was not looking in that direction, until I was startled by what seemed a softness, a feeling as of rather rough and coarse fur, and a sudden movement, as if the creature were twisting round its head to bite me. I regained complete consciousness in an instant, and I have some idea that I must have uttered a suppressed exclamation, for I noticed that Mr. Treasurer turned his head quickly in my direction. The impression of the unpleasant feeling was so strong that I found myself rubbing my hand upon my surplice. This accident led me to examine the figures after prayers more carefully than I had done before, and I realized for the first time with what skill they are executed.

'*Dec.* 6.—I do indeed miss Letitia's company. The evenings, after I have worked as long as I can at my *Defence*, are very trying. The house is too large for a lonely man, and visitors of any kind are too rare. I get an uncomfortable impression when going to my room that there *is* company of some kind. The fact is (I may as well formulate it to myself) that I hear voices. This, I am well aware, is a common symptom of incipient decay of the brain—and I believe that I should be less disquieted than I am if I had any suspicion that this was the cause. I have none—none whatever, nor is there anything in my family history to give colour to such an idea. Work, diligent work, and a punctual attention to the duties which fall to me is my best remedy, and I have little doubt that it will prove efficacious.

'*Jan.* 1.—My trouble is, I must confess it, increasing upon me. Last night, upon my return after midnight from the Deanery, I lit my candle to go upstairs. I was nearly at the top when something whispered to me, "Let me wish you a happy New Year." I could not be mistaken: it spoke distinctly and with a peculiar emphasis. Had I dropped my candle, as I all but did, I tremble to think what the consequences must have been. As it was, I managed to get up the last flight, and was quickly in my room with the door locked, and experienced no other disturbance.

'*Jan.* 15.—I had occasion to come downstairs last night to my work-room for my watch, which I had inadvertently left on my table when I went up to bed. I think I was at the top of the last flight when I had a sudden impression of a sharp whisper in my ear "*Take care.*" I clutched the balusters and naturally looked round at once. Of course, there was nothing. After a moment I went on—it was no good turning back—but I had as nearly as possible fallen: a cat—a large one by the feel of it—slipped between my feet, but again, of course, I saw nothing. It *may* have been the kitchen cat, but I do not think it was.

'*Feb.* 27.—A curious thing last night, which I should like to forget. Perhaps if I put it down here I may see it in its true proportion. I worked in the library from about 9 to 10. The hall and staircase seemed to be unusually full of what I can only call movement without sound: by this I mean that there seemed to be continuous going and coming, and that whenever I ceased writing to listen, or looked out into the hall, the stillness was absolutely unbroken. Nor, in going to my room at an earlier hour than usual—about half-past ten—was I conscious of anything that I could call a noise. It so happened that I had told John to come to my room for the letter to the bishop which I wished to have delivered early in the morning at the Palace. He was to sit up, therefore, and come for it when he heard me retire. This I had for the moment forgotten, though I had remembered to carry the letter with me to my room. But when, as I was winding up my watch, I heard a light tap at the door, and a low voice saying, "May I come in?" (which I most undoubtedly did hear), I recollected the fact, and took up the letter from my dressing-table, saying, "Certainly: come in." No one, however, answered my summons, and it was now that, as I strongly suspect, I committed an error: for I opened the door and held the letter out. There was certainly no one at that moment in the passage, but, in the instant of my standing there, the door at the end opened and John appeared carrying a candle. I asked him whether he had come to the door earlier; but am satisfied that he had not. I do not like the situation; but although my senses were very much on the alert, and though it was some time before I could sleep, I must allow that I perceived nothing further of an untoward character.'

With the return of spring, when his sister came to live with him for some months, Dr. Haynes's entries become more cheerful, and, indeed, no symptom of depression is discernible until the early part of September, when he was again left alone. And now, indeed, there is evidence that he was incommoded again, and that more pressingly. To this matter I will return in a moment, but I digress to put in a document which, rightly or wrongly, I believe to have a bearing on the thread of the story.

The account-books of Dr. Haynes, preserved along with his other papers, show, from a date but little later than that of his institution as archdeacon, a quarterly payment of £25 to J. L. Nothing could have been made of this, had it stood by itself. But I connect with it a very dirty and ill-written letter, which, like another that I have quoted, was in a pocket in the cover of a diary. Of date or postmark there is no vestige, and the decipherment was not easy. It appears to run:

Dr Sr.

I have bin expctin to her off you theis last wicks, and not Haveing done so must supose you have not got mine witch was saying how me and my man had met in with bad times this season all seems to go cross with us on the farm and which way to look for the rent we have no knowledge of it this been the sad case with us if you would have the great [liberality *probably, but the exact spelling defies reproduction*] to send fourty pounds otherwise steps will have to be took which I should not wish. Has you was the Means of me losing my place with Dr. Pulteney I think it is only just what I am asking and you know best what I could say if I was Put to it but I do not wish anything of that unpleasant Nature being one that always wish to have everything Pleasant about me.

Your obedt Servt,
JANE LEE.

About the time at which I suppose this letter to have been written there is, in fact, a payment of £40 to J. L.

We return to the diary:

'*Oct.* 22.—At evening prayers, during the Psalms, I had that same experience which I recollect from last year. I was resting my hand on one of the carved figures, as before (I usually avoid that of the cat now), and—I was going to have said—a change came over it, but that seems attributing too much importance to what must, after all, be due to some physical affection in myself: at any rate, the wood seemed to become chilly and soft as if made of wet linen. I can assign the moment at which I became sensible of this. The choir were singing the words (*Set thou an ungodly man to be ruler over him and*) *let Satan stand at his right hand.**

'The whispering in my house was more persistent to-night. I seemed not to be rid of it in my room. I have not noticed this before. A nervous man, which I am not, and hope I am not becoming, would have been much annoyed, if not alarmed, by it. The cat was on the stairs to-night. I think it sits there always. There *is* no kitchen cat.

'*Nov.* 15.—Here again I must note a matter I do not understand. I am much troubled in sleep. No definite image presented itself, but I was pursued by the very vivid impression that wet lips were whispering into my ear with great rapidity and emphasis for some time together. After this, I suppose, I fell asleep, but was awakened with a start by a feeling as if a hand were laid on my shoulder. To my intense alarm I found myself standing at the top of the lowest flight of the first staircase. The moon was shining brightly enough through the large window to let me see that there was a large cat on the second or third step. I can make no comment. I crept up to bed again, I do not know how. Yes, mine is a heavy burden. [Then follows a line or two which has been scratched out. I fancy I read something like "acted for the best."]'

Not long after this it is evident to me that the archdeacon's firmness began to give way under the pressure of these phenomena. I omit as unnecessarily painful and distressing the ejaculations and prayers which, in the months of December and January, appear for the first time and become increasingly frequent. Throughout this time, however, he is obstinate in clinging to his post. Why he did not plead ill-health and take refuge at Bath or Brighton I cannot tell; my impression is that it would have done him no good; that he was a man who, if he had confessed himself beaten by the annoyances, would have succumbed at once, and that he was conscious of this. He did seek to palliate them by inviting visitors to his house. The result he has noted in this fashion:

'*Jan.* 7.—I have prevailed on my cousin Allen to give me a few days, and he is to occupy the chamber next to mine.

'*Jan.* 8.—A still night. Allen slept well, but complained of the wind. My own experiences were as before: still whispering and whispering: what is it that he wants to say?

'*Jan.* 9.—Allen thinks this a very noisy house. He thinks, too, that my cat is an unusually large and fine specimen, but very wild.

'*Jan.* 10.—Allen and I in the library until 11. He left me twice to see what the maids were doing in the hall: returning the second time he told me he had seen one of them passing through the door at the end of the passage, and said if his wife were here she would soon get them into better order. I asked him what coloured dress the maid wore; he said grey or white. I supposed it would be so.

'*Jan.* 11.—Allen left me to-day. I must be firm.'

These words, *I must be firm*, occur again and again on subsequent days; sometimes they are the only entry. In these cases they are in an unusually large hand, and dug into the paper in a way which must have broken the pen that wrote them.

Apparently the archdeacon's friends did not remark any change in his behaviour, and this gives me a high idea of his courage and determination. The diary tells us nothing more than I have indicated of the last days of his life. The end of it all must be told in the polished language of the obituary notice:

'The morning of the 26th of February was cold and tempestuous. At an early hour the servants had occasion to go into the front hall of the residence occupied by the lamented subject of these lines. What was their horror upon observing the form of their beloved and respected master lying upon the landing of the principal staircase in an attitude which inspired the gravest fears. Assistance was procured, and an universal consternation was experienced upon the discovery that he had been the object of a brutal and a murderous attack. The vertebral column was fractured in more than one place. This might have been the result of a fall: it appeared that the stair-carpet was loosened at one point. But, in addition to this, there were injuries inflicted upon the eyes, nose and mouth, as if by the agency of some savage animal, which, dreadful to relate, rendered those features unrecognizable. The vital spark was, it is needless to add, completely extinct, and had been so, upon the testimony of respectable medical authorities, for several hours. The author or authors of this mysterious outrage are alike buried in mystery, and the most active conjecture has hitherto failed to suggest a solution of the melancholy problem afforded by this appalling occurrence.'

The writer goes on to reflect upon the probability that the writings of Mr. Shelley, Lord Byron, and M. Voltaire* may have been instrumental in bringing about the disaster, and concludes by hoping, somewhat vaguely, that this event may 'operate as an example to the rising generation'; but this portion of his remarks need not be quoted in full.

I had already formed the conclusion that Dr. Haynes was responsible for the death of Dr. Pulteney. But the incident connected with the carved figure of death upon the archdeacon's stall was a very perplexing feature. The conjecture that it had been cut out of the wood of the Hanging Oak was not difficult, but seemed impossible to substantiate. However, I paid a visit to Barchester, partly with the view of finding out whether there were any relics of the woodwork to be heard of. I was introduced by one of the canons to the curator of the local museum, who was, my friend said, more likely to be able to give me information on the point than anyone else. I told this gentleman of the description of certain carved figures and arms formerly on the stalls, and asked whether any had survived. He was able to show me the arms of Dean West and some other fragments. These, he said, had been got from an old resident, who had also once owned a figure— perhaps one of those which I was inquiring for. There was a very odd thing about that figure, he said. 'The old man who had it told me that he picked it up in a woodyard, whence he had obtained the still extant pieces, and had taken it home for his children. On the way home he was fiddling about with it and it came in two in his hands, and a bit of paper dropped out. This he picked up and, just noticing that there was writing on it, put it into his pocket, and subsequently into a vase on his mantelpiece. I was at his house not very long ago, and happened to pick up the vase and turn it over to see whether there were any marks on it, and the paper fell into my hand. The old man, on my handing it to him, told me the story I have told you, and said I might keep the paper. It was crumpled and rather torn, so I have mounted it on a card, which I have here. If you can tell me what it means I shall be very glad, and also, I may say, a good deal surprised.'

He gave me the card. The paper was quite legibly inscribed in an old hand, and this is what was on it:

> 'When I grew in the Wood
> I was water'd wth Blood
> Now in the Church I stand
> Who that touches me with his Hand
> If a Bloody hand he bear
> I councell him to be ware
> Lest he be fetcht away
> Whether by night or day,
> But chiefly when the wind blows high
> In a night of February.'

'This I drempt, 26 Febr. A° 1699.   JOHN AUSTIN.'

'I suppose it is a charm or a spell: wouldn't you call it something of that kind?' said the curator.

'Yes,' I said, 'I suppose one might. What became of the figure in which it was concealed?'

'Oh, I forgot,' said he. 'The old man told me it was so ugly and frightened his children so much that he burnt it.'

MARTIN'S CLOSE

❧❧❧

SOME few years back I was staying with the rector of a parish in the West,* where the society to which I belong owns property. I was to go over some of this land: and, on the first morning of my visit, soon after breakfast, the estate carpenter and general handy man, John Hill,* was announced as in readiness to accompany us. The rector asked which part of the parish we were to visit that morning. The estate map was produced, and when we had showed him our round, he put his finger on a particular spot. 'Don't forget,' he said, 'to ask John Hill about Martin's Close when you get there. I should like to hear what he tells you.' 'What ought he to tell us?' I said. 'I haven't the slightest idea,' said the rector, 'or, if that is not exactly true, it will do till lunch-time.' And here he was called away.

We set out; John Hill is not a man to withhold such information as he possesses on any point and you may gather from him much that is of interest about the people of the place and their talk. An unfamiliar word, or one that he thinks ought to be unfamiliar to you, he will usually spell—as c-o-b cob, and the like. It is not, however, relevant to my purpose to record his conversation before the moment when we reached Martin's Close. The bit of land is noticeable, for it is one of the smallest enclosures you are likely to see—a very few square yards, hedged in with quickset* on all sides, and without any gate or gap leading into it. You might take it for a small cottage garden long deserted, but that it lies away from the village and bears no trace of cultivation. It is at no great distance from the road, and is part of what is there called a moor, in other words, a rough upland pasture cut up into largish fields.

'Why is this little bit hedged off so?' I asked, and John Hill (whose answer I cannot represent as perfectly as I should like) was not at fault. 'That's what we call Martin's Close, sir: 'tes a curious thing 'bout that bit of land, sir: goes by the name of Martin's Close, sir. M-a-r-t-i-n Martin. Beg pardon, sir, did Rector tell you to make inquiry of me 'bout that, sir?' 'Yes, he did.' 'Ah, I thought so much, sir. I was tell'n Rector 'bout that last week, and he was very much interested. It 'pears there's a murderer buried there, sir, by the name of Martin. Old Samuel Saunders, that formerly lived yurr at what we call South-town, sir, he had a long tale 'bout that, sir: terrible murder done 'pon a young woman, sir. Cut her throat and cast her in the water down yurr.' 'Was he hung for it?' 'Yes, sir, he was hung just up yurr on the roadway, by what I've 'eard, on the Holy Innocents' Day,* many 'undred years ago, by the man that went by the name of the bloody judge: terrible red and bloody, I've 'eard.' 'Was his name Jeffreys,* do you think?' 'Might be possible 'twas—Jeffreys—J-e-f— Jeffreys. I reckon 'twas, and the tale I've 'eard many times from Mr. Saunders,—how this young man Martin—George Martin—was troubled before his crule action come to light by the young woman's sperit.' 'How was that, do you know?' 'No, sir, I don't exactly know how 'twas with it: but by what I've 'eard he was fairly tormented; and rightly tu. Old Mr. Saunders, he told a history regarding a cupboard down yurr in the New Inn.* According to what he related, this young woman's sperit come out of this cupboard: but I don't racollact the matter.'

This was the sum of John Hill's information. We passed on, and in due time I reported what I had heard to the Rector. He was able to show me from the parish account-books that a gibbet had been paid for in 1684, and a grave dug in the following year, both for the benefit of George Martin; but he was unable to suggest anyone in the parish, Saunders being now gone, who was likely to throw any further light on the story.

Naturally, upon my return to the neighbourhood of libraries, I made search in the more obvious places. The trial seemed to be nowhere reported. A newspaper of the time, and one or more news-letters, however, had some short notices, from which I learnt that, on the ground of local prejudice against the prisoner (he was described as a young gentleman of a good estate), the venue had been moved from Exeter to London; that Jeffreys had been the judge, and death the sentence, and that there had been some 'singular passages' in the evidence. Nothing further transpired till September of this year. A friend who knew me to be interested in Jeffreys then sent me a leaf torn out of a second-hand bookseller's catalogue with the entry: JEFFREYS, JUDGE: *Interesting old MS. trial for murder,** and so forth, from which I gathered, to my delight, that I could become pos-sessed, for a very few shillings, of what seemed to be a verbatim report, in shorthand, of the Martin trial. I telegraphed for the manuscript and got it. It was a thin bound volume, provided with a title written in longhand by someone in the eighteenth century, who had also added this note: 'My father, who took these notes in court, told me that the prisoner's friends had made interest with Judge Jeffreys that no report should be put out: he had intended doing this himself when times were better, and had shew'd it to the Revd. Mr. Glanvil,* who incourag'd his design very warmly, but death surpriz'd them both before it could be brought to an accomplishment.'

The initials W. G. are appended; I am advised that the original reporter may have been T. Gurney, who appears in that capacity in more than one State trial.

This was all that I could read for myself. After no long delay I heard of someone who was capable of deciphering the shorthand of the seventeenth century, and a little time ago the typewritten copy of the whole manuscript was laid before me. The portions which I shall communicate here help to fill in the very imperfect outline which subsists in the memories of John Hill and, I suppose, one or two others who live on the scene of the events.

The report begins with a species of preface, the general effect of which is that the copy is not that actually taken in court, though it is a true copy in regard to the notes of what was said; but that the writer has added to it some 'remarkable passages' that took place during the trial, and has made this present fair copy of the whole, intending at some favourable time to publish it; but has not put it into longhand, lest it should fall into the possession of unauthorized persons, and he or his family be deprived of the profit.

The report then begins:

This case came on to be tried on Wednesday, the 19th of November, between our sovereign lord the King, and George Martin Esquire, of (I take leave to omit some of the place-names), at a sessions of oyer and terminer* and gaol delivery, at the Old Bailey, and the prisoner, being in Newgate, was brought to the bar.

Clerk of the Crown. George Martin, hold up thy hand (which he did).

Then the indictment was read, which set forth that the prisoner 'not having the fear of God before his eyes, but being moved and seduced by the instigation of the devil, upon the 15th day of May, in the 36th year of our sovereign lord King Charles the Second,* with force and arms in the parish aforesaid, in and upon Ann Clark, spinster, of the same place, in the peace of God and of our said sovereign lord the King then and there being, feloniously, wilfully, and of your malice aforethought did make an assault and with a certain knife value a penny the throat of the said Ann Clark then and there did cut, of the which wound the said Ann Clark then and there did die, and the body of the said Ann Clark did cast into a certain pond of water situate in the same parish (with more that is not material to our purpose) against the peace of our sovereign lord the King, his crown and dignity.'

Then the prisoner prayed a copy of the indictment.

L. C. J. (Sir George Jeffreys). What is this? Sure you know that is never allowed. Besides, here is a plain indictment as ever I heard; you have nothing to do but to plead to it.

Pris. My lord, I apprehend there may be matter of law arising out of the indictment, and I would humbly beg the court to assign me counsel to consider of it. Besides, my lord, I believe it was done in another case: copy of the indictment was allowed.

L. C. J. What case was that?

Pris. Truly, my lord, I have been kept close prisoner ever since I came up from Exeter Castle, and no one allowed to come at me and no one to advise with.

L. C. J. But I say, what was that case you allege?

Pris. My lord, I cannot tell your lordship precisely the name of the case, but it is in my mind that there was such an one, and I would humbly desire——

L. C. J. All this is nothing. Name your case, and we will tell you whether there be any matter for you in it. God forbid but you should have anything that may be allowed you by law: but this is against law, and we must keep the course of the court.

Att.-Gen. (Sir Robert Sawyer).* My lord, we pray for the King that he may be asked to plead.

Cl. of Ct. Are you guilty of the murder whereof you stand indicated, or not guilty?

Pris. My lord, I would humbly offer this to the court. If I plead now, shall I have an opportunity after to except against the indictment?

L. C. J. Yes, yes, that comes after verdict: that will be saved to you, and counsel assigned if there be matter of law: but that which you have now to do is to plead.

Then after some little parleying with the court (which seemed strange upon such a plain indictment) the prisoner pleaded *Not Guilty*.

Cl. of Ct. Cul-prit.* How wilt thou be tried?
Pris. By God and my country.
Cl. of Ct. God send thee a good deliverance.
L. C. J. Why, how is this? Here has been a great to-do that you should not be tried at Exeter by your country, but be brought here to London, and now you ask to be tried by your country. Must we send you to Exeter again?
Pris. My lord, I understood it was the form.
L. C. J. So it is, man: we spoke only in the way of pleasantness. Well, go on and swear the jury.

So they were sworn. I omit the names. There was no challenging on the prisoner's part, for, as he said, he did not know any of the persons called. Thereupon the prisoner asked for the use of pen, ink, and paper, to which the L. C. J. replied: 'Ay, ay, in God's name let him have it.' Then the usual charge was delivered to the jury, and the case opened by the junior counsel for the King, Mr. Dolben.*
The Attorney-General followed:

May it please your lordship, and you gentlemen of the jury, I am of counsel for the King against the prisoner at the bar. You have heard that he stands indicted for a murder done upon the person of a young girl. Such crimes as this you may perhaps reckon to be not uncommon, and, indeed, in these times, I am sorry to say it, there is scarce any fact so barbarous and unnatural but what we may hear almost daily instances of it. But I must confess that in this murder that is charged upon the prisoner there are some particular features that mark it out to be such as I hope has but seldom if ever been per-petrated upon English ground. For as we shall make it appear, the person murdered was a poor country girl (whereas the prisoner is a gentleman of a proper estate) and, besides that, was one to whom Providence had not given the full use of her intellects, but was what is termed among us commonly an innocent or natural: such an one, therefore, as one would have supposed a gentleman of the prisoner's quality more likely to overlook, or, if he did notice her, to be moved to compassion for her unhappy condition, than to lift up his hand against her in the very horrid and barbarous manner which we shall show you he used.

Now to begin at the beginning and open the matter to you orderly: About Christmas of last year, that is the year 1683, this gentleman, Mr. Martin, having newly come back into his own country from the University of Cambridge, some of his neighbours, to show him what civility they could (for his family is one that stands in very good repute all over that country), entertained him here and there at their Christmas merrymakings, so that he was constantly riding to and fro, from one house to another, and sometimes, when the place of his destination was distant, or for other reason, as the unsafeness of the roads, he would be constrained to lie the night at an inn. In this way it happened that he came, a day or two after the Christmas, to the place where this young girl lived with her parents, and put up at the inn there, called the New Inn, which is, as I am informed, a house of good repute. Here was some dancing going on among the people of the place, and Ann Clark had been brought in, it seems, by her elder sister to look on; but being, as I have said, of weak understanding, and, besides that, very uncomely in her appearance, it was not likely she should take much part in the merriment; and accordingly was but standing by in a corner of the room. The prisoner at the bar, seeing her, one must suppose by way of a jest, asked her would she dance with him. And in spite of what her sister and others could say to prevent it and to dissuade her——

L. C. J. Come, Mr. Attorney, we are not set here to listen to tales of Christmas parties in taverns. I would not interrupt you, but sure you have more weighty matters than this. You will be telling us next what tune they danced to.

Att. My lord, I would not take up the time of the court with what is not material: but we reckon it to be material to show how this unlikely acquaintance begun: and as for the tune, I believe, indeed, our evidence will show that even that hath a bearing on the matter in hand.

L. C. J. Go on, go on, in God's name: but give us nothing that is impertinent.

Att. Indeed, my lord, I will keep to my matter. But, gentlemen, having now shown you, as I think, enough of this first meeting between the murdered person and the prisoner, I will shorten my tale so far as to say that from then on there were frequent meetings of the two: for the young woman was greatly tickled with having got hold (as she conceived it) of so likely a sweetheart, and he being once a week at least in the habit of passing through the street where she lived, she would be always on the watch for him; and it seems they had a signal arranged: he should whistle the tune that was played at the tavern: it is a tune, as I am informed, well known in that country, and has a burden, *'Madam, will you walk, will you talk with me?'**

L. C. J. Ay, I remember it in my own country, in Shropshire. It runs somehow thus, doth it not? [Here his lordship whistled a part of a tune, which was very observable, and seemed below the dignity of the court. And it appears he felt it so himself, for he said:] But this is by the mark, and I doubt it is the first time we have had dance-tunes in this court. The most part of the dancing we give occasion for is done at Tyburn.* [Looking at the prisoner, who appeared very much disordered.] You said the tune was material to your case, Mr. Attorney, and upon my life I think Mr. Martin agrees with you. What ails you, man? staring like a player that sees a ghost!

Pris. My lord, I was amazed at hearing such trivial, foolish things as they bring against me.

L. C. J. Well, well, it lies upon Mr. Attorney to show whether they be trivial or not: but I must say, if he has nothing worse than this he has said, you have no great cause to be in amaze. Doth it not lie something deeper? But go on, Mr. Attorney.

Att. My lord and gentlemen—all that I have said so far you may indeed very reasonably reckon as having an appearance of triviality. And, to be sure, had the matter gone no further than the humouring of a poor silly girl by a young gentleman of quality, it had been very well. But to proceed. We shall make it appear that after three or four weeks the prisoner became contracted to a young gentlewoman of that country, one suitable every way to his own condition, and such an arrangement was on foot that seemed to promise him a happy and a reputable living. But within no very long time it seems that this young gentlewoman, hearing of the jest that was going about that countryside with regard to the prisoner and Ann Clark, conceived that it was not only an unworthy carriage on the part of her lover, but a derogation to herself that he should suffer his name to be sport for tavern company: and so without more ado she, with the consent of her parents, signified to the prisoner that the match between them was at an end. We shall show you that upon the receipt of this intelligence the prisoner was greatly enraged against Ann Clark as being the cause of his misfortune (though indeed there was nobody answerable for it but himself), and that he made use of many outrageous expressions and threatenings against her, and subsequently upon meeting with her both abused her and struck at her with his whip: but she, being but a poor innocent, could not be persuaded to desist from her attachment to him, but would often run after him testifying with gestures and broken words the affection she had to him: until she was become, as he said, the very plague of his life. Yet, being that affairs in which he was now engaged necessarily took him by the house in which she lived, he could not (as I am willing to believe he would otherwise have done) avoid meeting with her from time to time. We shall further show you that this was the posture of things up to the 15th day of May in this present year. Upon that day the prisoner comes riding through the village, as of custom, and met with the young woman: but in place of passing her by, as he had lately done, he stopped, and said some words to her with which she appeared wonderfully pleased, and so left her; and after that day she was nowhere to be found, notwithstanding a strict search was made for her. The next time of the prisoner's passing through the place, her relations inquired of him whether he should know anything of her whereabouts; which he totally denied. They expressed to him their fears lest her weak intellects should have been upset by the attention he had showed her, and so she might have committed some rash act against her own life, calling him to witness the same time how often they had beseeched him to desist from taking notice of her, as fearing trouble might come of it: but this, too, he easily laughed away. But in spite of this light behaviour, it was noticeable in him that about this time his carriage and demeanour changed, and it was said of him that he seemed a troubled man. And here I come to a passage to which I should not dare to ask your attention, but that it appears to me to be founded in truth, and is supported by testimony deserving of credit. And, gentlemen, to my judgment it doth afford a great instance of God's revenge against murder, and that He will require the blood of the innocent.

*

[Here Mr. Attorney made a pause, and shifted with his papers: and it was thought remarkable by me and others, because he was a man not easily dashed.]

L. C. J. Well, Mr. Attorney, what is your instance?

Att. My lord, it is a strange one, and the truth is that, of all the cases I have been concerned in, I cannot call to mind the like of it. But to be short, gentlemen, we shall bring you testimony that Ann Clark was seen after this 15th of May, and that, at such time as she was so seen, it was impossible she could have been a living person.

[Here the people made a hum, and a good deal of laughter, and the Court called for silence, and when it was made]——

L. C. J. Why, Mr. Attorney, you might save up this tale for a week; it will be Christmas by that time, and you can frighten your cook-maids with it [at which the people laughed again, and the prisoner also, as it seemed]. God, man, what are you prating of—ghosts and Christmas jigs and tavern company—and here is a man's life at stake! (To the prisoner): And you, sir, I would have you know there is not so much occasion for you to make merry neither. You were not brought here for that, and if I know Mr. Attorney, he has more in his brief than he has shown yet. Go on, Mr. Attorney. I need not, mayhap, have spoken so sharply, but you must confess your course is something unusual.

Att. Nobody knows it better than I, my lord: but I shall bring it to an end with a round turn. I shall show you, gentlemen, that Ann Clark's body was found in the month of June, in a pond of water, with the throat cut: that a knife belonging to the prisoner was found in the same water: that he made efforts to recover the said knife from the water: that the coroner's quest brought in a verdict against the prisoner at the bar, and that therefore he should by course have been tried at Exeter: but that, suit being made on his behalf, on account that an impartial jury could not be found to try him in his own country, he hath had that singular favour shown him that he should be tried here in London. And so we will proceed to call our evidence.

Then the facts of the acquaintance between the prisoner and Ann Clark were proved, and also the coroner's inquest. I pass over this portion of the trial, for it offers nothing of special interest.

*

Sarah Arscott was next called and sworn.

Att. What is your occupation?

S. I keep the New Inn at ——.

Att. Do you know the prisoner at the bar?

S. Yes: he was often at our house since he come first at Christmas of last year.

Att. Did you know Ann Clark?

S. Yes, very well.

Att. Pray, what manner of person was she in her appearance?

S. She was a very short thick-made woman: I do not know what else you would have me say.

Att. Was she comely?

S. No, not by no manner of means: she was very uncomely, poor child! She had a great face and hanging chops and a very bad colour like a puddock.

L. C. J. What is that, mistress? What say you she was like?

S. My lord, I ask pardon; I heard Esquire Martin say she looked like a puddock in the face; and so she did.

L. C. J. Did you that? Can you interpret her, Mr. Attorney?

Att. My lord, I apprehend it is the country word for a toad.

L. C. J. Oh, a hop-toad! Ay, go on.

Att. Will you give an account to the jury of what passed between you and the prisoner at the bar in May last?

S. Sir, it was this. It was about nine o'clock the evening after that Ann did not come home, and I was about my work in the house; there was no company there only Thomas Snell, and it was foul weather. Esquire Martin came in and called for some drink, and I, by way of pleasantry, I said to him, 'Squire, have you been looking after your sweetheart?' and he flew out at me in a passion and desired I would not use such expressions. I was amazed at that, because we were accustomed to joke with him about her.

L. C. J. Who, her?

S. Ann Clark, my lord. And we had not heard the news of his being contracted to a young gentle-woman elsewhere, or I am sure I should have used better manners. So I said nothing, but being I was a little put out, I begun singing, to myself as it were, the song they danced to the first time they met, for I thought it would prick him. It was the same that he was used to sing when he came down the street; I have heard it very often: '*Madam, will you walk, will you talk with me?*' And it fell out that I needed something that was in the kitchen. So I went out to get it, and all the time I went on singing, something louder and more bold-like. And as I was there all of a sudden I thought I heard someone answering outside the house, but I could not be sure because of the wind blowing so high. So then I stopped singing, and now I heard it plain, saying, '*Yes, sir, I will walk, I will talk with you,*' and I knew the voice for Ann Clark's voice.

Att. How did you know it to be her voice?

S. It was impossible I could be mistaken. She had a dreadful voice, a kind of a squalling voice, in particular if she tried to sing. And there was nobody in the village that could counterfeit it, for they often tried. So, hearing that, I was glad, because we were all in an anxiety to know what was gone with her: for though she was a natural, she had a good disposition and was very tractable: and says I to myself, 'What, child! are you returned, then?' and I ran into the front room, and said to Squire Martin as I passed by, 'Squire, here is your sweetheart back again: shall I call her in?' and with that I went to open the door; but Squire Martin he caught hold of me, and it seemed to me he was out of his wits, or near upon. 'Hold, woman,' says he, 'in God's name!' and I know not what else: he was all of a shake. Then I was angry, and said I, 'What! are you not glad that poor child is found?' and I called to Thomas Snell and said, 'If the Squire will not let me, do you open the door and call her in.' So Thomas Snell went and opened the door, and the wind setting that way blew in and overset the two candles that was all we had lighted: and Esquire Martin fell away from holding me; I think he fell down on the floor, but we were wholly in the dark, and it was a minute or two before I got a light again: and while I was feeling for the fire-box, I am not certain but I heard someone step 'cross the floor, and I am sure I heard the door of the great cupboard that stands in the room open and shut to. Then, when I had a light again, I see Esquire Martin on the settle, all white and sweaty as if he had swounded away, and his arms hanging down; and I was going to help him; but just then it caught my eye that there was something like a bit of a dress shut into the cupboard door, and it came to my mind I had heard that door shut. So I thought it might be some person had run in when the light was quenched, and was hiding in the cupboard. So I went up closer and looked: and there was a bit of a black stuff cloak, and just below it an edge of a brown stuff dress, both sticking out of the shut of the door: and both of them was low down, as if the person that had them on might be crouched down inside.

Att. What did you take it to be?

S. I took it to be a woman's dress.

Att. Could you make any guess whom it belonged to? Did you know anyone who wore such a dress?

S. It was a common stuff, by what I could see. I have seen many women wearing such a stuff in our parish.

Att. Was it like Ann Clark's dress?

S. She used to wear just such a dress: but I could not say on my oath it was hers.

Att. Did you observe anything else about it?

S. I did notice that it looked very wet: but it was foul weather outside.

L. C. J. Did you feel of it, mistress?

S. No, my lord, I did not like to touch it.

L. C. J. Not like? Why that? Are you so nice that you scruple to feel of a wet dress?

S. Indeed, my lord, I cannot very well tell why: only it had a nasty ugly look about it.

L. C. J. Well, go on.

S. Then I called again to Thomas Snell, and bid him come to me and catch anyone that come out when I should open the cupboard door, 'for,' says I, 'there is someone hiding within, and I would know what she wants.' And with that Squire Martin gave a sort of a cry or a shout and ran out of the house into the dark, and I felt the cupboard door pushed out against me while I held it, and Thomas Snell helped me: but for all we pressed to keep it shut as hard as we could, it was forced out against us, and we had to fall back.

L. C. J. And pray what came out—a mouse?

S. No, my lord, it was greater than a mouse, but I could not see what it was: it fleeted very swift over the floor and out at the door.

L. C. J. But come; what did it look like? Was it a person?

S. My lord, I cannot tell what it was, but it ran very low, and it was of a dark colour. We were both daunted by it, Thomas Snell and I, but we made all the haste we could after it to the door that stood open. And we looked out, but it was dark and we could see nothing.

L. C. J. Was there no tracks of it on the floor? What floor have you there?

S. It is a flagged floor and sanded, my lord, and there was an appearance of a wet track on the floor, but we could make nothing of it, neither Thomas Snell nor me, and besides, as I said, it was a foul night.

L. C. J. Well, for my part, I see not—though to be sure it is an odd tale she tells—what you would do with this evidence.

Att. My lord, we bring it to show the suspicious carriage of the prisoner immediately after the disappearance of the murdered person: and we ask the jury's consideration of that; and also to the matter of the voice heard without the house.

Then the prisoner asked some questions not very material, and Thomas Snell was next called, who gave evidence to the same effect as Mrs. Arscott, and added the following:

Att. Did anything pass between you and the prisoner during the time Mrs. Arscott was out of the room?

Th. I had a piece of twist in my pocket.

Att. Twist of what?

Th. Twist of tobacco, sir, and I felt a disposition to take a pipe of tobacco. So I found a pipe on the chimney-piece, and being it was twist, and in regard of me having by an oversight left my knife at my house, and me not having over many teeth to pluck at it, as your lordship or anyone else may have a view by their own eyesight——

L. C. J. What is the man talking about? Come to the matter, fellow! Do you think we sit here to look at your teeth?

Th. No, my lord, nor I would not you should do, God forbid! I know your honours have better employment, and better teeth, I would not wonder.

L. C. J. Good God, what a man is this! Yes, I *have* better teeth, and that you shall find if you keep not to the purpose.

Th. I humbly ask pardon, my lord, but so it was. And I took upon me, thinking no harm, to ask Squire Martin to lend me his knife to cut my tobacco. And he felt first of one pocket and then of another and it was not there at all. And says I, 'What! have you lost your knife, Squire?' And up he gets and feels again and he sat down, and such a groan as he gave. 'Good God!' he says, 'I must have left it there.' 'But,' says I, 'Squire, by all appearance it is *not* there. Did you set a value on it,' says I, 'you might have it cried.' But he sat there and put his head between his hands and seemed to take no notice to what I said. And then it was Mistress Arscott come tracking back out of the kitchen place.

Asked if he heard the voice singing outside the house, he said 'No,' but the door into the kitchen was shut, and there was a high wind: but says that no one could mistake Ann Clark's voice.

Then a boy, William Reddaway, about thirteen years of age, was called, and by the usual questions, put by the Lord Chief Justice, it was ascertained that he knew the nature of an oath. And so he was sworn. His evidence referred to a time about a week later.

Att. Now, child, don't be frighted: there is no one here will hurt you if you speak the truth.

L. C. J. Ay, if he speak the truth. But remember, child, thou art in the presence of the great God of heaven and earth, that hath the keys of hell, and of us that are the king's officers, and have the keys of Newgate; and remember, too, there is a man's life in question; and if thou tellest a lie, and by that means he comes to an ill end, thou art no better than his murderer; and so speak the truth.

Att. Tell the jury what you know, and speak out. Where were you on the evening of the 23rd of May last?

L. C. J. Why, what does such a boy as this know of days. Can you mark the day, boy?

W. Yes, my lord, it was the day before our feast, and I was to spend sixpence there, and that falls a month before Midsummer Day.

One of the Jury. My lord, we cannot hear what he says.

L. C. J. He says he remembers the day because it was the day before the feast they had there, and he had sixpence to lay out. Set him up on the table there. Well, child, and where wast thou then?

W. Keeping cows on the moor, my lord.

But, the boy using the country speech, my lord could not well apprehend him, and so asked if there was anyone that could interpret him, and it was answered the parson of the parish was there, and he was accordingly sworn and so the evidence given. The boy said:

'I was on the moor about six o'clock, and sitting behind a bush of furze near a pond of water: and the prisoner came very cautiously and looking about him, having something like a long pole in his hand, and stopped a good while as if he would be listening, and then began to feel in the water with the pole: and I being very near the water—not above five yards—heard as if the pole struck up against something that made a wallowing sound, and the prisoner dropped the pole and threw himself on the ground, and rolled himself about very strangely with his hands to his ears, and so after a while got up and went creeping away.'

Asked if he had had any communication with the prisoner, 'Yes, a day or two before, the prisoner, hearing I was used to be on the moor, he asked me if I had seen a knife laying about, and said he would give sixpence to find it. And I said I had not seen any such thing, but I would ask about. Then he said he would give me sixpence to say nothing, and so he did.

L. C. J. And was that the sixpence you were to lay out at the feast?
W. Yes, if you please, my lord.

Asked if he had observed anything particular as to the pond of water, he said, 'No, except that it begun to have a very ill smell and the cows would not drink of it for some days before.'

Asked if he had ever seen the prisoner and Ann Clark in company together, he began to cry very much, and it was a long time before they could get him to speak intelligibly. At last the parson of the parish, Mr. Matthews, got him to be quiet, and the question being put to him again, he said he had seen Ann Clark waiting on the moor for the prisoner at some way off, several times since last Christmas.

Att. Did you see her close, so as to be sure it was she?
W. Yes, quite sure.
L. C. J. How quite sure, child?
W. Because she would stand and jump up and down and clap her arms like a goose (which he called by some country name: but the parson explained it to be a goose). And then she was of such a shape that it could not be no one else.
Att. What was the last time that you so saw her?

Then the witness began to cry again and clung very much to Mr. Matthews, who bid him not be frightened. And so at last he told this story: that on the day before their feast (being the same evening that he had before spoken of) after the prisoner had gone away, it being then twilight and he very desirous to get home, but afraid for the present to stir from where he was lest the prisoner should see him, remained some few minutes behind the bush, looking on the pond, and saw something dark come up out of the water at the edge of the pond farthest away from him, and so up the bank. And when it got to the top where he could see it plain against the sky, it stood up and flapped the arms up and down, and then run off very swiftly in the same direction the prisoner had taken: and being asked very strictly who he took it to be, he said upon his oath that it could be nobody but Ann Clark.

Thereafter his master was called, and gave evidence that the boy had come home very late that evening and been chided for it, and that he seemed very much amazed, but could give no account of the reason.

Att. My lord, we have done with our evidence for the King.

Then the Lord Chief Justice called upon the prisoner to make his defence; which he did, though at no great length, and in a very halting way, saying that he hoped the jury would not go about to take his life on the evidence of a parcel of country people and children that would believe any idle tale; and that he had been very much prejudiced in his trial; at which the L. C. J. interrupted him, saying that he had had singular favour shown to him in having his trial removed from Exeter, which the prisoner acknowledging, said that he meant rather that since he was brought to London there had not been care taken to keep him secured from interruption and disturbance. Upon which the L. C. J. ordered the Marshal to be called, and questioned him about the safe keeping of the prisoner, but could find nothing: except the Marshal said that he had been informed by the under-keeper that they had seen a person outside his door or going up the stairs to it: but there was no possibility the person should have got in. And it being inquired further what sort of person this might be, the Marshal could not speak to it save by hearsay, which was not allowed. And the prisoner, being asked if this was what he meant, said no, he knew nothing of that, but it was very hard that a man should not be suffered to be at quiet when his life stood on it. But it was observed he was very hasty in his denial. And so he said no more, and called no witnesses. Whereupon the Attorney-General spoke to the jury. [A full report of what he said is given, and, if time allowed, I would extract that portion in which he dwells on the alleged appearance of the murdered person: he quotes some authorities of ancient date, as St. Augustine *de cura pro mortuis gerenda** (a favourite book of reference with the old writers on the supernatural) and also cites some cases which may be seen in Glanvil's, but more conveniently in Mr. Lang's books.* He does not, however, tell us more of those cases than is to be found in print.]

The Lord Chief Justice then summed up the evidence for the jury. His speech, again, contains nothing that I find worth copying out: but he was naturally impressed with the singular character of the evidence, saying that he had never heard such given in his experience; but that there was nothing in law to set it aside, and that the jury must consider whether they believed these witnesses or not.

And the jury after a very short consultation brought the prisoner in Guilty.

So he was asked whether he had anything to say in arrest of judgment, and pleaded that his name was spelt wrong in the indictment, being Martin with an I, whereas it should be with a Y. But this was overruled as not material, Mr. Attorney saying, moreover, that he could bring evidence to show that the prisoner by times wrote it as it was laid in the indictment. And, the prisoner having nothing further to offer, sentence of death was passed upon him, and that he should be hanged in chains upon a gibbet near the place where the fact was committed, and that execution should take place upon the 28th December next ensuing, being Innocents' Day.

Thereafter the prisoner being to all appearance in a state of desperation, made shift to ask the L. C. J. that his relations might be allowed to come to him during the short time he had to live.

L. C. J. Ay, with all my heart, so it be in the presence of the keeper; and Ann Clark may come to you as well, for what I care.

At which the prisoner broke out and cried to his lordship not to use such words to him, and his lordship very angrily told him he deserved no tenderness at any man's hands for a cowardly butcherly murderer that had not the stomach to take the reward of his deeds: 'and I hope to God,' said he, 'that she *will* be with you by day and by night till an end is made of you.' Then the prisoner was removed, and, so far as I saw, he was in a swound, and the Court broke up.

I cannot refrain from observing that the prisoner during all the time of the trial seemed to be more uneasy than is commonly the case even in capital causes: that, for example, he was looking narrowly among the people and often turning round very sharply, as if some person might be at his ear. It was also very noticeable at this trial what a silence the people kept, and further (though this might not be otherwise than natural in that season of the year), what a darkness and obscurity there was in the court room, lights being brought in not long after two o'clock in the day, and yet no fog in the town.

It was not without interest that I heard lately from some young men who had been giving a concert in the village I speak of, that a very cold reception was accorded to the song which has been mentioned in this narrative: '*Madam, will you walk?*' It came out in some talk they had next morning with some of the local people that that song was regarded with an invincible repugnance; it was not so, they believed, at North Tawton,* but here it was reckoned to be unlucky. However, why that view was taken no one had the shadow of an idea.

MR. HUMPHREYS AND HIS INHERITANCE

愛

ABOUT fifteen years ago, on a date late in August or early in September, a train drew up at Wilsthorpe,* a country station in Eastern England. Out of it stepped (with other passengers) a rather tall and reasonably good-looking young man, carrying a handbag and some papers tied up in a packet. He was expecting to be met, one would say, from the way in which he looked about him: and he was, as obviously, expected. The stationmaster ran forward a step or two, and then, seeming to recollect himself, turned and beckoned to a stout and consequential person with a short round beard who was scanning the train with some appearance of bewilderment. 'Mr. Cooper,' he called out,—'Mr. Cooper, I think this is your gentleman'; and then to the passenger who had just alighted, 'Mr. Humphreys, sir? Glad to bid you welcome to Wilsthorpe. There's a cart from the Hall for your luggage, and here's Mr. Cooper, what I think you know.' Mr. Cooper had hurried up, and now raised his hat and shook hands. 'Very pleased, I'm sure,' he said, 'to give the echo to Mr. Palmer's kind words. I should have been the first to render expression to them but for the face not being familiar to me, Mr. Humphreys. May your residence among us be marked as a red-letter day, sir.' 'Thank you very much, Mr. Cooper,' said Humphreys, 'for your good wishes, and Mr. Palmer also. I do hope very much that this change of—er—tenancy—which you must all regret, I am sure—will not be to the detriment of those with whom I shall be brought in contact.' He stopped, feeling that the words were not fitting themselves together in the happiest way, and Mr. Cooper cut in, 'Oh, you may rest satisfied of that, Mr. Humphreys. I'll take it upon myself to assure you, sir, that a warm welcome awaits you on all sides. And as to any change of propriety* turning out detrimental to the neighbourhood, well, your late uncle——' And here Mr. Cooper also stopped, possibly in obedience to an inner monitor, possibly because Mr. Palmer, clearing his throat loudly, asked Humphreys for his ticket. The two men left the little station, and—at Humphreys' suggestion—decided to walk to Mr. Cooper's house, where luncheon was awaiting them.

The relation in which these personages stood to each other can be explained in a very few lines. Humphreys had inherited—quite unexpectedly—a property from an uncle: neither the property nor the uncle had he ever seen. He was alone in the world—a man of good ability and kindly nature, whose employment in a Government office for the last four or five years had not gone far to fit him for the life of a country gentleman. He was studious and rather diffident, and had few out-of-door pursuits except golf and gardening. To-day he had come down for the first time to visit Wilsthorpe and confer with Mr. Cooper, the bailiff, as to the matters which needed immediate attention. It may be asked how this came to be his first visit? Ought he not in decency to have attended his uncle's funeral? The answer is not far to seek: he had been abroad at the time of the death, and his address had not been at once procurable. So he had put off coming to Wilsthorpe till he heard that all things were ready for him. And now we find him arrived at Mr. Cooper's comfortable house, facing the parsonage, and having just shaken hands with the smiling Mrs. and Miss Cooper.

During the minutes that preceded the announcement of luncheon the party settled themselves on elaborate chairs in the drawing-room, Humphreys, for his part, perspiring quietly in the consciousness that stock was being taken of him.

'I was just saying to Mr. Humphreys, my dear,' said Mr. Cooper, 'that I hope and trust that his residence among us here in Wilsthorpe will be marked as a red-letter day.'

'Yes, indeed, I'm sure,' said Mrs. Cooper heartily, 'and many, many of them.'

Miss Cooper murmured words to the same effect, and Humphreys attempted a pleasantry about painting the whole calendar red, which, though greeted with shrill laughter, was evidently not fully understood. At this point they proceeded to luncheon.

'Do you know this part of the country at all, Mr. Humphreys?' said Mrs. Cooper, after a short interval. This was a better opening.

'No, I'm sorry to say I do *not*,' said Humphreys. 'It seems very pleasant, what I could see of it coming down in the train.'

'Oh, it *is* a pleasant part. Really, I sometimes say I don't know a nicer district, for the country; and the people round, too: such a quantity always going on. But I'm afraid you've come a little late for some of the better garden parties, Mr. Humphreys.'

'I suppose I have; dear me, what a pity!' said Humphreys, with a gleam of relief; and then, feeling that something more could be got out of this topic, 'But after all, you see, Mrs. Cooper, even if I could have been here earlier, I should have been cut off from them, should I not? My poor uncle's recent death, you know——'

'Oh dear, Mr. Humphreys, to be sure; what a dreadful thing of me to say!' (And Mr. and Miss Cooper seconded the proposition inarticulately.) 'What must you have thought? I *am* so sorry: you must really forgive me.'

'Not at all, Mrs. Cooper, I assure you. I can't honestly assert that my uncle's death was a great grief to me, for I had never seen him. All I meant was that I supposed I shouldn't be expected to take part for some little time in festivities of that kind.'

'Now, really it's very kind of you to take it in that way, Mr. Humphreys, isn't it, George? And you *do* forgive me? But only fancy! You never saw poor old Mr. Wilson!'

'Never in my life; nor did I ever have a letter from him. But, by the way, you have something to forgive *me* for. I've never thanked you, except by letter, for all the trouble you've taken to find people to look after me at the Hall.'

'Oh, I'm sure that was nothing, Mr. Humphreys; but I really do think that you'll find them give satisfaction. The man and his wife whom we've got for the butler and housekeeper we've known for a number of years: such a nice respectable couple, and Mr. Cooper, I'm sure, can answer for the men in the stables and gardens.'

'Yes, Mr. Humphreys, they're a good lot. The head gardener's the only one who's stopped on from Mr. Wilson's time. The major part of the employees, as you no doubt saw by the will, received legacies from the old gentleman and retired from their posts, and as the wife says, your housekeeper and butler are calculated to render you every satisfaction.'

'So everything, Mr. Humphreys, is ready for you to step in this very day, according to what I understood you to wish,' said Mrs. Cooper. 'Everything, that is, except company, and there I'm afraid you'll find yourself quite at a standstill. Only we did understand it was your intention to move in at once. If not, I'm sure you know we should have been only too pleased for you to stay here.'

'I'm quite sure you would, Mrs. Cooper, and I'm very grateful to you. But I thought I had really better make the plunge at once. I'm accustomed to living alone, and there will be quite enough to occupy my evenings—looking over papers and books and so on—for some time to come. I thought if Mr. Cooper could spare the time this afternoon to go over the house and grounds with me——'

'Certainly, certainly, Mr. Humphreys. My time is your own, up to any hour you please.'

'Till dinner-time, father, you mean,' said Miss Cooper. 'Don't forget we're going over to the Brasnetts'. And have you got all the garden keys?'

'Are you a great gardener, Miss Cooper?' said Mr. Humphreys. 'I wish you would tell me what I'm to expect at the Hall.'

'Oh, I don't know about a *great* gardener, Mr. Humphreys: I'm very fond of flowers—but the Hall garden might be made quite lovely, I often say. It's very old-fashioned as it is: and a great deal of shrubbery. There's an old temple, besides, and a maze.'

'Really? Have you explored it ever?'

'No-o,' said Miss Cooper, drawing in her lips and shaking her head. 'I've often longed to try, but old Mr. Wilson always kept it locked. He wouldn't even let Lady Wardrop into it. (She lives near here, at Bentley, you know, and she's a *great* gardener, if you like.) That's why I asked father if he had all the keys.'

'I see. Well, I must evidently look into that, and show you over it when I've learnt the way.'

'Oh, thank you so much, Mr. Humphreys! Now I shall have the laugh of Miss Foster (that's our rector's daughter, you know; they're away on their holiday now—such nice people). We always had a joke between us which should be the first to get into the maze.'

'I think the garden keys must be up at the house,' said Mr. Cooper, who had been looking over a large bunch. 'There is a number there in the library. Now, Mr. Humphreys, if you're prepared, we might bid good-bye to these ladies and set forward on our little tour of exploration.'

As they came out of Mr. Cooper's front gate, Humphreys had to run the gauntlet—not of an organized demonstration, but of a good deal of touching of hats and careful contemplation from the men and women who had gathered in somewhat unusual numbers in the village street. He had, further, to exchange some remarks with the wife of the lodge-keeper as they passed the park gates, and with the lodge-keeper himself, who was attending to the park road. I cannot, however, spare the time to report the progress fully. As they traversed the half-mile or so between the lodge and the house, Humphreys took occasion to ask his companion some question which brought up the topic of his late uncle, and it did not take long before Mr. Cooper was embarked upon a disquisition.

'It is singular to think, as the wife was saying just now, that you should never have seen the old gentleman. And yet—you won't misunderstand me, Mr. Humphreys, I feel confident, when I say that in my opinion there would have been but little congeniality betwixt yourself and him. Not that I have a word to say in deprecation—not a single word. I can tell you what he was,' said Mr. Cooper, pulling up suddenly and fixing Humphreys with his eye. 'Can tell you what he was in a nutshell, as the saying goes. He was a complete, thorough valentudinarian.* That describes him to a T. That's what he was, sir, a complete valentudinarian. No participation in what went on around him. I did venture, I think, to send you a few words of cutting from our local paper, which I took the occasion to contribute on his decease. If I recollect myself aright, such is very much the ghist of them. But don't, Mr. Humphreys,' continued Cooper, tapping him impressively on the chest,—'don't you run away with the impression that I wish to say aught but what is most creditable—*most* creditable—of your respected uncle and my late employer. Upright, Mr. Humphreys—open as the day; liberal to all in his dealings. He had the heart to feel and the hand to accommodate. But there it was: there was the stumbling-block—his unfortunate health—or, as I might more truly phrase it, his *want* of health.'

'Yes, poor man. Did he suffer from any special disorder before his last illness—which, I take it, was little more than old age?'

'Just that, Mr. Humphreys—just that. The flash flickering slowly away in the pan,' said Cooper, with what he considered an appropriate gesture,—'the golden bowl gradually ceasing to vibrate.* But as to your other question I should return a negative answer. General absence of vitality? yes: special complaint? no, unless you reckon a nasty cough he had with him. Why, here we are pretty much at the house. A handsome mansion, Mr. Humphreys, don't you consider?'

It deserved the epithet, on the whole: but it was oddly proportioned—a very tall red-brick house, with a plain parapet concealing the roof almost entirely. It gave the impression of a town house set down in the country; there was a basement, and a rather imposing flight of steps leading up to the front door. It seemed also, owing to its height, to desiderate wings, but there were none. The stables and other offices were concealed by trees. Humphreys guessed its probable date as 1770 or thereabouts.

The mature couple who had been engaged to act as butler and cook-housekeeper were waiting inside the front door, and opened it as their new master approached. Their name, Humphreys already knew, was Calton; of their appearance and manner he formed a favourable impression in the few minutes' talk he had with them. It was agreed that he should go through the plate and the cellar next day with Mr. Calton, and that Mrs. C. should have a talk with him about linen, bedding, and so on—what there was, and what there ought to be. Then he and Cooper, dismissing the Caltons for the present, began their view of the house. Its topography is not of importance to this story. The large rooms on the ground floor were satisfactory, especially the library, which was as large as the dining-room, and had three tall windows facing east. The bedroom prepared for Humphreys was immediately above it. There were many pleasant, and a few really interesting, old pictures. None of the furniture was new, and hardly any of the books were later than the seventies. After hearing of and seeing the few changes his uncle had made in the house, and contemplating a shiny portrait of him which adorned the drawing-room, Humphreys was forced to agree with Cooper that in all probability there would have been little to attract him in his predecessor. It made him rather sad that he could not be sorry— *dolebat se dolere non posse**—for the man who, whether with or without some feeling of kindliness towards his unknown nephew, had contributed so much to his well-being; for he felt that Wilsthorpe was a place in which he could be happy, and especially happy, it might be, in its library.

And now it was time to go over the garden: the empty stables could wait, and so could the laundry. So to the garden they addressed themselves, and it was soon evident that Miss Cooper had been right in thinking that there were possibilities. Also that Mr. Cooper had done well in keeping on the gardener. The deceased Mr. Wilson might not have, indeed plainly had not, been imbued with the latest views on gardening, but whatever had been done here had been done under the eye of a knowledgeable man, and the equipment and stock were excellent. Cooper was delighted with the pleasure Humphreys showed, and with the suggestions he let fall from time to time. 'I can see,' he said, 'that you've found your meatear here, Mr. Humphreys: you'll make this place a regular signosier* before very many seasons have passed over our heads. I wish Clutterham had been here—that's the head gardener—and here he would have been of course, as I told you, but for his son's being horse doover* with a fever, poor fellow! I should like him to have heard how the place strikes you.'

'Yes, you told me he couldn't be here to-day, and I was very sorry to hear the reason, but it will be time enough to-morrow. What is that white building on the mound at the end of the grass ride? Is it the temple Miss Cooper mentioned?'

'That it is, Mr. Humphreys—the Temple of Friendship. Constructed of marble brought out of Italy for the purpose, by your late uncle's grandfather. Would it interest you perhaps to take a turn there? You get a very sweet prospect of the park.'

The general lines of the temple were those of the Sibyl's Temple at Tivoli, helped out by a dome, only the whole was a good deal smaller. Some ancient sepulchral reliefs were built into the wall, and about it all was a pleasant flavour of the grand tour. Cooper produced the key, and with some difficulty opened the heavy door. Inside there was a handsome ceiling, but little furniture. Most of the floor was occupied by a pile of thick circular blocks of stone, each of which had a single letter deeply cut on its slightly convex upper surface. 'What is the meaning of these?' Humphreys inquired.

'Meaning? Well, all things, we're told, have their purpose, Mr. Humphreys, and I suppose these blocks have had theirs as well as another. But what that purpose is or was (Mr. Cooper assumed a didactic attitude here), I, for one, should be at a loss to point out to you, sir. All I know of them—and it's summed up in a very few words—is just this: that they're stated to have been removed by your late uncle, at a period before I entered on the scene, from the maze. That, Mr. Humphreys, is——'

'Oh, the maze!' exclaimed Humphreys. 'I'd forgotten that: we must have a look at it. Where is it?'

Cooper drew him to the door of the temple, and pointed with his stick. 'Guide your eye,' he said (somewhat in the manner of the Second Elder in Handel's 'Susanna'—*

'Far to the west direct your straining eyes
Where yon tall holm-tree rises to the skies.')

'Guide your eye by my stick here, and follow out the line directly
opposite to the spot where we're standing now, and I'll engage,
Mr. Humphreys, that you'll catch the archway over the entrance.
You'll see it just at the end of the walk answering to the one that leads
up to this very building. Did you think of going there at once? because
if that be the case, I must go to the house and procure the key. If you
would walk on there, I'll rejoin you in a few moments' time.'

Accordingly Humphreys strolled down the ride leading to the
temple, past the garden-front of the house, and up the turfy approach
to the archway which Cooper had pointed out to him. He was surprised to find that the whole maze was surrounded by a high wall, and
that the archway was provided with a padlocked iron gate; but then
he remembered that Miss Cooper had spoken of his uncle's objection
to letting anyone enter this part of the garden. He was now at the
gate, and still Cooper came not. For a few minutes he occupied himself in reading the motto cut over the entrance, '*Secretum meum mihi
et filiis domus meae,*'* and in trying to recollect the source of it. Then
he became impatient and considered the possibility of scaling the
wall. This was clearly not worth while; it might have been done if he
had been wearing an older suit: or could the padlock—a very old
one—be forced? No, apparently not: and yet, as he gave a final irritated kick at the gate, something gave way, and the lock fell at his feet.
He pushed the gate open, inconveniencing a number of nettles as he
did so, and stepped into the enclosure.

It was a yew maze, of circular form, and the hedges, long
untrimmed, had grown out and upwards to a most unorthodox
breadth and height. The walks, too, were next door to impassable.
Only by entirely disregarding scratches, nettle-stings, and wet, could
Humphreys force his way along them; but at any rate this condition
of things, he reflected, would make it easier for him to find his way
out again, for he left a very visible track. So far as he could remember,
he had never been in a maze before, nor did it seem to him now that
he had missed much. The dankness and darkness, and smell of
crushed goosegrass and nettles were anything but cheerful. Still, it
did not seem to be a very intricate specimen of its kind. Here he was
(by the way, was that Cooper arrived at last? No!) very nearly at the
heart of it, without having taken much thought as to what path he was

following. Ah! there at last was the centre, easily gained. And there was something to reward him. His first impression was that the central ornament was a sundial; but when he had switched away some portion of the thick growth of brambles and bindweed that had formed over it, he saw that it was a less ordinary decoration. A stone column about four feet high, and on the top of it a metal globe*— copper, to judge by the green patina—engraved, and finely engraved too, with figures in outline, and letters. That was what Humphreys saw, and a brief glance at the figures convinced him that it was one of those mysterious things called celestial globes, from which, one would suppose, no one ever yet derived any information about the heavens. However, it was too dark—at least in the maze—for him to examine this curiosity at all closely, and besides, he now heard Cooper's voice, and sounds as of an elephant in the jungle. Humphreys called to him to follow the track he had beaten out, and soon Cooper emerged panting into the central circle. He was full of apologies for his delay; he had not been able, after all, to find the key. 'But there!' he said, 'you've penetrated into the heart of the mystery unaided and unannealed,* as the saying goes. Well! I suppose it's a matter of thirty to forty years since any human foot has trod these precincts. Certain it is that I've never set foot in them before. Well, well! what's the old proverb about angels fearing to tread?* It's proved true once again in this case.' Humphreys' acquaintance with Cooper, though it had been short, was sufficient to assure him that there was no guile in this allusion, and he forbore the obvious remark, merely suggesting that it was fully time to get back to the house for a late cup of tea, and to release Cooper for his evening engagement. They left the maze accordingly, experiencing well-nigh the same ease in retracing their path as they had in coming in.

'Have you any idea,' Humphreys asked, as they went towards the house, 'why my uncle kept that place so carefully locked?'

Cooper pulled up, and Humphreys felt that he must be on the brink of a revelation.

'I should merely be deceiving you, Mr. Humphreys, and that to no good purpose, if I laid claim to possess any information whatsoever on that topic. When I first entered upon my duties here, some eighteen years back, that maze was word for word in the condition you see it now, and the one and only occasion on which the question ever arose within my knowledge was that of which my girl made mention

in your hearing. Lady Wardrop—I've not a word to say against her—
wrote applying for admission to the maze. Your uncle showed me the
note—a most civil note—everything that could be expected from
such a quarter. "Cooper," he said, "I wish you'd reply to that note on
my behalf." "Certainly, Mr. Wilson," I said, for I was quite inured to
acting as his secretary, "what answer shall I return to it?" "Well," he
said, "give Lady Wardrop my compliments, and tell her that if ever
that portion of the grounds is taken in hand I shall be happy to give
her the first opportunity of viewing it, but that it has been shut up
now for a number of years, and I shall be grateful to her if she kindly
won't press the matter." That, Mr. Humphreys, was your good
uncle's last word on the subject, and I don't think I can add anything
to it. Unless,' added Cooper, after a pause, 'it might be just this: that,
so far as I could form a judgment, he had a dislike (as people often
will for one reason or another) to the memory of his grandfather,
who, as I mentioned to you, had that maze laid out. A man of peculiar
tenets, Mr. Humphreys, and a great traveller. You'll have the opportunity, on the coming Sabbath, of seeing the tablet to him in our little
parish church; put up it was some long time after his death.'

'Oh! I should have expected a man who had such a taste for building to have designed a mausoleum for himself.'

'Well, I've never noticed anything of the kind you mention; and, in
fact, come to think of it, I'm not at all sure that his resting-place is
within our boundaries at all: that he lays in the vault I'm pretty confident is not the case. Curious now that I shouldn't be in a position to
inform you on that heading! Still, after all, we can't say, can we, Mr.
Humphreys, that it's a point of crucial importance where the pore
mortal coils are bestowed?'

At this point they entered the house, and Cooper's speculations
were interrupted.

Tea was laid in the library, where Mr. Cooper fell upon subjects
appropriate to the scene. 'A fine collection of books! One of the finest,
I've understood from connoisseurs, in this part of the country; splen-
did plates, too, in some of these works. I recollect your uncle showing
me one with views of foreign towns—most absorbing it was: got up
in first-rate style. And another all done by hand, with the ink as fresh
as if it had been laid on yesterday, and yet, he told me, it was the work
of some old monk hundreds of years back. I've always taken a keen
interest in literature myself. Hardly anything to my mind can

compare with a good hour's reading after a hard day's work; far better than wasting the whole evening at a friend's house—and that reminds me, to be sure. I shall be getting into trouble with the wife if I don't make the best of my way home and get ready to squander away one of these same evenings! I must be off, Mr. Humphreys.'

'And that reminds *me*,' said Humphreys, 'if I'm to show Miss Cooper the maze to-morrow we must have it cleared out a bit. Could you say a word about that to the proper person?'

'Why, to be sure. A couple of men with scythes could cut out a track to-morrow morning. I'll leave word as I pass the lodge, and I'll tell them, what'll save you the trouble, perhaps, Mr. Humphreys, of having to go up and extract them yourself: that they'd better have some sticks or a tape to mark out their way with as they go on.'

'A very good idea! Yes, do that; and I'll expect Mrs. and Miss Cooper in the afternoon, and yourself about half-past ten in the morning.'

'It'll be a pleasure, I'm sure, both to them and to myself, Mr. Humphreys. Good night!'

Humphreys dined at eight. But for the fact that it was his first evening, and that Calton was evidently inclined for occasional conversation, he would have finished the novel he had bought for his journey. As it was, he had to listen and reply to some of Calton's impressions of the neighbourhood and the season: the latter, it appeared, was seasonable, and the former had changed considerably—and not altogether for the worse—since Calton's boyhood (which had been spent there). The village shop in particular had greatly improved since the year 1870. It was now possible to procure there pretty much anything you liked in reason: which was a conveniency, because suppose anything was required of a suddent (and he had known such things before now), he (Calton) could step down there (supposing the shop to be still open), and order it in, without he borrered it of the Rectory, whereas in earlier days it would have been useless to pursue such a course in respect of anything but candles, or soap, or treacle, or perhaps a penny child's picture-book, and nine times out of ten it'd be something more in the nature of a bottle of whisky *you'd* be requiring; leastways—— On the whole Humphreys thought he would be prepared with a book in future.

The library was the obvious place for the after-dinner hours. Candle in hand and pipe in mouth, he moved round the room for

some time, taking stock of the titles of the books. He had all the pre-
disposition to take interest in an old library, and there was every
opportunity for him here to make systematic acquaintance with one,
for he had learned from Cooper that there was no catalogue save the
very superficial one made for purposes of probate. The drawing up of
a *catalogue raisonné** would be a delicious occupation for winter.
There were probably treasures to be found, too: even manuscripts, if
Cooper might be trusted.

As he pursued his round the sense came upon him (as it does upon
most of us in similar places) of the extreme unreadableness of a great
portion of the collection. 'Editions of Classics and Fathers, and
Picart's *Religious Ceremonies*, and the *Harleian Miscellany*, I suppose
are all very well, but who is ever going to read Tostatus Abulensis, or
Pineda on Job,* or a book like this?' He picked out a small quarto,
loose in the binding, and from which the lettered label had fallen off;
and observing that coffee was waiting for him, retired to a chair.
Eventually he opened the book. It will be observed that his condemnation of it rested wholly on external grounds. For all he knew it
might have been a collection of unique plays, but undeniably the outside was blank and forbidding. As a matter of fact, it was a collection
of sermons or meditations, and mutilated at that, for the first sheet
was gone. It seemed to belong to the latter end of the seventeenth
century. He turned over the pages till his eye was caught by a marginal note: '*A Parable of this Unhappy Condition*,' and he thought he
would see what aptitudes the author might have for imaginative composition. 'I have heard or read,' so ran the passage, 'whether in the
way of *Parable* or true *Relation* I leave my Reader to judge, of a Man
who, like *Theseus*, in the *Attick Tale*,* should adventure himself, into
a *Labyrinth* or *Maze*: and such an one indeed as was not laid out in the
Fashion of our *Topiary* artists of this Age, but of a wide compass, in
which, moreover, such unknown Pitfalls and Snares, nay, such ill
omened Inhabitants were commonly thought to lurk as could only be
encountered at the Hazard of one's very life. Now you may be sure
that in such a Case the Disswasions of Friends were not wanting.
"Consider of such-an-one" says a Brother "how he went the way you
wot of, and was never seen more." "Or of such another" says the
Mother "that adventured himself but a little way in, and from that
day forth is so troubled in his Wits that he cannot tell what he saw,
nor hath passed one good Night." "And have you never heard" cries

a Neighbour "of what Faces have been seen to look out over the *Palisadoes* and betwixt the Bars of the Gate?" But all would not do: the Man was set upon his Purpose: for it seems it was the common fireside Talk of that Country that at the Heart and Centre of this *Labyrinth* there was a Jewel of such Price and Rarity that would enrich the Finder thereof for his life: and this should be his by right that could persever to come at it. What then? *Quid multa?** The Adventurer pass'd the Gates, and for a whole day's space his Friends without had no news of him, except it might be by some indistinct Cries heard afar off in the Night, such as made them turn in their restless Beds and sweat for very Fear, not doubting but that their Son and Brother had put one more to the *Catalogue* of those unfortunates that had suffer'd shipwreck on that Voyage. So the next day they went with weeping Tears to the Clark of the Parish to order the Bell to be toll'd. And their Way took them hard by the gate of the *Labyrinth*: which they would have hastened by, from the Horrour they had of it, but that they caught sight of a sudden of a Man's Body lying in the Roadway, and going up to it (with what Anticipations may be easily figured) found it to be him whom they reckoned as lost: and not dead, though he were in a Swound most like Death. They then, who had gone forth as Mourners came back rejoycing, and set to by all means to revive their Prodigal. Who, being come to himself, and hearing of their Anxieties and their Errand of that Morning, "Ay" says he "you may as well finish what you were about: for, for all I have brought back the Jewel (which he shew'd them, and 'twas indeed a rare Piece) I have brought back that with it that will leave me neither Rest at Night nor Pleasure by Day." Whereupon they were instant with him to learn his Meaning, and where his Company should be that went so sore against his Stomach. "O" says he " 'tis here in my Breast: I cannot flee from it, do what I may." So it needed no Wizard to help them to a guess that it was the Recollection of what he had seen that troubled him so wonderfully. But they could get no more of him for a long Time but by Fits and Starts. However at long and at last they made shift to collect somewhat of this kind: that at first, while the Sun was bright, he went merrily on, and without any Difficulty reached the Heart of the *Labyrinth* and got the Jewel, and so set out on his way back rejoycing: but as the Night fell, *wherein all the Beasts of the Forest do move*, he begun to be sensible of some Creature keeping Pace with him and, as he thought, *peering and*

looking upon him from the next Alley to that he was in; and that when
he should stop, this Companion should stop also, which put him in
some Disorder of his Spirits. And, indeed, as the Darkness increas'd,
it seemed to him that there was more than one, and, it might be, even
a whole Band of such Followers: at least so he judg'd by the Rustling
and Cracking that they kept among the Thickets; besides that there
would be at a Time a Sound of Whispering, which seem'd to import
a Conference among them. But in regard of who they were or what
Form they were of, he would not be persuaded to say what he thought.
Upon his Hearers asking him what the Cries were which they heard
in the Night (as was observ'd above) he gave them this Account: That
about Midnight (so far as he could judge) he heard his Name call'd
from a long way off, and he would have been sworn it was his Brother
that so call'd him. So he stood still and hilloo'd at the Pitch of his
Voice, and he suppos'd that the *Echo*, or the Noyse of his Shouting,
disguis'd for the Moment any lesser sound; because, when there fell
a Stillness again, he distinguish'd a Trampling (not loud) of running
Feet coming very close behind him, wherewith he was so daunted
that himself set off to run, and that he continued till the Dawn broke.
Sometimes when his Breath fail'd him, he would cast himself flat on
his Face, and hope that his Pursuers might over-run him in the
Darkness, but at such a Time they would regularly make a Pause, and
he could hear them pant and snuff as it had been a Hound at Fault:*
which wrought in him so extream an Horrour of mind, that he would
be forc'd to betake himself again to turning and doubling, if by any
Means he might throw them off the Scent. And, as if this Exertion
was in itself not terrible enough, he had before him the constant Fear
of falling into some Pit or Trap, of which he had heard, and indeed
seen with his own Eyes that there were several, some at the sides and
other in the Midst of the Alleys. So that in fine (he said) a more
dreadful Night was never spent by Mortal Creature than that he had
endur'd in that *Labyrinth*; and not that Jewel which he had in his
Wallet, nor the richest that was ever brought out of the *Indies*, could
be a sufficient Recompence to him for the Pains he had suffered.

'I will spare to set down the further Recital of this Man's Troubles,
inasmuch as I am confident my Reader's Intelligence will hit the
Parallel I desire to draw. For is not this Jewel a just Emblem of the
Satisfaction which a Man may bring back with him from a Course of
this World's Pleasures? and will not the *Labyrinth* serve for an Image

of the World itself wherein such a Treasure (if we may believe the common Voice) is stored up?'

At about this point Humphreys thought that a little Patience would be an agreeable change, and that the writer's 'improvement' of his Parable might be left to itself. So he put the book back in its former place, wondering as he did so whether his uncle had ever stumbled across that passage; and if so, whether it had worked on his fancy so much as to make him dislike the idea of a maze, and determine to shut up the one in the garden. Not long afterwards he went to bed.

The next day brought a morning's hard work with Mr. Cooper, who, if exuberant in language, had the business of the estate at his fingers' ends. He was very breezy this morning, Mr. Cooper was: had not forgotten the order to clear out the maze—the work was going on at that moment: his girl was on the tentacles* of expectation about it. He also hoped that Humphreys had slept the sleep of the just, and that we should be favoured with a continuance of this congenial weather. At luncheon he enlarged on the pictures in the dining-room, and pointed out the portrait of the constructor of the temple and the maze. Humphreys examined this with considerable interest. It was the work of an Italian, and had been painted when old Mr. Wilson was visiting Rome as a young man. (There was, indeed, a view of the Colosseum in the background.) A pale thin face and large eyes were the characteristic features. In the hand was a partially unfolded roll of paper, on which could be distinguished the plan of a circular building, very probably the temple, and also part of that of a labyrinth. Humphreys got up on a chair to examine it, but it was not painted with sufficient clearness to be worth copying. It suggested to him, however, that he might as well make a plan of his own maze and hang it in the hall for the use of visitors.

This determination of his was confirmed that same afternoon; for when Mrs. and Miss Cooper arrived, eager to be inducted into the maze, he found that he was wholly unable to lead them to the centre. The gardeners had removed the guide-marks they had been using, and even Clutterham, when summoned to assist, was as helpless as the rest. 'The point is, you see, Mr. Wilson—I should say 'Umphreys—these mazes is purposely constructed so much alike, with a view to mislead. Still, if you'll foller me, I think I can put you right. I'll just put my 'at down 'ere as a starting-point.' He stumped off, and after five minutes brought the party safe to the hat again. 'Now that's a very peculiar thing,' he said, with a sheepish laugh. 'I made sure I'd left that 'at just over against a bramble-bush, and you can see for yourself there ain't no bramble-bush not in this walk at all. If you'll allow me, Mr. Humphreys—that's the name, ain't it, sir?—I'll just call one of the men in to mark the place like.'

William Crack arrived, in answer to repeated shouts. He had some difficulty in making his way to the party. First he was seen or heard in an inside alley, then, almost at the same moment, in an outer one. However, he joined them at last, and was first consulted without effect and then stationed by the hat, which Clutterham still considered it necessary to leave on the ground. In spite of this strategy, they spent the best part of three-quarters of an hour in quite fruitless wanderings, and Humphreys was obliged at last, seeing how tired Mrs. Cooper was becoming, to suggest a retreat to tea, with profuse apologies to Miss Cooper. 'At any rate you've won your bet with Miss Foster,' he said; 'you have been inside the maze; and I promise you the first thing I do shall be to make a proper plan of it with the lines marked out for you to go by.' 'That's what's wanted, sir,' said Clutterham, 'someone to draw out a plan and keep it by them. It might be very awkward, you see, anyone getting into that place and a shower of rain come on, and them not able to find their way out again; it might be hours before they could be got out, without you'd permit of me makin' a short cut to the middle: what my meanin' is, takin' down a couple of trees in each 'edge in a straight line so as you could git a clear view right through. Of course that'd do away with it as a maze, but I don't know as you'd approve of that.'

'No, I won't have that done yet: I'll make a plan first, and let you have a copy. Later on, if we find occasion, I'll think of what you say.'

Humphreys was vexed and ashamed at the fiasco of the afternoon, and could not be satisfied without making another effort that evening to reach the centre of the maze. His irritation was increased by finding it without a single false step. He had thoughts of beginning his plan at once; but the light was fading, and he felt that by the time he had got the necessary materials together, work would be impossible.

Next morning accordingly, carrying a drawing-board, pencils, compasses, cartridge paper, and so forth (some of which had been borrowed from the Coopers and some found in the library cupboards), he went to the middle of the maze (again without any hesitation), and set out his materials. He was, however, delayed in making a start. The brambles and weeds that had obscured the column and globe were now all cleared away, and it was for the first time possible to see clearly what these were like. The column was featureless, resembling those on which sundials are usually placed. Not so the globe. I have said that it was finely engraved with figures and inscriptions, and that on a first glance Humphreys had taken it for a celestial globe: but he soon found that it did not answer to his recollection of such things. One feature seemed familiar; a winged serpent—*Draco*—encircled it about the place which, on a terrestrial globe, is occupied by the equator: but on the other hand, a good part of the upper hemisphere was covered by the outspread wings of a large figure whose head was concealed by a ring at the pole or summit of the whole. Around the place of the head the words *princeps tenebrarum** could be deciphered. In the lower hemisphere there was a space hatched all over with cross-lines and marked as *umbra mortis*.* Near it was a range of mountains, and among them a valley with flames rising from it. This was lettered (will you be surprised to learn it?) *vallis filiorum Hinnom*.* Above and below *Draco* were outlined various figures not unlike the pictures of the ordinary constellations, but not the same. Thus, a nude man with a raised club was described, not as *Hercules* but as *Cain*. Another, plunged up to his middle in earth and stretching out despairing arms, was *Chore*, not *Ophiuchus*, and a third, hung by his hair to a snaky tree, was *Absolon*.* Near the last, a man in long robes and high cap, standing in a circle and addressing two shaggy demons who hovered outside, was described as *Hostanes magus** (a character unfamiliar to Humphreys). The scheme of the whole, indeed, seemed to be an assemblage of the patriarchs of evil, perhaps not uninfluenced by a study of Dante. Humphreys thought it an unusual exhibition of his great-grand-father's taste, but reflected that he had probably picked it up in Italy and had never taken the trouble to examine it closely: certainly, had he set much store by it, he would not have exposed it to wind and weather. He tapped the metal—it seemed hollow and not very thick—and, turning from it, addressed himself to his plan. After half an hour's work he found it was impossible to get on without using a clue: so he procured a roll of twine from Clutterham, and laid it out along the alleys from the entrance to the centre, tying the end to the ring at the top of the globe. This expedient helped him to set out a rough plan before luncheon, and in the afternoon he was able to draw it in more neatly. Towards tea-time Mr. Cooper joined him, and was much interested in his progress. 'Now this——' said Mr. Cooper, laying his hand on the globe, and then drawing it away hastily. 'Whew! Holds the heat, doesn't it, to a surprising degree, Mr. Humphreys. I suppose this metal—copper, isn't it?—would be an insulator or conductor, or whatever they call it.'

'The sun has been pretty strong this afternoon,' said Humphreys, evading the scientific point, 'but I didn't notice the globe had got hot. No—it doesn't seem very hot to me,' he added.

'Odd!' said Mr. Cooper. 'Now I can't hardly bear my hand on it. Something in the difference of temperament between us, I suppose. I dare say you're a chilly subject, Mr. Humphreys: I'm not: and there's where the distinction lies. All this summer I've slept, if you'll believe me, practically *in statu quo*,* and had my morning tub as cold as I could get it. Day out and day in—let me assist you with that string.'

'It's all right, thanks; but if you'll collect some of these pencils and things that are lying about I shall be much obliged. Now I think we've got everything, and we might get back to the house.'

They left the maze, Humphreys rolling up the clue as they went.

The night was rainy.

Most unfortunately it turned out that, whether by Cooper's fault or not, the plan had been the one thing forgotten the evening before. As was to be expected, it was ruined by the wet. There was nothing for it but to begin again (the job would not be a long one this time). The clue therefore was put in place once more and a fresh start made. But Humphreys had not done much before an interruption came in the shape of Calton with a telegram. His late chief in London wanted to consult him. Only a brief interview was wanted, but the summons was urgent. This was annoying, yet it was not really upsetting; there was a train available in half an hour, and, unless things went very cross, he could be back, possibly by five o'clock, certainly by eight. He gave the plan to Calton to take to the house, but it was not worth while to remove the clue.

All went as he had hoped. He spent a rather exciting evening in the library, for he lighted to-night upon a cupboard where some of the rarer books were kept. When he went up to bed he was glad to find that the servant had remembered to leave his curtains undrawn and his windows open. He put down his light, and went to the window which commanded a view of the garden and the park. It was a brilliant moonlight night. In a few weeks' time the sonorous winds of autumn would break up all this calm. But now the distant woods were in a deep stillness; the slopes of the lawns were shining with dew; the colours of some of the flowers could almost be guessed. The light of the moon just caught the cornice of the temple and the curve of its leaden dome, and Humphreys had to own that, so seen, these conceits of a past age have a real beauty. In short, the light, the perfume of the woods, and the absolute quiet called up such kind old associations in his mind that he went on ruminating them for a long, long time. As he turned from the window he felt he had never seen anything more complete of its sort. The one feature that struck him with a sense of incongruity was a small Irish yew, thin and black, which stood out like an outpost of the shrubbery, through which the maze was approached. That, he thought, might as well be away: the wonder was that anyone should have thought it would look well in that position.

However, next morning, in the press of answering letters and going over books with Mr. Cooper, the Irish yew was forgotten. One letter, by the way, arrived this day which has to be mentioned. It was from that Lady Wardrop whom Miss Cooper had mentioned, and it renewed the application which she had addressed to Mr. Wilson. She pleaded, in the first place, that she was about to publish a Book of Mazes, and earnestly desired to include the plan of the Wilsthorpe Maze, and also that it would be a great kindness if Mr. Humphreys could let her see it (if at all) at an early date, since she would soon have to go abroad for the winter months. Her house at Bentley was not far distant, so Humphreys was able to send a note by hand to her suggesting the very next day or the day after for her visit; it may be said at once that the messenger brought back a most grateful answer, to the effect that the morrow would suit her admirably.

The only other event of the day was that the plan of the maze was successfully finished.

This night again was fair and brilliant and calm, and Humphreys lingered almost as long at his window. The Irish yew came to his mind again as he was on the point of drawing his curtains: but either he had been misled by a shadow the night before, or else the shrub was not really so obtrusive as he had fancied. Anyhow, he saw no reason for interfering with it. What he *would* do away with, however, was a clump of dark growth which had usurped a place against the house wall, and was threatening to obscure one of the lower range of windows. It did not look as if it could possibly be worth keeping; he fancied it dank and unhealthy, little as he could see of it.

Next day (it was a Friday—he had arrived at Wilsthorpe on a Monday) Lady Wardrop came over in her car soon after luncheon. She was a stout elderly person, very full of talk of all sorts and particularly inclined to make herself agreeable to Humphreys, who had gratified her very much by his ready granting of her request. They made a thorough exploration of the place together; and Lady Wardrop's opinion of her host obviously rose sky-high when she found that he really knew something of gardening. She entered enthusiastically into all his plans for improvement, but agreed that it would be a vandalism to interfere with the characteristic laying-out of the ground near the house. With the temple she was particularly delighted, and, said she, 'Do you know, Mr. Humphreys, I think your bailiff must be right about those lettered blocks of stone. One of my mazes—I'm sorry to say the stupid people have destroyed it now—it was at a place in Hampshire—had the track marked out in that way. They were tiles there, but lettered just like yours, and the letters, taken in the right order, formed an inscription—what it was I forget—something about Theseus and Ariadne. I have a copy of it, as well as the plan of the maze where it was. How people can do such things! I shall never forgive you if you injure *your* maze. Do you know, they're becoming very uncommon? Almost every year I hear of one being grubbed up. Now, do let's get straight to it: or, if you're too busy, I know my way there perfectly, and I'm not afraid of getting lost in it; I know too much about mazes for that. Though I remember missing my lunch—not so very long ago either—through getting entangled in the one at Busbury. Well, of course, if you *can* manage to come with me, that will be all the nicer.'

After this confident prelude justice would seem to require that Lady Wardrop should have been hopelessly muddled by the Wilsthorpe maze. Nothing of that kind happened: yet it is to be doubted whether she got all the enjoyment from her new specimen that she expected. She was interested—keenly interested—to be sure, and pointed out to Humphreys a series of little depressions in the ground which, she thought, marked the places of the lettered blocks. She told him, too, what other mazes resembled his most closely in arrangement, and explained how it was usually possible to date a maze to within twenty years by means of its plan. This one, she already knew, must be about as old as 1780, and its features were just what might be expected. The globe, furthermore, completely absorbed her. It was unique in her experience, and she pored over it for long. 'I should like a rubbing of that,' she said, 'if it could possibly be made. Yes, I am sure you would be most kind about it, Mr. Humphreys, but I trust you won't attempt it on my account, I do indeed; I shouldn't like to take any liberties here. I have the feeling that it might be resented. Now, confess,' she went on, turning and facing Humphreys, 'don't you feel—haven't you felt ever since you came in here—that a watch is being kept on us, and that if we over-stepped the mark in any way there would be a—well, a pounce? No? *I* do; and I don't care how soon we are outside the gate.

'After all,' she said, when they were once more on their way to the house, 'it may have been only the airlessness and the dull heat of that place that pressed on my brain. Still, I'll take back one thing I said. I'm not sure that I shan't forgive you after all, if I find next spring that that maze has been grubbed up.'

'Whether or no that's done, you shall have the plan, Lady Wardrop. I have made one, and no later than to-night I can trace you a copy.'

'Admirable: a pencil tracing will be all I want, with an indication of the scale. I can easily have it brought into line with the rest of my plates. Many, many thanks.'

'Very well, you shall have that to-morrow. I wish you could help me to a solution of my block-puzzle.'

'What, those stones in the summer-house? That *is* a puzzle; they are in no sort of order? Of course not. But the men who put them down must have had some directions—perhaps you'll find a paper about it among your uncle's things. If not, you'll have to call in some-body who's an expert in cyphers.'

'Advise me about something else, please,' said Humphreys. 'That bush-thing under the library window: you would have that away, wouldn't you?'

'Which? That? Oh, I think not,' said Lady Wardrop. 'I can't see it very well from this distance, but it's not unsightly.'

'Perhaps you're right; only, looking out of my window, just above it, last night, I thought it took up too much room. It doesn't seem to, as one sees it from here, certainly. Very well, I'll leave it alone for a bit.'

Tea was the next business, soon after which Lady Wardrop drove off; but, half-way down the drive, she stopped the car and beckoned to Humphreys, who was still on the front-door steps. He ran to glean her parting words, which were: 'It just occurs to me, it might be worth your while to look at the underside of those stones. They *must* have been numbered, mustn't they? *Good*-bye again. Home, please.'

The main occupation of this evening at any rate was settled. The tracing of the plan for Lady Wardrop and the careful collation of it with the original meant a couple of hours' work at least. Accordingly, soon after nine Humphreys had his materials put out in the library and began. It was a still, stuffy evening; windows had to stand open, and he had more than one grisly encounter with a bat. These unnerving episodes made him keep the tail of his eye on the window. Once or twice it was a question whether there was—not a bat, but something more considerable—that had a mind to join him. How unpleasant it would be if someone had slipped noiselessly over the sill and was crouching on the floor!

The tracing of the plan was done: it remained to compare it with the original, and to see whether any paths had been wrongly closed or left open. With one finger on each paper, he traced out the course that must be followed from the entrance. There were one or two slight mistakes, but here, near the centre, was a bad confusion, probably due to the entry of the Second or Third Bat. Before correcting the copy he followed out carefully the last turnings of the path on the original. These, at least, were right; they led without a hitch to the middle space. Here was a feature which need not be repeated on the copy—an ugly black spot about the size of a shilling. Ink? No. It resembled a hole, but how should a hole be there? He stared at it with tired eyes: the work of tracing had been very laborious, and he was drowsy and oppressed. . . . But surely this was a very odd hole. It seemed to go not only through the paper, but through the table on which it lay. Yes, and through the floor below that, down, and still down, even into infinite depths. He craned over it, utterly bewildered. Just as, when you were a child, you may have pored over a square inch of counterpane until it became a landscape with wooded hills, and perhaps even churches and houses, and you lost all thought of the true size of yourself and it, so this hole seemed to Humphreys for the moment the only thing in the world. For some reason it was hateful to him from the first, but he had gazed at it for some moments before any feeling of anxiety came upon him; and then it did come, stronger and stronger—a horror lest something might emerge from it, and a really agonizing conviction that a terror was on its way, from the sight of which he would not be able to escape. Oh yes, far, far down there was a movement, and the movement was upwards—towards the surface. Nearer and nearer it came, and it was of a blackish-grey colour with more than one dark hole. It took shape as a face—a human face—a *burnt* human face: and with the odious writhings of a wasp creeping out of a rotten apple there clambered forth an appearance of a form, waving black arms prepared to clasp the head that was bending over them. With a convulsion of despair Humphreys threw himself back, struck his head against a hanging lamp, and fell.

There was concussion of the brain, shock to the system, and a long confinement to bed. The doctor was badly puzzled, not by the symptoms, but by a request which Humphreys made to him as soon as he was able to say anything. 'I wish you would open the ball in the maze.' 'Hardly room enough there, I should have thought,' was the best answer he could summon up; 'but it's more in your way than mine; my dancing days are over.' At which Humphreys muttered and turned over to sleep, and the doctor intimated to the nurses that the patient was not out of the wood yet. When he was better able to express his views, Humphreys made his meaning clear, and received a promise that the thing should be done at once. He was so anxious to learn the result that the doctor, who seemed a little pensive next morning, saw that more harm than good would be done by saving up his report. 'Well,' he said, 'I am afraid the ball is done for; the metal must have worn thin, I suppose. Anyhow, it went all to bits with the first blow of the chisel.' 'Well? go on, do!' said Humphreys impatiently. 'Oh! you want to know what we found in it, of course. Well, it was half full of stuff like ashes.' 'Ashes? What did you make of them?' 'I haven't thoroughly examined them yet; there's hardly been time: but Cooper's made up his mind—I dare say from something I said—that it's a case of cremation. . . . Now don't excite yourself, my good sir: yes, I must allow I think he's probably right.'

The maze is gone, and Lady Wardrop has forgiven Humphreys; in fact, I believe he married her niece. She was right, too, in her conjecture that the stones in the temple were numbered. There had been a numeral painted on the bottom of each. Some few of these had rubbed off, but enough remained to enable Humphreys to reconstruct the inscription. It ran thus:

'PENETRANS AD INTERIORA MORTIS.'*

Grateful as Humphreys was to the memory of his uncle, he could not quite forgive him for having burnt the journals and letters of the James Wilson who had gifted Wilsthorpe with the maze and the temple. As to the circumstances of that ancestor's death and burial no tradition survived; but his will, which was almost the only record of him accessible, assigned an unusually generous legacy to a servant who bore an Italian name.

Mr. Cooper's view is that, humanly speaking, all these many solemn events have a meaning for us, if our limited intelligence permitted of our disintegrating it, while Mr. Calton has been reminded of an aunt now gone from us, who, about the year 1866, had been lost for upwards of an hour and a half in the maze at Covent Gardens, or it might be Hampton Court.*

One of the oddest things in the whole series of transactions is that the book which contained the Parable has entirely disappeared. Humphreys has never been able to find it since he copied out the passage to send to Lady Wardrop.

THE RESIDENCE AT WHITMINSTER*

D R. ASHTON—Thomas Ashton, Doctor of Divinity—sat in his study, habited in a dressing-gown, and with a silk cap on his shaven head—his wig being for the time taken off and placed on its block on a side table. He was a man of some fifty-five years, strongly made, of a sanguine complexion, an angry eye, and a long upper lip. Face and eye were lighted up at the moment when I picture him by the level ray of an afternoon sun that shone in upon him through a tall sash window, giving on the west. The room into which it shone was also tall, lined with bookcases, and, where the wall showed between them, panelled. On the table near the doctor's elbow was a green cloth, and upon it what he would have called a silver standish—a tray with inkstands—quill pens, a calf-bound book or two, some papers, a church-warden pipe and brass tobacco-box, a flask cased in plaited straw, and a liqueur glass. The year was 1730, the month December, the hour somewhat past three in the afternoon.

I have described in these lines pretty much all that a superficial observer would have noted when he looked into the room. What met Dr. Ashton's eye when he looked out of it, sitting in his leather arm-chair? Little more than the tops of the shrubs and fruit-trees of his garden could be seen from that point, but the red-brick wall of it was visible in almost all the length of its western side. In the middle of that was a gate—a double gate of rather elaborate iron scroll-work, which allowed something of a view beyond. Through it he could see that the ground sloped away almost at once to a bottom, along which a stream must run, and rose steeply from it on the other side, up to a field that was park-like in character, and thickly studded with oaks, now, of course, leafless. They did not stand so thick together but that some glimpse of sky and horizon could be seen between their stems. The sky was now golden and the horizon, a horizon of distant woods, it seemed, was purple.

But all that Dr. Ashton could find to say, after contemplating this prospect for many minutes, was: 'Abominable!'

A listener would have been aware, immediately upon this, of the sound of footsteps coming somewhat hurriedly in the direction of the study: by the resonance he could have told that they were traversing a much larger room. Dr. Ashton turned round in his chair as the door opened, and looked expectant. The incomer was a lady—a stout lady in the dress of the time: though I have made some attempt at indicating the doctor's costume, I will not enterprise that of his wife—for it was Mrs. Ashton who now entered. She had an anxious, even a sorely distracted, look, and it was in a very disturbed voice that she almost whispered to Dr. Ashton, putting her head close to his, 'He's in a very sad way, love, worse, I'm afraid.' 'Tt—tt, is he really?' and he leaned back and looked in her face. She nodded. Two solemn bells, high up, and not far away, rang out the half-hour at this moment. Mrs. Ashton started. 'Oh, do you think you can give order that the minster clock be stopped chiming to-night? 'Tis just over his chamber, and will keep him from sleeping, and to sleep is the only chance for him, that's certain.' 'Why, to be sure, if there were need, real need, it could be done, but not upon any light occasion. This Frank, now, do you assure me that his recovery stands upon it?' said Dr. Ashton: his voice was loud and rather hard. 'I do verily believe it,' said his wife. 'Then, if it must be, bid Molly run across to Simpkins and say on my authority that he is to stop the clock chimes at sunset: and—yes—she is after that to say to my lord Saul that I wish to see him presently in this room.' Mrs. Ashton hurried off.

Before any other visitor enters, it will be well to explain the situation.

Dr. Ashton was the holder, among other preferments, of a prebend in the rich collegiate church of Whitminster, one of the foundations which, though not a cathedral, survived Dissolution and Reformation, and retained its constitution and endowments for a hundred years after the time of which I write. The great church, the residences of the dean and the two prebendaries, the choir and its appurtenances, were all intact and in working order. A dean who flourished soon after 1500 had been a great builder, and had erected a spacious quadrangle of red brick adjoining the church for the residence of the officials. Some of these persons were no longer required: their offices had dwindled down to mere titles, borne by clergy or lawyers in the town and neighbourhood; and so the houses that had been meant to accommodate eight or ten people were now shared among three—the dean and the two prebendaries. Dr. Ashton's included what had been the common parlour and the dining-hall of the whole body. It occupied a whole side of the court, and at one end had a private door into the minster. The other end, as we have seen, looked out over the country.

So much for the house. As for the inmates, Dr. Ashton was a wealthy man and childless, and he had adopted, or rather undertaken to bring up, the orphan son of his wife's sister. Frank Sydall was the lad's name: he had been a good many months in the house. Then one day came a letter from an Irish peer, the Earl of Kildonan* (who had known Dr. Ashton at college), putting it to the doctor whether he would consider taking into his family the Viscount Saul, the Earl's heir, and acting in some sort as his tutor. Lord Kildonan was shortly to take up a post in the Lisbon Embassy, and the boy was unfit to make the voyage: 'not that he is sickly,' the Earl wrote, 'though you'll find him whimsical, or of late I've thought him so, and to confirm this, 'twas only to-day his old nurse came expressly to tell me he was possess'd: but let that pass; I'll warrant you can find a spell to make all straight. Your arm was stout enough in old days, and I give you plenary authority to use it as you see fit. The truth is, he has here no boys of his age or quality to consort with, and is given to moping about in our raths* and graveyards: and he brings home romances that fright my servants out of their wits. So there are you and your lady forewarned.' It was perhaps with half an eye open to the possibility of an Irish bishopric (at which another sentence in the Earl's letter seemed to hint) that Dr. Ashton accepted the charge of my Lord Viscount Saul and of the 200 guineas a year that were to come with him.

So he came, one night in September. When he got out of the chaise that brought him, he went first and spoke to the postboy and gave him some money, and patted the neck of his horse. Whether he made some movement that scared it or not, there was very nearly a nasty accident, for the beast started violently, and the postilion being unready was thrown and lost his fee, as he found afterwards, and the chaise lost some paint on the gateposts, and the wheel went over the man's foot who was taking out the baggage. When Lord Saul came up the steps into the light of the lamp in the porch to be greeted by Dr. Ashton, he was seen to be a thin youth of, say, sixteen years old, with straight black hair and the pale colouring that is common to such a figure. He took the accident and commotion calmly enough, and expressed a proper anxiety for the people who had been, or might have been, hurt: his voice was smooth and pleasant, and without any trace, curiously, of an Irish brogue.

Frank Sydall was a younger boy, perhaps of eleven or twelve, but Lord Saul did not for that reject his company. Frank was able to teach him various games he had not known in Ireland, and he was apt at learning them; apt, too, at his books, though he had had little or no regular teaching at home. It was not long before he was making a shift to puzzle out the inscriptions on the tombs in the minster, and he would often put a question to the doctor about the old books in the library that required some thought to answer. It is to be supposed that he made himself very agreeable to the servants, for within ten days of his coming they were almost falling over each other in their efforts to oblige him. At the same time, Mrs. Ashton was rather put to it to find new maidservants; for there were several changes, and some of the families in the town from which she had been accustomed to draw seemed to have no one available. She was forced to go farther afield than was usual.

These generalities I gather from the doctor's notes in his diary and from letters. They are generalities, and we should like, in view of what has to be told, something sharper and more detailed. We get it in entries which begin late in the year, and, I think, were posted up all together after the final incident; but they cover so few days in all that there is no need to doubt that the writer could remember the course of things accurately.

On a Friday morning it was that a fox, or perhaps a cat, made away with Mrs. Ashton's most prized black cockerel, a bird without a single white feather on its body. Her husband had told her often enough that it would make a suitable sacrifice to Æsculapius;* that had discomfited her much, and now she would hardly be consoled. The boys looked everywhere for traces of it: Lord Saul brought in a few feathers, which seemed to have been partially burnt on the garden rubbish-heap. It was on the same day that Dr. Ashton, looking out of an upper window, saw the two boys playing in the corner of the garden at a game he did not understand. Frank was looking earnestly at something in the palm of his hand. Saul stood behind him and seemed to be listening. After some minutes he very gently laid his hand on Frank's head, and almost instantly thereupon, Frank suddenly dropped whatever it was that he was holding, clapped his hands to his eyes, and sank down on the grass. Saul, whose face expressed great anger, hastily picked the object up, of which it could only be seen that it was glittering, put it in his pocket, and turned away, leaving Frank huddled up on the grass. Dr. Ashton rapped on the window to attract their attention, and Saul looked up as if in alarm, and then springing to Frank, pulled him up by the arm and led him away. When they came in to dinner, Saul explained that they had been acting a part of the tragedy of Radamistus,* in which the heroine reads the future fate of her father's kingdom by means of a glass ball held in her hand, and is overcome by the terrible events she has seen. During this explanation Frank said nothing, only looked rather bewilderedly at Saul. He must, Mrs. Ashton thought, have contracted a chill from the wet of the grass, for that evening he was certainly feverish and disordered; and the disorder was of the mind as well as the body, for he seemed to have something he wished to say to Mrs. Ashton, only a press of household affairs prevented her from paying attention to him; and when she went, according to her habit, to see that the light in the boys' chamber had been taken away, and to bid them good night, he seemed to be sleeping, though his face was unnaturally flushed, to her thinking: Lord Saul, however, was pale and quiet, and smiling in his slumber.

Next morning it happened that Dr. Ashton was occupied in church and other business, and unable to take the boys' lessons. He therefore set them tasks to be written and brought to him. Three times, if not oftener, Frank knocked at the study door, and each time the doctor chanced to be engaged with some visitor, and sent the boy off rather roughly, which he later regretted. Two clergymen were at dinner this day, and both remarked—being fathers of families—that the lad seemed sickening for a fever, in which they were too near the truth, and it had been better if he had been put to bed forthwith: for a couple of hours later in the afternoon he came running into the house, crying out in a way that was really terrifying, and rushing to Mrs. Ashton, clung about her, begging her to protect him, and saying, 'Keep them off! keep them off!' without intermission. And it was now evident that some sickness had taken strong hold of him. He was therefore got to bed in another chamber from that in which he commonly lay, and the physician brought to him: who pronounced the disorder to be grave and affecting the lad's brain, and prognosticated a fatal end to it if strict quiet were not observed, and those sedative remedies used which he should prescribe.

We are now come by another way to the point we had reached before. The minster clock has been stopped from striking, and Lord Saul is on the threshold of the study.

'What account can you give of this poor lad's state?' was Dr. Ashton's first question. 'Why, sir, little more than you know already, I fancy. I must blame myself, though, for giving him a fright yesterday when we were acting that silly play you saw. I fear I made him take it more to heart than I meant.' 'How so?' 'Well, by telling him foolish tales I had picked up in Ireland of what we call the second sight.' '*Second* sight! What kind of sight might that be?' 'Why, you know our ignorant people pretend that some are able to foresee what is to come—sometimes in a glass, or in the air, maybe, and at Kildonan we had an old woman that pretended to such a power. And I dare say I coloured the matter more highly than I should: but I never dreamed Frank would take it so near as he did.' 'You were wrong, my lord, very wrong, in meddling with such superstitious matters at all, and you should have considered whose house you were in, and how little becoming such actions are to my character and person or to your own: but pray how came it that you, acting, as you say, a play, should fall upon anything that could so alarm Frank?' 'That is what I can hardly tell, sir: he passed all in a moment from rant about battles and lovers and Cleodora and Antigenes* to something I could not follow at all, and then dropped down as you saw.' 'Yes: was that at the moment when you laid your hand on the top of his head?' Lord Saul gave a quick look at his questioner—quick and spiteful—and for the first time seemed unready with an answer. 'About that time it may have been,' he said. 'I have tried to recollect myself, but I am not sure. There was, at any rate, no significance in what I did then.' 'Ah!' said Dr. Ashton, 'well, my lord, I should do wrong were I not to tell you that this fright of my poor nephew may have very ill consequences to him. The doctor speaks very despondingly of his state.' Lord Saul pressed his hands together and looked earnestly upon Dr. Ashton. 'I am willing to believe you had no bad intention, as assuredly you could have no reason to bear the poor boy malice: but I cannot wholly free you from blame in the affair.' As he spoke, the hurrying steps were heard again, and Mrs. Ashton came quickly into the room, carrying a candle, for the evening had by this time closed in. She was greatly agitated. 'O come!' she cried, 'come directly. I'm sure he is going.' 'Going? Frank? Is it possible? Already?' With some such incoherent words the doctor caught up a book of prayers from the table and ran out after his wife. Lord Saul stopped for a moment where he was. Molly, the maid, saw him bend over and put both hands to his face. If it were the last words she had to speak, she said afterwards, he was striving to keep back a fit of laughing. Then he went out softly, following the others.

Mrs. Ashton was sadly right in her forecast. I have no inclination to imagine the last scene in detail. What Dr. Ashton records is, or may be taken to be, important to the story. They asked Frank if he would like to see his companion, Lord Saul, once again. The boy was quite collected, it appears, in these moments. 'No,' he said, 'I do not want to see him; but you should tell him I am afraid he will be very cold.' 'What do you mean, my dear?' said Mrs. Ashton. 'Only that,' said Frank; 'but say to him besides that I am free of them now, but he should take care. And I am sorry about your black cockerel, Aunt Ashton; but he said we must use it so, if we were to see all that could be seen.'

Not many minutes after, he was gone. Both the Ashtons were grieved, she naturally most; but the doctor, though not an emotional man, felt the pathos of the early death: and, besides, there was the growing suspicion that all had not been told him by Saul, and that there was something here which was out of his beaten track. When he left the chamber of death, it was to walk across the quadrangle of the residence to the sexton's house. A passing bell, the greatest of the minster bells, must be rung, a grave must be dug in the minster yard, and there was now no need to silence the chiming of the minster clock. As he came slowly back in the dark, he thought he must see Lord Saul again. That matter of the black cockerel—trifling as it might seem—would have to be cleared up. It might be merely a fancy of the sick boy, but if not, was there not a witch-trial he had read, in which some grim little rite of sacrifice had played a part? Yes, he must see Saul.

I rather guess these thoughts of his than find written authority for them. That there was another interview is certain: certain also that Saul would (or, as he said, could) throw no light on Frank's words: though the message, or some part of it, appeared to affect him horribly. But there is no record of the talk in detail. It is only said that Saul sat all that evening in the study, and when he bid good night, which he did most reluctantly, asked for the doctor's prayers.

The month of January was near its end when Lord Kildonan, in the Embassy at Lisbon, received a letter that for once gravely disturbed that vain man and neglectful father. Saul was dead. The scene at Frank's burial had been very distressing. The day was awful in blackness and wind: the bearers, staggering blindly along under the flapping black pall, found it a hard job, when they emerged from the porch of the minster, to make their way to the grave. Mrs. Ashton was in her room—women did not then go to their kinsfolk's funerals—but Saul was there, draped in the mourning cloak of the time, and his face was white and fixed as that of one dead, except when, as was noticed three or four times, he suddenly turned his head to the left and looked over his shoulder. It was then alive with a terrible expression of listening fear. No one saw him go away: and no one could find him that evening. All night the gale buffeted the high windows of the church, and howled over the upland and roared through the woodland. It was useless to search in the open: no voice of shouting or cry for help could possibly be heard. All that Dr. Ashton could do was to warn the people about the college, and the town constables, and to sit up, on the alert for any news, and this he did. News came early next morning, brought by the sexton, whose business it was to open the church for early prayers at seven, and who sent the maid rushing upstairs with wild eyes and flying hair to summon her master. The two men dashed across to the south door of the minster, there to find Lord Saul clinging desperately to the great ring of the door, his head sunk between his shoulders, his stockings in rags, his shoes gone, his legs torn and bloody.

This was what had to be told to Lord Kildonan, and this really ends the first part of the story. The tomb of Frank Sydall and of the Lord Viscount Saul, only child and heir to William Earl of Kildonan, is one: a stone altar tomb in Whitminster churchyard.

Dr. Ashton lived on for over thirty years in his prebendal house, I do not know how quietly, but without visible disturbance. His successor preferred a house he already owned in the town, and left that of the senior prebendary vacant. Between them these two men saw the eighteenth century out and the nineteenth in; for Mr. Hindes, the successor of Ashton, became prebendary at nine-and-twenty and died at nine-and-eighty. So that it was not till 1823 or 1824 that anyone succeeded to the post who intended to make the house his home. The man who did so was Dr. Henry Oldys, whose name may be known to some of my readers as that of the author of a row of volumes labelled *Oldys's Works*, which occupy a place that must be honoured, since it is so rarely touched, upon the shelves of many a substantial library.

Dr. Oldys, his niece, and his servants took some months to transfer furniture and books from his Dorsetshire parsonage to the quadrangle of Whitminster, and to get everything into place. But eventually the work was done, and the house (which, though untenanted, had always been kept sound and weather-tight) woke up, and like Monte Cristo's mansion at Auteuil,* lived, sang, and bloomed once more. On a certain morning in June it looked especially fair, as Dr. Oldys strolled in his garden before breakfast and gazed over the red roof at the minster tower with its four gold vanes, backed by a very blue sky, and very white little clouds.

'Mary,' he said, as he seated himself at the breakfast-table and laid down something hard and shiny on the cloth, 'here's a find which the boy made just now. You'll be sharper than I if you can guess what it's meant for.' It was a round and perfectly smooth tablet—as much as an inch thick—of what seemed clear glass. 'It is rather attractive, at all events,' said Mary: she was a fair woman, with light hair and large eyes, rather a devotee of literature. 'Yes,' said her uncle, 'I thought you'd be pleased with it. I presume it came from the house: it turned up in the rubbish-heap in the corner.' 'I'm not sure that I do like it, after all,' said Mary, some minutes later. 'Why in the world not, my dear?' 'I don't know, I'm sure. Perhaps it's only fancy.' 'Yes, only fancy and romance, of course. What's that book, now—the name of that book, I mean, that you had your head in all yesterday?' '*The Talisman,** Uncle. Oh, if this should turn out to be a talisman, how enchanting it would be!' 'Yes, *The Talisman*: ah, well, you're welcome to it, whatever it is: I must be off about my business. Is all well in the house? Does it suit you? Any complaints from the servants' hall?' 'No, indeed, nothing could be more charming. The only *soupçon* of a complaint besides the lock of the linen closet, which I told you of, is that Mrs. Maple says she cannot get rid of the sawflies out of that room you pass through at the other end of the hall. By the way, are you sure you like your bedroom? It is a long way off from anyone else, you know.' 'Like it? To be sure I do; the farther off from you, my dear, the better. There, don't think it necessary to beat me: accept my apologies. But what are sawflies? Will they eat my coats? If not, they may have the room to themselves for what I care. We are not likely to be using it.' 'No, of course not. Well, what she calls sawflies are those reddish things like a daddy-long-legs,* but smaller,[1] and there are a great many of them perching about that room, certainly. I don't like them, but I don't fancy they are mischievous.' 'There seem to be several things you don't like this fine morning,' said her uncle, as he closed the door. Miss Oldys remained in her chair looking at the tablet, which she was holding in the palm of her hand. The smile that had been on her face faded slowly from it and gave place to an expression of curiosity and almost strained attention. Her reverie was broken by the entrance of Mrs. Maple, and her invariable opening, 'Oh, Miss, could I speak to you a minute?'

A letter from Miss Oldys to a friend in Lichfield, begun a day or two before, is the next source for this story. It is not devoid of traces of the influence of that leader of female thought in her day, Miss Anna Seward, known to some as the Swan of Lichfield.*

'My sweetest Emily will be rejoiced to hear that we are at length— my beloved uncle and myself—settled in the house that now calls us master—nay, master and mistress—as in past ages it has called so many others. Here we taste a mingling of modern elegance and hoary antiquity, such as has never ere now graced life for either of us. The town, small as it is, affords us some reflection, pale indeed, but veritable, of the sweets of polite intercourse: the adjacent country numbers amid the occupants of its scattered mansions some whose polish is annually refreshed by contact with metropolitan splendour, and others whose robust and homely geniality is, at times, and by way of contrast, not less cheering and acceptable. Tired of the parlours and drawing-rooms of our friends, we have ready to hand a refuge from the clash of wits or the small talk of the day amid the solemn beauties of our venerable minster, whose silver chimes daily "knoll us to prayer," and in the shady walks of whose tranquil graveyard we muse with softened heart, and ever and anon with moistened eye, upon the memorials of the young, the beautiful, the aged, the wise, and the good.'

Here there is an abrupt break both in the writing and the style.

'But my dearest Emily, I can no longer write with the care which you deserve, and in which we both take pleasure. What I have to tell

---

[1] Apparently the ichneumon fly (*Ophion obscurum*), and not the true sawfly, is meant.

you is wholly foreign to what has gone before. This morning my uncle brought in to breakfast an object which had been found in the garden; it was a glass or crystal tablet of this shape (a little sketch is given), which he handed to me, and which, after he left the room, remained on the table by me. I gazed at it, I know not why, for some minutes, till called away by the day's duties; and you will smile incredulously when I say that I seemed to myself to begin to descry reflected in it objects and scenes which were not in the room where I was. You will not, however, think it strange that after such an experience I took the first opportunity to seclude myself in my room with what I now half believed to be a talisman of mickle might. I was not disappointed. I assure you, Emily, by that memory which is dearest to both of us, that what I went through this afternoon transcends the limits of what I had before deemed credible. In brief, what I saw, seated in my bedroom, in the broad daylight of summer, and looking into the crystal depth of that small round tablet, was this. First, a prospect, strange to me, of an enclosure of rough and hillocky grass, with a grey stone ruin in the midst, and a wall of rough stones about it. In this stood an old, and very ugly, woman in a red cloak and ragged skirt, talking to a boy dressed in the fashion of maybe a hundred years ago. She put something which glittered into his hand, and he something into hers, which I saw to be money, for a single coin fell from her trembling hand into the grass. The scene passed: I should have remarked, by the way, that on the rough walls of the enclosure I could distinguish bones, and even a skull, lying in a disorderly fashion. Next, I was looking upon two boys; one the figure of the former vision, the other younger. They were in a plot of garden, walled round, and this garden, in spite of the difference in arrangement, and the small size of the trees, I could clearly recognize as being that upon which I now look from my window. The boys were engaged in some curious play, it seemed. Something was smouldering on the ground. The elder placed his hands upon it, and then raised them in what I took to be an attitude of prayer: and I saw, and started at seeing, that on them were deep stains of blood. The sky above was overcast. The same boy now turned his face towards the wall of the garden, and beckoned with both his raised hands, and as he did so I was conscious that some moving objects were becoming visible over the top of the wall—whether heads or other parts of some animal or human forms I could not tell. Upon the instant the elder boy turned sharply, seized the arm of the younger (who all this time had been poring over what lay on the ground), and both hurried off. I then saw blood upon the grass, a little pile of bricks, and what I thought were black feathers scattered about. That scene closed, and the next was so dark that perhaps the full meaning of it escaped me. But what I seemed to see was a form, at first crouching low among trees or bushes that were being threshed by a violent wind, then running very swiftly, and constantly turning a pale face to look behind him, as if he feared a pursuer: and, indeed, pursuers were following hard after him. Their shapes were but dimly seen, their number—three or four, perhaps—only guessed. I suppose they were on the whole more like dogs than anything else, but dogs such as we have seen they assuredly were not. Could I have closed my eyes to this horror, I would have done so at once, but I was helpless. The last I saw was the victim darting beneath an arch and clutching at some object to which he clung: and those that were pursuing him overtook him, and I seemed to hear the echo of a cry of despair. It may be that I became unconscious: certainly I had the sensation of awaking to the light of day after an interval of darkness. Such, in literal truth, Emily, was my vision—I can call it by no other name—of this afternoon. Tell me, have I not been the unwilling witness of some episode of a tragedy connected with this very house?'

The letter is continued next day. 'The tale of yesterday was not completed when I laid down my pen. I said nothing of my experiences to my uncle—you know, yourself, how little his robust common sense would be prepared to allow of them, and how in his eyes the specific remedy would be a black draught or a glass of port. After a silent evening, then—silent, not sullen—I retired to rest. Judge of my terror, when, not yet in bed, I heard what I can only describe as a distant bellow, and knew it for my uncle's voice, though never in my hearing so exerted before. His sleeping-room is at the farther extremity of this large house, and to gain access to it one must traverse an antique hall some eighty feet long, a lofty panelled chamber, and two unoccupied bedrooms. In the second of these—a room almost devoid of furniture—I found him, in the dark, his candle lying smashed on the floor. As I ran in, bearing a light, he clasped me in arms that trembled for the first time since I have known him, thanked God, and hurried me out of the room. He would say nothing of what had alarmed him. "To-morrow, to-morrow," was all I could get from him. A bed was hastily improvised for him in the room next to my own. I doubt if his night was more restful than mine. I could only get to sleep in the small hours, when daylight was already strong, and then my dreams were of the grimmest—particularly one which stamped itself on my brain, and which I must set down on the chance of dispersing the impression it has made. It was that I came up to my room with a heavy foreboding of evil oppressing me, and went with a hesitation and reluctance I could not explain to my chest of drawers. I opened the top drawer, in which was nothing but ribbons and handkerchiefs, and then the second, where was as little to alarm, and then, O heavens, the third and last: and there was a mass of linen neatly folded: upon which, as I looked with a curiosity that began to be tinged with horror, I perceived a movement in it, and a pink hand was thrust out of the folds and began to grope feebly in the air. I could bear it no more, and rushed from the room, clapping the door after me, and strove with all my force to lock it. But the key would not turn in the wards, and from within the room came a sound of rustling and bumping, drawing nearer and nearer to the door. Why I did not flee down the stairs I know not. I continued grasping the handle, and mercifully, as the door was plucked from my hand with an irresistible force, I awoke. You may not think this very alarming, but I assure you it was so to me.

'At breakfast to-day my uncle was very uncommunicative, and I think ashamed of the fright he had given us; but afterwards he inquired of me whether Mr. Spearman was still in town, adding that he thought that was a young man who had some sense left in his head. I think you know, my dear Emily, that I am not inclined to disagree with him there, and also that I was not unlikely to be able to answer his question. To Mr. Spearman he accordingly went, and I have not seen him since. I must send this strange budget of news to you now, or it may have to wait over more than one post.'

The reader will not be far out if he guesses that Miss Mary and Mr. Spearman made a match of it not very long after this month of June. Mr. Spearman was a young spark, who had a good property in the neighbourhood of Whitminster, and not unfrequently about this time spent a few days at the 'King's Head,' ostensibly on business. But he must have had some leisure, for his diary is copious, especially for the days of which I am telling the story. It is probable to me that he wrote this episode as fully as he could at the bidding of Miss Mary.

'Uncle Oldys (how I hope I may have the right to call him so before long!) called this morning. After throwing out a good many short remarks on indifferent topics, he said, "I wish, Spearman, you'd listen to an odd story and keep a close tongue about it just for a bit, till I get more light on it." "To be sure," said I, "you may count on me." "I don't know what to make of it," he said. "You know my bedroom. It is well away from everyone else's, and I pass through the great hall and two or three other rooms to get to it." "Is it at the end next the minster, then?" I asked. "Yes, it is: well, now, yesterday morning my Mary told me that the room next before it was infested with some sort of fly that the housekeeper couldn't get rid of. That may be the explanation, or it may not. What do you think?" "Why," said I, "you've not yet told me what has to be explained." "True enough, I don't believe I have; but by the by, what are these saw flies? What's the size of them?" I began to wonder if he was touched in the head. "What I call a sawfly," I said very patiently, "is a red animal, like a daddy-long-legs, but not so big, perhaps an inch long, perhaps less. It is very hard in the body, and to me"—I was going to say "particularly offensive," but he broke in, "Come, come; an inch or less. That won't do." "I can only tell you," I said, "what I know. Would it not be better if you told me from first to last what it is that has puzzled you, and then I may be able to give you some kind of an opinion." He gazed at me meditatively. "Perhaps it would," he said. "I told Mary only to-day that I thought you had some vestiges of sense in your head." (I bowed my acknowledgments.) "The thing is, I've an odd kind of shyness about talking of it. Nothing of the sort has happened to me before. Well, about eleven o'clock last night, or after, I took my candle and set out for my room. I had a book in my other hand—I always read something for a few minutes before I drop off to sleep. A dangerous habit: I don't recommend it: but *I* know how to manage my light and my bed curtains. Now then, first, as I stepped out of my study into the great hall that's next to it, and shut the door, my candle went out. I supposed I had clapped the door behind me too quick, and made a draught, and I was annoyed, for I'd no tinder-box nearer than my bedroom. But I knew my way well enough, and went on. The next thing was that my book was struck out of my hand in the dark: if I said twitched out of my hand it would better express the sensation. It fell on the floor. I picked it up, and went on, more annoyed than before, and a little startled. But as you know, that hall has many windows

without curtains, and in summer nights like these it's easy to see not
only where the furniture is, but whether there's anyone or anything
moving: and there was no one—nothing of the kind. So on I went
through the hall and through the audit chamber next to it, which also
has big windows, and then into the bedrooms which lead to my own,
where the curtains were drawn, and I had to go slower because of steps
here and there. It was in the second of those rooms that I nearly got
my *quietus*.* The moment I opened the door of it I felt there was something wrong. I thought twice, I confess, whether I shouldn't turn back
and find another way there is to my room rather than go through that
one. Then I was ashamed of myself, and thought what people call better of it, though I don't know about 'better' in this case. If I was to
describe my experience exactly, I should say this: there was a dry,
light, rustling sound all over the room as I went in, and then (you
remember it was perfectly dark) something seemed to rush at me, and
there was—I don't know how to put it—a sensation of long thin arms,
or legs, or feelers, all about my face, and neck, and body. Very little
strength in them, there seemed to be, but, Spearman, I don't think I
was ever more horrified or disgusted in all my life, that I remember:
and it does take something to put me out. I roared out as loud as I
could, and flung away my candle at random, and, knowing I was near
the window, I tore at the curtain and somehow let in enough light to
be able to see something waving which I knew was an insect's leg, by
the shape of it: but, Lord, what a size! Why, the beast must have been
as tall as I am. And now you tell me sawflies are an inch long or less.
What do you make of it, Spearman?"

' "For goodness' sake finish your story first," I said. "I never heard
anything like it." "Oh," said he, "there's no more to tell. Mary ran in
with a light, and there was nothing there. I didn't tell her what was
the matter. I changed my room for last night, and I expect for good."
"Have you searched this odd room of yours?" I said. "What do you
keep in it?" "We don't use it," he answered. "There's an old press
there, and some little other furniture." "And in the press?" said I. "I
don't know; I never saw it opened, but I do know that it's locked."
"Well, I should have it looked into, and, if you had time, I own to
having some curiosity to see the place myself." "I didn't exactly like
to ask you, but that's rather what I hoped you'd say. Name your time
and I'll take you there." "No time like the present," I said at once, for
I saw he would never settle down to anything while this affair was in

suspense. He got up with great alacrity, and looked at me, I am tempted to think, with marked approval. "Come along," was all he said, however; and was pretty silent all the way to his house. My Mary (as he calls her in public, and I in private) was summoned, and we proceeded to the room. The Doctor had gone so far as to tell her that he had had something of a fright there last night, of what nature he had not yet divulged; but now he pointed out and described, very briefly, the incidents of his progress. When we were near the important spot, he pulled up, and allowed me to pass on. "There's the room," he said. "Go in, Spearman, and tell us what you find." Whatever I might have felt at midnight, noonday I was sure would keep back anything sinister, and I flung the door open with an air and stepped in. It was a well-lighted room, with its large window on the right, though not, I thought, a very airy one. The principal piece of furniture was the gaunt old press of dark wood. There was, too, a four-post bedstead, a mere skeleton which could hide nothing, and there was a chest of drawers. On the window-sill and the floor near it were the dead bodies of many hundred sawflies, and one torpid one which I had some satisfaction in killing. I tried the door of the press, but could not open it: the drawers, too, were locked. Somewhere, I was conscious, there was a faint rustling sound, but I could not locate it, and when I made my report to those outside, I said nothing of it. But, I said, clearly the next thing was to see what was in those locked receptacles. Uncle Oldys turned to Mary. "Mrs. Maple," he said, and Mary ran off—no one, I am sure, steps like her—and soon came back at a soberer pace, with an elderly lady of discreet aspect.

'"Have you the keys of these things, Mrs. Maple?" said Uncle Oldys. His simple words let loose a torrent (not violent, but copious) of speech: had she been a shade or two higher in the social scale, Mrs. Maple might have stood as the model for Miss Bates.*

'"Oh, Doctor, and Miss, and you too, sir," she said, acknowledging my presence with a bend, "them keys! who was that again that come when first we took over things in this house—a gentleman in business it was, and I gave him his luncheon in the small parlour on account of us not having everything as we should like to see it in the large one— chicken, and apple-pie, and a glass of madeira—dear, dear, you'll say I'm running on, Miss Mary; but I only mention it to bring back my recollection; and there it comes—Gardner, just the same as it did last week with the artichokes and the text of the sermon. Now that

Mr. Gardner, every key I got from him were labelled to itself, and each and every one was a key of some door or another in this house, and sometimes two; and when I say door, my meaning is door of a room, not like such a press as this is. Yes, Miss Mary, I know full well, and I'm just making it clear to your uncle and you too, sir. But now there *was* a box which this same gentleman he give over into my charge, and thinking no harm after he was gone I took the liberty, knowing it was your uncle's property, to rattle it: and unless I'm most surprisingly deceived, in that box there was keys, but what keys, that, Doctor, is known Elsewhere, for open the box, no that I would not do."

'I wondered that Uncle Oldys remained as quiet as he did under this address. Mary, I knew, was amused by it, and he probably had been taught by experience that it was useless to break in upon it. At any rate he did not, but merely said at the end, "Have you that box handy, Mrs. Maple? If so, you might bring it here." Mrs. Maple pointed her finger at him, either in accusation or in gloomy triumph. "There," she said, "was I to choose out the very words out of your mouth, Doctor, them would be the ones. And if I've took it to my own rebuke one half a dozen times, it's been nearer fifty. Laid awake I have in my bed, sat down in my chair I have, the same you and Miss Mary gave me the day I was twenty year in your service, and no person could desire a better—yes, Miss Mary, but it *is* the truth, and well we know who it is would have it different if he could. 'All very well,' says I to myself, 'but pray, when the Doctor calls you to account for that box, what are you going to say?' No, Doctor, if you was some masters I've heard of and I was some servants I could name, I should have an easy task before me, but things being, humanly speaking, what they are, the one course open to me is just to say to you that without Miss Mary comes to my room and helps me to my recollection, which her wits *may* manage what's slipped beyond mine, no such box as that, small though it be, will cross your eyes this many a day to come."

' "Why, dear Mrs. Maple, why didn't you tell me before that you wanted me to help you to find it?" said my Mary. "No, never mind telling me why it was: let us come at once and look for it." They hastened off together. I could hear Mrs. Maple beginning an explanation which, I doubt not, lasted into the farthest recesses of the house-keeper's department. Uncle Oldys and I were left alone. "A valuable servant," he said, nodding towards the door. "Nothing goes wrong under her: the speeches are seldom over three minutes." "How will Miss Oldys manage to make her remember about the box?" I asked.

' "Mary? Oh, she'll make her sit down and ask her about her aunt's last illness, or who gave her the china dog on the mantelpiece— something quite off the point. Then, as Maple says, one thing brings up another, and the right one will come round sooner than you could suppose. There! I believe I hear them coming back already."

'It was indeed so, and Mrs. Maple was hurrying on ahead of Mary with the box in her outstretched hand, and a beaming face. "What was it," she cried as she drew near, "what was it as I said, before ever I come out of Dorsetshire to this place? Not that I'm a Dorset woman myself, nor had need to be. 'Safe bind, safe find,' and there it was in the place where I'd put it—what?—two months back, I dare say." She handed it to Uncle Oldys, and he and I examined it with some interest, so that I ceased to pay attention to Mrs. Ann Maple for the moment, though I know that she went on to expound exactly where the box had been, and in what way Mary had helped to refresh her memory on the subject.

'It was an oldish box, tied with pink tape and sealed, and on the lid was pasted a label inscribed in old ink, "The Senior Prebendary's House, Whitminster." On being opened it was found to contain two keys of moderate size, and a paper, on which, in the same hand as the label, was "Keys of the Press and Box of Drawers standing in the disused Chamber." Also this: "The Effects in this Press and Box are held by me, and to be held by my successors in the Residence, in trust for the noble Family of Kildonan, if claim be made by any survivor of it. I having made all the Enquiry possible to myself am of the opinion that that noble House is wholly extinct: the last Earl having been, as is notorious, cast away at sea, and his only Child and Heire deceas'd in my House (the Papers as to which melancholy Casualty were by me repos'd in the same Press in this year of our Lord 1753, 21 March). I am further of opinion that unless grave discomfort arise, such persons, not being of the Family of Kildonan, as shall become possess'd of these keys, will be well advised to leave matters as they are: which opinion I do not express without weighty and sufficient reason; and am Happy to have my Judgment confirm'd by the other Members of this College and Church who are conversant with the Events referr'd to in this Paper. Tho. Ashton, *S.T.P.*, *Præb. senr*. Will. Blake, *S.T.P.*, *Decanus*. Hen. Goodman, *S.T.B.*, *Præb. junr*."*

' "Ah!" said Uncle Oldys, "grave discomfort! So he thought there might be something. I suspect it was that young man," he went on, pointing with the key to the line about the "only Child and Heire." "Eh, Mary? The viscounty of Kildonan was Saul." "How *do* you know that, Uncle?" said Mary. "Oh, why not? it's all in Debrett*— two little fat books. But I meant the tomb by the lime walk. He's there. What's the story, I wonder? Do you know it, Mrs. Maple? and, by the way, look at your sawflies by the window there."

'Mrs. Maple, thus confronted with two subjects at once, was a little put to it to do justice to both. It was no doubt rash in Uncle Oldys to give her the opportunity. I could only guess that he had some slight hesitation about using the key he held in his hand.

' "Oh them flies, how bad they was, Doctor and Miss, this three or four days: and you, too, sir, you wouldn't guess, none of you! And how they come; too! First we took the room in hand, the shutters was up, and had been, I dare say, years upon years, and not a fly to be seen. Then we got the shutter bars down with a deal of trouble and left it so for the day, and next day I sent Susan in with the broom to sweep about, and not two minutes hadn't passed when out she come into the hall like a blind thing, and we had regular to beat them off her. Why, her cap and her hair, you couldn't see the colour of it, I do assure you, and all clustering round her eyes, too. Fortunate enough she's not a girl with fancies, else if it had been me, why only the tickling of the nasty things would have drove me out of my wits. And now there they lay like so many dead things. Well, they was lively enough on the Monday, and now here's Thursday, is it, or no, Friday. Only to come near the door and you'd hear them pattering up against it, and once you opened it, dash at you, they would, as if they'd eat you. I couldn't help thinking to myself, 'If you was bats, where should we be this night?' Nor you can't cresh 'em, not like a usual kind of a fly. Well, there's something to be thankful for, if we could but learn by it. And then this tomb, too," she said, hastening on to her second point to elude any chance of interruption, "of them two poor young lads. I say poor, and yet when I recollect myself, I was at tea with Mrs. Simpkins, the sexton's wife, before you come, Doctor and Miss Mary, and that's a family has been in the place, what? I dare say a hundred years in that very house, and could put their hand on any tomb or yet grave in all the yard and give you name and age. And his account of that young man, Mr. Simpkins's I mean to say—*well!"*

She compressed her lips and nodded several times. "Tell us, Mrs. Maple," said Mary. "Go on," said Uncle Oldys. "What about him?" said I. "Never was such a thing seen in this place, not since Queen Mary's times and the Pope and all," said Mrs. Maple. "Why, do you know he lived in this very house, him and them that was with him, and for all I can tell in this identical room" (she shifted her feet uneasily on the floor). "Who was with him? Do you mean the people of the house?" said Uncle Oldys suspiciously. "Not to call people, Doctor, dear no," was the answer; "more what he brought with him from Ireland, I believe it was. No, the people in the house was the last to hear anything of his goings-on. But in the town not a family but knew how he stopped out at night: and them that was with him, why, they were such as would strip the skin from the child in its grave; and a withered heart makes an ugly thin ghost,* says Mr. Simpkins. But they turned on him at the last, he says, and there's the mark still to be seen on the minster door where they run him down. And that's no more than the truth, for I got him to show it to myself, and that's what he said. A lord he was, with a Bible name of a wicked king, whatever his godfathers could have been thinking of." "Saul was the name," said Uncle Oldys. "To be sure it was Saul, Doctor, and thank you; and now isn't it King Saul that we read of raising up the dead ghost* that was slumbering in its tomb till he disturbed it, and isn't that a strange thing, this young lord to have such a name, and Mr. Simpkins's grandfather to see him out of his window of a dark night going about from one grave to another in the yard with a candle, and them that was with him following through the grass at his heels: and one night him to come right up to old Mr. Simpkins's window that gives on the yard and press his face up against it to find out if there was anyone in the room that could see him: and only just time there was for old Mr. Simpkins to drop down like, quiet, just under the window and hold his breath, and not stir till he heard him stepping away again, and this rustling-like in the grass after him as he went, and then when he looked out of his window in the morning there was treadings in the grass and a dead man's bone. Oh, he was a cruel child for certain, but he had to pay in the end, and after." "After?" said Uncle Oldys, with a frown. "Oh yes, Doctor, night after night in old Mr. Simpkins's time, and his son, that's our Mr. Simpkins's father, yes, and our own Mr. Simpkins too. Up against that same window, particular when they've had a fire of a chilly evening, with his face right on the panes, and his hands fluttering out, and his mouth open and shut, open and shut, for a minute or more, and then gone off in the dark yard. But open the window at such times, no, that they dare not do, though they could find it in their heart to pity the poor thing, that pinched up with the cold, and seemingly fading away to a noth-ink as the years passed on. Well, indeed, I believe it is no more than the truth what our Mr. Simpkins says on his own grandfather's word, 'A withered heart makes an ugly thin ghost.'" "I dare say," said Uncle Oldys suddenly: so suddenly that Mrs. Maple stopped short. "Thank you. Come away, all of you." "Why, *Uncle*," said Mary, "are you not going to open the press after all?" Uncle Oldys blushed, actu-ally blushed. "My dear," he said, "you are at liberty to call me a cow-ard, or applaud me as a prudent man, whichever you please. But I am neither going to open that press nor that chest of drawers myself, nor am I going to hand over the keys to you or to any other person. Mrs. Maple, will you kindly see about getting a man or two to move those pieces of furniture into the garret?" "And when they do it, Mrs. Maple," said Mary, who seemed to me—I did not then know why—more relieved than disappointed by her uncle's decision, "I have something that I want put with the rest; only quite a small packet."

'We left that curious room not unwillingly, I think. Uncle Oldys's orders were carried out that same day. And so,' concludes Mr. Spearman, 'Whitminster has a Bluebeard's chamber,* and, I am rather inclined to suspect, a Jack-in-the-box, awaiting some future occupant of the residence of the senior prebendary.'

THE DIARY OF MR. POYNTER

❦

T HE sale-room of an old and famous firm of book auctioneers in London is, of course, a great meeting-place for collectors, librarians, and dealers: not only when an auction is in progress, but perhaps even more notably when books that are coming on for sale are upon view. It was in such a sale-room that the remarkable series of events began which were detailed to me not many months ago by the person whom they principally affected—namely, Mr. James Denton, M.A., F.S.A., etc., etc., sometime of Trinity Hall, now, or lately, of Rendcomb Manor in the county of Warwick.*

He, on a certain spring day in a recent year, was in London for a few days upon business connected principally with the furnishing of the house which he had just finished building at Rendcomb. It may be a disappointment to you to learn that Rendcomb Manor was new; that I cannot help. There had, no doubt, been an old house; but it was not remarkable for beauty or interest. Even had it been, neither beauty nor interest would have enabled it to resist the disastrous fire which about a couple of years before the date of my story had razed it to the ground. I am glad to say that all that was most valuable in it had been saved, and that it was fully insured. So that it was with a comparatively light heart that Mr. Denton was able to face the task of building a new and considerably more convenient dwelling for himself and his aunt who constituted his whole *ménage*.

Being in London, with time on his hands, and not far from the sale-room at which I have obscurely hinted, Mr. Denton thought that he would spend an hour there upon the chance of finding, among that portion of the famous Thomas collection of MSS.,* which he knew to be then on view, something bearing upon the history or topography of his part of Warwickshire.

He turned in accordingly, purchased a catalogue and ascended to the sale-room, where, as usual, the books were disposed in cases and some laid out upon the long tables. At the shelves, or sitting about at the tables, were figures, many of whom were familiar to him. He exchanged nods and greetings with several, and then settled down to examine his catalogue and note likely items. He had made good progress through about two hundred of the five hundred lots—every now and then rising to take a volume from the shelf and give it a cursory glance—when a hand was laid on his shoulder, and he looked up. His interrupter was one of those intelligent men with a pointed beard and a flannel shirt, of whom the last quarter of the nineteenth century was, it seems to me, very prolific.

It is no part of my plan to repeat the whole conversation which ensued between the two. I must content myself with stating that it largely referred to common acquaintances, e.g., to the nephew of Mr. Denton's friend who had recently married and settled in Chelsea, to the sister-in-law of Mr. Denton's friend who had been seriously indisposed, but was now better, and to a piece of china which Mr. Denton's friend had purchased some months before at a price much below its true value. From which you will rightly infer that the conversation was rather in the nature of a monologue. In due time, however, the friend bethought himself that Mr. Denton was there for a purpose, and said he, 'What are you looking out for in particular? I don't think there's much in this lot.' 'Why, I thought there might be some Warwickshire collections, but I don't see anything under Warwick in the catalogue.' 'No, apparently not,' said the friend. 'All the same, I believe I noticed something like a Warwickshire diary. What was the name again? Drayton? Potter? Painter—either a P or a D, I feel sure.' He turned over the leaves quickly. 'Yes, here it is. Poynter. Lot 486. That might interest you. There are the books, I think: out on the table. Someone has been looking at them. Well, I must be getting on. Good-bye—you'll look us up, won't you? Couldn't you come this afternoon? we've got a little music about four. Well, then, when you're next in town.' He went off. Mr. Denton looked at his watch and found to his confusion that he could spare no more than a moment before retrieving his luggage and going for the train. The moment was just enough to show him that there were four largish volumes of the diary—that it concerned the years about 1710, and that there seemed to be a good many insertions in it of various kinds. It seemed quite worth while to leave a commission of five and twenty pounds for it, and this he was able to do, for his usual agent entered the room as he was on the point of leaving it.

That evening he rejoined his aunt at their temporary abode, which was a small dower-house not many hundred yards from the Manor. On the following morning the two resumed a discussion that had now lasted for some weeks as to the equipment of the new house. Mr. Denton laid before his relative a statement of the results of his visit to town—particulars of carpets, of chairs, of wardrobes, and of bedroom china. 'Yes, dear,' said his aunt, 'but I don't see any chintzes here. Did you go to——?' Mr. Denton stamped on the floor (where else, indeed, could he have stamped?). 'Oh dear, oh dear,' he said, 'the one thing I missed. I *am* sorry. The fact is I was on my way there and I happened to be passing Robins's.' His aunt threw up her hands. 'Robins's! Then the next thing will be another parcel of horrible old books at some outrageous price. I do think, James, when I am taking all this trouble for you, you might contrive to remember the one or two things which I specially begged you to see after. It's not as if I was asking it for myself. I don't know whether you think I get any pleasure out of it, but if so I can assure you it's very much the reverse. The thought and worry and trouble I have over it you have no idea of, and *you* have simply to go to the shops and order the things.' Mr. Denton interposed a moan of penitence. 'Oh, aunt——' 'Yes, that's all very well, dear, and I don't want to speak sharply, but you *must* know how very annoying it is: particularly as it delays the whole of our business for I can't tell how long: here is Wednesday—the Simpsons come to-morrow, and you can't leave them. Then on Saturday we have friends, as you know, coming for tennis. Yes, indeed, you spoke of asking them yourself, but, of course, I had to write the notes, and it is ridiculous, James, to look like that. We must occasionally be civil to our neighbours: you wouldn't like to have it said we were perfect bears. What was I saying? Well, anyhow it comes to this, that it must be Thursday in next week at least, before you can go to town again, and until we have decided upon the chintzes it is impossible to settle upon one single other thing.'

Mr. Denton ventured to suggest that as the paint and wallpapers had been dealt with, this was too severe a view: but this his aunt was not prepared to admit at the moment. Nor, indeed, was there any proposition he could have advanced which she would have found herself able to accept. However, as the day went on, she receded a little from this position: examined with lessening disfavour the samples and price lists submitted by her nephew, and even in some cases gave a qualified approval to his choice.

As for him, he was naturally somewhat dashed by the consciousness of duty unfulfilled, but more so by the prospect of a lawn-tennis party, which, though an inevitable evil in August, he had thought there was no occasion to fear in May. But he was to some extent cheered by the arrival on the Friday morning of an intimation that he had secured at the price of £12 10s. the four volumes of Poynter's manuscript diary, and still more by the arrival on the next morning of the diary itself.

The necessity of taking Mr. and Mrs. Simpson for a drive in the car on Saturday morning and of attending to his neighbours and guests that afternoon prevented him from doing more than open the parcel until the party had retired to bed on the Saturday night. It was then that he made certain of the fact, which he had before only suspected, that he had indeed acquired the diary of Mr. William Poynter, Squire of Acrington* (about four miles from his own parish)—that same Poynter who was for a time a member of the circle of Oxford antiquaries, the centre of which was Thomas Hearne,* and with whom Hearne seems ultimately to have quarrelled—a not uncommon episode in the career of that excellent man. As is the case with Hearne's own collections, the diary of Poynter contained a good many notes from printed books, descriptions of coins and other antiquities that had been brought to his notice, and drafts of letters on these subjects, besides the chronicle of everyday events. The description in the sale-catalogue had given Mr. Denton no idea of the amount of interest which seemed to lie in the book, and he sat up reading in the first of the four volumes until a reprehensibly late hour.

On the Sunday morning, after church, his aunt came into the study and was diverted from what she had been going to say to him by the sight of the four brown leather quartos on the table. 'What are these?' she said suspiciously. 'New, aren't they? Oh! are these the things that made you forget my chintzes? I thought so. Disgusting. What did you give for them, I should like to know? Over Ten Pounds? James, it is really sinful. Well, if you have money to throw away on this kind of thing, there *can* be no reason why you should not subscribe—and subscribe handsomely—to my anti-Vivisection League.* There is not, indeed, James, and I shall be very seriously annoyed if——. Who did you say wrote them? Old Mr. Poynter, of Acrington? Well, of course, there is some interest in getting together old papers about this neighbourhood. But Ten Pounds!' She picked up one of the volumes—not that which her nephew had been reading—and opened it at random, dashing it to the floor the next instant with a cry of disgust as an earwig fell from between the pages. Mr. Denton picked it up with a smothered expletive and said, 'Poor book! I think you're rather hard on Mr. Poynter.' 'Was I, my dear? I beg his pardon, but you know I cannot abide those horrid creatures. Let me see if I've done any mischief.' 'No, I think all's well: but look here what you've opened him on.' 'Dear me, yes, to be sure! how very interesting. Do unpin it, James, and let me look at it.'

It was a piece of patterned stuff about the size of the quarto page, to which it was fastened by an old-fashioned pin. James detached it and handed it to his aunt, carefully replacing the pin in the paper.

Now, I do not know exactly what the fabric was; but it had a design printed upon it, which completely fascinated Miss Denton. She went into raptures over it, held it against the wall, made James do the same, that she might retire to contemplate it from a distance: then pored over it at close quarters, and ended her examination by expressing in the warmest terms her appreciation of the taste of the ancient Mr. Poynter who had had the happy idea of preserving this sample in his diary. 'It is a most charming pattern,' she said, 'and remarkable too. Look, James, how delightfully the lines ripple. It reminds one of hair, very much, doesn't it? And then these knots of ribbon at intervals. They give just the relief of colour that is wanted. I wonder——' 'I was going to say,' said James with deference, 'I wonder if it would cost much to have it copied for our curtains.' 'Copied? how could you have it copied, James?' 'Well, I don't know the details, but I suppose that is a printed pattern, and that you could have a block cut from it in wood or metal.' 'Now, really, that is a capital idea, James. I am almost inclined to be glad that you were so—that you forgot the chintzes on Wednesday. At any rate, I'll promise to forgive and forget if you get this *lovely* old thing copied. No one will have anything in the least like it, and mind, James, we won't allow it to be sold. Now I *must* go, and I've totally forgotten what it was I came in to say: never mind, it'll keep.'

After his aunt had gone James Denton devoted a few minutes to examining the pattern more closely than he had yet had a chance of doing. He was puzzled to think why it should have struck Miss Denton so forcibly. It seemed to him not specially remarkable or pretty. No doubt it was suitable enough for a curtain pattern: it ran in vertical bands, and there was some indication that these were intended to converge at the top. She was right, too, in thinking that these main bands resembled rippling—almost curling—tresses of hair. Well, the main thing was to find out by means of trade directories, or otherwise, what firm would undertake the reproduction of an old pattern of this kind. Not to delay the reader over this portion of the story, a list of likely names was made out, and Mr. Denton fixed a day for calling on them, or some of them, with his sample.

The first two visits which he paid were unsuccessful: but there is luck in odd numbers. The firm in Bermondsey* which was third on his list was accustomed to handling this line. The evidence they were able to produce justified their being entrusted with the job. 'Our Mr. Cattell' took a fervent personal interest in it. 'It's 'eartrending, isn't it, sir,' he said, 'to picture the quantity of reelly lovely medeevial stuff of this kind that lays wellnigh unnoticed in many of our residential country 'ouses: much of it in peril, I take it, of being cast aside as so much rubbish. What is it Shakespeare says—unconsidered trifles.* Ah, I often say he 'as a word for us all, sir. I say Shakespeare, but I'm well aware all don't 'old with me there—I 'ad something of an upset the other day when a gentleman came in—a titled man, too, he was, and I think he told me he'd wrote on the topic, and I 'appened to cite out something about 'Ercules and the painted cloth.* Dear me, you never see such a pother. But as to this, what you've kindly confided to us, it's a piece of work we shall take a reel enthusiasm in achieving it out to the very best of our ability. What man 'as done, as I was observing only a few weeks back to another esteemed client, man can do, and in three to four weeks' time, all being well, we shall 'ope to lay before you evidence to that effect, sir. Take the address, Mr. 'Iggins, if you please.'

Such was the general drift of Mr. Cattell's observations on the occasion of his first interview with Mr. Denton. About a month later, being advised that some samples were ready for his inspection, Mr. Denton met him again, and had, it seems, reason to be satisfied with the faithfulness of the reproduction of the design. It had been finished off at the top in accordance with the indication I mentioned, so that the vertical bands joined. But something still needed to be done in the way of matching the colour of the original. Mr. Cattell had suggestions of a technical kind to offer, with which I need not trouble you. He had also views as to the general desirability of the pattern which were vaguely adverse. 'You say you don't wish this to be supplied excepting to personal friends equipped with a authorization from yourself, sir. It shall be done. I quite understand your wish to keep it exclusive: lends a catchit,* does it not, to the suite? What's every man's, it's been said, is no man's.'

'Do you think it would be popular if it were generally obtainable?' asked Mr. Denton.

'I 'ardly think it, sir,' said Cattell, pensively clasping his beard. 'I 'ardly think it. Not popular: it wasn't popular with the man that cut the block, was it, Mr. 'Iggins?'

'Did he find it a difficult job?'

'He'd no call to do so, sir; but the fact is that the artistic temperament—and our men are artists, sir, every one of them—true artists as much as many that the world styles by that term—it's apt to take some strange 'ardly accountable likes or dislikes, and here was an example. The twice or thrice that I went to inspect his progress: language I could understand, for that's 'abitual to him, but reel distaste for what I should call a dainty enough thing, I did not, nor am I now able to fathom. It seemed,' said Mr. Cattell, looking narrowly upon Mr. Denton, 'as if the man scented something almost Hevil in the design.'

'Indeed? did he tell you so? I can't say I see anything sinister in it myself.'

'Neether can I, sir. In fact I said as much. "Come, Gatwick," I said, "what's to do here? What's the reason of your prejudice—for I can call it no more than that?" But, no! no explanation was forthcoming. And I was merely reduced, as I am now, to a shrug of the shoulders, and a *cui bono*.* However, here it is,' and with that the technical side of the question came to the front again.

The matching of the colours for the background, the hem, and the knots of ribbon was by far the longest part of the business, and necessitated many sendings to and fro of the original pattern and of new samples. During part of August and September, too, the Dentons were away from the Manor. So that it was not until October was well in that a sufficient quantity of the stuff had been manufactured to furnish curtains for the three or four bedrooms which were to be fitted up with it.

On the feast of Simon and Jude* the aunt and nephew returned from a short visit to find all completed, and their satisfaction at the general effect was great. The new curtains, in particular, agreed to admiration with their surroundings. When Mr. Denton was dressing for dinner, and took stock of his room, in which there was a large amount of the chintz displayed, he congratulated himself over and over again on the luck which had first made him forget his aunt's commission and had then put into his hands this extremely effective means of remedying his mistake. The pattern was, as he said at dinner, so restful and yet so far from being dull. And Miss Denton—who, by the way, had none of the stuff in her own room—was much disposed to agree with him.

At breakfast next morning he was induced to qualify his satisfaction to some extent—but very slightly. 'There is one thing I rather regret,' he said, 'that we allowed them to join up the vertical bands of the pattern at the top. I think it would have been better to leave that alone.'

'Oh?' said his aunt interrogatively.

'Yes: as I was reading in bed last night they kept catching my eye rather. That is, I found myself looking across at them every now and then. There was an effect as if someone kept peeping out between the curtains in one place or another, where there was no edge, and I think that was due to the joining up of the bands at the top. The only other thing that troubled me was the wind.'

'Why, I thought it was a perfectly still night.'

'Perhaps it was only on my side of the house, but there was enough to sway my curtains and rustle them more than I wanted.'

That night a bachelor friend of James Denton's came to stay, and was lodged in a room on the same floor as his host, but at the end of a long passage, half-way down which was a red baize door, put there to cut off the draught and intercept noise.

The party of three had separated. Miss Denton a good first, the two men at about eleven. James Denton, not yet inclined for bed, sat him down in an arm-chair and read for a time. Then he dozed, and then he woke, and bethought himself that his brown spaniel, which ordinarily slept in his room, had not come upstairs with him. Then he thought he was mistaken: for happening to move his hand which hung down over the arm of the chair within a few inches of the floor, he felt on the back of it just the slightest touch of a surface of hair, and stretching it out in that direction he stroked and patted a rounded something. But the feel of it, and still more the fact that instead of a responsive movement, absolute stillness greeted his touch, made him look over the arm. What he had been touching rose to meet him. It was in the attitude of one that had crept along the floor on its belly, and it was, so far as could be recollected, a human figure. But of the face which was now rising to within a few inches of his own no feature was discernible, only hair. Shapeless as it was, there was about it so horrible an air of menace that as he bounded from his chair and rushed from the room he heard himself moaning with fear: and doubtless he did right to fly. As he dashed into the baize door that cut the passage in two, and—forgetting that it opened towards him—beat against it with all the force in him, he felt a soft ineffectual tearing at his back which, all the same, seemed to be growing in power, as if the hand, or whatever worse than a hand was there, were becoming more material as the pursuer's rage was more concentrated. Then he remembered the trick of the door—he got it open—he shut it behind him—he gained his friend's room, and that is all we need know.

It seems curious that, during all the time that had elapsed since the purchase of Poynter's diary, James Denton should not have sought an explanation of the presence of the pattern that had been pinned into it. Well, he had read the diary through without finding it mentioned, and had concluded that there was nothing to be said. But, on leaving Rendcomb Manor (he did not know whether for good), as he naturally insisted upon doing on the day after experiencing the horror I have tried to put into words, he took the diary with him. And at his seaside lodgings he examined more narrowly the portion whence the pattern had been taken. What he remembered having suspected about it turned out to be correct. Two or three leaves were pasted together, but written upon, as was patent when they were held up to the light. They yielded easily to steaming, for the paste had lost much of its strength and they contained something relevant to the pattern.

The entry was made in 1707.

'Old Mr. Casbury, of Acrington, told me this day much of young Sir Everard Charlett, whom he remember'd Commoner of University College,* and thought was of the same Family as Dr. Arthur Charlett, now master of yᵉ Coll. This Charlett was a personable young gent., but a loose atheistical companion, and a great Lifter, as they then call'd the hard drinkers, and for what I know do so now. He was noted, and subject to severall censures at different times for his extravagancies: and if the full history of his debaucheries had bin known, no doubt would have been expell'd yᵉ Coll., supposing that no interest had been imploy'd on his behalf, of which Mr. Casbury had some suspicion. He was a very beautiful person, and constantly wore his own Hair, which was very abundant, from which, and his loose way of living, the cant name for him was Absalom,* and he was accustom'd to say that indeed he believ'd he had shortened old David's days, meaning his father, Sir Job Charlett, an old worthy cavalier.

'Note that Mr. Casbury said that he remembers not the year of Sir Everard Charlett's death, but it was 1692 or 3. He died suddenly in October. [Several lines describing his unpleasant habits and reputed delinquencies are omitted.] Having seen him in such topping spirits the night before, Mr. Casbury was amaz'd when he learn'd the death. He was found in the town ditch, the hair as was said pluck'd clean off his head. Most bells in Oxford rung out for him, being a nobleman, and he was buried next night in St. Peter's in the East. But two years after, being to be moved to his country estate by his successor, it was said the coffin, breaking by mischance, proved quite full of Hair: which sounds fabulous, but yet I believe precedents are upon record, as in Dr. Plot's *History of Staffordshire*.*

'His chambers being afterwards stripp'd, Mr. Casbury came by part of the hangings of it, which 'twas said this Charlett had design'd expressly for a memoriall of his Hair, giving the Fellow that drew it a lock to work by, and the piece which I have fasten'd in here was parcel of the same, which Mr. Casbury gave to me. He said he believ'd there was a subtlety in the drawing, but had never discover'd it himself, nor much liked to pore upon it.'

The money spent upon the curtains might as well have been thrown into the fire, as they were. Mr. Cattell's comment upon what he heard of the story took the form of a quotation from Shakespeare. You may guess it without difficulty. It began with the words 'There are more things.'*

AN EPISODE OF CATHEDRAL HISTORY

❧❦

THERE was once a learned gentleman who was deputed to examine and report upon the archives of the Cathedral of Southminster.* The examination of these records demanded a very considerable expenditure of time: hence it became advisable for him to engage lodgings in the city: for though the Cathedral body were profuse in their offers of hospitality, Mr. Lake felt that he would prefer to be master of his day. This was recognized as reasonable. The Dean eventually wrote advising Mr. Lake, if he were not already suited, to communicate with Mr. Worby,* the principal Verger, who occupied a house convenient to the church and was prepared to take in a quiet lodger for three or four weeks. Such an arrangement was precisely what Mr. Lake desired. Terms were easily agreed upon, and early in December, like another Mr. Datchery* (as he remarked to himself), the investigator found himself in the occupation of a very comfortable room in an ancient and 'cathedraly' house.

One so familiar with the customs of Cathedral churches, and treated with such obvious consideration by the Dean and Chapter of this Cathedral in particular, could not fail to command the respect of the Head Verger. Mr. Worby even acquiesced in certain modifications of statements he had been accustomed to offer for years to parties of visitors. Mr. Lake, on his part, found the Verger a very cheery companion, and took advantage of any occasion that presented itself for enjoying his conversation when the day's work was over.

One evening, about nine o'clock, Mr. Worby knocked at his lodger's door. 'I've occasion,' he said, 'to go across to the Cathedral, Mr. Lake, and I think I made you a promise when I did so next I would give you the opportunity to see what it looks like at night time. It's quite fine and dry outside, if you care to come.'

'To be sure I will; very much obliged to you, Mr. Worby, for thinking of it, but let me get my coat.'

'Here it is, sir, and I've another lantern here that you'll find advisable for the steps, as there's no moon.'

'Anyone might think we were Jasper and Durdles,* over again, mightn't they?' said Lake, as they crossed the close, for he had ascertained that the Verger had read *Edwin Drood*.

'Well, so they might,' said Mr. Worby, with a short laugh, 'though I don't know whether we ought to take it as a compliment. Odd ways, I often think, they had at that Cathedral, don't it seem so to you, sir? Full choral matins at seven o'clock in the morning all the year round. Wouldn't suit our boys' voices nowadays, and I think there's one or two of the men would be applying for a rise if the Chapter was to bring it in—particular the alltoes.'

They were now at the south-west door. As Mr. Worby was unlocking it, Lake said, 'Did you ever find anybody locked in here by accident?'

'Twice I did. One was a drunk sailor; however he got in I don't know. I s'pose he went to sleep in the service, but by the time I got to him he was praying fit to bring the roof in. Lor'! what a noise that man did make! said it was the first time he'd been inside a church for ten years, and blest if ever he'd try it again. The other was an old sheep: them boys it was, up to their games. That was the last time they tried it on, though. There, sir, now you see what we look like; our late Dean used now and again to bring parties in, but he preferred a moonlight night, and there was a piece of verse he'd coat to 'em, relating to a Scotch cathedral,* I understand; but I don't know; I almost think the effect's better when it's all dark-like. Seems to add to the size and heighth. Now if you won't mind stopping somewhere in the nave while I go up into the choir where my business lays, you'll see what I mean.'

Accordingly Lake waited, leaning against a pillar, and watched the light wavering along the length of the church, and up the steps into the choir, until it was intercepted by some screen or other furniture, which only allowed the reflection to be seen on the piers and roof. Not many minutes had passed before Worby reappeared at the door of the choir and by waving his lantern signalled to Lake to rejoin him.

'I suppose it *is* Worby, and not a substitute,' thought Lake to himself, as he walked up the nave. There was, in fact, nothing untoward. Worby showed him the papers which he had come to fetch out of the Dean's stall, and asked him what he thought of the spectacle: Lake agreed that it was well worth seeing. 'I suppose,' he said, as they walked towards the altar-steps together, 'that you're too much used to going about here at night to feel nervous—but you must get a start every now and then, don't you, when a book falls down or a door swings to?'

'No, Mr. Lake, I can't say I think much about noises, not now-adays: I'm much more afraid of finding an escape of gas or a burst in the stove pipes than anything else. Still there have been times, years ago. Did you notice that plain altar-tomb there—fifteenth century we say it is, I don't know if you agree to that? Well, if you didn't look at it, just come back and give it a glance, if you'd be so good.' It was on the north side of the choir, and rather awkwardly placed: only about three feet from the enclosing stone screen. Quite plain, as the Verger had said, but for some ordinary stone panelling. A metal cross of some size on the northern side (that next to the screen) was the solitary feature of any interest.

Lake agreed that it was not earlier than the Perpendicular period:* 'but,' he said, 'unless it's the tomb of some remarkable person, you'll forgive me for saying that I don't think it's particularly noteworthy.'

'Well, I can't say as it is the tomb of anybody noted in 'istory,' said Worby, who had a dry smile on his face, 'for we don't own any record whatsoever of who it was put up to. For all that, if you've half an hour to spare, sir, when we get back to the house, Mr. Lake, I could tell you a tale about that tomb. I won't begin on it now; it strikes cold here, and we don't want to be dawdling about all night.'

'Of course I should like to hear it immensely.'

'Very well, sir, you shall. Now if I might put a question to you,' he went on, as they passed down the choir aisle, 'in our little local guide—and not only there, but in the little book on our Cathedral in the series*—you'll find it stated that this portion of the building was erected previous to the twelfth century. Now of course I should be glad enough to take that view, but—mind the step, sir—but, I put it to you—does the lay of the stone 'ere in this portion of the wall (which he tapped with his key), does it to your eye carry the flavour of what you might call Saxon masonry? No, I thought not; no more it does to me: now, if you'll believe me, I've said as much to those men—one's the librarian of our Free Libry here, and the other came down from London on purpose—fifty times, if I have once, but I might just as well have talked to that bit of stonework. But there it is, I suppose every one's got their opinions.'

The discussion of this peculiar trait of human nature occupied Mr. Worby almost up to the moment when he and Lake re-entered the former's house. The condition of the fire in Lake's sitting-room led to a suggestion from Mr. Worby that they should finish the evening in his own parlour. We find them accordingly settled there some short time afterwards.

Mr. Worby made his story a long one, and I will not undertake to tell it wholly in his own words, or in his own order. Lake committed the substance of it to paper immediately after hearing it, together with some few passages of the narrative which had fixed themselves *verbatim* in his mind; I shall probably find it expedient to condense Lake's record to some extent.

Mr. Worby was born, it appeared, about the year 1828. His father before him had been connected with the Cathedral, and likewise his grandfather. One or both had been choristers, and in later life both had done work as mason and carpenter respectively about the fabric. Worby himself, though possessed, as he frankly acknowledged, of an indifferent voice, had been drafted into the choir at about ten years of age.

It was in 1840 that the wave of the Gothic revival* smote the Cathedral of Southminster. 'There was a lot of lovely stuff went then, sir,' said Worby, with a sigh. 'My father couldn't hardly believe it when he got his orders to clear out the choir. There was a new dean just come in—Dean Burscough it was—and my father had been 'prenticed to a good firm of joiners in the city, and knew what good work was when he saw it. Crool it was, he used to say: all that beautiful wainscot oak, as good as the day it was put up, and garlands-like of foliage and fruit, and lovely old gilding work on the coats of arms and the organ pipes. All went to the timber yard—every bit except some little pieces worked up in the Lady Chapel, and 'ere in this overmantel.* Well—I may be mistook, but I say our choir never looked as well since. Still there was a lot found out about the history of the church, and no doubt but what it did stand in need of repair. There was very few winters passed but what we'd lose a pinnicle.' Mr. Lake expressed his concurrence with Worby's views of restoration, but owns to a fear about this point lest the story proper should never be reached. Possibly this was perceptible in his manner.

Worby hastened to reassure him, 'Not but what I could carry on about that topic for hours at a time, and do do when I see my opportunity. But Dean Burscough he was very set on the Gothic period, and nothing would serve him but everything must be made agreeable to that. And one morning after service he appointed for my father to meet him in the choir, and he came back after he'd taken off his robes in the vestry, and he'd got a roll of paper with him, and the verger that was then brought in a table, and they begun spreading it out on the table with prayer books to keep it down, and my father helped 'em, and he saw it was a picture of the inside of a choir in a Cathedral; and the Dean—he was a quick-spoken gentleman—he says, "Well, Worby, what do you think of that?" "Why," says my father, "I don't think I 'ave the pleasure of knowing that view. Would that be Hereford Cathedral,* Mr. Dean?" "No, Worby," says the Dean, "that's Southminster Cathedral as we hope to see it before many years." "In-deed, sir," says my father, and that was all he did say—leastways to the Dean—but he used to tell me he felt reelly faint in himself when he looked round our choir as I can remember it, all comfortable and furnished-like, and then see this nasty little dry picter, as he called it, drawn out by some London architect. Well, there I am again. But you'll see what I mean if you look at this old view.'

Worby reached down a framed print from the wall. 'Well, the long and the short of it was that the Dean he handed over to my father a copy of an order of the Chapter that he was to clear out every bit of the choir—make a clean sweep—ready for the new work that was being designed up in town, and he was to put it in hand as soon as ever he could get the breakers together. Now then, sir, if you look at that view, you'll see where the pulpit used to stand: that's what I want you to notice, if you please.' It was, indeed, easily seen; an unusually large structure of timber with a domed sounding-board, standing at the east end of the stalls on the north side of the choir, facing the bishop's throne. Worby proceeded to explain that during the alterations, services were held in the nave, the members of the choir being thereby disappointed of an anticipated holiday, and the organist in particular incurring the suspicion of having wilfully damaged the mechanism of the temporary organ that was hired at considerable expense from London.

The work of demolition began with the choir screen and organ loft, and proceeded gradually eastwards, disclosing, as Worby said, many interesting features of older work. While this was going on, the members of the Chapter were, naturally, in and about the choir a great deal, and it soon became apparent to the elder Worby—who could not help overhearing some of their talk—that, on the part of the senior Canons especially, there must have been a good deal of disagreement before the policy now being carried out had been adopted. Some were of opinion that they should catch their deaths of cold in the return-stalls, unprotected by a screen from the draughts in the nave: others objected to being exposed to the view of persons in the choir aisles, especially, they said, during the sermons, when they found it helpful to listen in a posture which was liable to misconstruction. The strongest opposition, however, came from the oldest of the body, who up to the last moment objected to the removal of the pulpit. 'You ought not to touch it, Mr. Dean,' he said with great emphasis one morning, when the two were standing before it: 'you don't know what mischief you may do.' 'Mischief?' it's not a work of any particular merit, Canon.' 'Don't call me Canon,' said the old man with great asperity, 'that is, for thirty years I've been known as Dr. Ayloff, and I shall be obliged, Mr. Dean, if you would kindly humour me in that matter. And as to the pulpit (which I've preached from for thirty years, though I don't insist on that), all I'll say is, I *know* you're doing wrong in moving it.' 'But what sense could there be, my dear Doctor, in leaving it where it is, when we're fitting up the rest of the choir in a totally different *style*? What reason could be given—apart from the look of the thing?' 'Reason! reason!' said old Dr. Ayloff; 'if you young men—if I may say so without any disrespect, Mr. Dean— if you'd only listen to reason a little, and not be always asking for it, we should get on better. But there, I've said my say.' The old gentleman hobbled off, and as it proved, never entered the Cathedral again. The season—it was a hot summer—turned sickly on a sudden. Dr. Ayloff was one of the first to go, with some affection of the muscles of the thorax, which took him painfully at night. And at many services the number of choirmen and boys was very thin.

Meanwhile the pulpit had been done away with. In fact, the sounding-board (part of which still exists as a table in a summer-house in the palace garden) was taken down within an hour or two of Dr. Ayloff's protest. The removal of the base—not effected without considerable trouble—disclosed to view, greatly to the exultation of the restoring party, an altar-tomb—the tomb, of course, to which Worby had attracted Lake's attention that same evening. Much fruitless research was expended in attempts to identify the occupant; from that day to this he has never had a name put to him. The structure had been most carefully boxed in under the pulpit-base, so that such slight ornament as it possessed was not defaced; only on the north side of it there was what looked like an injury; a gap between two of the slabs composing the side. It might be two or three inches across. Palmer, the mason, was directed to fill it up in a week's time, when he came to do some other small jobs near that part of the choir.

The season was undoubtedly a very trying one. Whether the church was built on a site that had once been a marsh, as was suggested, or for whatever reason, the residents in its immediate neighbourhood had, many of them, but little enjoyment of the exquisite sunny days and the calm nights of August and September. To several of the older people—Dr. Ayloff, among others, as we have seen—the summer proved downright fatal, but even among the younger, few escaped either a sojourn in bed for a matter of weeks, or at the least, a brooding sense of oppression, accompanied by hateful nightmares. Gradually there formulated itself a suspicion—which grew into a conviction—that the alterations in the Cathedral had something to say in the matter. The widow of a former old verger, a pensioner of the Chapter of Southminster, was visited by dreams, which she retailed to her friends, of a shape that slipped out of the little door of the south transept as the dark fell in, and flitted—taking a fresh direction every night—about the Close, disappearing for a while in house after house, and finally emerging again when the night sky was paling. She could see nothing of it, she said, but that it was a moving form: only she had an impression that when it returned to the church, as it seemed to do in the end of the dream, it turned its head: and then, she could not tell why, but she thought it had red eyes. Worby remembered hearing the old lady tell this dream at a tea-party in the house of the chapter clerk. Its recurrence might, perhaps, he said, be taken as a symptom of approaching illness; at any rate before the end of September the old lady was in her grave.

The interest excited by the restoration of this great church was not confined to its own county. One day that summer an F.S.A.,* of some celebrity, visited the place. His business was to write an account of the discoveries that had been made, for the Society of Antiquaries, and his wife, who accompanied him, was to make a series of illustrative drawings for his report. In the morning she employed herself in making a general sketch of the choir; in the afternoon she devoted herself to details. She first drew the newly-exposed altar-tomb, and when that was finished, she called her husband's attention to a beautiful piece of diaper-ornament* on the screen just behind it, which had, like the tomb itself, been completely concealed by the pulpit. Of course, he said, an illustration of that must be made; so she seated herself on the tomb and began a careful drawing which occupied her till dusk.

Her husband had by this time finished his work of measuring and description, and they agreed that it was time to be getting back to their hotel. 'You may as well brush my skirt, Frank,' said the lady, 'it must have got covered with dust, I'm sure.' He obeyed dutifully; but, after a moment, he said, 'I don't know whether you value this dress particularly, my dear, but I'm inclined to think it's seen its best days. There's a great bit of it gone.' 'Gone? Where?' said she. 'I don't know where it's gone, but it's off at the bottom edge behind here.' She pulled it hastily into sight, and was horrified to find a jagged tear extending some way into the substance of the stuff; very much, she said, as if a dog had rent it away. The dress was, in any case, hopelessly spoilt, to her great vexation, and though they looked everywhere, the missing piece could not be found. There were many ways, they concluded, in which the injury might have come about, for the choir was full of old bits of woodwork with nails sticking out of them. Finally, they could only suppose that one of these had caused the mischief, and that the workmen, who had been about all day, had carried off the particular piece with the fragment of dress still attached to it.

It was about this time, Worby thought, that his little dog began to wear an anxious expression when the hour for it to be put into the shed in the back yard approached. (For his mother had ordained that it must not sleep in the house.) One evening, he said, when he was just going to pick it up and carry it out, it looked at him 'like a Christian, and waved its 'and, I was going to say—well, you know 'ow they do carry on sometimes, and the end of it was I put it under my coat, and 'uddled it upstairs—and I'm afraid I as good as deceived my poor mother on the subject. After that the dog acted very artful with 'iding itself under the bed for half an hour or more before bed-time came, and we worked it so as my mother never found out what we'd done.' Of course Worby was glad of its company anyhow, but more particularly when the nuisance that is still remembered in Southminster as 'the crying' set in.

'Night after night,' said Worby, 'that dog seemed to know it was coming; he'd creep out, he would, and snuggle into the bed and cuddle right up to me shivering, and when the crying come he'd be like a wild thing, shoving his head under my arm, and I was fully near as bad. Six or seven times we'd hear it, not more, and when he'd dror out his 'ed again I'd know it was over for that night. What was it like, sir? Well, I never heard but one thing that seemed to hit it off. I happened to be playing about in the Close, and there was two of the Canons met and said "Good morning" one to another. "Sleep well last night?" says one—it was Mr. Henslow that one, and Mr. Lyall was the other. "Can't say I did," says Mr. Lyall, "rather too much of Isaiah xxxiv. 14* for me." "xxxiv. 14," says Mr. Henslow, "what's that?" "You call yourself a Bible reader!" says Mr. Lyall. (Mr. Henslow, you must know, he was one of what used to be termed Simeon's lot—pretty much what we should call the Evangelical party.)* "You go and look it up." I wanted to know what he was getting at myself, and so off I ran home and got out my own Bible, and there it was: "the satyr shall cry to his fellow." Well, I thought, is that what we've been listening to these past nights? and I tell you it made me look over my shoulder a time or two. Of course I'd asked my father and mother about what it could be before that, but they both said it was most likely cats: but they spoke very short, and I could see they was troubled. My word! that was a noise—'ungry-like, as if it was calling after someone that wouldn't come. If ever you felt you wanted company, it would be when you was waiting for it to begin again. I believe two or three nights there was men put on to watch in different parts of the Close; but they all used to get together in one corner, the nearest they could to the High Street, and nothing came of it.

'Well, the next thing was this. Me and another of the boys—he's in business in the city now as a grocer, like his father before him—we'd gone up in the choir after morning service was over, and we heard old Palmer the mason bellowing to some of his men. So we went up nearer, because we knew he was a rusty old chap and there might be some fun going. It appears Palmer'd told this man to stop up the chink in that old tomb. Well, there was this man keeping on saying he'd done it the best he could, and there was Palmer carrying on like all possessed about it. "Call that making a job of it?" he says. "If you had your rights you'd get the sack for this. What do you suppose I pay you your wages for? What do you suppose I'm going to say to the Dean and Chapter when they come round, as come they may do any time, and see where you've been bungling about covering the 'ole place with mess and plaster and Lord knows what?" "Well, master, I done the best I could," says the man; "I don't know no more than what you do 'ow it come to fall out this way. I tamped it right in the 'ole," he says, "and now it's fell out," he says, "I never see."

' "Fell out?" says old Palmer, "why it's nowhere near the place. Blowed out, you mean"; and he picked up a bit of plaster, and so did I, that was laying up against the screen, three or four feet off, and not dry yet; and old Palmer he looked at it curious-like, and then he turned round on me and he says, "Now then, you boys, have you been up to some of your games here?" "No," I says, "I haven't, Mr. Palmer; there's none of us been about here till just this minute"; and while I was talking the other boy, Evans, he got looking in through the chink, and I heard him draw in his breath, and he came away sharp and up to us, and says he, "I believe there's something in there. I saw something shiny." "What! I dare say!" says old Palmer; "well, I ain't got time to stop about there. You, William, you go off and get some more stuff and make a job of it this time; if not, there'll be trouble in my yard," he says.

'So the man he went off, and Palmer too, and us boys stopped behind, and I says to Evans, "Did you really see anything in there?" "Yes," he says, "I did indeed." So then I says, "Let's shove something in and stir it up." And we tried several of the bits of wood that was laying about, but they were all too big. Then Evans he had a sheet of music he'd brought with him, an anthem or a service, I forget which it was now, and he rolled it up small and shoved it in the chink; two or three times he did it, and nothing happened. "Give it me, boy," I said, and I had a try. No, nothing happened. Then, I don't know why I thought of it, I'm sure, but I stooped down just opposite the chink and put my two fingers in my mouth and whistled—you know the way— and at that I seemed to think I heard something stirring, and I says to Evans, "Come away," I says; "I don't like this." "Oh, rot," he says, "give me that roll," and he took it and shoved it in. And I don't think ever I see anyone go so pale as he did. "I say, Worby," he says, "it's caught, or else someone's got hold of it." "Pull it out or leave it," I says. "Come and let's get off." So he gave a good pull, and it came away. Leastways most of it did, but the end was gone. Torn off it was, and Evans looked at it for a second and then he gave a sort of a croak and let it drop, and we both made off out of there as quick as ever we could. When we got outside Evans says to me, "Did you see the end of that paper?" "No," I says, "only it was torn." "Yes, it was," he says, "but it was wet too, and black!" Well, partly because of the fright we had, and partly because that music was wanted in a day or two, and we knew there'd be a set-out about it with the organist, we didn't say nothing to anyone else, and I suppose the workmen they swept up the bit that was left along with the rest of the rubbish. But Evans, if you were to ask him this very day about it, he'd stick to it he saw that paper wet and black at the end where it was torn.'

After that the boys gave the choir a wide berth, so that Worby was not sure what was the result of the mason's renewed mending of the tomb. Only he made out from fragments of conversation dropped by the workmen passing through the choir that some difficulty had been met with, and that the governor—Mr. Palmer to wit—had tried his own hand at the job. A little later, he happened to see Mr. Palmer himself knocking at the door of the Deanery and being admitted by the butler. A day or so after that, he gathered from a remark his father let fall at breakfast that something a little out of the common was to be done in the Cathedral after morning service on the morrow. 'And I'd just as soon it was to-day,' his father added; 'I don't see the use of running risks.' ' "Father," I says, "what are you going to do in the Cathedral to-morrow?" And he turned on me as savage as I ever see him—he was a wonderful good-tempered man as a general thing, my poor father was. "My lad," he says, "I'll trouble you not to go picking up your elders' and betters' talk: it's not manners and it's not straight. What I'm going to do or not going to do in the Cathedral to-morrow is none of your business: and if I catch sight of you hanging about the place to-morrow after your work's done, I'll send you home with a flea in your ear. Now you mind that." Of course I said I was very sorry and that, and equally of course I went off and laid my plans with Evans. We knew there was a stair up in the corner of the transept which you can get up to the triforium, and in them days the door to it was pretty well always open, and even if it wasn't we knew the key usually laid under a bit of matting hard by. So we made up our minds we'd be putting away music and that, next morning while the rest of the boys was clearing off, and then slip up the stairs and watch from the triforium if there was any signs of work going on.

'Well, that same night I dropped off asleep as sound as a boy does, and all of a sudden the dog woke me up, coming into the bed, and thought I, now we're going to get it sharp, for he seemed more frightened than usual. After about five minutes sure enough came this cry. I can't give you no idea what it was like; and so near too—nearer than I'd heard it yet—and a funny thing, Mr. Lake, you know what a place this Close is for an echo, and particular if you stand this side of it. Well, this crying never made no sign of an echo at all. But, as I said, it was dreadful near this night; and on the top of the start I got with hearing it, I got another fright; for I heard something rustling outside in the passage. Now to be sure I thought I was done; but I noticed the dog seemed to perk up a bit, and next there was someone whispered outside the door, and I very near laughed out loud, for I knew it was my father and mother that had got out of bed with the noise. "Whatever is it?" says my mother. "Hush! I don't know," says my father, excited-like, "don't disturb the boy. I hope he didn't hear nothing."

'So, me knowing they were just outside, it made me bolder, and I slipped out of bed across to my little window—giving on the Close— but the dog he bored right down to the bottom of the bed—and I looked out. First go off I couldn't see anything. Then right down in the shadow under a buttress I made out what I shall always say was two spots of red—a dull red it was—nothing like a lamp or a fire, but just so as you could pick 'em out of the black shadow. I hadn't but just sighted 'em when it seemed we wasn't the only people that had been disturbed, because I see a window in a house on the left-hand side become lighted up, and the light moving. I just turned my head to make sure of it, and then looked back into the shadow for those two red things, and they were gone, and for all I peered about and started, there was not a sign more of them. Then come my last fright that night—something come against my bare leg—but that was all right: that was my little dog had come out of bed, and prancing about making a great to-do, only holding his tongue, and me seeing he was quite in spirits again, I took him back to bed and we slept the night out!

'Next morning I made out to tell my mother I'd had the dog in my room, and I was surprised, after all she'd said about it before, how quiet she took it. "Did you?" she says. "Well, by good rights you ought to go without your breakfast for doing such a thing behind my back: but I don't know as there's any great harm done, only another time you ask my permission, do you hear?" A bit after that I said something to my father about having heard the cats again. "*Cats?*" he says; and he looked over at my poor mother, and she coughed and he says, "Oh! ah! yes, cats. I believe I heard 'em myself."

'That was a funny morning altogether: nothing seemed to go right. The organist he stopped in bed, and the minor Canon he forgot it was the 19th day and waited for the *Venite*;* and after a bit the deputy he set off playing the chant for evensong, which was a minor; and then the Decani boys were laughing so much they couldn't sing, and when it came to the anthem the solo boy he got took with the giggles, and made out his nose was bleeding, and shoved the book at me what hadn't practised the verse and wasn't much of a singer if I had known it. Well, things was rougher, you see, fifty years ago, and I got a nip from the counter-tenor behind me that I remembered.

'So we got through somehow, and neither the men nor the boys weren't by way of waiting to see whether the Canon in residence— Mr. Henslow it was—would come to the vestries and fine 'em, but I don't believe he did: for one thing I fancy he'd read the wrong lesson for the first time in his life, and knew it. Anyhow, Evans and me didn't find no difficulty in slipping up the stairs as I told you, and when we got up we laid ourselves down flat on our stomachs where we could just stretch our heads out over the old tomb, and we hadn't but just done so when we heard the verger that was then, first shutting the iron porch-gates and locking the south-west door, and then the transept door, so we knew there was something up, and they meant to keep the public out for a bit.

'Next thing was, the Dean and the Canon come in by their door on the north, and then I see my father, and old Palmer, and a couple of their best men, and Palmer stood a talking for a bit with the Dean in the middle of the choir. He had a coil of rope and the men had crows. All of 'em looked a bit nervous. So there they stood talking, and at last I heard the Dean say, "Well, I've no time to waste, Palmer. If you think this'll satisfy Southminster people, I'll permit it to be done; but I must say this, that never in the whole course of my life have I heard such arrant nonsense from a practical man as I have from you. Don't you agree with me, Henslow?" As far as I could hear Mr. Henslow said something like "Oh well! we're told, aren't we, Mr. Dean, not to judge others?" And the Dean he gave a kind of sniff, and walked straight up to the tomb, and took his stand behind it with his back to the screen, and the others they come edging up rather gingerly. Henslow, he stopped on the south side and scratched on his chin, he did. Then the Dean spoke up: "Palmer," he says, 'which can you do easiest, get the slab off the top, or shift one of the side slabs?"

'Old Palmer and his men they pottered about a bit looking round the edge of the top slab and sounding the sides on the south and east and west and everywhere but the north. Henslow said something about it being better to have a try at the south side, because there was more light and more room to move about in. Then my father, who'd been watching of them, went round to the north side, and knelt down and felt of the slab by the chink, and he got up and dusted his knees and says to the Dean: "Beg pardon, Mr. Dean, but I think if Mr. Palmer'll try this here slab he'll find it'll come out easy enough. Seems to me one of the men could prise it out with his crow by means of this chink." "Ah! thank you, Worby," says the Dean; "that's a good suggestion. Palmer, let one of your men do that, will you?"

'So the man come round, and put his bar in and bore on it, and just that minute when they were all bending over, and we boys got our heads well over the edge of the triforium, there come a most fearful crash down at the west end of the choir, as if a whole stack of big timber had fallen down a flight of stairs. Well, you can't expect me to tell you everything that happened all in a minute. Of course there was a terrible commotion. I heard the slab fall out, and the crowbar on the floor, and I heard the Dean say, "Good God!"

'When I looked down again I saw the Dean tumbled over on the floor, the men was making off down the choir, Henslow was just going to help the Dean up, Palmer was going to stop the men (as he said afterwards) and my father was sitting on the altar step with his face in his hands. The Dean he was very cross. "I wish to goodness you'd look where you're coming to, Henslow," he says. "Why you should all take to your heels when a stick of wood tumbles down I cannot imagine"; and all Henslow could do, explaining he was right away on the other side of the tomb, would not satisfy him.

'Then Palmer came back and reported there was nothing to account for this noise and nothing seemingly fallen down, and when the Dean finished feeling of himself they gathered round—except my father, he sat where he was—and someone lighted up a bit of candle and they looked into the tomb. "Nothing there," says the Dean, "what did I tell you? Stay! here's something. What's this? a bit of music paper, and a piece of torn stuff—part of a dress it looks like. Both quite modern—no interest whatever. Another time perhaps you'll take the advice of an educated man"—or something like that, and off he went, limping a bit, and out through the north door, only as he went he called back angry to Palmer for leaving the door standing open. Palmer called out "Very sorry, sir," but he shrugged his shoulders, and Henslow says, "I fancy Mr. Dean's mistaken. I closed the door behind me, but he's a little upset." Then Palmer says, "Why, where's Worby?" and they saw him sitting on the step and went up to him. He was recovering himself, it seemed, and wiping his forehead, and Palmer helped him up on to his legs, as I was glad to see.

'They were too far off for me to hear what they said, but my father pointed to the north door in the aisle, and Palmer and Henslow both of them looked very surprised and scared. After a bit, my father and Henslow went out of the church, and the others made what haste they could to put the slab back and plaster it in. And about as the clock struck twelve the Cathedral was opened again and us boys made the best of our way home.

'I was in a great taking to know what it was had given my poor father such a turn, and when I got in and found him sitting in his chair taking a glass of spirits, and my mother standing looking anxious at him, I couldn't keep from bursting out and making confession where I'd been. But he didn't seem to take on, not in the way of losing his temper. "You was there, was you? Well, did you see it?" "I see everything, father," I said, "except when the noise came." "Did you see what it was knocked the Dean over?" he says, "that what come out of the monument? You didn't? Well, that's a mercy." "Why, what was it, father?" I said. "Come, you must have seen it," he says. "*Didn't* you see? A thing like a man, all over hair, and two great eyes to it?"

'Well, that was all I could get out of him that time, and later on he seemed as if he was ashamed of being so frightened, and he used to put me off when I asked him about it. But years after, when I was got to be a grown man, we had more talk now and again on the matter, and he always said the same thing. "Black it was," he'd say, "and a mass of hair, and two legs, and the light caught on its eyes."

'Well, that's the tale of that tomb, Mr. Lake; it's one we don't tell to our visitors, and I should be obliged to you not to make any use of it till I'm out of the way. I doubt Mr. Evans'll feel the same as I do, if you ask him.'

This proved to be the case. But over twenty years have passed by, and the grass is growing over both Worby and Evans; so Mr. Lake felt no difficulty about communicating his notes—taken in 1890—to me. He accompanied them with a sketch of the tomb and a copy of the short inscription on the metal cross which was affixed at the expense of Dr. Lyall to the centre of the northern side. It was from the Vulgate of Isaiah xxxiv., and consisted merely of the three words—

IBI CUBAVIT LAMIA.*

THE STORY OF A DISAPPEARANCE
AND AN APPEARANCE

❦

THE letters which I now publish were sent to me recently by a
person who knows me to be interested in ghost stories. There is
no doubt about their authenticity. The paper on which they are written, the ink, and the whole external aspect put their date beyond the
reach of question.

The only point which they do not make clear is the identity of the
writer. He signs with initials only, and as none of the envelopes of the
letters are preserved, the surname of his correspondent—obviously a
married brother—is as obscure as his own. No further preliminary
explanation is needed, I think. Luckily the first letter supplies all that
could be expected.

LETTER I

GREAT CHRISHALL,* *Dec.* 22, 1837.

MY DEAR ROBERT,—It is with great regret for the enjoyment I am
losing, and for a reason which you will deplore equally with myself,
that I write to inform you that I am unable to join your circle for this
Christmas: but you will agree with me that it is unavoidable when I
say that I have within these few hours received a letter from Mrs.
Hunt at B——,* to the effect that our Uncle Henry has suddenly and
mysteriously disappeared, and begging me to go down there immediately and join the search that is being made for him. Little as I, or you
either, I think, have ever seen of Uncle, I naturally feel that this is not
a request that can be regarded lightly, and accordingly I propose to go
to B—— by this afternoon's mail, reaching it late in the evening. I
shall not go to the Rectory, but put up at the King's Head, and to
which you may address letters. I enclose a small draft, which you will
please make use of for the benefit of the young people. I shall write
you daily (supposing me to be detained more than a single day) what
goes on, and you may be sure, should the business be cleared up in
time to permit of my coming to the Manor after all, I shall present

myself. I have but a few minutes at disposal. With cordial greetings to you all, and many regrets, believe me, your affectionate Bro.,

W. R.*

LETTER II

KING'S HEAD,* Dec. 23, '37.

MY DEAR ROBERT,—In the first place, there is as yet no news of Uncle H., and I think you may finally dismiss any idea—I won't say hope—that I might after all 'turn up' for Xmas. However, my thoughts will be with you, and you have my best wishes for a really festive day. Mind that none of my nephews or nieces expend any fraction of their guineas on presents for me.

Since I got here I have been blaming myself for taking this affair of Uncle H. too easily. From what people here say, I gather that there is very little hope that he can still be alive; but whether it is accident or design that carried him off I cannot judge. The facts are these. On Friday the 19th, he went as usual shortly before five o'clock to read evening prayers at the Church; and when they were over the clerk brought him a message, in response to which he set off to pay a visit to a sick person at an outlying cottage the better part of two miles away. He paid the visit, and started on his return journey at about half-past six. This is the last that is known of him. The people here are very much grieved at his loss; he had been here many years, as you know, and though, as you also know, he was not the most genial of men, and had more than a little of the *martinet* in his composition, he seems to have been active in good works, and unsparing of trouble to himself.

Poor Mrs. Hunt, who has been his housekeeper ever since she left Woodley,* is quite overcome: it seems like the end of the world to her. I am glad that I did not entertain the idea of taking quarters at the Rectory; and I have declined several kindly offers of hospitality from people in the place, preferring as I do to be independent, and finding myself very comfortable here.

You will, of course, wish to know what has been done in the way of inquiry and search. First, nothing was to be expected from investigation at the Rectory; and to be brief, nothing has transpired. I asked Mrs. Hunt—as others had done before—whether there was either any unfavourable symptom in her master such as might portend a sudden stroke, or attack of illness, or whether he had ever had reason to apprehend any such thing: but both she, and also his medical man, were clear that this was not the case. He was quite in his usual health. In the second place, naturally, ponds and streams have been dragged, and fields in the neighbourhood which he is known to have visited last, have been searched—without result. I have myself talked to the parish clerk and—more important—have been to the house where he paid his visit.

There can be no question of any foul play on these people's part. The one man in the house is ill in bed and very weak: the wife and the children of course could do nothing themselves, nor is there the shadow of a probability that they or any of them should have agreed to decoy poor Uncle H. out in order that he might be attacked on the way back. They had told what they knew to several other inquirers already, but the woman repeated it to me. The Rector was looking just as usual: he wasn't very long with the sick man—'He ain't,' she said, 'like some what has a gift in prayer; but there, if we was all that way, 'owever would the chapel people get their living?' He left some money when he went away, and one of the children saw him cross the stile into the next field. He was dressed as he always was: wore his bands*—I gather he is nearly the last man remaining who does so— at any rate in this district.

You see I am putting down everything. The fact is that I have nothing else to do, having brought no business papers with me; and, moreover, it serves to clear my own mind, and may suggest points which have been overlooked. So I shall continue to write all that passes, even to conversations if need be—you may read or not as you please, but pray keep the letters. I have another reason for writing so fully, but it is not a very tangible one.

You may ask if I have myself made any search in the fields near the cottage. Something—a good deal—has been done by others, as I mentioned; but I hope to go over the ground to-morrow. Bow Street* has now been informed, and will send down by tonight's coach, but I do not think they will make much of the job. There is no snow, which might have helped us. The fields are all grass. Of course I was on the *qui vive** for any indication to-day both going and returning; but there was a thick mist on the way back, and I was not in trim for wandering about unknown pastures, especially on an evening when bushes looked like men, and a cow lowing in the distance might have been the last trump. I assure you, if Uncle Henry had stepped out from among the trees in a little copse which borders the path at one place, carrying his head under his arm, I should have been very little more uncomfortable than I was. To tell you the truth, I was rather expecting something of the kind. But I must drop my pen for the moment: Mr. Lucas, the curate, is announced.

Later. Mr. Lucas has been, and gone, and there is not much beyond the decencies of ordinary sentiment to be got from him. I can see that he has given up any idea that the Rector can be alive, and that, so far as he can be, he is truly sorry. I can also discern that even in a more emotional person than Mr. Lucas, Uncle Henry was not likely to inspire strong attachment.

Besides Mr. Lucas, I have had another visitor in the shape of my Boniface*—mine host of the 'King's Head'—who came to see whether I had everything I wished, and who really requires the pen of a Boz* to do him justice. He was very solemn and weighty at first. 'Well, sir,' he said, 'I suppose we must bow our 'ead beneath the blow, as my poor wife had used to say. So far as I can gather there's been neither hide nor yet hair of our late respected incumbent scented out as yet; not that he was what the Scripture terms a hairy man* in any sense of the word.'

I said—as well as I could—that I supposed not, but could not help adding that I had heard he was sometimes a little difficult to deal with. Mr. Bowman looked at me sharply for a moment, and then passed in a flash from solemn sympathy to impassioned declamation. 'When I think,' he said, 'of the language that man see fit to employ to me in this here parlour over no more a matter than a cask of beer—such a thing as I told him might happen any day of the week to a man with a family—though as it turned out he was quite under a mistake, and that I knew at the time, only I was that shocked to hear him I couldn't lay my tongue to the right expression.'

He stopped abruptly and eyed me with some embarrassment. I only said, 'Dear me, I'm sorry to hear you had any little differences: I suppose my uncle will be a good deal missed in the parish?' Mr. Bowman drew a long breath. 'Ah, yes!' he said; 'your uncle! You'll understand me when I say that for the moment it had slipped my remembrance that he was a relative; and natural enough, I must say, as it should, for as to you bearing any resemblance to—to him, the notion of any such a thing is clean ridiculous. All the same, 'ad I 'ave bore it in my mind, you'll be among the first to feel, I'm sure, as I should have abstained my lips, or rather I should *not* have abstained my lips with no such reflections.'

I assured him that I quite understood, and was going to have asked him some further questions, but he was called away to see after some business. By the way, you need not take it into your head that he has anything to fear from the inquiry into poor Uncle Henry's disappearance—though, no doubt, in the watches of the night it will occur to him that *I* think he has, and I may expect explanations to-morrow.

I must close this letter: it has to go by the late coach.

LETTER III

Dec. 25, '37.

My Dear Robert,—This is a curious letter to be writing on Christmas Day, and yet after all there is nothing much in it. Or there may be—you shall be the judge. At least, nothing decisive. The Bow Street men practically say that they have no clue. The length of time and the weather conditions have made all tracks so faint as to be quite useless: nothing that belonged to the dead man—I'm afraid no other word will do—has been picked up.

As I expected, Mr. Bowman was uneasy in his mind this morning; quite early I heard him holding forth in a very distinct voice—purposely so, I thought—to the Bow Street officers in the bar, as to the loss that the town had sustained in their Rector, and as to the necessity of leaving no stone unturned (he was very great on this phrase) in order to come at the truth. I suspect him of being an orator of repute at convivial meetings.

When I was at breakfast he came to wait on me, and took an opportunity when handing a muffin to say in a low tone, 'I 'ope, sir, you recognize as my feelings towards your relative is not actuated by any taint of what you may call melignity—you can leave the room, Elizar, I will see the gentleman 'as all he requires with my own hands—I ask your pardon, sir, but you must be well aware a man is not always master of himself: and when that man has been 'urt in his mind by the application of expressions which I will go so far as to say 'ad not ought to have been made use of (his voice was rising all this time and his face growing redder); no, sir; and 'ere, if you will permit of it, I should like to explain to you in a very few words the exact state of the bone of contention. This cask—I might more truly call it a firkin—of beer——'

I felt it was time to interpose, and said that I did not see that it would help us very much to go into that matter in detail. Mr. Bowman acquiesced, and resumed more calmly:

'Well, sir, I bow to your ruling, and as you say, be that here or be it there, it don't contribute a great deal, perhaps, to the present question. All I wish you to understand is that I am as prepared as you are yourself to lend every hand to the business we have afore us, and—as I took the opportunity to say as much to the Orficers not three-quarters of an hour ago—to leave no stone unturned as may throw even a spark of light on this painful matter.'

In fact, Mr. Bowman did accompany us on our exploration, but though I am sure his genuine wish was to be helpful, I am afraid he did not contribute to the serious side of it. He appeared to be under the impression that we were likely to meet either Uncle Henry or the person responsible for his disappearance, walking about the fields, and did a great deal of shading his eyes with his hand and calling our attention, by pointing with his stick, to distant cattle and labourers. He held several long conversations with old women whom we met, and was very strict and severe in his manner, but on each occasion returned to our party saying, 'Well, I find she don't seem to 'ave no connexion with this sad affair. I think you may take it from me, sir, as there's little or no light to be looked for from that quarter; not without she's keeping something back intentional.'

We gained no appreciable result, as I told you at starting; the Bow Street men have left the town, whether for London or not I am not sure.

This evening I had company in the shape of a bagman,* a smartish fellow. He knew what was going forward, but though he has been on the roads for some days about here, he had nothing to tell of suspicious characters—tramps, wandering sailors or gipsies. He was very full of a capital Punch and Judy Show* he had seen this same day at W——,* and asked if it had been here yet, and advised me by no means to miss it if it does come. The best Punch and the best Toby dog, he said, he had ever come across. Toby dogs, you know, are the last new thing in the shows. I have only seen one myself, but before long all the men will have them.

Now why, you will want to know, do I trouble to write all this to you? I am obliged to do it, because it has something to do with another absurd trifle (as you will inevitably say), which in my present state of rather unquiet fancy—nothing more, perhaps—I have to put down. It is a dream, sir, which I am going to record, and I must say it is one of the oddest I have had. Is there anything in it beyond what the bagman's talk and Uncle Henry's disappearance could have suggested? You, I repeat, shall judge: I am not in a sufficiently cool and judicial frame to do so.

It began with what I can only describe as a pulling aside of curtains: and I found myself seated in a place—I don't know whether indoors or out. There were people—only a few—on either side of me, but I did not recognize them, or indeed think much about them. They never spoke, but, so far as I remember, were all grave and pale-faced and looked fixedly before them. Facing me there was a Punch and Judy Show, perhaps rather larger than the ordinary ones, painted with black figures on a reddish-yellow ground. Behind it and on each side was only darkness, but in front there was a sufficiency of light. I was 'strung up' to a high degree of expectation and looked every moment to hear the pan-pipes and the Roo-too-too-it. Instead of that there came suddenly an enormous—I can use no other word—an enormous single toll of a bell, I don't know from how far off—somewhere behind. The little curtain flew up and the drama began.

I believe someone once tried to re-write Punch as a serious tragedy;* but whoever he may have been, this performance would have suited him exactly. There was something Satanic about the hero. He varied his methods of attack: for some of his victims he lay in wait, and to see his horrible face—it was yellowish white, I may remark—peering round the wings made me think of the Vampyre in Fuseli's foul sketch.* To others he was polite and carneying—particularly to the unfortunate alien who can only say *Shallabalah*—though what Punch said I never could catch. But with all of them I came to dread the moment of death. The crack of the stick on their skulls, which in the ordinary way delights me, had here a crushing sound as if the bone was giving way, and the victims quivered and kicked as they lay. The baby—it sounds more ridiculous as I go on—the baby, I am sure, was alive. Punch wrung its neck, and if the choke or squeak which it gave were not real, I know nothing of reality.

The stage got perceptibly darker as each crime was consummated, and at last there was one murder which was done quite in the dark, so that I could see nothing of the victim, and took some time to effect. It was accompanied by hard breathing and horrid muffled sounds, and after it Punch came and sat on the foot-board and fanned himself and looked at his shoes, which were bloody, and hung his head on one side, and sniggered in so deadly a fashion that I saw some of those beside me cover their faces, and I would gladly have done the same. But in the meantime the scene behind Punch was clearing, and showed, not the usual house front, but something more ambitious—a grove of trees and the gentle slope of a hill, with a very natural—in fact, I should say a real—moon shining on it. Over this there rose slowly an object which I soon perceived to be a human figure with something peculiar about the head—what, I was unable at first to see. It did not stand on its feet, but began creeping or dragging itself across the middle distance towards Punch, who still sat back to it; and by this time, I may remark (though it did not occur to me at the moment) that all pretence of this being a puppet show had vanished. Punch was still Punch, it is true, but, like the others, was in some sense a live creature, and both moved themselves at their own will.

When I next glanced at him he was sitting in malignant reflection; but in another instant something seemed to attract his attention, and he first sat up sharply and then turned round, and evidently caught sight of the person that was approaching him and was in fact now very near. Then, indeed, did he show unmistakable signs of terror: catching up his stick, he rushed towards the wood, only just eluding the arm of his pursuer, which was suddenly flung out to intercept him. It was with a revulsion which I cannot easily express that I now saw more or less clearly what this pursuer was like. He was a sturdy figure clad in black, and, as I thought, wearing bands: his head was covered with a whitish bag.

The chase which now began lasted I do not know how long, now among the trees, now along the slope of the field, sometimes both figures disappearing wholly for a few seconds, and only some uncertain sounds letting one know that they were still afoot. At length there came a moment when Punch, evidently exhausted, staggered in from the left and threw himself down among the trees. His pursuer was not long after him, and came looking uncertainly from side to side. Then, catching sight of the figure on the ground, he too threw himself down—his back was turned to the audience—with a swift motion twitched the covering from his head, and thrust his face into that of Punch. Everything on the instant grew dark.

There was one long, loud, shuddering scream, and I awoke to find myself looking straight into the face of—what in all the world do you think? but—a large owl, which was seated on my window-sill immediately opposite my bed-foot, holding up its wings like two shrouded arms. I caught the fierce glance of its yellow eyes, and then it was gone. I heard the single enormous bell again—very likely, as you are saying to yourself, the church clock; but I do not think so—and then I was broad awake.

All this, I may say, happened within the last half-hour. There was no probability of my getting to sleep again, so I got up, put on clothes enough to keep me warm, and am writing this rigmarole in the first hours of Christmas Day. Have I left out anything? Yes; there was no Toby dog, and the names over the front of the Punch and Judy booth were Kidman and Gallop, which were certainly not what the bagman told me to look out for.

By this time, I feel a little more as if I could sleep, so this shall be sealed and wafered.

LETTER IV

Dec. 26, '37.

MY DEAR ROBERT,—All is over. The body has been found. I do not make excuses for not having sent off my news by last night's mail, for the simple reason that I was incapable of putting pen to paper. The events that attended the discovery bewildered me so completely that I needed what I could get of a night's rest to enable me to face the situation at all. Now I can give you my journal of the day, certainly the strangest Christmas Day that ever I spent or am likely to spend.

The first incident was not very serious. Mr. Bowman had, I think, been keeping Christmas Eve, and was a little inclined to be captious: at least, he was not on foot very early, and to judge from what I could hear, neither men or maids could do anything to please him. The latter were certainly reduced to tears; nor am I sure that Mr. Bowman succeeded in preserving a manly composure. At any rate, when I came downstairs, it was in a broken voice that he wished me the compliments of the season, and a little later on, when he paid his visit of ceremony at breakfast, he was far from cheerful: even Byronic, I might almost say, in his outlook on life.

'I don't know,' he said, 'if you think with me, sir; but every Christmas as comes round the world seems a hollerer thing to me. Why, take an example now from what lays under my own eye. There's my servant Eliza—been with me now for going on fifteen years. I thought I could have placed my confidence in Eliza, and yet this very morning—Christmas morning too, of all the blessed days in the year—with the bells a ringing and—and—all like that—I say, this very morning, had it not have been for Providence watching over us all, that girl would have put—indeed I may go so far to say, 'ad put the cheese on your breakfast-table——' He saw I was about to speak, and waved his hand at me. 'It's all very well for you to say, "Yes, Mr. Bowman, but you took away the cheese and locked it up in the cupboard," which I did, and have the key here, or if not the actual key, one very much about the same size. That's true enough, sir, but what do you think is the effect of that action on me? Why, it's no exaggeration for me to say that the ground is cut from under my feet. And yet when I said as much to Eliza, not nasty, mind you, but just firm-like, what was my return? "Oh," she says: "well," she says, "there wasn't no bones broke, I suppose." Well, sir, it 'urt me, that's all I can say: it 'urt me, and I don't like to think of it now.'

There was an ominous pause here, in which I ventured to say something like, 'Yes, very trying,' and then asked at what hour the church service was to be. 'Eleven o'clock,' Mr. Bowman said with a heavy sigh. 'Ah, you won't have no such discourse from poor Mr. Lucas as what you would have done from our late Rector. Him and me may have had our little differences, and did do, more's the pity.'

I could see that a powerful effort was needed to keep him off the vexed question of the cask of beer, but he made it. 'But I will say this, that a better preacher, nor yet one to stand faster by his rights, or what he considered to be his rights—however, that's not the question now—I for one, never set under. Some might say, "Was he a eloquent man?" and to that my answer would be: "Well, there you've a better right per'aps to speak of your own uncle than what I have." Others might ask, "Did he keep a hold of his congregation?" and there again I should reply, "That depends." But as I say—yes, Eliza, my girl, I'm coming—eleven o'clock, sir, and you inquire for the

King's Head pew.' I believe Eliza had been very near the door, and shall consider it in my vail.*

The next episode was church: I felt Mr. Lucas had a difficult task in doing justice to Christmas sentiments, and also to the feeling of disquiet and regret which, whatever Mr. Bowman might say, was clearly prevalent. I do not think he rose to the occasion. I was uncomfortable. The organ wolved*—you know what I mean: the wind died—twice in the Christmas Hymn, and the tenor bell, I suppose owing to some negligence on the part of the ringers, kept sounding faintly about once in a minute during the sermon. The clerk sent up a man to see to it, but he seemed unable to do much. I was glad when it was over. There was an odd incident, too, before the service. I went in rather early, and came upon two men carrying the parish bier back to its place under the tower. From what I overheard them saying, it appeared that it had been put out by mistake, by someone who was not there. I also saw the clerk busy folding up a moth-eaten velvet pall—not a sight for Christmas Day.

I dined soon after this, and then, feeling disinclined to go out, took my seat by the fire in the parlour, with the last number of *Pickwick*, which I had been saving up for some days. I thought I could be sure of keeping awake over this, but I turned out as bad as our friend Smith.* I suppose it was half-past two when I was roused by a piercing whistle and laughing and talking voices outside in the marketplace. It was a Punch and Judy—I had no doubt the one that my bagman had seen at W——. I was half delighted, half not—the latter because my unpleasant dream came back to me so vividly; but, anyhow, I determined to see it through, and I sent Eliza out with a crown-piece to the performers and a request that they would face my window if they could manage it.

The show was a very smart new one; the names of the proprietors, I need hardly tell you, were Italian, Foresta and Calpigi. The Toby dog was there, as I had been led to expect. All B—— turned out, but did not obstruct my view, for I was at the large first-floor window and not ten yards away.

The play began on the stroke of a quarter to three by the church clock. Certainly it was very good; and I was soon relieved to find that the disgust my dream had given me for Punch's onslaughts on his ill-starred visitors was only transient. I laughed at the demise of the Turncock, the Foreigner, the Beadle,* and even the baby. The only drawback was the Toby dog's developing a tendency to howl in the wrong place. Something had occurred, I suppose, to upset him, and something considerable: for, I forget exactly at what point, he gave a most lamentable cry, leapt off the footboard, and shot away across the market-place and down a side street. There was a stage-wait, but only a brief one. I suppose the men decided that it was no good going after him, and that he was likely to turn up again at night.

We went on. Punch dealt faithfully with Judy, and in fact with all comers; and then came the moment when the gallows was erected, and the great scene with Mr. Ketch* was to be enacted. It was now that something happened of which I can certainly not yet see the import fully. You have witnessed an execution, and know what the criminal's head looks like with the cap on. If you are like me, you never wish to think of it again, and I do not willingly remind you of it. It was just such a head as that, that I, from my somewhat higher post, saw in the inside of the show-box; but at first the audience did not see it. I expected it to emerge into their view, but instead of that there slowly rose for a few seconds an uncovered face, with an expression of terror upon it, of which I have never imagined the like. It seemed as if the man, whoever he was, was being forcibly lifted, with his arms somehow pinioned or held back, towards the little gibbet on the stage. I could just see the nightcapped head behind him. Then there was a cry and a crash. The whole showbox fell over backwards; kicking legs were seen among the ruins, and then two figures—as some said; I can only answer for one—were visible running at top speed across the square and disappearing in a lane which leads to the fields.

Of course everybody gave chase. I followed; but the pace was killing, and very few were in, literally, at the death. It happened in a chalk pit: the man went over the edge quite blindly and broke his neck. They searched everywhere for the other, until it occurred to me to ask whether he had ever left the market-place. At first everyone was sure that he had; but when we came to look, he was there, under the showbox, dead too.

But in the chalk pit it was that poor Uncle Henry's body was found, with a sack over the head, the throat horribly mangled. It was a peaked corner of the sack sticking out of the soil that attracted attention. I cannot bring myself to write in greater detail.

I forgot to say the men's real names were Kidman and Gallop. I feel sure I have heard them, but no one here seems to know anything about them.

I am coming to you as soon as I can after the funeral. I must tell you when we meet what I think of it all.

TWO DOCTORS

I T is a very common thing, in my experience, to find papers shut up in old books; but one of the rarest things to come across any such that are at all interesting. Still it does happen, and one should never destroy them unlooked at. Now it was a practice of mine before the war occasionally to buy old ledgers of which the paper was good, and which possessed a good many blank leaves, and to extract these and use them for my own notes and writings. One such I purchased for a small sum in 1911. It was tightly clasped, and its boards were warped by having for years been obliged to embrace a number of extraneous sheets. Three-quarters of this inserted matter had lost all vestige of importance for any living human being: one bundle had not. That it belonged to a lawyer is certain, for it is endorsed: *The strangest case I have yet met*, and bears initials, and an address in Gray's Inn.* It is only materials for a case, and consists of statements by possible witnesses. The man who would have been the defendant or prisoner seems never to have appeared. The *dossier* is not complete, but, such as it is, it furnishes a riddle in which the supernatural appears to play a part. You must see what you can make of it.

The following is the setting and the tale as I elicit it.

The scene is Islington* in 1718, and the time the month of June: a countrified place, therefore, and a pleasant season. Dr. Abell was walking in his garden one afternoon waiting for his horse to be brought round that he might set out on his visits for the day. To him entered his confidential servant, Luke Jennett, who had been with him twenty years.

'I said I wished to speak to him, and what I had to say might take some quarter of an hour. He accordingly bade me go into his study, which was a room opening on the terrace path where he was walking, and came in himself and sat down. I told him that, much against my will, I must look out for another place. He inquired what was my reason, in consideration I had been so long with him. I said if he would excuse me he would do me a great kindness, because (this appears to have been common form even in 1718) I was one that always liked to

have everything pleasant about me. As well as I can remember, he said
that was his case likewise, but he would wish to know why I should
change my mind after so many years, and, says he, "you know there
can be no talk of a remembrance of you in my will if you leave my
service now." I said I had made my reckoning of that.

'"Then," says he, "you must have some complaint to make, and if
I could I would willingly set it right." And at that I told him, not seeing how I could keep it back, the matter of my former affidavit and of
the bedstaff* in the dispensing-room, and said that a house where
such things happened was no place for me. At which he, looking very
black upon me, said no more, but called me fool, and said he would
pay what was owing me in the morning; and so, his horse being waiting, went out. So for that night I lodged with my sister's husband
near Battle Bridge* and came early next morning to my late master,
who then made a great matter that I had not lain in his house and
stopped a crown out of my wages owing.

'After that I took service here and there, not for long at a time, and
saw no more of him till I came to be Dr. Quinn's man at Dodds Hall
in Islington.'

There is one very obscure part in this statement—namely, the
reference to the former affidavit and the matter of the bedstaff. The
former affidavit is not in the bundle of papers. It is to be feared that it
was taken out to be read because of its special oddity, and not put
back. Of what nature the story was may be guessed later, but as yet no
clue has been put into our hands.

The Rector of Islington, Jonathan Pratt, is the next to step forward. He furnishes particulars of the standing and reputation of
Dr. Abell and Dr. Quinn, both of whom lived and practised in his
parish.

'It is not to be supposed,' he says, 'that a physician should be a
regular attendant at morning and evening prayers, or at the
Wednesday lectures, but within the measure of their ability I would
say that both these persons fulfilled their obligations as loyal members of the Church of England. At the same time (as you desire my
private mind) I must say, in the language of the schools, *distinguo*.*
Dr. A. was to me a source of perplexity, Dr. Q. to my eye a plain,
honest believer, not inquiring over closely into points of belief, but
squaring his practice to what lights he had. The other interested himself in questions to which Providence, as I hold, designs no answer to

be given us in this state: he would ask me, for example, what place I
believed those beings now to hold in the scheme of creation which by
some are thought neither to have stood fast when the rebel angels fell,
nor to have joined with them to the full pitch of their transgression.

'As was suitable, my first answer to him was a question, What warrant he had for supposing any such beings to exist? for that there was
none in Scripture I took it he was aware. It appeared—for as I am on
the subject, the whole tale may be given—that he grounded himself
on such passages as that of the satyr which Jerome tells us conversed
with Antony;* but thought too that some parts of Scripture might be
cited in support. "And besides," said he, "you know 'tis the universal
belief among those that spend their days and nights abroad, and I
would add that if your calling took you so continuously as it does me
about the country lanes by night, you might not be so surprised as I
see you to be by my suggestion." "You are then of John Milton's*
mind," I said, "and hold that

> Millions of spiritual creatures walk the earth
> Unseen, both when we wake and when we sleep."

' "I do not know," he said, "why Milton should take upon himself
to say 'unseen'; though to be sure he was blind when he wrote that.
But for the rest, why, yes, I think he was in the right." "Well," I said,
"though not so often as you, I am not seldom called abroad pretty
late; but I have no mind of meeting a satyr in our Islington lanes in all
the years I have been here; and if you have had the better luck, I am
sure the Royal Society* would be glad to know of it."

'I am reminded of these trifling expressions because Dr. A. took
them so ill, stamping out of the room in a huff with some such word
as that these high and dry parsons had no eyes but for a prayer-book
or a pint of wine.

'But this was not the only time that our conversation took a remarkable turn. There was an evening when he came in, at first seeming gay
and in good spirits, but afterwards as he sat and smoked by the fire
falling into a musing way; out of which to rouse him I said pleasantly
that I supposed he had had no meetings of late with his odd friends.
A question which did effectually arouse him, for he looked most
wildly, and as if scared, upon me, and said, "*You* were never there? I
did not see you. Who brought you?" And then in a more collected
tone, "What was this about a meeting? I believe I must have been in

a doze." To which I answered that I was thinking of fauns and centaurs in the dark lane, and not of a witches' Sabbath; but it seemed he took it differently.

'"Well," said he, "I can plead guilty to neither; but I find you very much more of a sceptic than becomes your cloth. If you care to know about the dark lane you might do worse than ask my housekeeper that lived at the other end of it when she was a child." "Yes," said I, "and the old women in the almshouse and the children in the kennel. If I were you, I would send to your brother Quinn for a bolus* to clear your brain." "Damn Quinn," says he; "talk no more of him: he has embezzled four of my best patients this month; I believe it is that cursed man of his, Jennett, that used to be with me, his tongue is never still; it should be nailed to the pillory if he had his deserts." This, I may say, was the only time of his showing me that he had any grudge against either Dr. Quinn or Jennett, and as was my business, I did my best to persuade him he was mistaken in them. Yet it could not be denied that some respectable families in the parish had given him the cold shoulder, and for no reason that they were willing to allege. The end was that he said he had not done so ill at Islington but that he could afford to live at ease elsewhere when he chose, and anyhow he bore Dr. Quinn no malice. I think I now remember what observation of mine drew him into the train of thought which he next pursued. It was, I believe, my mentioning some juggling tricks which my brother in the East Indies had seen at the court of the Rajah of Mysore.* "A convenient thing enough," said Dr. Abell to me, "if by some arrangement a man could get the power of communicating motion and energy to inanimate objects." "As if the axe should move itself against him that lifts it; something of that kind?" "Well, I don't know that that was in my mind so much; but if you could summon such a volume from your shelf or even order it to open at the right page."

'He was sitting by the fire—it was a cold evening—and stretched out his hand that way, and just then the fire-irons, or at least the poker, fell over towards him with a great clatter, and I did not hear what else he said. But I told him that I could not easily conceive of an arrangement, as he called it, of such a kind that would not include as one of its conditions a heavier payment than any Christian would care to make; to which he assented. "But," he said, "I have no doubt these bargains can be made very tempting, very persuasive. Still, you would not favour them, eh, Doctor? No, I suppose not."

'This is as much as I know of Dr. Abell's mind, and the feeling between these men. Dr. Quinn, as I said, was a plain, honest creature, and a man to whom I would have gone—indeed I have before now gone to him—for advice on matters of business. He was, however, every now and again, and particularly of late, not exempt from troublesome fancies. There was certainly a time when he was so much harassed by his dreams that he could not keep them to himself, but would tell them to his acquaintances and among them to me. I was at supper at his house, and he was not inclined to let me leave him at my usual time. "If you go," he said, "there will be nothing for it but I must go to bed and dream of the chrysalis." "You might be worse off," said I. "I do not think it," he said, and he shook himself like a man who is displeased with the complexion of his thoughts. "I only meant," said I, "that a chrysalis is an innocent thing." "This one is not," he said, "and I do not care to think of it."

'However, sooner than lose my company he was fain to tell me (for I pressed him) that this was a dream which had come to him several times of late, and even more than once in a night. It was to this effect, that he seemed to himself to wake under an extreme compulsion to rise and go out of doors. So he would dress himself and go down to his garden door. By the door there stood a spade which he must take, and go out into the garden, and at a particular place in the shrubbery, somewhat clear, and upon which the moon shone (for there was always in his dream a full moon), he would feel himself forced to dig. And after some time the spade would uncover something light-coloured, which he would perceive to be a stuff, linen or woollen, and this he must clear with his hands. It was always the same: of the size of a man and shaped like the chrysalis of a moth, with the folds showing a promise of an opening at one end.

'He could not describe how gladly he would have left all at this stage and run to the house, but he must not escape so easily. So with many groans, and knowing only too well what to expect, he parted these folds of stuff, or, as it sometimes seemed to be, membrane, and disclosed a head covered with a smooth pink skin, which breaking as the creature stirred, showed him his own face in a state of death. The telling of this so much disturbed him that I was forced out of mere compassion to sit with him the greater part of the night and talk with him upon indifferent subjects. He said that upon every recurrence of this dream he woke and found himself, as it were, fighting for his breath.'

Another extract from Luke Jennett's long continuous statement comes in at this point.

'I never told tales of my master, Dr. Abell, to anybody in the neighbourhood. When I was in another service I remember to have spoken to my fellow-servants about the matter of the bedstaff, but I am sure I never said either I or he were the persons concerned, and it met with so little credit that I was affronted and thought best to keep it to myself. And when I came back to Islington and found Dr. Abell still there, who I was told had left the parish, I was clear that it behoved me to use great discretion, for indeed I was afraid of the man, and it is certain I was no party to spreading any ill report of him. My master, Dr. Quinn, was a very just, honest man, and no maker of mischief. I am sure he never stirred a finger nor said a word by way of inducement to a soul to make them leave going to Dr. Abell and come to him; nay, he would hardly be persuaded to attend them that came, until he was convinced that if he did not they would send into the town for a physician rather than do as they had hitherto done.

'I believe it may be proved that Dr. Abell came into my master's house more than once. We had a new chambermaid out of Hertfordshire, and she asked me who was the gentleman that was looking after the master, that is Dr. Quinn, when he was out, and seemed so disappointed that he was out. She said whoever he was he knew the way of the house well, running at once into the study and then into the dispensing-room, and last into the bedchamber. I made her tell me what he was like, and what she said was suitable enough to Dr. Abell; but besides she told me she saw the same man at church, and someone told her that was the Doctor.

'It was just after this that my master began to have his bad nights, and complained to me and other persons, and in particular what discomfort he suffered from his pillow and bedclothes. He said he must buy some to suit him, and should do his own marketing. And accordingly brought home a parcel which he said was of the right quality, but where he bought it we had then no knowledge, only they were marked in thread with a coronet and a bird.* The women said they were of a sort not commonly met with and very fine, and my master said they were the comfortablest he ever used, and he slept now both soft and deep. Also the feather pillows were the best sorted and his head would sink into them as if they were a cloud: which I have myself remarked several times when I came to wake him of a morning, his face being almost hid by the pillow closing over it.

'I had never any communication with Dr. Abell after I came back to Islington, but one day when he passed me in the street and asked me whether I was not looking for another service, to which I answered I was very well suited where I was, but he said I was a tickleminded* fellow and he doubted not he should soon hear I was on the world again, which indeed proved true.'

Dr. Pratt is next taken up where he left off.

'On the 16th I was called up out of my bed soon after it was light—that is about five—with a message that Dr. Quinn was dead or dying. Making my way to his house I found there was no doubt which was the truth. All the persons in the house except the one that let me in were already in his chamber and standing about his bed, but none touching him. He was stretched in the midst of the bed, on his back, without any disorder, and indeed had the appearance of one ready laid out for burial. His hands, I think, were even crossed on his breast. The only thing not usual was that nothing was to be seen of his face, the two ends of the pillow or bolster appearing to be closed quite over it. These I immediately pulled apart, at the same time rebuking those present, and especially the man, for not at once coming to the assistance of his master. He, however, only looked at me and shook his head, having evidently no more hope than myself that there was anything but a corpse before us.

'Indeed it was plain to anyone possessed of the least experience that he was not only dead, but had died of suffocation. Nor could it be conceived that his death was accidentally caused by the mere folding of the pillow over his face. How should he not, feeling the oppression, have lifted his hands to put it away? whereas not a fold of the sheet which was closely gathered about him, as I now observed, was disordered. The next thing was to procure a physician. I had bethought me of this on leaving my house, and sent on the messenger who had come to me to Dr. Abell; but I now heard that he was away from home, and the nearest surgeon was got, who, however, could tell no more, at least without opening the body, than we already knew.

'As to any person entering the room with evil purpose (which was the next point to be cleared), it was visible that the bolts of the door were burst from their stanchions, and the stanchions broken away from the door-post by main force; and there was a sufficient body of witness, the smith among them, to testify that this had been done but a few minutes before I came. The chamber being, moreover, at the top of the house, the window was neither easy of access nor did it show any sign of an exit made that way, either by marks upon the sill or footprints below upon soft mould.'

The surgeon's evidence forms of course part of the report of the inquest, but since it has nothing but remarks upon the healthy state of the larger organs and the coagulation of blood in various parts of the body, it need not be reproduced. The verdict was 'Death by the visitation of God.'

Annexed to the other papers is one which I was at first inclined to suppose had made its way among them by mistake. Upon further consideration I think I can divine a reason for its presence.

It relates to the rifling of a mausoleum in Middlesex which stood in a park (now broken up), the property of a noble family which I will not name. The outrage was not that of an ordinary resurrection man. The object, it seemed likely, was theft. The account is blunt and terrible. I shall not quote it. A dealer in the North of London suffered heavy penalties as a receiver of stolen goods in connexion with the affair.

THE HAUNTED DOLLS' HOUSE

'I SUPPOSE you get stuff of that kind through your hands pretty often?' said Mr. Dillet, as he pointed with his stick to an object which shall be described when the time comes: and when he said it, he lied in his throat, and knew that he lied. Not once in twenty years—perhaps not once in a lifetime—could Mr. Chittenden, skilled as he was in ferreting out the forgotten treasures of half a dozen counties, expect to handle such a specimen. It was collectors' palaver, and Mr. Chittenden recognized it as such.

'Stuff of that kind, Mr. Dillet! It's a museum piece, that is.'

'Well, I suppose there are museums that'll take anything.'

'I've seen one, not as good as that, years back,' said Mr. Chittenden thoughtfully. 'But that's not likely to come into the market: and I'm told they 'ave some fine ones of the period over the water. No: I'm only telling you the truth, Mr. Dillet, when I say that if you was to place an unlimited order with me for the very best that could be got—and you know I 'ave facilities for getting to know of such things, and a reputation to maintain—well, all I can say is, I should lead you straight up to that one and say, "I can't do no better for you than that, sir."'

'Hear, hear!' said Mr. Dillet, applauding ironically with the end of his stick on the floor of the shop. 'How much are you sticking the innocent American buyer for it, eh?'

'Oh, I shan't be over hard on the buyer, American or otherwise. You see, it stands this way, Mr. Dillet—if I knew just a bit more about the pedigree——'

'Or just a bit less,' Mr. Dillet put in.

'Ha, ha! you will have your joke, sir. No, but as I was saying, if I knew just a little more than what I do about the piece—though anyone can see for themselves it's a genuine thing, every last corner of it, and there's not been one of my men allowed to so much as touch it since it came into the shop—there'd be another figure in the price I'm asking.'

'And what's that: five and twenty?'

'Multiply that by three and you've got it, sir. Seventy-five's my price.'

'And fifty's mine,' said Mr. Dillet.

The point of agreement was, of course, somewhere between the two, it does not matter exactly where—I think sixty guineas. But half an hour later the object was being packed, and within an hour Mr. Dillet had called for it in his car and driven away. Mr. Chittenden, holding the cheque in his hand, saw him off from the door with smiles, and returned, still smiling, into the parlour where his wife was making the tea. He stopped at the door.

'It's gone,' he said.

'Thank God for that!' said Mrs. Chittenden, putting down the teapot. 'Mr. Dillet, was it?'

'Yes, it was.'

'Well, I'd sooner it was him than another.'

'Oh, I don't know; he ain't a bad feller, my dear.'

'Maybe not, but in my opinion he'd be none the worse for a bit of a shake up.'

'Well, if that's your opinion, it's my opinion he's put himself into the way of getting one. Anyhow, *we* shan't have no more of it, and that's something to be thankful for.'

And so Mr. and Mrs. Chittenden sat down to tea.

And what of Mr. Dillet and of his new acquisition? What it was, the title of this story will have told you. What it was like, I shall have to indicate as well as I can.

There was only just room enough for it in the car, and Mr. Dillet had to sit with the driver: he had also to go slow, for though the rooms of the Dolls' House had all been stuffed carefully with soft cottonwool, jolting was to be avoided, in view of the immense number of small objects which thronged them; and the ten-mile drive was an anxious time for him, in spite of all the precautions he insisted upon. At last his front door was reached, and Collins, the butler, came out.

'Look here, Collins, you must help me with this thing—it's a delicate job. We must get it out upright, see? It's full of little things that mustn't be displaced more than we can help. Let's see, where shall we have it? (After a pause for consideration.) Really, I think I shall have to put it in my own room, to begin with at any rate. On the big table—that's it.'

It was conveyed—with much talking—to Mr. Dillet's spacious room on the first floor, looking out on the drive. The sheeting was unwound from it, and the front thrown open, and for the next hour or two Mr. Dillet was fully occupied in extracting the padding and setting in order the contents of the rooms.

When this thoroughly congenial task was finished, I must say that it would have been difficult to find a more perfect and attractive specimen of a Dolls' House in Strawberry Hill Gothic* than that which now stood on Mr. Dillet's large kneehole table, lighted up by the evening sun which came slanting through three tall sash-windows.

It was quite six feet long, including the Chapel or Oratory which flanked the front on the left as you faced it, and the stable on the right. The main block of the house was, as I have said, in the Gothic manner: that is to say, the windows had pointed arches and were surmounted by what are called ogival hoods, with crockets and finials* such as we see on the canopies of tombs built into church walls. At the angles were absurd turrets covered with arched panels. The Chapel had pinnacles and buttresses, and a bell in the turret and coloured glass in the windows. When the front of the house was open you saw four large rooms, bedroom, dining-room, drawing-room and kitchen, each with its appropriate furniture in a very complete state.

The stable on the right was in two storeys, with its proper complement of horses, coaches and grooms, and with its clock and Gothic cupola for the clock bell.

Pages, of course, might be written on the outfit of the mansion—how many frying-pans, how many gilt chairs, what pictures, carpets, chandeliers, four-posters, table linen, glass, crockery and plate it possessed; but all this must be left to the imagination. I will only say that the base or plinth on which the house stood (for it was fitted with one of some depth which allowed of a flight of steps to the front door and a terrace, partly balustraded) contained a shallow drawer or drawers in which were neatly stored sets of embroidered curtains, changes of raiment for the inmates, and, in short, all the materials for an infinite series of variations and refittings of the most absorbing and delightful kind.

'Quintessence of Horace Walpole, that's what it is: he must have had something to do with the making of it.' Such was Mr. Dillet's murmured reflection as he knelt before it in a reverent ecstasy. 'Simply wonderful! this is my day and no mistake. Five hundred pound coming in this morning for that cabinet which I never cared about, and now this tumbling into my hands for a tenth, at the very most, of what it would fetch in town. Well, well! It almost makes one afraid something'll happen to counter it. Let's have a look at the population, anyhow.'

Accordingly, he set them before him in a row. Again, here is an opportunity, which some would snatch at, of making an inventory of costume: I am incapable of it.

There were a gentleman and lady, in blue satin and brocade respectively. There were two children, a boy and a girl. There was a cook, a nurse, a footman, and there were the stable servants, two postilions, a coachman, two grooms.

'Anyone else? Yes, possibly.'

The curtains of the four-poster in the bedroom were closely drawn round all four sides of it, and he put his finger in between them and felt in the bed. He drew the finger back hastily, for it almost seemed to him as if something had—not stirred, perhaps, but yielded—in an odd live way as he pressed it. Then he put back the curtains, which ran on rods in the proper manner, and extracted from the bed a white-haired old gentleman in a long linen night-dress and cap, and laid him down by the rest. The tale was complete.

Dinner-time was now near, so Mr. Dillet spent but five minutes in putting the lady and children into the drawing-room, the gentleman into the dining-room, the servants into the kitchen and stables, and the old man back into his bed. He retired into his dressing-room next door, and we see and hear no more of him until something like eleven o'clock at night.

His whim was to sleep surrounded by some of the gems of his collection. The big room in which we have seen him contained his bed: bath, wardrobe, and all the appliances of dressing were in a commodious room adjoining: but his four-poster, which itself was a valued treasure, stood in the large room where he sometimes wrote, and often sat, and even received visitors. To-night he repaired to it in a highly complacent frame of mind.

There was no striking clock within earshot—none on the staircase, none in the stable, none in the distant church tower. Yet it is indubitable that Mr. Dillet was startled out of a very pleasant slumber by a bell tolling One.

He was so much startled that he did not merely lie breathless with wide-open eyes, but actually sat up in his bed.

He never asked himself, till the morning hours, how it was that, though there was no light at all in the room, the Dolls' House on the kneehole table stood out with complete clearness. But it was so. The effect was that of a bright harvest moon shining full on the front of a big white stone mansion—a quarter of a mile away it might be, and yet every detail was photographically sharp. There were trees about it, too—trees rising behind the chapel and the house. He seemed to be conscious of the scent of a cool still September night. He thought he could hear an occasional stamp and clink from the stables, as of horses stirring. And with another shock he realized that, above the house, he was looking, not at the wall of his room with its pictures, but into the profound blue of a night sky.

There were lights, more than one, in the windows, and he quickly saw that this was no four-roomed house with a movable front, but one of many rooms, and staircases—a real house, but seen as if through the wrong end of a telescope. 'You mean to show me something,' he muttered to himself, and he gazed earnestly on the lighted windows. They would in real life have been shuttered or curtained, no doubt, he thought; but, as it was, there was nothing to intercept his view of what was being transacted inside the rooms.

Two rooms were lighted—one on the ground floor to the right of the door, one upstairs, on the left—the first brightly enough, the other rather dimly. The lower room was the dining-room: a table was laid, but the meal was over, and only wine and glasses were left on the table. The man of the blue satin and the woman of the brocade were alone in the room, and they were talking very earnestly, seated close together at the table, their elbows on it: every now and again stopping to listen, as it seemed. Once *he* rose, came to the window and opened it and put his head out and his hand to his ear. There was a lighted taper in a silver candlestick on a sideboard. When the man left the window he seemed to leave the room also; and the lady, taper in hand, remained standing and listening. The expression on her face was that of one striving her utmost to keep down a fear that threatened to master her—and succeeding. It was a hateful face, too; broad, flat and sly. Now the man came back and she took some small thing from him and hurried out of the room. He, too, disappeared, but only for a moment or two. The front door slowly opened and he stepped out and stood on the top of the *perron*,* looking this way and that; then turned towards the upper window that was lighted, and shook his fist.

It was time to look at that upper window. Through it was seen a four-post bed: a nurse or other servant in an arm-chair, evidently sound asleep; in the bed an old man lying: awake, and, one would say, anxious, from the way in which he shifted about and moved his fingers, beating tunes on the coverlet. Beyond the bed a door opened. Light was seen on the ceiling, and the lady came in: she set down her candle on a table, came to the fireside and roused the nurse. In her hand she had an old-fashioned wine bottle, ready uncorked. The nurse took it, poured some of the contents into a little silver saucepan, added some spice and sugar from casters on the table, and set it to warm on the fire. Meanwhile the old man in the bed beckoned feebly to the lady, who came to him, smiling, took his wrist as if to feel his pulse, and bit her lip as if in consternation. He looked at her anxiously, and then pointed to the window, and spoke. She nodded, and did as the man below had done; opened the casement and listened—perhaps rather ostentatiously: then drew in her head and shook it, looking at the old man, who seemed to sigh.

By this time the posset* on the fire was steaming, and the nurse poured it into a small two-handled silver bowl and brought it to the bedside. The old man seemed disinclined for it and was waving it away, but the lady and the nurse together bent over him and evidently pressed it upon him. He must have yielded, for they supported him into a sitting position, and put it to his lips. He drank most of it, in several draughts, and they laid him down. The lady left the room, smiling good night to him, and took the bowl, the bottle and the silver saucepan with her. The nurse returned to the chair, and there was an interval of complete quiet.

Suddenly the old man started up in his bed—and he must have uttered some cry, for the nurse started out of her chair and made but one step of it to the bedside. He was a sad and terrible sight—flushed in the face, almost to blackness, the eyes glaring whitely, both hands clutching at his heart, foam at his lips.

For a moment the nurse left him, ran to the door, flung it wide open, and, one supposes, screamed aloud for help, then darted back to the bed and seemed to try feverishly to soothe him—to lay him down—anything. But as the lady, her husband, and several servants, rushed into the room with horrified faces, the old man collapsed under the nurse's hands and lay back, and the features, contorted with agony and rage, relaxed slowly into calm.

A few moments later, lights showed out to the left of the house, and a coach with flambeaux drove up to the door. A white-wigged man in black got nimbly out and ran up the steps, carrying a small leather trunk-shaped box. He was met in the doorway by the man and his wife, she with her handkerchief clutched between her hands, he with a tragic face, but retaining his self-control. They led the new-comer into the dining-room, where he set his box of papers on the table, and, turning to them, listened with a face of consternation at what they had to tell. He nodded his head again and again, threw out his hands slightly, declined, it seemed, offers of refreshment and lodging for the night, and within a few minutes came slowly down the steps, entering the coach and driving off the way he had come. As the man in blue watched him from the top of the steps, a smile not pleas-ant to see stole slowly over his fat white face. Darkness fell over the whole scene as the lights of the coach disappeared.

But Mr. Dillet remained sitting up in the bed: he had rightly guessed that there would be a sequel. The house front glimmered out again before long. But now there was a difference. The lights were in other windows, one at the top of the house, the other illuminating the range of coloured windows of the chapel. How he saw through these is not quite obvious, but he did. The interior was as carefully fur-nished as the rest of the establishment, with its minute red cushions on the desks, its Gothic stall-canopies, and its western gallery and pinnacled organ with gold pipes. On the centre of the black and white pavement was a bier: four tall candles burned at the corners. On the bier was a coffin covered with a pall of black velvet.

As he looked the folds of the pall stirred. It seemed to rise at one end: it slid downwards: it fell away, exposing the black coffin with its silver handles and name-plate. One of the tall candlesticks swayed and toppled over. Ask no more, but turn, as Mr. Dillet hastily did, and look in at the lighted window at the top of the house, where a boy and girl lay in two truckle-beds,* and a four-poster for the nurse rose above them. The nurse was not visible for the moment; but the father and mother were there, dressed now in mourning, but with very little sign of mourning in their demeanour. Indeed, they were laughing and talking with a good deal of animation, sometimes to each other, and sometimes throwing a remark to one or other of the children, and again laughing at the answers. Then the father was seen to go on tiptoe out of the room, taking with him as he went a white garment that hung on a peg near the door. He shut the door after him. A minute or two later it was slowly opened again, and a muffled head poked round it. A bent form of sinister shape stepped across to the truckle-beds, and suddenly stopped, threw up its arms and revealed, of course, the father, laughing. The children were in agonies of terror, the boy with the bedclothes over his head, the girl throwing herself out of bed into her mother's arms. Attempts at consolation followed—the parents took the children on their laps, patted them, picked up the white gown and showed there was no harm in it, and so forth; and at last putting the children back into bed, left the room with encouraging waves of the hand. As they left it, the nurse came in, and soon the light died down.

Still Mr. Dillet watched immovable.

A new sort of light—not of lamp or candle—a pale ugly light, began to dawn around the door-case at the back of the room. The door was opening again. The seer does not like to dwell upon what he saw entering the room: he says it might be described as a frog—the size of a man—but it had scanty white hair about its head. It was busy about the truckle-beds, but not for long. The sound of cries—faint, as if coming out of a vast distance—but, even so, infinitely appalling, reached the ear.

There were signs of a hideous commotion all over the house: lights moved along and up, and doors opened and shut, and running figures passed within the windows. The clock in the stable turret tolled one, and darkness fell again.

It was only dispelled once more, to show the house front. At the bottom of the steps dark figures were drawn up in two lines, holding flaming torches. More dark figures came down the steps, bearing, first one, then another small coffin. And the lines of torch-bearers with the coffins between them moved silently onward to the left.

The hours of night passed on—never so slowly, Mr. Dillet thought. Gradually he sank down from sitting to lying in his bed—but he did not close an eye: and early next morning he sent for the doctor.

The doctor found him in a disquieting state of nerves, and recommended sea-air. To a quiet place on the East Coast he accordingly repaired by easy stages in his car.

One of the first people he met on the sea front was Mr. Chittenden, who, it appeared, had likewise been advised to take his wife away for a bit of a change.

Mr. Chittenden looked somewhat askance upon him when they met: and not without cause.

'Well, I don't wonder at you being a bit upset, Mr. Dillet. What? yes, well, I might say 'orrible upset, to be sure, seeing what me and my poor wife went through ourselves. But I put it to you, Mr. Dillet, one of two things: was I going to scrap a lovely piece like that on the one 'and, or was I going to tell customers: 'I'm selling you a regular picture-palace-dramar in reel life of the olden time, billed to perform regular at one o'clock a.m.'? Why, what would you 'ave said yourself? And next thing you know, two Justices of the Peace in the back parlour, and pore Mr. and Mrs. Chittenden off in a spring cart to the County Asylum and everyone in the street saying, 'Ah, I thought it 'ud come to that. Look at the way the man drank!'—and me 'next door, or next door but one, to a total abstainer, as you know. Well, there was my position. What? Me 'ave it back in the shop? Well, what do *you* think? No, but I'll tell you what I will do. You shall have your money back, bar the ten pound I paid for it, and you make what you can.'

Later in the day, in what is offensively called the 'smoke-room' of the hotel, a murmured conversation between the two went on for some time.

'How much do you really know about that thing, and where it came from?'

'Honest, Mr. Dillet, I don't know the 'ouse. Of course, it came out of the lumber room of a country 'ouse—that anyone could guess. But I'll go as far as say this, that I believe it's not a hundred miles from this place. Which direction and how far I've no notion. I'm only judging by guess-work. The man as I actually paid the cheque to ain't one of my regular men, and I've lost sight of him; but I 'ave the idea that this part of the country was his beat, and that's every word I can tell you. But now, Mr. Dillet, there's one thing that rather physicks me.* That old chap,—I suppose you saw him drive up to the door—I thought so: now, would he have been the medical man, do you take it? My wife would have it so, but I stuck to it that was the lawyer, because he had papers with him, and one he took out was folded up.'

'I agree,' said Mr. Dillet. 'Thinking it over, I came to the conclusion that was the old man's will, ready to be signed.'

'Just what I thought,' said Mr. Chittenden, 'and I took it that will would have cut out the young people, eh? Well, well! It's been a lesson to me, I know that. I shan't buy no more dolls' houses, nor waste no more money on the pictures—and as to this business of poisonin' grandpa, well, if I know myself, I never 'ad much of a turn for that. Live and let live: that's bin my motto throughout life, and I ain't found it a bad one.'

Filled with these elevated sentiments, Mr. Chittenden retired to his lodgings. Mr. Dillet next day repaired to the local Institute, where he hoped to find some clue to the riddle that absorbed him. He gazed in despair at a long file of the Canterbury and York Society's* publications of the Parish Registers of the district. No print resembling the house of his nightmare was among those that hung on the staircase and in the passages. Disconsolate, he found himself at last in a derelict room, staring at a dusty model of a church in a dusty glass case: *Model of St. Stephen's Church, Coxham. Presented by J. Merewether, Esq., of Ilbridge House,* 1877. The work of his ancestor James Merewether, d.* 1786. There was something in the fashion of it that reminded him dimly of his horror. He retraced his steps to a wall map he had noticed, and made out that Ilbridge House was in Coxham Parish. Coxham was, as it happened, one of the parishes of which he had retained the name when he glanced over the file of printed registers, and it was not long before he found in them the record of the burial of Roger Milford, aged 76, on the 11th of September, 1757, and of Roger and Elizabeth Merewether, aged 9 and 7, on the 19th of the same month. It seemed worth while to follow up this clue, frail as it was; and in the afternoon he drove out to Coxham. The east end of the north aisle of the church is a Milford chapel, and on its north wall are tablets to the same persons; Roger, the elder, it seems, was distinguished by all the qualities which adorn 'the Father, the Magistrate, and the Man': the memorial was erected by his attached daughter Elizabeth, 'who did not long survive the loss of a parent ever solicitous for her welfare, and of two amiable children.' The last sentence was plainly an addition to the original inscription.

A yet later slab told of James Merewether, husband of Elizabeth, 'who in the dawn of life practised, not without success, those arts which, had he continued their exercise, might in the opinion of the most competent judges have earned for him the name of the British Vitruvius:* but who, overwhelmed by the visitation which deprived him of an affectionate partner and a blooming offspring, passed his Prime and Age in a secluded yet elegant Retirement: his grateful Nephew and Heir indulges a pious sorrow by this too brief recital of his excellences.'

The children were more simply commemorated. Both died on the night of the 12th of September.

Mr. Dillet felt sure that in Ilbridge House he had found the scene of his drama. In some old sketchbook, possibly in some old print, he may yet find convincing evidence that he is right. But the Ilbridge House of to-day is not that which he sought; it is an Elizabethan erection of the forties, in red brick with stone quoins and dressings.* A quarter of a mile from it, in a low part of the park, backed by ancient, stag-horned, ivy-strangled trees and thick undergrowth, are marks of a terraced platform overgrown with rough grass. A few stone balusters lie here and there, and a heap or two, covered with nettles and ivy, of wrought stones with badly-carved crockets. This, someone told Mr. Dillet, was the site of an older house.

As he drove out of the village, the hall clock struck four, and Mr. Dillet started up and clapped his hands to his ears. It was not the first time he had heard that bell.

Awaiting an offer from the other side of the Atlantic, the dolls' house still reposes, carefully sheeted, in a loft over Mr. Dillet's stables, whither Collins conveyed it on the day when Mr. Dillet started for the sea coast.

———————

[It will be said, perhaps, and not unjustly, that this is no more than a variation on a former story of mine called *The Mezzotint*. I can only hope that there is enough of variation in the setting to make the repetition of the *motif* tolerable.]

THE UNCOMMON PRAYER-BOOK

I

M R. DAVIDSON was spending the first week in January alone in a country town. A combination of circumstances had driven him to that drastic course: his nearest relations were enjoying winter sports abroad, and the friends who had been kindly anxious to replace them had an infectious complaint in the house. Doubtless he might have found someone else to take pity on him. 'But,' he reflected, 'most of them have made up their parties, and, after all, it is only for three or four days at most that I have to fend for myself, and it will be just as well if I can get a move on with my introduction to the Leventhorp Papers. I might use the time by going down as near as I can to Gaulsford and making acquaintance with the neighbourhood. I ought to see the remains of Leventhorp House, and the tombs in the church.'

The first day after his arrival at the Swan Hotel at Longbridge was so stormy that he got no farther than the tobacconist's. The next, comparatively bright, he used for his visit to Gaulsford, which interested him more than a little, but had no ulterior consequences. The third, which was really a pearl of a day for early January, was too fine to be spent indoors. He gathered from the landlord that a favourite practice of visitors in the summer was to take a morning train to a couple of stations westward, and walk back down the valley of the Tent, through Stanford St. Thomas and Stanford Magdalene,* both of which were accounted highly picturesque villages. He closed with this plan, and we now find him seated in a third-class carriage at 9.45 a.m., on his way to Kingsbourne Junction, and studying the map of the district.

One old man was his only fellow-traveller, a piping old man, who seemed inclined for conversation. So Mr. Davidson, after going through the necessary versicles and responses about the weather, inquired whether he was going far.

'No, sir, not far, not this morning, sir,' said the old man. 'I ain't only goin' so far as what they call Kingsbourne Junction. There isn't but two stations betwixt here and there. Yes, they calls it Kingsbourne Junction.'

'I'm going there, too,' said Mr. Davidson.

'Oh, indeed, sir; do you know that part?'

'No, I'm only going for the sake of taking a walk back to Longbridge, and seeing a bit of the country.'

'Oh, indeed, sir! Well, 'tis a beautiful day for a gentleman as enjoys a bit of a walk.'

'Yes, to be sure. Have you got far to go when you get to Kingsbourne?'

'No, sir, I ain't got far to go, once I get to Kingsbourne Junction. I'm agoin' to see my daughter, sir. She live at Brockstone. That's about two mile across the fields from what they call Kingsbourne Junction, that is. You've got that marked down on your map, I expect, sir.'

'I expect I have. Let me see, Brockstone, did you say? Here's Kingsbourne, yes; and which way is Brockstone—toward the Stanfords? Ah, I see it: Brockstone Court, in a park. I don't see the village, though.'

'No, sir, you wouldn't see no village of Brockstone. There ain't only the Court and the Chapel at Brockstone.'

'Chapel? Oh, yes, that's marked here, too. The Chapel; close by the Court, it seems to be. Does it belong to the Court?'

'Yes, sir, that's close up to the Court, only a step. Yes, that belong to the Court. My daughter, you see, sir, she's the keeper's wife now, and she live at the Court and look after things now the family's away.'

'No one living there now, then?'

'No, sir, not for a number of years. The old gentleman, he lived there when I was a lad; and the lady, she lived on after him to very near upon ninety years of age. And then she died, and them that have it now, they've got this other place, in Warwickshire I believe it is, and they don't do nothin' about lettin' the Court out; but Colonel Wildman, he have the shooting, and young Mr. Clark, he's the agent, he come over once in so many weeks to see to things, and my daughter's husband, he's the keeper.'

'And who uses the Chapel? just the people round about, I suppose.'

'Oh, no, no one don't use the Chapel. Why, there ain't no one to go. All the people about, they go to Stanford St. Thomas Church; but

my son-in-law, he go to Kingsbourne Church now, because the gentleman at Stanford, he have this Gregory singin',* and my son-in-
law, he don't like that; he say he can hear the old donkey brayin' any
day of the week, and he like something a little cheerful on the Sunday.'
The old man drew his hand across his mouth and laughed. 'That's
what my son-in-law say; he say he can hear the old donkey,' etc.,
*da capo.**

Mr. Davidson also laughed as honestly as he could, thinking meanwhile that Brockstone Court and Chapel would probably be worth
including in his walk; for the map showed that from Brockstone he
could strike the Tent Valley quite as easily as by following the main
Kingsbourne-Longbridge road. So, when the mirth excited by the
remembrance of the son-in-law's *bon mot* had died down, he returned
to the charge, and ascertained that both the Court and the Chapel
were of the class known as 'old-fashioned places,' and that the old
man would be very willing to take him thither, and his daughter
would be happy to show him whatever she could.

'But that ain't a lot, sir, not as if the family was livin' there; all the
lookin'-glasses is covered up, and the paintin's, and the curtains and
carpets folded away; not but what I dare say she could show you a
pair just to look at, because she go over them to see as the morth
shouldn't get into 'em.'

'I shan't mind about that, thank you; if she can show me the inside
of the Chapel, that's what I'd like best to see.'

'Oh, she can show you that right enough, sir. She have the key of
the door, you see, and most weeks she go in and dust about. That's a
nice Chapel, that is. My son-in-law, he say he'll be bound they didn't
have none of this Gregory singin' there. Dear! I can't help but smile
when I think of him sayin' that about th' old donkey. "I can hear him
bray," he say, "any day of the week"; and so he can, sir; that's true,
anyway.'

The walk across the fields from Kingsbourne to Brockstone was
very pleasant. It lay for the most part on the top of the country, and
commanded wide views over a succession of ridges, plough and
pasture, or covered with dark-blue woods—all ending, more or less
abruptly, on the right, in headlands that overlooked the wide valley of
a great western river. The last field they crossed was bounded by a
close copse, and no sooner were they in it than the path turned downward very sharply, and it became evident that Brockstone was neatly

fitted into a sudden and very narrow valley. It was not long before they had glimpses of groups of smokeless stone chimneys, and stone-tiled roofs, close beneath their feet; and, not many minutes after that, they were wiping their shoes at the back-door of Brockstone Court, while the keeper's dogs barked very loudly in unseen places, and Mrs. Porter, in quick succession, screamed at them to be quiet, greeted her father, and begged both her visitors to step in.

II

It was not to be expected that Mr. Davidson should escape being taken through the principal rooms of the Court, in spite of the fact that the house was entirely out of commission. Pictures, carpets, curtains, furniture, were all covered up or put away, as old Mr. Avery had said; and the admiration which our friend was very ready to bestow had to be lavished on the proportions of the rooms, and on the one painted ceiling, upon which an artist who had fled from London in the plague-year* had depicted the Triumph of Loyalty and Defeat of Sedition. In this Mr. Davidson could show an unfeigned interest. The portraits of Cromwell, Ireton, Bradshaw, Peters,* and the rest, writhing in carefully-devised torments, were evidently the part of the design to which most pains had been devoted.

'That were the old Lady Sadleir* had that paintin' done, same as the one what put up the Chapel. They say she were the first that went up to London to dance on Oliver Cromwell's grave.' So said Mr. Avery, and continued musingly, 'Well, I suppose she got some satisfaction to her mind, but I don't know as I should want to pay the fare to London and back just for that; and my son-in-law, he say the same; he say he don't know as he should have cared to pay all that money only for that. I was tellin' the gentleman as we come along in the train, Mary, what your 'Arry says about this Gregory singin' down at Stanford here. We 'ad a bit of a laugh over that, sir, didn't us?'

'Yes, to be sure we did; ha! ha!' Once again Mr. Davidson strove to do justice to the pleasantry of the keeper. 'But,' he said, 'if Mrs. Porter can show me the Chapel, I think it should be now, for the days aren't long, and I want to get back to Longbridge before it falls quite dark.'

Even if Brockstone Court has not been illustrated in *Rural Life**
(and I think it has not), I do not propose to point out its excellences

here; but of the Chapel a word must be said. It stands about a hundred yards from the house, and has its own little graveyard and trees about it. It is a stone building about seventy feet long, and in the Gothic style, as that style was understood in the middle of the seventeenth century. On the whole it resembles some of the Oxford college chapels as much as anything, save that it has a distinct chancel,* like a parish church, and a fanciful domed bell-turret at the south-west angle.

When the west door was thrown open, Mr. Davidson could not repress an exclamation of pleased surprise at the completeness and richness of the interior. Screen-work, pulpit, seating, and glass— all were of the same period; and as he advanced into the nave and sighted the organ-case with its gold embossed pipes in the western gallery, his cup of satisfaction was filled. The glass in the nave windows was chiefly armorial; and in the chancel were figure-subjects, of the kind that may be seen at Abbey Dore, of Lord Scudamore's work.*

But this is not an archæological review.

While Mr. Davidson was still busy examining the remains of the organ (attributed to one of the Dallams,* I believe), old Mr. Avery had stumped up into the chancel and was lifting the dust-cloths from the blue-velvet cushions of the stall-desks. Evidently it was here that the family sat.

Mr. Davidson heard him say in a rather hushed tone of surprise, 'Why, Mary, here's all the books open agin!'

The reply was in a voice that sounded peevish rather than surprised. 'Tt-tt-tt, well, there, I never!'

Mrs. Porter went over to where her father was standing, and they continued talking in a lower key. Mr. Davidson saw plainly that something not quite in the common run was under discussion; so he came down the gallery stairs and joined them. There was no sign of disorder in the chancel any more than in the rest of the Chapel, which was beautifully clean; but the eight folio Prayer-Books on the cushions of the stall-desks were indubitably open.

Mrs. Porter was inclined to be fretful over it. 'Whoever can it be as does it?' she said: 'for there's no key but mine, nor yet door but the one we come in by, and the winders is barred, every one of 'em; I don't like it, father, that I don't.'

'What is it, Mrs. Porter? Anything wrong?' said Mr. Davidson.

'No, sir, nothing reely wrong, only these books. Every time, pretty near, that I come in to do up the place, I shuts 'em and spreads the cloths over 'em to keep off the dust, ever since Mr. Clark spoke about it, when I first come; and yet there they are again, and always the same page—and as I says, whoever it can be as does it with the door and winders shut; and as I says, it makes anyone feel queer comin' in here alone, as I 'ave to do, not as I'm given that way myself, not to be frightened easy, I mean to say; and there's not a rat in the place—not as no rat wouldn't trouble to do a thing like that, do you think, sir?'

'Hardly, I should say; but it sounds very queer. Are they always open at the same place, did you say?'

'Always the same place, sir, one of the psalms it is, and I didn't particular notice it the first time or two, till I see a little red line of printing, and it's always caught my eye since.'

Mr. Davidson walked along the stalls and looked at the open books. Sure enough, they all stood at the same page: Psalm cix., and at the head of it, just between the number and the *Deus laudum*,* was a rubric, 'For the 25th day of April.' Without pretending to minute knowledge of the history of the Book of Common Prayer,* he knew enough to be sure that this was a very odd and wholly unauthorized addition to its text; and though he remembered that April 25 is St. Mark's Day, he could not imagine what appropriateness this very savage psalm could have to that festival. With slight misgivings he ventured to turn over the leaves to examine the title-page, and knowing the need for particular accuracy in these matters, he devoted some ten minutes to making a a line-for-line transcript of it. The date was 1653; the printer called himself Anthony Cadman.* He turned to the list of proper psalms for certain days; yes, added to it was that same inexplicable entry: *For the 25th day of April: the 109th Psalm.* An expert would no doubt have thought of many other points to inquire into, but this antiquary, as I have said, was no expert. He took stock, however, of the binding—a handsome one of tooled blue leather, bearing the arms that figured in several of the nave windows in various combinations.

'How often,' he said at last to Mrs. Porter, 'have you found these books lying open like this?'

'Reely I couldn't say, sir, but it's a great many times now. Do you recollect, father, me telling you about it the first time I noticed it?'

'That I do, my dear; you was in a rare taking, and I don't so much wonder at it; that was five year ago I was paying you a visit at

Michaelmas time, and you come in at tea-time, and says you, "Father, there's the books laying open under the cloths agin"; and I didn't know what my daughter was speakin' about, you see, sir, and I says, "Books?" just like that, I says; and then it all came out. But as Harry says,—that's my son-in-law, sir,—"whoever it can be," he says, "as does it, because there ain't only the one door, and we keeps the key locked up," he says, "and the winders is barred, every one on 'em. Well," he says, "I lay once I could catch 'em at it, they wouldn't do it a second time," he says. And no more they wouldn't, I don't believe, sir. Well, that was five year ago, and it's been happenin' constant ever since by your account, my dear. Young Mr. Clark, he don't seem to think much to it; but then he don't live here, you see, and 'tisn't his business to come and clean up here of a dark afternoon, is it?'

'I suppose you never notice anything else odd when you are at work here, Mrs. Porter?' said Mr. Davidson.

'No, sir, I do not,' said Mrs. Porter, 'and it's a funny thing to me I don't, with the feeling I have as there's someone settin' here—no, it's the other side, just within the screen—and lookin' at me all the time I'm dustin' in the gallery and pews. But I never yet see nothin' worse than myself, as the sayin' goes, and I kindly hope I never may.'

III

In the conversation that followed (there was not much of it), nothing was added to the statement of the case. Having parted on good terms with Mr. Avery and his daughter, Mr. Davidson addressed himself to his eight-mile walk. The little valley of Brockstone soon led him down into the broader one of the Tent, and on to Stanford St. Thomas, where he found refreshment.

We need not accompany him all the way to Longbridge. But as he was changing his socks before dinner, he suddenly paused and said half-aloud, 'By Jove, that is a rum thing!' It had not occurred to him before how strange it was that any edition of the Prayer-Book should have been issued in 1653, seven years before the Restoration, five years before Cromwell's death, and when the use of the book, let alone the printing of it, was penal. He must have been a bold man who put his name and a date on that title-page. Only, Mr. Davidson reflected, it probably was not his name at all, for the ways of printers in difficult times were devious.

As he was in the front hall of the Swan that evening, making some investigations about trains, a small motor stopped in front of the door, and out of it came a small man in a fur coat, who stood on the steps and gave directions in a rather yapping foreign accent to his chauffeur. When he came into the hotel, he was seen to be black-haired and pale-faced, with a little pointed beard, and gold pince-nez; altogether, very neatly turned out.

He went to his room, and Mr. Davidson saw no more of him till dinner-time. As they were the only two dining that night, it was not difficult for the newcomer to find an excuse for falling into talk; he was evidently wishing to make out what brought Mr. Davidson into that neighbourhood at that season.

'Can you tell me how far it is from here to Arlingworth?'* was one of his early questions; and it was one which threw some light on his own plans; for Mr. Davidson recollected having seen at the station an advertisement of a sale at Arlingworth Hall, comprising old furniture, pictures, and books. This, then, was a London dealer.

'No,' he said, 'I've never been there. I believe it lies out by Kingsbourne—it can't be less than twelve miles. I see there's a sale there shortly.'

The other looked at him inquisitively, and he laughed. 'No,' he said, as if answering a question, 'you needn't be afraid of my competing; I'm leaving this place to-morrow.'

This cleared the air, and the dealer, whose name was Homberger, admitted that he was interested in books, and thought there might be in these old country-house libraries something to repay a journey. 'For,' said he, 'we English have always this marvellous talent for accumulating rarities in the most unexpected places, ain't it?'

And in the course of the evening he was most interesting on the subject of finds made by himself and others. 'I shall take the occasion after this sale to look round the district a bit; perhaps you could inform me of some likely spots, Mr. Davidson?'

But Mr. Davidson, though he had seen some very tempting locked-up book-cases at Brockstone Court, kept his counsel. He did not really like Mr. Homberger.

Next day, as he sat in the train, a little ray of light came to illuminate one of yesterday's puzzles. He happened to take out an almanac-diary that he had bought for the new year, and it occurred to him to look at the remarkable events for April 25. There it was: 'St. Mark. Oliver Cromwell born, 1599.'

That, coupled with the painted ceiling, seemed to explain a good deal. The figure of old Lady Sadleir became more substantial to his imagination, as of one in whom love for Church and King had gradually given place to intense hate of the power that had silenced the one and slaughtered the other. What curious evil service was that which she and a few like her had been wont to celebrate year by year in that remote valley? and how in the world had she managed to elude authority? And again, did not this persistent opening of the books agree oddly with the other traits of her portrait known to him? It would be interesting for anyone who chanced to be near Brockstone on the twenty-fifth of April to look in at the Chapel and see if anything exceptional happened. When he came to think of it, there seemed to be no reason why he should not be that person himself; he, and if possible, some congenial friend. He resolved that so it should be.

Knowing that he knew really nothing about the printing of Prayer-Books, he realized that he must make it his business to get the best light on the matter without divulging his reasons. I may say at once that his search was entirely fruitless. One writer of the early part of the nineteenth century, a writer of rather windy and rhapsodical chat about books, professed to have heard of a special anti-Cromwellian issue of the Prayer-Book in the very midst of the Commonwealth period. But he did not claim to have seen a copy, and no one had believed him. Looking into this matter, Mr. Davidson found that the statement was based on letters from a correspondent who had lived near Longbridge; so he was inclined to think that the Brockstone Prayer-Books were at the bottom of it, and had excited a momentary interest.

Months went on, and St. Mark's Day came near. Nothing interfered with Mr. Davidson's plans of visiting Brockstone, or with those of the friend whom he had persuaded to go with him, and to whom alone he had confided the puzzle. The same 9.45 train which had taken him in January took them now to Kingsbourne; the same field-path led them to Brockstone. But to-day they stopped more than once to pick a cowslip; the distant woods and ploughed uplands were of another colour, and in the copse there was, as Mrs. Porter said, 'a regular charm of birds; why you couldn't hardly collect your mind sometimes with it.'

She recognized Mr. Davidson at once, and was very ready to do the honours of the Chapel. The new visitor, Mr. Witham, was as much struck by the completeness of it as Mr. Davidson had been. 'There can't be such another in England,' he said.

'Books open again, Mrs. Porter?' said Davidson, as they walked up to the chancel.

'Dear, yes, I expect so, sir,' said Mrs. Porter, as she drew off the cloths. 'Well, there!' she exclaimed the next moment, 'if they ain't shut! That's the first time ever I've found 'em so. But it's not for want of care on my part, I do assure you, gentlemen, if they wasn't, for I felt the cloths the last thing before I shut up last week, when the gentleman had done photografting the heast winder, and every one was shut, and where there was ribbons left, I tied 'em. Now I think of it, I don't remember ever to 'ave done that before, and per'aps, whoever it is, it just made the difference to 'em. Well, it only shows, don't it? if at first you don't succeed, try, try, try again.'

Meanwhile the two men had been examining the books, and now Davidson spoke.

'I'm sorry to say I'm afraid there's something wrong here, Mrs. Porter. These are not the same books.'

It would make too long a business to detail all Mrs. Porter's outcries, and the questionings that followed. The upshot was this. Early in January the gentleman had come to see over the Chapel, and thought a great deal of it, and said he must come back in the spring weather and take some photografts. And only a week ago he had drove up in his motoring car, and a very 'eavy box with the slides in it, and she had locked him in because he said something about a long explosion,* and she was afraid of some damage happening; and he says, no, not explosion, but it appeared the lantern what they take the slides with worked very slow; and so he was in there the best part of an hour and she come and let him out, and he drove off with his box and all and gave her his visiting-card, and oh, dear, dear, to think of such a thing! he must have changed the books and took the old ones away with him in his box.

'What sort of man was he?'

'Oh, dear, he was a small-made gentleman, if you can call him so after the way he've behaved, with black hair, that is if it was hair, and gold eye-glasses, if they was gold; reely, one don't know what to believe. Sometimes I doubt he weren't a reel Englishman at all, and yet he seemed to know the language, and had the name on his visiting-card like anybody else might.'

'Just so; might we see the card? Yes; T. W. Henderson, and an address somewhere near Bristol. Well, Mrs. Porter, it's quite plain this Mr. Henderson, as he calls himself, has walked off with your eight Prayer-Books and put eight others about the same size in place of them. Now listen to me. I suppose you must tell your husband about this, but neither you nor he must say one word about it to anyone else. If you'll give me the address of the agent,—Mr. Clark, isn't it?—I will write to him and tell him exactly what has happened, and that it really is no fault of yours. But, you understand, we must keep it very quiet; and why? Because this man who has stolen the books will of course try to sell them one at a time—for I may tell you they are worth a good deal of money—and the only way we can bring it home to him is by keeping a sharp look out and saying nothing.'

By dint of repeating the same advice in various forms, they succeeded in impressing Mrs. Porter with the real need for silence, and were forced to make a concession only in the case of Mr. Avery, who was expected on a visit shortly. 'But you may be safe with father, sir,' said Mrs. Porter. 'Father ain't a talkin' man.'

It was not quite Mr. Davidson's experience of him; still, there were no neighbours at Brockstone, and even Mr. Avery must be aware that gossip with anybody on such a subject would be likely to end in the Porters having to look out for another situation.

A last question was whether Mr. Henderson, so-called, had anyone with him.

'No, sir, not when he come he hadn't; he was working his own motoring car himself, and what luggage he had, let me see: there was his lantern and this box of slides inside the carriage, which I helped him into the Chapel and out of it myself with it, if only I'd knowed! And as he drove away under the big yew tree by the monument, I see the long white bundle laying on the top of the coach, what I didn't notice when he drove up. But he set in front, sir, and only the boxes inside behind him. And do you reely think, sir, as his name weren't Henderson at all? Oh, dear me, what a dreadful thing! Why, fancy what trouble it might bring to a innocent person that might never have set foot in the place but for that!'

They left Mrs. Porter in tears. On the way home there was much discussion as to the best means of keeping watch upon possible sales.

What Henderson-Homberger (for there could be no real doubt of the identity) had done was, obviously, to bring down the requisite number of folio Prayer-Books—disused copies from college chapels and the like, bought ostensibly for the sake of the bindings, which were superficially like enough to the old ones—and to substitute them at his leisure for the genuine articles. A week had now passed without any public notice being taken of the theft. He would take a little time himself to find out about the rarity of the books, and would ultimately, no doubt, 'place' them cautiously. Between them, Davidson and Witham were in a position to know a good deal of what was passing in the book-world, and they could map out the ground pretty completely. A weak point with them at the moment was that neither of them knew under what other name or names Henderson-Homberger carried on business. But there are ways of solving these problems.

And yet all this planning proved unnecessary.

IV

We are transported to a London office on this same 25th of April. We find there, within closed doors, late in the day, two police inspectors, a commissionaire, and a youthful clerk. The two latter, both rather pale and agitated in appearance, are sitting on chairs and being questioned.

'How long do you say you've been in this Mr. Poschwitz's employment? Six months? And what was his business? Attended sales in various parts and brought home parcels of books. Did he keep a shop anywhere? No? Disposed of 'em here and there, and sometimes to private collectors. Right. Now then, when did he go out last? Rather better than a week ago? Tell you where he was going? No? Said he was going to start next day from his private residence, and shouldn't be at the office—that's here, eh?—before two days; you was to attend as usual. Where is his private residence? Oh, that's the address, Norwood* way; I see. Any family? Not in this country? Now, then, what account do you give of what's happened since he came back? Came back on the Tuesday, did he? and this is the Saturday. Bring any books? One package; where is it? In the safe? You got the key? No, to be sure, it's open, of course. How did he seem when he got back—cheerful? Well, but how do you mean—curious? Thought he might be in for an illness: he said that, did he? Odd smell got in his nose, couldn't get rid of it; told you to let him know who wanted to see him before you let 'em in? That wasn't usual with him? Much the same all Wednesday, Thursday, Friday. Out a good deal; said he was going to the British Museum. Often went there to make inquiries in the way of his business. Walked up and down a lot in the office when he was in. Anyone call in on those days? Mostly when he was out. Anyone find him in? Oh, Mr. Collinson? Who's Mr. Collinson? An old customer; know his address? All right, give it us afterwards. Well, now, what about this morning? You left Mr. Poschwitz's here at twelve and went home. Anybody see you? Commissionaire, you did? Remained at home till summoned here. Very well.

'Now, commissionaire; we have your name—Watkins, eh? Very well, make your statement; don't go too quick, so as we can get it down.'

'I was on duty 'ere later than usual, Mr. Potwitch 'aving asked me to remain on, and ordered his lunching to be sent in, which came as ordered. I was in the lobby from eleven-thirty on, and see Mr. Bligh [the clerk] leave at about twelve. After that no one come in at all except Mr. Potwitch's lunching come at one o'clock and the man left in five minutes' time. Towards the afternoon I became tired of waitin' and I come upstairs to this first floor. The outer door what lead to the orfice stood open, and I come up to the plate-glass door here. Mr. Potwitch he was standing behind the table smoking a cigar, and he laid it down on the mantelpiece and felt in his trouser pockets and took out a key and went across to the safe. And I knocked on the glass, thinkin' to see if he wanted me to come and take away his tray; but he didn't take no notice, bein' engaged with the safe door. Then he got it open and stooped down and seemed to be lifting up a package off of the floor of the safe. And then, sir, I see what looked to be like a great roll of old shabby white flannel, about four to five feet high, fall for'ards out of the inside of the safe right against Mr. Potwitch's shoulder as he was stooping over; and Mr. Potwitch, he raised himself up as it were, resting his hands on the package, and gave a exclamation. And I can't hardly expect you should take what I says, but as true as I stand here I see this roll had a kind of a face in the upper end of it, sir. You can't be more surprised than what I was, I can assure you, and I've seen a lot in me time. Yes, I can describe it if you wish it, sir; it was very much the same as this wall here in colour [the wall had an earth-coloured distemper] and it had a bit of a band tied round underneath. And the eyes, well they was dry-like, and much as if there was two big spiders' bodies in the holes. Hair? no, I don't know as there was much hair to be seen; the flannel-stuff was over the top of the 'ead. I'm very sure it warn't what it should have been. No, I only see it in a flash, but I took it in like a photograft—wish I hadn't. Yes, sir, it fell right over on to Mr. Potwitch's shoulder, and this face hid in his neck,—yes, sir, about where the injury was,—more like a ferret going for a rabbit than anythink else; and he rolled over, and of course I tried to get in at the door; but as you know, sir, it were locked on the inside, and all I could do, I rung up everyone, and the surgeon come, and the police and you gentlemen, and you know as much as what I do. If you won't be requirin' me any more to-day I'd be glad to be getting off home; it's shook me up more than I thought for.'

'Well,' said one of the inspectors, when they were left alone; and 'Well?' said the other inspector; and, after a pause, 'What's the surgeon's report again? You've got it there. Yes. Effect on the blood like the worst kind of snake-bite; death almost instantaneous. I'm glad of that, for his sake; he was a nasty sight. No case for detaining this man Watkins, anyway; we know all about him. And what about this safe, now? We'd better go over it again; and, by the way, we haven't opened that package he was busy with when he died.'

'Well, handle it careful,' said the other; 'there might be this snake in it, for what you know. Get a light into the corners of the place, too. Well, there's room for a shortish person to stand up in; but what about ventilation?'

'Perhaps,' said the other slowly, as he explored the safe with an electric torch, 'perhaps they didn't require much of that. My word! it strikes warm coming out of that place! like a vault, it is. But here, what's this bank-like of dust all spread out into the room? That must have come there since the door was opened; it would seep it all away if you moved it—see? Now what do you make of that?'

'Make of it? About as much as I make of anything else in this case. One of London's mysteries this is going to be, by what I can see. And I don't believe a photographer's box full of large-size old-fashioned Prayer-Books is going to take us much further. For that's just what your package is.'

It was a natural but hasty utterance. The preceding narrative shows that there was, in fact, plenty of material for constructing a case; and when once Messrs. Davidson and Witham had brought their end to Scotland Yard, the join-up was soon made, and the circle completed.

To the relief of Mrs. Porter, the owners of Brockstone decided not to replace the books in the Chapel; they repose, I believe, in a safe-deposit in town. The police have their own methods of keeping certain matters out of the newspapers; otherwise, it can hardly be supposed that Watkins's evidence about Mr. Poschwitz's death could have failed to furnish a good many head-lines of a startling character to the press.

A NEIGHBOUR'S LANDMARK*

❧❧

HOSE who spend the greater part of their time in reading or writing books are, of course, apt to take rather particular notice of accumulations of books when they come across them. They will not pass a stall, a shop, or even a bedroom-shelf without reading some title, and if they find themselves in an unfamiliar library, no host need trouble himself further about their entertainment. The putting of dispersed sets of volumes together, or the turning right way up of those which the dusting housemaid has left in an apoplectic condition, appeals to them as one of the lesser Works of Mercy. Happy in these employments, and in occasionally opening an eighteenth-century octavo, to see 'what it is all about,' and to conclude after five minutes that it deserves the seclusion it now enjoys, I had reached the middle of a wet August afternoon at Betton Court*——

'You begin in a deeply Victorian manner,' I said; 'is this to continue?'

'Remember, if you please,' said my friend, looking at me over his spectacles, 'that I am a Victorian by birth and education, and that the Victorian tree may not unreasonably be expected to bear Victorian fruit. Further, remember that an immense quantity of clever and thoughtful Rubbish is now being written about the Victorian age. Now,' he went on, laying his papers on his knee, 'that article, "The Stricken Years," in *The Times* Literary Supplement* the other day,—able? of course it is able; but, oh! my soul and body, do just hand it over here, will you? it's on the table by you.'

'I thought you were to read me something you had written,' I said, without moving, 'but, of course——'

'Yes, I know,' he said. 'Very well, then, I'll do that first. But I *should* like to show you afterwards what I mean. However——' And he lifted the sheets of paper and adjusted his spectacles.

——at Betton Court, where, generations back, two country-house libraries had been fused together, and no descendant of either stock had ever faced the task of picking them over or getting rid of duplicates. Now I am not setting out to tell of rarities I may have discovered, of Shakespeare quartos bound up in volumes of political tracts, or anything of that kind, but of an experience which befell me in the course of my search—an experience which I cannot either explain away or fit into the scheme of my ordinary life.

It was, I said, a wet August afternoon, rather windy, rather warm. Outside the window great trees were stirring and weeping. Between them were stretches of green and yellow country (for the Court stands high on a hill-side), and blue hills far off, veiled with rain. Up above was a very restless and hopeless movement of low clouds travelling north-west. I had suspended my work—if you call it work—for some minutes to stand at the window and look at these things, and at the greenhouse roof on the right with the water sliding off it, and the Church tower that rose behind that. It was all in favour of my going steadily on; no likelihood of a clearing up for hours to come. I, therefore, returned to the shelves, lifted out a set of eight or nine volumes, lettered 'Tracts,' and conveyed them to the table for closer examination.

They were for the most part of the reign of Anne. There was a good deal of *The Late Peace, The Late War, The Conduct of the Allies*: there were also *Letters to a Convocation Man; Sermons preached at St. Michael's, Queenhithe; Enquiries into a late Charge of the* R*t.* R*ev. the Lord Bishop of Winchester* (or more probably Winton) *to his Clergy*:* things all very lively once, and indeed still keeping so much of their old sting that I was tempted to betake myself into an arm-chair in the window, and give them more time than I had intended. Besides, I was somewhat tired by the day. The Church clock struck four, and it really was four, for in 1889 there was no saving of daylight.*

So I settled myself. And first I glanced over some of the War pamphlets, and pleased myself by trying to pick out Swift by his style from among the undistinguished. But the War pamphlets needed more knowledge of the geography of the Low Countries than I had. I turned to the Church, and read several pages of what the Dean of Canterbury said to the Society for Promoting Christian Knowledge* on the occasion of their anniversary meeting in 1711. When I turned over to a Letter from a Beneficed Clergyman in the Country to the Bishop of C . . . .r, I was becoming languid, and I gazed for some moments at the following sentence without surprise:

'This Abuse (for I think myself justified in calling it by that name) is one which I am persuaded Your Lordship would (if 'twere known to you) exert your utmost efforts to do away. But I am also persuaded that you know no more of its existence than (in the words of the Country Song)

> "That which walks in Betton Wood
> Knows why it walks or why it cries." '*

Then indeed I did sit up in my chair, and run my finger along the lines to make sure that I had read them right. There was no mistake. Nothing more was to be gathered from the rest of the pamphlet. The next paragraph definitely changed the subject: 'But I have said enough upon this *Topick*' were its opening words. So discreet, too, was the namelessness of the Beneficed Clergyman that he refrained even from initials, and had his letter printed in London.

The riddle was of a kind that might faintly interest anyone: to me, who have dabbled a good deal in works of folk-lore, it was really exciting. I was set upon solving it—on finding out, I mean, what story lay behind it; and, at least, I felt myself lucky in one point, that, whereas I might have come on the paragraph in some College Library far away, here I was at Betton, on the very scene of action.

The Church clock struck five, and a single stroke on a gong followed. This, I knew, meant tea. I heaved myself out of the deep chair, and obeyed the summons.

My host and I were alone at the Court. He came in soon, wet from a round of landlord's errands, and with pieces of local news which had to be passed on before I could make an opportunity of asking whether there was a particular place in the parish that was still known as Betton Wood.

'Betton Wood,' he said, 'was a short mile away, just on the crest of Betton Hill, and my father stubbed up the last bit of it when it paid better to grow corn than scrub oaks. Why do you want to know about Betton Wood?'

'Because,' I said, 'in an old pamphlet I was reading just now, there are two lines of a country song which mention it, and they sound as if there was a story belonging to them. Someone says that someone else knows no more of whatever it may be—

> "Than that which walks in Betton Wood
> Knows why it walks or why it cries." '

'Goodness,' said Philipson, 'I wonder whether that was why . . . I must ask old Mitchell.' He muttered something else to himself, and took some more tea, thoughtfully.

'Whether that was why——?' I said.

'Yes, I was going to say, whether that was why my father had the Wood stubbed up. I said just now it was to get more plough-land, but I don't really know if it was. I don't believe he ever broke it up: it's rough pasture at this moment. But there's one old chap at least who'd remember something of it—old Mitchell.' He looked at his watch. 'Blest if I don't go down there and ask him. I don't think I'll take you,' he went on; 'he's not so likely to tell anything he thinks is odd if there's a stranger by.'

'Well, mind you remember every single thing he does tell. As for me, if it clears up, I shall go out, and if it doesn't, I shall go on with the books.'

It did clear up, sufficiently at least to make me think it worth while to walk up the nearest hill and look over the country. I did not know the lie of the land; it was the first visit I had paid to Philipson, and this was the first day of it. So I went down the garden and through the wet shrubberies with a very open mind, and offered no resistance to the indistinct impulse—was it, however, so very indistinct?—which kept urging me to bear to the left whenever there was a forking of the path. The result was that after ten minutes or more of dark going between dripping rows of box and laurel and privet, I was confronted by a stone arch in the Gothic style set in the stone wall which encircled the whole demesne. The door was fastened by a spring-lock, and I took the precaution of leaving this on the jar as I passed out into the road. That road I crossed, and entered a narrow lane between hedges which led upward; and that lane I pursued at a leisurely pace for as much as half a mile, and went on to the field to which it led. I was now on a good point of vantage for taking in the situation of the Court, the village, and the environment; and I leant upon a gate and gazed westward and downward.

I think we must all know the landscapes—are they by Birket Foster,* or somewhat earlier?—which, in the form of wood-cuts, decorate the volumes of poetry that lay on the drawing-room tables of our fathers and grandfathers—volumes in 'Art Cloth, embossed bindings'; that strikes me as being the right phrase. I confess myself an admirer of them, and especially of those which show the peasant leaning over a gate in a hedge and surveying, at the bottom of a downward slope, the village church spire—embosomed amid venerable trees, and a fertile plain intersected by hedgerows, and bounded by distant hills, behind which the orb of day is sinking (or it may be rising) amid level clouds illumined by his dying (or nascent) ray. The expressions employed here are those which seem appropriate to the pictures I have in mind; and were there opportunity, I would try to work in the Vale, the Grove, the Cot, and the Flood. Anyhow, they are beautiful to me, these landscapes, and it was just such a one that I was now surveying. It might have come straight out of 'Gems of Sacred Song, selected by a Lady' and given as a birthday present to Eleanor Philipson in 1852 by her attached friend Millicent Graves. All at once I turned as if I had been stung. There thrilled into my right ear and pierced my head a note of incredible sharpness, like the shriek of a bat, only ten times intensified—the kind of thing that makes one wonder if something has not given way in one's brain. I held my breath, and covered my ear, and shivered. Something in the circulation: another minute or two, I thought, and I return home. But I must fix the view a little more firmly in my mind. Only, when I turned to it again, the taste was gone out of it. The sun was down behind the hill, and the light was off the fields, and when the clock bell in the Church tower struck seven, I thought no longer of kind mellow evening hours of rest, and scents of flowers and woods on evening air; and of how someone on a farm a mile or two off would be saying 'How clear Betton bell sounds to-night after the rain!'; but instead images came to me of dusty beams and creeping spiders and savage owls up in the tower, and forgotten graves and their ugly contents below, and of flying Time and all it had taken out of my life. And just then into my left ear—close as if lips had been put within an inch of my head, the frightful scream came thrilling again.

There was no mistake possible now. It *was* from outside. 'With no language but a cry'* was the thought that flashed into my mind. Hideous it was beyond anything I had heard or have heard since, but I could read no emotion in it, and doubted if I could read any intelligence. All its effect was to take away every vestige, every possibility, of enjoyment, and make this no place to stay in one moment more. Of course there was nothing to be seen: but I was convinced that, if I waited, the thing would pass me again on its aimless, endless beat, and I could not bear the notion of a third repetition. I hurried back to the lane and down the hill. But when I came to the arch in the wall I stopped. Could I be sure of my way among those dank alleys, which would be danker and darker now! No, I confessed to myself that I was afraid: so jarred were all my nerves with the cry on the hill that I really felt I could not afford to be startled even by a little bird in a bush, or a rabbit. I followed the road which followed the wall, and I was not sorry when I came to the gate and the lodge, and descried Philipson coming up towards it from the direction of the village.

'And where have you been?' said he.

'I took that lane that goes up the hill opposite the stone arch in the wall.'

'Oh! did you? Then you've been very near where Betton Wood used to be: at least, if you followed it up to the top, and out into the field.'

And if the reader will believe it, that was the first time that I put two and two together. Did I at once tell Philipson what had happened to me? I did not. I have not had other experiences of the kind which are called super-natural, or -normal, or -physical, but, though I knew very well I must speak of this one before long, I was not at all anxious to do so; and I think I have read that this is a common case.

So all I said was: 'Did you see the old man you meant to?'

'Old Mitchell? Yes, I did; and got something of a story out of him. I'll keep it till after dinner. It really is rather odd.'

So when we were settled after dinner he began to report, faithfully, as he said, the dialogue that had taken place. Mitchell, not far off eighty years old, was in his elbow-chair. The married daughter with whom he lived was in and out preparing for tea.

After the usual salutations: 'Mitchell, I want you to tell me something about the Wood.'

'What Wood's that, Master Reginald?'

'Betton Wood. Do you remember it?'

Mitchell slowly raised his hand and pointed an accusing forefinger. 'It were your father done away with Betton Wood, Master Reginald, I can tell you that much.'

'Well, I know it was, Mitchell. You needn't look at me as if it were my fault.'

'Your fault? No, I says it were your father done it, before your time.'

'Yes, and I dare say if the truth was known, it was your father that advised him to do it, and I want to know why.'

Mitchell seemed a little amused. 'Well,' he said, 'my father were woodman to your father and your grandfather before him, and if he didn't know what belonged to his business, he'd oughter done. And if he did give advice that way, I suppose he might have had his reasons, mightn't he now?'

'Of course he might, and I want you to tell me what they were.'

'Well now, Master Reginald, whatever makes you think as I know what his reasons might 'a been I don't know how many year ago?'

'Well, to be sure, it is a long time, and you might easily have forgotten, if ever you knew. I suppose the only thing is for me to go and ask old Ellis what he can recollect about it.'

That had the effect I hoped for.

'Old Ellis!' he growled. 'First time ever I hear anyone say old Ellis were any use for any purpose. I should 'a thought you know'd better than that yourself, Master Reginald. What do you suppose old Ellis can tell you better'n what I can about Betton Wood, and what call have he got to be put afore me, I should like to know. His father warn't woodman on the place: he were ploughman—that's what he was, and so anyone could tell you what knows; anyone could tell you that, I says.'

'Just so, Mitchell, but if you know all about Betton Wood and won't tell me, why, I must do the next best I can, and try and get it out of somebody else; and old Ellis has been on the place very nearly as long as you have.'

'That he ain't, not by eighteen months! Who says I wouldn't tell you nothing about the Wood? I ain't no objection; only it's a funny kind of a tale, and 'taint right to my thinkin' it should be all about the parish. You, Lizzie, do you keep in your kitchen a bit. Me and Master Reginald wants to have a word or two private. But one thing I'd like to know, Master Reginald, what come to put you upon asking about it to-day?'

'Oh! well, I happened to hear of an old saying about something that walks in Betton Wood. And I wondered if that had anything to do with its being cleared away: that's all.'

'Well, you was in the right, Master Reginald, however you come to hear of it, and I believe I can tell you the rights of it better than anyone in this parish, let alone old Ellis. You see it came about this way: that the shortest road to Allen's Farm laid through the Wood, and when we was little my poor mother she used to go so many times in the week to the farm to fetch a quart of milk, because Mr. Allen what had the farm then under your father, he was a good man, and anyone that had a young family to bring up, he was willing to allow 'em so much in the week. But never you mind about that now. And my poor mother she never liked to go through the Wood, because there was a lot of talk in the place, and sayings like what you spoke about just now. But every now and again, when she happened to be late with her work, she'd have to take the short road through the Wood, and as sure as ever she did, she'd come home in a rare state. I remember her and my father talking about it, and he'd say, "Well, but it can't do you no harm, Emma," and she'd say, "Oh! but you haven't an idear of it, George. Why, it went right through my head," she says, "and I came over all bewildered-like, and as if I didn't know where I was. You see, George," she says, "it ain't as if you was about there in the dusk. You always goes there in the daytime, now don't you?" and he says: "Why, to be sure I do; do you take me for a fool?" And so they'd go on. And time passed by, and I think it wore her out, because, you understand, it warn't no use to go for the milk not till the afternoon, and she wouldn't never send none of us children instead, for fear we should get a fright. Nor she wouldn't tell us about it herself. "No," she says, "it's bad enough for me. I don't want no one else to go through it, nor yet hear talk about it." But one time I recollect she says, "Well, first it's a rustling-like all along in the bushes, coming very quick, either towards me or after me according to the time, and then there comes this scream as appears to pierce right through from the one ear to the other, and the later I am coming through, the more like I am to hear it twice over; but thanks be, I never yet heard it the three times." And then I asked her, and I says: "Why, that seems like someone walking to and fro all the time, don't it?" and she says, "Yes, it do, and whatever it is she wants, I can't think": and I says, "Is it a woman, mother?" and she says, "Yes, I've heard it is a woman."

'Anyway, the end of it was my father he spoke to your father, and told him the Wood was a bad wood. "There's never a bit of game in it, and there's never a bird's nest there," he says, "and it ain't no manner of use to you." And after a lot of talk, your father he come and see my mother about it, and he see she warn't one of these silly women as gets nervish about nothink at all, and he made up his mind there was somethink in it, and after that he asked about in the neighbourhood, and I believe he made out somethink, and wrote it down in a paper what very like you've got up at the Court, Master Reginald. And then he gave the order, and the Wood was stubbed up. They done all the work in the daytime, I recollect, and was never there after three o'clock.'

'Didn't they find anything to explain it, Mitchell? No bones or anything of that kind?'

'Nothink at all, Master Reginald, only the mark of a hedge and ditch along the middle, much about where the quickset hedge run now; and with all the work they done, if there had been anyone put away there, they was bound to find 'em. But I don't know whether it done much good, after all. People here don't seem to like the place no better than they did afore.'

'That's about what I got out of Mitchell,' said Philipson, 'and as far as any explanation goes, it leaves us very much where we were. I must see if I can't find that paper.'

'Why didn't your father ever tell you about the business?' I said.

'He died before I went to school, you know, and I imagine he didn't want to frighten us children by any such story. I can remember being shaken and slapped by my nurse for running up that lane towards the Wood when we were coming back rather late one winter afternoon: but in the daytime no one interfered with our going into the Wood if we wanted to—only we never did want.'

'Hm!' I said, and then, 'Do you think you'll be able to find that paper that your father wrote?'

'Yes,' he said, 'I do. I expect it's no farther away than that cup-board behind you. There's a bundle or two of things specially put aside, most of which I've looked through at various times, and I know there's one envelope labelled Betton Wood: but as there was no Betton Wood any more, I never thought it would be worth while to open it, and I never have. We'll do it now, though.'

'Before you do,' I said (I was still reluctant, but I thought this was perhaps the moment for my disclosure), 'I'd better tell you I think Mitchell was right when he doubted if clearing away the Wood had put things straight.' And I gave the account you have heard already: I need not say Philipson was interested. 'Still there?' he said. 'It's amazing. Look here, will you come out there with me now, and see what happens?'

'I will do no such thing,' I said, 'and if you knew the feeling, you'd be glad to walk ten miles in the opposite direction. Don't talk of it. Open your envelope, and let's hear what your father made out.'

He did so, and read me the three or four pages of jottings which it contained. At the top was written a motto from Scott's *Glenfinlas*,* which seemed to me well-chosen:

'Where walks, they say, the shrieking ghost.'

Then there were notes of his talk with Mitchell's mother, from which I extract only this much. 'I asked her if she never thought she saw anything to account for the sounds she heard. She told me, no more than once, on the darkest evening she ever came through the Wood; and then she seemed forced to look behind her as the rustling came in the bushes, and she thought she saw something all in tatters with the two arms held out in front of it coming on very fast, and at that she ran for the stile, and tore her gown all to flinders getting over it.'

Then he had gone to two other people whom he found very shy of talking. They seemed to think, among other things, that it reflected discredit on the parish. However, one, Mrs. Emma Frost, was prevailed upon to repeat what her mother had told her. 'They say it was a lady of title that married twice over, and her first husband went by the name of Brown, or it might have been Bryan ('Yes, there were Bryans at the Court before it came into our family,' Philipson put in), and she removed her neighbour's landmark: leastways she took in a fair piece of the best pasture in Betton parish what belonged by rights to two children as hadn't no one to speak for them, and they say years after she went from bad to worse, and made out false papers to gain thousands of pounds up in London, and at last they was proved in law to be false, and she would have been tried and put to death very like, only she escaped away for the time. But no one can't avoid the curse that's laid on them that removes the landmark, and so we take it she can't leave Betton before someone take and put it right again.'

At the end of the paper there was a note to this effect. 'I regret that I cannot find any clue to previous owners of the fields adjoining the Wood. I do not hesitate to say that if I could discover their representatives, I should do my best to indemnify them for the wrong done to them in years now long past: for it is undeniable that the Wood is very curiously disturbed in the manner described by the people of the place. In my present ignorance alike of the extent of the land wrongly appropriated, and of the rightful owners, I am reduced to keeping a separate note of the profits derived from this part of the estate, and my custom has been to apply the sum that would represent the annual yield of about five acres to the common benefit of the parish and to charitable uses: and I hope that those who succeed me may see fit to continue this practice.'

So much for the elder Mr. Philipson's paper. To those who, like myself, are readers of the State Trials it will have gone far to illuminate the situation. They will remember how between the years 1678 and 1684 the Lady Ivy, formerly Theodosia Bryan,* was alternately Plaintiff and Defendant in a series of trials in which she was trying to establish a claim against the Dean and Chapter of St. Paul's for a considerable and very valuable tract of land in Shadwell:* how in the last of those trials, presided over by L.C.J. Jeffreys, it was proved up to the hilt that the deeds upon which she based her claim were forgeries executed under her orders: and how, after an information for perjury and forgery was issued against her, she disappeared completely—so completely, indeed, that no expert has ever been able to tell me what became of her.

Does not the story I have told suggest that she may still be heard of on the scene of one of her earlier and more successful exploits?

*   *   *   *   *

'That,' said my friend, as he folded up his papers, 'is a very faithful record of my one extraordinary experience. And now——'

But I had so many questions to ask him, as for instance, whether his friend had found the proper owner of the land, whether he had done anything about the hedge, whether the sounds were ever heard now, what was the exact title and date of his pamphlet, etc., etc., that bed-time came and passed, without his having an opportunity to revert to the Literary Supplement of *The Times*.

———

[Thanks to the researches of Sir John Fox, in his book on *The Lady Ivie's Trial* (Oxford, 1929), we now know that my heroine died in her bed in 1695, having—heaven knows how—been acquitted of the forgery, for which she had undoubtedly been responsible.]

A VIEW FROM A HILL

H ow pleasant it can be, alone in a first-class railway carriage, on the first day of a holiday that is to be fairly long, to dawdle through a bit of English country that is unfamiliar, stopping at every station. You have a map open on your knee, and you pick out the villages that lie to right and left by their church towers. You marvel at the complete stillness that attends your stoppage at the stations, broken only by a footstep crunching the gravel. Yet perhaps that is best experienced after sundown, and the traveller I have in mind was making his leisurely progress on a sunny afternoon in the latter half of June.

He was in the depths of the country. I need not particularize further than to say that if you divided the map of England into four quarters, he would have been found in the south-western of them.*

He was a man of academic pursuits, and his term was just over. He was on his way to meet a new friend, older than himself. The two of them had met first on an official inquiry in town, had found that they had many tastes and habits in common, liked each other, and the result was an invitation from Squire Richards to Mr. Fanshawe which was now taking effect.

The journey ended about five o'clock. Fanshawe was told by a cheerful country porter that the car from the Hall had been up to the station and left a message that something had to be fetched from half a mile farther on, and would the gentleman please to wait a few minutes till it came back? 'But I see,' continued the porter, 'as you've got your bysticle, and very like you'd find it pleasanter to ride up to the 'All yourself. Straight up the road 'ere, and then first turn to the left—it ain't above two mile—and I'll see as your things is put in the car for you. You'll excuse me mentioning it, only I thought it were a nice evening for a ride. Yes, sir, very seasonable weather for the haymakers: let me see, I have your bike ticket. Thank you, sir; much obliged: you can't miss your road, etc., etc.'

The two miles to the Hall were just what was needed, after the day in the train, to dispel somnolence and impart a wish for tea. The Hall, when sighted, also promised just what was needed in the way of a quiet resting-place after days of sitting on committees and college-meetings. It was neither excitingly old nor depressingly new. Plastered walls, sash-windows, old trees, smooth lawns, were the features which Fanshawe noticed as he came up the drive. Squire Richards, a burly man of sixty odd, was awaiting him in the porch with evident pleasure.

'Tea first,' he said, 'or would you like a longer drink? No? All right, tea's ready in the garden. Come along, they'll put your machine away. I always have tea under the lime-tree by the stream on a day like this.'

Nor could you ask for a better place. Midsummer afternoon, shade and scent of a vast lime-tree, cool, swirling water within five yards. It was long before either of them suggested a move. But about six, Mr. Richards sat up, knocked out his pipe, and said: 'Look here, it's cool enough now to think of a stroll, if you're inclined? All right: then what I suggest is that we walk up the park and get on to the hill-side, where we can look over the country. We'll have a map, and I'll show you where things are; and you can go off on your machine, or we can take the car, according as you want exercise or not. If you're ready, we can start now and be back well before eight, taking it very easy.'

'I'm ready. I should like my stick, though, and have you got any field-glasses? I lent mine to a man a week ago, and he's gone off Lord knows where and taken them with him.'

Mr. Richards pondered. 'Yes,' he said, 'I have, but they're not things I use myself, and I don't know whether the ones I have will suit you. They're old-fashioned, and about twice as heavy as they make 'em now. You're welcome to have them, but *I* won't carry them. By the way, what do you want to drink after dinner?'

Protestations that anything would do were overruled, and a satisfactory settlement was reached on the way to the front hall, where Mr. Fanshawe found his stick, and Mr. Richards, after thoughtful pinching of his lower lip, resorted to a drawer in the hall-table, extracted a key, crossed to a cupboard in the panelling, opened it, took a box from the shelf, and put it on the table. 'The glasses are in there,' he said, 'and there's some dodge of opening it, but I've forgotten what it is. You try.' Mr. Fanshawe accordingly tried. There was no keyhole, and the box was solid, heavy and smooth: it seemed obvious that some part of it would have to be pressed before anything could happen. 'The corners,' said he to himself, 'are the likely places;

and infernally sharp corners they are too,' he added, as he put his thumb in his mouth after exerting force on a lower corner.

'What's the matter?' said the Squire.

'Why, your disgusting Borgia box* has scratched me, drat it,' said Fanshawe. The Squire chuckled unfeelingly. 'Well, you've got it open, anyway,' he said.

'So I have! Well, I don't begrudge a drop of blood in a good cause, and here are the glasses. They *are* pretty heavy, as you said, but I think I'm equal to carrying them.'

'Ready?' said the Squire. 'Come on then; we go out by the garden.'

So they did, and passed out into the park, which sloped decidedly upwards to the hill which, as Fanshawe had seen from the train, dominated the country. It was a spur of a larger range that lay behind. On the way, the Squire, who was great on earthworks, pointed out various spots where he detected or imagined traces of war-ditches and the like. 'And here,' he said, stopping on a more or less level plot with a ring of large trees, 'is Baxter's Roman villa.' 'Baxter?' said Mr. Fanshawe.

'I forgot; you don't know about him. He was the old chap I got those glasses from. I believe he made them. He was an old watch-maker down in the village, a great antiquary. My father gave him leave to grub about where he liked; and when he made a find he used to lend him a man or two to help him with the digging. He got a sur-prising lot of things together, and when he died—I dare say it's ten or fifteen years ago—I bought the whole lot and gave them to the town museum. We'll run in one of these days, and look over them. The glasses came to me with the rest, but of course I kept them. If you look at them, you'll see they're more or less amateur work—the body of them; naturally the lenses weren't his making.'

'Yes, I see they are just the sort of thing that a clever workman in a different line of business might turn out. But I don't see why he made them so heavy. And did Baxter actually find a Roman villa here?'

'Yes, there's a pavement turfed over, where we're standing: it was too rough and plain to be worth taking up, but of course there are drawings of it: and the small things and pottery that turned up were quite good of their kind. An ingenious chap, old Baxter: he seemed to have a quite out-of-the-way instinct for these things. He was invalu-able to our archæologists. He used to shut up his shop for days at a time, and wander off over the district, marking down places, where he scented anything, on the ordnance map; and he kept a book with fuller notes of the places. Since his death, a good many of them have been sampled, and there's always been something to justify him.'

'What a good man!' said Mr. Fanshawe.

'Good?' said the Squire, pulling up brusquely.

'I meant useful to have about the place,' said Mr. Fanshawe. 'But was he a villain?'

'I don't know about that either,' said the Squire; 'but all I can say is, if he was good, he wasn't lucky. And he wasn't liked: I didn't like him,' he added, after a moment.

'Oh?' said Fanshawe interrogatively.

'No, I didn't; but that's enough about Baxter: besides, this is the stiffest bit, and I don't want to talk and walk as well.'

Indeed it was hot, climbing a slippery grass slope that evening. 'I told you I should take you the short way,' panted the Squire, 'and I wish I hadn't. However, a bath won't do us any harm when we get back. Here we are, and there's the seat.'

A small clump of old Scotch firs crowned the top of the hill; and, at the edge of it, commanding the cream of the view, was a wide and solid seat, on which the two disposed themselves, and wiped their brows, and regained breath.

'Now, then,' said the Squire, as soon as he was in a condition to talk connectedly, 'this is where your glasses come in. But you'd better take a general look round first. My word! I've never seen the view look better.'

Writing as I am now with a winter wind flapping against dark windows and a rushing, tumbling sea within a hundred yards, I find it hard to summon up the feelings and words which will put my reader in possession of the June evening and the lovely English landscape of which the Squire was speaking.

Across a broad level plain they looked upon ranges of great hills, whose uplands—some green, some furred with woods—caught the light of a sun, westering but not yet low. And all the plain was fertile, though the river which traversed it was nowhere seen. There were copses, green wheat, hedges and pasture-land: the little compact white moving cloud marked the evening train. Then the eye picked out red farms and grey houses, and nearer home scattered cottages, and then the Hall, nestled under the hill. The smoke of chimneys was very blue and straight. There was a smell of hay in the air: there were wild roses on bushes hard by. It was the acme of summer.

After some minutes of silent contemplation, the Squire began to point out the leading features, the hills and valleys, and told where the towns and villages lay. 'Now,' he said, 'with the glasses you'll be able to pick out Fulnaker Abbey. Take a line across that big green field, then over the wood beyond it, then over the farm on the knoll.'

'Yes, yes,' said Fanshawe. 'I've got it. What a fine tower!'

'You must have got the wrong direction,' said the Squire; 'there's not much of a tower about there that I remember, unless it's Oldbourne Church that you've got hold of. And if you call that a fine tower, you're easily pleased.'

'Well, I do call it a fine tower,' said Fanshawe, the glasses still at his eyes, 'whether it's Oldbourne or any other. And it must belong to a largish church; it looks to me like a central tower—four big pinnacles at the corners, and four smaller ones between. I must certainly go over there. How far is it?'

'Oldbourne's about nine miles, or less,' said the Squire. 'It's a long time since I've been there, but I don't remember thinking much of it. Now I'll show you another thing.'

Fanshawe had lowered the glasses, and was still gazing in the Oldbourne direction. 'No,' he said, 'I can't make out anything with the naked eye. What was it you were going to show me?'

'A good deal more to the left—it oughtn't to be difficult to find. Do you see a rather sudden knob of a hill with a thick wood on top of it? It's in a dead line with that single tree on the top of the big ridge.'

'I do,' said Fanshawe, 'and I believe I could tell you without much difficulty what it's called.'

'Could you now?' said the Squire. 'Say on.'

'Why, Gallows Hill,' was the answer.

'How did you guess that?'

'Well, if you don't want it guessed, you shouldn't put up a dummy gibbet and a man hanging on it.'

'What's that?' said the Squire abruptly. 'There's nothing on that hill but wood.'

'On the contrary,' said Fanshawe, 'there's a largish expanse of grass on the top and your dummy gibbet in the middle; and I thought there was something on it when I looked first. But I see there's nothing—or is there? I can't be sure.'

'Nonsense, nonsense, Fanshawe, there's no such thing as a dummy gibbet, or any other sort, on that hill. And it's thick wood—a fairly young plantation. I was in it myself not a year ago. Hand me the glasses, though I don't suppose I can see anything.' After a pause: 'No, I thought not: they won't show a thing.'

Meanwhile Fanshawe was scanning the hill—it might be only two or three miles away. 'Well, it's very odd,' he said, 'it does look exactly like a wood without the glass.' He took it again. 'That *is* one of the oddest effects. The gibbet is perfectly plain, and the grass field, and there even seem to be people on it, and carts, or *a* cart, with men in it. And yet when I take the glass away, there's nothing. It must be something in the way this afternoon light falls: I shall come up earlier in the day when the sun's full on it.'

'Did you say you saw people and a cart on that hill?' said the Squire incredulously. 'What should they be doing there at this time of day, even if the trees have been felled? Do talk sense—look again.'

'Well, I certainly thought I saw them. Yes, I should say there were a few, just clearing off. And now—by Jove, it does look like something hanging on the gibbet. But these glasses are so beastly heavy I can't hold them steady for long. Anyhow, you can take it from me there's no wood. And if you'll show me the road on the map, I'll go there to-morrow.'

The Squire remained brooding for some little time. At last he rose and said, 'Well, I suppose that will be the best way to settle it. And now we'd better be getting back. Bath and dinner is my idea.' And on the way back he was not very communicative.

They returned through the garden, and went into the front hall to leave sticks, etc., in their due place. And here they found the aged butler Patten evidently in a state of some anxiety. 'Beg pardon, Master Henry,' he began at once, 'but someone's been up to mischief here, I'm much afraid.' He pointed to the open box which had contained the glasses.

'Nothing worse than that, Patten?' said the Squire. 'Mayn't I take out my own glasses and lend them to a friend? Bought with my own money, you recollect? At old Baxter's sale, eh?'

Patten bowed, unconvinced. 'Oh, very well, Master Henry, as long as you know who it was. Only I thought proper to name it, for I didn't think that box'd been off its shelf since you first put it there; and, if you'll excuse me, after what happened. . . .' The voice was lowered, and the rest was not audible to Fanshawe. The Squire replied with a few words and a gruff laugh, and called on Fanshawe to come and be shown his room. And I do not think that anything else happened that night which bears on my story.

Except, perhaps, the sensation which invaded Fanshawe in the small hours that something had been let out which ought not to have been let out. It came into his dreams. He was walking in a garden which he seemed half to know, and stopped in front of a rockery made of old wrought stones, pieces of window tracery from a church, and even bits of figures. One of these moved his curiosity: it seemed to be a sculptured capital with scenes carved on it. He felt he must pull it out, and worked away, and, with an ease that surprised him, moved the stones that obscured it aside, and pulled out the block. As he did so, a tin label fell down by his feet with a little clatter. He picked it up and read on it: 'On no account move this stone. Yours sincerely, J. Patten.' As often happens in dreams, he felt that this injunction was of extreme importance; and with an anxiety that amounted to anguish he looked to see if the stone had really been shifted. Indeed it had; in fact, he could not see it anywhere. The removal had disclosed the mouth of a burrow, and he bent down to look into it. Something stirred in the blackness, and then, to his intense horror, a hand emerged—a clean right hand in a neat cuff and coat-sleeve, just in the attitude of a hand that means to shake yours. He wondered whether it would not be rude to let it alone. But, as he looked at it, it began to grow hairy and dirty and thin, and also to change its pose and stretch out as if to take hold of his leg. At that he dropped all thought of politeness, decided to run, screamed and woke himself up.

This was the dream he remembered; but it seemed to him (as, again, it often does) that there had been others of the same import before, but not so insistent. He lay awake for some little time, fixing the details of the last dream in his mind, and wondering in particular what the figures had been which he had seen or half seen on the carved capital. Something quite incongruous, he felt sure; but that was the most he could recall.

Whether because of the dream, or because it was the first day of his holiday, he did not get up very early; nor did he at once plunge into the exploration of the country. He spent a morning, half lazy, half instructive, in looking over the volumes of the County Archæological

Society's transactions, in which were many contributions from Mr. Baxter on finds of flint implements, Roman sites, ruins of monastic establishments—in fact, most departments of archæology. They were written in an odd, pompous, only half-educated style. If the man had had more early schooling, thought Fanshawe, he would have been a very distinguished antiquary; or he might have been (he thus qualified his opinion a little later), but for a certain love of opposition and controversy, and, yes, a patronizing tone as of one possessing superior knowledge, which left an unpleasant taste. He might have been a very respectable artist. There was an imaginary restoration and elevation of a priory church which was very well conceived. A fine pinnacled central tower was a conspicuous feature of this; it reminded Fanshawe of that which he had seen from the hill, and which the Squire had told him must be Oldbourne. But it was not Oldbourne; it was Fulnaker Priory. 'Oh, well,' he said to himself, 'I suppose Oldbourne Church may have been built by Fulnaker monks, and Baxter has copied Oldbourne tower. Anything about it in the letter-press? Ah, I see it was published after his death—found among his papers.'

After lunch the Squire asked Fanshawe what he meant to do.

'Well,' said Fanshawe, 'I think I shall go out on my bike about four as far as Oldbourne and back by Gallows Hill. That ought to be a round of about fifteen miles, oughtn't it?'

'About that,' said the Squire, 'and you'll pass Lambsfield and Wanstone, both of which are worth looking at. There's a little glass at Lambsfield and the stone at Wanstone.'

'Good,' said Fanshawe, 'I'll get tea somewhere, and may I take the glasses? I'll strap them on my bike, on the carrier.'

'Of course, if you like,' said the Squire. 'I really ought to have some better ones. If I go into the town to-day, I'll see if I can pick up some.'

'Why should you trouble to do that if you can't use them yourself?' said Fanshawe.

'Oh, I don't know; one ought to have a decent pair; and—well, old Patten doesn't think those are fit to use.'

'Is he a judge?'

'He's got some tale: I don't know: something about old Baxter. I've promised to let him tell me about it. It seems very much on his mind since last night.'

'Why that? Did he have a nightmare like me?'

'He had something: he was looking an old man this morning, and he said he hadn't closed an eye.'

'Well, let him save up his tale till I come back.'

'Very well, I will if I can. Look here, are you going to be late? If you get a puncture eight miles off and have to walk home, what then? I don't trust these bicycles: I shall tell them to give us cold things to eat.'

'I shan't mind that, whether I'm late or early. But I've got things to mend punctures with. And now I'm off.'

*   *   *   *   *

It was just as well that the Squire had made that arrangement about a cold supper, Fanshawe thought, and not for the first time, as he wheeled his bicycle up the drive about nine o'clock. So also the Squire thought and said, several times, as he met him in the hall, rather pleased at the confirmation of his want of faith in bicycles than sympathetic with his hot, weary, thirsty, and indeed haggard, friend. In fact, the kindest thing he found to say was: 'You'll want a long drink to-night? Cider-cup do? All right. Hear that, Patten? Cider-cup, iced, lots of it.' Then to Fanshawe, 'Don't be all night over your bath.'

By half-past nine they were at dinner, and Fanshawe was reporting progress, if progress it might be called.

'I got to Lambsfield very smoothly, and saw the glass. It is very interesting stuff, but there's a lot of lettering I couldn't read.'

'Not with glasses?' said the Squire.

'Those glasses of yours are no manner of use inside a church—or inside anywhere, I suppose, for that matter. But the only places I took 'em into were churches.'

'H'm! Well, go on,' said the Squire.

'However, I took some sort of a photograph of the window, and I dare say an enlargement would show what I want. Then Wanstone; I should think that stone was a very out-of-the-way thing, only I don't know about that class of antiquities. Has anybody opened the mound it stands on?'

'Baxter wanted to, but the farmer wouldn't let him.'

'Oh, well, I should think it would be worth doing. Anyhow, the next thing was Fulnaker and Oldbourne. You know, it's very odd about that tower I saw from the hill. Oldbourne Church is nothing like it, and of course there's nothing over thirty feet high at Fulnaker, though you can see it had a central tower. I didn't tell you, did I? that Baxter's fancy drawing of Fulnaker shows a tower exactly like the one I saw.'

'So you thought, I dare say,' put in the Squire.

'No, it wasn't a case of thinking. The picture actually *reminded* me of what I'd seen, and I made sure it was Oldbourne, well before I looked at the title.'

'Well, Baxter had a very fair idea of architecture. I dare say what's left made it easy for him to draw the right sort of tower.'

'That may be it, of course, but I'm doubtful if even a professional could have got it so exactly right. There's absolutely nothing left at Fulnaker but the bases of the piers which supported it. However, that isn't the oddest thing.'

'What about Gallows Hill?' said the Squire. 'Here, Patten, listen to this. I told you what Mr. Fanshawe said he saw from the hill.'

'Yes, Master Henry, you did; and I can't say I was so much surprised, considering.'

'All right, all right. You keep that till afterwards. We want to hear what Mr. Fanshawe saw to-day. Go on, Fanshawe. You turned to come back by Ackford and Thorfield, I suppose?'

'Yes, and I looked into both the churches. Then I got to the turning which goes to the top of Gallows Hill; I saw that if I wheeled my machine over the field at the top of the hill I could join the home road on this side. It was about half-past six when I got to the top of the hill, and there was a gate on my right, where it ought to be, leading into the belt of plantation.'

'You hear that, Patten? A belt, he says.'

'So I thought it was—a belt. But it wasn't. You were quite right, and I was hopelessly wrong. I *cannot* understand it. The whole top is planted quite thick. Well, I went on into this wood, wheeling and dragging my bike, expecting every minute to come to a clearing, and then my misfortunes began. Thorns, I suppose; first I realized that the front tyre was slack, then the back. I couldn't stop to do more than try to find the punctures and mark them; but even that was hopeless. So I ploughed on, and the farther I went, the less I liked the place.'

'Not much poaching in that cover, eh, Patten?' said the Squire.

'No, indeed, Master Henry: there's very few cares to go——'

'No, I know: never mind that now. Go on, Fanshawe.'

'I don't blame anybody for not caring to go there. I know I had all the fancies one least likes: steps crackling over twigs behind me, indistinct people stepping behind trees in front of me, yes, and even a hand laid on my shoulder. I pulled up very sharp at that and looked round, but there really was no branch or bush that could have done it. Then, when I was just about at the middle of the plot, I was convinced that there was someone looking down on me from above—and not with any pleasant intent. I stopped again, or at least slackened my pace, to look up. And as I did, down I came, and barked my shins abominably on, what do you think? a block of stone with a big square hole in the top of it. And within a few paces there were two others just like it. The three were set in a triangle. Now, do you make out what they were put there for?'

'I think I can,' said the Squire, who was now very grave and absorbed in the story. 'Sit down, Patten.'

It was time, for the old man was supporting himself by one hand, and leaning heavily on it. He dropped into a chair, and said in a very tremulous voice, 'You didn't go between them stones, did you, sir?'

'I did *not*,' said Fanshawe, emphatically. 'I dare say I was an ass, but as soon as it dawned on me where I was, I just shouldered my machine and did my best to run. It seemed to me as if I was in an unholy evil sort of graveyard, and I was most profoundly thankful that it was one of the longest days and still sunlight. Well, I had a horrid run, even if it was only a few hundred yards. Everything caught on everything: handles and spokes and carrier and pedals— caught in them viciously, or I fancied so. I fell over at least five times. At last I saw the hedge, and I couldn't trouble to hunt for the gate.'

'There *is* no gate on my side,' the Squire interpolated.

'Just as well I didn't waste time, then. I dropped the machine over somehow and went into the road pretty near head-first; some branch or something got my ankle at the last moment. Anyhow, there I was out of the wood, and seldom more thankful or more generally sore. Then came the job of mending my punctures. I had a good outfit and I'm not at all bad at the business; but this was an absolutely hopeless case. It was seven when I got out of the wood, and I spent fifty minutes over one tyre. As fast as I found a hole and put on a patch, and blew it up, it went flat again. So I made up my mind to walk. That hill isn't three miles away, is it?'

'Not more across country, but nearer six by road.'

'I thought it must be. I thought I couldn't have taken well over the hour over less than five miles, even leading a bike. Well, there's my story: where's yours and Patten's?'

'Mine? I've no story,' said the Squire. 'But you weren't very far out when you thought you were in a graveyard. There must be a good few of them up there, Patten, don't you think? They left 'em there when they fell to bits, I fancy.'

Patten nodded, too much interested to speak. 'Don't,' said Fanshawe.

'Now then, Patten,' said the Squire, 'you've heard what sort of a time Mr. Fanshawe's been having. What do you make of it? Anything to do with Mr. Baxter? Fill yourself a glass of port, and tell us.'

'Ah, that done me good, Master Henry,' said Patten, after absorbing what was before him. 'If you really wish to know what were in my thoughts, my answer would be clear in the affirmative. Yes,' he went on, warming to his work, 'I should say as Mr. Fanshawe's experience of to-day were very largely doo to the person you named. And I think, Master Henry, as I have some title to speak, in view of me 'aving been many years on speaking terms with him, and swore in to be jury on the Coroner's inquest near this time ten years ago, you being then, if you carry your mind back, Master Henry, travelling abroad, and no one 'ere to represent the family.'

'Inquest?' said Fanshawe. 'An inquest on Mr. Baxter, was there?'

'Yes, sir, on—on that very person. The facts as led up to that occurrence was these. The deceased was, as you may have gathered, a very peculiar individual in 'is 'abits—in my idear, at least, but all must speak as they find. He lived very much to himself, without neither chick nor child, as the saying is. And how he passed away his time was what very few could orfer a guess at.'

'He lived unknown, and few could know when Baxter ceased to be,'* said the Squire to his pipe.

'I beg pardon, Master Henry, I was just coming to that. But when I say how he passed away his time—to be sure we know 'ow intent he was in rummaging and ransacking out all the 'istry of the neighbourhood and the number of things he'd managed to collect together— well, it was spoke of for miles round as Baxter's Museum, and many a time when he might be in the mood, and I might have an hour to spare, have he showed me his pieces of pots and what not, going back by his account to the times of the ancient Romans. However, you know more about that than what I do, Master Henry: only what I was a-going to say was this, as know what he might and interesting as he might be in his talk, there was something about the man—well, for one thing, no one ever remember to see him in church nor yet chapel at service-time. And that made talk. Our rector he never come in the house but once. "Never ask me what the man said"; that was all anybody could ever get out of *him*. Then how did he spend his nights, particularly about this season of the year? Time and again the labouring men'd meet him coming back as they went out to their work, and he'd pass 'em by without a word, looking, they says, like someone straight out of the asylum. They see the whites of his eyes all round. He'd have a fish-basket with him, that they noticed, and he always come the same road. And the talk got to be that he'd made himself some business, and that not the best kind—well, not so far from where you was at seven o'clock this evening, sir.

'Well, now, after such a night as that, Mr. Baxter he'd shut up the shop, and the old lady that did for him had orders not to come in; and knowing what she did about his language, she took care to obey them orders. But one day it so happened, about three o'clock in the afternoon, the house being shut up as I said, there come a most fearful to-do inside, and smoke out of the windows, and Baxter crying out seemingly in an agony. So the man as lived next door he run round to the back premises and burst the door in, and several others come too. Well, he tell me he never in all his life smelt such a fearful—well, odour, as what there was in that kitchen-place. It seem as if Baxter had been boiling something in a pot and overset it on his leg. There he laid on the floor, trying to keep back the cries, but it was more than he could manage, and when he seen the people come in—oh, he was in a nice condition: if his tongue warn't blistered worse than his leg it warn't his fault. Well, they picked him up, and got him into a chair, and run for the medical man, and one of 'em was going to pick up the pot, and Baxter, he screams out to let it alone. So he did, but he couldn't see as there was anything in the pot but a few old brown bones. Then they says "Dr. Lawrence'll be here in a minute, Mr. Baxter; he'll soon put you to rights." And then he was off again. He must be got up to his room, he couldn't have the doctor come in there and see all that mess—they must throw a cloth over it—anything— the tablecloth out of the parlour; well, so they did. But that must have been poisonous stuff in that pot, for it was pretty near on two months afore Baxter were about agin. Beg pardon, Master Henry, was you going to say something?'

'Yes, I was,' said the Squire. 'I wonder you haven't told me all this before. However, I was going to say I remember old Lawrence telling me he'd attended Baxter. He was a queer card, he said. Lawrence was up in the bedroom one day, and picked up a little mask covered with black velvet, and put it on in fun and went to look at himself in the glass. He hadn't time for a proper look, for old Baxter shouted out to him from the bed: "Put it down, you fool! Do you want to look through a dead man's eyes?" and it startled him so that he did put it down, and then he asked Baxter what he meant. And Baxter insisted on him handing it over, and said the man he bought it from was dead, or some such nonsense. But Lawrence felt it as he handed it over, and he declared he was sure it was made out of the front of a skull. He bought a distilling apparatus at Baxter's sale, he told me, but he could never use it: it seemed to taint everything, however much he cleaned it. But go on, Patten.'

'Yes, Master Henry, I'm nearly done now, and time, too, for I don't know what they'll think about me in the servants' 'all. Well, this business of the scalding was some few years before Mr. Baxter was took, and he got about again, and went on just as he'd used. And one of the last jobs he done was finishing up them actual glasses what you took out last night. You see he'd made the body of them some long time, and got the pieces of glass for them, but there was something wanted to finish 'em, whatever it was, I don't know, but I picked up the frame one day, and I says: "Mr. Baxter, why don't you make a job of this?" And he says, "Ah, when I've done that, you'll hear news, you will: there's going to be no such pair of glasses as mine when they're filled and sealed," and there he stopped, and I says: "Why, Mr. Baxter, you talk as if they was wine bottles: filled and sealed— why, where's the necessity for that?" "Did I say filled and sealed?" he says. "O, well, I was suiting my conversation to my company." Well, then come round this time of year, and one fine evening, I was pass- ing his shop on my way home, and he was standing on the step, very pleased with hisself, and he says: "All right and tight now: my best bit of work's finished, and I'll be out with 'em to-morrow." "What, fin- ished them glasses?" I says, "might I have a look at them?" "No, no," he says, "I've put 'em to bed for to-night, and when I do show 'em

you, you'll have to pay for peepin', so I tell you." And that, gentlemen, were the last words I heard that man say.

'That were the 17th of June, and just a week after, there was a funny
thing happened, and it was doo to that as we brought in "unsound
mind" at the inquest, for barring that, no one as knew Baxter in business could anyways have laid that against him. But George Williams,
as lived in the next house, and do now, he was woke up that same night
with a stumbling and tumbling about in Mr. Baxter's premises, and he
got out o' bed, and went to the front window on the street to see if
there was any rough customers about. And it being a very light night,
he could make sure as there was not. Then he stood and listened, and
he hear Mr. Baxter coming down his front stair one step after another
very slow, and he got the idear as it was like someone bein' pushed or
pulled down and holdin' on to everythin' he could. Next thing he hear
the street door come open, and out come Mr. Baxter into the street in
his day-clothes, 'at and all, with his arms straight down by his sides,
and talking to hisself, and shakin' his head from one side to the other,
and walking in that peculiar way that he appeared to be going as it
were against his own will. George Williams put up the window, and
hear him say: "O mercy, gentlemen!" and then he shut up sudden as
if, he said, someone clapped his hand over his mouth, and Mr. Baxter
threw his head back, and his hat fell off. And Williams see his face
looking something pitiful, so as he couldn't keep from calling out to
him: "Why, Mr. Baxter, ain't you well?" and he was goin' to offer
to fetch Dr. Lawrence to him, only he heard the answer: " 'Tis best
you mind your own business. Put in your head." But whether it were
Mr. Baxter said it so hoarse-like and faint, he never could be sure. Still
there weren't no one but him in the street, and yet Williams was that
upset by the way he spoke that he shrank back from the window and
went and sat on the bed. And he heard Mr. Baxter's step go on and up
the road, and after a minute or more he couldn't help but look out
once more and he see him going along the same curious way as before.
And one thing he recollected was that Mr. Baxter never stopped to
pick up his 'at when it fell off, and yet there it was on his head. Well,
Master Henry, that was the last anybody see of Mr. Baxter, leastways
for a week or more. There was a lot of people said he was called off on
business, or made off because he'd got into some scrape, but he was
well known for miles round, and none of the railway-people nor the
public-house people hadn't seen him; and then ponds was looked into

and nothink found; and at last one evening Fakes the keeper come down from over the hill to the village, and he says he seen the Gallows Hill planting black with birds, and that were a funny thing, because he never see no sign of a creature there in his time. So they looked at each other a bit, and first one says: "I'm game to go up," and another says: "So am I, if you are," and half a dozen of 'em set out in the evening time, and took Dr. Lawrence with them, and you know, Master Henry, there he was between them three stones with his neck broke.'

Useless to imagine the talk which this story set going. It is not remembered. But before Patten left them, he said to Fanshawe: 'Excuse me, sir, but did I understand as you took out them glasses with you to-day? I thought you did; and might I ask, did you make use of them at all?'

'Yes. Only to look at something in a church.'

'Oh, indeed, you took 'em into the church, did you, sir?'

'Yes, I did; it was Lambsfield church. By the way, I left them strapped on to my bicycle, I'm afraid, in the stable-yard.'

'No matter for that, sir. I can bring them in the first thing to-morrow, and perhaps you'll be so good as to look at 'em then.'

Accordingly, before breakfast, after a tranquil and well-earned sleep, Fanshawe took the glasses into the garden and directed them to a distant hill. He lowered them instantly, and looked at top and bottom, worked the screws, tried them again and yet again, shrugged his shoulders and replaced them on the hall-table.

'Patten,' he said, 'they're absolutely useless. I can't see a thing: it's as if someone had stuck a black wafer over the lens.'

'Spoilt my glasses, have you?' said the Squire. 'Thank you: the only ones I've got.'

'You try them yourself,' said Fanshawe, 'I've done nothing to them.'

So after breakfast the Squire took them out to the terrace and stood on the steps. After a few ineffectual attempts, 'Lord, how heavy they are!' he said impatiently, and in the same instant dropped them on to the stones, and the lens splintered and the barrel cracked: a little pool of liquid formed on the stone slab. It was inky black, and the odour that rose from it is not to be described.

'Filled and sealed, eh?' said the Squire. 'If I could bring myself to touch it, I dare say we should find the seal. So that's what came of his boiling and distilling, is it? Old Ghoul!'

'What in the world do you mean?'

'Don't you see, my good man? Remember what he said to the doctor about looking through dead men's eyes? Well, this was another way of it. But they didn't like having their bones boiled, I take it, and the end of it was they carried him off whither he would not. Well, I'll get a spade, and we'll bury this thing decently.'

As they smoothed the turf over it, the Squire, handing the spade to Patten, who had been a reverential spectator, remarked to Fanshawe: 'It's almost a pity you took that thing into the church: you might have seen more than you did. Baxter had them for a week, I make out, but I don't see that he did much in the time.'

'I'm not sure,' said Fanshawe, 'there is that picture of Fulnaker Priory Church.'

A WARNING TO THE CURIOUS

T HE place on the east coast which the reader is asked to consider is Seaburgh.* It is not very different now from what I remember it to have been when I was a child. Marshes intersected by dykes to the south, recalling the early chapters of *Great Expectations*;* flat fields to the north, merging into heath; heath, fir woods, and, above all, gorse, inland. A long sea-front and a street: behind that a spacious church of flint,* with a broad, solid western tower and a peal of six bells. How well I remember their sound on a hot Sunday in August, as our party went slowly up the white, dusty slope of road towards them, for the church stands at the top of a short, steep incline. They rang with a flat clacking sort of sound on those hot days, but when the air was softer they were mellower too. The railway ran down to its little terminus farther along the same road. There was a gay white windmill just before you came to the station, and another down near the shingle at the south end of the town, and yet others on higher ground to the north. There were cottages of bright red brick with slate roofs . . . but why do I encumber you with these commonplace details? The fact is that they come crowding to the point of the pencil when it begins to write of Seaburgh. I should like to be sure that I had allowed the right ones to get on to the paper. But I forgot. I have not quite done with the word-painting business yet.

Walk away from the sea and the town, pass the station, and turn up the road on the right. It is a sandy road, parallel with the railway, and if you follow it, it climbs to somewhat higher ground. On your left (you are now going northward) is heath, on your right (the side towards the sea) is a belt of old firs, wind-beaten, thick at the top, with the slope that old seaside trees have; seen on the skyline from the train they would tell you in an instant, if you did not know it, that you were approaching a windy coast. Well, at the top of my little hill, a line of these firs strikes out and runs towards the sea, for there is a ridge that goes that way; and the ridge ends in a rather well-defined mound commanding the level fields of rough grass, and a little knot of fir trees crowns it. And here you may sit on a hot spring day, very well content to look at blue sea, white windmills, red cottages, bright green grass, church tower, and distant martello tower* on the south.

As I have said, I began to know Seaburgh as a child; but a gap of a good many years separates my early knowledge from that which is more recent. Still it keeps its place in my affections, and any tales of it that I pick up have an interest for me. One such tale is this: it came to me in a place very remote from Seaburgh, and quite accidentally, from a man whom I had been able to oblige—enough in his opinion to justify his making me his confidant to this extent.

I know all that country more or less (he said). I used to go to Seaburgh pretty regularly for golf in the spring. I generally put up at the 'Bear,'* with a friend—Henry Long it was, you knew him perhaps— ('Slightly,' I said) and we used to take a sitting-room and be very happy there. Since he died I haven't cared to go there. And I don't know that I should anyhow after the particular thing that happened on our last visit.

It was in April, 19—, we were there, and by some chance we were almost the only people in the hotel. So the ordinary public rooms were practically empty, and we were the more surprised when, after dinner, our sitting-room door opened, and a young man put his head in. We were aware of this young man. He was rather a rabbity anæmic subject—light hair and light eyes—but not unpleasing. So when he said: 'I beg your pardon, is this a private room?' we did not growl and say: 'Yes, it is,' but Long said, or I did—no matter which: 'Please come in.' 'Oh, may I?' he said, and seemed relieved. Of course it was obvious that he wanted company; and as he was a reasonable kind of person—not the sort to bestow his whole family history on you—we urged him to make himself at home. 'I dare say you find the other rooms rather bleak,' I said. Yes, he did: but it was really too good of us, and so on. That being got over, he made some pretence of reading a book. Long was playing Patience, I was writing. It became plain to me after a few minutes that this visitor of ours was in rather a state of fidgets or nerves, which communicated itself to me, and so I put away my writing and turned to at engaging him in talk.

After some remarks, which I forget, he became rather confidential. 'You'll think it very odd of me' (this was the sort of way he began), 'but the fact is I've had something of a shock.' Well, I recommended a drink of some cheering kind, and we had it. The waiter coming in made an interruption (and I thought our young man seemed very jumpy when the door opened), but after a while he got back to his woes again. There was nobody he knew in the place, and he did happen to know who we both were (it turned out there was some common acquaintance in town), and really he did want a word of advice, if we didn't mind. Of course we both said: 'By all means,' or 'Not at all,' and Long put away his cards. And we settled down to hear what his difficulty was.

'It began,' he said, 'more than a week ago, when I bicycled over to Froston,* only about five or six miles, to see the church; I'm very much interested in architecture, and it's got one of those pretty porches with niches and shields. I took a photograph of it, and then an old man who was tidying up in the churchyard came and asked if I'd care to look into the church. I said yes, and he produced a key and let me in. There wasn't much inside, but I told him it was a nice little church, and he kept it very clean, "but," I said, "the porch is the best part of it." We were just outside the porch then, and he said, "Ah, yes, that is a nice porch; and do you know, sir, what's the meanin' of that coat of arms there?"

'It was the one with the three crowns,* and though I'm not much of a herald, I was able to say yes, I thought it was the old arms of the kingdom of East Anglia.

'"That's right, sir," he said, "and do you know the meanin' of them three crowns that's on it?"

'I said I'd no doubt it was known, but I couldn't recollect to have heard it myself.

'"Well, then," he said, "for all you're a scholard, I can tell you something you don't know. Them's the three 'oly crowns what was buried in the ground near by the coast to keep the Germans from landing—ah, I can see you don't believe that. But I tell you, if it hadn't have been for one of them 'oly crowns bein' there still, them Germans would a landed here time and again, they would. Landed with their ships, and killed man, woman and child in their beds. Now then, that's the truth what I'm telling you, that is; and if you don't believe me, you ast the rector. There he comes: you ast him, I says."

'I looked round, and there was the rector, a nice-looking old man, coming up the path; and before I could begin assuring my old man, who was getting quite excited, that I didn't disbelieve him, the rector struck in, and said: "What's all this about, John? Good day to you, sir. Have you been looking at our little church?"

'So then there was a little talk which allowed the old man to calm down, and then the rector asked him again what was the matter.

'"Oh," he said, "it warn't nothink, only I was telling this gentleman he'd ought to ast you about them 'oly crowns."

'"Ah, yes, to be sure," said the rector, "that's a very curious matter, isn't it? But I don't know whether the gentleman is interested in our old stories, eh?"

'"Oh, he'll be interested fast enough," says the old man, "he'll put his confidence in what you tells him, sir; why, you known William Ager yourself, father and son too."

'Then I put in a word to say how much I should like to hear all about it, and before many minutes I was walking up the village street with the rector, who had one or two words to say to parishioners, and then to the rectory, where he took me into his study. He had made out, on the way, that I really was capable of taking an intelligent interest in a piece of folk-lore, and not quite the ordinary tripper. So he was very willing to talk, and it is rather surprising to me that the particular legend he told me has not made its way into print before. His account of it was this: "There has always been a belief in these parts in the three holy crowns. The old people say they were buried in different places near the coast to keep off the Danes or the French or the Germans. And they say that one of the three was dug up a long time ago, and another has disappeared by the encroaching of the sea, and one's still left doing its work, keeping off invaders. Well, now, if you have read the ordinary guides and histories of this county, you will remember perhaps that in 1687 a crown, which was said to be the crown of Redwald, King of the East Angles, was dug up at Rendlesham,* and alas! alas! melted down before it was even properly described or drawn. Well, Rendlesham isn't on the coast, but it isn't so very far inland, and it's on a very important line of access. And I believe that is the crown which the people mean when they say that one has been dug up. Then on the south you don't want me to tell you where there was a Saxon royal palace which is now under the sea,* eh? Well, there was the second crown, I take it. And up beyond these two, they say, lies the third."

'"Do they say where it is?" of course I asked.

'He said, "Yes, indeed, they do, but they don't tell," and his manner did not encourage me to put the obvious question. Instead of that I waited a moment, and said: "What did the old man mean when he said you knew William Ager, as if that had something to do with the crowns?"

' "To be sure," he said, "now that's another curious story. These Agers—it's a very old name in these parts, but I can't find that they were ever people of quality or big owners—these Agers say, or said, that their branch of the family were the guardians of the last crown. A certain old Nathaniel Ager was the first one I knew—I was born and brought up quite near here—and he, I believe, camped out at the place during the whole of the war of 1870.* William, his son, did the same, I know, during the South African War.* And young William, *his* son, who has only died fairly recently, took lodgings at the cottage nearest the spot, and I've no doubt hastened his end, for he was a consumptive, by exposure and night watching. And he was the last of that branch. It was a dreadful grief to him to think that he was the last, but he could do nothing, the only relations at all near to him were in the colonies. I wrote letters for him to them imploring them to come over on business very important to the family, but there has been no answer. So the last of the holy crowns, if it's there, has no guardian now."

'That was what the rector told me, and you can fancy how interesting I found it. The only thing I could think of when I left him was how to hit upon the spot where the crown was supposed to be. I wish I'd left it alone.

'But there was a sort of fate in it, for as I bicycled back past the churchyard wall my eye caught a fairly new gravestone, and on it was the name of William Ager. Of course I got off and read it. It said "of this parish, died at Seaburgh, 19—, aged 28." There it was, you see. A little judicious questioning in the right place, and I should at least find the cottage nearest the spot. Only I didn't quite know what was the right place to begin my questioning at. Again there was fate: it took me to the curiosity-shop down that way—you know—and I turned over some old books, and, if you please, one was a prayer-book of 1740 odd, in a rather handsome binding—I'll just go and get it, it's in my room.'

He left us in a state of some surprise, but we had hardly time to exchange any remarks when he was back, panting, and handed us the book opened at the fly-leaf, on which was, in a straggly hand:

'Nathaniel Ager is my name and England is my nation,
Seaburgh is my dwelling-place and Christ is my Salvation,
When I am dead and in my Grave, and all my bones are rotton,
I hope the Lord will think on me when I am quite forgotton.'

This poem was dated 1754, and there were many more entries of Agers, Nathaniel, Frederick, William, and so on, ending with William, 19—.

'You see,' he said, 'anybody would call it the greatest bit of luck. *I* did, but I don't now. Of course I asked the shopman about William Ager, and of course he happened to remember that he lodged in a cottage in the North Field and died there. This was just chalking the road for me. I knew which the cottage must be: there is only one sizable one about there. The next thing was to scrape some sort of acquaintance with the people, and I took a walk that way at once. A dog did the business for me: he made at me so fiercely that they had to run out and beat him off, and then naturally begged my pardon, and we got into talk. I had only to bring up Ager's name, and pretend I knew, or thought I knew something of him, and then the woman said how sad it was him dying so young, and she was sure it came of him spending the night out of doors in the cold weather. Then I had to say: "Did he go out on the sea at night?" and she said: "Oh, no, it was on the hillock yonder with the trees on it." And there I was.

'I know something about digging in these barrows.* I've opened many of them in the down country. But that was with owner's leave, and in broad daylight and with men to help. I had to prospect very carefully here before I put a spade in: I couldn't trench across the mound, and with those old firs growing there I knew there would be awkward tree roots. Still the soil was very light and sandy and easy, and there was a rabbit hole or so that might be developed into a sort of tunnel. The going out and coming back at odd hours to the hotel was going to be the awkward part. When I made up my mind about the way to excavate I told the people that I was called away for a night, and I spent it out there. I made my tunnel: I won't bore you with the details of how I supported it and filled it in when I'd done, but the main thing is that I got the crown.'

Naturally we both broke out into exclamations of surprise and interest. I for one had long known about the finding of the crown at Rendlesham and had often lamented its fate. No one has ever seen an Anglo-Saxon crown—at least no one had. But our man gazed at us with a rueful eye. 'Yes,' he said, 'and the worst of it is I don't know how to put it back.'

'Put it back?' we cried out. 'Why, my dear sir, you've made one of the most exciting finds ever heard of in this country. Of course it ought to go to the Jewel House at the Tower.* What's your difficulty? If you're thinking about the owner of the land, and treasure-trove, and all that, we can certainly help you through. Nobody's going to make a fuss about technicalities in a case of this kind.'

Probably more was said, but all he did was to put his face in his hands, and mutter: 'I don't know how to put it back.'

At last Long said: 'You'll forgive me, I hope, if I seem impertinent, but are you *quite* sure you've got it?' I was wanting to ask much the same question myself, for of course the story did seem a lunatic's dream when one thought over it. But I hadn't quite dared to say what might hurt the poor young man's feelings. However, he took it quite calmly—really, with the calm of despair, you might say. He sat up and said: 'Oh, yes, there's no doubt of that: I have it here, in my room, locked up in my bag. You can come and look at it if you like: I won't offer to bring it here.'

We were not likely to let the chance slip. We went with him; his room was only a few doors off. The boots was just collecting shoes in the passage: or so we thought: afterwards we were not sure. Our visitor—his name was Paxton—was in a worse state of shivers than before, and went hurriedly into the room, and beckoned us after him, turned on the light, and shut the door carefully. Then he unlocked his kit-bag, and produced a bundle of clean pocket-handkerchiefs in which something was wrapped, laid it on the bed, and undid it. I can now say I *have* seen an actual Anglo-Saxon crown. It was of silver— as the Rendlesham one is always said to have been—it was set with some gems, mostly antique intaglios and cameos,* and was of rather plain, almost rough workmanship. In fact, it was like those you see on the coins and in the manuscripts. I found no reason to think it was later than the ninth century. I was intensely interested, of course, and I wanted to turn it over in my hands, but Paxton prevented me. 'Don't *you* touch it,' he said, 'I'll do that.' And with a sigh that was, I declare to you, dreadful to hear, he took it up and turned it about so that we could see every part of it. 'Seen enough?' he said at last, and we nodded. He wrapped it up and locked it in his bag, and stood looking at us dumbly. 'Come back to our room,' Long said, 'and tell us what the trouble is.' He thanked us, and said: 'Will you go first and see if—if the coast is clear?' That wasn't very intelligible, for our proceedings hadn't been, after all, very suspicious, and the hotel, as I said, was practically empty. However, we were beginning to have inklings of—we didn't know what, and anyhow nerves are infectious. So we did go, first peering out as we opened the door, and fancying (I found we both had the fancy) that a shadow, or more than a shadow—but it made no sound—passed from before us to one side as we came out into the passage. 'It's all right,' we whispered to Paxton—whispering seemed the proper tone—and we went, with him between us, back to our sitting-room. I was preparing, when we got there, to be ecstatic about the unique interest of what we had seen, but when I looked at Paxton I saw that would be terribly out of place, and I left it to him to begin.

'What *is* to be done?' was his opening. Long thought it right (as he explained to me afterwards) to be obtuse, and said: 'Why not find out who the owner of the land is, and inform——' 'Oh, no, no!' Paxton broke in impatiently, 'I beg your pardon: you've been very kind, but don't you see it's *got* to go back, and I daren't be there at night, and daytime's impossible. Perhaps, though, you don't see: well, then, the truth is that I've never been alone since I touched it.' I was beginning some fairly stupid comment, but Long caught my eye, and I stopped. Long said: 'I think I do see, perhaps: but wouldn't it be—a relief—to tell us a little more clearly what the situation is?'

Then it all came out: Paxton looked over his shoulder and beckoned to us to come nearer to him, and began speaking in a low voice: we listened most intently, of course, and compared notes afterwards, and I wrote down our version, so I am confident I have what he told us almost word for word. He said: 'It began when I was first prospecting, and put me off again and again. There was always somebody—a man—standing by one of the firs. This was in daylight, you know. He was never in front of me. I always saw him with the tail of my eye on the left or the right, and he was never there when I looked straight for him. I would lie down for quite a long time and take careful observations, and make sure there was no one, and then when I got up and began prospecting again, there he was. And he began to give me hints, besides; for wherever I put that prayer-book—short of locking it up, which I did at last—when I came back to my room it was always out on my table open at the fly-leaf where the names are, and one of my razors across it to keep it open. I'm sure he just can't open my bag, or something more would have happened. You see, he's light and weak, but all the same I daren't face him. Well, then, when I was making the tunnel, of course it was worse, and if I hadn't been so keen I should have dropped the whole thing and run. It was like someone scraping at my back all the time: I thought for a long time it was only soil dropping on me, but as I got nearer the—the crown, it was unmistakable. And when I actually laid it bare and got my fingers into the ring of it and pulled it out, there came a sort of cry behind me—oh, I can't tell you how desolate it was! And horribly threatening too. It spoilt all my pleasure in my find—cut it off that moment. And if I hadn't been the wretched fool I am, I should have put the thing back and left it. But I didn't. The rest of the time was just awful. I had hours to get through before I could decently come back to the hotel. First I spent time filling up my tunnel and covering my tracks, and all the while he was there trying to thwart me. Sometimes, you know, you see him, and sometimes you don't, just as he pleases, I think: he's there, but he has some power over your eyes. Well, I wasn't off the spot very long before sunrise, and then I had to get to the junction for Seaburgh, and take a train back. And though it was daylight fairly soon, I don't know if that made it much better. There were always hedges, or gorse-bushes, or park fences along the road—some sort of cover, I mean—and I was never easy for a second. And then when I began to meet people going to work, they always looked behind me very strangely: it might have been that they were surprised at seeing anyone so early; but I didn't think it was only that, and I don't now: they didn't look exactly at *me*. And the porter at the train was like that too. And the guard held open the door after I'd got into the carriage—just as he would if there was somebody else coming, you know. Oh, you may be very sure it isn't my fancy,' he said with a dull sort of laugh. Then he went on: 'And even if I do get it put back, he won't forgive me: I can tell that. And I was so happy a fortnight ago.' He dropped into a chair, and I believe he began to cry.

We didn't know what to say, but we felt we must come to the rescue somehow, and so—it really seemed the only thing—we said if he was so set on putting the crown back in its place, we would help him. And I must say that after what we had heard it did seem the right thing. If these horrid consequences had come on this poor man, might there not really be something in the original idea of the crown having some curious power bound up with it, to guard the coast? At least, that was my feeling, and I think it was Long's too. Our offer was very welcome to Paxton, anyhow. When could we do it? It was nearing half-past ten. Could we contrive to make a late walk plausible to the hotel people that very night? We looked out of the window: there was a brilliant full moon—the Paschal moon.* Long undertook to tackle the boots and propitiate him. He was to say that we should not be much over the hour, and if we did find it so pleasant that we stopped out a bit longer we would see that he didn't lose by sitting up. Well, we were pretty regular customers of the hotel, and did not give much trouble, and were considered by the servants to be not under the mark in the way of tips; and so the boots *was* propitiated, and let us out on to the sea-front, and remained, as we heard later, looking after us. Paxton had a large coat over his arm, under which was the wrapped-up crown.

So we were off on this strange errand before we had time to think how very much out of the way it was. I have told this part quite shortly on purpose, for it really does represent the haste with which we settled our plan and took action. 'The shortest way is up the hill and through the churchyard,' Paxton said, as we stood a moment before the hotel looking up and down the front. There was nobody about—nobody at all. Seaburgh out of the season is an early, quiet place. 'We can't go along the dyke by the cottage, because of the dog,' Paxton also said, when I pointed to what I thought a shorter way along the front and across two fields. The reason he gave was good enough. We went up the road to the church, and turned in at the churchyard gate. I confess to having thought that there might be some lying there who might be conscious of our business: but if it was so, they were also conscious that one who was on their side, so to say, had us under surveillance, and we saw no sign of them. But under observation we felt we were, as I have never felt it at another time. Specially was it so when we passed out of the churchyard into a narrow path with close high hedges, through which we hurried as Christian did through that Valley;* and so got out into open fields. Then along hedges, though I would sooner have been in the open, where I could see if anyone was visible behind me; over a gate or two, and then a swerve to the left, taking us up on to the ridge which ended in that mound.

As we neared it, Henry Long felt, and I felt too, that there were what I can only call dim presences waiting for us, as well as a far more actual one attending us. Of Paxton's agitation all this time I can give you no adequate picture: he breathed like a hunted beast, and we could not either of us look at his face. How he would manage when we got to the very place we had not troubled to think: he had seemed so sure that that would not be difficult. Nor was it. I never saw anything like the dash with which he flung himself at a particular spot in the side of the mound, and tore at it, so that in a very few minutes the greater part of his body was out of sight. We stood holding the coat and that bundle of handkerchiefs, and looking, very fearfully, I must admit, about us. There was nothing to be seen: a line of dark firs behind us made one skyline, more trees and the church tower half a mile off on the right, cottages and a windmill on the horizon on the left, calm sea dead in front, faint barking of a dog at a cottage on a gleaming dyke between us and it: full moon making that path we know across the sea: the eternal whisper of the Scotch firs just above us, and of the sea in front. Yet, in all this quiet, an acute, an acrid consciousness of a restrained hostility very near us, like a dog on a leash that might be let go at any moment.

Paxton pulled himself out of the hole, and stretched a hand back to us. 'Give it to me,' he whispered, 'unwrapped.' We pulled off the handkerchiefs, and he took the crown. The moonlight just fell on it as he snatched it. We had not ourselves touched that bit of metal, and I have thought since that it was just as well. In another moment Paxton was out of the hole again and busy shovelling back the soil with hands that were already bleeding. He would have none of our help, though. It was much the longest part of the job to get the place to look undisturbed: yet—I don't know how—he made a wonderful success of it. At last he was satisfied, and we turned back.

We were a couple of hundred yards from the hill when Long suddenly said to him: 'I say, you've left your coat there. That won't do. See?' And I certainly did see it—the long dark overcoat lying where the tunnel had been. Paxton had not stopped, however: he only shook his head, and held up the coat on his arm. And when we joined him, he said, without any excitement, but as if nothing mattered any more: 'That wasn't my coat.' And, indeed, when we looked back again, that dark thing was not to be seen.

Well, we got out on to the road, and came rapidly back that way. It was well before twelve when we got in, trying to put a good face on it, and saying—Long and I—what a lovely night it was for a walk. The boots was on the look-out for us, and we made remarks like that for his edification as we entered the hotel. He gave another look up and down the seafront before he locked the front door, and said: 'You didn't meet many people about, I s'pose, sir?' 'No, indeed, not a soul,' I said; at which I remember Paxton looked oddly at me. 'Only I thought I see someone turn up the station road after you gentle-men,' said the boots. 'Still, you was three together, and I don't sup-pose he meant mischief.' I didn't know what to say; Long merely said 'Good night,' and we went off upstairs, promising to turn out all lights, and to go to bed in a few minutes.

Back in our room, we did our very best to make Paxton take a cheerful view. 'There's the crown safe back,' we said; 'very likely you'd have done better not to touch it' (and he heavily assented to that), 'but no real harm has been done, and we shall never give this away to anyone who would be so mad as to go near it. Besides, don't you feel better yourself? I don't mind confessing,' I said, 'that on the way there I was very much inclined to take your view about—well, about being followed; but going back, it wasn't at all the same thing, was it?' No, it wouldn't do: '*You've* nothing to trouble yourselves about,' he said, 'but I'm not forgiven. I've got to pay for that miser-able sacrilege still. I know what you are going to say. The Church might help. Yes, but it's the body that has to suffer. It's true I'm not feeling that he's waiting outside for me just now. But——' Then he stopped. Then he turned to thanking us, and we put him off as soon as we could. And naturally we pressed him to use our sitting-room next day, and said we should be glad to go out with him. Or did he play golf, perhaps? Yes, he did, but he didn't think he should care about that to-morrow. Well, we recommended him to get up late and sit in our room in the morning while we were playing, and we would have a walk later in the day. He was very submissive and *piano** about it all: ready to do just what we thought best, but clearly quite certain in his own mind that what was coming could not be averted or palli-ated. You'll wonder why we didn't insist on accompanying him to his home and seeing him safe into the care of brothers or someone. The fact was he had nobody. He had had a flat in town, but lately he had made up his mind to settle for a time in Sweden, and he had disman-tled his flat and shipped off his belongings, and was whiling away a fortnight or three weeks before he made a start. Anyhow, we didn't see what we could do better than sleep on it—or not sleep very much, as was my case—and see what we felt like to-morrow morning.

We felt very different, Long and I, on as beautiful an April morn-ing as you could desire; and Paxton also looked very different when we saw him at breakfast. 'The first approach to a decent night I seem ever to have had,' was what he said. But he was going to do as we had settled: stay in probably all the morning, and come out with us later. We went to the links; we met some other men and played with them in the morning, and had lunch there rather early, so as not to be late back. All the same, the snares of death overtook him.

Whether it could have been prevented, I don't know. I think he would have been got at somehow, do what we might. Anyhow, this is what happened.

We went straight up to our room. Paxton was there, reading quite peaceably. 'Ready to come out shortly?' said Long, 'say in half an hour's time?' 'Certainly,' he said: and I said we would change first, and perhaps have baths, and call for him in half an hour. I had my bath first, and went and lay down on my bed, and slept for about ten minutes. We came out of our rooms at the same time, and went together to the sitting-room. Paxton wasn't there—only his book. Nor was he in his room, nor in the downstair rooms. We shouted for him. A servant came out and said: 'Why, I thought you gentlemen was gone out already, and so did the other gentleman. He heard you a-calling from the path there, and run out in a hurry, and I looked out of the coffee-room window, but I didn't see you. 'Owever, he run off down the beach that way.'

Without a word we ran that way too—it was the opposite direction to that of last night's expedition. It wasn't quite four o'clock, and the day was fair, though not so fair as it had been, so there was really no reason, you'd say, for anxiety: with people about, surely a man couldn't come to much harm.

But something in our look as we ran out must have struck the servant, for she came out on the steps, and pointed, and said, 'Yes, that's the way he went.' We ran on as far as the top of the shingle bank, and there pulled up. There was a choice of ways: past the houses on the sea-front, or along the sand at the bottom of the beach, which, the tide being now out, was fairly broad. Or of course we might keep along the shingle between these two tracks and have some view of both of them; only that was heavy going. We chose the sand, for that was the loneliest, and someone *might* come to harm there without being seen from the public path.

Long said he saw Paxton some distance ahead, running and waving his stick, as if he wanted to signal to people who were on ahead of him. I couldn't be sure: one of these sea-mists was coming up very quickly from the south. There was someone, that's all I could say. And there were tracks on the sand as of someone running who wore shoes; and there were other tracks made before those—for the shoes sometimes trod in them and interfered with them—of someone not in shoes. Oh, of course, it's only my word you've got to take for all this: Long's dead, we'd no time or means to make sketches or take casts, and the next tide washed everything away. All we could do was to notice these marks as we hurried on. But there they were over and over again, and we had no doubt whatever that what we saw was the track of a bare foot, and one that showed more bones than flesh.

The notion of Paxton running after—after anything like this, and supposing it to be the friends he was looking for, was very dreadful to us. You can guess what we fancied: how the thing he was following might stop suddenly and turn round on him, and what sort of face it would show, half-seen at first in the mist—which all the while was getting thicker and thicker. And as I ran on wondering how the poor wretch could have been lured into mistaking that other thing for us, I remembered his saying, 'He has some power over your eyes.' And then I wondered what the end would be, for I had no hope now that the end could be averted, and—well, there is no need to tell all the dismal and horrid thoughts that flitted through my head as we ran on into the mist. It was uncanny, too, that the sun should still be bright in the sky and we could see nothing. We could only tell that we were now past the houses and had reached that gap there is between them and the old martello tower. When you are past the tower, you know, there is nothing but shingle for a long way—not a house, not a human creature, just that spit of land,* or rather shingle, with the river on your right and the sea on your left.

But just before that, just by the martello tower, you remember there is the old battery, close to the sea. I believe there are only a few blocks of concrete left now: the rest has all been washed away, but at this time there was a lot more, though the place was a ruin. Well, when we got there, we clambered to the top as quick as we could to take breath and look over the shingle in front if by chance the mist would let us see anything. But a moment's rest we must have. We had run a mile at least. Nothing whatever was visible ahead of us, and we were just turning by common consent to get down and run hopelessly on, when we heard what I can only call a laugh: and if you can understand what I mean by a breathless, a lungless laugh, you have it: but I don't suppose you can. It came from below, and swerved away into the mist. That was enough. We bent over the wall. Paxton was there at the bottom.

You don't need to be told that he was dead. His tracks showed that he had run along the side of the battery, had turned sharp round the corner of it, and, small doubt of it, must have dashed straight into the open arms of someone who was waiting there. His mouth was full of sand and stones, and his teeth and jaws were broken to bits. I only glanced once at his face.

At the same moment, just as we were scrambling down from the battery to get to the body, we heard a shout, and saw a man running down the bank of the martello tower. He was the caretaker stationed there, and his keen old eyes had managed to descry through the mist that something was wrong. He had seen Paxton fall, and had seen us a moment after, running up—fortunate this, for otherwise we could hardly have escaped suspicion of being concerned in the dreadful business. Had he, we asked, caught sight of anybody attacking our friend? He could not be sure.

We sent him off for help, and stayed by the dead man till they came with the stretcher. It was then that we traced out how he had come, on the narrow fringe of sand under the battery wall. The rest was shingle, and it was hopelessly impossible to tell whither the other had gone.

What were we to say at the inquest? It was a duty, we felt, not to give up, there and then, the secret of the crown, to be published in every paper. I don't know how much you would have told; but what we did agree upon was this: to say that we had only made acquaintance with Paxton the day before, and that he had told us he was under some apprehension of danger at the hands of a man called William Ager. Also that we had seen some other tracks besides Paxton's when we followed him along the beach. But of course by that time everything was gone from the sands.

No one had any knowledge, fortunately, of any William Ager living in the district. The evidence of the man at the martello tower freed us from all suspicion. All that could be done was to return a verdict of wilful murder by some person or persons unknown.

Paxton was so totally without connections that all the inquiries that were subsequently made ended in a No Thoroughfare. And I have never been at Seaburgh, or even near it, since.

AN EVENING'S ENTERTAINMENT

❧

NOTHING is more common form in old-fashioned books than the description of the winter fireside, where the aged grandam narrates to the circle of children that hangs on her lips story after story of ghosts and fairies, and inspires her audience with a pleasing terror. But we are never allowed to know what the stories were. We hear, indeed, of sheeted spectres with saucer eyes, and—still more intriguing—of 'Rawhead and Bloody Bones'* (an expression which the Oxford Dictionary traces back to 1550), but the context of these striking images eludes us.

Here, then, is a problem which has long obsessed me; but I see no means of solving it finally. The aged grandams are gone, and the collectors of folklore began their work in England too late to save most of the actual stories which the grandams told. Yet such things do not easily die quite out, and imagination, working on scattered hints, may be able to devise a picture of an evening's entertainment, such an one as Mrs. Marcet's *Evening Conversations*, Mr. Joyce's *Dialogues on Chemistry*, and somebody else's *Philosophy in Sport made Science in Earnest*, aimed at extinguishing by substituting for Error and Superstition the light of Utility and Truth;* in some such terms as these:

Charles: I think, papa, that I now understand the properties of the lever, which you so kindly explained to me on Saturday; but I have been very much puzzled since then in thinking about the pendulum, and have wondered why it is that, when you stop it, the clock does not go on any more.

Papa: (You young sinner, have you been meddling with the clock in the hall? Come here to me! *No, this must be a gloss that has somehow crept into the text*.) Well, my boy, though I do not wholly approve of your conducting without my supervision experiments which may possibly impair the usefulness of a valuable scientific instrument, I will do my best to explain the principles of the pendulum to you. Fetch me a piece of stout whipcord from the drawer in my study, and ask cook to be so good as to lend you one of the weights which she uses in her kitchen.

And so we are off.

How different the scene in a household to which the beams of Science have not yet penetrated! The Squire, exhausted by a long day after the partridges, and replete with food and drink, is snoring on one side of the fireplace. His old mother sits opposite to him knitting, and the children (Charles and Fanny, not Harry and Lucy: they would never have stood it) are gathered about her knee.

Grandmother: Now, my dears, you must be very good and quiet, or you'll wake your father, and you know what'll happen then.

Charles: Yes, I know: he'll be woundy* cross-tempered and send us off to bed.

Grandmother (stops knitting and speaks with severity): What's that? Fie upon you, Charles! that's not a way to speak. Now I *was* going to have told you a story, but if you use such-like words, I shan't. (*Suppressed outcry:* 'Oh, granny!') Hush! hush! Now I believe you *have* woke your father!

Squire (thickly): Look here, mother, if you can't keep them brats quiet——

Grandmother: Yes, John, yes! it's too bad. I've been telling them if it happens again, off to bed they shall go.

Squire relapses.

Grandmother: There, now, you see, children, what did I tell you? you *must* be good and sit still. And I'll tell you what: to-morrow you shall go a-black-berrying, and if you bring home a nice basketful, I'll make you some jam.

Charles: Oh yes, granny, do! and I know where the best blackberries are: I saw 'em to-day.

Grandmother: And where's that, Charles?

Charles: Why, in the little lane that goes up past Collins's cottage.

Grandmother (laying down her knitting): Charles! whatever you do, don't you dare to pick one single blackberry in that lane. Don't you *know*—but there, how should you—what was I thinking of? Well, anyway, you mind what I say——

Charles and Fanny: But why, granny? Why shouldn't we pick 'em there?

Grandmother: Hush! hush! Very well then, I'll tell you all about it, only you mustn't interrupt. Now let me see. When I was quite a little girl that lane had a bad name, though it seems people don't remember about it now. And one day—dear me, just as it might be to-night—I told my poor mother when I came home to my supper—a summer evening it was—I told her where I'd been for my walk, and how I'd come back down that lane, and I asked her how it was that there were currant and gooseberry bushes growing in a little patch at the top of the lane. And oh, dear me, such a taking as she was in! She shook me and she slapped me, and says she, 'You naughty, naughty child, haven't I forbid you twenty times over to set foot in that lane? and here you go dawdling down it at night-time,' and so forth, and when she'd finished I was almost too much taken aback to say anything: but I did make her believe that was the first I'd ever heard of it; and that was no more than the truth. And then, to be sure, she was sorry she'd been so short with me, and to make up she told me the whole story after my supper. And since then I've often heard the same from the old people in the place, and had my own reasons besides for thinking there was something in it.

Now, up at the far end of that lane—let me see, is it on the right- or the left-hand side as you go up?—the left-hand side—you'll find a little patch of bushes and rough ground in the field, and something like a broken old hedge round about, and you'll notice there's some old gooseberry and currant bushes growing among it—or there used to be, for it's years now since I've been up that way. Well, that means there was a cottage stood there, of course; and in that cottage, before I was born or thought of, there lived a man named Davis. I've heard that he wasn't born in the parish, and it's true there's nobody of that name been living about here since I've known the place. But however that may be, this Mr. Davis lived very much to himself and very seldom went to the public-house, and he didn't work for any of the farmers, having as it seemed enough money of his own to get along. But he'd go to the town on market-days and take up his letters at the post-house where the mails called. And one day he came back from market, and brought a young man with him; and this young man and he lived together for some long time, and went about together, and whether he just did the work of the house for Mr. Davis, or whether Mr. Davis was his teacher in some way, nobody seemed to know. I've heard he was a pale, ugly young fellow and hadn't much to say for himself. Well, now, what did those two men do with themselves? Of course I can't tell you half the foolish things that the people got into their heads, and we know, don't we, that you mustn't speak evil when you aren't sure it's true, even when people are dead and gone. But as

I said, those two were always about together, late and early, up on the downland and below in the woods: and there was one walk in particular that they'd take regularly once a month, to the place where you've seen that old figure cut out in the hill-side;* and it was noticed that in the summertime when they took that walk, they'd camp out all night, either there or somewhere near by. I remember once my father— that's your great-grandfather—told me he had spoken to Mr. Davis about it (for it's his land he lived on) and asked him why he was so fond of going there, but he only said: 'Oh, it's a wonderful old place, sir, and I've always been fond of the old-fashioned things, and when him (that was his man he meant) and me are together there, it seems to bring back the old times so plain.' And my father said, 'Well,' he said, 'it may suit *you*, but *I* shouldn't like a lonely place like that in the middle of the night.' And Mr. Davis smiled, and the young man, who'd been listening, said, 'Oh, we don't want for company at such times,' and my father said he couldn't help thinking Mr. Davis made some kind of sign, and the young man went on quick, as if to mend his words, and said, 'That's to say, Mr. Davis and me's company enough for each other, ain't we, master? and then there's a beautiful air there of a summer night, and you can see all the country round under the moon, and it looks so different, seemingly, to what it do in the daytime. Why, all them barrows on the down——'

And then Mr. Davis cut in, seeming to be out of temper with the lad, and said, 'Ah yes, they're old-fashioned places, ain't they, sir? Now, what would you think was the purpose of them?' And my father said (now, dear me, it seems funny, doesn't it, that I should recollect all this: but it took my fancy at the time, and though it's dull perhaps for you, I can't help finishing it out now), well, he said, 'Why, I've heard, Mr. Davis, that they're all graves, and I know, when I've had occasion to plough up one, there's always been some old bones and pots turned up. But whose graves they are, I don't know: people say the ancient Romans were all about this country at one time, but whether they buried their people like that I can't tell.' And Mr. Davis shook his head, thinking, and said, 'Ah, to be sure: well they look to me to be older-like than the ancient Romans, and dressed different— that's to say, according to the pictures the Romans was in armour, and you didn't never find no armour, did you, sir, by what you said?' And my father was rather surprised and said, 'I don't know that I mentioned anything about armour, but it's true I don't remember to have found any. But you talk as if you'd seen 'em, Mr. Davis,' and they both of them laughed, Mr. Davis and the young man, and Mr. Davis said, 'Seen 'em, sir? that would be a difficult matter after all these years. Not but what I should like well enough to know more about them old times and people, and what they worshipped and all.' And my father said, 'Worshipped? Well, I dare say they worshipped the old man on the hill.' 'Ah, indeed!' Mr. Davis said, 'well, I shouldn't wonder,' and my father went on and told them what he'd heard and read about the heathens and their sacrifices: what you'll learn some day for yourself, Charles, when you go to school and begin your Latin. And they seemed to be very much interested, both of them; but my father said he couldn't help thinking the most of what he was saying was no news to them. That was the only time he ever had much talk with Mr. Davis, and it stuck in his mind, particularly, he said, the young man's word about *not wanting for company*: because in those days there was a lot of talk in the villages round about—why, but for my father interfering, the people here would have ducked an old lady for a witch.

Charles: What does that mean, granny, ducked an old lady for a witch? Are there witches here now?

Grandmother: No, no, dear! why, what ever made me stray off like that? No, no, that's quite another affair. What I was going to say was that the people in other places round about believed that some sort of meetings went on at night-time on that hill where the man is, and that those who went there were up to no good. But don't you interrupt me now, for it's getting late. Well, I suppose it was a matter of three years that Mr. Davis and this young man went on living together: and then all of a sudden, a dreadful thing happened. I don't know if I ought to tell you. (*Outcries of* 'Oh yes! yes, granny, you must,' etc.). Well, then, you must promise not to get frightened and go screaming out in the middle of the night. ('No, no, we won't, of course not!') One morning very early towards the turn of the year, I think it was in September, one of the woodmen had to go up to his work at the top of the long covert just as it was getting light; and just where there were some few big oaks in a sort of clearing deep in the wood he saw at a distance a white thing that looked like a man through the mist, and he was in two minds about going on, but go on he did, and made out as he came near that it *was* a man, and more than that, it was Mr. Davis's young man: dressed in a sort of white gown he was, and hanging by his neck to the limb of the biggest oak, quite, quite dead: and near his feet there lay on the ground a hatchet all in a gore of blood. Well, what a terrible sight that was for anyone to come upon in that lonely place! This poor man was nearly out of his wits: he dropped everything he was carrying and ran as hard as ever he could straight down to the Parsonage, and woke them up and told what he'd seen. And old Mr. White, who was the parson then, sent him off to get two or three of the best men, the blacksmith and the church-wardens and what not, while he dressed himself, and all of them went up to this dreadful place with a horse to lay the poor body on and take it to the house. When they got there, everything was just as the wood-man had said: but it was a terrible shock to them all to see how the corpse was dressed, specially to old Mr. White, for it seemed to him to be like a mockery of the church surplice that was on it, only, he told my father, not the same in the fashion of it. And when they came to take down the body from the oak tree they found there was a chain of some metal round the neck and a little ornament like a wheel* hanging to it on the front, and it was very old looking, they said. Now in the meantime they had sent off a boy to run to Mr. Davis's house and see whether he was at home; for of course they couldn't but have their suspicions. And Mr. White said they must send too to the con-stable of the next parish, and get a message to another magistrate (he was a magistrate himself), and so there was running hither and thither. But my father as it happened was away from home that night, otherwise they would have fetched him first. So then they laid the body across the horse, and they say it was all they could manage to keep the beast from bolting away from the time they were in sight of the tree, for it seemed to be mad with fright. However, they managed to bind the eyes and lead it down through the wood and back into the village street; and there, just by the big tree where the stocks are, they found a lot of the women gathered together, and this boy whom they'd sent to Mr. Davis's house lying in the middle, as white as paper, and not a word could they get out of him, good or bad. So they saw there was something worse yet to come, and they made the best of their way up the lane to Mr. Davis's house. And when they got near that, the horse they were leading seemed to go mad again with fear, and reared up and screamed, and struck out with its forefeet and the man that was leading it was as near as possible being killed, and the dead body fell off its back. So Mr. White bid them get the horse away as quick as might be, and they carried the body straight into the living-room, for the door stood open. And then they saw what it was that had given the poor boy such a fright, and they guessed why the horse went mad, for you know horses can't bear the smell of dead blood.

There was a long table in the room, more than the length of a man, and on it there lay the body of Mr. Davis. The eyes were bound over with a linen band and the arms were tied across the back, and the feet were bound together with another band. But the fearful thing was that the breast being quite bare, the bone of it was split through from the top downwards with an axe! Oh, it was a terrible sight; not one there but turned faint and ill with it, and had to go out into the fresh air. Even Mr. White, who was what you might call a hard nature of a man, was quite overcome and said a prayer for strength in the garden.

At last they laid out the other body as best they could in the room, and searched about to see if they could find out how such a frightful thing had come to pass. And in the cupboards they found a quantity of herbs and jars with liquors, and it came out, when people that understood such matters had looked into it, that some of these liquors were drinks to put a person asleep. And they had little doubt that that wicked young man had put some of this into Mr. Davis's drink, and then used him as he did, and, after that, the sense of his sin had come upon him and he had cast himself away.

Well now, you couldn't understand all the law business that had to be done by the coroner and the magistrates; but there was a great coming and going of people over it for the next day or two, and then the people of the parish got together and agreed that they couldn't bear the thought of those two being buried in the churchyard alongside of Christian people; for I must tell you there were papers and writings found in the drawers and cupboards that Mr. White and some other clergymen looked into; and they put their names to a paper that said these men were guilty, by their own allowing, of the dreadful sin of idolatry; and they feared there were some in the neighbouring places that were not free from that wickedness, and called upon them to repent, lest the same fearful thing that was come to these men should befall them also; and then they burnt those writings. So then, Mr. White was of the same mind as the parishioners, and late one evening twelve men that were chosen went with him to that evil house, and with them they took two biers made very roughly for the purpose and two pieces of black cloth, and down at the cross-road, where you take the turn for Bascombe and Wilcombe,* there were other men waiting with torches, and a pit dug, and a great crowd of people gathered together from all round about. And the men that went to the cottage went in with their hats on their heads, and four of them took the two bodies and laid them on the biers and covered them over with the black cloths, and no one said a word, but they bore them down the lane, and they were cast into the pit and covered over with stones and earth, and then Mr. White spoke to the people that were gathered together. My father was there, for he had come back when he heard the news, and he said he never should forget the strangeness of the sight, with the torches burning and those two black things huddled together in the pit, and not a sound from any of the people, except it might be a child or a woman whimpering with the fright. And so, when Mr. White had finished speaking, they all turned away and left them lying there.

They say horses don't like the spot even now, and I've heard there was something of a mist or a light hung about for a long time after, but I don't know the truth of that. But this I do know, that next day my father's business took him past the opening of the lane, and he saw three or four little knots of people standing at different places along it, seemingly in a state of mind about something; and he rode up to them, and asked what was the matter. And they ran up to him and said, 'Oh, Squire, it's the blood! Look at the blood!' and kept on like that. So he got off his horse and they showed him, and there, in four places, I think it was, he saw great patches in the road, of blood: but he could hardly see it was blood, for almost every spot of it was covered with great black flies, that never changed their place or moved. And that blood was what had fallen out of Mr. Davis's body as they bore it down the lane. Well, my father couldn't bear to do more than just take in the nasty sight so as to be sure of it, and then he said to one of those men that was there, 'Do you make haste and fetch a basket or a barrow full of clean earth out of the churchyard and spread it over these places, and I'll wait here till you come back.' And very soon he came back, and the old man that was sexton with him, with a shovel and the earth in a hand-barrow: and they set it down at the first of the places and made ready to cast the earth upon it; and as soon as ever they did that, what do you think? the flies that were on it rose up in the air in a kind of a solid cloud and moved off up the lane towards the house, and the sexton (he was parish clerk as well) stopped and looked at them and said to my father, 'Lord of flies,* sir,' and no more would he say. And just the same it was at the other places, every one of them.

Charles: But what did he mean, granny?

Grandmother: Well, dear, you remember to ask Mr. Lucas when you go to him for your lesson to-morrow. I can't stop now to talk about it: it's long past bed-time for you already. The next thing was, my father made up his mind no one was going to live in that cottage again, or yet use any of the things that were in it: so, though it was one of the best in the place, he sent round word to the people that it was to be done away with, and anyone that wished could bring a faggot to the burning of it; and that's what was done. They built a pile of wood in the living-room and loosened the thatch so as the fire could take good hold, and then set it alight; and as there was no brick, only the chimney-stack and the oven, it wasn't long before it was all gone. I seem to remember seeing the chimney when I was a little girl, but that fell down of itself at last.

Now this that I've got to is the last bit of all. You may be sure that for a long time the people said Mr. Davis and that young man were seen about, the one of them in the wood and both of them where the house had been, or passing together down the lane, particularly in the spring of the year and at autumn-time. I can't speak to that, though if we were sure there are such things as ghosts, it would seem likely that people like that wouldn't rest quiet. But I can tell you this, that one evening in the month of March, just before your grandfather and I were married, we'd been taking a long walk in the woods together and picking flowers and talking as young people will that are courting; and so much taken up with each other that we never took any particular notice where we were going. And on a sudden I cried out, and your grandfather asked what was the matter. The matter was that I'd felt a sharp prick on the back of my hand, and I snatched it to me and saw a black thing on it, and struck it with the other hand and killed it. And I showed it him, and he was a man who took notice of all such things, and he said, 'Well, I've never seen ought like that fly before,' and though to my own eye it didn't seem very much out of the common, I've no doubt he was right.

And then we looked about us, and lo and behold if we weren't in the very lane, just in front of the place where that house had stood, and, as they told me after, just where the men set down the biers a minute when they bore them out of the garden gate. You may be sure we made haste away from there; at least, I made your grandfather come away quick, for I was wholly upset at finding myself there; but he would have lingered about out of curiosity if I'd have let him. Whether there was anything about there more than we could see I shall never be sure: perhaps it was partly the venom of that horrid fly's bite that was working in me that made me feel so strange; for, dear me, how that poor arm and hand of mine did swell up, to be sure! I'm afraid to tell you how large it was round! and the pain of it, too! Nothing my mother could put on it had any power over it at all, and it wasn't till she was persuaded by our old nurse to get the wise man over at Bascombe to come and look at it, that I got any peace at all. But he seemed to know all about it, and said I wasn't the first that had been taken that way. 'When the sun's gathering his strength,' he said, 'and when he's in the height of it, and when he's beginning to lose his hold, and when he's in his weakness, them that haunts about that lane had best to take heed to themselves.' But what it was he bound on my arm and what he said over it, he wouldn't tell us. After that I soon got well again, but since then I've heard often enough of people suffering much the same as I did; only of late years it doesn't seem to happen but very seldom: and maybe things like that do die out in the course of time.

But that's the reason, Charles, why I say to you that I won't have you gathering me blackberries, no, nor eating them either, in that lane; and now you know all about it, I don't fancy you'll want to yourself. There! Off to bed you go this minute. What's that, Fanny? A light in your room? The idea of such a thing! You get yourself undressed at once and say your prayers, and perhaps if your father doesn't want me when he wakes up, I'll come and say good night to you. And you, Charles, if I hear anything of you frightening your little sister on the way up to your bed, I shall tell your father that very moment, and you know what happened to you the last time.

The door closes, and granny, after listening intently for a minute or two, resumes her knitting. The Squire still slumbers.

THERE WAS A MAN DWELT
BY A CHURCHYARD

❧

T HIS, you know, is the beginning of the story about sprites and goblins which Mamilius,* the best child in Shakespeare, was telling to his mother the queen, and the court ladies, when the king came in with his guards and hurried her off to prison. There is no more of the story; Mamilius died soon after without having a chance of finishing it. Now what was it going to have been? Shakespeare knew, no doubt, and I will be bold to say that I do. It was not going to be a new story: it was to be one which you have most likely heard, and even told. Everybody may set it in what frame he likes best. This is mine:

There was a man dwelt by a churchyard. His house had a lower story of stone and an upper one of timber. The front windows looked out on the street and the back ones on the churchyard. It had once belonged to the parish priest, but (this was in Queen Elizabeth's days) the priest was a married man and wanted more room; besides, his wife disliked seeing the churchyard at night out of her bedroom window. She said she saw—but never mind what she said; anyhow, she gave her husband no peace till he agreed to move into a larger house in the village street, and the old one was taken by John Poole, who was a widower, and lived there alone. He was an elderly man who kept very much to himself, and people said he was something of a miser.

It was very likely true: he was morbid in other ways, certainly. In those days it was common to bury people at night and by torchlight: and it was noticed that whenever a funeral was toward, John Poole was always at his window, either on the ground floor or upstairs, according as he could get the better view from one or the other.

There came a night when an old woman was to be buried. She was fairly well to do, but she was not liked in the place. The usual thing was said of her, that she was no Christian, and that on such nights as Midsummer Eve and All Hallows,* she was not to be found in her house. She was red-eyed and dreadful to look at, and no beggar ever knocked at her door. Yet when she died she left a purse of money to the Church.

There was no storm on the night of her burial; it was fair and calm. But there was some difficulty about getting bearers, and men to carry the torches, in spite of the fact that she had left larger fees than common for such as did that work. She was buried in woollen, without a coffin. No one was there but those who were actually needed—and John Poole, watching from his window. Just before the grave was filled in, the parson stooped down and cast something upon the body—something that clinked—and in a low voice he said words that sounded like 'Thy money perish with thee.' Then he walked quickly away, and so did the other men, leaving only one torch-bearer to light the sexton and his boy while they shovelled the earth in. They made no very neat job of it, and next day, which was a Sunday, the church-goers were rather sharp with the sexton, saying it was the untidiest grave in the yard. And indeed, when he came to look at it himself, he thought it was worse than he had left it.

Meanwhile John Poole went about with a curious air, half exulting, as it were, and half nervous. More than once he spent an evening at the inn, which was clean contrary to his usual habit, and to those who fell into talk with him there he hinted that he had come into a little bit of money and was looking out for a somewhat better house. 'Well, I don't wonder,' said the smith one night, 'I shouldn't care for that place of yours. I should be fancying things all night.' The landlord asked him what sort of things.

'Well, maybe somebody climbing up to the chamber window, or the like of that,' said the smith. 'I don't know—old mother Wilkins that was buried a week ago to-day, eh?'

'Come, I think you might consider of a person's feelings,' said the landlord. 'It ain't so pleasant for Master Poole, is it now?'

'Master Poole don't mind,' said the smith. 'He's been there long enough to know. I only says it wouldn't be my choice. What with the passing bell, and the torches when there's a burial, and all them graves laying so quiet when there's no one about: only they say there's lights—don't you never see no lights, Master Poole?'

'No, I don't never see no lights,' said Master Poole sulkily, and called for another drink, and went home late.

That night, as he lay in his bed upstairs, a moaning wind began to play about the house, and he could not go to sleep. He got up and crossed the room to a little cupboard in the wall: he took out of it something that clinked, and put it in the breast of his bedgown. Then he went to the window and looked out into the churchyard.

Have you ever seen an old brass in a church with a figure of a person in a shroud? It is bunched together at the top of the head in a curious way. Something like that was sticking up out of the earth in a spot of the churchyard which John Poole knew very well. He darted into his bed and lay there very still indeed.

Presently something made a very faint rattling at the casement. With a dreadful reluctance John Poole turned his eyes that way. Alas! Between him and the moonlight was the black outline of the curious bunched head. . . . Then there was a figure in the room. Dry earth rattled on the floor. A low cracked voice said 'Where is it?' and steps went hither and thither, faltering steps as of one walking with difficulty. It could be seen now and again, peering into corners, stooping to look under chairs; finally it could be heard fumbling at the doors of the cupboard in the wall, throwing them open. There was a scratching of long nails on the empty shelves. The figure whipped round, stood for an instant at the side of the bed, raised its arms, and with a hoarse scream of 'YOU'VE GOT IT!'——

At this point H.R.H. Prince Mamilius (who would, I think, have made the story a good deal shorter than this) flung himself with a loud yell upon the youngest of the court ladies present, who responded with an equally piercing cry. He was instantly seized upon by H.M. Queen Hermione, who, repressing an inclination to laugh, shook and slapped him very severely. Much flushed, and rather inclined to cry, he was about to be sent to bed: but, on the intercession of his victim, who had now recovered from the shock, he was eventually permitted to remain until his usual hour for retiring; by which time he too had so far recovered as to assert, in bidding good night to the company, that he knew another story quite three times as dreadful as that one, and would tell it on the first opportunity that offered.

RATS

〰〰

'And if you was to walk through the bedrooms now, you'd see the ragged, mouldy bedclothes a-heaving and a-heaving like seas.' 'And a-heaving and a-heaving with what?' he says. 'Why, with the rats under 'em.'*

B UT was it with the rats? I ask, because in another case it was not. I cannot put a date to the story, but I was young when I heard it, and the teller was old. It is an ill-proportioned tale, but that is my fault, not his.

It happened in Suffolk, near the coast. In a place where the road makes a sudden dip and then a sudden rise; as you go northward, at the top of that rise, stands a house on the left of the road. It is a tall red-brick house, narrow for its height; perhaps it was built about 1770. The top of the front has a low triangular pediment with a round window in the centre. Behind it are stables and offices, and such garden as it has is behind them. Scraggy Scotch firs are near it: an expanse of gorse-covered land stretches away from it. It commands a view of the distant sea from the upper windows of the front. A sign on a post stands before the door; or did so stand, for though it was an inn of repute once, I believe it is so no longer.

To this inn came my acquaintance, Mr. Thomson, when he was a young man, on a fine spring day, coming from the University of Cambridge, and desirous of solitude in tolerable quarters and time for reading. These he found, for the landlord and his wife had been in service and could make a visitor comfortable, and there was no one else staying in the inn. He had a large room on the first floor commanding the road and the view, and if it faced east, why, that could not be helped; the house was well built and warm.

He spent very tranquil and uneventful days: work all the morning, an afternoon perambulation of the country round, a little conversation with country company or the people of the inn in the evening over the then fashionable drink of brandy and water, a little more reading and writing, and bed; and he would have been content that

this should continue for the full month he had at disposal, so well was
his work progressing, and so fine was the April of that year—which
I have reason to believe was that which Orlando Whistlecraft*
chronicles in his weather record as the 'Charming Year.'

One of his walks took him along the northern road, which stands
high and traverses a wide common, called a heath. On the bright
afternoon when he first chose this direction his eye caught a white
object some hundreds of yards to the left of the road, and he felt it
necessary to make sure what this might be. It was not long before he
was standing by it, and found himself looking at a square block of
white stone fashioned somewhat like the base of a pillar, with a square
hole in the upper surface. Just such another you may see at this day
on Thetford Heath.* After taking stock of it he contemplated for
a few minutes the view, which offered a church tower or two, some
red roofs of cottages and windows winking in the sun, and the expanse
of sea—also with an occasional wink and gleam upon it—and so
pursued his way.

In the desultory evening talk in the bar, he asked why the white
stone was there on the common.

'A old-fashioned thing, that is,' said the landlord (Mr. Betts), 'we
was none of us alive when that was put there.' 'That's right,' said
another. 'It stands pretty high,' said Mr. Thomson, 'I dare say a sea-
mark was on it some time back.' 'Ah! yes,' Mr. Betts agreed, 'I 'ave
'eard they could see it from the boats; but whatever there was, it's fell
to bits this long time.' 'Good job too,' said a third, ' 'twarn't a lucky
mark, by what the old men used to say; not lucky for the fishin', I
mean to say.' 'Why ever not?' said Thomson. 'Well, I never see it
myself,' was the answer, 'but they 'ad some funny ideas, what I mean,
peculiar, them old chaps, and I shouldn't wonder but what they made
away with it theirselves.'

It was impossible to get anything clearer than this: the company,
never very voluble, fell silent, and when next someone spoke it was of
village affairs and crops. Mr. Betts was the speaker.

Not every day did Thomson consult his health by taking a country
walk. One very fine afternoon found him busily writing at three
o'clock. Then he stretched himself and rose, and walked out of his
room into the passage. Facing him was another room, then the stair-
head, then two more rooms, one looking out to the back, the other to
the south. At the south end of the passage was a window, to which he

went, considering with himself that it was rather a shame to waste such a fine afternoon. However, work was paramount just at the moment; he thought he would just take five minutes off and go back to it; and those five minutes he would employ—the Bettses could not possibly object—to looking at the other rooms in the passage, which he had never seen. Nobody at all, it seemed, was indoors; probably, as it was market day, they were all gone to the town, except perhaps a maid in the bar. Very still the house was, and the sun shone really hot; early flies buzzed in the window-panes. So he explored. The room facing his own was undistinguished except for an old print of Bury St. Edmunds; the two next him on his side of the passage were gay and clean, with one window apiece, whereas his had two. Remained the south-west room, opposite to the last which he had entered. This was locked; but Thomson was in a mood of quite indefensible curiosity, and feeling confident that there could be no damaging secrets in a place so easily got at, he proceeded to fetch the key of his own room, and when that did not answer, to collect the keys of the other three. One of them fitted, and he opened the door. The room had two windows looking south and west, so it was as bright and the sun as hot upon it as could be. Here there was no carpet, but bare boards; no pictures, no washing-stand, only a bed, in the farther corner: an iron bed, with mattress and bolster, covered with a bluish check counterpane. As featureless a room as you can well imagine, and yet there was something that made Thomson close the door very quickly and yet quietly behind him and lean against the window-sill in the passage, actually quivering all over. It was this, that under the counterpane someone lay, and not only lay, but stirred. That it was some *one* and not some *thing* was certain, because the shape of a head was unmistakable on the bolster; and yet it was all covered, and no one lies with covered head but a dead person; and this was not dead, not truly dead, for it heaved and shivered. If he had seen these things in dusk or by the light of a flickering candle, Thomson could have comforted himself and talked of fancy. On this bright day that was impossible. What was to be done? First, lock the door at all costs. Very gingerly he approached it and bending down listened, holding his breath; perhaps there might be a sound of heavy breathing, and a prosaic explanation. There was absolute silence. But as, with a rather tremulous hand, he put the key into its hole and turned it, it rattled, and on the instant a stumbling padding tread was heard coming towards the door. Thomson fled like a rabbit to his room and locked himself in: futile enough, he knew it was; would doors and locks be any obstacle to what he suspected? but it was all he could think of at the moment, and in fact nothing happened; only there was a time of acute suspense—followed by a misery of doubt as to what to do. The impulse, of course, was to slip away as soon as possible from a house which contained such an inmate. But only the day before he had said he should be staying for at least a week more, and how if he changed plans could he avoid the suspicion of having pried into places where he certainly had no business? Moreover, either the Bettses knew all about the inmate, and yet did not leave the house, or knew nothing, which equally meant that there was nothing to be afraid of, or knew just enough to make them shut up the room, but not enough to weigh on their spirits: in any of these cases it seemed that not much was to be feared, and certainly so far he had had no sort of ugly experience. On the whole the line of least resistance was to stay.

Well, he stayed out his week. Nothing took him past that door, and, often as he would pause in a quiet hour of day or night in the passage and listen, and listen, no sound whatever issued from that direction. You might have thought that Thomson would have made some attempt at ferreting out stories connected with the inn—hardly perhaps from Betts, but from the parson of the parish, or old people in the village; but no, the reticence which commonly falls on people who have had strange experiences, and believe in them, was upon him. Nevertheless, as the end of his stay drew near, his yearning after some kind of explanation grew more and more acute. On his solitary walks he persisted in planning out some way, the least obtrusive, of getting another daylight glimpse into that room, and eventually arrived at this scheme. He would leave by an afternoon train—about four o'clock. When his fly was waiting, and his luggage on it, he would make one last expedition upstairs to look round his own room and see if anything was left unpacked, and then, with that key, which he had contrived to oil (as if that made any difference!), the door should once more be opened, for a moment, and shut.

So it worked out. The bill was paid, the consequent small talk gone through while the fly was loaded: 'pleasant part of the country—been very comfortable, thanks to you and Mrs. Betts—hope to come back some time,' on one side: on the other, 'very glad you've found satisfaction, sir, done our best—always glad to 'ave your good word—very much favoured we've been with the weather, to be sure.' Then, 'I'll just take a look upstairs in case I've left a book or something out—no, don't trouble, I'll be back in a minute.' And as noiselessly as possible he stole to the door and opened it. The shattering of the illusion! He almost laughed aloud. Propped, or you might say sitting, on the edge of the bed was—nothing in the round world but a scarecrow! A scarecrow out of the garden, of course, dumped into the deserted room. . . . Yes; but here amusement ceased. Have scarecrows bare bony feet? Do their heads loll on to their shoulders? Have they iron collars and links of chain about their necks? Can they get up and move, if never so stiffly, across a floor, with wagging head and arms close at their sides? and shiver?

The slam of the door, the dash to the stair-head, the leap downstairs, were followed by a faint. Awaking, Thomson saw Betts standing over him with the brandy bottle and a very reproachful face. 'You shouldn't a done so, sir, really you shouldn't. It ain't a kind way to act by persons as done the best they could for you.' Thomson heard words of this kind, but what he said in reply he did not know. Mr. Betts, and perhaps even more Mrs. Betts, found it hard to accept his apologies and his assurances that he would say no word that could damage the good name of the house. However, they *were* accepted. Since the train could not now be caught, it was arranged that Thomson should be driven to the town to sleep there. Before he went the Bettses told him what little they knew. 'They says he was landlord 'ere a long time back, and was in with the 'ighwaymen that 'ad their beat about the 'eath. That's how he come by his end: 'ung in chains, they say, up where you see that stone what the gallus stood in. Yes, the fishermen made away with that, I believe, because they see it out at sea and it kep' the fish off, according to their idea. Yes, we 'ad the account from the people that 'ad the 'ouse before we come. "You keep that room shut up," they says, "but don't move the bed out, and you'll find there won't be no trouble." And no more there 'as been; not once he haven't come out into the 'ouse, though what he may do now there ain't no sayin'. Anyway, you're the first I know on that's seen him since we've been 'ere: I never set eyes on him myself, nor don't want. And ever since we've made the servants' rooms in the stablin', we ain't 'ad no difficulty that way. Only I do 'ope, sir, as you'll keep a close tongue, considerin' 'ow an 'ouse do get talked about': with more to this effect.

The promise of silence was kept for many years. The occasion of my hearing the story at last was this: that when Mr. Thomson came to stay with my father it fell to me to show him to his room, and instead of letting me open the door for him, he stepped forward and threw it open himself, and then for some moments stood in the doorway holding up his candle and looking narrowly into the interior. Then he seemed to recollect himself and said: 'I beg your pardon. Very absurd, but I can't help doing that, for a particular reason.' What that reason was I heard some days afterwards, and you have heard now.

AFTER DARK IN THE PLAYING FIELDS

❧❧

THE hour was late and the night was fair. I had halted not far
from Sheeps' Bridge* and was thinking about the stillness, only
broken by the sound of the weir, when a loud tremulous hoot just
above me made me jump. It is always annoying to be startled, but I
have a kindness for owls. This one was evidently very near: I looked
about for it. There it was, sitting plumply on a branch about twelve
feet up. I pointed my stick at it and said, 'Was that you?' 'Drop it,'
said the owl. 'I know it ain't only a stick, but I don't like it. Yes, of
course it was me: who do you suppose it would be if it warn't?'

We will take as read the sentences about my surprise. I lowered the
stick. 'Well,' said the owl, 'what about it? If you will come out here of
a Midsummer evening like what this is, what do you expect?' 'I beg
your pardon,' I said, 'I should have remembered. May I say that I
think myself very lucky to have met you to-night? I hope you have
time for a little talk?' 'Well,' said the owl ungraciously, 'I don't know
as it matters so particular to-night. I've had me supper as it happens,
and if you ain't too long over it—ah-h-h!' Suddenly it broke into a
loud scream, flapped its wings furiously, bent forward and clutched its
perch tightly, continuing to scream. Plainly something was pulling
hard at it from behind. The strain relaxed abruptly, the owl nearly fell
over, and then whipped round, ruffling up all over, and made a vicious
dab at something unseen by me. 'Oh, I *am* sorry,' said a small clear
voice in a solicitous tone. 'I made sure it was loose. I do hope I didn't
hurt you.' 'Didn't 'urt me?' said the owl bitterly. 'Of course you 'urt
me, and well you know it, you young infidel. That feather was no more
loose than—oh, if I could git at you! Now I shouldn't wonder but
what you've throwed me all out of balance. Why can't you let a person
set quiet for two minutes at a time without you must come creepin' up
and—well, you've done it this time, anyway. I shall go straight to 'ead-
quarters and'—(finding it was now addressing the empty air)—'why,
where have you got to now? Oh, it is too bad, that it is!'

'Dear me!' I said, 'I'm afraid this isn't the first time you've been
annoyed in this way. May I ask exactly what happened?'

'Yes, you may ask,' said the owl, still looking narrowly about as it spoke, 'but it 'ud take me till the latter end of next week to tell you. Fancy coming and pulling out anyone's tail feather! 'Urt me something crool, it did. And what for, I should like to know? Answer me that! Where's the *reason* of it?'

All that occurred to me was to murmur, 'The clamorous owl that nightly hoots and wonders at our quaint spirits.' I hardly thought the point would be taken, but the owl said sharply: 'What's that? Yes, you needn't to repeat it. I 'eard. And I'll tell you what's at the bottom of it, and you mark my words.' It bent towards me and whispered, with many nods of its round head: 'Pride! stand-offishness! that's what it is! *Come not near our fairy queen*'* (this in a tone of bitter contempt). 'Oh, dear no! we ain't good enough for the likes of them. Us that's been noted time out of mind for the best singers in the Fields: now, ain't that so?'

'Well,' I said, doubtfully enough, '*I* like to hear you very much: but, you know, some people think a lot of the thrushes and nightingales and so on; you must have heard of that, haven't you? And then, perhaps—of course I don't know—perhaps your style of singing isn't exactly what they think suitable to accompany their dancing, eh?'

'I should kindly 'ope not,' said the owl, drawing itself up. 'Our family's never give in to dancing, nor never won't neither. Why, what ever are you thinkin' of!' it went on with rising temper. 'A pretty thing it would be for me to set there hiccuppin' at them'—it stopped and looked cautiously all round it and up and down and then continued in a louder voice—'them little ladies and gentlemen. If it ain't sootable for them, I'm very sure it ain't sootable for me. And' (temper rising again) 'if they expect me never to say a word just because they're dancin' and carryin' on with their foolishness, they're very much mistook, and so I tell 'em.'

From what had passed before I was afraid this was an imprudent line to take, and I was right. Hardly had the owl given its last emphatic nod when four small slim forms dropped from a bough above, and in a twinkling some sort of grass rope was thrown round the body of the unhappy bird, and it was borne off through the air, loudly protesting, in the direction of Fellows' Pond.* Splashes and gurgles and shrieks of unfeeling laughter were heard as I hurried up. Something darted away over my head, and as I stood peering over the bank of the pond, which was all in commotion, a very angry and dishevelled owl scrambled heavily up the bank, and stopping near my feet shook itself and flapped and hissed for several minutes without saying anything I should care to repeat.

Glaring at me, it eventually said—and the grim suppressed rage in its voice was such that I hastily drew back a step or two—' 'Ear that? Said they was very sorry, but they'd mistook me for a duck. Oh, if it ain't enough to make anyone go reg'lar distracted in their mind and tear everything to flinders for miles round.' So carried away was it by passion, that it began the process at once by rooting up a large beakful of grass, which alas! got into its throat; and the choking that resulted made me really afraid that it would break a vessel. But the paroxysm was mastered, and the owl sat up, winking and breathless but intact.

Some expression of sympathy seemed to be required; yet I was chary of offering it, for in its present state of mind I felt that the bird might interpret the best-meant phrase as a fresh insult. So we stood looking at each other without speech for a very awkward minute, and then came a diversion. First the thin voice of the pavilion clock, then the deeper sound from the Castle quadrangle, then Lupton's Tower, drowning the Curfew Tower* by its nearness.

'What's that?' said the owl, suddenly and hoarsely. 'Midnight, I should think,' said I, and had recourse to my watch. 'Midnight?' cried the owl, evidently much startled, 'and me too wet to fly a yard! Here, you pick me up and put me in the tree; don't, I'll climb up your leg, and you won't ask me to do that twice. Quick now!' I obeyed. 'Which tree do you want?' 'Why, my tree, to be sure! Over there!' It nodded towards the Wall. 'All right. Bad-calx* tree do you mean?' I said, beginning to run in that direction. ' 'Ow should I know what silly names you call it? The one what 'as like a door in it. Go faster! They'll be coming in another minute.' 'Who? What's the matter?' I asked as I ran, clutching the wet creature, and much afraid of stumbling and coming over with it in the long grass. '*You'll* see fast enough,' said this selfish bird. 'You just let me git on the tree, *I* shall be all right.'

And I suppose it was, for it scrabbled very quickly up the trunk with its wings spread and disappeared in a hollow without a word of thanks. I looked round, not very comfortably. The Curfew Tower was still playing St. David's tune* and the little chime that follows, for the third and last time, but the other bells had finished what they had to say, and now there was silence, and again the 'restless changing weir'* was the only thing that broke—no, that emphasized it.

Why had the owl been so anxious to get into hiding? That of course was what now exercised me. Whatever and whoever was coming, I was sure that this was no time for me to cross the open field: I should do best to dissemble my presence by staying on the darker side of the tree. And that is what I did.

*   *   *   *   *

All this took place some years ago, before summertime came in.* I do sometimes go into the Playing Fields at night still, but I come in before true midnight. And I find I do not like a crowd after dark—for example at the Fourth of June fireworks.* You see—no, you do not, but I see—such curious faces: and the people to whom they belong flit about so oddly, often at your elbow when you least expect it, and looking close into your face, as if they were searching for someone— who may be thankful, I think, if they do not find him. 'Where do they come from?' Why, some, I think, out of the water, and some out of the ground. They look like that. But I am sure it is best to take no notice of them, and not to touch them.

Yes, I certainly prefer the daylight population of the Playing Fields to that which comes there after dark.

WAILING WELL

❧

In the year 19— there were two members of the Troop of Scouts attached to a famous school, named respectively Arthur Wilcox and Stanley Judkins. They were the same age, boarded in the same house, were in the same division, and naturally were members of the same patrol. They were so much alike in appearance as to cause anxiety and trouble, and even irritation, to the masters who came in contact with them. But oh how different were they in their inward man, or boy!

It was to Arthur Wilcox that the Head Master said, looking up with a smile as the boy entered chambers, 'Why, Wilcox, there will be a deficit in the prize fund if you stay here much longer! Here, take this handsomely bound copy of the *Life and Works of Bishop Ken*,* and with it my hearty congratulations to yourself and your excellent parents.' It was Wilcox again, whom the Provost noticed as he passed through the playing fields, and, pausing for a moment, observed to the Vice-Provost,* 'That lad has a remarkable brow!' 'Indeed, yes,' said the Vice-Provost. 'It denotes either genius or water on the brain.'

As a Scout, Wilcox secured every badge and distinction for which he competed. The Cookery Badge, the Map-making Badge, the Life-saving Badge, the Badge for picking up bits of newspaper, the Badge for not slamming the door when leaving pupil-room, and many others. Of the Life-saving Badge I may have a word to say when we come to treat of Stanley Judkins.

You cannot be surprised to hear that Mr. Hope Jones* added a special verse to each of his songs, in commendation of Arthur Wilcox, or that the Lower Master burst into tears when handing him the Good Conduct Medal in its handsome claret-coloured case: the medal which had been unanimously voted to him by the whole of Third Form. Unanimously, did I say? I am wrong. There was one dissentient, Judkins *mi.*,* who said that he had excellent reasons for acting as he did. He shared, it seems, a room with his major. You cannot, again, wonder that in after years Arthur Wilcox was the first, and so far the only boy, to become Captain of both the School and of the

Oppidans,* or that the strain of carrying out the duties of both positions, coupled with the ordinary work of the school, was so severe
that a complete rest for six months, followed by a voyage round the
world, was pronounced an absolute necessity by the family doctor.

It would be a pleasant task to trace the steps by which he attained
the giddy eminence he now occupies; but for the moment enough of
Arthur Wilcox. Time presses, and we must turn to a very different
matter: the career of Stanley Judkins—Judkins *ma*.

Stanley Judkins, like Arthur Wilcox, attracted the attention of the
authorities; but in quite another fashion. It was to him that the Lower
Master* said, with no cheerful smile, 'What, again, Judkins? A very
little persistence in this course of conduct, my boy, and you will have
cause to regret that you ever entered this academy. There, take that,
and that, and think yourself very lucky you don't get that and that!' It
was Judkins, again, whom the Provost had cause to notice as he
passed through the playing fields, when a cricket ball struck him with
considerable force on the ankle, and a voice from a short way off
cried, 'Thank you, cut-over!' 'I think,' said the Provost, pausing for a
moment to rub his ankle, 'that that boy had better fetch his cricket
ball for himself!' 'Indeed, yes,' said the Vice-Provost, 'and if he
comes within reach, I will do my best to fetch him something else.'

As a Scout, Stanley Judkins secured no badge save those which he
was able to abstract from members of other patrols. In the cookery
competition he was detected trying to introduce squibs into the Dutch
oven of the next-door competitors. In the tailoring competition he
succeeded in sewing two boys together very firmly, with disastrous
effect when they tried to get up. For the Tidiness Badge he was dis-
qualified, because, in the Midsummer schooltime, which chanced to
be hot, he could not be dissuaded from sitting with his fingers in the
ink: as he said, for coolness' sake. For one piece of paper which he
picked up, he must have dropped at least six banana skins or orange
peels. Aged women seeing him approaching would beg him with tears
in their eyes not to carry their pails of water across the road. They
knew too well what the result would inevitably be. But it was in the
life-saving competition that Stanley Judkins's conduct was most
blameable and had the most far-reaching effects. The practice, as you
know, was to throw a selected lower boy, of suitable dimensions, fully
dressed, with his hands and feet tied together, into the deepest part of
Cuckoo Weir,* and to time the Scout whose turn it was to rescue him.

On every occasion when he was entered for this competition Stanley Judkins was seized, at the critical moment, with a severe fit of cramp, which caused him to roll on the ground and utter alarming cries. This naturally distracted the attention of those present from the boy in the water, and had it not been for the presence of Arthur Wilcox the death-roll would have been a heavy one. As it was, the Lower Master found it necessary to take a firm line and say that the competition must be discontinued. It was in vain that Mr. Beasley Robinson* represented to him that in five competitions only four lower boys had actually succumbed. The Lower Master said that he would be the last to interfere in any way with the work of the Scouts; but that three of these boys had been valued members of his choir, and both he and Dr. Ley* felt that the inconvenience caused by the losses outweighed the advantages of the competitions. Besides, the correspondence with the parents of these boys had become annoying, and even distressing: they were no longer satisfied with the printed form which he was in the habit of sending out, and more than one of them had actually visited Eton and taken up much of his valuable time with complaints. So the life-saving competition is now a thing of the past.

In short, Stanley Judkins was no credit to the Scouts, and there was talk on more than one occasion of informing him that his services were no longer required. This course was strongly advocated by Mr. Lambart:* but in the end milder counsels prevailed, and it was decided to give him another chance.

So it is that we find him at the beginning of the Midsummer Holidays of 19— at the Scouts' camp in the beautiful district of W (or X) in the country of D (or Y).*

It was a lovely morning, and Stanley Judkins and one or two of his friends—for he still had friends—lay basking on the top of the down. Stanley was lying on his stomach with his chin propped on his hands, staring into the distance.

'I wonder what that place is,' he said.

'Which place?' said one of the others.

'That sort of clump in the middle of the field down there.'

'Oh, ah! How should I know what it is?'

'What do you want to know for?' said another.

'I don't know: I like the look of it. What's it called? Nobody got a map?' said Stanley. 'Call yourselves Scouts!'

'Here's a map all right,' said Wilfred Pipsqueak, ever resourceful, 'and there's the place marked on it. But it's inside the red ring. We can't go there.'

'Who cares about a red ring?' said Stanley. 'But it's got no name on your silly map.'

'Well, you can ask this old chap what it's called if you're so keen to find out.' 'This old chap' was an old shepherd who had come up and was standing behind them.

'Good mornin, young gents,' he said, 'you've got a fine day for your doin's, ain't you?'

'Yes, thank you,' said Algernon de Montmorency, with native politeness. 'Can you tell us what that clump over there's called? And what's that thing inside it?'

'Course I can tell you,' said the shepherd. 'That's Wailin' Well, that is. But you ain't got no call to worry about that.'

'Is it a well in there?' said Algernon. 'Who uses it?'

The shepherd laughed. 'Bless you,' he said, 'there ain't from a man to a sheep in these parts uses Wailin' Well, nor haven't done all the years I've lived here.'

'Well, there'll be a record broken to-day, then,' said Stanley Judkins, 'because I shall go and get some water out of it for tea!'

'Sakes alive, young gentleman!' said the shepherd in a startled voice, 'don't you get to talkin' that way! Why, ain't your masters give you notice not to go by there? They'd ought to have done.'

'Yes, they have,' said Wilfred Pipsqueak.

'Shut up, you ass!' said Stanley Judkins. 'What's the matter with it? Isn't the water good? Anyhow, if it was boiled, it would be all right.'

'I don't know as there's anything much wrong with the water,' said the shepherd. 'All I know is, my old dog wouldn't go through that field, let alone me or anyone else that's got a morsel of brains in their heads.'

'More fool them,' said Stanley Judkins, at once rudely and ungrammatically. 'Who ever took any harm going there?' he added.

'Three women and a man,' said the shepherd gravely. 'Now just you listen to me. I know these 'ere parts and you don't, and I can tell you this much: for these ten years last past there ain't been a sheep fed in that field, nor a crop raised off of it—and it's good land, too. You can pretty well see from here what a state it's got into with brambles and suckers and trash of all kinds. *You've* got a glass, young gentleman,' he said to Wilfred Pipsqueak, 'you can tell with that anyway.'

'Yes,' said Wilfred, 'but I see there's tracks in it. Someone must go through it sometimes.'

'Tracks!' said the shepherd. 'I believe you! Four tracks: three women and a man.'

'What d'you mean, three women and a man?' said Stanley, turning over for the first time and looking at the shepherd (he had been talking with his back to him till this moment: he was an ill-mannered boy).

'Mean? Why, what I says: three women and a man.'

'Who are they?' asked Algernon. 'Why do they go there?'

'There's some p'r'aps could tell you who they *was*,' said the shepherd, 'but it was afore my time they come by their end. And why they goes there still is more than the children of men can tell: except I've heard they was all bad 'uns when they was alive.'

'By George, what a rum thing!' Algernon and Wilfred muttered: but Stanley was scornful and bitter.

'Why, you don't mean they're deaders? What rot! You must be a lot of fools to believe that. Who's ever seen them, I'd like to know?'

'*I've* seen 'em, young gentleman!' said the shepherd, 'seen 'em from near by on that bit of down: and my old dog, if he could speak, he'd tell you he've seen 'em, same time. About four o'clock of the day it was, much such a day as this. I see 'em, each one of 'em, come peerin' out of the bushes and stand up, and work their way slow by them tracks towards the trees in the middle where the well is.'

'And what were they like? Do tell us!' said Algernon and Wilfred eagerly.

'Rags and bones, young gentlemen: all four of 'em: flutterin' rags and whity bones. It seemed to me as if I could hear 'em clackin' as they got along. Very slow they went, and lookin' from side to side.'

'What were their faces like? Could you see?'

'They hadn't much to call faces,' said the shepherd, 'but I could seem to see as they had teeth.'

'Lor'!' said Wilfred, 'and what did they do when they got to the trees?'

'I can't tell you that, sir,' said the shepherd. 'I wasn't for stayin' in that place, and if I had been, I was bound to look to my old dog: he'd gone! Such a thing he never done before as leave me; but gone he had, and when I came up with him in the end, he was in that state he didn't know me, and was fit to fly at my throat. But I kep' talkin' to him, and after a bit he remembered my voice and came creepin' up like a child askin' pardon. I never want to see him like that again, nor yet no other dog.'

The dog, who had come up and was making friends all round, looked up at his master, and expressed agreement with what he was saying very fully.

The boys pondered for some moments on what they had heard: after which Wilfred said: 'And why's it called Wailing Well?'

'If you was round here at dusk of a winter's evening, you wouldn't want to ask why,' was all the shepherd said.

'Well, I don't believe a word of it,' said Stanley Judkins, 'and I'll go there next chance I get: blowed if I don't!'

'Then you won't be ruled by me?' said the shepherd. 'Nor yet by your masters as warned you off? Come now, young gentleman, you don't want for sense, I should say. What should I want tellin' you a pack of lies? It ain't sixpence to me anyone goin' in that field: but I wouldn't like to see a young chap snuffed out like in his prime.'

'I expect it's a lot more than sixpence to you,' said Stanley. 'I expect you've got a whisky still or something in there, and want to keep other people away. Rot I call it. Come on back, you boys.'

So they turned away. The two others said, 'Good evening' and 'Thank you' to the shepherd, but Stanley said nothing. The shepherd shrugged his shoulders and stood where he was, looking after them rather sadly.

On the way back to the camp there was great argument about it all, and Stanley was told as plainly as he could be told all the sorts of fools he would be if he went to the Wailing Well.

That evening, among other notices, Mr. Beasley Robinson asked if all maps had got the red ring marked on them. 'Be particular,' he said, 'not to trespass inside it.'

Several voices—among them the sulky one of Stanley Judkins— said, 'Why not, sir?'

'Because not,' said Mr. Beasley Robinson, 'and if that isn't enough for you, I can't help it.' He turned and spoke to Mr. Lambart in a low voice, and then said, 'I'll tell you this much: we've been asked to warn Scouts off that field. It's very good of the people to let us camp here at all, and the least we can do is to oblige them—I'm sure you'll agree to that.'

Everybody said, 'Yes, sir!' except Stanley Judkins, who was heard to mutter, 'Oblige them be blowed!'

Early in the afternoon of the next day, the following dialogue was heard. 'Wilcox, is all your tent there?'

'No, sir, Judkins isn't!'

'That boy is *the* most infernal nuisance ever invented! Where do you suppose he is?'

'I haven't an idea, sir.'

'Does anybody else know?'

'Sir, I shouldn't wonder if he'd gone to the Wailing Well.'

'Who's that? Pipsqueak? What's the Wailing Well?'

'Sir, it's that place in the field by—well, sir, it's in a clump of trees in a rough field.'

'D'you mean inside the red ring? Good heavens! What makes you think he's gone there?'

'Why, he was terribly keen to know about it yesterday, and we were talking to a shepherd man, and he told us a lot about it and advised us not to go there: but Judkins didn't believe him, and said he meant to go.'

'Young ass!' said Mr. Hope Jones, 'did he take anything with him?'

'Yes, I think he took some rope and a can. We did tell him he'd be a fool to go.'

'Little brute! What the deuce does he mean by pinching stores like that! Well, come along, you three, we must see after him. Why can't people keep the simplest orders? What was it the man told you? No, don't wait, let's have it as we go along.'

And off they started—Algernon and Wilfred talking rapidly and the other two listening with growing concern. At last they reached that spur of down overlooking the field of which the shepherd had spoken the day before. It commanded the place completely; the well inside the clump of bent and gnarled Scotch firs was plainly visible, and so were the four tracks winding about among the thorns and rough growth.

It was a wonderful day of shimmering heat. The sea looked like a floor of metal. There was no breath of wind. They were all exhausted when they got to the top, and flung themselves down on the hot grass.

'Nothing to be seen of him yet,' said Mr. Hope Jones, 'but we must stop here a bit. You're done up—not to speak of me. Keep a sharp look-out,' he went on after a moment, 'I thought I saw the bushes stir.'

'Yes,' said Wilcox, 'so did I. Look . . . no, that can't be him. It's somebody though, putting their head up, isn't it?'

'I thought it was, but I'm not sure.'

Silence for a moment. Then:

'That's him, sure enough,' said Wilcox, 'getting over the hedge on the far side. Don't you see? With a shiny thing. That's the can you said he had.'

'Yes, it's him, and he's making straight for the trees,' said Wilfred.

At this moment Algernon, who had been staring with all his might, broke into a scream.

'What's that on the track? On all fours—O, it's the woman. O, don't let me look at her! Don't let it happen!' And he rolled over, clutching at the grass and trying to bury his head in it.

'Stop that!' said Mr. Hope Jones loudly—but it was no use. 'Look here,' he said, 'I must go down there. You stop here, Wilfred, and look after that boy. Wilcox, you run as hard as you can to the camp and get some help.'

They ran off, both of them. Wilfred was left alone with Algernon, and did his best to calm him, but indeed he was not much happier himself. From time to time he glanced down the hill and into the field. He saw Mr. Hope Jones drawing nearer at a swift pace, and then, to his great surprise, he saw him stop, look up and round about him, and turn quickly off at an angle! What could be the reason? He looked at the field, and there he saw a terrible figure—something in ragged black—with whitish patches breaking out of it: the head, perched on a long thin neck, half hidden by a shapeless sort of blackened sun-bonnet. The creature was waving thin arms in the direction of the rescuer who was approaching, as if to ward him off: and between the two figures the air seemed to shake and shimmer as he had never seen it: and as he looked, he began himself to feel something of a waviness and confusion in his brain, which made him guess what might be the effect on someone within closer range of the influence. He looked away hastily, to see Stanley Judkins making his way pretty quickly towards the clump, and in proper Scout fashion; evidently picking his steps with care to avoid treading on snapping

sticks or being caught by arms of brambles. Evidently, though he saw
nothing, he suspected some sort of ambush, and was trying to go
noiselessly. Wilfred saw all that, and he saw more, too. With a sudden
and dreadful sinking at the heart, he caught sight of someone among
the trees, waiting: and again of someone—another of the hideous
black figures—working slowly along the track from another side of
the field, looking from side to side, as the shepherd had described it.
Worst of all, he saw a fourth—unmistakably a man this time—rising
out of the bushes a few yards behind the wretched Stanley, and painfully, as it seemed, crawling into the track. On all sides the miserable
victim was cut off.

Wilfred was at his wits' end. He rushed at Algernon and shook
him. 'Get up,' he said. 'Yell! Yell as loud as you can. Oh, if we'd got
a whistle!'

Algernon pulled himself together. 'There's one,' he said, 'Wilcox's:
he must have dropped it.'

So one whistled, the other screamed. In the still air the sound carried. Stanley heard: he stopped: he turned round: and then indeed a
cry was heard more piercing and dreadful than any that the boys on
the hill could raise. It was too late. The crouched figure behind
Stanley sprang at him and caught him about the waist. The dreadful
one that was standing waving her arms waved them again, but in
exultation. The one that was lurking among the trees shuffled forward, and she too stretched out her arms as if to clutch at something
coming her way; and the other, farthest off, quickened her pace and
came on, nodding gleefully. The boys took it all in in an instant of
terrible silence, and hardly could they breathe as they watched the
horrid struggle between the man and his victim. Stanley struck with
his can, the only weapon he had. The rim of a broken black hat fell off
the creature's head and showed a white skull with stains that might be
wisps of hair. By this time one of the women had reached the pair,
and was pulling at the rope that was coiled about Stanley's neck.
Between them they overpowered him in a moment: the awful screaming ceased, and then the three passed within the circle of the clump
of firs.

Yet for a moment it seemed as if rescue might come. Mr. Hope
Jones, striding quickly along, suddenly stopped, turned, seemed to
rub his eyes, and then started running *towards* the field. More: the
boys glanced behind them, and saw not only a troop of figures from

the camp coming over the top of the next down, but the shepherd running up the slope of their own hill. They beckoned, they shouted, they ran a few yards towards him and then back again. He mended his pace.

Once more the boys looked towards the field. There was nothing. Or, was there something among the trees? Why was there a mist about the trees? Mr. Hope Jones had scrambled over the hedge, and was plunging through the bushes.

The shepherd stood beside them, panting. They ran to him and clung to his arms. 'They've got him! In the trees!' was as much as they could say, over and over again.

'What? Do you tell me he've gone in there after all I said to him yesterday? Poor young thing! Poor young thing!' He would have said more, but other voices broke in. The rescuers from the camp had arrived. A few hasty words, and all were dashing down the hill.

They had just entered the field when they met Mr. Hope Jones. Over his shoulder hung the corpse of Stanley Judkins. He had cut it from the branch to which he found it hanging, waving to and fro. There was not a drop of blood in the body.

On the following day Mr. Hope Jones sallied forth with an axe and with the expressed intention of cutting down every tree in the clump, and of burning every bush in the field. He returned with a nasty cut in his leg and a broken axe-helve.* Not a spark of fire could he light, and on no single tree could he make the least impression.

I have heard that the present population of the Wailing Well field consists of three women, a man, and a boy.

The shock experienced by Algernon de Montmorency and Wilfred Pipsqueak was severe. Both of them left the camp at once; and the occurrence undoubtedly cast a gloom—if but a passing one—on those who remained. One of the first to recover his spirits was Judkins *mi*.

Such, gentlemen, is the story of the career of Stanley Judkins, and of a portion of the career of Arthur Wilcox. It has, I believe, never been told before. If it has a moral, that moral is, I trust, ovbious: if it has none, I do not well know how to help it.

THE EXPERIMENT

A NEW YEAR'S EVE GHOST STORY

(*Full Directions will be found at the End*)

❦

THE Reverend Dr. Hall was in his study making up the entries for the year in the parish register: it being his custom to note baptisms, weddings and burials in a paper book as they occurred, and in the last days of December to write them out fairly in the vellum book that was kept in the parish chest.

To him entered his housekeeper, in evident agitation. 'Oh, sir,' said she, 'whatever do you think? The poor Squire's gone!'

'The Squire? Squire Bowles? What are you talking about, woman? Why, only yesterday——.'

'Yes, I know, sir, but it's the truth. Wickem, the clerk, just left word on his way down to toll the bell—you'll hear it yourself in a minute. There now, just listen.'

Sure enough the sound broke on the still night—not loud, for the Rectory did not immediately adjoin the churchyard. Dr. Hall rose hastily.

'Terrible, terrible,' he said. 'I must see them at the Hall at once. He seemed so greatly better yesterday.' He paused. 'Did you hear any word of the sickness having come this way at all? There was nothing said in Norwich. It seems so sudden.'

'No, indeed, sir, no such thing. Just caught away with a choking in his throat, Wickem says. It do make one feel—well, I'm sure I had to set down as much as a minute or more, I come over that queer when I heard the words—and by what I could understand they'll be asking for the burial very quick. There's some can't bear the thought of the cold corpse laying in the house, and——.'

'Yes: well, I must find out from Madam Bowles herself or Mr. Joseph. Get me my cloak, will you? Ah, and could you let Wickem know that I desire to see him when the tolling is over?' He hurried off.

*

'In an hour's time he was back and found Wickem waiting for him. 'There is work for you, Wickem,' he said, as he threw off his cloak, 'and not overmuch time to do it in.'

'Yes, sir,' said Wickem, 'the vault to be opened to be sure——.'

'No, no, that's not the message I have. The poor Squire, they tell me, charged them before now not to lay him in the chancel. It was to be an earth grave in the yard, on the north side.' He stopped at an inarticulate exclamation from the clerk. 'Well?' he said.

'I ask pardon, sir,' said Wickem in a shocked voice, 'but did I understand you right? No vault, you say, and on the north side? Tt-tt-! Why the poor gentleman must a been wandering.'

'Yes, it does seem strange to me, too,' said Dr. Hall, 'but no, Mr. Joseph tells me it was his father's—I should say stepfather's— clear wish, expressed more than once, and when he was in good health. Clean earth and open air. You know, of course, the poor Squire had his fancies, though he never spoke of this one to me. And there's another thing. Wickem. No coffin.'

'Oh dear, dear, sir,' said Wickem, yet more shocked. 'Oh, but that'll make sad talk, that will, and what a disappointment for Wright, too! I know he'd looked out some beautiful wood for the Squire, and had it by him years past.'

'Well, well, perhaps the family will make it up to Wright in some way,' said the Rector, rather impatiently, 'but what you have to do is to get the grave dug and all things in a readiness—torches from Wright you must not forget—by ten o'clock to-morrow night. I don't doubt but there will be somewhat coming to you for your pains and hurry.'

'Very well, sir, if those be the orders, I must do my best to carry them out. And should I call in on my way down and send the women up to the Hall to lay out the body, sir?'

'No: that, I think—I am sure—was not spoken of. Mr. Joseph will send, no doubt, if they are needed. No, you have enough without that. Good-night, Wickem. I was making up the registers when this doleful news came. Little had I thought to add such an entry to them as I must now.'

All things had been done in decent order. The torchlighted cortège had passed from the Hall through the park, up the lime avenue to the top of the knoll on which the church stood. All the village had been there, and such neighbours as could be warned in the few hours available. There was no great surprise at the hurry.

Formalities of law there were none then, and no one blamed the stricken widow for hastening to lay her dead to rest. Nor did anyone look to see her following in the funeral train. Her son Joseph—only issue of her first marriage with a Calvert of Yorkshire—was the chief mourner.

There were, indeed, no kinsfolk on Squire Bowles's side who could have been bidden. The will, executed at the time of the Squire's second marriage, left everything to the widow.

And what was 'everything'? Land, house, furniture, pictures, plate were all obvious. But there should have been accumulations in coin, and beyond a few hundreds in the hands of agents—honest men and no embezzlers—cash there was none. Yet Francis Bowles had for years received good rents and paid little out. Nor was he a reputed miser; he kept a good table, and money was always forthcoming for the moderate spendings of his wife and stepson. Joseph Calvert had been maintained ungrudgingly at school and college.

What, then, had he done with it all? No ransacking of the house brought any secret hoard to light; no servant, old or young, had any tale to tell of meeting the Squire in unexpected places at strange hours. No, Madam Bowles and her son were fairly non-plussed. As they sat one evening in the parlour discussing the problem for the twentieth time:

'You have been at his books and papers, Joseph, again today, haven't you?'

'Yes, mother, and no forwarder.'

'What was it he would be writing at, and why was he always sending letters to Mr. Fowler at Gloucester?'

'Why, you know he had a maggot about the Middle State of the Soul. 'Twas over that he and that other were always busy. The last thing he wrote would be a letter that he never finished. I'll fetch it. . . . Yes, the same song over again.

'"Honoured friend,—I make some slow advance in our studies, but I know not well how far to trust our authors. Here is one lately come my way who will have it that for a time after death the soul is under control of certain spirits as Raphael, and another whom I doubtfully read as Nares,* but still so near to this state of life that on prayer to them he may be free to come and disclose matters to the living. Come, indeed, he must, if he be rightly called, the manner of which is set forth in an experiment. But having come, and once opened his mouth, it may chance that his summoner shall see and hear more than of the hid treasure which it is likely he bargained for; since the experiment puts this in the forefront of things to be enquired. But the eftest* way is to send you the whole, which herewith I do; copied from a book of recipes which I had of good Bishop Moore.'"*

Here Joseph stopped, and made no comment, gazing on the paper. For more than a minute nothing was said, then Madam Bowles, drawing her needle through her work and looking at it, coughed and said, 'There was no more written?'

'No, nothing, mother.'

'No? Well, it is strange stuff. Did ever you meet this Mr. Fowler?'

'Yes, it might be once or twice, in Oxford, a civil gentleman enough.'

'Now I think of it,' said she, 'it would be but right to acquaint him with—with what has happened: they were close friends. Yes, Joseph, you should do that: you will know what should be said. And the letter is his, after all.'

'You are in the right, mother, and I'll not delay it.' And forthwith he sat down to write.

From Norfolk to Gloucester was no quick transit. But a letter went, and a larger packet came in answer; and there were more evening talks in the panelled parlour at the Hall. At the close of one, these words were said: 'To-night, then, if you are certain of yourself, go round by the field path. Ay, and here is a cloth will serve.'

'What cloth is that, mother? A napkin?'

'Yes, of a kind: what matter?' So he went out by the way of the garden, and she stood in the door, musing, with her hand on her mouth. Then the hand dropped and she said half aloud: 'If only I had not been so hurried! But it was the face cloth, sure enough.'

It was a very dark night, and the spring wind blew loud over the black fields: loud enough to drown all sounds of shouting or calling. If calling there was, there was no voice, nor any that answered, nor any that regarded—yet.

Next morning, Joseph's mother was early in his chamber. 'Give me the cloth,' she said, 'the maids must not find it. And tell me, tell me, quick!'

Joseph, seated on the side of the bed with his head in his hands, looked up at her with bloodshot eyes. 'We have opened his mouth,' he said. 'Why in God's name did you leave his face bare?'

'How could I help it? You know how I was hurried that day? But do you mean you saw it?'

Joseph only groaned and sunk his head in his hands again. Then, in a low voice, 'He said you should see it, too.'

With a dreadful gasp she clutched at the bedpost and clung to it. 'Oh, but he's angry,' Joseph went on. 'He was only biding his time, I'm sure. The words were scarce out of my mouth when I heard like the snarl of a dog in under there.' He got up and paced the room. 'And what can we do? He's free! And I daren't meet him! I daren't take the drink and go where he is! I daren't lie here another night. Oh, why did you do it? We could have waited.'

'Hush,' said his mother: her lips were dry. ' 'Twas you, you know it, as much as I. Besides, what use in talking? Listen to me: 'tis but six o'clock. There's money to cross the water: such as they can't follow. Yarmouth's not so far, and most night boats sail for Holland, I've heard. See you to the horses. I can be ready.'

Joseph stared at her. 'What will they say here?'

'What? Why, cannot you tell the parson we have wind of property lying in Amsterdam which we must claim or lose? Go go; or if you are not man enough for that, lie here again to-night.' He shivered and went.

That evening after dark a boatman lumbered into an inn on Yarmouth Quay, where a man and a woman sat, with saddle-bags on the floor by them.

'Ready, are you, mistress and gentleman?' he said. 'She sails before the hour, and my other passenger he's waitin' on the quay. Be there all your baggage?' and he picked up the bags.

'Yes, we travel light,' said Joseph. 'And you have more company bound for Holland?'

'Just the one,' said the boatman, 'and he seem to travel lighter yet.'

'Do you know him?' said Madam Bowles: she laid her hand on Joseph's arm, and they both paused in the doorway.

'Why no, but for all he's hooded I'd know him again fast enough, he have such a cur'ous way of speakin', and I doubt you'll find he know you, by what he said. "Goo you and fetch 'em out," he say, "and I'll wait on 'em here," he say, and sure enough he's a-comin' this way now.'

Poisoning of a husband was petty treason then, and women guilty of it were strangled at the stake and burnt. The Assize records of Norwich tell of a woman so dealt with and of her son hanged thereafter, convict on their own confession, made before the Rector of their parish, the name of which I withhold, for there is still hid treasure to be found there.

Bishop Moore's book of recipes is now in the University Library at Cambridge, marked Dd 11, 45, and on the leaf numbered 144 this is written:

An experiment most ofte proved true, to find out tresure hidden in the ground, theft, manslaughter, or anie other thynge. Go to the grave of a ded man, and three tymes call hym by his nam at the hed of the grave, and say. Thou, N., N., N., I coniure the, I require the, and I charge the, by thi Christendome that thou takest leave of the Lord Raffael and Nares and then askest leave this night to come and tell me trewlie of the tresure that lyith hid in such a place. Then take of the earth of the grave at the dead bodyes hed and knitt it in a lynnen clothe and put itt under thi right eare and sleape theruppon: and wheresoever thou lyest or slepest, that night he will com and tell thee trewlie in waking or sleping.

THE MALICE OF INANIMATE OBJECTS

❦

THE Malice of Inanimate Objects is a subject upon which an old friend of mine was fond of dilating, and not without justification. In the lives of all of us, short or long, there have been days, dreadful days, on which we have had to acknowledge with gloomy resignation that our world has turned against us. I do not mean the human world of our relations and friends: to enlarge on that is the province of nearly every modern novelist. In their books it is called 'Life' and an odd enough hash it is as they portray it. No, it is the world of things that do not speak or work or hold congresses and conferences. It includes such beings as the collar stud, the inkstand, the fire, the razor, and, as age increases, the extra step on the staircase which leads you either to expect or not to expect it. By these and such as these (for I have named but the merest fraction of them) the word is passed round, and the day of misery arranged. Is the tale still remembered of how the Cock and Hen went to pay a visit to Squire Korbes?* How on the journey they met with and picked up a number of associates, encouraging each with the announcement:

'To Squire Korbes we are going
For a visit is owing.'

Thus they secured the company of the Needle, the Egg, the Duck, the Cat, possibly—for memory is a little treacherous here—and finally the Millstone: and when it was discovered that Squire Korbes was for the moment out, they took up positions in his mansion and awaited his return. He did return, wearied no doubt by a day's work among his extensive properties. His nerves were first jarred by the raucous cry of the Cock. He threw himself into his armchair and was lacerated by the Needle. He went to the sink for a refreshing wash and was splashed all over by the Duck. Attempting to dry himself with the towel he broke the Egg upon his face. He suffered other indignities from the Hen and her accomplices, which I cannot now recollect, and finally, maddened with pain and fear, rushed out by the back door and had his brains dashed out by the Millstone that had perched itself in the appropriate place. 'Truly,' in the concluding words of the story, 'this Squire Korbes must have been either a very wicked or a very unfortunate man.' It is the latter alternative which I incline to accept. There is nothing in the preliminaries to show that any slur rested on his name, or that his visitors had any injury to avenge. And will not this narrative serve as a striking example of that Malice of which I have taken upon me to treat? It is, I know, the fact that Squire Korbes's visitors were not all of them, strictly speaking, inanimate. But are we sure that the perpetrators of this Malice are really inanimate either? There are tales which seem to justify a doubt.

Two men of mature years were seated in a pleasant garden after breakfast. One was reading the day's paper, the other sat with folded arms, plunged in thought, and on his face were a piece of sticking plaster and lines of care. His companion lowered his paper. 'What,' said he, 'is the matter with you? The morning is bright, the birds are singing, I can hear no aeroplanes or motor bikes.'

'No,' replied Mr. Burton, 'it is nice enough, I agree, but I have a bad day before me. I cut myself shaving and split my tooth powder.'

'Ah,' said Mr. Manners, 'some people have all the luck,' and with this expression of sympathy he reverted to his paper. 'Hullo,' he exclaimed, after a moment, 'here's George Wilkins dead! You won't have any more bother with him, anyhow.'

'George Wilkins?' said Mr. Burton, more than a little excitedly, 'Why, I didn't even know he was ill.'

'No more he was, poor chap. Seems to have thrown up the sponge and put an end to himself. Yes,' he went on, 'it's some days back: this is the inquest. Seemed very much worried and depressed, they say. What about, I wonder? Could it have been that will you and he were having a row about?'

'Row?' said Mr. Burton angrily, 'there was no row: he hadn't a leg to stand on: he couldn't bring a scrap of evidence. No, it may have been half-a-dozen things: but Lord! I never imagined he'd take anything so hard as that.'

'I don't know,' said Mr. Manners, 'he was a man, I thought, who did take things hard: they rankled. Well, I'm sorry, though I never saw much of him. He must have gone through a lot to make him cut his throat. Not the way I should choose, by a long sight. Ugh! Lucky he hadn't a family, anyhow. Look here, what about a walk round before lunch? I've an errand in the village.'

Mr. Burton assented rather heavily. He was perhaps reluctant to give the inanimate objects of the district a chance of getting at him. If so, he was right. He just escaped a nasty purl over the scraper at the top of the steps: a thorny branch swept off his hat and scratched his fingers, and as they climbed a grassy slope he fairly leapt into the air with a cry and came down flat on his face. 'What in the world?' said his friend coming up. 'A great string, of all things! What business— Oh, I see—belongs to that kite' (which lay on the grass a little farther up). 'Now if I can find out what little beast has left that kicking about, I'll let him have it—or rather I won't, for he shan't see his kite again. It's rather a good one, too.' As they approached, a puff of wind raised the kite and it seemed to sit up on its end and look at them with two large round eyes painted red, and, below them, three large printed red letters, I.C.U. Mr. Manners was amused and scanned the device with care. 'Ingenious,' he said, 'it's a bit off a poster, of course: I see! Full Particulars, the word was.' Mr. Burton on the other hand was not amused, but thrust his stick through the kite. Mr. Manners was inclined to regret this. 'I dare say it serves him right,' he said, 'but he'd taken a lot of trouble to make it.'

'Who had?' said Mr. Burton sharply. 'Oh, I see, you mean the boy.'

'Yes, to be sure, who else? But come on down now: I want to leave a message before lunch. As they turned a corner into the main street, a rather muffled and choky voice was heard to say 'Look out! I'm coming.' They both stopped as if they had been shot.

'Who *was* that?' said Manners. 'Blest if I didn't think I knew'— then, with almost a yell of laughter he pointed with his stick. A cage with a grey parrot in it was hanging in an open window across the way. 'I *was* startled, by George: it gave you a bit of a turn, too, didn't it?' Burton was inaudible. 'Well, I shan't be a minute: you can go and make friends with the bird.' But when he rejoined Burton, that unfortunate was not, it seemed, in trim for talking with either birds or men; he was some way ahead and going rather quickly. Manners paused for an instant at the parrot window and then hurried on laughing more than ever. 'Have a good talk with Polly?' said he, as he came up.

'No, of course not,' said Burton, testily. 'I didn't bother about the beastly thing.'

'Well, you wouldn't have got much out of her if you'd tried,' said Manners. 'I remembered after a bit; they've had her in the window for years: she's stuffed.' Burton seemed about to make a remark, but suppressed it.

Decidedly this was not Burton's day out. He choked at lunch, he broke a pipe, he tripped in the carpet, he dropped his book in the pond in the garden. Later on he had or professed to have a telephone call summoning him back to town next day and cutting short what should have been a week's visit. And so glum was he all the evening that Manners' disappointment in losing an ordinarily cheerful companion was not very sharp.

At breakfast Mr. Burton said little about his night: but he did intimate that he thought of looking in on his doctor. 'My hand's so shaky,' he said, 'I really daren't shave this morning.'

'Oh, I'm sorry,' said Mr. Manners, 'my man could have managed that for you: but they'll put you right in no time.'

Farewells were said. By some means and for some reason Mr. Burton contrived to reserve a compartment to himself. (The train was not of the corridor type.) But these precautions avail little against the angry dead.

I will not put dots or stars, for I dislike them, but I will say that apparently someone tried to shave Mr. Burton in the train, and did not succeed overly well. He was however satisfied with what he had done, if we may judge from the fact that on a once white napkin spread on Mr. Burton's chest was an inscription in red letters: GEO. W. FECI.*

Do not these facts—if facts they are—bear out my suggestion that there is something not inanimate behind the Malice of Inanimate Objects? Do they not further suggest that when this malice begins to show itself we should be very particular to examine and if possible rectify any obliquities in our recent conduct? And do they not, finally, almost force upon us the conclusion that, like Squire Korbes, Mr. Burton must have been either a very wicked or a singularly unfortunate man?

A VIGNETTE

Y OU are asked to think of the spacious garden of a country rec- tory,* adjacent to a park of many acres, and separated therefrom by a belt of trees of some age which we knew as the Plantation. It is but about thirty or forty yards broad. A close gate of split oak leads to it from the path encircling the garden, and when you enter it from that side you put your hand through a square hole cut in it and lift the hook to pass along to the iron gate which admits to the park from the Plantation. It has further to be added that from some windows of the rectory, which stands on a somewhat lower level than the Plantation, parts of the path leading thereto, and the oak gate itself can be seen. Some of the trees, Scotch firs and others, which form a backing and a surrounding, are of considerable size, but there is noth- ing that diffuses a mysterious gloom or imparts a sinister flavour— nothing of melancholy or funereal associations. The place is well clad, and there are secret nooks and retreats among the bushes, but there is neither offensive bleakness nor oppressive darkness. It is, indeed, a matter for some surprise when one thinks it over, that any cause for misgivings of a nervous sort have attached itself to so normal and cheerful a spot, the more so, since neither our childish mind when we lived there nor the more inquisitive years that came later ever nosed out any legend or reminiscence of old or recent unhappy things.

Yet to me they came, even to me, leading an exceptionally happy wholesome existence, and guarded—not strictly but as carefully as was any way necessary—from uncanny fancies and fear. Not that such guarding avails to close up all gates. I should be puzzled to fix the date at which any sort of misgiving about the Plantation gate first visited me. Possibly it was in the years just before I went to school, possibly on one later summer afternoon of which I have a faint memory, when I was coming back after solitary roaming in the park, or, as I bethink me, from tea at the Hall:* anyhow, alone, and fell in with one of the villagers also homeward bound just as I was about to turn off the road on to the track leading to the Plantation. We broke off our talk with 'good nights', and when I looked back at him after a minute or so I was just a little surprised to see him standing still and looking after me. But no remark passed, and on I went. By the time I was within the iron gate and outside the park, dusk had undoubtedly come on; but there was no lack yet of light, and I could not account to myself for the questionings which certainly did rise as to the presence of anyone else among the trees, questionings to which I could not very certainly say 'No', nor, I was glad to feel, 'Yes', because if there were anyone they could not well have any business there. To be sure, it is difficult, in anything like a grove, to be quite certain that nobody is making a screen out of a tree trunk and keeping it between you and him as he moves round it and you walk on. All I can say is that if such an one was there he was no neighbour or acquaintance of mine, and there was some indication about him of being cloaked or hooded. But I think I may have moved at a rather quicker pace than before, and have been particular about shutting the gate. I think, too, that after that evening something of what Hamlet calls a 'gain-giving'* may have been present in my mind when I thought of the Plantation. I do seem to remember looking out of a window which gave in that direction, and questioning whether there was or was not any appearance of a moving form among the trees. If I did, and perhaps I did, hint a suspicion to the nurse the only answer to it will have been 'the hidea of such a thing!' and an injunction to make haste and get into my bed.

Whether it was on that night or a later one that I seem to see myself again in the small hours gazing out of the window across moonlit grass and hoping I was mistaken in fancying any movement in that half-hidden corner of the garden, I cannot now be sure. But it was certainly within a short while that I began to be visited by dreams which I would much rather not have had—which, in fact, I came to dread acutely; and the point round which they centred was the Plantation gate.

As years go on it but seldom happens that a dream is disturbing. Awkward it may be, as when, while I am drying myself after a bath, I open the bedroom door and step out on to a populous railway platform and have to invent rapid and flimsy excuses for the deplorable *déshabille*. But such a vision is not alarming, though it may make one despair of ever holding up one's head again. But in the times of which I am thinking, it did happen, not often, but oftener than I liked, that the moment a dream set in I knew that it was going to turn out ill, and that there was nothing I could do to keep it on cheerful lines.

Ellis the gardener might be wholesomely employed with rake and spade as I watched at the window; other familiar figures might pass and repass on harmless errands; but I was not deceived. I could see that the time was coming when the gardener and the rest would be gathering up their properties and setting off on paths that led homeward or into some safe outer world, and the garden would be left—to itself, shall we say, or to denizens who did not desire quite ordinary company and were only waiting for the word 'all clear' to slip into their posts of vantage.

Now, too, was the moment near when the surroundings began to take on a threatening look; that the sunlight lost power and a quality of light replaced it which, though I did not know it at the time, my memory years after told me was the lifeless pallor of an eclipse. The effect of all this was to intensify the foreboding that had begun to possess me, and to make me look anxiously about, dreading that in some quarter my fear would take a visible shape. I had not much doubt which way to look. Surely behind those bushes, among those trees, there was motion, yes, and surely—and more quickly than seemed possible—there was motion, not now among the trees, but on the very path towards the house. I was still at the window, and before I could adjust myself to the new fear there came the impression of a tread on the stairs and a hand on the door. That was as far as the dream got, at first; and for me it was far enough. I had no notion what would have been the next development, more than that it was bound to be horrifying.

That is enough in all conscience about the beginning of my dreams. A beginning it was only, for something like it came again and again; how often I can't tell, but often enough to give me an acute distaste for being left alone in that region of the garden. I came to fancy that I could see in the behaviour of the village people whose work took them that way an anxiety to be past a certain point, and moreover a welcoming of company as they approached that corner of the park. But on this it will not do to lay overmuch stress, for, as I have said, I could never glean any kind of story bound up with the place.

However, the strong probability that there had been one once I cannot deny.

I must not by the way give the impression that the whole of the Plantation was haunted ground. There were trees there most admirably devised for climbing and reading in; there was a wall, along the top of which you could walk for many hundred yards and reach a frequented road, passing farmyard and familiar houses; and once in the park, which had its own delights of wood and water, you were well out of range of anything suspicious—or, if that is too much to say, of anything that suggested the Plantation gate.

But I am reminded, as I look on these pages, that so far we have had only preamble, and that there is very little in the way of actual incident to come, and that the criticism attributed to the devil when he sheared the sow is like to be justified. What, after all, was the outcome of the dreams to which without saying a word about them I was liable during a good space of time? Well, it presents itself to me thus. One afternoon—the day being neither overcast nor threatening—I was at my window in the upper floor of the house. All the family were out. From some obscure shelf in a disused room I had worried out a book, not very recondite: it was, in fact, a bound volume of a magazine in which were contained parts of a novel.* I know now what novel it was, but I did not then, and a sentence struck and arrested me. Someone was walking at dusk up a solitary lane by an old mansion in Ireland, and being a man of imagination he was suddenly forcibly impressed by what he calls 'the aerial image of the old house, with its peculiar malign, scared, and skulking aspect' peering out of the shade of its neglected old trees. The words were quite enough to set my own fancy on a bleak track. Inevitably I looked and looked with apprehension, to the Plantation gate. As was but right it was shut, and nobody was upon the path that led to it or from it. But as I said a while ago, there was in it a square hole giving access to the fastening; and through that hole, I could see—and it struck like a blow on the diaphragm—something white or partly white. Now this I could not bear, and with an access of something like courage—only it was more like desperation, like determining that I must know the worst—I did steal down and, quite uselessly, of course, taking cover behind bushes as I went, I made progress until I was within range of the gate and the hole. Things were, alas! worse than I had feared; through that hole a face was looking my way. It was not monstrous, not pale, fleshless, spectral. Malevolent I thought and think it was; at any rate the eyes were large and open and fixed. It was pink and, I thought, hot, and just above the eyes the border of a white linen drapery hung down from the brows.

There is something horrifying in the sight of a face looking at one out of a frame as this did; more particularly if its gaze is unmistakably fixed upon you. Nor does it make the matter any better if the expression gives no clue to what is to come next. I said just now that I took this face to be malevolent, and so I did, but not in regard of any positive dislike or fierceness which it expressed. It was, indeed, quite without emotion: I was only conscious that I could see the whites of the eyes all round the pupil, and that, we know, has a glamour of madness about it. The immovable face was enough for me. I fled, but at what I thought must be a safe distance inside my own precincts I could not but halt and look back. There was no white thing framed in the hole of the gate, but there was a draped form shambling away among the trees.

Do not press me with questions as to how I bore myself when it became necessary to face my family again. That I was upset by something I had seen must have been pretty clear, but I am very sure that I fought off all attempts to describe it. Why I make a lame effort to do it now I cannot very well explain: it undoubtedly has had some formidable power of clinging through many years to my imagination. I feel that even now I should be circumspect in passing that Plantation gate; and every now and again the query haunts me: Are there here and there sequestered places which some curious creatures still frequent, whom once on a time anybody could see and speak to as they went about on their daily occasions, whereas now only at rare intervals in a series of years does one cross their paths and become aware of them; and perhaps that is just as well for the peace of mind of simple people.

APPENDIX

M. R. JAMES ON GHOST STORIES

From the Preface to *Ghost Stories of an Antiquary* (1904)

I WROTE these stories at long intervals, and most of them were read to patient friends, usually at the season of Christmas. One of these friends [James McBryde] offered to illustrate them, and it was agreed that, if he would do that, I would consider the question of publishing them. Four pictures he completed, which will be found in this volume, and then, very quickly and unexpectedly, he was taken away. This is the reason why the greater part of the stories are not provided with illustrations. Those who knew the artist will understand how much I wished to give a permanent form even to a fragment of his work; others will appreciate the fact that here a remembrance is made of one in whom many friendships centred. The stories themselves do not make any very exalted claim. If any of them succeed in causing their readers to feel pleasantly uncomfortable when walking along a solitary road at nightfall, or sitting over a dying fire in the small hours, my purpose in writing them will have been attained.

From the Preface to *More Ghost Stories of an Antiquary* (1911)

Some years ago I promised to publish a second volume of ghost stories when a sufficient number of them should have been accumulated. That time has arrived, and here is the volume. It is, perhaps, unnecessary to warn the critic that in evolving the stories I have not been possessed by that austere sense of the responsibility of authorship which is demanded of the writer of fiction in this generation; or that I have not sought to embody in them any well-considered scheme of 'psychical' theory. To be sure, I have my ideas as to how a ghost story ought to be laid out if it is to be effective. I think that, as a rule, the setting should be fairly familiar and the majority of the characters and their talk such as you may meet or hear any day. A ghost story of which the scene is laid in the twelfth or thirteenth century may succeed in being romantic or poetical: it will never put the reader into the position of saying to himself, 'If I'm not very careful, something of this kind may happen to me!' Another requisite, in my opinion, is that the ghost should be malevolent or odious: amiable and helpful apparitions are all very well in fairy tales or in local legends, but I have no use for them in a fictitious ghost story. Again, I feel that the technical terms of 'occultism,' if they are not very carefully handled, tend to put the mere ghost story (which is all that I am attempting) upon a quasi-scientific plane, and to call into play faculties quite other than the imaginative. I am well aware that mine is a nineteenth- (and not a twentieth-) century conception of this class of tale; but were not the prototypes of all the best ghost stories written in the sixties and seventies?

However, I cannot claim to have been guided by any very strict rules. My stories have been produced (with one exception) at successive Christmas seasons. If they serve to amuse some readers at the Christmas-time that is coming—or at any time whatever—they will justify my action in publishing them.

From the Introduction to V. H. Collins (ed.), *Ghosts and Marvels* (Oxford, 1924)

Often have I been asked to formulate my views about ghost stories and tales of the marvellous, the mysterious, the supernatural. Never have I been able to find out whether I had any views that could be formulated. The truth is, I suspect, that the *genre* is too small and special to bear the imposition of far-reaching principles. Widen the question, and ask what governs the construction of short stories in general, and a great deal might be said, and has been said. There are, of course, instances of whole novels in which the supernatural governs the plot; but among them are few successes. The ghost story is, at its best, only a particular sort of short story, and is subject to the same broad rules as the whole mass of them. Those rules, I imagine, no writer ever consciously follows. In fact, it is absurd to talk of them as rules; they are qualities which have been observed to accompany success.

Some such qualities I have noted, and while I cannot undertake to write about broad principles, something more concrete is capable of being recorded. Well, then: two ingredients most valuable in the concocting of a ghost story are, to me, the atmosphere and the nicely managed crescendo. I assume, of course, that the writer will have got his central idea before he undertakes the story at all. Let us, then, be introduced to the actors in a placid way; let us see them going about their ordinary business, undisturbed by forebodings, pleased with their surroundings; and into this calm environment let the ominous thing put out its head, unobtrusively at first, and then more insistently, until it holds the stage. It is not amiss sometimes to leave a loophole for a natural explanation; but, I would say, let the loophole be so narrow as not to be quite practicable. Then, for the setting. The detective story cannot be too much up-to-date: the motor, the telephone, the aeroplane, the newest slang, are all in place there. For the ghost story a slight haze of distance is desirable. 'Thirty years ago,'

'Not long before the war,' are very proper openings. If a really remote date be chosen, there is more than one way of bringing the reader in contact with it. The finding of documents about it can be made plausible; or you may begin with your apparition and go back over the years to tell the cause of it; or (as in 'Schalken the Painter')* you may set the scene directly in the desired epoch, which I think is hardest to do with success. On the whole (though not a few instances might be quoted against me) I think that a setting so modern that the ordinary reader can judge of its naturalness for himself is preferable to anything antique. For some degree of actuality is the charm of the best ghost stories; not a very insistent actuality, but one strong enough to allow the reader to identify himself with the patient; while it is almost inevitable that the reader of an antique story should fall into the position of the mere spectator.

'Stories I Have Tried to Write'

First published in *The Touchstone*, 2 (30 Nov. 1929), 46–7
Reprinted in *The Collected Ghost Stories of M. R. James* (1931), 643–7

I have neither much experience nor much perseverance in the writing of stories—I am thinking exclusively of ghost stories, for I never cared to try any other kind—and it has amused me sometimes to think of the stories which have crossed my mind from time to time and never materialized properly. Never properly: for some of them I have actually written down, and they repose in a drawer somewhere. To borrow Sir Walter Scott's most frequent quotation, 'Look on (them) again I dare not.'* They were not good enough. Yet some of them had ideas in them which refused to blossom in the surroundings I had devised for them, but perhaps came up in other forms in stories that did get as far as print. Let me recall them for the benefit (so to style it) of somebody else.

There was the story of a man travelling in a train in France.* Facing him sat a typical Frenchwoman of mature years, with the usual moustache and a very confirmed countenance. He had nothing to read but an antiquated novel he had bought for its binding—*Madame de Lichtenstein** it was called. Tired of looking out of the window and studying his *vis-à-vis*, he began drowsily turning the pages, and paused at a conversation between two of the characters. They were discussing an acquaintance, a woman who lived in a largish house at Marcilly-le-Hayer. The house was described, and—here we were coming to a point—the mysterious disappearance of the woman's husband. Her name was mentioned, and my reader couldn't help thinking he knew it in some other connexion. Just then the train stopped at a country station, the traveller, with a start, woke up from a doze—the book open in his hand—the woman opposite him got out, and on the label of her bag he read the name that had seemed to be in his novel. Well, he went on to Troyes, and from there he made excursions, and one of these took him—at lunch-time—to—yes, to Marcilly-le-Hayer.* The hotel in the Grande Place faced a three-gabled house of some pretensions. Out of it came a well-dressed woman *whom he had seen before.* Conversation with the waiter. Yes, the lady was a widow, or so it was believed. At any rate nobody knew what had become of her husband. Here I think we broke down. Of course, there was no such conversation in the novel as the traveller thought he had read.

Then there was quite a long one about two undergraduates spending Christmas in a country house that belonged to one of them. An uncle, next heir to the estate, lived near. Plausible and learned Roman priest, living with the uncle, makes himself agreeable to the young men. Dark walks home at night after dining with the uncle. Curious disturbances as they pass through the shrubberies. Strange, shapeless tracks in the snow round the house, observed in the morning. Efforts to lure away the companion and isolate the proprietor and get him to come out after dark. Ultimate defeat and death of the priest, upon whom the Familiar, baulked of another victim, turns.

Also the story of two students of King's College, Cambridge,* in the sixteenth century (who were, in fact, expelled thence for magical practices), and their nocturnal expedition to a witch at Fenstanton, and of how, at the turning to Lolworth, on the Huntingdon* road, they met a company leading an unwilling figure whom they seemed to know. And of how, on arriving at Fenstanton, they learned of the witch's death, and of what they saw seated upon her newly-dug grave.

These were some of the tales which got as far as the stage of being written down, at least in part. There were others that flitted across the mind from time to time, but never really took shape. The man, for instance (naturally a man with *something* on his mind), who, sitting in his study one evening, was startled by a slight sound, turned hastily, and saw a certain dead face looking out from between the window curtains: a dead face, but with living eyes. He made a dash at the curtains and tore them apart. A pasteboard mask fell to the floor. But there was no one there, and the eyes of the mask were but eyeholes. What was to be done about that?

There is the touch on the shoulder that comes when you are walking quickly homewards in the dark hours, full of anticipation of the warm room and bright fire, and when you pull up, startled, what face or no-face do you see?

Similarly, when Mr. Badman had decided to settle the hash of Mr. Goodman and had picked out just the right thicket by the roadside from which to fire at him, how came it exactly that when Mr. Goodman and his unexpected friend actually did pass, they found Mr. Badman weltering in the road? He was able to tell them something of what he had found waiting for him—even beckoning to him—in the thicket: enough to prevent them from looking into it themselves. There are possibilities here, but the labour of constructing the proper setting has been beyond me.

There may be possibilities, too, in the Christmas cracker, if the right people pull it, and if the motto which they find inside has the right message on it. They will probably leave the party early, pleading indisposition; but very likely a *previous engagement of long standing* would be the more truthful excuse.

In parenthesis, many common objects may be made the vehicles of retribution, and where retribution is not called for, of malice. Be careful how you handle the packet you pick up in the carriage-drive, particularly if it contains nail-parings and hair. Do not, in any case, bring it into the house. It may not be alone . . . (Dots are believed by many writers of our day to be a good substitute for effective writing. They are certainly an easy one. Let us have a few more . . . . . .)

Late on Monday night a toad came into my study: and, though nothing has so far seemed to link itself with this appearance, I feel that it may not be quite prudent to brood over topics which may open the interior eye to the presence of more formidable visitants. Enough said.

'Some Remarks on Ghost Stories'
The Bookman (December 1929), 169–72

Very nearly all the ghost stories of old times claim to be true narratives of remarkable occurrences. At the outset I must make it clear that with these—be they ancient, medieval or post-medieval—I have nothing to do, any more than I have with those chronicled in our own days. I am concerned with a branch of fiction; not a large branch, if you look at the rest of the tree, but one which has been astonishingly fertile in the last thirty years. The avowedly fictitious ghost story is my subject, and that being understood I can proceed.

In the year 1854 George Borrow narrated to an audience of Welshmen, 'in the tavern of Gutter Vawr, in the county of Glamorgan,' what he asserted to be 'decidedly the best ghost story in the world.' You may read this story either in English, in Knapp's notes to *Wild Wales*,* or in Spanish, in a recent edition with excellent pictures (*Las Aventuras de Pánfilo*). The source is Lope de Vega's *El Peregrino en su patria*,* published in 1604. You will find it a remarkably interesting specimen of a tale of terror written in Shakespeare's lifetime, but I shall be surprised if you agree with Borrow's estimate of it. It is nothing but an account of a series of nightmares experienced by a wanderer who lodges for a night in a 'hospital,' which had been deserted because of hauntings. The ghosts come in crowds and play tricks with the victim's bed. They quarrel over cards, they squirt water at the man, they throw torches about the room. Finally they steal his clothes and disappear; but next morning the clothes are where he put them when he went to bed. In fact they are rather goblins than ghosts.

Still, here you have a story written with the sole object of inspiring a pleasing terror in the reader; and as I think, that *is* the true aim of the ghost story.

As far as I know, nearly two hundred years pass before you find the literary ghost story attempted again. Ghosts of course figure on the stage, but we must leave them out of consideration. Ghosts are the subject of quasi-scientific research in this country at the hands of Glanville, Beaumont* and others; but these collectors are out to prove theories of the future life and the spiritual world. Improving treatises, with illustrative instances, are written on the Continent, as by Lavater.* All these, if they do afford what our ancestors called amusement (Dr. Johnson decreed that *Coriolanus* was 'amusing'), do so by a side-wind. *The Castle of Otranto* is perhaps the progenitor of the ghost story as a literary genre, and I fear that it is merely amusing in the modern sense. Then we come to Mrs. Radcliffe, whose ghosts are far better of their kind, but with exasperating timidity are all explained away; and to Monk Lewis, who in the book which gives him his nickname is odious and horrible without being impressive. But Monk Lewis* was responsible for better things than he could produce himself. It was under his auspices that Scott's verse first saw the light: among the *Tales of Terror and Wonder* are not only some of his translations, but 'Glenfinlas' and the 'Eve of St. John,' which must always rank as fine ghost stories. The form into which he cast them was that of the ballads which he loved and collected, and we must not forget that the ballad is in the direct line of ancestry of the ghost story. Think of 'Clerk Saunders,' 'Young Benjie,' the 'Wife of Usher's Well.' I am tempted to enlarge on the *Tales of Terror*, for the most part supremely absurd, where Lewis holds the pen, and jigs along with such stanzas as:

> All present then uttered a terrified shout;
> 　All turned with disgust from the scene.
> The worms they crept in, and the worms they crept out,
> And sported his eyes and his temples about,
> 　While the spectre addressed Imogene.

But proportion must be observed.

If I were writing generally of horrific books which include supernatural appearances, I should be obliged to include Maturin's *Melmoth*,* and doubtless imitations of it which I know nothing of. But *Melmoth* is a long—a cruelly long—book, and we must keep our eye on the short prose ghost story in the first place. If Scott is not the creator of this, it is to him that we owe two classical specimens—'Wandering Willie's Tale' and the 'Tapestried Chamber.' The former we know is an episode in a novel; anyone who searches the novels of succeeding years will certainly find (as we, alas, find in *Pickwick* and *Nicholas Nickleby*!) stories of this type foisted in; and possibly some of them may be good enough to deserve reprinting. But the real happy hunting ground, the proper habitat of our game is the magazine, the annual, the periodical publication destined to amuse the family circle. They came up thick and fast, the magazines, in the thirties and forties, and many died young. I do not, having myself sampled the task, envy the devoted one who sets out to examine the files, but it is not rash to promise him a measure of success. He will find ghost stories; but of what sort? Charles Dickens will tell us. In a paper from *Household Words*, which will be found among *Christmas Stories* under the name of 'A Christmas Tree' (I reckon it among the best of Dickens's occasional writings), that great man takes occasion to run through the plots of the typical ghost stories of his time. As he remarks, they are 'reducible to a very few general types and classes; for ghosts have little originality, and "walk" in a beaten track.' He gives us at some length the experience of the nobleman and the ghost of the beautiful young housekeeper who drowned herself in the park two hundred years before; and, more cursorily, the indelible bloodstain, the door that will not shut, the clock that strikes thirteen, the phantom coach, the compact to appear after death, the girl who meets her double, the cousin who is seen at the moment of his death far away in India, the maiden lady who 'really did see the Orphan Boy.' With such things as these we are still familiar. But we have rather forgotten—and I for my part have seldom met—those with which he ends his survey: 'Legion is the name of the German castles where we sit up alone to meet the spectre— where we are shown into a room made comparatively cheerful for our reception' (more detail, excellent of its kind, follows), 'and where, about the small hours of the night, we come into the knowledge of divers supernatural mysteries. Legion is the name of the haunted German students, in whose society we draw yet nearer to the fire, while the schoolboy in the corner opens his eyes wide and round, and flies off the footstool he has chosen for his seat, when the door accidentally blows open.'

As I have said, this German stratum of ghost stories is one of which I know little; but I am confident that the searcher of magazines will penetrate to it. Examples of the other types will accrue, especially when he reaches the era of Christmas Numbers, inaugurated by Dickens himself. His Christmas Numbers are not to be confused with his *Christmas Books*, though the latter led on to the former. Ghosts are not absent from these, but I do not call the *Christmas Carol* a ghost story proper; while I do assign that name to the stories of the Signalman and the Juryman (in 'Mugby Junction' and 'Dr. Marigold').

These were written in 1865 and 1866, and nobody can deny that they conform to the modern idea of the ghost story. The setting and the personages are those of the writer's own day; they have nothing antique about them. Now this mode is not absolutely essential to success, but it is characteristic of the majority of successful stories: the belted knight who meets the spectre in the vaulted chamber and has to say 'By my halidom', or words to that effect, has little actuality about him. Anything, we feel, might have happened in the fifteenth century. No; the seer of ghosts must talk something like me, and be dressed, if not in my fashion, yet not too much like a man in a pageant, if he is to enlist my sympathy. Wardour Street has no business here.

If Dickens's ghost stories are good and of the right complexion, they are not the best that were written in his day. The palm must I think be assigned to J. S. Le Fanu, whose stories of 'The Watcher' (or 'The Familiar'), 'Mr. Justice Harbottle,' 'Carmilla,' are unsurpassed, while 'Schalken the Painter,' 'Squire Toby's Will,' the haunted house in 'The House by the Churchyard,' 'Dickon the Devil,' 'Madam Crowl's Ghost,' run them very close. Is it the blend of French and Irish in Le Fanu's descent and surroundings that gives him the knack of infusing ominousness into his atmosphere? He is anyhow an artist in words; who else could have hit on the epithets in this sentence: 'The aerial image of the old house for a moment stood before her, with its peculiar malign, scared and skulking aspect.' Other famous stories of Le Fanu there are which are not quite ghost stories—'Green Tea' and 'The Room in the Dragon Volant'; and yet another, 'The Haunted Baronet,' not famous, not even known but to a few, contains some admirable touches, but somehow lacks proportion. Upon mature consideration, I do not think that there are better ghost stories anywhere than the best of Le Fanu's; and among these I should give the first place to 'The Familiar' (*alias* 'The Watcher').

Other famous novelists of those days tried their hand—Bulwer Lytton* for one. Nobody is permitted to write about ghost stories without mentioning 'The Haunters and the Haunted.' To my mind it is spoilt by the conclusion; the Cagliostro element (forgive an inaccuracy) is alien. It comes in with far better effect (though in a burlesque guise) in Thackeray's one attempt in this direction—'The Notch in the Axe,' in the *Roundabout Papers*. This to be sure begins by being a skit partly on Dumas, partly on Lytton; but as Thackeray warmed to his work he got interested in the story and, as he says, was quite sorry to part with Pinto in the end. We have to reckon too with Wilkie Collins. *The Haunted Hotel*, a short novel, is by no means ineffective; grisly enough, almost, for the modern American taste.

Rhoda Broughton, Mrs. Riddell, Mrs. Henry Wood, Mrs. Oliphant*— all these have some sufficiently absorbing stories to their credit. I own to reading not infrequently 'Featherston's Story' in the fifth series of *Johnny Ludlow*, to delighting in its domestic flavour and finding its ghost very convincing. (*Johnny Ludlow*, some young persons may not know, is by Mrs. Henry Wood.) The religious ghost story, as it may be called, was never done better than by Mrs. Oliphant in 'The Open Door' and 'A Beleaguered City'; though there is a competitor, and a strong one, in Le Fanu's 'Mysterious Lodger.'

Here I am conscious of a gap; my readers will have been conscious of many previous gaps. My memory does in fact slip on from Mrs. Oliphant to Marion Crawford* and his horrid story of 'The Upper Berth,' which (with 'The Screaming Skull' some distance behind) is the best in his collection of *Uncanny Tales*, and stands high among ghost stories in general.

That was I believe written in the late eighties. In the early nineties comes the deluge, the deluge of the illustrated monthly magazines, and it is no longer possible to keep pace with the output either of single stories or of volumes of collected ones. Never was the flow more copious than it is to-day, and it is only by chance that one comes across any given example. So nothing beyond scattering and general remarks can be offered. Some whole novels there have been which depend for all or part of their interest on ghostly matter. There is *Dracula*, which suffers by excess. (I fancy, by the way, that it must be based on a story in the fourth volume of Chambers's *Repository*,* issued in the fifties.) There is *Alice-for-Short*,* in which I never cease to admire the skill with which the ghost is woven into the web of the tale. But that is a very rare feat.

Among the collections of short stories, E. F. Benson's* three volumes rank high, though to my mind he sins occasionally by stepping over the line of legitimate horridness. He is however blameless in this aspect as compared with some Americans, who compile volumes called *Not At Night** and the like. These are merely nauseating, and it is very easy to be nauseating. I, *moi qui vous parle*, could undertake to make a reader physic-ally sick, if I chose to think and write in terms of the Grand Guignol. The authors of the stories I have in mind tread, as they believe, in the steps of Edgar Allan Poe and Ambrose Bierce* (himself sometimes unpardonable), but they do not possess the force of either.

Reticence may be an elderly doctrine to preach, yet from the artistic point of view I am sure it is a sound one. Reticence conduces to effect, blatancy ruins it, and there is much blatancy in a lot of recent stories. They drag in sex too, which is a fatal mistake; sex is tiresome enough in the novels; in a ghost story, or as the backbone of a ghost story, I have no patience with it.

At the same time don't let us be mild and drab. Malevolence and terror, the glare of evil faces, 'the stony grin of unearthly malice,' pursuing forms in darkness, and 'long-drawn, distant screams,' are all in place, and so is a modicum of blood, shed with deliberation and carefully husbanded; the weltering and wallowing that I too often encounter merely recall the methods of M. G. Lewis.

Clearly it is out of the question for me to begin upon a series of 'short notices' of recent collections; but an illustrative instance or two will be to the point. A. M. Burrage,* in *Some Ghost Stories*, keeps on the right side of the line, and if about half of his ghosts are amiable, the rest have their terrors, and no mean ones. H. R. Wakefield,* in *They Return at Evening* (a good title) gives us a mixed bag, from which I should remove one or two that leave a nasty taste. Among the residue are some admirable pieces, very inventive. Going back a few years I light on Mrs. Everett's *The Death Mask*,* of a rather quieter tone on the whole, but with some excellently conceived stories. Hugh Benson's *Light Invisible* and *Mirror of Shalott* are too ecclesiastical. K. and Hesketh Prichard's 'Flaxman Low'* is most ingenious and successful, but rather over-technically 'occult.' It seems impertinent to apply the same criticism to Algernon Blackwood,* but 'John Silence' is surely open to it. Mr. Elliott O'Donnell's* multitudinous volumes I do not know whether to class as narratives of fact or exercises in fiction. I hope they may be of the latter sort, for life in a world managed by his gods and infested by his demons seems a risky business.

So I might go on through a long list of authors; but the remarks one can make in an article of this compass can hardly be illuminating. The reading of many ghost stories has shown me that the greatest successes have been scored by the authors who can make us envisage a definite time and place, and give us plenty of clear-cut and matter-of-fact detail, but who, when the climax is reached, allow us to be just a little in the dark as to the working of their machinery. We do not want to see the bones of their theory about the supernatural.

All this while I have confined myself almost entirely to the English ghost story. The fact is that either there are not many good stories by foreign writers, or (more probably) my ignorance has veiled them from me. But I should feel myself ungrateful if I did not pay a tribute to the supernatural tales of Erckmann–Chatrian.* The blend of French with German in them, comparable to the French–Irish blend in Le Fanu, has produced some quite first-class romance of this kind. Among longer stories, 'La

Maison Forestière' (and, if you will, 'Hugues le Loup'); among shorter ones 'Le Blanc et le Noir,' 'Le Rêve du Cousin Elof' and 'L'Œil Invisible' have for years delighted and alarmed me. It is high time that they were made more accessible than they are.

There need not be any peroration to a series of rather disjointed reflections. I will only ask the reader to believe that, though I have not hitherto mentioned it, I have read *The Turn of the Screw.**

'Ghosts—Treat Them Gently!'
Evening News (17 April 1931)

What first interested me in ghosts? This I can tell you quite definitely. In my childhood I chanced to see a toy Punch and Judy set, with figures cut out in cardboard. One of these was The Ghost. It was a tall figure habited in white with an unnaturally long and narrow head, also surrounded with white, and a dismal visage.

Upon this my conceptions of a ghost were based, and for years it permeated my dreams.

Other questions—why I like ghost stories, or what are the best, or why they are the best, or a recipe for writing such things—I have never found it easy to be so positive about. Clearly, however, the public likes them. The recrudescence of ghost stories in recent years is notable: it corresponds, of course, with the vogue of the detective tale.

The ghost story can be supremely excellent in its kind, or it may be deplorable. Like other things, it may err by excess or defect. Bram Stoker's *Dracula* is a book with very good ideas in it, but—to be vulgar—the butter is spread far too thick. Excess is the fault here: to give an example of erring by defect is difficult, because the stories that err in that way leave no impression on the memory.

I am speaking of the literary ghost story here. The story that claims to be 'veridical' (in the language of the Society of Psychical Research) is a very different affair. It will probably be quite brief, and will conform to some one of several familiar types. This is but reasonable, for, if there be ghosts—as I am quite prepared to believe—the true ghost story need do no more than illustrate their normal habits (if normal is the right word), and may be as mild as milk.

The literary ghost, on the other hand, has to justify his existence by some startling demonstration, or, short of that, must be furnished with a background that will throw him into full relief and make him the central feature.

Since the things which the ghost can effectively do are very limited in number, ranging about death and madness and the discovery of secrets, the setting seems to me all-important, since in it there is the greatest opportunity for variety.

It is upon this and upon the first glimmer of the appearance of the supernatural that pains must be lavished. But we need not, we should not, use all the colours in the box. In the infancy of the art we needed the haunted castle on a beetling rock to put us in the right frame: the tendency is not yet extinct, for I have but just read a story with a mysterious mansion on a desolate height in Cornwall and a gentleman practising the worst sort of magic. How often, too, have ruinous old houses been described or shown to me as fit scenes for stories!

'Can't you imagine some old monk or friar wandering about this long gallery?' No, I can't.

I know Harrison Ainsworth* could: *The Lancashire Witches* teems with Cistercians and what he calls votaresses in mouldering vestments, who glide about passages to very little purpose. But these fail to impress. Not that I have not a soft corner in my heart for *The Lancashire Witches*, which—ridiculous as much of it is—has distinct merits as a story.

It cannot be said too often that the more remote in time the ghost is the harder it is to make him effective, always supposing him to be the ghost of a dead person. Elementals and such-like do not come under this rule.

Roughly speaking, the ghost should be a contemporary of the seer. Such was the elder Hamlet and such Jacob Marley. The latter I cite with confidence and in despite of critics, for, whatever may be urged against some parts of *A Christmas Carol*, it is, I hold, undeniable that the introduction, the advent, of Jacob Marley is tremendously effective.

And be it observed that the setting in both these classic examples is contemporary and even ordinary. The ramparts of the Kronborg and the chambers of Ebenezer Scrooge were, to those who frequented them, features of every-day life.

But there are exceptions to every rule. An ancient haunting can be made terrible and can be invested with actuality, but it will tax your best endeavours to forge the links between past and present in a satisfying way. And in any case there must be ordinary level-headed modern persons—Horatios—on the scene, such as the detective needs his Watson or his Hastings* to play the part of the lay observer.

Setting or environment, then, is to me a principal point, and the more readily appreciable the setting is to the ordinary reader the better. The other essential is that our ghost should make himself felt by gradual stirrings diffusing an atmosphere of uneasiness before the final flash or stab of horror.

Must there be horror? you ask. I think so. There are but two really good ghost stories I know in the language wherein the elements of beauty and pity dominate terror. They are Lanoe Falconer's* 'Cecilia de Noel' and Mrs. Oliphant's 'The Open Door.' In both there are moments of horror; but in both we end by saying with Hamlet: 'Alas, poor ghost!' Perhaps my limit of two stories is overstrict; but that these two are by very much the best of their kind I do not doubt.

On the whole, then, I say you must have horror and also malevolence. Not less necessary, however, is reticence. There is a series of books I have read, I think American in origin, called *Not at Night* (and with other like titles), which sin glaringly against this law. They have no other aim than that of Mr. Wardle's Fat Boy.*

Of course, all writers of ghost stories do desire to make their readers' flesh creep; but these are shameless in their attempts. They are unbelievably crude and sudden, and they wallow in corruption. And if there is a theme that ought to be kept out of the ghost story, it is that of the charnel house. That and sex, wherein I do not say that these *Not at Night* books deal, but certainly other recent writers do, and in so doing spoil the whole business.

To return from the faults of ghost stories to their excellence. Who, do I think, has best realized their possibilities? I have no hesitation in saying that it is Joseph Sheridan Le Fanu. In the volume called *In a Glass Darkly* are four stories of paramount excellence, 'Green Tea,' 'The Familiar,' 'Mr Justice Harbottle,' and 'Carmilla.' All of these conform to my requirements: the settings are quite different, but all *seen* by the writer; the approaches of the supernatural nicely graduated; the climax adequate. Le Fanu was a scholar and poet, and these tales show him as such. It is true that he died as long ago as 1873, but there is wonderfully little that is obsolete in his manner.

Of living writers I have some hesitation in speaking, but on any list that I was forced to compile the names of E. F. Benson, Blackwood, Burrage, De la Mare* and Wakefield would find a place.

But, although the subject has its fascinations, I see no use in being pontifical about it. These stories are meant to please and amuse us. If they do so, well; but, if not, let us relegate them to the top shelf and say no more about it.

Preface to *The Collected Ghost Stories of M. R. James* (1931)

In accordance with a fashion which has recently become common, I am issuing my four volumes of ghost stories under one cover, and appending to them some matter of the same kind.

I am told they have given pleasure of a certain sort to my readers: if so, my whole object in writing them has been attained, and there does not seem to be much reason for prefacing them by a disquisition upon how I came to write them. Still, a preface is demanded by my publishers, and it may as well be devoted to answering questions which I have been asked.

First, whether the stories are based on my own experience? To this the answer is No: except in one case, specified in the text, where a dream furnished a suggestion. Or again, whether they are versions of other people's experiences? No. Or suggested by books? This is more difficult to answer concisely. Other people have written of dreadful spiders—for instance, Erckmann-Chatrian in an admirable story called *L'Araignée Crabe**—and of pictures which came alive: the State Trials give the language of Judge Jeffreys and the courts at the end of the seventeenth century: and so on. Places have been more prolific in suggestion: if anyone is curious about my local settings, let it be recorded that S. Bertrand de Comminges and Viborg are real places: that in *Oh, Whistle, and I'll come to you*, I had Felixstowe in mind; in *A School Story*, Temple Grove, East Sheen; in *The Tractate Middoth*, Cambridge University Library; in *Martin's Close*, Sampford Courtenay in Devon: that the cathedrals of Barchester and Southminster were blends of Canterbury, Salisbury, and Hereford: that Herefordshire was the imagined scene of *A View from a Hill*, and Seaburgh in *A Warning to the Curious* is Aldeburgh in Suffolk.

I am not conscious of other obligations to literature or local legend, written or oral, except in so far as I have tried to make my ghosts act in ways not inconsistent with the rules of folklore. As for the fragments of ostensible erudition which are scattered about my pages, hardly anything in them is not pure invention; there never was, naturally, any such book as that which I quote in the *Treasure of Abbot Thomas*.

Other questioners ask if I have any theories as to the writing of ghost stories. None that are worthy of the name or need to be repeated here: some thoughts on the subject are in a preface to *Ghosts and Marvels*. [*The World's Classics*, Oxford, 1924.] There is no receipt for success in this form of fiction more than in any other. The public, as Dr. Johnson said, are the ultimate judges: if they are pleased, it is well; if not, it is no use to tell them why they ought to have been pleased.

Supplementary questions are: Do I believe in ghosts? To which I answer that I am prepared to consider evidence and accept it if it satisfies me. And lastly, Am I going to write any more ghost stories? To which I fear I must answer, Probably not.

Since we are nothing if not bibliographical nowadays, I add a paragraph or two setting forth the facts about the several collections and their contents.

'Ghost Stories of an Antiquary' was published (like the rest) by Messrs. Arnold in 1904. The first issue had four illustrations by the late James McBryde. In this volume *Canon Alberic's Scrap-book* was written in 1894 and printed soon after in the *National Review*: *Lost Hearts* appeared in the *Pall Mall Magazine*. Of the next five stories, most of which were read to friends at Christmas-time at King's College, Cambridge, I only recollect that I wrote *Number 13* in 1899, while *The Treasure of Abbot Thomas* was composed in summer 1904.

The second volume, 'More Ghost Stories,' appeared in 1911. The first six of the seven tales it contains were Christmas productions, the very first (*A School Story*) having been made up for the benefit of the King's College Choir School. *The Stalls of Barchester Cathedral* was printed in the *Contemporary Review*: *Mr. Humphreys and his Inheritance* was written to fill up the volume.

'A Thin Ghost and Others' was the third collection, containing five stories and published in 1919. In it, *An Episode of Cathedral History* and *The Story of a Disappearance and an Appearance* were contributed to the *Cambridge Review*.

Of six stories in 'A Warning to the Curious,' published in 1925, the first, *The Haunted Dolls' House*, was written for the library of Her Majesty the Queen's Dolls' House, and subsequently appeared in the *Empire Review*. *The Uncommon Prayer-book* saw the light in the *Atlantic Monthly*, the title-story in the *London Mercury*, and another, I think *A Neighbour's Landmark*, in an ephemeral called *The Eton Chronic*. Similar ephemerals were responsible for all but one of the appended pieces (not all of them strictly stories), whereof one, *Rats*, composed for *At Random*, was included by Lady Cynthia Asquith in a collection entitled *Shudders*. The exception, *Wailing Well*, was written for the Eton College troop of Boy Scouts, and read at their camp-fire at Worbarrow Bay in August, 1927. It was then printed by itself in a limited edition by Robert Gathorne Hardy and Kyrle Leng at the Mill House Press, Stanford Dingley.

Four or five of the stories have appeared in collections of such things in recent years, and a Norse version of four from my first volume, by Ragnhild Undset, was issued in 1919 under the title of *Aander og Trolddom*.*

EXPLANATORY NOTES

ABBREVIATIONS

CGS	*Collected Ghost Stories* (1931)
Cox I	Michael Cox, *M. R. James: An Informal Portrait* (1986)
Cox II	*Casting the Runes and Other Ghost Stories*, ed. Michael Cox (1987)
E&K	*Eton and King's* (1926)
EB	*Encyclopaedia Britannica*
GSA	*Ghost Stories of an Antiquary* (1904)
Joshi I	*Count Magnus and Other Ghost Stories*, ed. S. T. Joshi (2005)
Joshi II	*The Haunted Doll's House and Other Ghost Stories* (2006)
KCL	King's College Library, Cambridge
LTF	*Montague Rhodes James: Letters to a Friend*, ed. Gwendolen McBryde (1956)
Lubbock	S. G. Lubbock, *Montague Rhodes James* (1939)
MGSA	*More Ghost Stories of an Antiquary* (1911)
Pfaff	R. W. Pfaff, *Montague Rhodes James* (1980)
PT	*A Pleasing Terror*, ed. Christopher and Barbara Roden (2001)
S&N	*Suffolk and Norfolk* (1930)
SOED	*Shorter Oxford English Dictionary*
TG	*A Thin Ghost and Others* (1919)
WTC	*A Warning to the Curious* (1925)

Quotations from the Bible are from the King James Version, unless otherwise stated, and quotations from Shakespeare are from the Riverside edition.

CANON ALBERIC'S SCRAP-BOOK

Written between spring 1892, when MRJ first visited St Bertrand de Comminges, and October 1893, when it was read, with 'Lost Hearts', to the Chitchat Society at Cambridge. Originally entitled 'A Curious Story', though MRJ's handwritten manuscript is untitled. Renamed 'The Scrap-book of Canon Alberic' for its first publication in *The National Review*, 25 (March 1895), 132–41. Modified to its current form for *GSA*, reprinted in *CGS*. Manuscript in KCL, MS MRJ:A/1.

  3 *ST. BERTRAND DE COMMINGES*: a tiny habitation (population 237 in 1999) in the Haute-Garonne region of southern France, very near the Spanish border. Once a way-station for pilgrims on the route to Santiago de Compostela, St Bertrand is spectacularly situated, perched high in the foothills of the Pyrenees. The town is dominated by the enormous Romanesque cathedral of St Bertrand, dating from the twelfth

century, when Bertrand de l'Isle was ordained as the first bishop of the Comminges. Bertrand was canonized in 1309 by his successor as bishop of Comminges, Bertrand de Got, later Pope Clement V. MRJ first visited St Bertrand in 1892, along with Armitage Robinson and Arthur Shipley (Cox I, 106), and wrote an account of the cathedral, including a sketch which records the position of the stuffed crocodile, which he sent to his parents:

> S. Bertrand de Comminges . . . is a tiny walled town on a steep hill. But the snow which was some inches deep prevented our walking round it. We could only examine the cathedral: it is a splendid church, without aisles and short. You see the whole length from the door. There is no proper nave. The stalls which are like those at Auch form a separate enclosure inside the church into which you can't see. In the corner of the nave is a splendid organ case of XVI cent with nearly all the inside gone. A splendid 14th century cope of English work in the treasury with all sorts of scenes on it. Beautiful cloisters and altogether a sweet place. (*PT*, 15)

He revisited the Comminges in 1899 and again in 1901, as part of his annual bicycling holiday, in which he attempted to visit all the cathedrals of France (he saw all but four). Pfaff (p. 114) speculates that MRJ may have visited St Bertrand as early as 1887.

3 *verger or sacristan*: *SOED* defines *verger* as 'one whose duty it is to take care of the interior of a church, and to act as attendant', and *sacristan* as 'the sexton of a parish church', that is, an attendant and a gravedigger.

4 *Dennistoun*: originally 'Anderson' in both MS and *National Review*, though changed to Dennistoun for *GSA*. Dennistoun makes a cameo reappearance in 'The Mezzotint', while Mr Anderson is the protagonist of 'Number 13'.

St. Bertrand's ivory crozier . . . the dusty stuffed crocodile: both still on display in the cathedral. The crozier is made from a narwhal tusk, and the crocodile is a souvenir brought back by a returning crusader.

the stalls, the enormous dilapidated organ, the choir-screen of Bishop John de Mauléon: Jean de Mauléon, bishop of Comminges from 1523 to 1551, oversaw the construction of these, the most distinctive features of the cathedral's interior. The stalls, sixty-seven in all, are magnificently carved, and culminate in a wonderfully intricate depiction of the Tree of Jesse. The organ is no longer dilapidated—it was completely restored to its spectacular Renaissance glory in 1974. The huge choir-screen completely bisects the cathedral's nave and aisles.

How St. Bertrand delivered a man whom the Devil long sought to strangle: this specific painting is fictional, though the tomb of St Bertrand is behind the altar, and it is adorned by a series of paintings depicting the saint's miracles.

5 *Angelus*: 'A devotional exercise commemorating the Incarnation, in which the Angelic Salutation is thrice repeated, said by Roman Catholics, at morning, noon, and sunset, at the sound of a bell' (*SOED*).

amateur des vieux livres: 'lover of old books'.

6 *a stupid missal of Plantin's printing, about 1580*: a missal is a book containing the mass. Christoph Plantin (*c.*1520–89) was a French printer and typographical pioneer, based in Antwerp from 1549. Publisher of numerous Bibles and other ecclesiastical works; best known for the *Biblia Polyglotta* (*Polyglot Bible*), 1569–72. MRJ visited the Musée Plantin-Moretus in Antwerp in April 1891, and examined 'an early illuminated Sedalius 10th century' (Cox II, 301). Joshi I (p. 260) asserts that Plantin was 'a secret member of a heretical mystical sect', whose works he published privately.

Alberic de Mauléon: fictional, though characteristically embedded in layers of genuine factual information.

7 *antiphoner*: a book containing antiphons, that is, 'A versicle or sentence sung by one choir in response to another' (*SOED*).

late in the seventeenth century: 'early in the xviiith century' in MS.

Psalter: a copy of the Psalms, for liturgical use.

uncial writing: early Latin and Greek manuscript writing, comprised of large, rounded letters, not joined together.

Papias 'On the Words of Our Lord': Papias (second century) was bishop of Hierapolis in Phrygia, Asia Minor (near modern Erzurum, Turkey). *On the Words of Our Lord* (often translated as *Explanation of the Sayings of the Lord*) now exists only in fragments, excerpted in the writings of Irenaeus and Eusebius (a severe critic), but is nevertheless considered an important account of the beginnings of the Church. In *The Wanderings and Homes of Manuscripts* (London: SPCK, 1919), MRJ writes: 'It is almost a relief that catalogues [of ancient English libraries] do not tell us of supremely desirable things, such as Papias on the Oracles of the Lord or the complete Histories and Annals of Tacitus' (p. 76).

8 *in the north-west angle of the cloister was a cross drawn in gold paint*: the cloisters contain the tombs of many of the canons of St Bertrand. Intriguingly, the tomb at the north-west angle of the cloister is broken open.

Mr. Minor-Canon Quatremain in "Old St. Paul's": a novel of 1841 by William Harrison Ainsworth, set during the London plague and fire of 1665–6. Minor Canon Thomas Quatremain believes he has discovered the location of buried treasure in Old St Paul's Cathedral (destroyed by fire in 1666) by use of astrological divination.

a Biblical scene: Cox suggests that the picture may echo Raphael's cartoon *The Death of Ananias*, which is in the Victoria and Albert Museum (called the South Kensington Museum in the 1890s) (Cox II, 301). Julia Briggs (*Night Visitors: The Rise and Fall of the English Ghost Story* (London,

1977), 130) speculates that the demon may be based on a crouching figure in Breughel's *The Fall of the Rebel Angels*.

8 *King Solomon*: according to the *Testament of Solomon* (written between the fifth and first centuries BCE), Solomon commanded a number of demons, including some obstructing the building of the Temple in Jerusalem, by means of a ring given to him by the archangel Michael. The *Testament* established Solomon's reputation as a mage and an exorcist.

9 *lecturer on morphology*: morphology is the science of biological form. This may be an oblique reference to Arthur Shipley, who had accompanied MRJ to St Bertrand in 1892, and was university lecturer on the advanced morphology of invertebrata at Cambridge from 1894 to 1908 (Cox II, 302).

10 *Gehazi*: see 2 Kings 5. The prophet Elisha cures Naaman, captain of the Syrian host, of leprosy, and declines any payment for this. Gehazi, Elisha's servant, follows after Naaman, to 'take somewhat of him', and is given two silver talents and two changes of garment. When Elisha discovers this, he curses Gehazi: 'The leprosy therefore of Naaman shall cleave unto thee, and unto they seed forever. And he went out from his presence a leper as white as snow.'

12 *'Deux fois je l'ai vu; mille fois je l'ai senti'*: 'Two times I have seen it; a thousand times I have felt it.'

13 *Ecclesiasticus*: Ecclesiasticus (Sirach) 39: 28: 'There are winds that have been created for vengeance, and in their anger they scourge heavily' (Revised Standard Version).

Isaiah: see Isaiah 34: 13–14:

> And thorns shall come up in her palaces, nettles and brambles in the fortresses thereof: and it shall be an habitation of dragons, and a court for owls.
>
> The wild beasts of the desert shall also meet with the wild beasts of the island, and the satyr shall cry to his fellow, and the screech-owl also shall rest there, and find for herself a place of rest.

Wentworth Collection at Cambridge: fictional version of the Fitzwilliam Museum, of which MRJ was curator.

Versicle: 'One of a series of short sentences, said or sung antiphonically in divine service; *spec.* one said by the officiant and followed by the RESPONSE of the congregation or people' (*SOED*). See also the notes to p. 7: *Antiphoner* and *Psalter*.

Psalm: Whoso dwelleth (xci.): Psalm 91: 'He that dwelleth in the secret place of the most High shall abide under the shadow of the Almighty.' See particularly verses 5–6:

> Thou shalt not be afraid of the terror by night, nor for the arrow that flieth by day.

Nor for the pestilence that walketh in darkness; nor for the destruction that wasteth at noonday.

'Gallia Christiana': an encyclopedia of the bishops and abbots of France, first compiled by Claude Robert in 1626.

Sammarthani: Dionysius Sammarthanus, or Denys de Sainte-Marthe (1650–1725), a Benedictine monk who began the revision of the *Gallia Christiana* in the early eighteenth century.

LOST HEARTS

Composed between July 1892 (when MRJ visited St Michan's church in Dublin) and October 1893, when it was read to the Chitchat Society along with 'Canon Alberic's Scrap-book'. First published in the *Pall Mall Magazine*, 7/32 (December 1895), 639–47. Reprinted in *GSA*: 'Lost Hearts' was not originally intended as part of the volume, but was added by MRJ specifically in response to publisher Edward Arnold's request, 'Are there any more ghost stories? Those sent would only make a slim volume, and if there was half as much or as much again it would be a great advantage' (KCL MS MRJ:D/Arnold). Published again in *CGS*. Manuscript in KCL MS MRJ:A/2.

14 *Aswarby Hall, in the heart of Lincolnshire*: a real house, though not answering to MRJ's description. Aswarby Hall, in the village of Aswarby, Lincolnshire, was originally a Tudor manor house, and was extensively modernized in 1836. It was demolished in 1951—only the entrance gates remain.

15 *the Mysteries*: the Eleusinian Mysteries. Secret Greek rites taught by the goddess Demeter, who had lived disguised as a nurse in the home of King Celeus of the city of Eleusis, as recounted in the Homeric *Hymn to Demeter*. As initiation ceremonies into the cult of Demeter and Persephone, the Mysteries were enacted every year, and were considered the most important of all Classical rites.

the Orphic poems: poems attributed to Orpheus, of which only two examples survive, the epic *Argonautica Orphica* (fifth–sixth century BCE) and a corpus of hymns (2–300 CE). These works were supposedly recited as part of the Eleusinian Mysteries. See M. L. West, *The Orphic Poems* (Oxford: Oxford University Press, 1983). Recalling a period of illness as a schoolboy in 1879, MRJ wrote, 'I think the last straw was reading a lot of the Orphic Hymns (fifty of them) at a sitting'—but, he noted, 'they taught me a good many words so I will not repent of my evil ways' (Cox I, 33).

Mithras: originally, an Iranian warrior deity, slayer of the sacred bull, from whose blood came all animals and plants useful to man. Mithraic religion, based like the Eleusinian Mysteries on initiation ceremonies, flourished particularly amongst the Roman legions, and was for a time the major rival to Christianity, which adopted a number of its beliefs and practices.

15 *the Neo-Platonists*: modification of Platonic philosophy for the Roman world, most notably in the work of Plotinus (205–70). Very influential for Christian and Islamic theology until the Renaissance. Roden and Roden have plausibly argued that Mr Abney may in part be based on the Neoplatonic intellectual Thomas Taylor (1758–1835), translator of the Orphic poems (*The Mystical Initiations of Hymns of Orpheus*, 1787), and author of *A Dissertation on the Eleusinian and Bacchic Mysteries* (1791), and note that 'a legend, surely apocryphal, persisted to the effect that Taylor had performed at his home a bloody sacrifice to the Ancient Gods' (*PT*, 18).

Gentleman's Magazine . . . Critical Museum: the *Gentleman's Magazine* was the first general periodical in England, a compendium of comment, opinion, news, and scholarship for the educated general reader. First published in London in 1731 by Edward Cave ('Sylvanus Urban'), it ran until 1907. The *Critical Museum* is fictitious.

17 *'urdy-gurdy*: a hurdy-gurdy is a stringed musical instrument played by turning a handle, particularly associated with European folk music.

St. Michan's Church in Dublin: seventeenth-century parish church in the Smithfield area of Dublin. The vaults contain the mummified remains of 'four anonymous citizens of uncertain age—dried out, we are told, by the high tannic acid content of this once-forested marshy site': Catherine Casey, *The Buildings of Ireland: Dublin* (New Haven and London: Yale University Press, 2005), 241. MRJ visited St Michan's in 1892, and found the vaults 'horrid' and their inhabitants 'a nightmare' (Cox I, 107). The MS version glosses St Michan's vaults as '[famous for their preservative properties]'.

18 *Censorinus*: Latin grammarian, third century; author of *De Die Natali* (*The Birthday Book*).

19 *the rat that could speak*: Charles Dickens was one of MRJ's favourite novelists, and this is a reference to Dickens's story of Mr Chips, a shipwright who sells his soul to the Devil 'for an iron pot and a bushel of tenpenny nails and half a ton of copper and a rat that could speak', which offers a comic parallel to the Faustian themes of 'Lost Hearts'. The story first appeared as part of the 'Nurse's Stories' in *All the Year Round* (8 September 1760), and was reprinted in *The Uncommercial Traveller* (1861).

20 *March 24, 1812*: MS has 'the 24th of March 1811'—an obvious mistake as this is six months before Stephen arrives at Aswarby, though the MS repeats this date later in the story, and so it may be that the date in the opening sentence is the erroneous one.

22 *Simon Magus . . . Clementine Recognitions*: another Faustian allusion. Simon Magus first appears in Acts 8: 9–24, as a Samaritan sorcerer who converts to Christianity, but then attempts to bribe the Apostles in exchange for being given the power of the Holy Ghost (hence 'simony', the traffic in sacred objects). Simon's mythological afterlife, as a false

messiah and as the founder of post-Christian Gnosticism, is very rich. A number of Church Fathers identified him as the archetypal heretic, or even as the source of all heresies. The *Clementine Recognitions*, a narrative of the life of St Clement, bishop of Rome (first century), contains an account of Simon as a rogue disciple John the Baptist, who claimed to have been able to create life. This was a major source for the development of the Faust myth.

Hermes Trismegistus: 'Thrice Great Hermes', a conflation of the Greek god Hermes and the Egyptian god Thoth, both gods of writing and magic, and thus believed to be the source of Hermetic philosophy and religion, which emphasizes arcane or secret textual knowledge (of the kind possessed here by Mr Abney). According to some traditions, Hermes Trismegistus was a human mage.

twelve years: *CGS* and Joshi I (p. 23) both read 'twenty-one years'. This is a transcription of a mistake in the original MS, which reads 'below the age of 21 years', when it should obviously read 'below the age of 12 years', as Mr Abney's insistence on knowing the precise date of Stephen's twelfth birthday makes plain.

corpora vilia: plural of *corpus vile*, an expendable experimental subject.

The remains of the first two subjects, at least, it will be well to conceal: this implies, rather strangely, that the mutilated bodies of Phoebe have remained *unconcealed* at Aswarby Hall for respectively twenty and seven years. Have they, as the allusion to St Michan's vaults might imply, been preserved?

the psychic portion of the subjects . . . ghosts: a belief common in spiritualist thinking, enormously influential in late Victorian England.

THE MEZZOTINT

First published in *GSA*, reprinted in *CGS*. Eton College Library MS 368A.

24 *Dennistoun*: the protagonist of 'Canon Alberic's Scrap-book'. 'Anderson' in MS.

an art museum at another University: MS reads 'an art museum at a sister university'. The Ashmolean Museum at Oxford University—later in the story referred to as the Ashleian Museum at Bridgeford University. The MS has 'Oxford' instead of 'Bridgeford'.

the Shelburnian Library: the Bodleian Library, Oxford University.

Mr. J. W. Britnell: 'Mr. E. V. Daniells' (and sometimes 'Daniell') in the MS.

25 *mezzotint*: 'A method of engraving on copper or steel, in which the surface of the plate is first roughened uniformly, the lights and half-lights being then produced by scraping away the "nap" thus formed, and the untouched parts giving the deepest shadows' (*SOED*).

26 '*A. W. F. sculpsit*': 'A. W. F. he carved it'.

—*ssex*: the MS tries both '—folk' and '—shire' before settling on '—ssex'.

Professor Binks: MS adds '(it seems a good enough name for a man in his position)'.

28 *sported the doors of both sets of rooms*: in university slang, 'sporting the oak' meant closing the door to one's rooms (Cox II, 305).

29 *Canterbury College*: there is no Canterbury College at Oxford, though both Christ Church and St John's have Canterbury quadrangles.

30 *Garwood*: 'Gregory' in MS.

31 *skip*: a college servant. Technically, in Oxford, Robert Filcher would have been Mr Williams's scout; in Cambridge, his gyp; and only in Trinity College Dublin, his skip.

Phasmatological Society: that is, the Society for the Study of Ghosts (from the Greek *phasma*, ghost). This is MRJ's own invention, though it is likely to be modelled on the high-profile Society for Psychical Research (SPR), founded in 1882 to investigate the veracity of spiritual and paranormal phenomena. The SPR itself grew out of the Cambridge Ghost Society, which is very close to James's Phasmatological Society.

32 *Door Bible*: a Bible containing the celebrated illustrations of Gustave Doré (1832–83), a French artist renowned for his horrific and phantasmagoric images; first published in 1866.

33 *Murray's Guide to Essex*: Richard J. King, *Handbook for Essex, Suffolk, Norfolk and Cambridgeshire* (London: John Murray, 1870). Anningley Hall is fictitious.

like the man in Tess of the D'Urbervilles: in Thomas Hardy's *Tess of the D'Urbervilles* (1891), Tess's father, Jack Durbeyfield, (correctly) believes himself to be a dispossessed member of the ancient D'Urberville family.

34 *north side of the church*: see MRJ's 'Ghost Stories', written whilst still at Eton: 'A "belated wanderer" . . . pitched his camp in a churchyard. He laid himself down under a buttress on the north side of the building, and in blissful ignorance of the fact that he was surrounded by the graves of murderers and suicides (who were there, as is often the case, buried on the north side of the church), he fell asleep' (Joshi I, 247). Mrs Mothersole, the witch from 'The Ash-Tree', is also buried on the north side of the church, as is Squire Bowles in 'The Experiment'.

spes ultima gentis: 'last hope of his family'.

Sadducean Professor of Ophiology: MRJ's coinage, meaning 'Professor of Serpents'. The Sadducees were a priestly Jewish caste 'which say that there is no resurrection' (Matthew 22: 23), and who believed in 'neither angel nor spirit' (Acts 23: 8); they were admonished by Christ for their denial of the supernatural (Matthew 22: 29–33). The connection with serpents is from Matthew 4: 7: 'But when [John the Baptist] saw the Pharisees and Sadducees come to his baptism, he said unto them, O generation of vipers, who hath warned you to flee from the wrath to come?' MS has the more straightforward 'Professor of Biology', to which the word 'Sadducean' has been added.

THE ASH-TREE

First published in *GSA*, reprinted in *CGS*. MS not located, though included in a Sotheby's sale, 9 November 1936 (*PT*, 50).

35 *Castringham Hall*: fictitious, though its location has led to suggestions that it may have been modelled on Livermere Hall, a seventeenth-century house on whose lands James lived as a boy, in Livermere Rectory (*PT*, 39). MRJ's last published story, 'A Vignette', opens with a description of Livermere Rectory.

36 *auto-da-fé*: 'act of the faith': the public burning of a heretic by the Inquisition.

Mrs. Mothersole: 'Mothersole' is a local Suffolk name. There are a number of Mothersoles buried in Great Livermere churchyard.

Sir Matthew Fell: a fictional conflation of two figures notorious for their activities during the seventeenth-century witch trials, and with particular connections to Bury St Edmunds (see note below). The first is Matthew Hopkins (*c.*1620–47), the infamous 'Witchfinder General' (a title he bestowed on himself), responsible for the execution of eighteen people in one day in the Bury witch trial of 1645. The second is Sir Matthew Hale (1609–76), an MP and judge who presided over witch trials in Bury in 1662, where two elderly widows, Amy Denny and Rose Cullender, were found guilty of witchcraft and hanged. 'Fell' has numerous meanings relevant to the story: the past tense of the verb 'to fall'; 'a cutting down of timber'; 'the line of termination of a web, formed by the last weft-thread'; 'fierce, savage, cruel, ruthless'; 'dire, intensely painful or destructive'; 'full of spirit, doughty'; 'shrewd, clever, cunning' (*SOED*).

gathering sprigs 'from the ash-tree near my house': the ash tree has numerous folkloric and mythological meanings. According to some traditions, the witch's broomstick was made of ash.

Bury St. Edmunds: town in Suffolk, 5 miles from MRJ's childhood home in Livermere. *S&N* has a lengthy description of Bury (and particularly its celebrated Abbey), which is described as 'the most attractive town in Suffolk' (p. 42). As the location of the Suffolk county assizes, witch trials did take place in Bury in the seventeenth century.

39 *ring of Pope Borgia*: Rodrigo Borgia (1431–1503), patriarch of the notorious Renaissance family; made Pope Alexander VI in 1492, reputedly through bribery and murder—also the means by which he maintained his power. Allegedly murdered rivals and enemies, including numerous cardinals, by means of a ring and a chalice, both containing arsenic.

drawing the Sortes: the *Sortes Sanctorum*, or 'lots of the saints'; bibliomancy. Divination by means of consulting a book, usually the Bible, at random, and interpreting the messages of the scripture. The instance here refers to Charles I's alleged divination by means of a copy of Virgil's *Aeneid* (the *sortes Vergilianae*, common in early modern England; in the medieval period, Virgil had acquired a considerable reputation as a necromancer) in the Bodleian Library in 1642, on the eve of the English Civil War, a story which survives in a number of different forms. The passage consulted was:

> And when, at length, the cruel war shall cease,
> On hard conditions may he buy his peace:
> Nor let him, then, enjoy supreme command;
> But fall, untimely, by some hostile hand,
> And lie unburied on the barren sand!

Charles's forces lost the war to Cromwell's republican army, and he was executed in 1649.

40 *Luke ... Isaiah ... Job ... blood*: respectively, excerpts from the Parable of the Barren Fig Tree; a prophecy of the destruction of Babylon; and an account of the eagle's diet of human carrion ('Her young ones also suck up blood: and where the slain are, there is she').

Popish Plot: alleged Catholic plot to assassinate Charles II, fabricated by the Anglican clergyman Titus Oates in 1678, in an attempt to inflame anti-Catholic hysteria.

41 *Sibyl's temple at Tivoli*: Tivoli (Roman Tibur) is in Lazio, just east of Rome. Amongst its many architectural monuments is the Temple of the Tiburtine Sybil.

42 *Bishop of Kilmore*: the diocese of Kilmore is in County Cavan. Kilmore survives as a Catholic bishopric; the Anglican Church of Ireland amalgamated the diocese in 1841 to form the bishopric of Kilmore, Elphin, and Ardagh. Kilmore (from the Irish Cill Mhór) is a very common Irish place name, though it is possible that MRJ chose it here as a pun, 'kill more'.

43 *Clare Hall in Cambridge*: Cambridge college founded in 1326; changed its name to Clare College in 1856.

Polyænus: second-century Macedonian writer; author of the eight-volume *Stratagems of War*.

44 *"Thou shalt seek me in the morning, and I shall not be"*: not from Chronicles, but from Job 7: 21: 'And why dost thou not pardon my transgression, and take away mine iniquity? for now I shall sleep in the dust; and thou shalt seek me in the morning, but I shall not be.'

NUMBER 13

First published in *GSA*, reprinted in *CGS*. Manuscript (incomplete) in KCL MS MRJ:A/3. In the Preface to *CGS*, MRJ claimed 'I only recollect that I wrote "Number 13" in 1899', which was the date of his first visit to

Denmark. It seems more likely that the story was written in 1900, after the second visit, when MRJ stayed in Viborg. May have been read for the first time at Christmas 1903 (Cox I, 133). The MS version contains the following rejected opening, in faint, pencilled handwriting which is often near-indecipherable:

> Too few Englishmen travel in Jutland. Too few that is if we are taking the unselfish view that the pleasantest part of the [earth] would right [*sic*] be visited by the largest possible number of people: not one too few, on the other hand if we are explaining what are most likely our genuine feeling [*sic*] that there ought to be certain parts of this earth kept sacred from the mass of tourists. Still I am not really apprehensive that Jutland will ever become a crowded tourist resort. Its beauties are of a tranquil, a tame, a melancholy kind. Its literature is luckily not popularized by translations, and its sights in the way of [smudged word], galleries and museums are few. I am therefore the less afraid that I shall do it the disservice of bringing the curse of trippers and hotel coupons [?] upon it by singing its praises. Perhaps the story that I am about to tell may even have the opposite effect.

48 *Viborg*: 'Sacred Hill'. Early capital of Jutland, Denmark, and originally a centre of pagan worship; largely rebuilt after a fire of 27 June 1726. MRJ first visited Denmark in 1899 on a cycling holiday with his friends James McBryde and Will Stone. The three did not stay in Viborg that year, but did when they returned to Denmark in 1900. 'Perhaps', MRJ wrote in *E&K*, 'the expeditions I made in [McBryde's] company to Denmark and Sweden . . . were the most blissful that I ever had' (p. 144). The idea for 'Number 13' 'was suggested by Will Stone' (Lubbock, 32).

Hald: south-west of Viborg; Bishop Jörgen Friis was imprisoned in Hald Castle (see note to p. 51).

Finderup: King Erik Glipping (Erik V of Denmark) was mysteriously murdered in Finderup in 1286; Marsk Stig Andersen was amongst those convicted of the murder, though the details remain unclear.

Preisler's . . . the Phœnix . . . the Golden Lion: the first two are, or were, genuine Viborg hotels: MRJ stayed in Preisler's in August 1900. The Golden Lion is fictitious.

Sognekirke . . . Raadhuus: parish church and city hall.

Mr. Anderson: the original name of Dennistoun, protagonist of 'Canon Alberic's Scrap-book'. May be used as an allusion to Hans Christian Andersen, whom MRJ greatly admired, and translated in 1930: 'Hans Andersen and the old ballads had already prepared me to find in Denmark what I daresay a great many people do not look for there—a land of romance' (*E&K*, 144). May also carry a concealed echo of the 'Marsk Stig [Andersen]' mentioned above.

Rigsarkiv: public archive or record office.

48 *last days of Roman Catholicism in the country*: Denmark officially became Lutheran in 1536; Viborg played a central role in the Danish Reformation, under the leadership of Hans Tausen (1494–1561). 'Number 13' implies a connection between Catholicism and occultism, or even satanism—see the reference to 'the gross corruption and superstition of the Babylonish Church'; and like 'Lost Hearts' it makes allusion to the Faust myth: 'he practised secret and wicked arts, and had sold his soul to the enemy'.

49 *'1 Bog Mose, Cap. 22'*: 1st Book of Moses [that is, Genesis], chapter 22; the story of Abraham and Isaac. The great Danish philosopher Søren Kierkegaard (1813–55) used this passage as the starting point for his existentialist masterwork *Fear and Trembling* (1843).

bagmen: commercial travellers.

51 *Bishop Jörgen Friis*: last Catholic bishop of Viborg, from 1521 to 1536. Expelled from the see by the Reformation leader Hans Tausen, and imprisoned in his own dungeon at Hald Castle (see note to p. 48), 1536–8. 'Jörgen Friis' is amended in MS, corrected from MRJ's own spelling, 'Friisen'.

Troldmand: 'troll man'; a sorcerer. McBryde wrote and illustrated his *The Story of a Troll-hunt* as 'a monument of this journey' to Denmark (*E&K*, 144).

terrier: 'A register of landed property . . . an inventory of property or goods' (*SOED*).

52 *stuepige*: chambermaid.

54 *There was no Number 13 at all*: MS follows this with a deleted sentence: 'Well, I can only say that I must have been drunk [;] there is no other explanation. Drunk or dreaming: and I never do either.'

Scarlet Woman: the Whore of Babylon. See Revelation 17: 4–5:

> And the woman was arrayed in purple and scarlet colour, and decked with gold and precious stones and pearls, having a golden cup in her hands full of abominations and filthiness of her fornication:
>
> And upon her forehead was a name written, MYSTERY, BABYLON THE GREAT, THE MOTHER OF HARLOTS AND ABOMINATIONS OF THE EARTH.

Reformation exegesis often identified the Whore of Babylon with the Roman Catholic Church.

casus belli: cause of war.

Baekkelund: the reference is unclear, though may refer to a café or restaurant. Baekke is some 40 miles south of Hald. Baekkelund is a Norwegian surname.

55 *Aarhuus*: city in eastern Jutland, some 25 miles south-west of Viborg.

Silkeborg: 20 miles south of Viborg.

57 *Emily in the Mysteries of Udolpho*: Emily St Aubert, the heroine of Ann Radcliffe's classic Gothic novel *The Mysteries of Udolpho* (1794), is, like

all Radcliffe's heroines, much given to the composition of impromptu verses. MRJ makes particular reference here to the beginning of chapter 7: 'and while she leaned out of her window . . . her ideas arranged themselves in the following lines . . .'.

59 *'omnis spiritus laudet Dominum'*: from the closing verse of the last of the Psalms (Psalm 150: 6): 'Let everything that hath breath praise the Lord.'

61 *palæographer*: a scholar of ancient writing.

Hans Sebald Beham: 1500–50; German engraver and illustrator.

62 *Upsala*: Uppsala; Swedish city, which MRJ visited in 1901.

Daniel Salthenius: 1701–51. MRJ wrote that he had seen in Uppsala 'two contracts with the devil written (and signed in blood) in 1718 by Daniel Salthenius, who was condemned to death for writing them. He escaped and died Professor of Divinity at Königsberg' (Cox I, 110).

COUNT MAGNUS

Written 1901 or 1902; first published in *GSA*; reprinted in *CGS*. KCL MS MRJ:A/4 contains only one page of a draft version of the story.

63 *Horace Marryat's . . . Danish Isles*: Horace Marryat, *Journal of a Residence in Jutland, the Danish Isles, and Copenhagen* (2 vols., 1860). Marryat also wrote *One Year in Sweden: Including a Visit to the Isle of Gotland* (2 vols., 1862).

Pantechnicon fire: the Pantechnicon was an enormous (2 acres of space) warehouse for storing furniture in Motcombe Street, Belgravia, London; destroyed by fire, 14 February 1874. 'Pantechnicon' (Greek for 'all the crafts') is now used to refer to any large furniture-removal van.

64 *Råbäck*: MRJ visited Råbäck on his trip to Sweden with McBryde, August 1901.

Dahlenberg's Suecia antiqua et moderna: Erik Jönsson, Count Dahlbergh, *Suecia Antiqua et Hodierna* (Sweden Ancient and Modern), 3 vols. (1660–1716). A celebrated collection of engravings of Swedish architecture and landscape, compiled by Dahlbergh; in part aimed to display Sweden as a modern world power.

De la Gardie: a prominent Swedish noble family. Magnus Gabriel de la Gardie (1622–86) was variously Lord High Treasurer, Lord High Chancellor, and Lord High Steward of Sweden.

65 *mausoleum*: MRJ visited the De la Gardie mausoleum at the Cistercian abbey of Varnhem in August 1901 (Cox II, 310).

67 *Black Pilgrimage*: the 'Black Pilgrimage' to Chorazin may have been MRJ's invention, but it has subsequently been taken up by a number of writers and occultists. For a study of this, see Rosemary Pardoe and Jane Nicholls, 'The Black Pilgrimage' (*PT*, 601–8).

67 *Skara*: small cathedral city in southern Sweden, which MRJ visited in 1901.

The book of the Phœnix . . . and so forth: The *Book of the Phoenix* is a fictitious work of alchemical writing; *The Book of the Thirty Words* is also fictitious. Cox II (311) identifies the *Book of the Toad* with Trinity MS 1399, *Bufo Gradiens* ('Toad Passant'). According to Jewish tradition, Miriam, the sister of Moses, was an alchemist: see Raphael Patai, *The Jewish Alchemists: A History and Source Book* (Princeton: Princeton University Press, 1994), chs. 5 and 6. The *Turba Philosophorum* ('Assembly of the Philosophers') is a Latin alchemical text reputedly dating to the twelfth century, but first published in 1572; translated into English by Arthur Edward Waite in 1896 as *The Turba Philosophorum, or Assembly of the Sages*.

'Liber nigræ peregrinationis': 'Book of the Black Pilgrimage'.

68 *Chorazin*: a city in Galilee rebuked by Christ for its faithlessness: see Matthew 11: 20–2. Because of this condemnation, Chorazin became identified as the birthplace of the Antichrist, a tradition which seems to have its origin in the seventh-century *Apocalypse of Pseudo-Methodius*, a significant text for medieval eschatology—as MRJ, author of numerous studies of Latin apocalypses, certainly knew: he had written the entry on 'Man of Sin and Antichrist' for Hastings's *Dictionary of the Bible* (1898–1902), iii. 226–8, which makes reference to Pseudo-Methodius (*PT*, 604).

'of the air': the 'Prince of the Air' is Satan; see Ephesians 2: 2: 'Wherein in time past ye walked according to the course of this world, according to the prince of the power of the air, the spirit that now worketh in the children of disobedience.' For an analysis of Satan as ruler of the air (hence his iconographic wings), see Jeffrey Burton Russell, *The Devil: Perceptions of Evil from Antiquity to Primitive Christianity* (Ithaca, NY, and London: Cornell University Press, 1977), 246.

71 *devil-fish*: generic term for 'various large and formidable fishes'; usually refers to angler fish, but in this context most likely 'the octopus, cuttlefish or other cephalopod' (*SOED*).

73 *Skåne . . . Trollhättan*: Skåne is the southernmost province of Sweden. Trollhättan is a city in southern Sweden, near Skara; its name, which means 'Trolls' hoods', is clearly significant in the context of the story's hooded demon. See also note to p. 51: *Troldmand*.

On referring to No. 13, I find that he is a Roman priest in a cassock: see the connections between Roman Catholicism and devil-worship in 'Number 13', James's other Scandinavian story.

74 *Harwich*: major port in Essex, very near to Felixstowe (see note to p. 76: *Burnstow*).

Belchamp St. Paul: a village in north Essex, very near the Suffolk border.

'OH, WHISTLE, AND I'LL COME TO YOU, MY LAD'

Probably written 1903; first read Christmas 1903. First published in *GSA*; reprinted in *CGS*. MS in the King's School, Canterbury. The title is from a 1793 song by Robert Burns:

> O whistle, an' I'll come to you, my lad;
> O whistle, an' I'll come to you, my lad:
> Tho' father and mither should baith gae mad,
> O whistle, an' I'll come to you, my lad.

76 *Professor of Ontography ... St. James's College*: the Professor of Ontography is James's coinage, though it means something like 'Professor of Reality' (fittingly, given Parkins's avowed materialism). St James's is a fictional Oxbridge college.

Burnstow: a fictional version of Felixstowe, Suffolk, as MRJ notes in the Preface to *CGS*. See also 'The Tractate Middoth', p. 134, where William Garrett travels to Burnstow-on-Sea.

Templars' preceptory: 'A subordinate community of the Knights Templars; the estate or manor supporting this, or its buildings' (*SOED*). There is no such preceptory at Felixstowe.

the Long: the long summer university vacation.

78 *Dr. Blimber*: Dr Blimber is the principal of the Brighton school to which young Paul Dombey is sent in Dickens's *Dombey and Son*. The quotation here is misremembered, or imagined—as the story's note attests, 'Mr Rogers was wrong'.

79 *Disney*: an allusion to the Disney Professor of Archaeology at Cambridge University, endowed in 1851. MRJ applied unsuccessfully for this chair when it became vacant in 1892.

80 *round churches*: the Templars did build round churches, such as Holy Sepulchre in Cambridge, or Temple church in the Inns of Court, London.

feræ naturæ: of a wild nature.

81 *martello tower ... Aldsey*: Martello towers are small defensive forts and watchtowers built along the British and Irish coastline (and across the British Empire) during and after the Napoleonic Wars. Aldsey is fictional, though there are a number of Martello towers in and around Felixstowe.

'Now I saw in my dream ... meet him': another misremembered quotation. This is from the account of Christian meeting the fiend Apollyon ('the Destroyer') in John Bunyan's *The Pilgrim's Progress*:

> Then I saw in my Dream, that these good Companions (when *Christian* was gone down to the bottom of the Hill) gave him a loaf of Bread, a bottle of Wine, and a cluster of Raisins; and then he went on his way.

> But now in this Valley of *Humiliation* poor *Christian* was hard put to it, for he had gone but a little way before he espied a foul *Fiend* coming over the field to meet him; his name is *Apollyon*. (Bunyan, *The Pilgrim's Progress*, ed. N. H. Keeble (Oxford and New York: Oxford World's Classics, 1984), 46)

82 *boots*: a servant responsible for cleaning shoes.

Belshazzar: see Daniel 5 for the story of Belshazzar's Feast. The Babylonian (Chaldean) king Belshazzar, son of Nebuchadnezzar, hosts an opulent feast, during which an invisible hand writes on the wall the words 'MENE, MENE, TEKEL, UPHARSIN', which no one can understand except the prophet Daniel, who interprets the words to mean 'God hath numbered thy kingdom, and finished it. . . . Thou art weighed in the balances, and art found wanting. . . . Thy kingdom is divided, and given to the Medes and Persians.' That night, Belshazzar is killed; his kingdom is conquered by Darius the Median.

'I ought to be able to make it out': understandably, there is some dispute as to what 'FUR FLA FLE BIS' means. 'Fur Flabis Flebis' can be translated as 'Thief, you will blow, you will weep'; 'Furbis Flabis Flebis' as 'You will blow, you will weep, you will go mad'. MRJ's Eton tutor H. E. Luxmoore recalled hearing the story as 'Fur flebis' when it was read at Christmas 1903 along with 'Number 13' (Cox II, 312). It is probably safest to leave this as an ambiguous reference rather than commit to any one interpretation. The swastikas surrounding 'QUIS EST ISTE QUI UENIT [VENIT]' ('Who is this who is coming?') are in this context an ancient symbol prevalent in Eastern religions, though also adopted by Christianity.

84 *Experto crede*: 'Believe one who has experienced it' (or 'one who knows').

86 *'like some great bourdon in a minster tower'*: a long-unidentified quotation, though given the story's recurring interest in misquotation and ambiguous interpretation, it may well be invented (in which case, mischievously, MRJ himself would be the 'minor poet' here). A bourdon is the bass-stop of an organ.

87 *cleek*: iron golf club.

88 *Feast of St. Thomas the Apostle*: 21 December. St Thomas is famously, like Parkins, 'doubting', a rational materialist forced to confront the evidence of the supernatural when he sees the risen Christ.

THE TREASURE OF ABBOT THOMAS

Written in the summer of 1904, when MRJ was researching the stained glass at Ashridge Park. First published in *GSA*, and written specifically in response to publisher Edward Arnold's request for more ghost stories to expand the collection to 60,000 words (KCL MS MRJ:D/Arnold). Reprinted in *CGS*. Eton College Library MS 365.

94 *'Sertum Steinfeldense Norbertinum'*: this is a fictional work by a fictional author, though the Premonstratensian abbey at Steinfeld (in the Eiffel

mountains, in the district of North Rhine-Westphalia in the far west of Germany) is real. In 1802, after its dissolution, the abbey's sixteenth-century stained glass was removed and sold: some of it went to East Anglia, as the story suggests, while much of it was bought by Lord Brownlow for Ashridge Park, Hertfordshire, and is now in the Victoria and Albert Museum. In 1906, MRJ wrote a study of this, *Notes of Glass in Ashridge Chapel*, which he researched in July 1904: this is the 'private chapel—no matter where' mentioned later, and the story is obviously the product of the same research.

95 *Job, John, and Zechariah*: initially 'Solomon, John and Paul' in MS.

Vulgate: the Bible in Latin.

There is a place . . . hidden: Job 28: 1: 'there is . . . a place for gold where it is fined [refined]', though here recast as 'There is a place for gold where it is hidden' ['absconditur'].

96 *sad perplexity*: the phrase is from Wordsworth's 'Tintern Abbey':

> And now, with gleams of half-extinguished thought,
> With many recognitions dim and faint,
> And somewhat of a sad perplexity,
> The picture of the mind revives again.

There may be a parallel suggested here, very faintly, between Tintern and Steinfeld abbeys.

clerestory: 'The upper part of the nave, choir, and transepts of any large church, containing a series of windows, clear to the roofs of the aisles, admitting light to the central parts of the building' (*SOED*).

Abbot Thomas von Eschenhausen: fictional, though perhaps based on Abbot Johannes Trithemius (see note to p. 103); the earliest stained glass from Steinfeld does date from around 1520.

They have on their raiment a writing which no man knoweth: a conflation of parts of two verses: Revelation 19: 16 ('And he hath on his vesture and on his thigh, a name written . . .') and Revelation 19: 12 ('and he had a name written, which no man knew, but he himself').

Upon one stone are seven eyes: Zechariah 3: 9: 'For behold the stone that I have laid before Joshua; upon one stone shall be seven eyes: behold, I will engrave the graving thereof, saith the LORD of hosts, and I will remove the iniquity of that land in one day.'

97 *Parsbury*: fictional, but presumably intended to be in Hertfordshire.

Cobblince: Koblenz, in the Rhineland, western Germany.

98 *I have never visited Steinfeld myself*: MRJ's *Notes of Glass in Ashridge Chapel* makes it clear that MRJ had never visited Steinfeld: 'There is an account of Steinfeld in the Gallia Christiana, vol. III (Diocese of Cologne). I have not yet hit on any modern guide which will tell me whether there are any remains of it [the glass] at the present day' (Cox II, 315).

101 *Turk's head broom*: a round-headed brush.

103 *"Steganographia"* . . . *"Cryptographia"* . . . *"de Augmentis Scientiarium"*: the first two are landmark works in the history of cryptography and code. Johannes Trithemius (born Johann Heidenberg, 1462–1516), abbot of Sponheim (in the Rhineland, very near Koblenz), was reputed to be an occultist and black magician. His *Steganographia* (written 1499, published 1606), written in code, was long believed to be a work of black magic, though it is in fact a study of cryptography ('steganography' means 'concealed writing'). 'Cryptographia' is the *Cryptomenytices et Cryptographiae* (1624) by Gustavus Selenus, a pseudonym for Augustus the Younger (1579–1666), duke of Brunswick-Lüneberg in central Germany. Selenus also wrote an important study of chess, *Chess, or the King's Game* (1616). *De Augmentis Scientiarum* (1623) is the expanded Latin version of Francis Bacon's *Advancement of Learning*; volume vi contains a brief account of cryptography. Bacon devised a method of steganography which is still used, and still called the 'Baconian cipher'.

104 *Gare à qui la touche*: 'Beware whoever touches it'. Originally part of the coronation ceremony of the Lombard kings: 'Dieu me la donne, gare à qui la touche' ('God gives it [the Iron Crown of Lombardy] to me; beware whoever touches it').

105 *of Eliezer and Rebekah, and of Jacob opening the well for Rachel*: both stories featuring wells. In Genesis 24, Abraham sends Eliezer, his 'eldest servant', to find a wife for his son Isaac; Eliezer meets Rachel 'by a well of water' in the city of Nahor, Mesopotamia. In Genesis 29, Jacob meets Rachel at the well of Haran:

> And he looked, and behold a well in the field, and, lo, there were three flocks lying by it; for out of that well they watered the flocks: and a great stone was upon the well's mouth.
>
> And thither were all the flocks gathered: and they rolled the stone from the well's mouth, and watered the sheep, and put the stone again upon the well's mouth in his place (Genesis 29: 2–3)

A SCHOOL STORY

First read 28 December 1906; written for the students of King's College Choir School. First published in *MGSA*; reprinted in *CGS*. KCL MS MRJ:A/5.

111 *the Strand and Pearson's*: two magazines, both established in the 1890s, and both specializing in popular fiction. Abridged versions of some of MRJ's stories were published without his knowledge in *Pearson's* in the 1930s. MS version reads 'Now a days the *Strand* would be a large contributor.'

Berkeley Square: 50 Berkeley Square, Mayfair: 'the most haunted house in London', whose residents included former prime minister George Canning;

now the home of Maggs Brothers antiquarian booksellers (who, interestingly, obtained the MRJ manuscripts for KCL). The house is the subject of a number of ghost stories, including Rhoda Broughton's 'The Truth, the Whole Truth, and Nothing but the Truth' (1868), where it appears as '32 —— Street, May Fair'. Caryl Brahms's comic take on the legend, *No Nightingales* (1944), was filmed as *The Ghosts of Berkeley Square* (1947).

112 *The school I mean was near London*: based on MRJ's own preparatory school, Temple Grove, in East Sheen, Richmond, London, to which he went in 1873.

His name was Sampson: this sentence not in MS, where his name is rendered variously as 'Sampson' and 'Simpson'.

113 *meminiscimus patri meo*: bad schoolboy Latin attempt at 'I remember my father'.

THE ROSE GARDEN

First published in *MGSA*; reprinted in *CGS*. MS Fitzwilliam Museum, Cambridge.

118 *Westfield Hall, in the county of Essex*: fictional, but obviously intended to lie somewhere between the Essex towns of Maldon and Chelmsford, which are about 5 miles apart.

122 *a very odd disjointed sort of dream*: in *The Gothic Quest* (1939), Montague Summers wrote that 'the late Dr M. R. James told me that one of his Ghost Stories—I am not sure which, but I rather fancy it might be *The Rose Garden*—was suggested to him by his recollection of a peculiarly vivid dream' (Cox II, 318).

126 *Roothing*: the Rodings, or Roothings, are a group of eight villages in Essex, a number of which contain distinctive Norman churches. The name is derived from the Anglo-Saxon *Hroðingas*, named for their founder, Hroða. There is no village of Priors Roothing, though there is an Abbess Roding.

Fifth of November mask: the fifth of November is Guy Fawkes's Night, in which an effigy of Guy Fawkes is traditionally burned on a bonfire to commemorate the unsuccessful Gunpowder Plot to blow up Parliament in 1605.

127 *Sir —— ——, Lord Chief Justice under Charles II*: probably Sir William Scroggs (1623–83), the Lord Chief Justice notorious for his savage conducting of the 'Popish Plot' trials of 1679–81 (see also note to p. 40), culminating in the trial and execution of Oliver Plunket, archbishop of Armagh, in 1681.

128 *quieta non movere*: do not disturb quiet things—or, let sleeping dogs lie.

THE TRACTATE MIDDOTH

First published in *MGSA*; reprinted in *CGS*. KCL MS MRJ:A/6.

129 *Piccadilly weepers*: long side whiskers, fashionable in the 1860s.

a certain famous library: Cambridge University Library.

129 *Talmud: Tractate Middoth . . . 1707*: the Talmud (Hebrew for study or learning) is a collection of Jewish commentaries and interpretative writings on oral and scriptural laws, comprising the Mishna (laws) and Gemara (commentary). The Middot ('measurement') is the tenth Mishnahic tractate of the Order of Kodashim ('Holy Things'), the Fifth Order of the Mishna, dealing with the religious ceremony of the Temple of Jerusalem. The Middot itself describes the measurements of the Second Temple of Jerusalem. Nachmanides, or Nahmanides, was the pseudonym of the Catalan rabbi and sage Moses Ben Nahman (1194–1270), a celebrated commentator on the Talmud—although the specific volume referred to here may be fictional.

137 *Dundreary*: Lord Dundreary, a character in Tom Taylor's hit play *Our American Cousin* (1858), sported a spectacular set of Piccadilly weepers.

139 *a track*: that is, 'Trac.', the abbreviated form of Tractate.

140 *Bretfield Manor*: Bredfield is a village in Suffolk; the Jacobean Bredfield House (destroyed in the Second World War) was the birthplace of Edward Fitzgerald (1809–83), translator of *The Rubáiyát of Omar Khayyám*.

CASTING THE RUNES

First published in *MGSA*; reprinted in *CGS*. British Library MS Egerton 3141.

145 *ut supra*: 'as stated above'.

  Mr. Karswell: it is often assumed that Karswell is based on the notorious occultist, sex magician, and dissident member of the Order of the Golden Dawn, Aleister Crowley, the self-proclaimed 'Great Beast'. Although Crowley was a student at Trinity College Cambridge, in the 1890s, there is no evidence that MRJ knew anything about him, let alone based the character upon him.

146 *Lufford Abbey, Warwickshire*: fictional.

148 *John's*: St John's College, Cambridge.

150 *There is nothing to be added by way of description of him to what we have heard already*: the MS follows this with an excised passage: 'though he is a principal character in this tale it is enough to know that he was of middle age and size [height], bearded, of regular habits, with a turn for investigations genealogical, topographical, and antiquarian; a familiar figure in the Reading Room and the Select MSS Room of the Museum, and at the Record Office, by no means uninteresting or uninterested in life, but one who had never experienced any deep convulsion of his being.'

  Pyretic Saline: Lamplough's Pyretic Saline was a popular Victorian health tonic.

  John Harrington, F.S.A., of The Laurels, Ashbrooke: FSA is Fellow of the Society of Antiquaries. There are Ashbrookes in Sunderland and Northern Ireland, but this particular Ashbrooke is fictional.

Three months were allowed: MS has 'after six months', amended to 'after three months'.

153 *Harley 3586*: the Harley Collection is a major collection of early books and documents housed in the British Library, and gathered by Robert Harley (1661–1724) and his son Edward Harley (1689–1741). MS Harley 3586 is a collection of two monastic registers from the fourteenth century, and two letters in English, both written in 1676, one (11 December) by the antiquarian and lexicographer Thomas Blount (1618–79), and one (26 October) by Thomas Goad of Balliol College, Oxford. It may be a fortuitous accident that MRJ chose this MS, but he may also have conflated this Thomas Goad with his older namesake (1576–1638), a seventeenth-century theologian who was, like MRJ himself, a scholar of Eton and a scholar and Fellow of King's (and the son of a provost of King's). This conjunction of seventeenth-century antiquarians and theologians seems on balance, given MRJ's interests in this area, to be suggestive.

154 *Dr. Watson, his medical man*: perhaps a joking allusion to Sherlock Holmes's famous associate.

hors de combat: 'out of the fight'; disabled from fighting.

ptomaine poisoning: food poisoning, which was believed to be caused by 'ptomaines', alkaloids (chemical compounds) found in decaying food. The discovery of bacteria and the successive formulations of the germ theory of disease across the second half of the nineteenth century had made the theory of ptomaine poisoning obsolete by the time James was writing.

158 *Runic letters*: ancient alphabet, most commonly associated with Scandinavian and Anglo-Saxon writing; often carrying or implying magical qualities.

Golden Legend: influential collection of saints' lives, compiled by Jacobus de Voragine around 1260.

159 *Golden Bough*: monumental work of comparative anthropology and religion published between 1890 and 1915 by Sir James George Frazer (1854–1941). One of the towering intellectual achievements of Edwardian Britain. MRJ was highly sceptical of the whole project of comparative mythography: see Introduction, p. xv.

160 *'black spot'*: the symbol of a death sentence, delivered by pirates in Robert Louis Stevenson's *Treasure Island* (1883).

a woodcut of Bewick's: Thomas Bewick (1753–1828): English wood engraver, best known for his illustrations of birds, and of Aesop's *Fables*; the particular woodcut described here is fictional.

'Ancient Mariner': Samuel Taylor Coleridge's 'The Rime of the Ancient Mariner' (1798), ll. 448–51.

162 *Cook's*: Thomas Cook and Son was the pioneering nineteenth-century travel agency, specializing in package tours.

163 *'Lord Warden'*: this was a real Dover hotel, in which MRJ stayed on his way to and from France (Cox II, 322).

Joanne's Guide: Hachette's *Guides Joannes* were the forerunners to the famous *Blue Guides*, which began publication in 1918.

164 *St. Wulfram's Church at Abbeville*: a church which MRJ had visited on a number of occasions during his trips to France.

THE STALLS OF BARCHESTER CATHEDRAL

First published in the *Contemporary Review*, 97/35 (April 1910), 449–60; reprinted in *MGSA* and *CGS*. Location of MS unknown, though sold at Sotheby's 9 November 1936 (*PT*, 178).

165 *Barchester*: MRJ borrowed this fictional English city from the Barsetshire novels (1855–67) of Anthony Trollope. In the Preface to *CGS*, he writes that 'the cathedrals of Barchester and Southminster [in "An Episode of Cathedral History"] were blends of Canterbury, Salisbury, and Hereford'.

Ranxton-sub-Ashe . . . Lichfield: the former is fictional, the latter a city in Staffordshire in the English midlands, perhaps most famous as the birthplace of Samuel Johnson.

Prebend . . . Precentor: a prebend or prebendiary is a stipendiary canon, paid out of cathedral revenues. A precentor directs the singing of a congregation.

the Argonautica of Valerius Flaccus . . . Life of Joshua: the Roman poet Gaius Valerius Flaccus' unfinished *Argonautica* (*c*. CE 70) is a free Latin adaptation of Appolonius of Rhodes's Greek epic of Jason and the Argonauts, composed in the third century BCE. Joshua was the leader of the tribes of Israel after the death of Moses (see the Old Testament books of Numbers and Joshua), who ordered the destruction of Jericho.

167 *Cyrus*: probably an epic on the life of the Persian emperor Cyrus the Great (*c*.600–530 BCE), who has a revered place in Old Testament history for his liberation of the Israelites from Babylon: on Cyrus' edict, they were returned to the Holy Land, and commanded to rebuild the Temple in Jerusalem (see Ezra 6: 3–5).

Bell's Cathedral Series: a celebrated multi-volume series of guides to English and Welsh cathedrals, published from the 1890s.

Sir Gilbert Scott: Sir George Gilbert Scott (1811–78), major Victorian architect, most closely associated with the Gothic revival.

168 *triforium . . . reredos . . . baldacchino*: triforium: 'a gallery or arcade in the wall over the arches at the sides of the nave and choir, and sometimes of the transepts, in some large churches' (*SOED*). Reredos: decorated screen behind a church altar. Baldacchino: a structure in the form of a canopy, placed above an altar.

169 *Second Epistle to the Thessalonians*: 2 Thessalonians 2: 7: 'For the mystery of iniquity doth already work: only he who now letteth will let, until he be taken out of the way.'

170 *join with the aged Israelite in the canticle*: a reference to the Nunc Dimittis of Simeon in Luke 2: 29–31, which begins with the verse 'Lord, now lettest thou thy servant depart in peace, according to thy will.' This is the canticle prescribed for Evensong in the Book of Common Prayer.

the genus Mus: a mouse.

Tartarean: Tartarus was the hell of Greek mythology, an abyss of torment and punishment.

171 *"friar of orders gray"*: a snatch of song sung by Petruchio in Shakespeare's *The Taming of the Shrew* (IV. i. 145–6): 'It was the friar of orders grey, | As he forth walked on his way.' The grey friars are the Franciscans.

172 *Magnificat*: Luke 1: 46–55. The song of Mary on her visitation to Elizabeth, mother of John the Baptist, sung when the baby leaps for joy in his mother's womb, and beginning 'My soul doth magnify the Lord.' Like the Nunc Dimittis, it is sung at Evensong in the Anglican liturgy.

175 *Set thou an ungodly man . . . right hand*: Psalm 109: 6: a curse.

Set thou a wicked man over him, and let Satan stand at his right hand.
    When he shall be judged, let him be condemned: and let his prayer become sin.
    Let his days be few, and let another take his office. (Psalm 109: 6–8)

176 *Mr. Shelley, Lord Byron, and M. Voltaire*: all adduced here as anticlerical freethinkers and radicals, and from the story's 1818 perspective, all controversial or scandalous modern figures.

MARTIN'S CLOSE

First published in *MGSA*; reprinted in *CGS*. Eton College Library MS 368.

179 *a parish in the West*: Sampford Courtenay in Devon, according to MRJ's Preface to *CGS*. King's College owned property in this village, which MRJ visited in 1893 (Cox I, 103).

John Hill: 'John Ward' in MS.

quickset: a hedge of living plants, specifically hawthorn.

180 *Holy Innocents' Day*: 28 December, date of the commemoration of the massacre of the innocents, the children of Bethlehem killed by the order of King Herod: see Matthew 2: 16–18.

Jeffreys: George Jeffreys, 1st Baron of Wem (1645–89), popularly known as 'the Hanging Judge'. Lord Chief Justice from 1683; notorious for his conducting of the 'Bloody assizes' of 1685 following the Duke of

Monmouth's failed rebellion. Lord Chancellor from 1685. Arrested following the accession to the throne of William of Orange in 1688; died in the Tower of London, 1689.

180 *New Inn*: an actual hotel in Sampford Courtenay, dating back to the sixteenth or seventeenth century.

Interesting old MS. trial for murder: MRJ was himself a keen and knowledgeable reader of seventeenth-century court transcripts, and in 1929 he wrote the Preface to the Clarendon Press edition of *Lady Ivie's Trial*. See also 'The Ash-Tree' and 'A Neighbour's Landmark' for fictional reflections of this interest.

181 *Revd. Mr. Glanvil*: Joseph Glanvill (1636–80—and thus dead some four years before the date of this story). English clergyman and intellectual, chaplain to Charles II from 1672. Most famous as a defender of the reality of witchcraft and the supernatural; attacked the experimental scientific method across a number of volumes.

oyer and terminer: 'legal term of Anglo-French origin, meaning "to hear and determine", applied in England to one of the commissions by which a judge of assize sits' (*EB*).

182 *upon the 15th day of May . . . King Charles the Second*: 15 May 1684. Although Charles II did not ascend to the throne until 1660, the date here is counted from the execution of Charles I in 1649, and thus disregards the intervening period of Cromwell's Republic.

Robert Sawyer: 1633–92; Attorney General for England and Wales, and Speaker of the House of Commons.

183 *Cul-prit*: according to legal tradition, 'culprit' is a compound of *cul* (short for *culpable*, guilty) and *pri(s)t*, 'ready': 'it is supposed that when the prisoner had pleaded Not Guilty, the Clerk of the Court replied with *'Culpable, prest daverrer notre bille'*, i.e. 'Guilty, ready to aver our indictment' (*SOED*). One word, 'culprit', in MS.

Mr. Dolben: William Dolben (*c.*1627–94); judge, celebrated (or notorious) for presiding over the trials of many of those implicated in the Popish Plot, including Oliver Plunket.

185 *'Madam, will you walk, will you talk with me?'*: the refrain of a popular English folk song, which closes with the lines: 'Thou shalt give me the keys of my heart, | And we shall be married till death do us part.' For the song, its history and melody, see Lucy Broadwood and J. A. Fuller Maitland, *English County Songs* (London: Leadenhall Press, 1893), who note that 'In many [versions] the lady's cupidity is at last excited by some especially magnificent offer, and, on her consenting, the man refuses to have anything to do with her.' This is the conclusion which seems likely to underlie the events of 'Martin's Close'.

Tyburn: near Marble Arch, London; a site of executions until the eighteenth century. The notorious 'Tyburn Tree' was a triple gallows for the execution of multiple felons.

195 *St. Augustine de cura pro mortuis gerenda*: 'On care to be had for the dead', a treatise on funerary rites, written *c.*421 by St Augustine of Hippo (354–430).

    Mr. Lang's books: Andrew Lang (1844–1912), prolific Scottish folklorist and man of letters; one of the founders of the Society for Psychical Research; author of numerous high-profile books on the supernatural, including *Cock Lane and Common Sense* (1894).

196 *North Tawton*: Devon, very near to Sampford Courtenay.

MR. HUMPHREYS AND HIS INHERITANCE

First published in *MGSA*: in the Preface to *CGS*, MRJ claims that the story 'was written to fill up the volume'. Reprinted in *CGS*. Eton College Library MS 366. In a letter of 3 January 1912 to his friend Arthur Hort, MRJ explained his conception of the story:

> As far as I can give it the explanation is this. That old Mr Wilson who made the maze had remained in the globe with his ashes, quiescent as long as the gate was not opened. When they opened it and laid out the clue, and left the gate open, he woke up and came out. It was he who was mistaken on two successive nights for an Irish yew and a growth against the house wall, and on the last evening he made himself visible to his descendant creeping up as it were out of unknown depths and emerging at the appropriate spot—the centre of the plan of the maze. (Cox II, 324)

KCL MS MRJ A/11 is a draft of a story that features a protagonist called 'John Humphreys' who inherits a property; it has a few small, circumstantial parallels with 'Mr Humphreys' (most notably its reference to an Irish yew, which recurs here), though it is essentially a different story. The fragment is reproduced in *PT*, 429–39, under the title 'John Humphreys'.

197 *Wilsthorpe*: a village in the southern part of Lincolnshire, very near the Norfolk border. Its branch-line railway station was built in 1860.

    change of propriety: the first of Mr Cooper's many malapropisms; he means 'change of proprietorship'.

201 *valentudinarian*: valetudinarian; hypochondriac.

    'the golden bowl gradually ceasing to vibrate': Ecclesiastes 12: 6–7:

> Or ever the silver cord be loosed, or the golden bowl be broken, or the pitcher be broken at the fountain, or the wheel be broken at the cistern.
>   Then shall the dust return to the earth as it was: and the spirit shall return unto God who gave it.

202 *dolebat se dolere non posse*: 'grieved that he could not grieve'.

203 *meatear . . . signosier*: métier (calling); cynosure (centre of attention, guiding star).

203 *horse doover*: a conflation of *hors de combat* (out of action) with an over-literal translation of *hors d'œuvre* (out of work).

Handel's 'Susanna': oratorio by George Frideric Handel (catalogue no. HWV 66), composed 1748. The libretto is probably by the Irish librettist Newburgh Hamilton. The quotation slightly misremembers the Second Elder's lines in iii.i.61: 'Far to the west direct your straining eyes, | Where yon tall holm tree darts into the skies.'

204 *'Secretum meum mihi et filiis domus meae'*: 'My secret is for me and the sons of my house'. Martin Hughes suggests that this may be 'A paraphrase of Isaiah 24: 16 (Vulgate): *secretum meum mihi secretum mihi vae mihi* ("I have my secret, I have my secret, woe is me")': 'A Maze of Secrets in a Story by M. R. James', *Durham University Journal*, 85:54/1 (January 1993), 81–93.

205 *A stone column about four feet high, and on the top of it a metal globe*: Pardoe and Nicholls suggest that 'MRJ may have got the idea of a globe in a maze from the ancient turf maze at Hilton, near Cambridge, which has a stone globe on a pedestal in the middle' (*PT*, 596).

unannealed: 'unaneled' means 'Not having received extreme unction [ie, the Last Rites]' (*SOED*). Whilst this cannot be what Mr Cooper intends, it is nevertheless relevant to the story's concerns with mortality and funeral rites.

angels fearing to tread: 'For fools rush in where angels fear to tread': Alexander Pope, *An Essay on Criticism* (1711), l. 625.

208 *catalogue raisonné*: descriptive catalogue.

Picart's Religious Ceremonies . . . the Harleian Miscellany . . . Tostatus Abulensis . . . Pineda on Job: Bernard Picart (1673–1733) was a French engraver best known for his *Cérémonies et costumes de tous les peoples du monde* (10 vols., 1723–43). *The Harleian Miscellany* (1744–6) contained selections from the library of Edward Harley, 2nd Earl of Oxford (1689–1741). *Tostatus Abulensis*: Alonso Fernandez de Madrigal (*c.*1400–55), known as Alonso Tostado. Bishop of Avila and prolific biblical exegete. John de Pineda (1558–1637), Spanish Jesuit theologian and exegete; *Commentariorum in Job Libri Tredecim* (1597–1601).

like Theseus, in the Attick Tale: the tale of Theseus, who slew the Minotaur in the Labyrinth of Knossos, and thus helped free Attica (that part of Greece containing Athens) from the bondage of King Minos.

209 *Quid multa?*: 'What more?', or 'Need I say more?'

210 *a Hound at Fault*: a hound which has lost the scent of its prey.

211 *tentacles*: tenterhooks.

213 *princeps tenebrarum*: 'the Prince of Darkness'; the Devil.

umbra mortis: the shadow of death.

vallis filiorum Hinnom: 'the valley of the sons of Hinnom', or Gehenna. A valley near Jerusalem, the site of the altar of Tophet at which children were burned in sacrifice to the fire-god Moloch (2 Kings 23: 10). Gehenna became synonymous with hell, a place of fiery torment.

Cain . . . Chore . . . Ophiuchus . . . Absolon: Cain slew his brother Abel and was exiled, anathematized, to the Land of Nod to the East of Eden (Genesis 4: 1–17). Chore, or Core, is a variant spelling of Korah, the son of Izhar, who led a rebellion against Moses. The rebels were punished by being swallowed by the earth (Numbers 16: 1–35), in a manner clearly resonant for the thematic concerns of 'Mr Humphreys'. Ophiuchus, 'The Snake Holder', is a constellation of stars. Absalom (Absolon) was the favourite son of King David, who led a rebellion against his father, and is slain by Joab at the battle of the Woods of Ephraim, after getting tangled 'in the thick boughs of a great oak' (2 Samuel 13–19). Cain, Korah, and Absalom are linked here as doomed rebels, or as those who set themselves against the word of God.

Hostanes magus: Hostanes was the legendary mage of the Persian emperor Xerxes I (486–465 BCE). According to the *Octavius* of Marcus Minucius Felix (second–third century), Hostanes was 'The foremost of these Magi both in eloquence and art. . . . The same Hostanes also has told us of earthly demons, wandering spirits, the enemies of mankind.' *The Fathers of the Church: Tertullian, Apologetical Works and Minucius Felix, Octavius*, trans. Rudolph Arbesmann, Emily Joseph Daly, and Edward A. Quain (New York: Catholic University of America, 1950), 379.

214 *in statu quo*: Mr Cooper means that he sleeps practically naked. This is probably a malapropic rendering of *in flagrante delicto*—literally 'in a blazing wrong', and usually translated idiomatically as 'caught red-handed'; it is likely that Cooper is alluding to its connection with sexual impropriety, 'to be caught in the act', 'in a compromising position'.

220 '*PENETRANS AD INTERIORA MORTIS*': 'Penetrating to the inner places of death'; from Proverbs 7: 27 (Vulgate): 'viae inferi domus eius penetrantes interiora mortis'; 'Her house is the way to hell, going down to the chambers of death'.

Covent Gardens . . . Hampton Court: In his first example, Mr Calton is mistaken: there is no maze at Covent Garden (in central London), though Inigo Jones's great piazza is at the centre of a warren of streets. Hampton Court has the most famous of all English mazes, constructed between 1689 and 1695 for William I by George London and Henry Wise.

THE RESIDENCE AT WHITMINSTER

First published in *TG*; reprinted in *CGS*. MS not located.

221 *Whitminster*: fictitious, though there is coincidentally a village with this name in Gloucestershire. Cathedral staff who live in the cathedral close are referred to as being 'in residence'.

223 *Earl of Kildonan*: fictitious Irish title.

223 *raths*: a rath is an Irish term, originally meaning a hill fort, and common as a prefix to place names.

224 *Æsculapius*: Roman god of medicine (deriving from his Greek counterpart Asclepius).

225 *Radamistus*: Rhadamistus, an Iberian prince, ruler of Armenia (CE 51–5). An episode in Tacitus' *Annals* (12.51) in which Rhadamistus stabs his pregnant wife Zenobia and commits her body to the river Araxes rather than surrender her to enemy forces (an event which she miraculously survives) provided a popular basis for operas. Handel was a particular favourite of MRJ, and it seems likely that his *Radamisto* (1720, with a libretto by Nicola Francesco Haym) is being alluded to here, though Pietro Metastasio's libretto *Zenobia* was twice set to music (by Giovanni Bononcini in 1737 and J. A. Hasse in 1761). Fittingly, given this story's Irish resonances, the Irish dramatist Arthur Murphy's *Zenobia: A Tragedy* was performed in the Theatre Royal, Drury Lane, in 1796.

226 *Cleodora and Antigenes*: Cleodora may refer to the nymph Kleodora, who saw the future by means of throwing pebbles (which would link with the story's theme of supernatural divination), or to one of the Danaides, the fifty daughters of Danaüs, betrothed to the fifty sons of Aegyptus, who, on the command of their father, each (except for one, Hypermnestra) beheaded their husbands on their wedding nights. William Smith's *Dictionary of Greek and Roman Biography and Mythology* (1870) lists numerous Antigenes, including four separate doctors, which might be intended as an allusive echo of Aesculapius (see note to p. 224), though given the reference in the sentence to 'battles', this Antigenes seems most likely to be Alexander the Great's general, burned alive by his enemy Antigonus in 316 BCE. The reference in both cases seems to be to shockingly violent murders.

229 *Monte Cristo's mansion at Auteuil*: in Alexandre Dumas's *The Count of Monte Cristo* (1844), the hero Edmond Dantès resides in Auteuil, now in the sixteenth arrondissement of Paris.

The Talisman: 1825 novel by Sir Walter Scott, the second of his 'Tales of the Crusaders'. The talisman of the title has miraculous curative powers, which Saladin, disguised as a physician, uses to cure the ailing Richard the Lionheart.

230 *sawflies . . . daddy-long-legs*: the sawfly is a very common insect of the family Tenthredinoidea. The daddy-long-legs is an English colloquial term for the crane fly. Fittingly given the story's theme, the *ichneumon* of MRJ's note is a notorious parasite wasp, which injects its young into the body of a host, from where it eats its way out.

Anna Seward . . . the Swan of Lichfield: 1747–1809; popular English poet. Sir Walter Scott was her literary executor.

235 *I nearly got my quietus*: I nearly died.

236 *Miss Bates*: a voluble spinster from Jane Austen's *Emma* (1815).

238 *S.T.P. ... Præb. Junr.* S.T.P. = Sacrosanctae Theologiae Professor (Professor of Sacred Theology). *S.T.B.* = Sacrae Theologiae Baccalaureus (Bachelor of Sacred Theology). *Præb. senr.* = Praebenda senior (Senior Prebendary). *Præb. junr.* = Praebenda junior (Junior Prebendary). *Decanus* = Dean.

239 *Debrett*: John Debrett (1753–1822), *Debrett's Baronetage of England* (first published 1803), a guide to the British and Irish peerage.

240 *a withered heart makes an ugly thin ghost*: source of the collection's title, *A Thin Ghost and Others*.

King Saul that we read of raising up the dead ghost: in 1 Samuel 28: 7–20 the Witch of Endor raises Samuel's ghost at Saul's behest.

241 *Bluebeard's chamber*: in Perrault's fairy tale, the serial murderer Bluebeard keeps the corpses of his wives in a forbidden chamber in his castle.

THE DIARY OF MR. POYNTER

First published in *TG*; reprinted in *CGS*. MS not located.

242 *Mr. James Denton ... in the county of Warwick*: F.S.A. = Fellow of the Society of Antiquaries (of which MRJ became a member in the mid-1890s). Trinity Hall is a Cambridge college, founded 1350. Rendcomb Manor is fictitious.

Thomas collection of MSS.: fictitious.

245 *Acrington*: fictitious.

Thomas Hearne: 1678–1735; English antiquarian noted for his editions of medieval chronicles; assistant librarian, Bodleian Library, Oxford University (1699–1715). The quarrels to which MRJ refers here probably allude to his opposition to George I, to whom he refused to take the oath of allegiance—for which reason he lost his position in the Bodleian.

anti-Vivisection League: opposition to vivisection (animal experimentation) was a prominent radical cause in the late Victorian period. The high-profile Anti-Vivisection Society was founded by Frances Power Cobbe in 1875.

247 *Bermondsey*: a district of Southwark, on the south bank of the Thames, London. In the nineteenth century, Bermondsey was a notoriously rough area of docks, warehouses, and slums.

unconsidered trifles: 'a snapper-up of unconsidered trifles': Shakespeare, *The Winter's Tale*, IV.ii.26.

'Ercules and the painted cloth: this reference remains slightly cryptic, though it seems to be part of an allusion by Mr Cattell to the ongoing debate as to the real authorship of Shakespeare's plays. Cox II (p. 327) believes it to be a misquotation of *Henry IV, Part 1*, IV.ii.25: 'slaves as ragged as Lazarus in the painted cloth'. Rosemary Pardoe, perhaps more plausibly, identifies the reference as the pageant scene from *Love's*

Labour's Lost, v.ii.575–6: 'You will be scrap'd out of the painted cloth for this', after which the Boy (Moth) enters dressed as Hercules. See Pardoe, 'Hercules and the Painted Cloth', *Ghosts and Scholars*, 31 (2000), 49–50.

248 *catchit*: cachet.

cui bono: 'to whose benefit?' A legal term implying guilt on behalf of the person with most to gain from committing the crime. Given Mr Cattell's propensity for malapropisms (which he shares with very many of MRJ's working-class characters), it seems likely that he means to say something else.

the feast of Simon and Jude: 28 October.

252 *Commoner of University College*: University College is the oldest of the Oxford Colleges, founded 1249 (St Edmund Hall, founded 1226, gained full college status in 1957). A commoner is a student who pays for his own commons (dinner)—that is, one who does not hold a scholarship or exhibition.

251 *Absalom*: son of King David, renowned for his beauty, who rebelled unsuccessfully against his father's rule: see 2 Samuel 13–18. 2 Samuel 15: 25–6 makes specific reference to the beauty and lustre of Absalom's hair:

> But in all Israel there was none to be so much praised as Absalom for his beauty: from the sole of his foot even to the crown of his head there was no blemish in him.
> And when he polled his head [i.e. cut his hair], (for it was at every year's end that he polled it, because the hair was heavy on him, therefore he polled it:) he weighed the hair of his head at two hundred shekels after the king's weight.

Given the story's background in seventeenth-century antiquarianism and monarchical controversies, this may carry a veiled allusion to John Dryden's satirical allegory 'Absalom and Achitophel' (1681), which uses the Absalom story to recount the history of the Popish Plot of 1678 (a favourite subject of MRJ's—see 'The Ash-Tree' and 'The Rose Garden') and the ongoing events which were to culminate in the Monmouth Rebellion of 1685, in which the Protestant Duke of Monmouth attempted to overthrow the Catholic James II.

Dr. Plot's History of Staffordshire: Robert Plot (1640–96), *The Natural History of Staffordshire* (1686). Like Everard Charlett, Plot was a commoner at University College Oxford; he was also first keeper of the Ashmolean Museum, and first professor of chemistry at the University of Oxford.

'There are more things': Shakespeare, *Hamlet*, I.v.166–7: 'There are more things in heaven and earth, Horatio, | Than are dreamt of in your philosophy'.

AN EPISODE OF CATHEDRAL HISTORY

First published in the *Cambridge Review* (10 June 1914); reprinted in *TG* and *CGS*. KCL MS MRJ:A/7. MS dated 1911, in MRJ's hand. First read 18 May 1913, according to A. C. Benson: 'Monty read us a very good ghost story, with an admirable verger very humorously portrayed—the ghost part weak' (Cox II, 328).

252 *Southminster*: fictitious, but in the Preface to *CGS*, MRJ notes that 'the cathedrals of Barchester [in "The Stalls of Barchester Cathedral"] and Southminster were blends of Canterbury, Salisbury, and Hereford'.

Mr. Worby: there are a number of Worbys buried in the churchyard at Great Livermere, including one in the grave next door to MRJ's father.

Mr. Datchery: Dick Datchery is the name adopted by a mysterious character in *The Mystery of Edwin Drood*, whose identity is not revealed in Dickens's unfinished last work. MRJ was a great admirer of Dickens, and wrote an article on *Drood*, 'The Edwin Drood Syndicate', for the *Cambridge Review* (November–December 1905). MRJ believed that Datchery was actually Edwin Drood himself in disguise. *Drood*'s setting of a provincial English cathedral city, Cloisterham (Rochester), has clear resonances for this story. In *E&K*, MRJ recalls that 'Six of us, calling ourselves the *Edwin Drood Syndicate*, went down early in July of 1909 to Rochester to examine the possibilities of various theories on the spot' (p. 141). One of the six was Henry Jackson, who went on to write a study, *About Edwin Drood* (1911).

253 *Jasper and Durdles*: more Droodiana. John Jasper is Edwin Drood's uncle, precentor of Cloisterham cathedral, and prime candidate for the role of the novel's villain; Durdles is a bibulous stonemason. In chapter 3 of *Drood*, Jasper and Durdles walk through the crypt of Cloisterham cathedral, discussing the provenance and manufacture of tombs.

a Scotch Cathedral: Cox II (p. 329) identifies this as a reference to Scott's *The Lord of the Isles* (1813):

> If thou would'st view fair Melrose aright,
> Go visit it by the pale moonlight;
> For the gay beams of lightsome day
> Gild, but to flount, the ruins of grey.

254 *Perpendicular period*: late medieval Gothic architecture, flourishing from *c.*1350 to 1500, characterized by vertical lines and large, elaborate stained glass. Canterbury Cathedral, one of the models for Southminster, is partly Perpendicular, as is King's College Chapel, and parts of Hereford Cathedral.

the series: Bell's Cathedral Series: influential guidebooks to English and Welsh Cathedrals, published 1836–1932.

255 *Gothic revival*: rediscovery of medieval architectural forms, particularly popular across the nineteenth century, hence 'Victorian Gothic'. MRJ

was strongly opposed to Victorian restoration of ecclesiastical architecture to its 'original' forms.

255 *Lady Chapel . . . overmantel*: 'Lady Chapel': typically the largest and most important chapel within a church; dedicated to the Virgin Mary. 'Overmantel': 'A piece of ornamental cabinet work, often including a mirror, placed over a mantelpiece' (*SOED*); a characteristically Victorian design.

256 *Hereford Cathedral*: a major example of Victorian Gothic restoration. Following the collapse of the Western Tower in 1786, Hereford Cathedral was restored in three phases across the nineteenth century, by James Wyatt, Lewis Nockalls Cottingham, and George Gilbert Scott.

258 *F.S.A.*: see note to p. 242.

259 *diaper-ornament*: diamond-patterned textile work.

260 *Isaiah xxxiv. 14*: see note to p. 13. The demons of these two stories are virtually identical (one has yellow eyes, the other red), and are both imprisoned within cathedrals. Could 'Canon Alberic' 's demon be the fellow to whom this satyr cries, 'as if it were calling after someone that wouldn't come'?

Simeon's lot . . . the Evangelical party: Charles Simeon (1759–1836), leading Evangelical preacher in the Church of England, and like MRJ both an Old Etonian and a Fellow of King's. From the mid-eighteenth century, the Evangelical movement was influential within Anglicanism, calling for social and clerical reform, and for a greater sacralization of the Church of England; in part, it was a response to the rise of Methodism and other Dissenting Protestant faiths in the eighteenth century. MRJ's father, an Anglican clergyman, was an Evangelical strongly influenced by Simeon.

264 *Venite*: a canticle sung in the Anglican liturgy of Morning Prayer, consisting of Psalm 95, which opens, 'O come, let us sing unto the Lord' ('Venite, exultemus domino'). It is one of the Psalms ordered for Morning Prayer on the nineteenth day of the month, according to the Book of Common Prayer. The *Decani boys* are the choristers on the Dean's (south) side of the choir; opposite them, on the Precentor's (north) side are the *Cantoris*.

267 *IBI CUBAVIT LAMIA*: 'The screech owl also shall rest there' (KJV), or perhaps more appropriately 'there shall the night hag alight' (RSV); from the Vulgate of Isaiah 34: 14 (see note to p. 13 for the King James translation): 'et occurrent daemonia onocentauris et pilosus clamabit alter ad alterum ibi cubavit lamia et invenit sibi requiem'. The lamia was a Greek succubus or night demon who devoured children, and gained particular cultural currency in the nineteenth century as a vampiric femme fatale. Thus, importantly, 'Cathedral History' 's demon is *female* (as opposed to its male counterpart in 'Canon Alberic').

THE STORY OF A DISAPPEARANCE AND
AN APPEARANCE

First published in the *Cambridge Review* (4 June 1913); reprinted in *TG* and *CGS*. KCL MS MRJ:A/8. S. G. Lubbock, present at the first reading, records that 'the silence which fell when the grim story ended was broken by the voice of Luxmoore: "Were there envelopes in those days?"' (Lubbock, 39).

268 *GREAT CHRISHALL*: the villages of Great Chishill and Chrishall, which share a common etymology, are a mile or so apart, one either side of the Cambridgeshire–Essex border.

B——: 'Bicester' in the MS; a town north of Oxford.

269 *W. R.*: MS follows this with a deleted sentence: 'P. S. Perhaps I ought not to joke about what may turn out a tragedy: but I can't help thinking that Uncle H's figure is not very well adapted to the vanishing trick.'

KING'S HEAD, Dec. 23, '37: MS reads 'King's Head, Bicester Dec. 23. '37'. There is still a King's Head in Bicester.

Woodley: a town in Berkshire, about 30 miles from Bicester.

270 *bands*: 'A pair of strips . . . hanging down in front, as part of clerical, legal or academic dress' (*SOED*).

Bow Street: the Bow Street Runners, the first organized, professional London police force, was established by Henry Fielding in 1749.

on the qui vive: on the lookout (from a French sentinel's call, 'Long live who?').

271 *Boniface*: the landlord in George Farquhar's play *The Beaux' Stratagem* (1707).

Boz: the pen name of Charles Dickens in his early years as a writer; *Sketches by Boz* was a collection of short pieces published to great success in 1836, the year before this story is set.

what the Scripture terms a hairy man: Genesis 27: 11, from the story of Jacob and Esau: 'And Jacob said to Rebekah his mother, Behold, Esau my brother is a hairy man, and I am a smooth man.'

273 *bagman*: a commercial traveller. This may be another allusion to early Dickens: 'The Story of the Bagman's Uncle' is a ghost story which comprises chapter 49 of *The Pickwick Papers* (1837). On 26 December, the narrator reads 'the last number of *Pickwick*'.

Punch and Judy Show: the specifics of the Punch and Judy show are important to this story. Punch and Judy is an English puppet show derived from the Italian *commedia dell'arte*, and featuring the violent, anarchic, stick-wielding Mr Punch (shortened from Punchinello), who bests a series of stock characters, traditionally including his wife Judy, a policeman, a crocodile, various foreigners, a baby, Toby the Dog (often, as here, a real dog, dressed in a ruff), Jack Ketch the Hangman, and even the Devil himself. The first reference to Punchinello in England is by Samuel Pepys, whose diary records seeing a show on 9 May 1662.

273 *W——*: MS reads 'Brackley', a town in Northamptonshire, a few miles up the road from Bicester.

274 *I believe someone once tried to re-write Punch as a serious tragedy*: John Payne Collier (1789–1883), *The Tragical Comedy or Comical Tragedy of Punch and Judy* (1828). This was published as part of Collier's critical study *Punch and Judy: A Short History with the Original Dialogue*, with illustrations by the Dickensian illustrator George Cruickshank.

the Vampyre in Fuseli's foul sketch: a reference to *The Nightmare* (1781) by Henry Fuseli (Johann Heinrich Füssli, 1741–1825), one of the iconic paintings of Romanticism, depicting a goblin or incubus squatting on the chest of a sleeping woman.

Shallabalah: another Dickensian allusion, from *The Old Curiosity Shop*, chapter 16: 'the foreign gentleman who not being familiar with the language is unable in the representation to express his ideas other than by the utterance of the word "Shallabalah" three distinct times'.

278 *vail*: gratuity or tip.

The organ wolved: 'Wolve: Of an organ: To give forth a hollow wailing sound like the howl of a wolf, from deficient wind-supply' (*SOED*).

our friend Smith: possibly a personal reference, to MRJ's Old Etonian friend (and former member of the Chitchat Society), Henry Babington Smith.

Turncock . . . beadle: a turncock is 'A waterworks official who turns on the water from the mains to the supply-pipes' (*SOED*). Not a stock Punch and Judy character, but MRJ perhaps meant to write 'turnkey' (jailer), a character who does feature in Punch and Judy. A beadle is a minor official of the court or church, charged with keeping order.

279 *Mr. Ketch*: Jack Ketch (d. 1686), executioner in the reign of Charles II; afterwards a proverbial name for all executioners.

TWO DOCTORS

First published in *TG*; reprinted in *CGS*. MS not located.

281 *Gray's Inn*: Holborn, London; one of the four Inns of Court, the centres of London's legal profession.

Islington: a suburb of north London; certainly no longer 'a countrified place'.

282 *bedstaff*: 'A stick used in some way about a bed, formerly handy as a weapon' (*SOED*). The 'matter of the bedstaff', repeated on three occasions in the story, presumably refers to Dr Abell's 'power of communicating motion and energy into inanimate objects', such as the poker on p. 284.

Battle Bridge: Battle Bridge Field is west of Gray's Inn Road, London.

distinguo: 'I differentiate'; a term used to draw distinctions in argument in medieval scholasticism. See Ignacio Angelleli, 'The Techniques of Disputation in the History of Logic', *Journal of Philosophy*, 67/20 (October 1970), 800–15.

283 *the satyr which Jerome tells us conversed with Antony*: St Jerome (*c.*347–420), Church Father, translator of the Bible into Latin (the Vulgate). In his *Life of St Paul the Hermit*, Jerome records how St Antony discourses with a satyr and a centaur, whose language he finds himself miraculously able to speak. The satyr asks Antony for his blessing.

John Milton's: the quotation is from *Paradise Lost*, iv.677–8.

Royal Society: the Royal Society of London for the Improvement of Natural Knowledge, learned scientific society, founded 1662.

284 *bolus*: a large, round pill or tablet.

Mysore: city in Karnataka, southern India. According to Hindu legend, Mysore was once ruled by the demon Mahishasura.

286 *a coronet and a bird*: presumably the heraldic symbols of the 'noble family' of Middlesex from whose mausoleum the bedsheets (or shroud) were stolen.

287 *tickleminded*: this might simply mean sensitive or easily upset, though the *SOED* defines 'tickle-brain' as 'potent liquor', and so this might imply alcoholism.

THE HAUNTED DOLLS' HOUSE

Written for the library of Queen Mary's Doll's House in Windsor, designed by Sir Edwin Lutyens in 1920. Other tiny works in the library were by Arthur Conan Doyle, Hilaire Belloc, Thomas Hardy, and others. See Mary Stewart-Wilson and David Cripps, *Queen Mary's Doll's House* (London: Ebury Press, 1996). First published in the *Empire Review* (February 1923), reprinted in *WTC* and *CGS*. MS not located.

291 *Strawberry Hill Gothic*: Horace Walpole (1717–97), author of *The Castle of Otranto* (1764), generally reckoned to be the first Gothic novel in English, acquired Strawberry Hill, near Richmond, west London, in 1748, and renovated it in spectacular neo-Gothic style. 'Strawberry Hill Gothic' became an influential architectural mode for the nineteenth-century Gothic revival in architecture.

ogival hoods . . . crockets . . . finials: ogival hoods: 'Having the form or outline of an ogive or pointed ("Gothic") arch' (*SOED*); crockets: 'small ornaments, usually in the form of buds or curled leaves, placed on the the insides of pinnacles, canopies, etc., in Gothic architecture' (*SOED*); a finial is 'An ornament placed upon the apex of a roof, pediment, or gable, or upon each corner of a tower' (*SOED*).

294 *perron*: 'A platform, ascended by steps, in front of a church, mansion, etc., and upon which the door or doors open' (*SOED*).

294 *posset*: a drink made of hot milk, alcohol, and spices, used as a cold remedy.

295 *truckle-beds*: beds on castors or tracks, for storage underneath another bed when not in use.

297 *physicks me*: 'To physic' means 'To dose with . . . a purgative', or 'To treat with remedies' (*SOED*); but here in its colloquial usage, meaning something like 'to puzzle' or 'to confound'.

298 *Canterbury and York Society's*: society for the publication of episcopal and archepiscopal records, founded 1904.

Coxham . . . Ilbridge House: both fictitious.

Vitruvius: Marcus Vitruvius Pollo (first century BCE), Roman architect and engineer. His *De Architectura* was rediscovered in the Renaissance, and became the most important sourcebook for neoclassical architecture. Thus, Roger Merewether's interest in Gothic runs totally counter to his training as a neoclassical architect, and can be said here to represent his unconscious, unofficial, or murderous self.

299 *quoins and dressings*: quoins are the stoneworkings at the external angles of a building; dressings are 'projecting mouldings on a surface' (*SOED*). This new building is neither neo-Classical nor neo-Gothic, but 'an Elizabethan erection of the [eighteen-] forties'.

THE UNCOMMON PRAYER-BOOK

First published in the *Atlantic Monthly*, 127/6 (June 1921), 756–65. Reprinted in *WTC* and *CGS*. Eton College Library MS 367.

300 *Gaulsford . . . Leventhorp House . . . Longbridge . . . the valley of the Tent . . . Stanford St. Thomas and Stanford Magdalene*: these are fictitious places, though Cox II (p. 331) suggests that the story is set in the valley of the Teme, near the English–Welsh border in Herefordshire and Worcestershire. The Teme flows through both Stanford Bridge and Stanford-on-Teme. MS has 'the Leventhorp house'; *Atlantic Monthly* has 'the Leventhorp House'.

302 *Gregory singin'*: Gregorian chanting, or plainsong. Associated with the Oxford Movement in the nineteenth century, and thus a sign of High Church Anglicanism.

da capo: literally 'from the top', used in music to signify 'repeat from the beginning'.

303 *the plague-year*: 1665–6, when bubonic plague may have killed as many as 100,000 Londoners. Daniel Defoe published a fictionalized record, *The Journal of the Plague Year*, in 1722.

Cromwell, Ireton, Bradshaw, Peters: all notable figures in the Parliamentary cause during the English Civil War (1641–51), all condemned for regicide. Oliver Cromwell (1599–1658) was leader of the Parliamentary army and Lord Protector of England, 1653–8. Henry Ireton (1611–51),

Cromwell's son-in-law, was a general in the Parliamentary army. John Bradshaw (1602–59) was the judge who presided over the trial of Charles I, and later Lord President of the Council of State of the English Republic. Hugh Peters (1598–1660) was a celebrated Cromwellite preacher.

Lady Sadleir: Lady Anne Sadleir (1585–1671/2). Literary patron and major donor to the library of Trinity College Cambridge, which MRJ had catalogued from 1897.

Rural Life: a disguised version of *Country Life*.

304 *chancel*: the eastern part of a church, where the priest officiates.

Abbey Dore, of Lord Scudamore's work: Dore Abbey is a Cistercian abbey in Herefordshire, of which MRJ was particularly fond, calling it in his book *Abbeys* (London: Great Western Railway, 1925) 'the most surprising and delightful of all the places I have to write about' (p. 116). MRJ visited Dore on a number of occasions whilst staying with Gwendolen McBryde in nearby Woodford (*LTF*, 18). The Scudamores are an old Herefordshire family, closely connected with Dore Abbey. John Scudamore (1601–71), 1st Viscount Scudamore of Sligo, and 'an enthusiastic churchman of the Laudian type' (MRJ, *Abbeys*, 116), restored and reconsecrated Dore Abbey in 1633–4.

the Dallams: a dynasty of seventeenth-century organ builders. Thomas Dallam (*c*.1575–1630) built the organ at King's College Cambridge in 1605–6.

305 *Psalm cix. . . . Deus laudum*: Psalm 109 ('Hold not thy peace, O God of my praise') is indeed a 'very savage psalm', a curse, which MRJ also uses in 'The Stalls of Barchester Cathedral'. The Latin translation of the beginning of Psalm 109 should read '*Deus laudem*'.

Book of Common Prayer: book containing the order of Anglican church services, first produced in the aftermath of the Reformation. Published in a number of different versions between 1549 and 1622. The Book of Common Prayer was suppressed between 1553 and 1558, in the reign of the Catholic Mary I, and it is from this period (1553) that the Uncommon Prayer-Book dates.

Anthony Cadman: fictitious.

307 *Arlingworth*: fictitious.

309 *long explosion*: long exposure; one of MRJ's characteristic working-class malapropisms.

311 *Norwood*: a district of south London.

A NEIGHBOUR'S LANDMARK

First published in the *Eton Chronic* (17 March 1924), 4–10. Reprinted in *WTC* and *CGS*. The final paragraph was added for the *CGS* publication. MS not located.

315 *A Neighbour's Landmark*: a commination (or recital of divine threats against sinners) from the Book of Common Prayer: 'Cursed is he that removeth his neighbour's land-mark.' Derived from Deuteronomy 19: 14: 'Thou shalt not remove thy neighbour's landmark, which they of old time have set in thine inheritance, which thou shalt inherit in the land that the Lord thy God giveth thee to possess it.'

Betton Court: fictitious.

"The Stricken Years," in the Times Literary Supplement: there is no such article, but this may be MRJ, himself 'a Victorian by birth and education', disparaging the revisionist biographical studies of Lytton Strachey's *Eminent Victorians* (1918) as 'clever and thoughtful Rubbish . . . written about the Victorian age'. Strachey was equally unimpressed by MRJ: see Introduction, p. xiv.

316 *The Late Peace, The Late War . . . to his Clergy*: some of these tracts and pamphlets are genuine. *The Conduct of the Allies and of the Late Ministry in Beginning and Carrying on the Present War* (1711) is a pamphlet by Jonathan Swift criticizing the Whig government for its involvement in the War of the Spanish Succession (1701–14). *The Late Peace* and *The Late War*, though impossible to identify precisely, are very likely pamphlets also referring to the War of the Spanish Succession. *A Letter to a Convocation Man* (1696) is a celebrated religious tract by Francis Atterbury (1663–1732), bishop of Rochester, calling for ecclesiastical reform of the Church of England. *St Michael Queenhithe* was a church in the City of London, rebuilt by Wren after the Great Fire of 1666, but demolished in 1876. Sir Jonathan Trelawny (1650–1721), a patron of Francis Atterbury and the convocation movement, was bishop of Winchester from 1706 until his death.

no saving of daylight: daylight saving time was adopted in Britain in 1916, following the tireless advocacy of William Willett.

the Society for Promoting Christian Knowledge: SPCK; the oldest Anglican mission agency, founded in 1698 by Thomas Bray to 'counteract the growth of vice and immorality'.

317 *"That which walks . . . cries"*: this couplet was praised by the distinguished Cambridge classicist and poet A. E. Housman as 'good poetry' (Cox I, 145).

318 *Birket Foster*: Myles Birket Foster (1825–99), illustrator most famous for depicting country scenes.

319 *'With no language but a cry'*: Tennyson, *In Memoriam A. H. H.* (1849), 54:20.

324 *Scott's Glenfinlas*: 'Glenfinlas, or Lord Ronald's Coronach' is a supernatural ballad by Sir Walter Scott, first published in Matthew Lewis's miscellany *Tales of Wonder* (1800):

> O aid me, then, to seek the pair
> Whom, loitering in the woods, I lost;

Alone, I dare not venture there,
Where walks, they say, the shrieking ghost.

MRJ wrote that Scott's 'Glenfinlas' and 'The Eve of St John' 'must always rank as fine ghost stories' ('Some Remarks on Ghost Stories'). East Anglian folklore makes reference to two ghosts of shrieking women, in Aylmerton and Sheringham (both in Norfolk): see J. Westwood and J. Simpson, *The Lore of the Land* (London: Penguin 2005), 489, 514.

325 *Lady Ivy, formerly Theodosia Bryan*: MRJ was particularly interested in seventeenth-century trials, and in 1929 wrote the Preface for Sir John Fox's edition of *The Lady Ivie's Trial* (Oxford, 1929).

Shadwell: in the East End of London.

A VIEW FROM A HILL

First published in the *London Mercury*, 12/67 (May 1925), 17–30; reprinted in *WTC* and *CGS*. MS not located.

326 *in the south-western of them*: all of the place names in the story are fictitious, but MRJ wrote in the Preface to *CGS* 'that Herefordshire was the imagined scene of "A View from a Hill"'.

328 *Borgia box*: a reference to the notoriety of the Borgias as poisoners: see note to p. 39. This anticipates the observation that 'it must have been poisonous stuff in the pot' that is boiled down to make the glasses.

337 *'He lived unknown, and few could know when Baxter ceased to be'*: cf. Wordsworth, 'She Dwelt Among the Untrodden Ways': 'She lived unknown, and few could know | When Lucy ceased to be'.

A WARNING TO THE CURIOUS

First published in the *London Mercury*, 12/70 (August 1925), 354–65; reprinted in *WTC* and *CGS*. MS in Pierpont Morgan Library, New York.

343 *Seaburgh*: fictionalized version of Aldeburgh, on the Suffolk coast, rendered here with meticulous accuracy. MRJ spent part of his childhood here, visiting his paternal grandmother, and returned often throughout his life, and especially in later years. 'Aldeburgh . . . has a special charm for those who, like myself, have known it from childhood; but I do not find it easy to put that charm into words' (*S&N*, 102).

Great Expectations: the opening chapters of Dickens's 1861 novel are memorably set on the Essex marshes, not far down the coast from Aldeburgh.

a spacious church of flint: 'Characteristic of East Anglian churches is the use of flint: plain flint, knapped smooth, forms the beautiful surfaces of many towers and walls, and flint and stone panelling adorns the bases of towers and porches and runs along below the battlements of aisles' (*S&N*, 7). The 'dignified and spacious' (*S&N*, 104) parish church of St Peter and St Paul at Aldeburgh is made of flint, and stands on a hill above the town. The poet George Crabbe was curate of this church from 1781, and set his classic work *Peter Grimes* (made into an opera by another Aldeburgh resident, Benjamin Britten) in Slaughden, a fishing village half a mile south of Aldeburgh, which was completely lost to the sea in 1936.

344 *martello tower*: Aldeburgh's Martello tower began construction in 1806. It is the largest of many Martello towers on the East Anglian coast, and the only one in a clover-leaf shape.

the '*Bear*': fictionalized version of the White Lion, Aldeburgh, where MRJ liked to stay.

345 *Froston*: a conjunction of Friston (which does not have crowns on the porch of its church) and Theberton (which does); both are a few miles from Aldeburgh.

three crowns: although depicted on churches and pub signs throughout the region, the Three Crowns are not 'the old arms of the kingdom of East Anglia', but 'unauthorized arms unofficially identified with the region' (Westwood and Simpson, *The Lore of the Land*, 683).

346 *the crown of Redwald, King of the East Angles, was dug up at Rendlesham*: Raedwald (d. 616–17) was the first king of the East Angles, believed by some to be buried at Sutton Hoo (Rendlesham), Suffolk, site of the greatest of all Anglo-Saxon architectural finds, fully excavated by Basil Brown in 1939. John Kirby's *A Topographical and Historical Description of the County of Suffolk* (Woodbridge, 1839) makes reference to the work of the historian William Camden (1551–1623): 'The editor of Cambden [*sic*] adds, "It is said that in digging here about thirty years since, there was found an ancient silver crown, weighing about sixty ounces, which was thought to have belonged to Redwald; or some other king of the East Angles; but it was sold, and melted down' (p. 123). Westwood and Simpson (*The Lore of the Land*, 682) place the date of this discovery as 1687.

a Saxon royal palace, which is now under the sea: Dunwich, Suffolk—the ancient capital of East Anglia, lost to the sea between 1286 and 1328.

347 *the war of 1870*: the Franco-Prussian War of 1870–1. Britain was not a combatant, but it is relevant here given the crowns' specific purpose of warding off German invasion.

South African War: the Boer War of 1899–1902.

348 *barrows*: burial mounds, as famously can be seen at Sutton Hoo.

349 *Jewel House at the Tower*: the British Crown Jewels are housed in the Tower of London.

intaglios and cameos: intaglios are engraved gems; cameos are the opposite, gems with relief carvings. Westwood and Simpson (*The Lore of the Land* 682) describe these details as 'almost certainly anachronistic'.

352 *Paschal moon*: Easter moon.

   as Christian did through that Valley: the Valley of Humiliation in Bunyan's *Pilgrim's Progress*: see note to p. 81.

354 *piano*: 'soft'; a musical notation.

356 *spit of land*: Orford Ness, a spit of land some 9 miles long, running south along the coast from Aldeburgh.

AN EVENING'S ENTERTAINMENT

First published in *WTC*, reprinted in *CGS*. Composed to make up the final story in *WTC*; very likely it is to this story that MRJ refers when he writes to Gwendolen McBryde on 3 October 1925: 'The ghost story book is finished. I had to write another one instead of the one I was at, which would not come out' (*LTF*, 135).

358 *'Rawhead and Bloody Bones'*: *OED* defines 'Raw-head' as 'A bugbear or bogeyman, typically imagined as having a head in the form of a skull, or one whose flesh has been stripped of its skin, invoked to frighten children. Also occas.: a skull. Freq. used in conjunction with *bloody-bones*'. 'Bloody-bones' appears to date from 1548, when it appeared in *The Wyll of the deuyll, and last testament*, an anti-Catholic tract published by Humfrey Powell (d. *c*.1566): 'Our faythfull Secretaryes, Hobgoblyn and Blooddybone.' As a conjunction, 'Rawhead and Bloody Bones' makes its first appearance in John Jeffere's *Buggbears* (*c*.1564): 'Hob Goblin, Rawhead, & bloudibone the ouglie hagges Bugbeares, & helhoundes, and hecate the nyght mare.'

   Mrs. Marcet . . . Utility and Truth: these are all explanatory scientific works. Jane Haldimand Marcet (1769–1858) wrote a series of *Conversations* on science and political economy; given the context, MRJ would seem to be referring here to *Conversations on Chemistry, Intended More Especially for the Female Sex* (1805). The others are *Dialogues in Chemistry, Intended for the Instruction and Entertainment of Young People* (1809) by the Unitarian minister Jeremiah Joyce (1763–1816); and *Philosophy in Sport Made Science in Earnest: Being an Attempt to Illustrate the First Principles on Natural Philosophy by the Aid of Popular Toys and Sports* (1827), by John Ayrton Paris (*c*.1785–1856).

359 *woundy*: extremely, excessively.

361 *that old figure cut out in the hill-side*: probably the Cerne Abbas Giant, an enormous, priapic figure cut into the chalk hillside at Cerne Abbas, Dorset, and generally taken to be a pagan fertility god. In *Abbeys*, MRJ wrote: 'That [Cerne Abbey] is really old I have little doubt; I have always supposed that it was set up here as a counterblast to the worship of the wicked old giant who is portrayed on the side of Trendle Hill just beyond the Abbey. He is surely of very great antiquity, and is perhaps the most striking monument of the early paganism of the country. Whether he is British or Saxon, who shall say? Some have thought that he represents

what Caesar describes—a wicker figure in which troops of victims were enclosed and then burnt to death. On this hypothesis the figure would have been marked out by a palisade of wattles on the ground, and the victims, bound, crowded into the enclosure. In any case, here must have been an important heathen sanctuary, and a fit place consequently for champions of the new religion to set their standard' (p. 149).

363 *a little ornament like a wheel*: the pagan 'sun wheel', a symbol of the cycle of the year, and thus of fertility, invoked at the end of the story by the Wise Man of Bascombe: 'When the sun's gathering his strength . . . and when he's in the height of it, and when he's beginning to lose his hold, and when he's in his weakness, them that haunts about that lane had best take heed to themselves.'

365 *Bascombe and Wilcombe*: both fictitious.

366 *Lord of flies*: Beelzebub (more properly Beelzebul), often taken as a translation from the Hebrew for 'Lord of the Flies', refers variously to the Devil himself, or to a prince of hell. 'Baal-zebub, the god of Ekron', a Philistine deity, appears in 2 Kings 1: 2–6. Beelzebub is 'the prince of devils' in Matthew 12: 24 and Mark 3: 22, and 'the chief of the devils' in Luke 11: 15.

THERE WAS A MAN DWELT BY A CHURCHYARD

First published in the Eton magazine *Snapdragon* (6 December 1924), 4–5; reprinted in *CGS*. MS not located.

368 *Mamilius*: *The Winter's Tale*, ii.i.25–31. Mamilius is the son of Leontes and Hermione, and starts a story which begins 'There was a man dwelt by a churchyard', only to be interrupted when Leontes breaks in with guards and imprisons Hermione on suspicion of infidelity. Mamilius dies shortly afterwards, of a broken heart. It is this passage which gives the play its title, when Mamilius says, 'A sad tale's best for winter. I have one of sprites and goblins.' In his introduction to *Ghosts and Marvels*, ed. V. H. Collins (London: Oxford University Press, 1924), MRJ writes that this passage 'justifies all ghost stories, and puts them in their proper place'.

Midsummer Eve and All Hallows: Midsummer Eve (23 June) and All Hallows, or Halloween (31 October), are both amongst the dates associated with the Witches' Sabbath.

RATS

First published in the Eton magazine *At Random* (23 March 1929), 12–14; reprinted in Lady Cynthia Asquith's anthology *Shudders* (1929), and *CGS*. MS not located.

371 *'And if . . . rats under 'em'*: from Charles Dickens, 'Tom Tiddler's Ground', a Christmas story published in *All the Year Round* (1861).

372 *Orlando Whistlecraft*: 1810–93; meteorologist; author of *The Climate of England* (1840), *The Magnificent and Notably Hot Summer of 1846* (1847), *The Weather Record of 1856* (1857), and *Whistlecraft's Weather Almanac* (annually, 1856–84). Like MRJ, a native of Suffolk.

Thetford Heath: Norfolk; 'of Thetford I will not treat now, only pausing to note that not far from the Bury road, on the west side, you may catch sight of a block of stone on the heath which I have always taken to be a gibbet: certainly the locality would have suited highwaymen' (*S&N*, 65–6).

AFTER DARK IN THE PLAYING FIELDS

First published in the Eton magazine *College Days* (28 June 1924), 311–12, 314; reprinted in *CGS*. MS not located.

377 *Sheeps' Bridge*: the whole story is set in Eton, and relies heavily on a specific knowledge of the school's geography. Sheep's Bridge goes over the Jordan on the Playing Fields. There are a number of weirs nearby.

378 *'The clamorous owl . . . spirits'* . . . *'Come not near our fairy queen'*: both quotations are from *A Midsummer Night's Dream*: II.ii.6–7, 12.

Fellows' Pond: on the Playing Fields, near Sheep's Bridge.

379 *Castle quadrangle . . . Lupton's Tower . . . Curfew Tower*: Lupton's Tower is the central feature of Lupton's Range in the Eton School Yard, built by Henry Redman in 1520, and named after Roger Lupton, provost of Eton from 1503 to 1535. The Quadrangle and the Curfew Tower are both features of nearby Windsor Castle.

Bad-calx: a reference to the Eton Wall Game, a ball game whose rules were drawn up in 1849. The game is traditionally played on College Field, between two goals known as 'Good Calx'—a doorway at one end of the field—and 'Bad Calx'—an ancient elm tree near Fellows' Pond, whose stump was removed in 1994.

St. David's tune: 'St David's' is #140 in the *Eton College Hymn Book* (3rd edn., 1995), which notes 'Present form of melody in T. Ravenscroft's *Psalter*, 1621'. The hymn is sung to words by James Montgomery (1771–1854), which open 'Lift up your heads, ye gates of brass'.

380 *'restless changing weir'*: William Morris, 'The Earthly Paradise':

> The sheep-bells and the restless changing weir,
> All little sounds made musical and clear
> Beneath a sky that burning August gives;
> While yet the thought of glorious summer lives.

before summer-time came in: before 1916, when daylight saving time was adopted: see note to p. 316.

Fourth of June fireworks: the 'Fourth of June' is Eton's foremost celebration day, in honour of its greatest patron, King George III, who was born on this day in 1738 (actually 24 May according to the Julian Calendar still in operation in Britain until 1752). The celebration is no longer held on 4 June, but on the Wednesday before the first week in June.

WAILING WELL

First read at a camp of Eton Boy Scouts in Warbarrow Bay, Dorset, 27 July 1927. MRJ's obituary in the *Eton College Chronicle* (18 June 1936) records that, after hearing the story, 'several boys had a somewhat disturbed night, as the scene of the story was quite close to Camp' (Cox I, 208). First published as a self-standing story (Mill House Press, 1928; a print run of 157 copies); reprinted in *CGS*. MS not located.

381   *Bishop Ken*: Thomas Ken (1637–1711), bishop of Bath and Wells; one of seven nonjuring bishops tried for seditious libel when they refused to take an oath of allegiance to William and Mary in 1688; removed from his bishopric in 1691.

     Head Master . . . Provost . . . Vice-Provost: given that the story names actual members of the Eton staff of 1927, then the headmaster would be Cyril Alington, the provost MRJ himself, and the vice-provost Hugh Macnaghten. As Alington wrote, MRJ and Macnaghten did not get on: 'Both wrote books about Eton, and neither could endure to read the other's work, for Hugh thought Monty frivolous and Monty knew Hugh to be sentimental. The one [MRJ] went to bed very late and rose as late as decency permitted: the other retired soon after dusk, and was up with the lark, and I need hardly say that it was the early riser who was the most uncharitable in his judgement of his colleague's idiosyncracies' (Cox I, 214). This may account for the slightly cruel portrait of the vice-provost here.

     Mr. Hope Jones: William Hope-Jones, housemaster at Eton, known as 'Ho Jo', and author of the scouting song 'The Woad Ode'.

     Judkins mi.: 'Judkins minor', Judkins the younger; as opposed to his older brother '*Judkins ma.*': 'Judkins major'.

382   *Oppidans*: non-scholarship pupils at Eton, who board in the town rather than in the school itself.

     Lower Master: Sir Clarence Henry Kennett Marten (1872–1948), lower master, 1925; vice-provost, 1929; provost, 1945; knighted on the steps of the College Chapel, 1945.

     Cuckoo Weir: Cuckoo Weir Stream, where Eton swimming tests took place until the 1950s. There are a number of weirs around Eton's grounds: see note to p. 377.

383   *Mr. Beasley Robinson*: A. C. Beasley Robinson, Eton master.

     Dr. Ley: Henry George Ley (1887–1962), organist and composer; precentor (music master) at Eton, 1926.

     Mr. Lambart. Julian Lambart, Eton master.

the beautiful district of W (or X) in the county of D (or Y): Worbarrow Bay, Dorset.

390 *axe-helve*: axe-handle.

THE EXPERIMENT

First published in the *Morning Post*, 31 December 1931. MS not located.

393 *Raphael . . . Nares*: 'Raphael (Hebrew: "God heals"), noted in the apocryphal book of Tobit as God's envoy, the healer of Tobit's blindness, and conqueror of the demon Asmodeus, is called in the apocryphal *First Book of Enoch* (20:17) "the angel of the spirits of men" ' (*EB*). Nares is Latin for 'nostrils'. Steve Duffy, 'Nares', *Ghosts and Scholars*, 31 (2000), 50, suggests that Nares is a demon who steals the breath (and thus the soul) from the dying body.

394 *eftest*: readiest, most convenient. The source is Shakespeare's *Much Ado About Nothing*, IV.ii.38: 'Yea, marry, that's the eftest way.'

Bishop Moore: John Moore (1646–1714), bishop of Ely. Possessor of a vast library of some 30,000 books and manuscripts, donated in 1715 to Cambridge University Library by King George I, who had acquired it after Moore's death for £6,450. This collection is now known as the Royal Library.

THE MALICE OF INANIMATE OBJECTS

First published in the Eton magazine *The Masquerade* (June 1932). MS in 'private hands' (Cox II, 335).

397 *Squire Korbes*: MRJ here recounts the Grimms' fairytale, 'Squire Korbes'.

400 *GEO. W. FECI*: 'George Wilkins made this'.

A VIGNETTE

First published posthumously in the *London Mercury*, 35 (November 1936), 18–22. The story is prefaced by the following passage, by the editor, R. A. Scott James:

'A Vignette' is undoubtedly the last ghost story written by the late Dr. M. R. James, provost of Eton, and probably his last piece of continuous writing intended for the Press. It came into being in this way. Mr. Owen Hugh Smith was good enough to ask Dr. James to try to recapture the mood in which he wrote *Ghost Stories of an Antiquary*, and to let me have something in a similar vein for the Christmas number of *The London Mercury* (1935). The answer was that he would do his best. On December 12th of that year he sent off to me the manuscript, written in pencil, from The Lodge, Eton College, with the following letter:

I am ill satisfied with what I enclose. It comes late and is short and ill written. There have been a good many events conspiring to keep it back, besides a growing inability. So pray don't use it unless it has some quality I do not see in it.

I send it because I was enjoined to do something by Mr. Owen Hugh Smith.

It was then too late for our Christmas number, or, indeed, for the January number; so it was agreed that it should be held over till one of the closing months of this year.

At the moment of going to press, I see it announced that the original manuscripts of his *Ghost Stories* are to appear at a Sotheby's sale on November 9th (written on foolscap paper). The original of 'A Vignette,' of course, is not among them. Like the others, it is written on lined foolscap.'

MS not located.

401 *a country rectory*: this is a depiction of Great Livermere rectory, Suffolk, where MRJ lived as a child.

the Hall: Livermere Hall, a seventeenth-century house, demolished in 1923: 'Livermere Hall is gone, and many oaks in its park are cut down. "It must needs be that," let us say, changes "come." But village and park have some beauty left' (*S&N*, 71).

402 *what Hamlet calls a 'gain-giving'*: misgiving; *Hamlet*, V.ii.215–16: 'It is but foolery, but it is such a gain-giving, as would perhaps trouble a woman.'

404 *parts of a novel*: J. Sheridan Le Fanu's *The House by the Churchyard*, serialized in the *Dublin University Magazine*, 1861–3: 'As the aerial aspect of the house stood before her with its peculiar, malign, scared and skulking aspect, as if it had drawn back in shame and guilt under the melancholy old elms among the tall hemlock and nettles.' There is some dispute as to whether the correct word here is 'scared' or 'sacred': MRJ clearly believed the latter, which he uses on both occasions that he quotes the passage, here and in his essay 'Some Remarks on Ghost Stories'.

APPENDIX: M. R. JAMES ON GHOST STORIES

408 *'Schalken the Painter'*: 'Strange Event in the Life of Schalken the Painter', 1839 ghost story by Sheridan Le Fanu, inspired by the work of the Dutch painter Godfried Schalcken (1643–1706).

'Look on (them) again I dare not': not Scott, but Shakespeare's Scottish play: *Macbeth* II.ii.49.

There was the story of a man travelling in a train in France: a fragment of this story survives in KCL: MS MRJ A/10.

Madame de Lichtenstein: Caroline de Lichtenfeld in the MS, that is, *Caroline de Lichfield, ou Mémoires d'une famille prussienne* (1786), by the Swiss novelist and translator Isabelle de Montolieu (1751–1832), one of the most important European novels of the late eighteenth century.

409 *Marcilly-le-Hayer*: small town in the Aube region of northern France.

the story of two students of King's College, Cambridge: a draft of this exists in manuscript form: Cambridge University Library MS Add.7484.l.27 & 28b; it was published as 'The Fenstanton Witch' in *Ghosts and Scholars*, 12 (1990).

Fenstanton . . . Lolworth . . . Huntingdon: Fenstanton and Lolworth are both villages just north of Cambridge; Huntingdon as a market town in Cambridgeshire, and formerly the county town of Huntingdonshire.

410 *Wild Wales*: 1862 work by the Norfolk novelist and travel writer George Borrow (1803–81).

Lope de Vega's El Peregrino en su patria: 'The Pilgrim in his own Country', work of fiction by the Spanish dramatist and poet (1562–1635).

411 *Glanville, Beaumont*: for Joseph Glanvill, see note to p. 181. John Beaumont (*c.*1636–1701), *An Historical, Physiological and Theological Treatise of Spirits* (1705).

Lavater: Johann Kasper Lavater (1741–1801), Swiss poet.

The Castle of Otranto . . . Mrs. Radcliffe . . . Monk Lewis: the most influential examples of eighteenth-century Gothic fiction: *The Castle of Otranto* (1764) by Horace Walpole (1717–97); Ann Radcliffe (1764–1823), author of *The Mysteries of Udolpho* (1794) and others; Matthew Lewis (1775–1819), author of *The Monk* (1796). Lewis's influential compendium of ghost stories and folklore, *Tales of Wonder*, was published in 1801.

Maturin's Melmoth: Charles Maturin, *Melmoth the Wanderer* (1820); influential Gothic novel written by a Dublin Anglican clergyman.

413 *Bulwer Lytton*: Edward Bulwer-Lytton (1803–73), politician and prolific novelist.

414 *Rhoda Broughton, Mrs. Riddell, Mrs. Henry Wood, Mrs. Oliphant*: Rhoda Broughton (1840–1920); Charlotte Riddell (1832–1906); Mrs Henry Wood (Ellen Price) (1814–87); Margaret Oliphant (1825–97). All Victorian novelists and ghost-story writers.

Marion Crawford: Francis Marion Crawford (1854–1909), American novelist and writer of supernatural fiction.

Chambers's Repository: *Chambers' Repository of Instructive and Amusing Papers*: a popular compendium, published in numerous volumes from the 1850s.

Alice-for-Short: 1907 novel by the Arts and Crafts potter and designer William Frend de Morgan (1839–1917).

414 *E. F. Benson*: 1867–1914; ghost-story writer, and younger brother of MRJ's friend A. C. Benson.

Not At Night: an anthology series published in twelve volumes from 1925 to 1937, with stories largely drawn from the pulp magazine *Weird Tales*. It was edited by the horror writer Christine Campbell Thompson (1897–1985).

Ambrose Bierce: 1842–*c*.1913; American writer, author of *The Devil's Dictionary* (1911).

415 *A. M. Burrage*: Alfred McLelland Burrage (1889–1956), ghost-story writer; *Some Ghost Stories* (1927).

H. R. Wakefield: H. Russell Wakefield (*c*.1890–1964), ghost-story writer; *They Return at Evening* (1928).

Mrs. Everett's The Death Mask: H. D. Everett (Mrs Theo Douglas), *The Death Mask and other ghosts* (1920).

K. and Hesketh Prichard's 'Flaxman Low': Katherine O'Brien Ryall Prichard (1852–1935) and her son, Hesketh Vernon Hesketh-Prichard (1876–1922); *The Experiences of Flaxman Low* (1899).

Algernon Blackwood: 1869–1951; *John Silence: Physician Extraordinary* (1908).

Elliott O'Donnell: 1872–1965; Irish ghost-story writer.

Erckmann–Chatrian: Émile Erckmann (1822–99) and Alexandre Chatrian (1826–90), joint authors of many ghost stories.

416 *The Turn of the Screw*: classic 1898 ghost story by Henry James.

417 *Harrison Ainsworth*: William Harrison Ainsworth (1805–82), Lancashire novelist; *The Lancashire Witches* (1848).

Hastings: Captain Arthur Hastings is Hercule Poirot's sidekick in the long-running series of detective novels by Agatha Christie.

418 *Lanoe Falconer's*: pseudonym of Mary Elizabeth Hawker (1892–1908); *Cecilia de Noël* (1891).

Mr. Wardle's Fat Boy: the Fat Boy in Dickens's *Pickwick Papers* says, 'I wants to make your flesh creep.'

De la Mare: Walter De la Mare (1873–1956); writer and poet.

419 *L'Araignée Crabe*: 'The Crab Spider'. For Erckmann–Chatrian, see note to p. 415.

420 *Aander og Trolddom*: Norwegian for 'Spirits and Magic'.